For Mary, Josh and Alysha;
almost always with patience, understanding
and words to the wise.

Also By Scott K Bywater

Genesis Makers

*e*Volution

by

Scott K Bywater

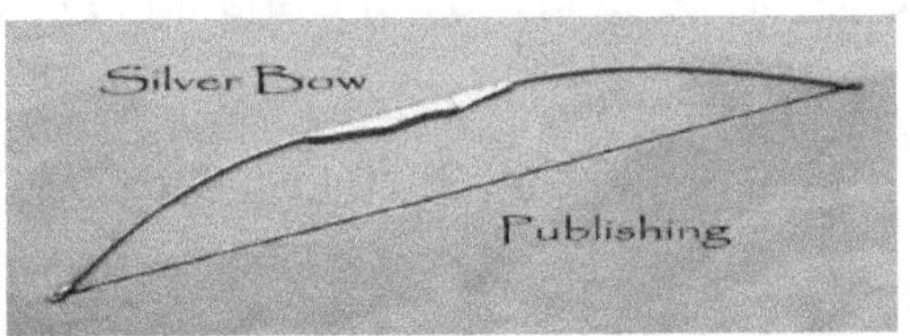

720 Sixth Street, Unit # 5
New Westminster, BC V3L 3C5
CANADA

Title: eVOLUTION
Author: Scott K. Bywater
Cover Art: "User Space" by Joshua Nicholas Bywater
Layout and Design: Candice James
Editing: Candice James

ISBN 9781774031025 (softcover)
ISBN 9781774031032 (e-book)
© 2020 Silver Bow Publishing

Library and Archives Canada Cataloguing in Publication

Title: Evolution / by Scott K. Bywater.
Names: Bywater, Scott K., 1962- author.
Identifiers: Canadiana (print) 20200312510 | Canadiana (ebook) 20200312545 | ISBN 9781774031025 (softcover) | ISBN 9781774031032 (EPUB)
Classification: LCC PR9619.4.B99 E96 2020 | DDC 823/.92—dc23

Contents

Prologue – Godrock ... 7

Afterword -Renewal ... 384

Prologue

Godrock
"Do ya' feel lucky, punk?" — *Clint Eastwood, Dirty Harry*

The ice-storm exploded from the Transantarctic Mountains with nothing more than snowdrifts and a few lonely outcrops to slow it. Penguins and leopard seals loved this place but for humans it was like being thrust onto a harsh alien world where none of the trimmings of the lower latitudes applied - bar a few hardy souls who thrived on toil and challenge, Antarctica sucked.

Glancing out in the near darkness he narrowed his eyes, 'Jesus Christ,' Roeffel said, 'is this going to give out…like ever?' He put his head in his hands, pulling his snow mask away from his face. Despite the freezing temperature, his face was flushed with blood, sweat thick on his top lip. He yelled to be heard above the deafening wind, whistling and howling at a hundred and thirty clicks, making comms almost impossible, life pretty much the same.

Each of them was cowering inside their Zima sleds with the insulated canopies zipped almost to the top, their makeshift homes lashed together with elastic rope but still the wind drove them forward on the ice. The anchors kept slipping so they'd given up and accepted the inevitable creep. Maybe it'd push 'em all the way back to Byrd Base and safety, Roeffel said to himself, grunting and closing his eyes, wishing time would speed up and get it the hell over with. Could just as easily send them plummeting into a blue-ice crevasse where they'd remain forever, well, until fucking hell froze over, he mused idly, realising with a frosty snort that they were there already. Listening to the guttural roar, the constant pummelling of ice crystals on fabric, he knew this was only going to end one way if the storm didn't break soon.

Roeffel, Rick and Ravi kicked off their long-planned trek two weeks before, setting off from Marie Byrd in late November, a pretty good time to enjoy the notorious comforts of the seventy-fifth parallel. They had all the gadgets and emergency gear they reckoned would deliver a measure of comfort and safety. They knew this place was a death trap for the unprepared and underprepared, Ravi shook his head, mentally adding the prepared to the list. And the goddamn unlucky.

Their armoury boasted a heated Intel Ultrabook and a Yellowbrick Sat Phone that bounced off the low orbit Iridium network, providing connectivity across their entire journey. That is except when the satellite bastardry dropped out as it had now. Each of them had handheld Garmin GPS units complete with three-option emergency beacons and every other geek feature they could afford on their limited post-grad budget. Yet they were being completely screwed over by the worst blizzard they'd ever had the misfortune of confronting. Katabatic gravity flows were whipping up killer wind chill despite their canopy protection and personal three-layer Gore-Tex insulation. Pain from slowly freezing flesh was becoming unbearable.

The emergency beacon was punched a day ago but they knew there was no hope of extraction until the storm lost some of its grunt. Their two-way comms with the ground-station at McMurdo was cactus and now there was nothing but harrowing amplitude static. So, there was little choice than to sit it out, hoping like hell they didn't die in the meantime. Ravi knew it would be line ball, giving them maybe another day, maybe half that, he wasn't sure.

Ravi was sure Rick had hypothermia and it was a decent way on. His stupor was obvious when he unzipped his canopy until it was splayed to the elements like it was a summer's night. 'Christ Rick, what are you doing man?' Ravi said helplessly, staring at the pitiable sight from a couple of metres away. The idiot was struggling to get out of his carbon-fibre capsule and jump into the blizzard but his clumsy attempts had him on his back. If it wasn't life and death it would've been comical. 'Jesus, zip it up dude,' Ravi said, screaming, '…you're going to fucking kill yourself!' He shouted as loud as he could, hoping it might snap him out of whatever mania was gripping him. Rick didn't hear him, maybe ignored him. 'Dumb fuck,' he said to himself, sighing heavily, scratching at oozing sores around his cracked lips. Rick had vanished inside his canopy again, the flap still wide open, flailing like a flag in a wind tunnel.

'Where are we Ravi?' He said, shrieking through the tiny slit in his sled cover. Ravi peered into the icefall, barely able to see him even though he was so close. Their three heavy-duty polar sleds were tightly lashed together but were being tossed around relentlessly, wind roaring like jet engines. 'No change!' He yelled hoarsely, bewildered by the stupid question. Ravi had checked his GPS ten minutes ago and they'd only moved courtesy of the driving wind since. Did he think they were out there hauling their sleds in the dark? Must be tripping, Ravi muddled vaguely, barely able to move his fingers and toes, in his mind's eyes they'd turned into solid plates of flesh.

'Repeat' Roeffel said in a wavering voice. Ravi sensed his own confusion growing, distantly noting that Roeffel must be bad, not as bad as Rick but bad enough and he wasn't far away himself, he knew the signs. Dizziness was rolling through his mind as though the world outside was lopsided, watching breath troll from his mouth in short frosty puffs, mesmerised. GPS coordinates were a dim memory so he unzipped the backpack at his feet, snatching at the Garmin several times before he finally grabbed it. Why the hell didn't Roeffel check his own damn unit instead of screwing with him? 'Lazy fuck,' he said almost inaudibly, seeing the rock they'd found just before hearing the wind and icefall scream down the Transantarctic Mountains. Man, it was shiny he mooned dreamily, admiring the silvery reflection in the dim light. Whoa, swee-eet, he thought hazily, staring vaguely at it for a few seconds.

Not long after leaving the geographic South Pole on their voyage home, they'd found it sticking proudly out of the glacier like a burnt finger. It was silvery black and contrasted starkly with the paleness of the ice. Rick had grabbed his pick to try and coax it out by chipping away some ice around its base. Roeffel surprised by bending down and pulling it out as easy as a spoon from warm butter. Motherfucker, Rick had blurted, thinking Excalibur while he gazed at Roeffel's bedraggled smile behind his white frosted whiskers. It was almost like it had been placed there deliberately, just for them, because no way in shit they could have missed it.

Rick was a sharp field geologist but even he struggled to identify the minerals, telling them they were, um…metallic. Der, Roeffel had mocked, grinning at him with an index finger poking his temple, thanking him for the bleeding obvious. The matrix was igneous, he knew that much, full of greenish flecks which Rick said was pyroxene. The metallic stuff was sphalerite, galena or maybe both he eventually said, scratching his chin uncertainly. Location was the real kicker because what the hell was it doing on the glacier so far from the central mountains or any other outcropping piece of dirt? They were clueless on that one and not even Rick the rockhound had a decent theory apart from glacial creep over a few million years from location fuck knows. Anyway, the glacier was moving toward the mountains so that seemed to mess up his theory and the odds of it sitting up on its end, being exposed on a surface that received a metre of icefall each year must have been vanishingly small. Laws of probability, Ravi had chided a little curiously, banging Rick on the back, telling him if it's possible, it'll happen somewhere, and somewhere was right here, right now apparently. A week earlier or later, it would've been covered by ice so go figure he thought, running the numbers in his head. An hour after they picked it off the ice they were engulfed in the freezing, cyclonic nightmare from which there seemed no escape.

Roeffel's voice snapped him back. 'Position, now!' He said, feeling tight in the chest.

Ravi glanced cloudily at the GPS, eyes widening visibly behind his acrylic goggles. 'Oh c-crap,' he said brokenly, staring doe-like at the temperature gauge. 'Minus seventy-three.' He'd keep that to himself. Fuck, he thought grimly. 'We're um, eight clicks west of mag-pole,' he yelled back, swallowing ice as he spoke, feeling it sticking in his throat like a wedge.

How far to the next EQ dump?' Roeffel asked weakly, bringing a shaky hand to his forehead, convinced they didn't have a prayer. The wind was now officially ridiculous, coming from everywhere, rhythmically pushing and pulling them in waves, leaving them addled, verging on sea sickness. The ferocity was like nothing any of them had come close to, setting the standard for a true holiday adventure, he mulled humourlessly, feeling drunk or stoned, maybe both, adding to the dread.

Gawking at the GPS numbers on Webmaps, the shock caused the words to stick in his throat, '…er, ah, distance to EQ3 is, uh…five clicks,' he said, feeling his mind thicken into glutinous lumps. It might as well be on the Moon Ravi told himself, coughing to clear his throat. Suddenly he heard Roeffel screaming at Rick to "get back in the motherfucking sled". 'Oh you have to be—', Ravi said, tilting his head, watching the insane scene play out in the ice-filled dimness. Rick's clothes were off and he was running against the wind, being flung along the ice on his back, away into the darkness of the storm, a hypothermia induced paroxysm, like a sports-field streaker. Rick was butt naked in conditions that would snap freeze him like a shrimp on a trawler boat.

'You're fucking kidding me!' Ravi shrieked, shaking his head sharply, trying to right his mind and effort some sort of plan but there was nothing there. His mind was mush, everything was unravelling and he was shaking violently which he knew was his body's futile attempt at generating heat. He'd seen the horrible blackness on his fingers and toes, the agony on his top lip and both ears. Ravi screamed, crying in anguish, wheezing painful breaths through lips now split like burnt franks. 'Shit, shit, fuck!' He yelled inside the confines of his frozen coffin, bashing the interior with his fists, unable to hold back the panic in his cold addled mind. He could sense blood being sucked deeper into his body as his brain struggled to keep his vital organs running. Muscles were cramping in a final act of torture. He could feel his heartbeat becoming erratic as chilled nerve endings started repelling electrical currents. Ravi was struck by a primal desire to burrow into the ice to find some sort of refuge but it was a transient thought. They were fucked and he knew it with a harrowing richness, despite his stupor. Staring sluggishly at the ice-storm, Ravi imagined a field of cotton candy in a hurricane, sweetly pink in the meagre light that managed to penetrate the steely storm clouds.

Rick was gone, Roeffel had hypothermia and was probably dead as well or dying. Ravi was losing his sense of self as dizziness and confusion blunted his higher brain. Not long now he told himself with an odd calmness, staring wanly at the ferocity outside his tiny shelter. Shelter he sighed, chewing on the ill-gotten word. This tenuous canvass bag hardly qualified as life-saving although he wasn't sure what would. Maybe one of the EMUs the astronauts wore on their EVAs he dreamed distantly, that'd do it. All snug and secure, surrounded by rivulets of warm water with the killer conditions outside nary a worry. Smiling broadly at the idea he drifted into a sleepless slumber, a prelude to shutdown, a welcome escape from the pain of living.

An almighty surge of gravity driven wind screamed from the highlands, destroying everything in its path. Sleds were ripped from one another, Ravi and Roeffel were wrenched from their canopies and sent sprawling into the icefall. They were dead in minutes.

Five minutes later the winds ground to a halt and the orange torso of the Sun peeked cheekily through the clouds as they rapidly thinned near the horizon. Mt Kirkpatrick was suddenly clear to the east and it was a sight to see.

Coincidence was a bitch.

1. Antarctica

**"Every luxury must be paid for, and everything is a luxury,
starting with being in this world."** *— Cesare Pavese*

Descending into the soupy atmosphere there were glimpses of a colossal landmass through the patchy clouds, stretching like an exquisitely stippled canvass, horizon to horizon, deep cracks, abyssal cliffs dividing the supercontinent into hulking slices of real estate.

Continuing toward the surface, a multi-storied rainforest luxuriated in the steam and humidity and in places, where the twisted vines and undergrowth thinned, large creatures and smaller agile critters swarmed. To an observer this was a planet among planets, plentiful, vibrant, lucky in every respect - warmth from a friendly star, a Moon sufficiently large to draw generous tides, the sky alive with flying animals, gliding on richly oxygenated currents.

The landmass was a fertile paradise but for parts of it the days of plenty were under threat. Channels and fissures were being cleaved away by molten rock, driving pieces of the mighty jigsaw apart, eventually allowing egress to a mighty ocean that lapped its shores.

Even at an achingly slow pace, thousands of millennia would bring a global reworking, pushing slices of the great continent to less amenable climes. Chunks of the landscape would creep into a freezing, windswept nightmare, buried alive by kilometre deep glaciers, banished to the outer 'burbs and fated to support little more than a kiss of moss and a sweep of lichen for millions of years.

But the bleakness and desolation hid fabulous deposits of oil and gas, enormous reserves of coal and fortunes in pipe-born diamonds and precious metals. If the ice and isolation weren't enough to deter the hoards, there was a small detail known as the Madrid Protocol, a dream killer for anyone thinking about doing anything unscientific down South. The protocol was a global heads of agreement outlawing anything to do with exploration or mining, even thinking about it until 2048.

The great southern land was under the most stringent lock and key. Killer conditions, arse-end of the world and global law had it tied up in knots for generations. It was rightly assumed that mining would never be allowed at the Pole until the global economy hinged on whatever might lie under its pristine white skirt. No one in the know thought the Antarctic freeze would soften any time before the middle of the millennium. Maybe.

Bedrock at the South Pole had been hidden from view for more than sixty million years in the east and slightly more than half that in the remote wilderness of the west. Mankind had never laid eyes on it, bar some radar, microwave and ASCAR images that were milky and vague at best. Real detail, touch and feel stuff was zero. The "big island" of Antarctica to the east was buried by ice flows soon after the Chicxlulub event doomed the Dinosaurs. In fact, humans had a better grip on the vagaries of Mars and, a little perversely, knew more about the hidden lunar far side and even distant Titan than landfall at the South Pole. Along with some of the abyssal trenches of the deep oceans, the hard surface of Antarctica was the last great mystery on the planet. Many on Earth wondered about the secrets of a landscape that was conveniently hidden by a barrier of ice that at depth was harder than steel.

2. Rhodium

**"It wasn't curiosity that killed the goose who laid the golden egg,
but an insatiable greed that devoured common sense." — *E.A. Bucchianeri***

Carson Becker's mining empire grew from a dingy room full of empty beer cans to a corporate Gargantua in two short years. A modest public float raising funds for a promising tenement led to the discovery of a southern El Dorado that spelt out rich beyond the dreams of avarice in a perfect mineralogical symphony. Cutting into the first cave of sardine-like metal, the grandeur of the deposit became clear to the muckers drilling the first spiral decline, almost popping Becker's heart when he got the news that so defied the humble drilling results. Unlike the nearby Olympic Dam deposit, this one was high grade, near surface and colossal…striking straight down and crammed with finely spun platinum, gold and rare earth's, intermingled with massive, primary strata bound copper and uranium. It was an explorer's wet dream and stock markets devoured the company whole, rocketing shares from pocket change to over a hundred bucks a pop. Becker Resources NL morphed into a Fortune 500 Company overnight, a billion shares trading in a single day of breathtaking market chaos, leaving the blue chippers drifting aimlessly in its wake. Not bad for a Company previously worth a few cents. Everybody wanted in. The Company was promptly worth the GDP of a G20 and Becker himself was handed a personal fortune he couldn't spend in a dozen lifetimes.

***

Becker's eyes grew wider as he gazed at the specimen, losing focus and glaring over at the dishevelled map of Antarctica stuck ingloriously on the wall. 'Fuck,' he said to himself harshly, not sure who it was aimed at, maybe everyone, the Pole itself or just life as he now knew it.

Becker was standing and fidgeting, shaking his head almost imperceptibly, impatience and desire obvious to those who knew him well. Hyperfocus it was called and he didn't need some quack with a caduceus symbol stencilled on his forehead to tell him. He hated WebMD but it would have to do - it told him he met all five criteria, also the majors for Asperger's, even a few for Tourette's. Christ, he thought, scraping his forehead with a knuckle, what a goddamn screw up.

The only time he spoke with his signature vigour was when he eyeballed *"the specimen"*, better known as the shit-rock to most. Becker had deified it, installing it as the guest of honour in perpetuity, to be revered and prostrated before by all who happened upon it. He was a pain in the arse and the rock was a fucking curse, that was the measured opinion from his executive team.

The specimen was mixed up with the frozen belongings of an exploration team who'd tried vainly to haul themselves back from Valkyrie Dome in West Antarctica, having apparently stumbled upon Becker's godrock in the process. He'd later acquired it from a private collector just as his IPO was closing.

Eyes burning with fever, greenback fever Becker figured, the dealer whispered behind his hand that it was native silver, maybe bismuth from the South Pole. "Ssshh" he'd spat under his breath, eyes darting around as though the CIA had bugged every inch of his back-alley junkyard.

Nervously fiddling with a crucifix around his neck, he said it was unique…worth a King's ransom as a specimen "you know". Becker didn't know shit. He wasn't sure what it was but he sure as hell knew what it wasn't. The dealer was a jerk, it was all he could do not to laugh in his pious face but he held it in, playing along, paying him his ten grand and watching the dude's eyes almost drop from his skull. Becker had no idea that its real value was light years beyond his wildest, whisky filled reveries.

As it turned out, the rock was a mix of pyroxene and plagioclase, clearly part of some spectacularly mineralised reef that Becker felt certain was a one-off. He agreed with the idiot dealer on that score because woven in and around the worthless parts of the rock were grains of native platinum with hexagonal chunks of osmium. Pretty frigging amazing in itself but it was like quartz hosting gold, no-good gangue destined for the mullock heap. The thing about the rock that made his heart pound was the shiny globs of something that peered back at him like shining eyes. To Becker's expletive driven disbelief, the spectroscope identified the silvery gloop as rhodium, by a fair margin the most valuable thing on the planet. His feverish research told him it only occurred as slivers or flecks in other rare earth's, never as nuggets as big as a pinkie.

Becker had heaved in several shuddering breaths when it hit home, thumping his forehead with a fist in case he was dreaming, fighting to register what his eyes were telling him. If this piece of rock-candy was typical of where it came from, well he couldn't even imagine the riches, more importantly, the fame it might deliver. Every muscle in his body tightened like piano wire, black spots dancing behind his eyes, washing out his vision. It'd make Grimwald's Hill look like a two-bit garage sale. He gasped between bursts of adrenaline that made him want to scream and holler, maybe even fall to his knees in prayer. Even the storied Tsumeb and Broken Hill deposits would seem like low-grade jokes not worth the fuel to crack the outcrop.

The rock was never far from his thinking, rolling around in his brain, never finding a like-shaped hole to drop into. The years following Becker's breakout discovery were so chaotic the rock got shoved further back in his mind, but never forgotten. What made it such a mind-fuck was the source, and as his sworn enemy Murphy and his grating law had so sanctimoniously determined, it was smack-bang in the middle of an icy hellscape, imprisoned by a mining ban equivalent to a death sentence. The dark, custodial document barred every nation on Earth for the rest of Becker's life, leaving his dreams screwed, broken, gone, pulverised into molecular dust.

With his Company settled and the manic acquisitions and exploration were at a pause, Becker felt obsession come back hard, prickling interminably front and centre in his brain. Desire was swelling in his loins like an ornery dog suddenly in heat, frantically looking for anything that moved. In the depths of night, he occasionally imagined grabbing his rockhammer and parachuting onto the ice from his Kamov chopper.

Becker's HQ was spitting distance from the Opera House in Sydney, staring over the harbour and iconic arch in the biggest city down under, a glass edifice bearing the Company's name in bold, glitzy 3D letters. Driving south over the Harbour Bridge it was the first thing in your face, *Becker Resources NL* and unless you were legally blind it was a confronting eyesore, undeniably a massive personal jerk off. No narcissism Becker dismissed smugly to those accusing. Hey, it's the Company name, check the ASX, I can't stick lies up there, deal with it. Classic Becker.

The boardroom was perched on the twenty-fifth floor with space for twenty suits around a daunting oak table so highly polished it was like a bloody mirror-ball. The oak monster was purely for show because he only needed room for two, the only ones he trusted, Connie and Joe. The rest of the Board were Muppets, installed to satisfy Stock Exchange compliance and the hordes of investors that irritated the hell out of him. The Board got the intel he wanted them to get and not a zac more. Becker pulled the reins, ruled the purse strings, made the decisions and the Board accepted this because he paid them a dump truck full of money to do whatever they were told, without the option of asking why. His money, his rules.

***

Becker shifted anxiously in his seat, fidgeting with a pen in one hand, drumming his fingers on the keyboard with the other. Connie and Joe sat opposite, studying him, eyebrows slightly raised, Connie the suggestion of an eye roll. Becker was sighing, making odd noises in his throat, glaring at a slightly crumpled geological map of Antarctica, seemingly waiting for it to give up its secrets of its own volition.

Connie's raven hair was a straight black bob, cropped at the jawline, framing her delicate features that men found tough to reconcile with her straight up, no bullshit charm. Becker's athletic background was barely a memory, the rigours of business and too many meals on the run packing on the pounds and hiding the rest. Slim and muscled, Connie occasionally jabbed a finger at Becker with derision, the stiff finger and accusing eyes directed toward his expansive midriff were enough to seriously piss him off. She had triplets and worked damn hard to keep them but for Becker, his abs were a blind orebody, kind of there, but well concealed.

'Jesus Christ,' he said abruptly, glancing up from the map, eyes blood-shot causing Connie to do a double take, wondering if this guy ever slept. Tilting his head, he was lured back to the map like a trout to a butter worm. 'They could've picked it up anywhere between Valkyrie and where they dropped dead,' Becker said, rubbing his temple, then scraping a finger through knotted hair. 'We've got GPS data…we know they barely got beyond the Pole, never made it to Valkyrie but—'

Connie couldn't believe she had to listen to this drivel all over again, rubbing an eyelid, trying to work out his messed-up brain. 'Why does it even matter?' She said, groaning, 'cause it's not gonna mean shit even if you do find out where they got it.' Connie felt herself flush, seeing the infuriating longing in Becker's eyes as he scowled at the moth-eaten map spread roughly over the table. You absolute twat, she thought, crossing her arms roughly, thinking *Groundhog Day*, wincing as the mindless charade repeated itself, again.

'Just forget it,' Joe said, averting his eyes. 'Focus on what we've got going at Maranga with the locals.' He tried to massage Becker's addled mind in a different direction.

Becker spun his head around, peering at Joe wide-eyed, making him sway back a bit. 'Are you serious? Tell me you're not. Let the registrars deal with it, I pay them what I pay 'em to deal with this indigenous title crap.' Gazing back at the map, then at Connie he sighed heavily, pulling at the hair near his temple. His face softened slightly, knowing he was screwed without them, needing them on side. He put his hands up defensively, 'look, okay, we need to find out where it came from' he paused momentarily, turning his head and looking at the specimen in the centre of the table, then calmly continued, '…to give me, you know, some measure of, uh…closure.' A deep, dark worry line dug into his forehead above the bridge of his nose. 'Damn it, I can't function, I can't sleep, Jesus, I can't piss straight.' He jerked his head up at the ceiling, seemingly seeking help from someone a little higher up on the food chain.

'You're an atheist, there's nothing up there for you,' Connie said, flashing a sour grin. 'You gotta be kidding with this, it's nuts, stupid, a boy's own pipe-dream. You've got a continent of wilderness down there and most of it's under territorial claim.' Her chest felt heavy as she vented at Becker who seemed to have seriously lost whatever tenuous grip he had on reality. Incredibly, he was getting worse, more manic, more obsessive, high maintenance, call it what you like. He was turning into a fanatical, card-carrying nutjob.

'But that's what makes it so intriguing,' Becker said, whispering with an intensity bordering on pyrexia. His eyes gleamed, conjuring images of chambers crammed with rhodium crystals dangling like stalactites from the roof. And he could run along merrily, picking the low hanging fruit and stuffing them in his backpack like it was a bloody strawberry farm. Connie could see he was tripping. Becker didn't look up from the map, continuing to study the ice sheet west of Mt Kirkpatrick. 'Their route was through Marie Byrd in the west,' he said, touching the map and pointing with his index finger, 'the only time they stepped into territorial whatever was in the final thirty clicks when they made it past the Pole.' Connie studied him amused at how wired he was. She could see how the dynorphins in his stupid brain were roused every time he sized up his pornographic rock that got him off so good. He didn't give a crap about his Company or the billions he had hiding in tax havens around the globe. Becker didn't have eyes for anything but *the thing*, seizing his tiny brain to the exclusion of all else. Connie watched him, seeing a bully in a sandpit, refusing to share his toys and every kid who didn't back off got a squirrel grip, a headlock or both. Becker's arrogance was reaching new levels and it was combined with an insufferable egomania, narcissism and look-at-fucking-me glare. Not surprisingly it left him with almost no friends and many who just straight out despised him.

Squinting, he weighed her up, 'there's no way it came from near the Pole, it had to have come from closer, nearer the Transantarctic Mountains, maybe in MBL, you know, unclaimed land.' Glancing back at the map, he stuck his jaw out, surveying it for the umpteenth time.

Connie studied his dopey face again, feeling pressure and heat swelling in her core. The need to vent was overwhelming, she needed to scream, shout, maybe beat her fists on the boardroom table or better, on his big dumb forehead. Connie drew a rasping breath. 'So what?' She said, 'get real would you, it doesn't matter if it's claimed, unclaimed or has a goddamn sign on it saying, *"come get some"*. You understand the Madrid Protocol, right? That piece of rock you want to shag might as well have come from Venus…nobody is allowed to do shit in Antarctica bar research and feeding the fucking penguins.' She clenched and unclenched her fists, turning to Joe who shrugged, rolling his eyes submissively to the floor. Joe loved the way Connie gave Becker what he needed, raw un-edited truth, executing it with a perfect balance of angst and sarcasm. He also loved the way Connie looked and he knew Becker agreed although he'd never admit it. Connie was sexy, brilliant, motivated, didn't take crap from anyone. Rank, position or any other arbitrary station in life didn't mean jack to her.

'Oh God, whatever Con,' Becker said without malice, 'the real problem is that it might have been severed from a reef, carried a thousand clicks away, then spat out by the glacial reduction. That's the twist we can never know.' Turning around he eyeballed Connie and Joe, toe tapping an anxious beat on the carpet. His irritating look-at-me face had melted away, replaced by something more supplicating.

Jesus, this'll be good, Connie told herself, seeing the sudden weather change. She felt a thud of dread as the muscles in her stomach clenched, watching his galling face grow serious.

'Look I'm just gonna come out and say it because I can't go on like this anymore.' The colour in his face had deepened so much she thought he might have a stroke right there and then. Connie was idly trying to recall her first aid training in case he collapsed like a lead weight, started foaming at the mouth, started dying.

Connie caught Joe's eye, visibly grimacing. Shit, she thought, feeling her hands go clammy, he's going to fucking say it. Becker was obsessive-compulsive but the insanity of the idea rattling around in his thick head, unspoken but clearly in there, was bordering on insanity and corporate bloody suicide.

After a pause, Becker edged closer to them, speaking in a sunken growl that had recaptured its belligerence. 'I've had a team in Antarctica for two weeks who have—'

Connie's body spasmed, her eyes narrowing to a flinty stare, 'you fucking what?' She said, baring her teeth. 'Why didn't you tell—'

'Just hear me out,' Becker snapped, raising his arms aggressively, 'they've been running airborne surveys over MBL with UAV drones, magnetometry, induced polarisation and the like, looking for magnetic anomalies under the ice.'

'Oh, brilliant Carson, Joe murmured sarcastically, eyes darting everywhere but at Becker. 'I mean, you didn't bother to discuss it…to tell us?' He glanced at Becker quickly, looking away at the floor, then at Connie, lifting a puzzled eyebrow.

Connie just groaned, muttering expletives under her breath, realising what a godforsaken nightmare this was descending into.

'I didn't because I wanted to protect you, plausible deniability and all that…you know. Anyway, I knew what you'd say.' He gazed off in the distance, face hardening. 'This is happening… so best you get on and deal with it.' He turned on his heels, swaggering over to the boardroom table, sitting down roughly, stroking his chin as he pulled his thoughts together. 'The western survey is complete, results are due tomorrow, that's why I'm telling you now. It's starting to get real. Expedition was headed by Bagley, he tells me they might have, uh…found something.' Becker's eyes sparkled. 'He's waiting on formal mag interpretations to confirm gravity results.'

'Fuck me,' Connie said, curling her mouth into a bitter sneer. 'What about the Company, the investors, if the market finds out you'll be crucified, in the media, on the Exchanges, the share price will implode, market cap will vanish—'

'Screw 'em,' Becker said fiercely, pointing a finger at Connie. 'You only live once and by Christ I am going to chase this until it's done, with or without you.' Shifting his weight sharply, he said, '…the train is leaving.' He raised both arms defiantly, glaring at Connie, appraising her reaction. 'You on or off? I need both of you with me.' His face was like an eroded cliff, steeply lined and seriously confronting as he shifted his gaze to Joe, tightening muscles in his jaw.

Joe felt suddenly warm, tiny beads of sweat standing out on his forehead and top lip. Neither of them needed to speak or waste a molecule of mind to make a decision. Turning back to Becker, Connie snorted, shaking her head minutely. Joe stared at him deadpan, speechless.

'No…no way this is happening,' she said, closing her mouth tightly, her heart suddenly throbbing in her neck disconcertingly. Peeking at Joe, he nodded subtly. 'We're out, there's too much at stake, no way,' Connie added, feeling a desire to physically hurt him, 'our futures are this fucking Company, our shareholding will be junk if the ASX or New York gets wind of this.' She glared at him, daring him to punch out a smart-arse answer. 'You get that… right, you know, comprendo?' Selfish prick, she thought contemptuously.

Becker stared at them blankly, saying nothing, cocking a single eyebrow. He eventually exhaled loudly, 'okay, I got it,' he said, loping over to the door, opening it and leaving the boardroom, closing the door gently with a dull click.

Joe and Connie locked eyes for a long moment, sharing the madness, baffled by Becker's disregard for everything he'd worked so hard for, correcting herself immediately, everything they'd all worked so hard for.

'Did that actually happen?' Joe finally said, grabbing the sides of his head in exasperation. 'Is he seriously going to put the whole lot at risk – the company, the shareholding, the wealth, shit…even his freedom?' He stared woodenly while his mind did the sums, carrying the one, getting only gibberish and infinities. 'If he gets, er, I mean when he gets caught he'll end up in San Quentin for a decent stretch.' He couldn't resist a smirk, picturing Becker in an orange jumpsuit surrounded by a gang of eager suitors. Serve him bloody right he told himself amusingly. 'Arrogant arsehole,' Joe muttered, struggling to process it. Illegal, illogical…it was all Becker.

Connie shuffled a few steps forward, then back, replaying the irrational events in her mind. 'I knew he was obsessive but honest to God, this is so far beyond that, he's clinical, terminal or fucking something.' She pulled at her hair wistfully, wrapping a few locks around a finger. 'He's going to screw everything up – shares in the Company will be worth less than bat shit. Then the goddamn vultures will gut it.' She suddenly looked vulnerable as she pondered her future. If the oaf got his way it would likely be a rather bleak, depressing and penniless existence.

Rolling Becker's delusional words around, they pondered the financial juggernaut they'd built - Government payoffs, deft blind turns with all manner of regulators, drilling 24/7, mucking in the mud, pegging questionable leases and tenements, it was demanding, tricky and dangerous, physically and legally. But now this. Trying to talk him down was all they could think of but then they remembered it was Becker. Once he'd steeled his mind on something, especially this thing that had a mortgage on his soul, well, talking was just escaping air, barely whispers in a windstorm.

During his rise to riches, Becker sprinted at life with an arrogance and balls-out ego that served him well when aligned with a considered business plan and a "generally" principled approach, courtesy of Joe and Connie. But now it was just raw audacity free of any redeeming qualities at all, based entirely on a tunnel-visioned obsession. The goose wanted to square off against international law over a rock that came from some mystical reef buried in a land of rainbows and teddy bears. The chances of it being part of the splinters of rock and dirt that peeked above the ice were vanishingly small. Wishful, delusional thinking, Connie reckoned. She was sure he expected this so-called reef to be waiting for him in the mountains like a fucking hotdog stand and all he needed to do was shoo away a few penguins, maybe a unicorn or two and unfold his operation in broad daylight. He was a seriously egotistical dick. Likeable maybe, a decent Ocker bloke sure, knew his minerals and rocks, but it didn't change the fact he was a selfish prick.

Connie was pondering the game plan, glancing around nervously, looking at her watch, trying to come up with something to back themselves out of this Freudian nightmare. If Becker's hopes materialised, if the expedition team found this godforsaken anomaly, did they wrestle him to the ground, lock him up, maybe keep him prisoner until he confessed his insanity…maybe send him to some rehab unit for the criminally self-involved? She sighed, exhaling bitterly at the idea, almost laughing out loud. They could hold him until he was a hundred, nothing would change. Maybe they'd have to resign themselves to it, let him go, but a distant thought was bubbling in her mind, making her feel queasy. She closed her eyes tightly, biting her lip, searching for something a little less repugnant.

3. Anomaly

"Only those who dare to fail greatly can ever achieve greatly." — *Robert F. Kennedy*

Becker's drones had surveyed eighty percent of Marie Byrd Land using electric B3 Aeroscouts that executed a software-driven grid pattern covering the entire route travelled by the ill-fated explorers. It was tough, even for UAVs, the western shield of the southern continent was the coldest, wildest, most hazardous place on the planet, home to violent katabatic winds and needle-sharp ice storms that could shred a man before he was afforded the dignity of dying from wind chill.

The B3s used cutting-edge data acquisition systems, onboard GPS computers and fluxgate magnetometers that drew in conductivity from the land below. While the ice got in the way, they still penetrated several hundred metres into the frozen ground, giving perfect scalar calibration of massive objects that might be hidden below. Becker was sure his orebody extended all the way to the surface because if it didn't how the hell did the specimen come loose and end up all lonely on the ice? If his suspicions were right, then any penetration by their EMAR birds would be enough. What no one was sure about was location. Maybe it wasn't in the west, maybe it was in the east within one of the territorial occupations or maybe it arrived inside a meteorite and there was no orebody at all. He called bullshit on that one, enough geeks had droned on about Oort Clouds and solar system leftovers to convince him it simply didn't fit the bill. Meteorites were iron and nickel, sometimes with silicates thrown in for good measure. That said, he grudgingly conceded the likelihood that any source rock was buried under kilometres of ice and nowhere near the ice-free mountains, as he so desperately wanted.

Becker grew to despise sleeping because he would inevitably drift off into one of his rhodium-inspired nightmares that no amount of clonazepam was able to stop or even take the edge off. Glorious dreams gave him a boost but it was the drop-dead failures that seemed to play out in wrenching detail.

During Becker's darker contemplations he saw the deposit totally beyond reach, located within briefly ascending strata that spat the specimen out and was then thrust down into the molten bowels of the mantle, into geological oblivion.

*   *   *

Becker sat behind his laptop, wringing his hands, feeling like time was barely crawling, watching the clock as it perversely ticked in slo-mo, waiting for the goddamn email. It was almost like an out of body experience, he saw himself from above, the front, to the side, as though his entire existence had been leading up to this moment. Becker's anticipation was cat-like; he could feel his heart pounding on his ribs, throbbing painfully in his throat.

'Come on you son of a bitch,' he said impatiently, glaring at his Inbox, daring the cyberspace bastardry to remain empty. Connie and Joe were still in the building, he'd seen them huddled in the corner of the twenty-fifth floor breakout, whispering like addled teenagers, talking about him he knew, and in less than glowing terms no doubt. Fuck 'em he thought, pinching his mouth, certain he could do it without them, in the next breath knowing how much bullshit that was.

The message he was willing to arrive was from GeoTek Engineering in Turkey, masters in high-tech remote sensing, expensive as hell but worth every cent…he hoped. Becker was confident that if his orebody was there, this mob would find it. If it wasn't there he was screwed no matter who was doing the looking. He'd paid Geo twenty times their normal fee to execute a covert, in-and-out mission using low flying, camouflaged drones with an encrypted uplink to the Molniya Satellite Network. In terms of the survey, all had gone well and now he was waiting in white-knuckle terror for the aeromagnetic and gravity flux data. Doubts and fears were gathering momentum, Becker knew odds were steeply against him, he'd done the math a thousand times, understanding how far behind the eight-ball he really was. He was no fool; it was frigging Antarctica for Christ's sake! Exuding bullish conviction to Joe and Connie was critical to the plan, but the reality in his mind was far from it. With no priors, no precedents it always meant piss poor odds and generally trouble, especially when it was illegal under protocols signed off by every G20 nation on Earth.

A sudden beep made Becker jerk in his seat, sending a bolt of electricity rifling up his spine, a yelp giving way to a gurgle of terror. He drew in a deep breath and held his hands out, steadying himself as perspiration pimpled his forehead. Becker stared hazily at the email, gritting his teeth as his encryption programme worked to make sense of the jumbled lines of letters and characters. It was from GeoTek, a PDF file attached titled innocuously "Ant Survey Run – MBL".

'Holy sweet fuck,' he said under his breath, feeling light headed. 'Well here goes nothing,' he said almost inaudibly, clicking on the attachment, bringing up an Antarctic profile with lines of narration set out beneath it. Becker squinted blindly, struggling to focus, opening his eyes as wide as he could then letting them relax. The graph showed Total Field Magnetic Data, broadly from West to East across Marie Byrd Land. His eyes were straining in their sockets, drawn to an anomaly at Latitude 79.78, Longitude -142.66 East. The lines rose steeply upward, narrated with "dB/dt Z ch. 5 to 22".   Becker froze, body and soul slowing to a crawl, it took a moment to sink into his thickened head. 'M-My God,' he eventually said haltingly. 'My God,' he repeated louder, starting to digest the summary below the profile. It referred to a TEM anomaly, interpreted to be of interest, defined as a vertically inclined plate, recommendation to core drill, assay, determine character, composition.

'Interpreted to be of interest?' He bellowed, jumping to his feet, 'of fucking interest? You bet your sweet arse it's of interest,' he said, whooping it up, fist pumping as he backed away from the laptop. The desire, the elation hit him like an ore train, his pulse almost maxing out in his neck. GeoTek was his first thought, he needed to speak with them, no hang on, Connie, she had to come first.

'Where are those two idiots?' Becker said, taking short strides, grabbing his cell, punching "Captain" on his call list. She answered after a few rings.

'Oh God, yes?' She said acidly, rolling her eyes at Joe.

'Grab Joe, get in here. I've got something to show you.'

'Sorry…you are?' Connie said deadpan.

'Very funny, now get in here,' he said, hanging up, smirking wryly. He smacked the side of the chair, raising both arms in a victory salute. 'I fucking knew it!' He yelled, quickly tempering his outburst, knowing there was much to do. Hyper focussed he might have been but he knew damn well there were endless unknowns to grapple with, risks too numerous to count, variables, possibilities, unfathomables. But the first non-negotiable was marked with a big fucking tick. There was something down there, albeit under kilometres of ancient glacial ice, hard as hell at depth.

Becker's Polar anomaly was undeniably real, his low flying Aeroscouts had identified a Transient Electromagnetic Anomaly the size of five football fields sitting on and deep within the frozen bedrock.

Becker was like a well-worn book to Connie and by his tone she figured something had him squarely by the cajones. She swore to herself after hanging up, butterflies buzzing in her stomach, hearing nothing but the thwack of her own heart. Dragging Joe reluctantly from his perked coffee they set off, neither of them keen to clap eyes on his smug dial. Although perversely intrigued they were mostly fearful because it was bad news they wanted from GeoTek - that they went, looked, found zip. That would be news to party to, but by his boorish tone they knew otherwise, Connie carving her hands through her hair as she brooded over uncountable misgivings.

Strolling into his office, she buzzed air through her lips, seeing him in typical Becker pose, standing like a storefront dummy, squinting myopically at the map as though he was searching for detail that simply wasn't there.

'God, give it a rest, you'll wear it out if you keep gawking at it,' Connie said, glancing irritably at Joe. His face had *look at me* plastered all over it and was crying out to be slapped.

Becker grinned, swanning over to his laptop, almost gliding in self-satisfaction. Damn it, she thought, balling her fists and digging her fingernails into her palms.

'I've received the summary survey report from GeoTek, you might find it rather interesting,' he said softly, almost in passing, trying hard to act casual.

They didn't have to look at the damn report. Becker's cocky expression was enough, the cat that ate the bloody canary, yellow feathers may as well have been sticking out of his gob. Connie's heart sank further as she mulled over the ugly truth, feeling a need to grab something to steady herself.

Joe glanced over Becker's shoulder at the laptop, startled by the imagery on the screen, sighting an EMAR peak vividly defined under the ice. 'Jesus Christ,' he said shrilly, before he had a chance to think, looking at Connie sheepishly, seeing the scowl on her face and shrugging. He couldn't help it. Joe hated to admit it but he was intrigued by the magnetic profile dancing on Becker's screen. Connie was irritated with Joe and pissed off with Becker, seeing only lifestyle annihilation painted on the terminal like a vivid Monet abstraction.

Becker finally turned from the map, taking a measured breath. 'I'm going to speak to GeoTek and activate the Dig and Test protocol.'

Connie's nostrils flared, eyeing him head on, weighing up the planning that had already gone into this criminal endeavour. 'Are you actually serious?' She jerked her head up, wincing, 'you mean you have a mission planned, like…already? You've only just received the damn report.' She glared at him sideways, struggling to take it in, wondering what else she didn't know about.

'Come on Con, you know me better than that. I've had this planned for six months on the hunch we'd find something. I've thought of everything, including keeping it a secret from you two wieners.' He smiled broadly with a brief finger jab, snorting derisively.

She felt the back of her neck grow warm. 'Screw you,' she said, jerking her head away, once again not sure if she shouldn't just get up and start walking.

'Base Camp is good to go,' he continued, talking over the top of her muttering, 'along with all the drilling equipment, incline transport, lighting, camouflage shields, specialist personnel and the like,' he said, smiling airily as he casually listed them off. 'Everything is organised, paid for, nothing has been left to chance. GeoTek has been paid way over ticket to coordinate the expedition, all they're waiting on is a go/no go.'

'No go,' Connie said with a glaring lack of enthusiasm, realising full well the decision was made. Not a thing she or Joe said would make a speck of difference, threatening, pleading or simply pointing out the madness, all useless, wasted energy. Her need for physical violence was gaining impetus as the only solution.

'How do you plan to get there and not raise suspicion?' Joe asked timidly, peeking at Connie, 'Just sail in, unpack a rig, start hacking through the ice?'

'I'd say that'd be the size of it,' Connie snorted, flashing a cold smile, 'well thought through…great plan Becker.'

He paused momentarily, fighting to avoid giving Connie an expletive ridden response. 'Sit down, I'll tell you,' he said as gently as he could muster, ignoring the growing tension in his body and their galling negativity. 'I told you I'd thought of everything and I mean it. The plan is to covertly transport everything to Marie Bird Land which is unpopulated, territorially unclaimed. The drilling rig is a digital sublimator, a sonic thermal resonance unit able to decrystallise ice directly into vapour as it descends. Everything will be hidden under ice-shields, we'll be invisible from the air, uh…mostly invisible from the ground.' Becker's voice caught on his words as he described his plan of attack on the southern continent. 'Everything has been considered, no expense spared.'

'Famous last fucking words,' she said, still feeling like whacking him in the moosh. 'I remember what happened the last time I heard that shit.'

'Play nice Connie,' Becker said, serving her a short-lived grin. She turned away deliberately, got up and motioned Joe over to the bar area in the corner of Becker's sprawling office. Connie rubbed her forehead, wrinkling her nose, chewing on something clearly distasteful.

Gazing at Joe, her eyes were brown and hypnotic, like a pensive barn owl. 'We can't stop him you know, he'll go, it doesn't matter what we do or say. Have a look at him, only death or locking the jerk up will stop him…he's totally wired on this thing.'

Joe nodded knowingly. 'He thinks his data is a mandate so yeah, he's going alright, nothing'll stop him, not us, not the law—'

Connie's mind had been sprinting for minutes now, running the numbers, coming up with an answer that terrified her. It wasn't an answer…it was a fucking nightmare. That said, she'd known what they needed to do for a while now and had been battling to put on a brave face, and swallow the nasty taste in her mouth.

Connie's words to Joe were whispered almost without sound so Becker couldn't hear them. Joe eyed her, seeing the emotional wrestle, feeling his heart pound high in his chest. 'If we don't agree to help him, 'she started with a tremor, 'we're as screwed as we'd be if we didn't. Apart from the legal stuff our financial positions will be junk if he gets made. Make no mistake, he'll be caught because he's so blinded there'll be screw ups and plenty of 'em.' Peering at Becker she could see him mitred to the laptop, still poring over the damn report, basically making eyes at it like some dotty teen. Connie ran a hand over her face, looking back at Joe, 'the nutjob reckons he's thought of everything but no way, he's got gold fever…we know what that means right?' She raised a narrow eyebrow at him. 'How many times have we seen it? He'll go hard, fast, shortcuts here, oversight there…he'll screw it up inside a day down there, maybe on the way there. I mean, there's so many moving parts in this hair-brained scheme, chaos will bite him in the arse.' Connie's voice was growing husky and strained, 'anything with so many unknowns is fucked from the get-go.' The colour in her face drained away and she looked suddenly exhausted as the knowing set in.

'Then why the hell get involved?' Joe asked flatly, 'we should distance ourselves, protect ourselves from the fallout.'

'Jesus,' Connie said a bit too loudly, '…you're not getting it. Listen to me. To protect ourselves we need to watch him, go with him, provide oversight on what goes down over there. Even if we don't go we're party to it – he's told us, we know about it, it's illegal, we're keeping quiet. Either way we're screwed. Plausible deniability has left the building.'

Joe looked at her blankly. 'Shit,' he muttered after it sunk in, realising his fate had been pretty much decided. Christ, he said to himself, feeling an ache in his temple. 'Maybe we should expose him, go to the authorities,' he said in a bluster, eyeing Connie uneasily, knowing she'd never turn on him. As much as he irritated her, that is, annoyed the bloody shit out of her, that would never happen, and he couldn't do it either. They'd been through so much as a team, the thought of outing him to the Feds wasn't an option, but still they needed to consider every eventuality didn't they? Joe racked his brain but came up with nothing, raising his arms, softly shaking his head.

'We go,' she said pensively, 'we go, we come back, put the whole thing behind us.' Having said it she did have one major question for him and the answer better come back no or she'd club him. Connie nodded at Joe and they stealthily ambled back toward Becker who was watching them like a hawk, steeling himself for more irksome negatives.

'Well?' He asked sharply, looking directly at Connie, mulling over which way it might go. He knew she was the ringleader, the decision maker, the lead juror as it were. Joe would follow like he always did.

Connie looked him in the eye, studying. 'So, let me ask you this,' she said slightly irritated, 'If we go, somehow manage to get there undetected, set up, remain invisible, dig through kilometres of glacier, find the anomaly, crack it, test it, work out its size, get the assay results…what then?' She screwed her face up, snapping her head toward him. 'Are you seriously planning to mine the bloody thing because if you are…the first part is fucking child's play.' She had both hands firmly on hips, glowering at him. 'It'll go from improbable to a one-way ticket to the big house or the nuthouse, maybe both, in what order I don't know. I mean, help me out here - do you want to prove up a mineral deposit or do you actually, honestly expect to mine it in a country that has a fuck-off sign posted by every G8 on Earth?' She peered at him with contempt, daring him to respond in the wrong way. Connie actually had serious concerns for his mental state. Was he really that much of a whack job?

'Blood-pressure Con...breathe, in, out, relax, you know the drill,' he said acidly, smiling cautiously, taking a short step backward.

Connie let out a loud sigh and held her forehead. 'Oh Jesus,' she wheezed, realising there wasn't going to be a denial, just confirmation of the depth of his insanity.

Becker was unrepentant, continuing in a flood, quite matter-of-factly. 'Phase one is proving the deposit, phase two is mining the deposit, and believe me it can be—'

Sweet Jesus, she thought as he started speaking. The pressure in her throat was too much. This guy was stone cold bonkers. 'It can't be done!' Connie shrieked, crossing her arms roughly across her chest and feeling the thump of her heart, maintaining a menacing glare at Becker who didn't flinch.

'Just hear me out!' He fired back just as loud. Connie's mouth was still open and it stayed open as though Becker's words had physically attacked her. Taking a calming breath, he continued in a more measured voice, 'okay...look, so rhodium ore will be sorted sub-ice, the high-grade shipped back once a month in our research vessel, the Mondiali. We transfer it to Mangala ore-trains that empty at Port Warren, ship the rhodium back to Mangala then finally, back to Warren with the Mangala copper and gold.' He lifted an eyebrow, 'did you know that Mangala will report a rhodium find in the next year or so? It's a rare earth mine so all is kosher.' The other eyebrow lifted as well, both going higher, testifying to his brilliance.

Connie scrutinised him mutely for a few seconds before giving it to him. Any self-control had been ruined by his obsessive disdain for logic and his infuriating, ill-conceived bluster. 'Oh, this is not happening,' she said, cradling her head, then lifting her chin to eyeball him, wondering what rusted gears were turning inside that bulbous head of his. 'That is such unmitigated horseshit I don't even know where to begin. It's such convoluted lunacy...look I know you have some smarts about mining but you're so blinded you're not thinking straight.' Fucking right angles she meant to say. Connie pushed her head toward him sharply, 'hello?' Connie felt like knocking on his head, fully expecting sawdust to career from his ears. Sighing long and heavy, she said, 'for a start, the pyroxene matrix is foreign to the geology up there...how many people will you need to bankroll to pull it off, and what about collectors? They'll get hold of them, no mine in the world has ever stopped specimen leakage. They'll know straight away it's not Mangala matrix, then it's over.' She cocked her head at him, disbelieving. 'The idea is beyond crazy, it's got so many missing pieces, holes, chasms in it...I...Jesus.' Connie stopped and studied him with contemptuous amusement. 'The fact that you're even considering this is...I don't know what it is. Exploration is nuts. Okay, it's possible...but seriously, mining? That's dead-set insanity.'

'Risk and reward Connie,' he said confidently. 'Risk and—'

'It's all fucking risk,' she snapped. 'There won't be a reward, just a goddamn gaol term, financial destruction and personal humiliation.' She'd had enough, he'd fallen off whatever grid he had a tenuous grip on, there was no point wasting breath. Bloody jerk, she said to herself bitterly, pondering again whether she should just up and go, keep going until she was on the other side of the Harbour Bridge. Then she'd turn around, flip the bird and catch a ferry to the airport. Connie backed away from him and walked over to the far wall.

'I'll say it again for those not listening,' Becker declared loudly, 'you only live once and I ain't departing without rolling the dice.' He ambled deliberately back to the map of Antarctica, angling his head toward Marie Byrd in the west, blocking out the irritating white noise in the corner. Becker was sure she had something stuck up her arse, she was so effing tedious and unimaginative. 'Take a risk girl,' he said, knowing he should let it slide for a bit but screw it he thought, repeating what he said before. 'You only live once, right?'

'Yeah, and I'll be goddamned if I want to spend it bankrupt in bloody lock up,' Connie said, watching Joe then pulling her eyes back to Becker who looked so much like a street corner nutter, all wild hair, blazing eyes, bullshit opinions. Despite it all, Connie knew what the way forward was, at least for his so-called Phase 1. Phase 2 was a steaming cow pat that was so on the nose it was indescribable. No way it could be allowed to happen. Connie bit her lip, trying to keep her voice under control, feeling a deep sense of wrongness. 'If we go we have equal say in what happens over there.' It wasn't a question.

Becker's face spread into a boyish grin, 'of course, you both have equal say, equal rights, you'll always have my ear,' he said, eyeing Connie hopefully, squirming a bit, 'I need you guys on my side…on my team.' Becker pushed home an inferred advantage, standing straighter, rocking back on his heels, waiting for the final judgement, holding his breath.

Connie took a few measured breaths, glancing up at the CCTV cam on the ceiling. She looked at the wooden plaque that was slightly askew on the wall and was reminded how much she liked the short verse.

"Geology gave us the immensity of time
and taught us how little of it our own species has occupied."

She always thought it was odd that a biologist and pop-scientist like SJ Gould would end up penning her favourite quote. Blinking almost in slow motion she zoned back to Becker who was watching her, surveying her cautiously. Oh God she thought, the words were coming out, she could feel them in her throat, jagged, chaffing. 'This is stupid, dangerous, suicidal but you know what Becker…we'll go.' She glanced at Joe who looked seriously pained. 'Against all our instincts we'll go, if only to stop you from making Becker fuck ups and coming back in ankle chains and handcuffs.'

Becker smiled slowly and broadly. 'Not much of an acceptance speech but it'll do,' he said, holding up a thumb.

'Don't push it, we're going for us, not you, best you remember that.'

'Committed to memory,' Becker said, touching his ear, 'anyway, let's have a drink, celebrate the union!' His mouth twisted into a cock-eyed grin that spoke to deep satisfaction.

Connie half-smiled, half-sneered back at him. This big boned goose was an arrogant shit with a ballistic dose of OCD but she couldn't help admiring the bastard. If he wanted something, apparently he was irresistible.

Becker grabbed three glasses, pouring a generous slug of expensive whisky in each.

'I need some detail on Phase 1 Becker, so I can start a risk assessment,' Connie said a little shakily, not sure where to start but the when had to be right now. Having committed in voice, she was immediately dazed by the possibilities, the nightmares that might lie ahead of them. Connie would focus on the broader hazards, then work her way down the ever-steepening cliff toward the probable disaster below. Thin ice, she knew, chewing on the irony frostily. Connie had already visualised so many perils they were clotting in her mind like an over-floured pie. Afterall, their support network was premised on a truckload of US dollars Becker had thrown at GeoTek which gave her zero comfort. 'Your boys from Turkey will do your bidding because you've paid them so much coin but you understand that Joe and I, we're not like that, right?' She flashed a cold smile, feeling seriously conflicted about their decision to go. 'We're going to assess every detail of your little op, without the lip service. Hopefully we'll stop you and your site team from fucking things up too badly.'

'Sure, since you put it so quaintly, absolutely,' he said, rolling his eyes. 'I'll send you the full mission layout and ops schedule by email, but I can run through it now if you like.'

Connie bent her head slightly forward, 'I wanna see detail, the mission specs, not listen to you drone on about the false positives.' She squinted at him scornfully.

Becker pretended to look hurt, 'hey, no fair. I'll give you an unbiased summary, no more, no less…no lies. You can look at the reports later, cross-check me on the bullshit meter.'

'Fine, whatever,' Connie conceded, 'but I'll need another dram of your million-dollar whisky first.'

Becker reached for the bottle, throwing a decent slug into her glass. Joe watched them curiously. She and Becker were like an old married couple although Connie was decades younger and a shitload better looking.

Draining his glass, Becker wiped his mouth, feeling a buzz from the alcohol. He smiled warmly at Connie who stared back vacantly, waiting for his rundown of this so-called plan his overpaid pals in Eurasia had devised. 'Right,' he said, nodding seriously, 'we fly into Marie Bird in a converted C-17 Globemaster I picked up from the Soviets—'

'…W-wait, what, fly in?' Joe said, interrupting, 'I assumed you'd be boating in…what will something that big land on?' He felt a muscle in his jaw twitch as he battled with the image, visualising a metal block dropping onto ice-cream. 'That's a big arse plane.'

Becker smiled again, raising his chin smugly, 'all organised Joe, we have a two-kilometre blue-ice runway topped with snow pavement, facing into the katabatic winds of the glacier. We're good to land with a weight of four hundred and fifty thousand pounds. It's a drop and go – they land, stop, we demount, go. Then we're on our own in every sense, so self-sufficiency is paramount.' He peeked expectantly at Connie, hoping she was impressed with all the forethought, but she was looking down at her hands, nibbling on her bottom lip, looking tense, squirming, counting the risks, already out of fingers and toes.

Becker continued in a flood of words, 'by the time we land, the shields and base camp will be in place. It's all quite remarkable,' he said, thrusting his chest out proudly. 'The shields are snow-coloured woven aramid fibres, that's sort of like Kevlar to you civvies. It'll protect us and mask our movements. We can work freely without concern, no one will see us from the air or from more than a few hundred metres away on the ground.'

Joe and Connie both snorted, almost in unison. They could see Becker had it all boxed up in his mind, a cute little package with a pink bow tied right on top, all colourful and cute.

'It's all donuts and sprinkles … right,' Connie said in a sharply sarcastic tone.

'Trust me,' Becker said with his mouth pushed slightly up, looking relaxed.

'I trust that you have OCD and you can't help yourself.'

He groaned something unintelligible.

'Because we're going doesn't mean we agree with any of this,' she said, giving an exaggerated eye roll, then meeting his gaze squarely.

Becker took a moment to draw a decent breath and settle a bit, pretty sure going harder right now would end in a painful escalation. 'Okay, okay… just understand that everything's been planned for,' he said calmly, firmly. 'There'll be a team of ten onsite when we arrive, eight engineers from GeoTek and two rockhounds, Ronnie Lehman and Vernon.'

'Shit, you roped them in on this?' Joe said in a higher vocal pitch, 'I can't believe it…how much did you pay them? They're not risk takers, in fact they're safety wowsers really.'

'I paid them plenty but they were pretty damn excited when I explained all this, and delighted when I asked them to sign up,' Becker said smugly, giving Connie a subtle wink.

'Pretty damn excited to be millionaires you mean,' Connie murmured, tapping a foot, ticked off by Becker's ability to just buy whatever, whoever he wanted.

'So I encouraged them with a bit of green, big deal…it's business, that's how it rolls.'

'It's criminal is what it is.'

'I buy things, it's what I do.'

'Yeah well, situation normal then,' Connie added, wrinkling her nose, 'if you've got it … use it, leave your morals at the door, right?'

'Buying their services is not a crime, just a means to an end,' Becker shot back irritably.

'Oh God, I get that, but this here is a crime,' she said, flourishing her arms in the direction of his laptop. 'And while I'm struggling to believe it, Joe and I are onboard and if we manage to pull it off, well that's just your dumb luck.'

Becker cleared his throat roughly, looking briefly heavenward, despite Connie's religious protestations. 'It'll take three days to drill to bedrock assuming the sonic system does what GeoTek has promised. They've guaranteed it you know—'

'Oh seriously, wake up you oaf. How can you possibly guarantee what you don't understand?' Connie said with incredulity, 'it's not—'

'Any fucking way,' Becker interrupted loudly, 'then they'll install the portable light towers and the electric Inclinator car that will run on Santoprene tracks all the way to ground zero.'

'A car? Seriously Becker, on a descent that steep? Have you got any—'

'It's a funicular,' he said wearily, 'you know, like a cable car, the carriage stays horizontal even though the slope is, well…half way to straight down I guess.'

'And this one's special, right?' Connie lifted an eyebrow quizzically.

'Well yeah,' he said, 'very special, actually, comes with all the trimmings money can buy, except air conditioning.' He grinned sarcastically. 'So, at ground zero a small chamber will be bored out and we'll set up the corer, the bedrock EMAR system and see what we've got.' Becker turned and gazed wistfully at his rock, Connie could see the primal desire wipe the smugness from his face, leaving only a lingering frustration.

'So that's it,' Becker finished up, 'you can read the PDF which sets everything out in detail but remember, nothing leaves the building, paper, electronic, whatever. It's encrypted to our private keys but we can't take any chances. Secrecy is paramount.'

***

Becker needed to phone GeoTek, give them the go for Phase 1 and transfer the entire one hundred and fifty million into their Jersey bank account. They'd guaranteed a start date thirty days after that, per the confidential heads of agreement, the only copy buried in his hidden basement safe.

'Everything will be there when we arrive,' Becker said, 'food, accommodation, equipment, snow-gear. Nothing has been overlooked.'

'Yep, well we'll see, you can keep saying that, it's the eating that counts,' Connie said, shuffling slowly toward the door.

'Always the pragmatist Con. Have faith and you shall be rewarded,' he drawled loudly, having consumed too much of his top shelf liquor.

Connie stopped, turning back to him, unable to restrain herself. 'Rewarded with what? A one-way ticket to prison, to bankruptcy…food stamps? Get a bloody grip,' she said testily, stepping through the door and disappearing.

Joe was next to her, struggling to keep up as she marched off down the corridor, his vision blurring and then fading in and out. 'What have we done?' He puffed, holding his forehead, continuing toward their offices, struggling with the scope of what lay before them at the south of the planet.

'We've done what we had to do,' Connie said evenly. 'I don't want to do it any more than you but if we don't it's gonna end in a tragedy on so many levels.' She glanced at him, tilting her head from side to side. 'With both of us on board he's got a chance, more importantly Joe, we've got a chance.'

'What about this Phase 2 stuff?' Joe said, disbelief squeezed into the furrows on his face. 'Surely he can't be serious with that.' Joe knew it was madness that could never be allowed to see the light of day.

'That can't happen…won't happen,' Connie said flatly, 'I mean, disguising the rhodium as Mangala ore? Finding it, proving it might work if we're really lucky but mining and moving the ore, nu-uh. If we can't talk him out of it he's on his own. Chances of that working are zero. I'll out him to the Feds on that one…fucking watch me.' She blew out her cheeks, rattling her lips. This was a find only mission to free the fool of his demonic possession, if it was there or not, this was a once only exorcism.

They eyed each other deliberately, mutely attesting to the extent of Becker's mania - the OCD, craziness or whatever it was derailing his higher brain. The part of his noodle supposedly there to balance risk and reward was clearly dead or at best a cream-puff weakling, totally shut out by his Hippocampus. Becker didn't seem to give a crap if it landed him in gaol or left him penniless.

Connie reached her office and waved bye to Joe distractedly. She collapsed into her chair and gazed at the picture of her and Becker, shoulder to shoulder, smiling in front of the massive hole in the ground that was the Maranga Superpit near Coober Pedy. Her world started to spin, her eyes prickling with moisture. 'What happened to you Carson?' She said out loud to herself, laying her head back and closing her eyes, agonising over events that would start unfolding in less than a month. Opening the PDF attachment, she saw "Mission 45" in big bold print at the top. 'Christ,' Connie breathed, feeling her pulse thud unpleasantly in her throat as she scrutinised the plot for the horror story Becker was about to drop them into.

4. Mission 45

"Adventure is just bad planning" ~ *Roald Amundsen*

The first glimpse of their Antarctic transport hadn't failed to impress, because, like Joe had so succinctly put it, it was a big arse plane. The three of them walked along the tarmac toward the rear cargo hatch, four Pratt & Whitney engines performing ear-rattling run-up as they approached. The hatch was fully deployed and rested on the runway like a giant metal tongue in the early morning heat, and it was a killer, the fourth scorcher in a row to hit Australia's largest city.

Connie was bug-eyed at the aircraft, a gorgeous clean-skin C-17 Globemaster III, fully fifty-three metres in length and a similar dimension across the wings, pure alpine in colour, perfectly matched to their icy destination. She was struggling to believe this goliath would actually land on top of the ice and not have its wheels sink hopelessly into it, ripping it apart. The C-17 was normally deployed for strategic airlifts but this beauty was on its way to execute the worst crime ever committed on the South Pole. With a chest thud that shook her entire body, she realised it was piracy, pure and simple, something she'd never considered. Connie the Pirate, she brooded, vaguely amused, wondering half seriously if it was too late to sprint back to the departure lounge and hide among the baggage, seeking diplomatic immunity from the crazy fuck called Becker.

The three of them stepped over the gentle ridge of the cargo hatch and walked up the incline into a huge silver tunnel packed with hundreds of crates and boxes. Connie saw folded seats along either side of the cabin, noticing how spartan and unpadded they were, mentally bracing for a disagreeable flight. She could feel her mind spinning, gawking at the equipment, stewing on where she was, what would be waiting for them when the damn thing landed.

'Got it for a song,' Becker said with a satisfied smile. 'Soviets sold it for ninety million,' he scoffed, 'it's only three years old, less than half price…chlen golova!' He laughed to himself. 'That's Russian for dickheads…I'd have paid a hundred and twenty.'

'You really are quite the negotiator,' Connie said thinly.

'Appreciate it,' he said with a smirk and a wink. 'Although negotiating with Ivan is like shooting goldfish in a bowl, no skill required, just US dollars,' he chuckled more indulgently, looking for all the world like he was propped on a bar stool sharing a few drinks with his mates, not a frigging care in the world. Connie couldn't believe how calm he was. Here they were about to sail off on some bootless errand to rape a country under generational quarantine and he was cracking jokes like a bozo jetting off on a Caribbean holiday.

Becker motioned them to the metal seats, showing them how to buckle up using the army style belts and a few minutes later the cockpit door opened with a loud crack, allowing egress to a rather rotund pilot who strode toward them ominously. 'We'll be taking off in seven minutes Mr Becker, you all belted, good to go?'

'Absolutely, good to go,' Becker confirmed, 'don't forget the snow chains after take-off,' he added unnecessarily.

'Baz is looking forward to it,' the plump man said, grinning knowingly.

'Yeah right,' Becker replied lightly, conscious of what a rotten job it was.

To make sure the plane had enough stopping power on the ice, one of the pilots had to descend into the wheel wells after take-off and manually fix snow chains to half of the eighteen tires. A sweaty two-hour nightmare in a pressurised suit that Becker wouldn't wish it on his worst enemy.

'Shit,' Connie blurted, startled by the sudden thud of the cargo flap as it lifted off the tarmac and started closing with a loud, hydraulic whir. It shut tight with a metallic thump as they started taxiing toward the head of the runway.

Joe felt a little out of breath, uncomfortably so, as his brain buzzed and his heart punched a gentle beat in the back of his throat. Apart from despising flying, it was what lay at the end of the journey that was the kicker. They knew a lot about the mission from the expedition manifesto prepared by GeoTek but it was ground truthing he knew would bring the real horror. Nothing was certain, not in a wilderness as lethal as the west of Antarctica. Angling his neck back he rested it on the metal superstructure of the cabin, battling with his mind.

Connie hated flying even more than Joe, especially in something as sterile and empty as this monster. Everyone from her mum to her ex-boyfriend had told her a hundred times it was safer than driving a car or crossing the goddamn road. Yeah, yeah, whatever, she would reply churlishly, that was all fine and dandy, but in a car, you didn't plummet for ten minutes in a death dive, contemplating your demise along with hundreds of other screaming idiots. That is until you collided with the ground and were burnt alive in jet fuel. Cop that she'd fire back! Air travel was for assholes who wanted to run the odds on dying in the worst way imaginable.

Connie copied Joe and lay her head on the cold metal wall of the plane, closing her eyes, wanting to sleep or at least give her emotions a breather. Becker was back to his normal self, staring like a hoot owl at his love buddy, the shapely geological map of Antarctica. On it he'd scrawled in black letters; Lat N 79.78 Long E 142.66 with a red circle marking the centre of the anomaly, where the EMAR response peaked. He hadn't blinked, moved or even stirred an eyebrow for as long as she'd been watching him; bereft of anything suggesting life. She was sure he used the map for a blanket at night, and maybe other things she didn't want to contemplate. It was his cherished companion, ironically moth eaten and stained like an old pirate map.

'Becker…look at me,' Connie said softly, 'you're gonna bore straight through that map if you don't stop mooning at it. And I'll be left to pick up the pieces, hand you tissues and the like.' She grinned at him, wiggling her eyebrows.

Becker was about to respond when his cell rang.

'Becker,' he said aggressively.

'Hello Peter.' Becker glanced at Connie and mouthed Weems as he listened to the voice on the other end. Among other things, Peter Weems was an experimental physicist and head of the GeoTek team at Byrd Base. Becker sucked in a breath and held it, then blew it out loudly, frowning steeply at his cell. Momentary silence was broken by his thunderous voice. 'For fuck's sake! What about the Yeti Robot – you used it, right?' He placed his hand on his forehead which was suddenly burnished red. 'Oh Jesus, to save time…really? You were told to follow safety protocols to the fucking letter, now we're about to start…we lose three men?' He shook his head in disbelief, peering out the window blindly as the plane gathered speed up the runway. 'Shit!' He yelled, looking mortified. 'Shit, shit shit!' He pounded a fist into his thigh, glowering at his phone.

Connie's heart lurched as she processed it. Three dead…was the mission done already? She immediately recalled Becker's cheap claims that everything had been planned for. What a crock of shit, in Antarctica or anywhere for that matter, planning only mitigated risk. Unplannables bite you on the arse, plan, no plan, best strategy ever, whatever. And what the hell was a Yeti Robot?

'Okay Peter, we'll be there in five hours, just follow the goddamn rules.' He ended the call, reluctantly looking at Joe, then Connie. 'Do not fucking say I told you so because this is one of those things you can't plan for…rookie stupidity.'

'I told you so Becker, I really did,' Connie said, ignoring him, drawing her lips back in a snarl. 'I fucking *so* told you so.'

'Seriously, how could they screw it up so bad?' He said, massaging the bridge of his nose. 'Frigging idiots. Three of the crew were ground-truthing trig calcs for the decline so it hits bedrock at peak EMAR. No virgin ground is walked on, breathed on without the Yeti Robot doing it first. It's got ground penetrating radar that detects crevasses, slides and the like, but did the dumb fuckers use it?' He looked vacantly at Connie, searching for an answer, blinking rapidly. 'No, these boys knew better, they just trotted onto the glacier like they wanted to chuck a footy around…fell through the ice, kept falling for another five hundred metres. They wanted to save time and nobody stopped them, can you believe that shit?' Becker threw his hands up, fists balled, 'all of 'em, including those three, were trained to watch out for each other, guard against dumb decisions. We have redundancies to prevent stupidity…so what the hell happened down there?' He swung his head from side to side and expelled a huge, cranky sigh.

'What happened you ask?' Connie said, nodding slowly, 'well…you happened Becker.' She looked directly at him, eyes narrow and accusing.

'This is what we were talking about,' Joe said. 'You can plan this stuff to whatever level of detail you like but there's too much chaos going on to guarantee anything. There's unpredictable elements, stuff that just happens, interplays of factors, conditions, probability that could have any number of outcomes.'

'You're screwed Becker,' Connie said with a malicious sneer, 'that's what he's trying to say, he's just too polite to drop it on you.' She shrugged, smiling at Joe, mouthing "sorry".

'Bullshit,' Becker responded, curling his lip threateningly. Small setbacks happen, I get that, so should you. Nothing in the field is perfect—'

'Small setback, she said, regarding him with distaste. 'My God…you're serious, aren't you? Three men, three men are gone…that's almost ten percent of your entire team.' She glared at him, mouth agape, her huge brown eyes radiating contempt.

'We can cover them – it's not a problem.'

'Oh for the love of, do you even care that these men are dead, on *your* mission…on *your* ham-fisted watch?'

Becker didn't fight back because he was happy to relent, and she was at least partially right, not to mention ready to beat him to death. That said, Connie's righteous posturing pissed him off because she knew the risks of exploration as well as he did. Legal, illegal, it didn't matter, risks were risks. When safeguards were broken, people died, especially in Antarctica because the environment was so hazardous. It was one thing on a mine site but this was a whole other world of hurt if you bent the rules. Basically, it was take care, respect the place, follow the rules, or you were screwed. Screwed meant dead.

5. Base Camp

"It was like visiting Disneyland, Las Vegas and Mars simultaneously" ~ *Victor Boyarsky*

Becker gawked at Connie, a smile ruffling the corners of his mouth, 'take a gander,' he said, waving his arms a little, then stabbing at the glass.

Connie took a deep breath, trying to steady herself as she caught her first glimpse of the white continent, stunned by the breathtaking view from her window.

They were flying over broken ice sheets that looked like they'd been shattered into pieces with a mighty hammer, stretching for hundreds of kilometres, and veiled by the haze of distance was Antarctica itself; colossal, incredible, the last true wilderness on the planet. And they were going there to dig the damn thing up, kilometres of it, with a tunnel that would impale the glacier at forty-five degrees. Pirating, Connie needed no reminder, shifting slightly in her seat.

Taking in the incredible, pristine virginity, Joe couldn't believe what their mission would soon have them doing. It seemed so wrong on so many levels...sort of like slaughtering a seal cub and defiantly crying research. Maybe they could club a few penguins to death while they were there, do the job properly.

In the distance, they saw a vaguely geometric form start to take shape in the whiteout, becoming gradually clearer as they approached, incised into the landscape like an ancient Nazca line. It was the airstrip but it was way too conspicuous Connie reckoned, suddenly feeling like the plane was closing in on her. This was supposed to be an op as covert as they came, so like…what the hell? She felt exposed and anxious as though eyes were all over them, waiting for their monster to drop so they could haul them away to lock up at McMurdo. Connie closed her eyes, deliberately slowing her breathing and gripping the sides of her seat until her knuckles went white, waiting for catastrophe.

'Welcome to Basecamp,' Becker said with a gleam in his eye, pointing through the window nearest to Connie.

Joe looked and saw squat, there was ice, some boulders, a dark outcropping of rock in the distance but that was it. 'Um, where?' He said, puzzled, figuring it was camouflaged from the air but sure that there would be at least some sign of it, especially from this close.

'Well I guess that means they did a good job.' Becker said, glancing at Connie with an expectant look, brows riding high.

'Oh Jesus, you want a compliment, maybe a slap on the back? We can't see it so…are you sure it's there?' She said, turning her mouth down. 'Maybe your GeoTek boys are hamming it up in Costa Rica, spending your hard earned money on tequila and fighting cocks.' Her sarcastic smile was right in his face now. 'Or maybe it's in the wrong place…next to McMurdo…oops,' she said, putting a finger to her lips.

'You know it Con. Look…down there,' he said, pointing with his eyes this time. 'It's there, trust me.'

'Okay mister wizard,' Connie taunted, 'what about the bloody runway? It's more obvious than your lack of humility. If we can see it so can anyone else.' Her voice was edged with uncertainty.

'Relax, we're in Marie Byrd, there's no one within hundreds of clicks of this place, as soon as they drop and go, the boys will cover it over…everything's been considered.'

She continued to glare doubtfully, murmuring expletives under her breath as Becker's hollow words bounced around the metal interior of the plane. 'I'll remind you of that when things turn sour.' Connie broke away, looking through the window at the pale surface, wondering if this Byrd Base was really down there like he said. It was just unbroken whiteness for as far as she could see. It beggared belief.

Bobbing his head around, Joe was surveying the airstrip nervously as his doubts grew. 'You sure we can land this thing down there…looks pretty, uh…soft,' he said, avoiding eye contact.

Glancing at Connie he could see she wasn't doing much better than he was. Neither of them seriously expected to land in one piece, it just seemed so unlikely that something this massive could skid along on top of the ice and not sink in like a fork through cheesecake.

Connie's hands were trembling so she clutched them tightly together, squashing them between her knees. 'You sure this'll work?' She gave Becker a nervous half-glance.

'Piece of piss,' Becker shot back calmly. 'These things have landed in the mountains in Afghanistan and Kathmandu, the ice down there is rock hard, trust me. These guys can land in places you wouldn't think are possible, they hardly ever crash,' Becker said, grinning sideways at Connie, chuckling ever so slightly.

She ignored him, tilting her head down at the metal floor, clenching her core muscles tight. Arsehole, she thought, hating him for being so irritatingly calm. She jumped as the whir of the wing flaps rumbled through the fuselage, increasing camber and lift as the plane readied itself for a low speed landing. She lurched again when the wheels seemed to explode into place beneath them. 'Fuck, shit,' she blurted, holding both hands even tighter between her legs, staring down at the floor again. 'If this fucker crashes Becker I'm using you as a human shield.' Her face was ashen as the blood drained away.

'Happy with that,' he grinned back, delighting in her terror.

The huge plane slowed alarmingly, pitching steeply and banking to the left. The pilot adjusted the ailerons to yaw the plane into the runway, wings-down in a sideslip approach to counter the savage crosswinds.

'Is this normal?' Connie said shakily as the plane continued to bank steeply. The noise inside was horrendous. She tried to swallow the acid in her throat, ending up coughing violently.

'Right out of the polar handbook,' Becker shouted back. 'This is how they do it down here. Just breathe, relax. Wheels down in one minute.'

The plane touched down with only the slightest bump as though they'd pushed into only slightly yielding ice on landing. In reality, the snow pavement wasn't much softer than concrete thanks to the positive weather conditions that allowed the layers of pavement to crystallise and bond with the hard blue-ice glacier.

The rear cargo hatch was already deploying as the plane taxied slowly back to the top of the runway, carefully avoiding the tyre tracks that were left on landing. Men appeared from nowhere in thick white Arctic parkers, gathering crates in a scene of manic activity, moving them off the plane and onto large snowmobiles. Connie assumed these were the transports to basecamp, wherever the hell that was. She flung her head around again, still seeing nothing, just ice everywhere and men dressed in white. Connie was sweating despite the cold.

Departing the plane in single file, Connie was instantly overwhelmed by the up-close and personal vista of Antarctica, the clear blue sky, dazzling whiteness of the ice, the burnished chocolate mountains that punctuated the horizon ahead of them.

'It's amazing Joe, I mean I knew it would be beautiful from the pictures, but not like this.' She pressed her fingers into her cheeks and slowly shook her head in disbelief.

'Er, yeah, stunning,' he said distractedly, shoving his hands deep into his pockets, '…but like, where the hell is basecamp?' Joe didn't give a rat's ass about the view, he just wanted cover from whoever might be watching them, maybe waiting for them to dig themselves deep enough to prove their criminal guilt beyond doubt.

Becker came striding over, pointing at the air above Connie's shoulder. 'Over there. Come,' he said, gesturing them to follow, punching through the shallow ice until a contrast gradually gathered form.

'The shielding is, well…pretty awesome I guess,' Connie conceded, walking within a few metres of what looked like a huge cream coloured entry.

The structure was composed of four shields overlapping above the base itself, supported by six smaller shields that locked under the top structure, weaving around the base to the ground. It looked like a tremendous white mollusc with an intricate multi-layered shell that had somehow been picked up and dropped onto the ice.

Becker bent down and pulled up the roller door with a grunt, walking inside to something that on first sight seemed impossible. Joe likened it to opening the door of the Tardis for the first time and finding an entire world inside something the size of a phone box. To be confronted with so much space and commotion in the midst of "nothing" was quite incredible. From a few tens of metres away it was invisible but now it was like Atlantis had magically bubbled up from the depths of the glacier.

Connie opened her mouth and kept it open as she got her first gawp at the chamber within, seeing Becker doting like a proud father, pointing here and there, gloating and crowing. 'How on Earth did you do all this?' She hoisted a single eyebrow, her mind spiralling as she fought to take it all in and process it. Becker had his tongue out, rubbing his thumb against his two forefingers. 'Money, of course, why did I ask?' She said, smacking her forehead lightly. No way she thought it was going to be like this though, her mind's-eye told her it'd be some ramshackle tumbledown, but this was so much more than that, a lush, fertile mirage in a harsh desert wilderness, except this was as real as it got.

The showstopper was a gleaming white behemoth recumbent in the middle of the hidden expanse. "Mother fuck" was all Connie could come up with, sinking into stunned silence as she grappled with the dizzying image. Front and centre was the superstructure of a mighty A380 Airbus, the colour of freshly driven snow, clipped of its wings, a tremendous flightless bird prostrate on the icy tundra. Around it were hundreds of crates of food, tonnes of mechanical equipment including two massive fuel-powered generators, polar clothing on several racks, and everything else needed for their extended stay on the glacier.

'The Airbus is our Palazzo de Pole,' Becker quipped with a crooked smile, pleased that he'd impressed with basecamp, more so because it was organised in such a ridiculously short time. 'Come,' he repeated eagerly, gesturing with a flourish as he started tracking toward the side of the aircraft, leaving shallow footprints in the ice. 'We've got the upper deck, the crew have the lower deck. Look around, no expense spared, especially for you two…first class all the way.'

'I see you secured the penthouse Becker,' Connie taunted, 'I'll try and be surprised.'

Hey, you got it too, it ain't just me up there,' he said, all smiles and sparkling eyes. Christ, Connie pondered, scraping a hand through her hair and sighing. All this positivity made her deeply uneasy. The single, only reason to smile and mean it was when they disembarked back in Sydney, everything else should be game face. The Pole was no place for levity and backslapping, at least until the reason you were there was under lock and key, then she could look forward to placing her two size fours back on Australian soil, smiling, and fucking meaning it.

Walking into the lower section, they could see the aircraft had been gutted and given a major work over. Thick insulation covered the entire inside of the aircraft, separate rooms created for living, working, eating and even a bloody rec room with billiard tables! A similar setup existed on the upper level although the makeover was considerably more luxurious with soft chairs, fur-lined bed clothes and a miniature electric heater in each compartment.

Becker ushered them to a room on the top deck where they found Peter Weems waiting for them, a painfully thin man with cavernous wrinkles in his forehead and bushy eyebrows that were nigh on comical. His age was indeterminate, he could've been fifty, maybe eighty but one thing Joe was sure of, this dude had to be an undertaker, maybe moonlighting as one. Ops Manager by day, bury the bodies at night, no dramas.

Weems spoke with an air of authority, appearing calm and intelligent which Connie was grateful for because this is the last place you needed an inexperienced junior or an overconfident goofball directing things. She had a supersized image of Becker in mind when she visualised goofball. Simple association she knew.

'What about the men?' Becker asked, lifting his chin sternly.

'Bodies are gone,' Weems said with little emotion, 'the crevasse was so deep we had to use ranging radar to find 'em. They're almost half a click down, frozen solid like sea ice.'

'Jesus,' Connie said, lowering her head, 'poor sods.'

Stupid sods,' Weems said without empathy, peering curiously at Connie. 'If you don't follow the rules out there you're done. There's no second chances, unless you do things by the numbers, this place is a goddamn death trap.'

Becker tapped in, 'Good advice, you two best take note, it could save your lives out there. In here we're fine, subsurface ice is monitored around the clock by microwave sensors and altimeters but when we get under the ice and outside the compound, remember those words.'

Connie was silent, unhappy with Weems lack of empathy but relieved to hear Becker's words of caution. Serious Becker was way more comforting than the other dick, she mused, as a thunderous roar rumbled over the base, the C-17 clawing its way back into the sky and soaring above the rocky peaks that separated the western ice mass from the east. She was surprised it was back in the air already, recalling the hundreds of crates and other crap that had been aboard; a little disconcerted that the only way off the Pole had just left in a massive spray of jet fuel and ice. She visualised the runway being hastily covered over, pushing her clammy hands fully into her pockets, gulping involuntarily, her freezing breath catching in her throat as she surveyed their unnerving isolation.

'Okay Pete, what do you say?' Becker said, craning his head forward and nodding.

'I say we're go for Phase I,' he said, looking down his nose. 'Everything's ready, all the infrastructure's complete, drilling rig's assembled, tested, signed off, all systems are nominal. Deployment for tomorrow morning is as scheduled.' He squinted, peering around the room, adjusting his collar. 'Drilling to bedrock should take two days, that's eight kilometres in forty-eight hours.' He glared at each of them in turn. Undertaker smacked back at Joe again, forcing him to shake his head to try and lose the image. Weems summoned a brittle smile. 'The sublimation rig is incredible, the engineers tested it on the blue ice rise over by Josh's Bluff and it was like a hot knife through butter, just steam and a bloody big hole,' he said with as much enthusiasm as they'd heard from this strange, severe man.

'That rig is our ace in the hole,' Becker said, grinning at Connie, fairly beaming with pride.

Connie's half smile descended into a scowl as she watched him enthuse over his little toy like the job was already done. Bozo Becker was back. 'We haven't even started and you're acting like we've actually achieved something,' Connie said, looking away briefly with calculated disdain. 'For Christ's sake would you get real, everything's in front of us, not a goddamn thing has been accomplished.' She stabbed him with her eyes. 'You need to get serious and stay serious or we'll all die out here, or get nabbed by the bloody Feds.'

Becker rocked back a bit on his heels, appraising her quizzically. 'Well yes ma'am,' he said, saluting her crisply, clicking his heels together, stifling a smirk unsuccessfully.

'Arsehole,' she spat with zero humour. It was starting, she knew it. They were fucked.

Tunnelling through more than two kilometres of ice at a forty-five-degree angle meant the length of the decline would be slightly over eight kilometres. Once complete and fitted with the tracks and the base-camp vehicle, the Inclinator could travel at twelve clicks per hour if maxed, taking around fifty minutes to travel from surface to bedrock base. Of course that was assuming all went well, which meant no disasters and there were so many possibilities. So they needed to be slow, meticulous, careful with everything they did, keep Becker on a short leash and hope to God they had a massive dose of luck.

'So what, we just hang around while the drill does its thing?' Connie said, 'like for two days…and do what?' She crossed her arms, a little nonplussed. 'There better be a tennis court or golf course out there.' Looking at him she chewed the inside of her cheek, grinning oh so faintly.

'You suck at ball sports so I didn't bother...your ex told me that,' Becker bubbled sarcastically. Chalk one up for me he thought, flashing Connie a cheeky grin.

'Funny,' she murmured, looking irritated but keeping her mouth shut, too busy pondering the next two days in this godforsaken deep freeze.

'Funny and true,' he said, with a strange expression on his face, 'like Penang, remember cocktails at the pool bar with those lawyers. Arrested for nudity...now that's funny and true,' Becker said, waving a hand at her, still smiling widely, ignoring Joe who looked mortified, shaking his head, trying to warn him off.

'You fucking prat Becker,' she said, squaring him up with a hateful stare, wondering why he'd brought it up. It was no joke and he damn well knew it. Even so many years later it still played on her mind. She'd gotten drunk, disrobed on the beach for a dare, Becker's fucking dare, and in the greatest humiliation of her life, been caught by the local Polis. Connie was hauled off to a crowded cell in Georgetown full of local drunks and other smelly itinerants. The thing she remembered most wasn't the dank smell or the groping, it was the kid who looked so different from the rest of them, disturbingly so. He wore crisp dark clothing and stood motionless in the corner of the cell, staring at her with the most starkly blue eyes she'd ever seen. When Becker's fumbling attempts finally got her released, he was still there and she heard him speak but the voice seemed way too mature. The kid couldn't have been more than fifteen but he spoke like a well to do adult, slightly posh accent, British maybe. 'You deserve it,' he'd said in his polished English, adding, 'look at the chaos, disorder, confusion.' He paused momentarily while his eyes intensified to a laser-blue and that's the one thing she'd never forget, the incredible colour, the deepest, most intricate shades of blue imaginable. 'Do you understand what you have done?' He said, the only movement, the rhythmic swirling in his eyes. No one turned or paid the slightest attention to him even though the voice was distinct against the background of chattering Bahasa. He stuck out like the proverbial black sheep, his age, the stark black clothing, eyes, but no one reacted, no one seemed to know he was there, except her. Connie asked the grizzled guard who came to collect her why he was in a cell with grown men and the reply was initially puzzling, then downright terrifying. The guard didn't see him, saying there was "no boy, no boy", proceeding to yap at her, calling her mad, laughing uproariously while pointing his index finger in her face and bustling her up the dark, dirty corridor. Tipsy she may have been but Connie knew damn well what she saw, it stayed with her to this day, a perplexing, troubling memory. The words the kid spoke meant nothing but they were imprinted on her temporal lobe like universal ink.

'Okay, it was a joke, supposed to be, poor taste I get it. Sorry I brought it up. The uh...boy, right?' Becker was annoyed with himself because he knew how much it freaked her out. She was drunk, imagined something and the rest was history. Becker pulled his hand across his face and continued, trying to paint over his boorish screw up. 'So, uh...while the drilling's happening and the decline transport is being installed, we'll be taking specialist advice on machinery operation, troubleshooting, safety protocols, things like that. Joe, you'll be operating the portable diamond corer, Connie, you'll have the spectrometer, ground EMAR and microwave setup.' He smiled boyishly at them, 'so there's plenty of work to do over the next few days...no golf or tennis I'm afraid.'

'Bummer,' Joe said, shooting him a measured grin. 'Need to work on my short game.'

'You just need to work on your game, period,' Becker taunted.

He shook his head, smirking, 'just putting it out there.'

Connie was gazing at the ground and heard none of the to and fro's, stewing over the kid's words in the cellblock, for maybe the hundredth time. She knew it wasn't imagined, no way it was. But if no one else saw him, did that prove it was some hallucinatory meltdown, that her sense of reality was, well...wrong? As a person with some scientific background she had to concede that; but no way she shot back. He was real, her brain was definitive on it, Becker could go fuck himself. And there was something else in there too, a tiny shrill voice stuck between reality and dream state that she couldn't escape, wedged between her reasoning and memory, telling her quite clearly that she was going to die.

*   *   *

34

Day and night were irrelevant at the South Pole. The concepts lost meaning south of the seventy-fifth parallel, their servitude over sleep and wakefulness a distant memory, courtesy of Earth's tilt and where it happened to be on its lonely shuffle around the Sun. It was still Sun up and Sun down but it took its own good time to get around to it.

Connie and Joe continued to be amazed and a little disconcerted by the strange motion of the Sun in the sky, seeming more like an alien star than their own friendly life-giver. Becker had deliberately planned their assault during the permanent daylight of summer and while sometimes it teased with a sliver of torso slipping beneath the horizon, it always popped back up like a cork in the ocean.

Connie purred over the gorgeous sunset colours that came and went, so counter-intuitive to the "normal" world back home. She was grateful they weren't here in winter when months of dusk stretched across the continent with just the ghostly glow of a dawn that never seemed to come.

Their first "day" saw a vicious ice storm descend on the compound and even though the shields were designed to give passage to most of the wind and half the ice, the manual pulley system that freed the build-up was hammering away all night. The poor buggers on the outside had a very uncomfortable time of it. They divided their time between yanking on the white leather release straps before the buildup of ice became too heavy, and then machining away the drifts around the base of the vertical shields.

The next morning, Connie descended the stairs with Joe, seeing a perfectly cloud free sky in the part they could see. It was beautiful, the contrast of the sky and the ice, almost warm at nearly two degrees Celsius. Connie peered through the mesh of the compound at the deep blue sky, feeling the slight warmth in the Sun, her mouth twitching with amusement. 'Bust out the budgie smugglers,' she said brightly, watching her breath condense and disappear in front of her, thinking how perverse it was that this should be considered "warm". Connie looked back at Joe, seeing his brooding expression, watching him rub both temples while staring dreamily at the horizon.

'Hello…anyone home?'

Joe blinked heavily, rocking from one leg to the other, 'er, um yeah,' he said, breathing in shallow gasps. 'You know, uh, this is stupid but it's, uh…getting real.' His pupils were oddly dilated. 'I spent most of last night, uh…thinking this thing through. I barely slept a wink with all the wind, the ice and the like. This here,' he said, peering around wide-eyed, taking a few uncertain steps, 'it won't work, I just don't think it can. You just need to do the math…the odds are so small, Jesus, think about it.' His eyes were riveted on her face, then rolled slowly up to the sky. 'We're in the middle of the harshest unclaimed territory anywhere, using brand new tech, doing it illegally, and I won't even mention immorally.' His eyes burnt from lack of sleep, 'and they're just the bigger issues. If you dig into the detail, well, that's a recipe for clinical anxiety…insomnia.' Joe swore quietly under his breath, feeling his teeth start to chatter. 'People trek through this area you know, rarely, but it happens. What if we're sprung? What happens if there's a knock at the door…explorers or science-types wandering past, like the ones that found his stupid rock? Does Mr all prepared Becker have a contingency plan for that?' He gently rubbed his eyes with the tips of his gloved fingers. 'Does he pay them off and what happens if they tell him to sod off? Do we detain them, and what happens when we're done and need to leave?' Joe gazed at her in blank despair. 'I mean, maybe he'll chuck 'em down the crevasse with the others.' He didn't believe any of it but there were so many loose ends, so much elbow room for disaster it bordered on the incomprehensible. 'And you wonder why I didn't fucking sleep?' He could feel his muscles tense and twitch under his thick clothing.

Connie looked him full in the eye, screwing her face up and sniffing indignantly. 'God, look at you Joe.' She shook her head testily. 'Did you even read the bloody manifest?' Connie asked, knowing he hadn't; clearly hadn't.

'Well uh, yeah…some of it.'

'Well if you'd read all of it you'd know that officially, to anyone who needs to know, such as your random drop-ins, we're a private research team.' She squinted with derision at the hypocrisy of the words. 'We're drilling ice cores to locate sub-glacial lakes that might have microbial potential, quantifying the biodiversity down there. Becker even has a bunch of pretty handouts for any curious explorers who come a knocking. So relax Joe,' she pointed outward to the ice, 'just chill.' She gave him a half smile, patting him gently on the shoulder. 'Read the bloody manifest!'

Joe nodded his head in contrition. 'I'm not big on fiction but I'll read it…sure.'

Becker emerged from the aircraft, descended the stairs two at a time and motored over to them, all whiskers and teeth.

'Morning legends,' he said, the grin blossoming into a broad face splitter. 'You okay Joe? He asked, studying his face, 'you don't look so good, you used the goggles I left for you?'

Joe grunted something, making no eye contact with Becker, looking down at his hands.

'Sleeping while the Sun's out takes a bit of getting used to. It might be dim out, but the reflection off the ice is a killer for sleeping habits,' Becker offered happily.

'I'm fine, thanks,' Joe returned wearily, feeling a bit better knowing there was a contingency of sorts in place, in case some randoms happened along. His anxiety levels were through the roof but eased ever so slightly, his heartbeat, the knot in his throat dialling down just a little bit.

'Drilling's about to start,' Becker said, slapping Joe on the shoulder, pointing in the direction of a heavily partitioned area near the edge of the compound. They could see a break in the ice and beyond it, the glistening gut of freshly cut glacier.

Walking over, both of them goggled at the sheer size of the damn thing, Connie's mouth falling open as she stared at the sapphire beauty of the chasm. Her heart took an almighty leap and started pounding wildly as she realised it would soon enough be the entrance to their world…beneath the mighty glacier. They saw a roughly square hole fully ten metres across, five metres deep and at the bottom was what looked like a brand-new drilling rig taking up about half the floor space. Brightly painted in glossy yellow and red it was vivid against the paleness of the ice, hardly camouflaged Connie thought, but beneath the mesh she assumed, hoped it was invisible. A fibreglass ladder with deeply ribbed steps led from where they were standing to the bottom of the hole.

The sonic rig looked like nothing they'd seen before, hardly unexpected given that the technology was pretty much brand new, costing Becker a hefty sum to acquire. The drill head was massive, angling at the wall of the crater at about forty-five degrees to the perpendicular. The thing was on tractor tracks with a formidable strip of sharp silver spikes to manacle it to the slippery, steep ice face. Black cables ran everywhere, along with one red and two green cables connected to a tremendous metal spool sitting central to a giant metal girder not far from where they were standing. Becker proudly stabbed at its ten thousand metres of electrical cable, which Connie likened to a gargantuan ball of multicoloured wool.

Once the rig had excavated the main tunnel, it would exit the decline and start building the bedrock chamber. It was then that the polymer tracks would be laid by the HPU. This was Becker's hydraulic pressure unit originally developed for the extensions of the Koffiefontein diamond mine in South Africa, designed to remotely set tracks for the ore trains so they could climb the highly inclined chutes that joined the crystal stopes to the surface. The twin tracks were joined together by criss-crossing polymer rods and would be sent down the tunnel by the HPU and self-set using explosive bolts. That was the theory anyway. Becker had poached a guy called Nolan Steyn from the Koffiefontein who'd done it before so there was a level of confidence, although ice was way different from deeply weathered granite and dolerite. Steyn had mapped, modelled and tested it in Greenland on a small scale, reporting excitedly by Sat phone, "Gaan naai 'n koei" which Becker initially took to be very good news indeed, based on the excitement in his voice. The follow up report was most satisfactory, although why Steyn had told him to "go fuck a cow" in Afrikaans, he'd never found out. Strange guy, that was all he knew.

***

36

'Looks like some sci-fi something or other,' Connie mused, marvelling at the deeply grooved drill head. 'Like some bizarre laser weapon.'

'Bizarre sonic weapon,' Becker corrected with a sigh. 'Sound not light Connie, get it right…geez,' he said, grinning disarmingly at her.

'Christ, Becker, now you're a tech guru correcting me on science? Is that what you think?'

'That's what I know,' he ambled over to a table that had schematics and plans plastered all over it, secured neatly by a glass plate to stop the winds scattering them to all points of the glacier.

Four men were gently tending to the rig as though it were as delicate and needy as a newborn, pawing over LED displays for the drill head, the drifters, clamps, the critical endothermal unit and the drill feed systems. One tech was pulling out the breakers, checking each one studiously, then reinserting them as if they were filled with nitro. So far everything physically able to be monitored was operating to expectation. All Becker took from it was that no one was running around shouting fire or fuck, which made him breathe easier.

The drill would be guided automatically by GPS and GLONASS SatNav which allowed the rig to be targeted to the centimetre, critical in contacting the peak of the anomaly. And once they hit bedrock the unit would be off-railed and piloted manually by basecamp, remote controlled to quarry the small chamber they'd need to perform the geo testing and analysis.

As Steyn had so eloquently reported, continuing to throw in strange language between the facts, everything had been executed successfully in a similar "Koppen ET" climatic test environment. But would the experience be the same two kilometres under the ice? That was what kept Becker awake at night, and when he was asleep it was at the hub of his dreams and awful nightmares. What if they got down there and nothing worked, what if everything just, well…failed, refused to operate the way it was supposed to and sat there under the ice like a few tonnes of scrap? It wasn't like they could send a bunch of techs down the tunnel to fix whatever went wrong. It had to work first time, or they were finished, the whole mission would be dust. He'd return home with nothing to show for the hundreds of millions he'd pissed away, having to somehow resign himself to a lifetime of bitter regret, an unbearable hell he knew. Maybe he'd just hunker down in the tunnel and let himself freeze into a block of ice and wait until some arsehole thawed him out like a chicken wing in a million years time. At least he'd be free of the incessant, unfulfilled craving. He snorted, coughing out a pale exhalation of air, heart in mouth, wondering what their voyage into the guts of this place was really going to be like.

One of the men gave a thumbs up sign to Becker who immediately fired it back with interest. 'Okay, we're good,' Becker boomed. 'Give it juice.' His face was a wrinkled hive of concentration as he waited for something to go horribly wrong, trying to be upbeat, but his confidence had evaporated into the glacier.

Connie studied him nervously, for the first time seeing lines of worry cross his face, clenching her jaw to stave off a chuckle. 'So, you leave it to the last second to actually weigh up the risks, I mean to realise there are risks?' She eyed him with a glimmer of disbelief. 'Jesus, your humanity's showing Becker…careful.'

'Stow the bullshit,' he snapped, staring at the rig, 'just cross everything you've got, we can't afford a screw up, not now, not at the beginning. If this new tech works, bloody ripper. If it fails, we're cooked. At best our timelines will be blown to shit, at worst no tunnel.' He wrestled with the chilling implications of a serious fuck up.

Connie was conflicted because she wasn't sure if failure at this point mightn't be a good thing. But if it did fail, she'd have to deal with Becker who would be insufferable, frustrated, angry, unfulfilled – an egocentric, whining nightmare for the rest of his life, and her life. She honestly couldn't decide which way she wanted it to go.

The lead engineer stepped up, sucked in a shoulder heaving breath and then pressed the big green button, his trailing exhalation clouding the instrument panel for a brief second. Becker gasped when the drill head finally started rotating, lighting up into reds, yellows and eventually blues. They could sense rather than hear a sound but it gradually became higher in pitch, quickly mellowing and disappearing, leaving only the sound of the wind whistling over the glacier.

Connie watched Becker opening and closing his mouth soundlessly. 'Is it, uh…good?' She asked, scratching her mouth with thumb and forefinger, hearing nothing but the sounds of nature.

'It's fine,' Becker said, grinning tightly, 'the resonance, um…the frequency is way beyond our hearing, if you can hear it then there is something wrong. It sends dogs nuts.' He cocked an eyebrow at Connie, grinning mischievously, nodding in her direction.

'Oh, LOL Becker. Lucky it doesn't piss off big gorillas with OCD, right?'

He smirked coldly, shifting his gaze back pensively to his expensive toy in the hole. Deep down he was terrified it might stall somewhere in the tunnel, maybe detonate in a spray of acrid black smoke and pieces of colourful metal. Rubbing the nape of his neck he could feel tension in his muscles, the skin drawn tight on his face as his mind wandered. He knew the last thing the team needed was an impatient hothead under the ice. Connie would say it was his persona del mar and it was damn hard to argue, but he was trying to change, although under pressure, well, he wasn't sure. The mission cried out for a cool, composed leader, because he could see the fear, strike that, terror in their eyes. If he let himself go down the same path, it wasn't going to end well for any of them.

The drill head and its beetle-like carapace disappeared slowly as it sublimated "first ice", excavating the very head of the decline and spewing a dense cloud of vapour into the atmosphere. The engineers frantically set about fitting a telescopic chute to the end of the tunnel so the vapour vented toward the top of the compound. With the constant wind that tormented the flat glacier of Marie Bird they thought, rightly or wrongly, that the escaping mist would be invisible to distant eyes.

Standing at the safety fence, Becker was like an iron effigy, sweating profusely, watching the rig vanish from view as it dug its burrow, hopefully on the way to landfall.

'Only eight clicks to go,' Joe said, barely a whisper above the driving wind. He pictured the hauntingly dark journey to bedrock, ancient strata that hadn't seen the Sun or the kiss of wind and rain for almost forty million years. Jesus Christ, he fevered, thumbing his ear nervously. Blood started pounding in his temples at the idea of such a profound disconnect…such a profound reconnect. Joe wondered what it would be like when they descended through the narrow, frozen tunnel, seeing something akin to the most starless space, black hole black. He was at the ops briefing yesterday, was silent throughout and left it perspiring, nauseous and scared witless. He wasn't even sure he could do it.

The Inclinator techs would roll out kilometres of Santoprene track that would connect basecamp to bedrock and once it was secured with the Inclinator car in place, Connie and Joe would reluctantly embark on a voyage of epically terrifying proportions. Riding through a tunnel three metres wide, lit only by helmet lights and those of the car they were travelling in, until over two kilometres of tough-as-steel pack ice lay above their heads. Numbingly claustrophobic didn't seem to be a strong enough description. And if there was a technical failure and all the lights went out? She didn't even want to contemplate that hideous scenario. It would be panic, chaos and a slow horrible death because no one could save them. They might as well be stranded in outer space because seriously, climbing kilometres of ice-tunnel pitched upward at forty-five degrees with only a slippery black cable or even slipperier polymer tracks to grab on to? All of it in darkness where the absence of light would be as total as it was ever going to get. Hardly bloody likely she told herself, almost hyperventilating at the thought, feeling an urge to run across the glacier and find someone to hand herself in to, wave down a chopper, toboggan to McMurdo maybe. That was her standard panic-response, the primal flight thing…just run, keep running until whatever it was, was left behind. Of course down there the whole "run for your life" thing was a hopeless joke. As was fighting. All that would be left was acceptance…oh and dying. Hard.

'Anyone, uh, scared of, uh…tight, dark spaces?' Connie said unblinking, rocked by mental images, struggling to comprehend why she hadn't thought it through in more detail before. 'I've been in a few mine shafts in my time, even ones where we've lost power so I know what it's like. I've just never really given this whole ice tunnel *whatsit* the proper focus, and to be honest, I wish I hadn't now.' Connie's feelings were written all over her face, carved in delicate lines snaking across her forehead.

'Piece of cake,' Becker said, grinning widely despite his own grave reservations about the sub-ice journey. He shrugged matter-of-factly, 'if you want something bad enough, a bit of, discomfort is part of the deal,' he said, hiding a deep dread, punched by a racing pulse.

'I don't want it badly or otherwise,' Connie said, snorting, 'so like…how do you justify my discomfort?' She wanted out of this place, back home to Sydney, to the real world of sunshine, commerce and not breaking the fucking law. When they'd reluctantly consented to the hair-brained venture she hadn't really gripped the reality of what they'd be doing. Illegalities and perils aside, digging through the ice, looking for an orebody, maybe even testing it was a few inches short of a death wish, but on paper it sounded sort of okay. But now that she had her feet on the ground, confronted by an ice-hole that looked like the entrance to hell, she was under no illusions. Connie was scared, pure and simple.

'I'll look after you Con, don't sweat it. I put our chances of returning at around fifty-fifty,' Becker teased, saluting her derisively. His grin was so wide it stretched almost ear to ear, splitting his smug face in half.

'Reassuring,' Connie whispered, knowing the official manifest said ninety-ten, which she didn't think created a hell of a lot of confidence either. Ten percent chance of dying under the ice. Just brilliant, she said silently, mulling over the distasteful odds, holding a hand over her stomach, almost feeling it churning through her parka.

Staring down at the ground, Joe looked ready to faint or vomit; maybe both simultaneously. He doubted all over again whether he could do it, scratching the bridge of his nose hard with a fingernail as he chucked it around. Of course, he knew there was no choice, he was in way too deep to pull out now, it would threaten the entire mission so he'd just have to suck it up, hope like hell he didn't die.

***

A chunk of vapour trailing rock appeared from space, grew smaller and seconds later sliced into the atmosphere of the dusty orange world in a fiery hail of ablating nickel and iron. Striking the planet near the smooth, circular plain of Lunae Planus, it detonated in a blistering pall of bedrock and duricrust, impact debris already visible as a mighty crimson stain bleeding into space from equatorial Mars. Although small by astronomical standards, the meteor collided with enough energy to blast a billion tonnes of rock and dirt from the planet, much of it escaping its meagre gravity, racing inward, hastened by the pull of the Sun. One piece of stony conglomerate about twenty metres across tumbled end over end in the direction of Earth's Newtonian free-fall around Sol. Travelling at thirteen kilometres per second it would reach the blue planet in a little over sixty days.

None of the planet's remote sensors would detect it until it started to disintegrate in the thermosphere. If nothing changed, it would strike at a shallow angle of less than twenty degrees, detonating near the bottom of the stratosphere with the explosive power of a small nuke.

39

6. Bedrock Chase

"Somewhere, something incredible is waiting to be known." ~ *Carl Sagan*

They watched the video stream as the rig continued to cut its way through ice toward bedrock buried far below. Twelve hundred and thirty-four metres of solid ice had been sublimated directly into water vapour - pressurised, de-phased and dispatched over the Marie Byrd glacier as a mighty grey cloud.

Becker felt a tiny measure of elation, nodding his head positively. 'You know, theory and testing are one thing Quincy but to do it at the arse end of the world…it's amazing. Another kilometre and the bonus is yours my friend.' Quincy managed a tight smile, picturing dollar signs, Pacific islands…the rig dead in the tunnel! His smile faded abruptly, knowing how much could still go south. In this business, nothing was done until it was done.

Becker also thought better of it, putting it out of his mind because getting ahead of yourself was only inviting the M-word which was way more odious than the F-word, but a voice in his head reckoned luck might be on their side. Apart from the idiots in the crevasse, everything was pretty much on track. They were more than half way through the tunnel dig without major fault. The sublimation rig had performed superbly although he was fatalistic about that continuing. Few fledgling technologies were reliable in their formative stages…bugs, breakdowns, unexpected stuff were part of the game. The unsettling facial tic and dark throbbing vein in Quincy's forehead were constant reminders of what could happen. Still, every metre of vacated ice was a step up the ladder, a step closer to the prize he hoped like sweet fuck was real.

Quincy Arnett was the sonic sublimation guru and lead on the ice-drilling phase of the expedition. Computer programming was his game, a Fourth-Gen compiler employed by Microsoft until Becker made him an offer he couldn't refuse. He handed Quincy a signed cheque and a pen, told him to fill in the rest. The poor fellow had almost collapsed in front of him.

***

Becker suddenly stiffened, instantly muddled by the noise, unable to think, not knowing where to look or what to do. Connie instinctively ducked and threw her arms up, inching out from under the canvass covered ops-room, peering fearfully though the broad weave polyester. She expected to see massive thunderheads and lightning but there was only benign blue sky, the Sun shining weakly to the west. Spinning to Becker, he saw her brown eyes wide open, bulging, ready to drop.

'What the hell?' Becker yelled, tossing his head around, searching.

The sound was so painfully loud their second thought was an explosive weapon or maybe an F24 breaking the sound barrier…repeatedly.

Becker's face slackened, then he planted his legs wide, raising his arms at the sky, 'no, no,' he moaned, pacing around fitfully, watching fireballs screaming through the atmosphere, trailing rippling yellow fire that sounded like thunderous popcorn. Becker was muttering expletives, curling an arm protectively over his head, realising it could derail everything they'd set in motion. 'Motherfucker,' he started ranting wildly, tramping around the other three, scowling at the fiery fragments raining from the sky. He felt like hitting something, chiding his stupidity for even thinking about luck being on his side, knowing it was just laying out the red carpet for Murphy who just waltzed in and unbuckled his pants.

One of the pieces of talus just missed the apex of the shields, smashing into the ice a few hundred metres from the compound. Becker was still looking around manically, darting eyes over the ice, at the sky. 'What're the stone motherless odds?' His face was red and blotchy with rage, eyes brutal as he stared skyward, brooding over the most damnable luck imaginable.

'Holy shit,' Joe said, gazing at a smoking hole in the ice, fully five metres across when it first hit. The vaporised ice closed in on itself pretty quickly, leaving only a dirty, water filled depression.

'Meteors,' Connie said, stating the painfully obvious, seeing the last of the fireballs slam into the glacier like fiery metal pellets, leaving a series of short-lived craters and clouds of steam.

Everything was suddenly still and quiet but Becker's face confirmed an imminent eruption as he limbered up his shoulders, seemingly readying for a showdown on the glacier.

'Jesus H…fuck!' He spat, still pacing back and forth in jerky steps, coming to a halt, drawing a long breath, then spinning around to Connie. 'We need to crank this up,' he said loudly and quickly. 'Remote sensors'll pick up the shockwave, they'll be all over it.' He shot Joe a fierce look, 'we're gonna be overrun with media….and bloody meteor hunters,' he added, holding his head with both hands, groaning, scraping both temples with his thumbs. 'This is just great…of all the half-arsed, piece of shit things to happen——. 'He stopped abruptly and lowered his head, breathing in and out a few times, screwing his face up. Becker lifted his head in disbelief. 'Do you know what a Strewn field is? Well fuck me if we're not smack bang in the middle of one, and half the frigging world will be trying to find it.'

'Half the world?' Connie said disdainfully, rolling her eyes. 'It's just a bloody meteorite.'

Joe looked at her and lifted a shoulder. 'No, Becker's right, pieces of this thing could be worth more than gold. There's thousands of them out there, hunters all across the world, they just sit around waiting for this stuff to happen and when it does they're packed, ready to go.' He turned to Becker warily, 'although the fact that it happened in Antarctica should give us more lead time I guess.'

'Sooo,' Connie said slowly, '…what do we do?' Pack up, run before anyone has time to get here?' She hoped that would be it, they could just get the hell out of this frozen nightmare. 'I mean, we can just uncover the strip, recall the transport, bug out before we're made, right? You know, avoid being thrown into federal prison for a decade.' She folded her arms roughly across her chest.

'No!' Becker yelled sharply, causing Connie and Joe to flinch and look straight at him. 'We just ramp everything up, shorten time frames and yes, take a few more risks. We need to get the chamber dug, get our testing done and confirm the deposit, then,' he paused, holding one wagging finger up, '…we get out of here.' Becker closed his eyes, desperately searching for the right way.

Connie turned away deliberately, then looked back at Becker, scowling, 'are you, Jesus…take a few more risks? What the hell are we doing now? We're not on a Boy's Own down here you know.' She eyed him furiously, 'I mean, how much dodgier can this get?' She flicked her eyes up at Joe, then slitted them at Becker accusingly. 'So how long do we have until this place becomes effing meteor central?'

Becker took a step backward, 'well, best guess, maybe forty-eight hours, we're isolated down here but make no mistake, some'll find a way to get here quick. These pricks are nuts.' He turned away, cursing under his breath.

Connie glanced at Becker curiously. 'Like you right? 'Psychotic, unbalanced…obsessed, sounds like— '

'Quincy!' Becker shouted, 'get over here,' he said, ignoring Connie's blather.

Quincy raised an eyebrow at Connie, walking slowly over to where Becker had resumed shuffling back and forth like a wild animal cornered in a cage.

'You need to get that chamber dug,' Becker said, invading his personal space and smelling his cheap cologne, 'ramp it up, two metres a second, you said it could do that, right?' It wasn't a question.

Quincy's eyes opened wider than they already were, wondering again who this chump with the chequebook thought he was. 'Look, I said it could do one-point-five for a short period, not two, and not two continually. If sublimation fails and it starts producing water we're screwed. The electronics bay is water resistant not waterproof, your mission will be over before it's started, if we can't get— '

'Jesus Quincy, can it physically do it? Forget the maybes, what ifs, the technical mumbo-jumbo,' he said, frowning at him, flaring his nostrils and daring him to quote more *maybe* horseshit.

Connie turned to Becker, lifting her eyes, 'there's my old mate, look at you, all hidden behind that risk mitigation and "be a better boss" crap. Didn't take much to bring you back did it?' She returned his glare then broke off, turning away abruptly.

'It took a fucking meteor actually,' Becker said defensively, 'the plan was always flexible, event based because the unexpected was always to be expected. But seriously, a meteorite?' He slapped his forehead lightly with his palm. 'Of all the dumb luck, but it's happened so we need to adapt.'

'Flexible and event based…hmmm,' Connie said, nodding. 'Have you considered that bugging out might be a better option, a safer, more considered response…to that?' Connie was thrusting her finger at the battle-scarred glacier, quickly realising she might as well be addressing the ice-shelf itself.

'Whatever,' he growled, shifting his eyes to Quincy, gripping a hand under his chin. 'Two metres a second, get it done,' he said. 'How long will it take to excavate the chamber once we're at bedrock?'

'Three hours give or take, assuming there's no problems…electrical failures, breakdowns, stuff like that.'

'Okay, go,' Becker said gruffly. 'Once it's done, I'll get the decline crew going on track placement. Then we set the Inclinator in place and we go.' He looked at each of them, one eyebrow higher than the other. 'Let's get all the equipment in the hole so it's ready to be onboarded. Be back here at 1030 hours.' Becker straightened himself, rolled his shoulders and looked at them stonily. 'This is it guys…the moment we've been waiting for.' Soon as he said it, he regretted it.

Connie may as well have stuck her tongue squarely in his face, the frosty smile making his blood run cold. 'Hang on,' she said bitterly, 'indulge me, the moment we've been waiting for?' She studied him closely, narrowing her eyes as though searching for some sign of intelligence. 'Christ, you can't be serious, we may as well be frigging hostages,' she said unflinchingly, taking a step in his direction.

Joe agreed but stayed silent, he wasn't in the mood for a pitched battle with Becker right now, feeling more like curling into a ball in his quarters and barricading the door.

'Um, by memory I reckon you agreed to come. I didn't hold a gun to your head.'

'You may as well have. We came to protect you from yourself, and us from you!' Connie sneered. 'For God's sake, there's a vested interest you know, if you fail we're all screwed. That's why we're here. Like I said, hostages to your stinking ego and obsession. Want me to go on?'

Becker's anger faded and finally a smile broke over his face. 'Well then, thanks for coming. How's that?' He shrugged submissively, not really sure how to respond, just knowing he had to keep his cool, most of all needing to shut her down.

'Oh God, let's just get on and do it,' Connie said, walking over to the edge of the compound, looking anxiously over the ice at the anaemic Sun lying just to the east of Mt Kirkpatrick, a towering chocolate and cream edifice in the distance. Connie worked to snapshot the picture in her mind, shuddering at the reality of the outside world being relegated to a memory. Their fate lay under the glacier, like it or not because Becker would never give up, not even meteors and the prospect of capture had put him off or given him a moment's pause about continuing. Pissed him off definitely; but a reality check? No fucking way.

Joe raised his head to the dim sky, praying to any God that might be listening to let the drill fail. Or better, have the military descend on the place, arrest everyone and haul them away, by sack truck if necessary. He even thought of phoning in an anonymous tip-off but Becker had the only Sat phone. Joe had already tried his cell, knowing it wouldn't work but hoping for a miracle. The inevitability of it all was now a horrible, mind-altering reality.

***

The three of them were at the head of the decline, ogling the forbidding entrance to their bedrock passage which presented like a section of moist gut, recently severed, shining with the fluids of life. Connie could only see darkness and horror, the embodiment of all her phobias. Although fear of being crushed in an ice-tunnel collapse and slowly freezing to death in pitch darkness was hardly a phobia, she figured, just plain being human.

Their transport would be efforted by a rather innocuous Funicular car attached to the hard-as-steel polymer rails, staying horizontal even though its descent was at forty-five degrees through its unique elevator and angled lift design. Becker had seen it before but still thought it quite ingenious.

Quincy had been ordered to override the speed governor so they could manually trim the rate of decline and by trim Becker meant speed the damn thing up wherever he could. Connie and Joe just grunted, knowing words of protest were futile – they'd given up trying to reel in Becker's disdain for their lives.

The loading crew had just about finished cramming the Funicular with machinery and sustenance packs, telescopic lighting towers and the quintessential asset, the Portaloo. It looked thoroughly out of place but as Connie had said, it was the most essential piece of equipment. Being stuck in a cavern bounded on every side by rock hard ice, living on dehydrated nutrients high in protein, thickeners and other gut churning additives without a chemical loo…well that was a nightmare no one wanted to live. Connie had spent time with Becker on mine sites, wincing as she recalled how his digestive system chugged and gurgled on his steady diet of meat and more meat. Having experienced the horror of not getting to the loo first in the morning, well…she was convinced a rotting corpse had little on Becker's evil, morning ablutions.

He had an army-style VHF walky-talky that could connect to basecamp if it had a clear line of sight with the other unit. When Becker hit *Talk*, a beeper would sound that Weems had strung up to a steel girder on the ice, connected to a high wattage globe that would flash an alert signal. He could then walk down to the head of the tunnel with the Walkie and converse with the car below.

'Okay you two, game faces,' Becker said, staring at them gravely. Apprehensive he was, just like them, but trying like hell to appear calm and assured, desperate for some Klonopin or maybe a shot of something alcoholic to take the edge off, temper his excitement, anxiety, allow him to focus.

'We'll be fine,' Connie said, staring at him with huge unblinking eyes, swallowing heavily, 'won't we?'

'Um, n-no doubt,' he said brokenly, irritated by his lack of composure. 'We've got an incredibly stable tunnel, GPR says so, that's ground penetrating radar. We just have to get down there, see what we've got. It's going to be challenging but it's under control.' His face belied his words, creased with worry, the imminence of the mission filling him with unexpected angst.

'Becker, you're allowed to be scared,' Connie said softly. 'It's okay.'

'Yeah, uh, right,' he said uneasily. 'You and Joe being here, well…you know.'

'We know. Just get us out of there alive, oh…and with sanity intact.'

All of them were covered head to toe in extreme element thermal protection, which raised one of the ironies because once they got nearer bedrock, temperature would start to rise due to geothermal heat transfer. It would be far from warm but unlike the hellish wind chill on the surface, they would be working in almost sublime conditions of only minus two or three Celsius. And no wind! It'd be like a bloody pleasure cruise Becker quipped with a wry smile, knowing the reality would be anything but.

Stepping up, they jammed into the forward compartment of the car, which was about two metres square, damn squeezy for three people in thick clothing, made worse by the Grizzly sized

Becker. Behind them lay all the equipment they needed, carefully slotted in and tightly harnessed to avoid damage on the way down.

Gazing into the inky depths, Connie saw with dismay how dark it got so quickly, descending almost immediately into a complete absence of light. She sensed a tingling in her extremities, a disconcerting pumping and clenching of her organs as breathlessness and panic started cutting into her. Her deeper mind slid image after image past her visual cortex, the lot of them getting progressively more disturbing, filling her with the need to run, unable to think of anything but getting out. She saw herself die, buried in an avalanche of ice and rock, unable to move even a finger or toe. Crushed, snap frozen, suffocated, a more agonising hell she couldn't imagine.

Punching the *On* button, Becker gasped in relief as he heard the electric motor engage immediately, pushing the car along the shiny black runner tracks. Twin-lights at the front sparked to life, angled downward into the guts of the tunnel, providing light as they descended. The illumination was actually better than they'd expected, revealing the amazingly smooth sides of a squarish shaft that to Connie's shuddersome disbelief, extended eight thousand odd metres into the stone motherless darkness, and at the end was the dead heart of the ancient continent. She held the guardrail in a death grip, feeling the prickle of every unpleasant emotion rolled into one overpowering sense of doom.

Connie looked behind them, seeing the bright light of basecamp slowly receding, fighting to ignore the stomach punch of claustrophobia as the dying light from the polar plateau receded. 'How long,' she said, turning suddenly to Becker, the helmet lights illuminating their vacant, buttery features. Becker's eyes were wired, there didn't seem to be any fear or even anxiety that she could see but Connie was sure she saw lines of worry in his face before they left. Now there was just wide-eyed lust to get to his mother loving bedrock.

'If we maintain this pace,' Becker said, 'we should reach landfall in around fifty minutes.' His eyes were straining to make out any detail, playing human statue at the head of the car as though drenched in quick dry cement, fixed there like a hood ornament.

About ten minutes in they heard a single rifle shot grow to a continuous wave of skin crawling dissonance everywhere around them, ear-splitting and deeply echoing in the enclosed space.

'Oh Christ,' Connie screamed as the horror of the noise fed into her mind, spinning around as adrenaline kicked in, searching wildly for cracks in the ice, fissures that would push open, releasing tonnes of splintered blue ice that would trap them for eternity. Blood pounded in her brain, blocking out any hope of rational thought. Please was the only word Connie had and she screamed it out loud, tensing every muscle in her body, wild animal fear flickering in her eyes as she stared back at the dim light of salvation. Incredibly, the cracking got louder, pealing from every surface, now physically painful, making her weak in the legs, loose in the bowels. Becker didn't move, pushing his arms out to steady himself, waiting for what seemed like an inevitable, life ending tunnel collapse. Joe was unsteady, moaning and whimpering, taking short, drunken steps.

'What the hell's happening?' Connie yelled, staring into space, waiting for death to come.

'Just wait,' Becker said harshly, palms outstretched, gesturing calm. His comment was directed as much at himself as the others. To him it summed up the piss poor safety protocols designed by GeoTek, apparently dooming the mission to failure before it even got off its arse. Fuckers, he thought, baring his teeth, wanting so desperately to bounce their ill-gotten cheque.

'We have to turn back!' Joe bellowed, struggling to be heard over the cracking and splintering that pounded them in concussive waves.

Just wait! Becker felt his legs cramp. That's all they could do. Wait. Hope they didn't die.

Joe and Connie stared desperately at Becker who was silent, seemingly concentrating on something. 'Becker!' Connie shrieked, trying to break his stupor, watching the walls of the tunnel but seeing no suggestion of instability, despite the hellish noise thundering through the ice.

Before Becker could turn around he yelled, 'ice shelf!' His eyes shining and alive with hope. Inching closer, Joe and Connie were only a few inches from his nose, smelling the garlic, stale on his breath.

'For Christ's sake listen,' Becker said. 'The noise is from the ice shelf, probably Ross.' He paused to suck in some cold air. 'Remember what Weems said? Noise travels way faster through ice than air…that's why it sounds so close…so loud. It's not the bloody tunnel so relax.' Becker sighed loudly, 'it's not the tunnel,' he whispered, drawing in several deep breaths to compose himself.

Their eyes settled back in their sockets as they digested what he was saying. 'Jesus,' Connie almost sobbed, feeling herself loosen up ever so slightly, giving Joe a stiff-necked nod, making a brave attempt to smile. They were still breathing, the tunnel still intact and she was trying to take solace in it but was struggling. Sort of like fronting a firing squad, seeing the first volley of bullets miraculously miss. Her heart would soar with elation but then you suddenly realise the Captain has a service revolver to finish the job…no matter how lucky you were, there would never be a reprieve. Connie wondered if that's what was happening here, dodge one peril, get taken down by the next, or the one after that. Gasping dismally, she peered ahead, not processing or registering a thought.

Over the next ten minutes the sound of the cracking diminished, eventually subsiding completely into silence. Now there was just the whir of the GE motor, the gentle rubbing of the wheels on polymer and the sound of the gentle breeze wafting through the tunnel from above.

Joe tried to focus on the tasks he had once they arrived at bedrock but his mind was rooted on the probability of never getting there. They had no right being here, inside this ice tunnel with no visible means of support apart from the tensile strength of the glacier itself. And like Connie, he felt a deep certainty that he would die badly, either on the way down, on the way back, or maybe in the dingy chamber itself. He holed up in the corner where the guardrails met and closed his eyes tightly.

Connie was letting her gaze wander, losing focus, but was snapped back by something just beyond the reach of the Inclinator's lights, breathing in sharply. It should have been pitch dark but now it didn't seem to be. There was a vague kiss of luminance on the walls of the tunnel - it was there and then it wasn't. Connie's heart started punching her breastbone, watching it abruptly come, then go, wondering if it was an illusion, maybe a stress related mirage type thing. Straining her eyes, she fought to focus, blinking several times, squinting through slits…was her brain playing tricks?

Ahead of the lights, in the pitch-black reaches of the tunnel, Connie could definitely see a contrast radiating from the surface ice of the tunnel and it was everywhere, the sides, above and below. Holy shit she told herself, feeling a chill across her shoulders. I can see colours!

'Um…what is that?' She said pensively, pointing a gloved finger straight ahead. Becker and Joe were already peering at it, glancing seesaw like at each other. He slowed the passage of the car, stopping it about ten metres short of the strange glow, the whir of the electrics disappearing, leaving only an eerie silence. All they could hear was their own ragged breathing, heartbeats unnervingly loud in their ears.

Light was sparkling in the darkness as though gemstones were exposed in the ice and fluorescing under a UV light. Staring at it, they had the same question - before the rig rolled through and did its business this was solid glacier. Go figure Connie said to herself, rhythmically squeezing her hands together, hearing voices of doom gathering in her mind.

Becker re-engaged the motor and inched up to the light, having the troubling feeling that whatever it was might be alive. The how's and whys made little sense but there it was, animation where there shouldn't be any. Joe's eyes were like boiled eggs in the torchlight as he suddenly stopped blinking and his mouth fell open. 'Bioluminant,' he said, pushing his head forward, now face to face with it, stretching his arm out and making to pick at it.

'Joe, no!' Connie snapped, waving him back. 'It could be anything, it might be full of something toxic…lethal maybe. This ice is millions of years old and pro-quo so is that shit you're about to fondle.' Connie searched his face, aghast at his lack of mind.

'Oh for…just relax, it's algae, it's fine,' Joe said, touching it deliberately, bringing his finger up to his Mine Arc light, studying it as closely as he could. 'Blue-green algae,' he said softly as though a loud voice might scare it off. 'Looks a bit like the gear they pulled out up near Hawaii, lights up using chemicals, you know, no Sun required.' A rueful grin flashed across his face.

Connie thought about it for a second. 'Well that's all fine, but what chemicals are down here except ice, uh…hydrogen and oxygen?' She wrinkled her brow, almost closing one eye, 'and how the hell did it get here when we just dug the damn hole, it can't live in solid ice.' Connie puzzled over what seemed like a scientific nonsense, her heart tap-tapping in her throat.

'We'll get a sample on the way back,' Becker said dismissively as he re-engaged the motor. With a slight jerk, they resumed the journey toward landfall, leaving the ebb and flow of blues, reds and greens behind them. Connie glanced nervously over her shoulder, struck by how much the supposed algae resembled very out of place Christmas lights.

Joe was picking at Connie's question, which had also been his. 'We must have woken it up,' he said quietly. 'Maybe it was frozen in the ice, brought back by the drill and the moisture when it went past.' Joe patted his chin, intrigued.

Becker was peeved by the irrelevant discussion and Joe could see he didn't give a rat's ass about anything a molecule off-plan. His brain was totally routed to the end of the Inclinator's journey. Mineral discovery, fame, was his focus, science discovery could come later or never, he wasn't fussed.

***

Weems finally found time to sit down and view the video stream from the rig as it hit bedrock. He wanted to check out vision of the testing chamber to ensure all was in order. According to the data feed it had all been completed a few hours ago and to his surprise, been a great success. "Five by Five" Hoffman had piped with a grin. They now had a thumping big chamber more than two clicks under the ice, just waiting for Becker and his team to arrive and do whatever the hell they were going to do. It was his job to get them there, after that, he didn't give a shit. He quickly conceded he did give a shit, because if Becker found his booty, he'd receive an incentive payment on top of the bonus he'd already pocketed, not like Quincy or Weems but pretty damn good all the same.

All of it was achieved with a remarkable 3D landscape-modelling program, allowing rig specialist Hoffman to shape the cavern remotely with his "thawographics" software, developed specially for the mission. The dig was orchestrated by real-time data combining SatNav, GPS and sublimation efficiency data, taken with glacier chemistry, which was basically the ice-to-contaminant ratio keeping the risk of collapse to virtually zero.

They'd given up on the grainy vision from the Canon at the front of the rig after only a few minutes. The resolution, supposed to stand up in poor light was in Weems' words, "worse than shit". This was the first opportunity he'd had to check out film capture and he was damn excited at being among the first to clap eyes on the bedrock Nature had concealed from the world for so many millions of years. More than that, he wanted to see if there was any sign of this so-called element 45 orebody that had Becker strung up by the balls.

'Jesus, hit fast forward,' Weems said sharply, 'maybe the signal noise'll clean up a bit, if there's any sign of this rhodium I wanna be the one to tell the fool.' He could only imagine his reaction, it'd be pure gold. Pure rhodium he corrected with a malicious smile. In his mind, he saw Becker clutching his chest, shuddering, lurching, then carking it under the ice just metres from the prize he so wantonly craved. Such dark, pleasant irony he mused, then he remembered he hadn't been paid yet, giving him pause on the whole dying thing.

Hoffman punched a few keystrokes to set the digital feed racing forward, then hit Play. 'Okay, here we go but the image ain't any clearer boss.'

'Nothing else you can do?' Weems asked him narrowly.

'Nup,' Hoffman said, 'The STOIK is maxed on every corrector, the adaptive algorithm is top of the wozza but that's the best it'll do…it was crap to start with, now it's just shite.' He grinned sideways at him, giving Weems his best "suck it up" look, turning back to the video, chuckling into his thick whiskers.

46

The video showed the rig take its first cut through the tunnel wall that would ultimately morph into Becker's testing pit. Clouds of dim pixelating mist obscured the vision but front and centre were the first stirrings of a space being opened up.

Hoffman was studying the software panel, wondering what else he could do to bring the image up a bit, suddenly edging closer and studying the bottom of the video, blinking rapidly, aware of a sudden lump in his throat. He couldn't immediately identify it or explain it but there was something there, a different, brighter lustre, different texture. Despite the crummy resolution he could see it wasn't ice or rock. He turned to Weems expecting him to be staring at the screen but instead, the idiot was poring over his cellphone. Hoffman sighed, breathing a profanity, pausing the feed.

'Boss…hello?' He snapped his fingers. 'Look…look,' he urged loudly, pointing to the bottom of the screen, his index finger touching the stilled image.

Weems face first vacant, melted into puzzlement then quickly to excitement. 'Woo fucken hoo,' he said, slapping his thighs with both hands, smiling crookedly at Hoffman. 'That's it…the old prick was right! Jesus Christ, it's there Hoff…it's actually there.' His eyes were bloated, staring unfocussed at the image, then back at Hoffman. 'Ha!' He snapped like a gunshot,' tipping his head back, *'you sweet, beautiful orebody'* he thought joyously, his whole face creasing into a mercurial smile, visualising dollars signs and zeros and everything that would come with it.

Hoffman studied Weems curiously, trying to work out what whoopee weed this whack job was on. Attention to detail was his thing but he was failing his own test big time. Clearly the fool was seeing only what he wanted to see.

'You think that's um, rhodium?' Hoffman asked, eyeballing him severely.

'Well it ain't bedrock brother!' His smile was beaming.

'Boss, well yes I agree, but for God's sake…look closer.' He jabbed his head forward, hitting the Play button to resume normal feed. Weems saw Hoffman's puzzled expression, so he pulled his chair closer, placing a hand on his forehead, blocking out glare from the fluoro's above.

Weems stared, face paling, he peered at the screen. It was blurry but clear enough.

'This, er…can't be can it?' He whispered closemouthed, eyes stretching wide then narrowing to focus, turning his head this way and that, grunting.

'No boss,' he said, locking eyes with Weems, having absolutely nothing to add.

'How long till they get there?' Weems asked uneasily, coughing to loosen the congestion in his throat.

'Not long,' Hoffman said, 'thirty minutes, maybe less.'

'Shit,' Weems muttered, wondering if he should warn them or just let it unfold. It's not like Becker would turn back. In fact, he'd tell us to go screw ourselves and go harder and faster. Weems eyes were glazed as he leered at the screen, rolling the detail around in his brain and coming up with zero.

The image that hung in front of them had just enough visual quality to tell them that what they had locked onto had absolutely no business being beneath the ice in Antarctica.

***

'It might be millions of years old,' Connie said, watching with grim fascination as the last vestiges of light from the algae disappeared in the darkness above. Peering toward basecamp she likened the view to the night sky with a single star smack bang in the middle of it. Soon after they'd started out it was huge but now it was a tiny white dwarf, distant, dim and forlorn she thought, feeling a sweep of hopelessness well-up inside. If anything went wrong, help would have to descend from that diminutive light above. She realised bleakly that it might as well have to come from a different world because the chances of anyone rescuing them while they were alive was probably zero.

7. Approach

"I believe alien life is quite common in the universe, although intelligent life is less so. Some say it has yet to appear on planet Earth." ~- *Stephen Hawking*

'Nine minutes,' Becker said, reading the countdown timer on his wristwatch, factoring in the irksome delay caused by the algae. Looking around he gently massaged his chest, knowing he needed to calm down, rocked by his heart falling out of rhythm every few thwumps. It's just metal he said to himself…just rhodium he repeated several times, but he knew how much shit that was even before he mouthed the stupid words. If what they were coming upon was anything like the specimen back in Sydney it would become the stuff of legend, a godlike El Dorado that everything else would be compared to for the rest of eternity. Becker reckoned he could smell the minerally scent of rhodium in the crisp air, rubbish he knew, but there it was, real, undeniable, a seducing feeling to be close to something so tantalising, and fattened to a thumping obsession by more than a decade of dreaming.

They heard static followed by a voice, maybe two voices. 'Becker, you there? Pick up.' It was Weems on the two-way, sounding out of breath, conveying an urgency that made them uneasy.

Becker snatched at the radio. 'Of course I'm here.' His heart was thudding in the back of his throat. No more screw-ups he screamed to himself, hoping some other dumb fucker hadn't fallen down a crevasse.

Weems said, 'well, er, we've been watching the video feed from the rig and...hang on, Jesus, Hoff shut up.' Weems sounded edgy. 'There's something down there …in the chamber.'

Backer flicked a glance at Connie who was already staring anxiously at the radio, then him, having clearly heard the words relayed on speaker. She gazed with eyes that were almost bovine, hypnotically moist in the light.

'An outcrop…of mineralisation you mean?' He asked with hopeful words but sounding mostly puzzled.

Joe was glaring at Becker, wondering what sort of idiot, one-track mind he had because surely, he realised any outcrop would've been eroded by the glacier like, tens of millions of years ago! The ice would've sheared it off, carried it a thousand clicks away. For someone in the mining business he was seriously deluded, Joe thought, clenching his mouth tight to avoid snapping at him.

'No,' Weems said loudly. 'The video stream is no good but, well…we can't see any bedrock down there...as in there's no apparent rock at all.'

Becker saw lights flashing in front of his eyes, spots and dots, making him dizzy and woozy. Turning to Connie he screwed his face up. 'What the hell are you talking about…no rock? The rig hit something hard beneath the ice at exactly the right depth. We know that from the onboard diagnostics, I saw the density profile, it was totally in order.'

'Um, well yes it hit something hard, but I'll say it again, it doesn't look like bedrock.'

Becker felt like his world was falling apart, the lights behind his eyelids melding into a flood of fizzing sparks. Weems wasn't making sense. 'So okay genius, what did we hit then?' He was confused, frustration pushing him off-balance. Nothing was adding up. Had Weems screwed up the trig calcs and led them to some false basement that was only detached strata floating above genuine landfall?

'No Carson, shit, listen, the rig is definitely on bedrock but it's, well, it looks like it's covered with something solid, uh, reflective. Something shiny.'

Connie and Joe were silent, taking it all in, putting the few pieces they had together but their brains couldn't attach anything reasonable to what Weems was saying. Low light bogey, Joe reckoned, happens all the time.

Becker was fighting with one hope that really ought to be impossible but it was all he could dredge up from the chaos. If it was true, he knew it would take incredible to a staggering new height.

His face felt bitterly cold, way colder than it should have been, and he was pretty sure all the blood had drained away, given up on his brain and gone to feed his organs where it could do some good.

'You still there?' Weems prompted.

'Yep. Um…could it be rhodium?' Becker asked, heart in mouth. 'Like pure metal. Could the top of the orebody be an enriched layer of it, a solid secondary surface deposit maybe…pure reworked native metal? He felt wobbly, imagining the epic nature of such a deposit. Christ, he dreamed, it'd make King Solomon's mines look like a quartzite mill.

'It's not rhodium,' Weems said cautiously, trying to bring him down gradually. 'Uh, are you copying me okay?'

'Copy you fine,' Becker confirmed curiously. 'Why?'

'Just wanna make sure, look Becker, this vitreous whatever we're looking at has a pattern. The stuff we're looking at has lines of curvature incised in it…as in circles.' Weems took a rattling breath, exhaling slowly. 'We think they're cut into it although they could be just surface markings we can't tell from here. We reckon it extends beyond the chamber…well beyond it.'

Becker's eyes nearly fell out of his skull. Blood was erupting in his temples, making him feel light-headed. 'Fuck me,' he growled, scraping his fingernails down his cheek. 'What is going…are you sure Weems?' Becker said, staring fixedly at Connie, deep in formless thought.

'I'm looking at it…it's grainy but they're there…definitely there.'

Joe's mind was swirling, mainly with shadowy questions. Incised lines. Circles? He puzzled over how that might be, what screwed up process could have created them? None that he was familiar with, none that he'd ever heard of, like ever.

Connie's mouth was still hanging open, gasping in small spurts like a beached fish, baffled by the extraordinary words from Byrd Base.

'Glacial striations?' Joe said weakly, knowing it didn't fit the bill. No way it was that.

'You said circular, right?' Becker asked Weems. 'Do you mean sort of circular or circular?'

Weems took another deep breath and released it, sighing loudly over the Walkie. 'They look pretty damn perfect on the screen here, seem to be evenly spaced too. We can only see a few of them but there's definitely more under the ice if the pattern continues.'

Becker's helmet light lit up the lines of tension in his face. 'For fuck's sake,' he boomed.

'What happened to event management and adapting, your words right?' Connie said accusingly. 'Did you forget what you already preached, what did you call it, "Becker Gospel"?'

'Yeah, well, I've done enough of that already.' He lifted his goggles, wiping his red-rimmed eyes, 'Will this complicate our testing Peter?' He added with an understated fury.

'Um, well, I'm not sure,' Weems replied, sounding a bit shocked. 'Carson, we have no idea what this is. It may be your metal, but I really don't think so. It might be something of extreme archaeological significance, although how it would get under the ice is well…uh, who knows I guess. But you'll need to take care when you get there okay? Things are dicey enough already. If you go smashing something historically significant they'll string you up.'

'Who the hell is they?' Becker said impatiently, massaging his brow.

'Christ…the Feds, military, the frigging UN, they'll be lining up.'

'If we're made they'll string me up anyway,' Becker said casually. 'They can't do it twice.'

Connie chuckled slightly, 'extreme care and Carson Becker?' She chided, picturing a vat of oil and water, knowing there wasn't the slightest hope of either accepting the other.

Becker ignored Connie, more concerned with Weems, wanting to tell him to go clean his fucking glasses, but he held onto it. 'Righto,' he said, adding, 'any sign of meteor chasers?'

'None yet,' Weems said, 'but they're coming, make no mistake. We've had all manner of planes fly over, so the choppers won't be far behind.'

'Shit…okay.' Becker terminated the call, peering at Connie wordlessly. 'Circular patterns,' he mused out loud, grimacing. 'Could that possibly be natural?' He said, hoping it was, conceding he was no landform expert. Maybe there was some obscure glacial process that might be responsible, some local erosional force, unseen, undescribed. They were two kilometres down, so hey, anything was possible he guessed, feeling a disconcerting looseness in his gut. He thought of the Portaloo, another good reason to get to bedrock quickly.

Connie had been pushing the words around since Weems uttered them, his shaky claim of under ice curios was absurd. No way humans had been down here before. Circles were the most mathematically pure objects in the Universe, but striations that were circular, parallel and reducing in size, and were embedded in something lustrous, possibly metallic, could any of that be natural? Hardly bloody likely Connie concluded, chewing on her bottom lip, battling to come up with an answer that was reasonable. She turned her head up at Becker. 'Natural? I can't see how,' she said doubtfully, 'although Weems did say the video quality was poor so maybe it's a visual anomaly, a relic, a low light something. I reckon we'll find nothing but bedrock and rhodium Becker,' she offered, smiling, knowing he'd love that. And for what it was worth, it made her feel better too.

'Damn straight,' he shot back, grinning widely, his mind refilling with dream inspired images of a metallic elē ganache under the ice. Despite their pitched battles, Connie was Becker's rock. If she said it, he believed her, whether he fessed up or not.

Joe heard what Connie said and wasn't so sure. Circular grooves were either there or not and he doubted whether low light would make a zac of difference. Weems was an intelligent guy, not prone to making ill-founded judgements so if he believed it, well, they at least needed to take it seriously. Joe was straining to come up with any sort of reasonable answer for it, glacial striation, hydrothermal activity, acidic flow, ablation? No, a definite no to each one as he listed them off, sensing something gnawing at him. If the grooves were vaguely parallel it could be explained by the glacier picking up rocks and etching the bedrock as it scraped its way toward sea level. But if the grooves were parallel and circular, well fuck knows was all he had, and as a geophysicist he should have a hell of a lot more than that. Joe's mind was condensing into things he only half understood.

Connie saw Joe drift off, he hadn't blinked, changed expression or seemingly breathed for nearly two minutes. 'Hey sleepy…what's up?' She snapped her fingers sharply in front of his face.

Joe blinked and eventually focussed. 'Um, yeah sorry.' He ran his hand over his face and rested his arm on his hip. 'Look, I don't buy that Weems saw some low light figment,' he whispered, almost without moving his mouth. 'You and I know how he operates, Becker was clear on it. He's never made a mistake or bad judgement in his life, and he seemed pretty damn certain what he saw, there were no ifs or buts.'

'Or candy nuts,' Connie added with a mischievous grin.

'R-really?' Joe said with a piercing stare, 'this is deadly serious.' He nodded sharply at her. 'It could be anything down there. I mean, it's not enough that we're here breaking the law, might be killed at any moment, now we've stumbled on something…fucking something.' Joe flexed his shoulders, wondering how many black cats Becker had crushed beneath the wheels of his Hummer.

'So what?' Connie said, cupping her mouth, realising she'd spoken too loudly.

'Yes, down,' Joe muttered urgently, bowing his head.

'It is what it is,' she said, 'we'll see if he's right or wrong when we get there. She peered over at Becker and shrugged, slightly amused. He wouldn't have heard them if they'd used a megaphone and then cracked him over the head with it. Every one of his senses was directed at the tunnel ahead, searching, waiting for his fairy dust chamber to materialise from the gloom.

Joe drew in a grating breath, blowing it out through his mouth. 'I get that, but if Weems is right then think about it, we've got maybe unnatural incisions down there, and the surface hasn't seen clear air…like in forever.' He was only centimetres from her nose and she could see every muscle in his face pulled taut. Connie's jaw suddenly dropped open, she'd been so terrified by the tunnel and the prospect of death, she hadn't properly weighed up what Joe was saying. Connie had been so myopically focussed on not dying, but now, she pored over it, eyes widening, goose bumps rising on the back of her neck, the knowing settling in.

Joe continued, darting his eyes furtively to Becker, shifting back to Connie, '…and if the incisions are circles reducing in diameter, then, what's the likelihood it would sit on top of the mag anomaly?' He shook his head, continuing to digest the facts, if they actually were facts at all.

'The likelihood is zero,' Connie said, her voice trailing off into baffled silence.

Joe eyed her nervously up and down. 'Yes, the likelihood is zero,' he agreed, lifting a shoulder gently. 'This metal or whatever it is…is the TEM anomaly. The circular patterns, he said it was reflective, vitreous, if it's rhodium or not rhodium, it must be what the Aeroscouts saw. If Weems is reading it right then Becker's going to be seriously cut, angry…angrier.'

Connie's heart was pounding an uneasy rhythm. 'So you think it's artificial…i-is that it?' She stammered under her breath, 'cut by someone?' Her mouth stayed open well after the words escaped, her eyes huge.

'Or something,' Joe said, gazing into her eyes with a strange expression. 'There were no humans when all this was free of ice, not even primates I don't think…just mammals, marsupials, lizards, things like that.'

'Jesus Christ,' Connie breathed, tracing her fingers around her mouth and nose. The journey through the tunnel was taking on a massive air of unreality, taken to a brand-new level of weirdness by Weems description of some inexplicable metal something.

Joe was physically jolted by another thought that elbowed its way roughly between the others. He knew the glaciers in Antarctica had been hacking at the landscape for eons, digesting hundreds of metres of bedrock over all those millions of years. That was geologic fact, leaving him perplexed and struggling to find the right words. 'Uh, Connie,' Joe said falteringly, his mind wrestling with the growing improbability. 'Help me out here. If the glaciers have eroded the bedrock for so long…how is it that grooves, gouges or even a metallic surface could survive that?'

Her brow squeezed into shadowy creases. 'Dunno, maybe the whole thing extends down, like really deep.' Connie gave a confused shrug. 'Just park it, let's wait, see what's there,' she offered, tapping a finger against her lips thoughtfully.

Joe's final thought was that maybe Weems had gotten it wrong after all, that for the first time in his careful, studious life he'd screwed it up big time. But Joe knew that Hoffman and his lead engineer were in the room as well and they clearly agreed with him. All of them had seen it, none had dissented.

Straining and squinting, they searched for any visual sign of the chamber that should have been at least dimly lit by the lights from the rig inside, but there was nothing but blackness beyond the Inclinator's lights.

Joe felt like an explorer at the bow of a ship coming upon a strange new land in the middle of a Moonless night, Becker the point guard, scouring the water ahead for danger. Not surprisingly he was first to see it.

His arm sprung from his body, index finger slashing through the air. 'Look!' He barked like a rifle shot. 'There…light!' He thrust his head forward, slitting his eyes. 'That has to be it, I'll be goddamned…we actually made it.' He leant perilously over the guardrail, 'we damn well made it,' he repeated louder, bouncing around the car, making it rock a little, whooping it up. 'Motherfucker!' He trumpeted, continuing to point at the light, a diffuse yellow radiance licking the walls of the tunnel below.

'Christ almighty,' Connie said, hanging on as tight as she could, 'you'll derail us before we even get there.'

'Come here you bastard,' he boomed, ignoring her. 'Bedrock Base!' Becker's words echoed eerily in the half-light of the tunnel.

Starting as a gentle glimmer, it grew into a tunnel-sized wall of light as they approached, now less than half a click away, a dim pall of primrose, sparkling and glinting off the coarse blue glacier walls.

8. Artefact

"Where there is mystery, it is generally supposed there must be evil."
~ *George Gordon Byron*

Becker felt a hot, pulsing pain in his chest and thought for a second he was dying, but it quickly abated after a few measured breaths. '…just stress,' he murmured to himself, breathing in and out a few more times, convincing himself the pain wouldn't return. Becker said the words with less confidence than he'd hoped, 'here we go guys…time for some ground truthing.' He brought the car to a rather abrupt stop, leaving it just short of the end of the tracks. The downward pitch of the tunnel had levelled out in the last two hundred metres, allowing Becker to reduce the Funicular's incline to almost horizontal, not far off the ice which was now barely metres above bedrock.

The ice-chamber was only metres ahead, sharply to the left at about forty degrees, the entrance a metre or so below the dense blue ice they were standing on. Becker's heart had finally reduced in size a bit but was still thudding against his soft palate.

The Funicular had quite simply run out of tracks, an odd sight because the polymer rails didn't stop at the dead-end of the primary tunnel but instead ran themselves up the vertical ice wall, secured there with the same explosive bolts that held it securely to the ground. Given that the HPU had sent down over eight clicks of tracks it had gotten it amazingly spot on, a few extra metres was all it amounted to. This gave Becker a lift after Weems nailed them with his maddening report.

'Grab what you can and let's go,' Becker said impatiently, anxiety swelling into mild hysteria, 'we need to move…now.' He drew a series of slow inhalations deep into his lungs, steeling himself.

Each of them grabbed the pieces of equipment they were trained to use, or at least those bits they could carry in one trip. Connie grabbed the bag holding the spectrometer, Joe the metal frame for the core driller and Becker carried some of the metal housing for the Portaloo. Connie watched him with an ironic sneer, thinking how fitting it was, watching him grapple with the bulky toilet panels, knowing he'd be the number one ticket holder by virtue of usage. She idly pondered the lack of airflow in the chamber, squashing her nose up, sensing danger on several fronts.

Surveying the unsettling entrance, Weems' unexpected words were funnelling into an unnerving sense of foreboding that seemed to be telling them the next few steps might be the most impactful of their lives, in any number of ways.

'Okay, we're good?' Becker said, nodding at Joe and Connie who stared blankly without reply, peering hesitantly at the blue-ice entrance that looked pretty much like an entrance to hell.

Access to the chamber was a rough-hewn hole in the tunnel wall about two metres wide and a similar distance high with a ramp of sorts leading down to ground zero, to what should have been bedrock… had to be bedrock, Becker hoped. Fucking Weems, he spat silently, realising he was tapping his foot almost in time with his pulse, which was almost maxing out.

'Damn this gear is heavy,' Connie said, already puffing from exertion. 'If we're going in, let's get on and do it, otherwise this stuff gets dropped and stays where it falls.'

Becker turned, and carrying a box of electrical cables and switches, disappeared into the chamber.

Connie realised this was it. Somehow, they'd defied the odds and managed to reel in the object of Becker's obsession and arrived at the most isolated place on the planet…alive. Joe pursed his lips, giving a perfunctory shrug, accepting the inevitable, blowing out a cloud of pale vapour as he started forward. 'Well I'll be fucked,' he said in a hoarse whisper.

The scene that greeted them was completely unlike the icy cavern they'd visualised in their minds. It was eerily beautiful, serene and big like a frozen auditorium, an ice rink maybe, a panorama of shining blue and white. An irregularly shaped cavity about twenty metres long, sort of rectangular in shape, with the roof about two metres above Becker's head; and sitting on the far side was the sublimation rig with its drill head looking like a brightly illuminated ice-cream cone.

Surrounding them was something sort of expected but still searingly unexpected, exposed for all to see, no longer just a bunch of vague adjectives, verbs and nouns, it was under them, tangible and as real as anything got. What Weems reported as grainy vision of a metallic surface of some kind was indisputably real and totally, unutterably incredible.

Becker accepted the bizarre scene wordlessly at first, fighting hard to process what he was seeing, head bobbing around like a turkey, studying something that looked perversely like regular metal. 'Holy Mother of God,' he finally blustered, vacancy quickly giving way to dazed astonishment, his head bent at a strange angle as he gawked at the floor of the cavern, asking himself the question. As in…how could it be here, curvature, shine, incisions, it was preposterous. Nothing clicked in his mind beyond a simplistic profanity…what the fuck? It didn't make a lick of sense.

Connie's irises were roundly in view, spidery veins and all, arms wrapped around her torso, lips with the suggestion of a tremor. 'Down h-here, it can't be, I d-don't…it's amazing.' She turned full circle to establish some perspective on its size, drumming the side of her head softly with gloved fingers as she moved haltingly on the strange surface.

Joe was pretty much frozen…it was incredible, nuts, call it what you like, he felt like he'd been hit with a shovel. Peering down and then up, exchanging pensive glances, they were stewing on the same imponderable, what the hell had they gotten themselves into?

In front of them, under them, around them was a metal-like mass with perfectly formed lines cut into it, just like Weems had said, about two metres apart, seemingly extending well beyond the narrow confines of the chamber. Their thick polar boots should have been perched on andesite volcanics of the Antarctic bedrock but they clearly were not.

What struck them most was how incredibly new it looked, which seemed as unlikely as it being here in the first place, because sitting above them were gigatonnes of ice dragging house size slabs of broken rock across it, the most destructive sandpaper imaginable. Yet it was free of any signs of scratching or scouring, like an antimony alloy that had been spat out all shiny and new, barely having had time to cure.

Joe finally dragged his eyes off the floor, gawking at Becker, pearly whites exposed and shining in the dim light. 'This is, well…incredible, but um, what, how and shit…who? I mean, this didn't get down here by itself.' He gave a paper-thin smile and rolled his eyes almost imperceptibly. 'The ice, the distance, the engineering, I mean, seriously.' Joe stood up straight, staring upward, breathing noisily through his nose.

Becker bent down and ran his hand warily over it. 'I have no frigging idea on any of that,' he said sharply, tiring of the bullshit banter, raking his forehead roughly with the gnarly skin on the back of his hand. 'Where is my bedrock?' He said, glaring at the ground, seemingly aggrieved at what was blocking the way to the glorious source of his mag profile.

Connie blew a loud sigh through her teeth, 'you know, maybe this is some secret basement type thing built by one of the territory owners. Perhaps our US buddies have created a more secure, Area 51 under the ice here. Their base isn't far away at McMurdo,' she said, hearing the daft words and sighing again, talking lower and slower. 'It'd be funny because it's gotta be the most secure location ever, and we found it. Becker and his little team of fortune hunters.' Connie's grin was faint, passing quickly.

'Jesus, wouldn't the DoD be pissed,' Joe said. 'They'd lock us up, swallow the key, or just straight out kill us…you know, just a few more defence related sanctions buried in the ice.'

Becker was silent and hadn't heard a thing. He was still glowering at the same piece of metal basement, chastising it under his breath. 'Where is my fucking bedrock?' He repeated, louder this time, flitting his eyes around the chamber, searching for rock but seeing only ice and shiny *whatever-it-was* everywhere he looked.

Connie turned away from Joe, clenching her teeth. 'Jesus, screw your bedrock okay,' she said, gesturing sharply with her right hand. 'Are you seriously that blind? We have a situation here and look at you, can't see the bloody forest for the trees.'

Becker looked straight through Connie, still agonising over what was under him. 'Where does this thing start and finish?' He said, cracking a knuckle on one hand, glaring down mercilessly. 'Maybe we can get to bedrock by excavating more ice— '

'Oh God, brilliant idea,' she said, wanting to kick him in the arse to knock him out of his insufferable mania but knowing it would be wasted energy. 'Look, we try and work out what it is…then we worry about your precious bedrock.' She curled her lip savagely, hitting him head on with an icy glare.

Becker's mouth was wide open as he stared openly at this dogmatic woman. 'Why the hell do you think we came here?' He was taking short, erratic steps, groaning and muttering as he went. 'And what're the odds some fucking metal plug thing melted over the top of my deposit? I mean for Christ's sake there's noth— '

'Your deposit? Connie said, rocking her head back. 'Sorry, is your name printed on the ground somewhere?' She pierced him with another icy stare, dumfounded at his sheer audacity. Now the oaf claimed ownership of something sitting in the largest nature preserve on the planet where possession of anything was a pipe dream. A territorial claim was the best you could do, giving you rights to bugger all except occupation, bird watching and peering through a bloody microscope. Pure Becker, all-balls no brains, look at me persona.

Joe stepped quietly over to where Becker and Connie were trading insults, hoping some science might distract them for a bit. 'Okay, so based on the vector of these curves, I reckon the diameter of the one here,' he pointed with his palm, 'is about a hundred and fifty metres. That means the centre…like the bulls-eye of this thing should be about half that far to the east of here.'

Becker stood taller. 'That means the shortest route to bedrock is to the west.' So let's start.'

'You and your bedrock should get a fucking room,' Connie snapped, jabbing a finger at him viciously. 'Stop with the bedrock talk, first the circles, then the bedrock.' Her eyes were burning with fury and Becker returned it, crimson flushing his face as he circled her like a shark.

'Who the hell is in charge of this mission?' He yelled, his face now looking almost purple. 'I'll give you two guesses but you're not gonna need 'em.' Becker was still scowling, daring her to keep it up.

'Majority rules down here, Joe and I say it's our call, not yours.' Becker shifted his glare squarely to Joe who nodded hesitantly at Connie, zero eye contact with Becker.

'So it's bloody mutiny…Jesus Christ,' he muttered, smirking coldly. 'We don't have time for this, topside'll be buzzing with meteor hunters and media soon enough.' HIs expression went blank, seeing Connie's iron mug and realising she wasn't budging, probably ever and despite it all, he needed them. 'Fine, whatever, have it your way but I want a drill core, underneath this…stuff. Then it's your call, you can do what you like.' Becker's eyes were suddenly pleading, eyebrows dropping with the "poor me" he played so well.

Connie saw Joe shrug reluctantly and raise his eyes. 'God…okay,' she said, 'you got yourself a real bedrock addiction there Becker.'

After ten minutes of prep the lightweight diamond rig stood proudly on the flat metal surface with enough rods to get to about fifty metres, but there was no time for that. According to the EMAR survey, the anomaly extended right to the surface so they should only need to top it once they got through the plate.

Joe pushed back the safety arm and locked it with a loud click, firing up the supercapacitor engine, the reverb off the walls created an endless feedback loop that was painful and added to the general sense of confusion in the chamber. The drill they were using was a state of the art Yanmar unit, "kick-arse, top of the line" was Becker's proud summary as he patted the damn thing like an obedient puppy.

Joe glanced at Becker and gulped visibly, getting the go to "rip it up", looking down at the piece of the anomaly in the drill's crosshairs, nervously gripping the lever that would connect the circuits to propel the diamond bit downward.

'Christ, go!' Becker hammered impatiently, 'for God's sake do it.' His eyes were almost on stalks as he waited for it to reach into his target rock, to penetrate it and give him something he could touch and feel.

Joe punched the lever and the drill head descended slowly to the surface, Becker's eyes growing even wider as he followed it down, staring like an expectant father, blown away by the scene he never thought he'd see. It was history, right here, now, it had to be rhodium, the specimen had to come from this massive magnetic profile. There were no other EM peaks anywhere near the projected transit line of the explorers. Every geophysical pointer, marker, possibility led right here to where they were standing.

His vision swam as he watched the rig fight with the strange surface, vibrating wildly and worse, seeing blue smoke eventually billowing from the power unit at the rear. Jesus fuck, Becker screamed to himself, seeing the ominous vapour wafting through the chamber. Nightmares about equipment failure were slamming into him at exactly the wrong time, thinking M-word but refusing to give it a molecule of oxygen.

'Shut it down,' Connie yelled. 'Off!'

Becker glared at Joe murderously, flicking his hand across his throat. He slammed a fist into his palm, sending a gunshot echoing through the freezing air. 'Is there some goddamn curse on me?' Becker pounded his fist on his thigh this time. 'Does some Gypsy bitch have me as a fucking Voodoo doll? This was supposed to be the best drill money could buy,' he paused, catching his breath, sharply lifting a hand to his forehead, 'what a load of pre-purchase, stitch-me-up bullshit.' He felt like screaming, hitting something, someone, mainly the slick prick who sold him the unit amid a bluster of best-practice crap. Here he was in the place he'd dreamed about for so long and now a technical hitch with a brand-new rig might destroy the whole goddamn lot. 'Jesus, damn it!' He spat, almost dancing on the spot, rolling his eyes up to the icy roof, stewing on the wrongness of it all.

The drill bit was stationary in its sleeve, still smoking and smelling red hot, cooling off slowly in the freezing chamber. With the unit turned off there was just the slightest sound of water flowing somewhere, underneath them, like a gently flowing stream.

Joe raised his eyes, looking like he'd just seen the ghost of Boo Berry. The diamond bit was gone, eroded down to the nub like a spent pencil.

'Oh you are kidding me,' Becker moaned pitiably, punching the metal softly with his knuckles, openly staring at the spot where the bit hit the surface, expecting some sort of hole, a depression at least, some marks in anger certainly. There was no indication of abrasion, the metal alloy, if that's what it was, showed not the slightest bit of surface stress. The spot where the drill had been trying to bore into still looked shiny and brand new like the rest of it.

'Is the entire fucking Universe against me?' He said furiously, feeling the anger thicken in his throat, throwing a death stare at Connie. 'What is this stuff? I'm on site, good to go and what do I have to deal with?' Becker was unblinking, rocking a little. 'A goddamn iron plate that a high-speed drill can't lay a glove on. He crunched his teeth together, twisting his head slowly side to side. Motherfucking piece of shit! This can't be wha— '

Connie interrupted, 'Jesus, relax Becker, you'll have a bloody aneurism, and it's not an iron plate, trust me. Joe, you're the rock guy, what do you reckon?'

Joe was surveying it closely, rubbing his glove across it, knocking on it, searching for anything familiar. Mineralogically speaking it looked solid but with a finely spun, maybe densely crystallised structure, a bit like a pure native metal. But they were soft and malleable, had some give in them - this stuff was perversely the opposite. 'It's pretty much non-acoustic too,' Joe said, frowning at it. 'Hitting it with a boot does nothing, no noise, it's like knocking on rubber…but it's hard like proper metal.' His eyes were alive, puzzled at the way expectation was being violated. 'It's um, like whacking an anvil with a hammer and getting nothing but crickets. This stuff is crazy,' he said, his green eyes narrowing thoughtfully. 'It's gotta be an experimental hybrid of some sort…not very helpful I know but that's about all I've got. Maybe your idea wasn't so barmy,' he said glancing at Connie with a hint of amusement.

'Area 51 you mean…wait, 52, right? She lifted an eyebrow, exhaling with the slightest scrape of humour, 'doubt it Joe, I mean, come on.'

Becker swiped a hand over his face, down his chin, taking mincing steps, watching Joe closely. 'What about the drill Einstein?' He said menacingly, ogling him from a few feet away.

Joe was taken aback by his hostility, how the hell could he be held responsible but then he remembered it was Becker; lashing out was his thing when stuff didn't go as planned. 'Well, uh, it should cut through everything but itself,' he offered timidly. 'Anything lower on Moh's scale should be abraded, simple as that, I honestly don't know what it could be, I can guess but I don't— '

'Oh well let me think for a minute…of course, guess!' Becker said, flinging both arms in front of his face as though catching a football. 'Just give us what you have for Christ sake.'

'It's not much, but I've heard of graphite that's been, like…superheated in meteorites.' He wrinkled his brow, fighting to recall the detail. 'Um, the heat forms diamond but it's got a hex structure so it's actually a lot harder than diamond. But this stuff here isn't just harder than diamond…it's completely impervious. No matter how hard something is, it should show at least a burn mark from the abraded carbon in the bit.' He cleared his throat nervously, peering down at the metal.

'So that means what?' Connie said, feeling an ache in her stomach. 'Maybe it really is some screwy experiment.'

Becker rolled his eyes, 'get real would you,' he said, trying to check his irritation.

'I'm not hearing any pearls of wisdom from you, what do you think? All I've heard is iron plate, I reckon Joe and I are closer than that.'

Lifting his eyebrows high, Becker gawked at her. 'What do I think? Oh, that's easy…I'm being done over by some twisted whatever that has me by the nuts and is slowly squeezing them until they burst like goddamn walnuts.' He had one finger on each temple, rubbing gently, pursing his mouth irritably. 'You know, things are probably turning to shit topside so we need to move.'

'Move how?' Connie said, leaning forward. 'You keeping up with events down here, like paying attention?'

Becker was looking down intently, oblivious to what Connie was saying. 'Christ, this is unbelievable,' he said, a little subdued. 'I thought maybe we might get sprung, maybe a killer storm, a cave in or the Inclinator gets stuck…but this? Seriously, this is…I don't know what it is but it's not bloody fair.' He gazed at her then closed his eyes tight, wishing the nightmare would just go away.

All the details were slowly gelling in Joe's mind, shuffling here, spinning there, rearranging like a Rubik's Cube until everything clicked into the right sequence to add up to something logical. With it came a warm, tingling sensation near the base of his neck like a static relay had just connected and was sparking to life. This thing was under kilometres of ice and had to be at least thirty million years old, he reasoned, because after that bedrock was vacuum-packed by frozen water. A flush of adrenaline exploded into his brain, making him gasp out loud.

Becker pushed his hand roughly through his hair. 'So what now?' He said, hanging his head a little, 'how do we punch through this stuff?' He looked from one to the other, desperate for an idea, a theory, a complete guess. Raised eyes, gently shaking heads told him all he needed to know. 'Damn it,' he spluttered, seeing his decade long dream blowing away like dust in the wind.

' C'mon Becker, there's nothing more we can do. This thing,' she said, banging her foot on it, 'isn't going to be cut by us so, you know what? Just suck it up.'

'Suck it up? Really…that's the best you've got?'

'In these circumstances, yep, that's what I've got,' Connie said, flashing a cold smile, having had quite enough of his sandbox and toy soldiers crap.

'Brilliant advice,' he said.

'Look, there's nothing you or Joe or I can do about it…nothing will cut through this stuff.'

'I didn't do all this to be denied now,' Becker groaned in self-pity. 'We're right here on top of the damn thing, it's like this deposit, if that's what's under here has been deliberately covered to protect it, you know…to keep me out!' He swatted his mouth with his fingers, fighting to keep control of himself.

'Wah Wah, grow up, it is what it is,' Connie said with zero charity, looking away abruptly and deliberately.

'Don't give me that shit, you of all people know what this means, how much I've spent, the years of planning and— '

'Oh fuck me, you got your bat and ball all packed over there?' She said with no hint of humour. 'Look what I've done, look what I've spent, everything coming out of your gob starts with "I".' She broke again from his stare, walking over to the far wall that was bathed in light from the Inclinator car. Becker watched her amble off, grudgingly conceding how good she looked from behind. Proportion, muscles - that did it for him. Becker was losing his mind, he'd just confirmed it.

Joe didn't want to say it but he felt like he had to. Becker intimidated him to the point of losing most of his higher mental function but he had to do it, and it wasn't all bad news. In fact it could be construed as, well…rather good.

Standing and clearing his throat quietly he walked a few paces toward the rig and said, 'er Carson, I um…don't think there's any rhodium here, or anything else for that matter, uh…apart from what we're standing on.'

Becker almost did a double take, breathing 'fuck me' and then louder, 'you too Joe, you in for a pound as well? Okay, give me what you've got, both barrels, bring it on both of you, expedition assassination…go for it.' He waved both hands toward his chest, 'bring it, take your best fucking shot my friend,' he said, resigned to more demoralising home truths whistling past his ears.

'I'm not trying to make things worse,' he said, holding his palms up defensively. 'I just think things are becoming clearer. This plate of stuff, might be what your EMAR birds identified, not the deposit you figured it was. I mean, think about it, what's the likelihood of this thing sitting on top of a deposit of the world's rarest metal?' Joe stared at him warily, waiting for a rush of blood and profanity from Becker. He didn't think it was coming because as he reeled off his words, Becker's face was collapsing further, like the final crush of neutrons before they surrendered to the inevitability of a black hole. Every syllable was a grenade that dug a brand-new furrow in his brow, unbricking his hope, pretty much his reason for being and he suddenly looked like he might cry.

'Oh sweet Jesus,' Becker said, arms limply at his sides, seeing the logic in what he was saying, reluctantly conceding that Joe's words made horrible sense.

'It's not all bad,' Joe said, 'if this stuff is as unusual as we think, I mean we can't even touch it with our diamond-bit, then maybe it's way more important than any regular rhodium find, uh…if rhodium can be called regular of course.' The last thing he wanted to do was dis Becker's rhodium because that was like urinating on Church grounds, sullying the holy water with soda pop.

'Use Becker-speak Joe, replace important with valuable and fame and he'll get it just fine, right? I mean it could be, should be crazy valuable. Maybe even more so than your stupid rhodium. 'Connie snarled.

'Hey!' Becker snapped, spinning his head around, 'careful there *Missy*,' knowing how much it pissed her off when he called her that, a name reserved for special occasions.

'Careful you,' she returned with a sharp finger jab, eyeing him stonily.

Becker paused for a moment, chucking Joe's words around, sucking his mouth in and nodding slightly. 'You might be right, goddamn it, of course you are. This stuff might be the most significant discovery in the history of what…geology, chemistry, physics…you name it.' His eyes were blazing as he fought to connect his voice with his rambling mind. 'God, it could be worth, well who knows, right? The whole bloody world will beat a path to my door…er, I mean our door,' he glanced giddily at Connie, pulling at his ear. 'We could name our own price, this would make us famous…like the chick that discovered uranium, you know, what's her name?' Becker had a glassy, glazed look, like a nutter with a sandwich board.

'Madame Curie you mean?' Joe said, 'she discovered radium.'

'Yeah that's the one, she's famous, a name in the history books, right?'

'And died in the process…radiation poisoning. Slow, very ugly.'

'Shit,' Becker exclaimed, glancing sidelong at the metal, there's no chance this might be…'

'There's every chance,' Connie chimed in, stifling her mirth perfectly. 'When your hair starts falling out we'll know for sure, and trust me, that'd be quite the look with your huge melon.'

'I think you'll be fine,' Joe said, giving Connie a cautionary smile. 'It must be an alloy of some sort, tough, atomically very dense.'

'Of course then there's the small issue of how you might remove it or if you can remove it,' Connie said, pondering Becker's assignment of "value" to it. 'Good luck trying to cut it into pieces,' she quipped, regarding him with contempt, to which Becker scowled and blew her a kiss.

'Hope you brought your Swiss Army Knife.'

We'll figure something out smart-arse, maybe we can melt it or find the edge and pry it off the bedrock or something like— '

'Anyway,' Joe interrupted quietly, 'let's get the light towers up, fire up the sub. We need to get rid of the ice to the east so we can get a look at the middle of this thing.' He looked around tentatively at the cave. 'We'll have to keep the ceiling low to minimise vapour but it's still going to get mighty steamy in here.'

Connie glanced at Becker, 'better put your water wings on, you know you can't swim.'

'Yeah well, I can float,' he said, wincing, adding angrily, 'give it a bloody rest.'

'When we get home and we're safe I'll give it a rest,' she said, folding her arms against her chest. Hiding her emotions was becoming more difficult as she looked anxiously toward the west, where Joe reckoned the centre of the thing had to be. Sarcasm would only take her so far.

It was already damp in the chamber due to normal bedrock liquefaction but the rig's ability to turn ice into vapour would create clouds of condensation in the still air. Moist was about to get very wet indeed and only a few minutes in, groundwater was already inches deep and vapour swathing the cavern like a Shanghai smog. Heat from the endothermal unit and steam from the sublimation combined to raise temperatures above freezing point, making them uncomfortably hot in their thick G-Tek thermals. If they discarded the waterproofs and got wet though, they'd freeze to death or get frostbite when the temperature fell again.

***

Joe was sitting on the back of the sub, piloting it manually, reckoning the centre of the metallic structure had to be close, if only based on the steepening curvature of the lines.

'Do you want to answer the damn thing?' Connie said. Becker's radiophone had been pumping out static on and off for five minutes now. 'Weems wants to speak to you…might be important.'

'I'll speak to him when I need something.'

Connie squinted at him narrowly. 'Nice management style, learn that from the Soviets?'

'Jesus, not now, take a break,' he said, waving her away as he surveyed the additional acreage of metal they were opening up, doing the sums on tonnage and value, coming up with a number he could barely process. If they could somehow manage to move this stuff and if it was as unique as he reckoned, his fame, well… move over Columbus, Amundsen, hold the door Neil…I'm comin' through.

Connie ignored his incessant babblings about buying a line of islands in the Pacific and maybe Hawaii or Majorca with the change. Joe knew this stuff wasn't going anywhere. Becker could fantasize all he liked but that's all it would ever be, ego driven delusion that was English for Becker, Joe snuffled, picturing his smug dial in the medical book for reference.

Connie, like any right-minded person, naturally assumed it would be virginal ground they were clearing of ice down here, like the first boot print on Mars or the Moon, no place you'd expect to find some odd, artificial object staring back at you. The Pole was just as untouched by humans as the planets, in fact more so she figured because this place was sight unseen, no NASA robots had ever trundled across it or even spied this place properly. She frowned and clenched her jaw, wondering what might have been around before the big freeze set in…it was absolutely clear that something trod these shores tens of millions of years ago because the anomaly sure as hell didn't spirit itself here. Connie felt her heart start drumming an uneasy rhythm as everything around her started gathering an unsettling rigour. It had been in there for a while and for her, like Joe, the clues were starting to snap into place like jigsaw pieces.

***

Joe stopped the rig to let the air clear a bit, hopping off to check out the ground they'd opened up. 'Man this thing is big,' he said, gazing at the intricately carved surface, getting a better grip on its awesome dimensions. 'The rings are reducing so we agree there has to be a centre point, like a bulls-eye right?' He looked at Connie expectantly. 'So, uh…what do you figure is there?' He spoke slowly, pregnantly, 'in the middle of the whole thing I mean.' Joe's eyes grew wider as he spoke, unblinking.

'Does there have to be a middle?' Connie said in a faltering tone, assuming there did but not entirely sure. Maybe the pattern would change at some point.

'Connie please,' Joe said mockingly. 'The curvatures are decreasing so it means there'll eventually be a point of axis with a circle around it and no more within.' He shook his head almost imperceptibly, 'the only unknown is the size, math says so.'

Connie shot her old friend a disarming smile, 'you're the geek Joe, if you say it's so then okay.' She watched him fidget with his clothing, averting his eyes, looking down at his ruby red gloves. Joe was brilliant in his field and a top-notch guy but he lacked the conviction to really succeed in a business sense. He was a follower without the natural instinct to be a leader in exploration, possibly anything else, and worse, he seemed to expect failure from just about everything he did. Becker was so far left of Joe it wasn't funny, and he scared the crap out of him, reducing Joe oft-times to a sweaty, heart pounding muddle. Connie found their interactions comical at times, if Becker didn't pay him what he did, which was a shitload over sticker, Joe would've walked years ago.

'Okay,' Becker said warily, 'air is good, let's rig up, find this dartboard of yours.'

'Bulls-eye, the centre is the bulls-eye,' Joe corrected politely.

'Whatever, just find the bloody centre,' he shot back harshly, 'the clock is ticking!'

Connie twisted her mouth at Joe, nodding, giving him the familiar *"ignore the prick"* look.

Joe had chucked around all the options and was now pretty sure he knew what they were dealing with. Doubts were circling but only because the verdict was so unnerving…deranged really. Joe was surprised Connie hadn't crunched the numbers and come to a similar conclusion, or maybe she had, and like him was too afraid to give it air, to actually voice it out loud. Maybe he was wrong but if he was right, well…his brain told him he needed to keep it simple. Dig toward the final curvature, see if there were answers, and if there were, assess them coolly and carefully. Changing tack, he winced, picturing an empty circle…a prosaic metallic centrepiece without detail or even the slightest whiff of a deeper meaning. Weighing it up all over again Joe's heart raced, breath hard to draw, like a hand was closing around his throat. Was this thing supposed to remain hidden. Were they doing precisely the wrong thing by stripping away what might be a carefully designed veil? He agonised over it but realised the question was so moot it was almost amusing. Becker wouldn't be dissuaded and nor would he, the curiosity to know had him hooked and it even prevailed over the

59

fear of dying horribly under the ice. The bulls-eye was now the prize - rhodium was off the table, replaced by something of greater magnitude.

Joe jumped back on the rig and fired it up, studying the last circle-line, believing the next would be around thirty metres across, breathing deeply, releasing a long, slow exhalation between his teeth. He tasted something strange in his mouth, metallic, salty, hot, a sensation new to him. Licking his lips he swallowed carefully, steadying himself, looking down at the silver driveshaft of the vehicle. He pushed the machine very slowly forward amid a burst of moist white vapour, another curvature coming and going, chewing ice from the plate's surface up to a patchy ceiling of about two and a half metres.

Every muscle in his body was pulled tight as he steeled his mind, bracing himself for this to be the one…but If it was, it was no different to the others, just plain silver-grey metal broken by a circumferential incision. He'd convinced himself the centre would be barren of answers, they'd do all this work, end up with nothing but endless questions and no possibility of closure, of finding out why…how his thing was here. It would remain some unsolvable architectural enigma left under the ice to haunt humanity forever, something to be prodded and evaluated, theorised over by generations of geeks for the rest of time.

Joe sighted something ahead and his fingers opened by reflex, dropping the rig's hand controller, a burst of adrenaline shooting through him. Powering down the rig he killed the engine, plunging the chamber into deafening silence broken only by the slooshing of running water. His eyes pushed out so that the rims were clearly visible. 'Connie, um, Becker,' he slurred without blinking or moving his head.

The other two were rigid, staring fish-eyed, seeing it at the same time as Joe who stammered something in gibberish, glancing around sharply, wrestling with a thousand formless thoughts. Blood pulsed in his neck, a disconcerting thud near his voice box. Slowly moving off the rig he inched in step with the other two, eyes roaming the partially denuded ice ahead of them. The thing was still sealed inside the ice but was translucent, clear enough so they could see it pretty well.

Connie's hair prickled on her body, the visual made her gasp out for air. 'Oh my, ' she whispered grabbing Becker's arm. 'What, uh…um?' Her words wound down like a dying battery.

Becker just stared. If he was breathing no one could tell.

Observable through the crumbling wall of ice was something resembling a colossal halide globe, a bit like a giant shining eyeball, Becker reckoned, unconsciously searching for cover, darting his eyes around without moving his head. It was so unexpected but what was expected, none of them had a ghost of an answer to that one. Not this though, Connie thought. The reality was they'd unearthed a highly radiant object and that was it, at least right now. She looked around for something to steady herself on, seeing Joe's head tilted at a funny angle as he eyed it, watching an odd flicker within, maybe some sort of complexity, density or structure. Joe stepped slowly around it, making a nervous humming sound, certain it was way more than just a source of light.

Becker finally pushed a breath of air through his throat, 'okay, look…just stay calm,' he said, pressing his hands out spastically a few times. 'Just stay where you are,' he puffed, his forehead now beaded with perspiration. He stared vacuously at the imperious light, lines of sweat dripping down his cheeks.

'We're fine,' Connie said uncertainly, off-put by a strange fluttering in her stomach as she studied what was poking rather innocuously through the ice. 'It's you that looks ready to pack it in, take a few breaths.' She nodded at him and he reciprocated with a couple of gasping breaths. Jesus, the man for every situation she mused with a derisive grunt.

'Uh, I'm…good,' Becker croaked, angling his head like Joe, straining to make sense of what he was looking at.

'Joe, lose the rest of the ice,' Connie said, taking a few short steps toward it, peering more closely. She flashed Becker a wry grin, 'hey, maybe there's a brand name on it, shit, or a US flag, you know NASA,' she crinkled her nose then quickly regained a sober expression. 'Joe – go!'

The rig made short work of removing the rest of the ice, leaving the hemispherical object exposed, naked, unexplainable and most of all *'wrong'*. The thing was entombed under kilometres of glacial ice, at depth as hard as a high tensile alloy, and apparently doing its thing, shining like a buried star for God knew how long. It was simple in outline, mathematically pure, it clearly could have been anything, but the one thing they did know was it gave off light, but no heat whatsoever.

So there you have it they thought, the centre of the great circle was filled with bright white light that had distinct structure, shape and maybe some internal complexity. A smaller, black hemisphere lay about a metre away, just to the left of where they were standing, like a basketball cut in half. Apart from the big one being a light source, both were without any immediate signs of utility, at least as they would define it.

What wasn't lost on them was the growing discomfort that couldn't be ignored. Joe tentatively embraced it, albeit silently, because collectively it tallied to something not covered by the human playbook. The seemingly impenetrable metal, the unexplainable, likely impossible location, and of course the jewel in the crown, the weird hemisphere of radiance shining in the middle like an inscrutable egg yolk. Taken together, it told them unequivocally that this was a universe away from some steeply covert Government experiment.

Joe turned from the light, gazing at Connie then shifting his glazed expression to Becker.

'Um, you okay Joe?' Connie said, knowing he had something to say.

His expression was grim as he watched her. 'You know, right? He said the words with an awed undertone, inclining his head the other way as he said it.

'No idea,' Connie said, lying. She had an involuntary resistance to even thinking it, and no fucking way she'd be the first to say it.

Joe looked from Connie to Becker and back again, shaking his head reluctantly. 'Okay…you know what it isn't then? They glanced over Joe's shoulder at the glowing object.

'This can't be from Earth,' Joe stated matter of factly. They shifted their gaze back to him with no change in expression. Becker pursed his lips, nodding his head in agreement. Even he'd managed to get it by a simple process of elimination.

'Can't be,' Connie said, forking a hand through her hair nervously. 'No way it's the Russians or Americans, the Chinese or anyone else...no way, not down here.'

Joe said quietly, 'do you know what it would take to get this thing down here? No way it's possible, no way it's ours.'

'Of course it's fucking not,' Connie said, 'no one on Earth has the tech to do this. I mean we're down here but this thing was surrounded by solid glacier with no signs of interruption to the ice.' She saw Joe staring dumbly at the object, the light reflecting in his unblinking eyes.

Becker squeezed his eyebrows together sceptically, 'it's the most obvious answer but how do we know what sort of crazy stuff they're doing out in Nevada or at that Lab Twelve place in Russia you told us about? There's all sorts of mad shit going on out there…like you said, mysterious objects in the sky, people disappearing, stuff like that.'

'For God's sake snap out of it,' Connie said, 'if you think humans could do this then you're even more stupid than you look. Joe – help me out will you.'

'I'm just throwing it out there,' Becker said defensively, 'I get that it's not ours.'

Joe cleared his throat, 'uh, this has to be the work of something off-planet, not us, not humans, but as to what, well…it could be an artefact or a "tell all" of some kind. You know, put here for us when we'd acquired some smarts.'

Connie turned slowly to Becker, twisting her mouth, sneering.

Joe continued, ignoring both of them, 'this location ticks all the boxes. We only found it by advanced remote sensing using radar and gravimetrics.'

Becker stared at Joe, deadpan, rubbing a hand over his chin stubble. 'Fuck me,' he said.

'I get the whole artefact thing,' Connie said, 'but why…to let them know if we're officially a threat so they can send off a flotilla to wipe us out?'

'More likely to let them know when it's worthwhile making contact,' Joe said stiffly, clenching his jaw nervously, roaming his eyes around, looking terrified.

'Well, we're all in it together,' Connie soothed, knowing she wasn't doing any better, her heart pounding somewhere it shouldn't be, too high, too low, it seemed to be everywhere.

Nodding, Joe said, 'so that's when meaningful dialogue could be had, I mean it's hardly worth trying to communicate with savages I guess.'

Connie smirked and winked playfully at Becker, repeating the dose, 'well I guess they won't be talking to you.'

Becker gave her a hard smile, 'Just focus.'

She eyed him warily, 'no comeback? Christ, you really are rattled.'

'Well okay smart-arse, answer me this, how did they get this thing here? How could anyone get this under kilometres of ice without disturbing it? Or did they dig the ice out and pack it back like a fucking sandcastle?' Thinking about it, Becker thought it sounded sort of plausible, 'but wouldn't there be some indication, some evidence of their tampering?' He looked quizzically at Connie and Joe, both of them looking as puzzled as he felt.

'I've been wondering about that,' Joe said, moving closer. 'I reckon it depends on whether we're supposed to do something to activate it. You know, to have it do whatever it was put here to do, assuming it has a purpose. Maybe mobilising it requires an act of significant cognitive strength that would demonstrate our technical ability'

Becker had zoned out and was now scowling at Joe, minutely shaking his head.

Connie crossed her arms, 'Are you really that challenged?' then, seriously 'Joe?'

'What I'm saying is, if this is just an object that tells them we've found it, it would need to be hidden somewhere and require a technical capability for us to actually find it. With me Carson?'

'So far,' he said. He wasn't sure but he went with it anyway, refusing to look at Connie who managed to hold her tongue.

'Like I said, the other scenario is that the object needs to be activated somehow. Not just located but triggered to do something.'

Becker was scratching his face with all his fingers on one hand.

Joe lifted his shoulders, all of this was guesswork, figuring he was probably wrong about everything, logic was fine up to a point but it was only human logic and who even knew if that was "logical" in the broader sense of the Universe. Having the slightest insight into how an off-planet mind worked was pie in the sky stuff. He was uncomfortably certain that human assumptions wouldn't hold up in the deeper recesses of space. Logic was relative, had to be…but was that simply being logical? He rubbed an eye, feeling like he was trapped in an infinite feedback loop.

'Hello…Joe?' Connie said sharply, seeing him drift off.

Joe blinked, squinting narrowly, knowing what had to happen. This was a one-time opportunity and scared, terrified maybe, no way in shit was he going to pass on it. 'We need to see what this thing is about, try and understand it, work out what makes it tick.'

Connie looked at him sideways, 'but if this thing needs complex action to activate it then it shouldn't be buried out of sight, right?'

'Well, yes.' Joe said, sounding unsure, 'it's just an opinion that could be completely wrong of course. Maybe we only need to touch one of them, we don't know yet.' His eyes sparkled as he nibbled on what he'd just said, brows squeezed into a protruding ridge above his eyes.

Connie sighed, 'so why the hell is it stuck down here?'

'Alf Wegener,' Joe breathed, spreading his hands thoughtfully, apparently throwing her a bone as he continued stewing over the few facts they had.

Becker was irritated by the meaningless byplay. 'Oh for God's sake…Alf what? Look, can we focus? Time is ticking…it's no time for fucking parlour games.'

Joe took a step back, blinking several times in a hurry. 'Look, I don't know, nobody does, but I think maybe it was created to be found without too much difficulty but things happened that weren't, um…anticipated. Maybe they didn't try and understand it carefully enough or maybe it didn't matter. A civilisation capable of creating this thing, well perhaps they don't make mistakes and I'm the one screwing up.' Joe gulped, scratching at his ear until it turned beet red. 'Shit…who knows,' he snapped, feeling muddled, 'we only have our own shitty little minds to work with here.'

'Cut to the chase will you,' Becker implored, 'just give us what you have…we have zero time. We need to do something, find something, get topside ASAP or we're done. So speak freely, in bloody English!'

'I agree with Becker, much as it hurts,' Connie said. 'Spill it Joe.' Becker's radiophone squawked again. 'You're going to have to answer that eventually,' Connie said.

'First things first…Joe?' Becker said, craning his head aggressively at him.

'My opinion only… right? What the makers of this, uh…thing didn't factor in I think was continental drift. Antarctica used to be the central jig in a massive continent that existed yonks ago…hundreds of millions of years I think.' He could see Becker's eyes start to glaze over. 'Carson stay with me, I can't dumb it down any more.'

'Hey, watch it, I'm not made of stone,' he fired back. 'How do you know all this crap anyway?'

'You seriously don't know I have a geophysics Doctorate from Flinders Uni? You employed me yourself.'

'I, um, just wasn't sure all this stuff was part of that I guess.'

'You goose Becker,' Connie snorted. 'People not your strong point, right?'

'And your degree is in what Professor?' Becker countered, blowing her a kiss.

'Common sense…school of life, stuff like that,' she sneered. 'The same subjects you failed and continue to fail daily.'

'Go,' Becker said, jerking his head at him, turning away from Connie.

'So the continent started to break up. India went one way, Australia the other and the middle piece, Antarctica, went south until it reached the bottom of the world. The ice in the west from memory is around thirty million years old and that's what's sitting above us. This thing wasn't supposed to be hidden but the drifting continents shunted it into a deep freeze, hid it more profoundly than they, whoever the hell they are, could have imagined I think.'

'Surely this is an advanced race though,' Connie said, perplexed, 'shouldn't they have foreseen continental drift, changing climate and so on?'

'That's what I thought but maybe they don't have it, remember, Earth is probably the only planet in the solar system with plate tectonics. Maybe it's really rare.'

'Doubt it,' Connie said, but knew it couldn't be ruled out. Venus likely had it, some of the moons of Saturn and Jupiter possibly.

'These are all guesses,' Joe conceded, staring distantly at the metallic ground.

'It was just dumb luck we found this thing, right?' Becker said, shifting his gaze to the shining object, still finding it all quite implausible.

'Yeah well that's right,' Joe replied, 'this thing ended up so completely buried it should never have been found…like not ever. Sitting under all this ice in a mining embargoed continent.' He looked at Becker hesitantly, 'it's one in a…well pick your own number really.'

'It just needed old money-bags, all-nuts Becker to find it,' Connie said with an acid grin. 'Just ignore all the rules and treaties and go digging around for Yamashita's Gold under the ice.'

Becker's features lightened. 'You know, you're right Connie, I might be responsible for one of the greatest scientific finds in history, I hadn't thought that far ahead.' He smiled broadly at her and she returned with a stiff tongue poking right at him.

'Just dumb luck, and that suits you down to the ground.'

Joe jumped in to head off another stoush. 'Carson, you need to report this to Weems,' he said seriously, he's been trying to get you for an hour at least.' He looked at his watch, gasping. 'Jesus, we've been down here five hours!'

Becker grabbed the Motorola from his belt holster and headed for the tunnel, walking into darkness with only his helmet light for illumination. Becker was about to hit the blue Call button when he caught something echoing in the distance, up in the coalmine darkness of the tunnel. Becker stopped breathing, narrowing his eyes but it was way too dark. The light from his helmet only extended a few metres up the incline, ending in a dead straight line. 'What the hell,' he said under his breath, scanning the blackness ahead, seeing nothing, feeling his heart beat faster. 'Joe, Connie…come here,' he said tensely, fighting to slow his breathing.

'Probably can't operate the radiophone,' she muttered to Joe who nodded vague agreement. Walking into the tunnel they saw Becker peering fixedly into the depths of the darkness. 'There's something up there,' he breathed without turning to look at them. They both froze, staring into the silent inky blackness.

'Have you gone mad?' Connie said loudly, hearing the echo die, replaced by the beating of her own heart. 'You think a penguin has waddled down to say hey?'

'Ssshh,' he said urgently…listen.' He had his finger to his mouth, eyes as wide as they could go, staring openly.

Connie's eyes suddenly bugged open when a scratching, scraping sound rose in the tunnel ahead, rebounding harshly off the ice. 'Jesus Christ,' she whispered with a spray of white breath, her face melting into a strange frown… part focus, part fear. 'Something is coming down the tunnel, um, but…how?' She felt heavy in her legs as she wrestled with a question she had no answer to.

'How can that be?' Joe said apprehensively, 'the only car is in the chamber; you sure as hell can't walk down that slope.'

The scraping sound appeared close but it was hard to tell; the noise was everywhere, echoing off the walls and floor. Connie's pulse was tapping a beat in her mouth, Joe was jerking his head around, searching, sizing up the unearthly noise, having no reasonable answer.

'You don't suppose they're here already do you,' Connie said, not believing it but equally not discounting anything. The coincidence between locating the object and the strange noise emerging in the tunnel, well that was troubling indeed.

'Turn your lights off,' Becker said quietly. 'Maybe we can get a look at it.'

'Perhaps it's a polar bear that smells you Becker,' Connie said, suppressing a giggle.

'North Pole,' Joe reminded her.

'Dumb arse,' Becker said distantly, still straining to see any detail ahead.

'Turn your geek off for five minutes,' Connie said to Joe. 'It's the principle, not the literal.

'Can't bear to be wrong can you,' Becker teased, turning and grinning insufferably, leaning forward. 'Bear, get it?'

Connie eyed him scornfully, pondering his idiot state of mind.

Joe turned off his light, joining the others in the murkiness and although the light from the chamber bled into the tunnel it was still pitch dark a couple of metres in. After her eyes adjusted, the thing emerged into the half-light and Connie saw it. She yelped and edged back toward the chamber, seeing a point of light approaching, a single bright lens amid the nothingness.

Joe had moved back with Connie, leaving Becker in front. 'Um, well…it seems to be moving down the Inclinator tracks,' he said shakily, watching something writhing and twisting behind the optic, definitely heading their way.

Becker suddenly threw his head forward, blinking, and slitting his eyes, 'oh you're kidding me,' he said, sighing heavily, striding forward into the gloom.

'Well, well,' Joe said, feeling himself decompress a bit, dabbing sweat from his forehead with a glove.

Connie watched nervously, trying to make sense of the bizarre scene. Were they trying to get away from something topside?

A few metres away was an ice sled, heavily converted with metal flanges, allowing it to slide or more likely bump along the polymer rails. Sitting atop it was Quincy, hands coated with some sort of slimy goo, in his right hand a rappel handle and a makeshift metal brake attached to both flanges. Quincy's eyes were massive, like some poor soul pulled half-alive from a horrible aviation accident. He'd clearly had a hell of a time of it, scraping and shuddering down the steeply angled tunnel.

'What the hell?' Becker said curiously, stunned by his sudden appearance, 'and what is that crap all over your hands?' The poor bloke looked and smelt like he'd backstroked through an EXXON runoff pool.

Quincy's shoulders were heaving as he dragged in air, exhausted from the exertion of the dark and tormenting descent. 'It's...uh...drill lubricant...uh, had to apply it every few hundred metres or so to, uh...keep it moving over the tracks.' He took several gasping breaths, groaning and getting up from the sled. 'Jesus what a fucking nightmare,' he added through more guttural breaths that shook his body.

'So why are you here?' Becker repeated urgently, 'is there trouble topside?' His eyes were wild, waiting on the worst news possible.

'I'm here because you ignored protocol and didn't answer your fucking phone,' he said angrily, puffing. The microwave sensors...altimeters said the tunnel was fine so there was only one answer...you.'

'We were, er, otherwise engaged, I was about to call you when I heard your little buggy approaching.'

'You asked if there is trouble topside. If you'd taken my call you'd already know that we're in some serious shit. We've been made...it's over.' He eyed him squarely, face dripping perspiration. 'We're done Carson.'

Becker's face collapsed into a twisted, lined mess as he searched Quincy's face for several seconds. 'What...fuck...how?' He demanded roughly. 'It's been less than a day since the meteor exploded, it's not enough— '

'Well apparently it was enough time,' he interrupted, speaking louder. 'The media's all over the place...maggots on a fucking corpse. They're hanging from the rafters up there. The first chopper arrived three hours ago, it almost landed on top of us. Seriously, it's insane. Four more choppers arrived soon after. There's tents everywhere, snowmobiles cutting up the place, and drones for Christ's sake...doing low altitude magnetic shit looking for pieces of the stupid rock.'

'You used the cover plan, right?' Becker said, barely concealing his rage, staring severely at Quincy, feeling nauseous.

'The British media that found us laughed in our faces. They saw your moniker on some of the documents, started quoting Antarctic treaties and well...Weems folded like a cheap suit. He didn't tell them about the rhodium but he said you were, er...exploring.'

'Fucking Weems,' Becker said savagely. 'Are they still on site?'

'They've gone, but they reported us to UNEP, the UN's environmental protection monkeys. They're sending an enforcement team from New Zealand to Scott Base and then on to us, this will be news by tomorrow, global bloody news, from Russia to anywhere you can think of.'

Becker's lips pulled back, exposing crooked front teeth. 'Fuck!' He screamed. 'I'm screwed. That goddamn meteor, seriously, what are the chances?' He was almost doing a war dance on the spot, trying to think through a haze of anger. 'That pencil necked, tea-totalling arsehole. What are the odds,' he repeated, 'one in what? What's the biggest fucking number you can think of?'

'Googolplex,' Joe said idly.

'Okay one in fucking Googolplex then...that's the odds. Goddamn that idiot Weems. I'm going to ruin the bastard. His bonus, his payment...they're smoke.'

'I say this with the utmost respect,' Connie said, deadpan, trying her best to be serious, 'I don't think he's the one that needs to worry about being ruined. We're all in the shit but yours is way deeper...bottomless I would venture.'

'Shit,' Becker said more quietly this time, still trying to think of something. 'What do we do…is there anything we can do?' Eyes darting, he said it to no one in particular but was happy to take anything from anybody at this point.

Joe dropped his shoulders. 'We're done,' he said. 'Even if we go topside, get away before the MPs and Feds arrive, they know we were here.'

Connie's brow softened and relaxed into something less severe. 'I think there may, and I stress *'may'* be a way out,' Connie said uncertainly. 'It's not perfect but it's a plan.' She looked at him knowingly, nodding, breaking into a cold smile. 'You're welcome.'

He was impassive. 'I'll thank you after I hear it…if it's not some half-arsed suicide plan.'

'Like a mission to dig up the South Pole you mean?'

'Give it a rest.'

'Maybe I won't tell you.' She looked away in mock annoyance.

'For God's sake, now isn't the time to be screwing around,' Becker said pleadingly.

'Let's go back to the chamber, I think Quincy might like to see what we, uh…found. Then I'll tell you.'

Walking out of the tunnel and back into the muted light of the cavern, Quincy had no idea what to expect but the scene that dropped into place nearly blew his heart. Edging onto the polished metal he peered like a startled possum at the incisions, stroking his chin as he went, following the lines of curvature, ending up staring at the hemisphere of light, belching bright white light from the final elemental circle.

'Good sweet God…why didn't you tell me about this? This is…I'm not sure what words to use.' He glanced up with eyes radiating genuine, unfettered awe. 'Uh…is this is what I think it is?'

'What do you think it is?' Connie asked curiously, eyeballing Quincy who was standing there silently, still searching for words.

'We agree it's off-world,' Joe said, 'and no way in hell it's anything made by us.'

'Um so, alien...that's what you're saying…alien?' He said incredulously, inching up to it in short steps, arms slightly out to the side. 'Motherfucker,' he whispered to it, gently snuffling air through his nose, shocked by its simplistic facade. His overriding thought was what manner of thing had designed it, rendered the contours, cut the incisions, and why had they placed it on our world?

'Okay Connie, hit me with that idea of yours,' Becker said, holding still anxiously, hoping her acerbic smarts had come up with something real, because at the moment he was neck-deep in it. Life was unravelling, his billionaire business empire sinking into the blue ice chamber, so blinded was he by the chase he'd never seriously considered failing. He was so consumed by the need to just get out and do it he'd pretty much ignored everybody and now that he was confronting it, it was painful as he mulled over what he might have done to his friends. Fuck the investors and the Board, they could take a hike. He looked around, cursing himself, wondering why it took a massive screw up to make him see what was so obvious to everyone else. Connie had been right all along, he was being a dickhead… was a dickhead.

Connie surveyed Becker briefly, 'well as I see it, it's pretty simple,' she started, upbeat. 'In the context of humanity at least, this discovery is probably unrivalled. If it's what we think it is, it'll make its discoverers famous.' She raised her hands in an expansive gesture, squinting with a hint of drama. 'There was never any mineral deposit here, we know that now.' Joe and Becker nodded tentatively, curious about the direction she was taking. 'The anomaly found by gravity magnetics was this uh…object, pure and simple. You with me Becker?'

'Uh, yep I guess, keep going.' His eyes were eager, expression still haunted, but slightly more hopeful.

'So you were never hunting a mineral deposit, you were hunting something of far more significance. You wanted to fund the expedition, then reveal the artefact to the world.' Connie stopped momentarily, stifling a giggle, grinning. 'It was your gift to humanity,' she sighed, unable to hold back a full-blown snort.

Becker's face lit up and a smile beamed across his face. 'Jesus, I'm a goddamn philanthropist!' He said jubilantly, quickly deciding he loved it. 'Now that's a story…it's bloody genius.' He peered at Joe who shrugged hesitantly, nodding anyway.

'It's a little brittle but I'm not sure how they could definitively disprove it,' she said, tilting her head thoughtfully.

Becker thought about it some more. 'What about the expedition summaries, documentation and such, that's a game breaker if they get hold of them,' he said, wrinkling his brow.

'No it isn't - that was the cover story to keep it quiet if someone got too close. Look, the story is that you had the feeling there was something of scientific interest under the ice. You didn't know how or why but they were the dreams, the feeling you'd had for a decade. So you did some exploring and yes technically it was illegal but it was all for the benefit of the planet. You were searching for something of science, not material worth.' Connie coughed, nearly choking on the words. 'There's no mineral deposit here so no one can claim self-interest,' Connie said, pausing, mulling it further. Becker and no self-interest; it was a sentence steeped in madness. 'Jesus what a load of steaming horseshit,' she piped with a mocking grin.

'I love it,' Becker said, 'it's a beaut and it craps all over the truth. Quincy, Joe?'

'It's got more holes than a…uh, you know, uh…but it'll do,' Joe said, 'that's as good as it gets I suppose.'

Quincy nodded agreement. 'Simple, difficult to disprove.'

'Give me your radiophone,' Connie said gruffly, 'I'll tell Weems, make sure he toes the line if anyone returns before we get topside. I'll get him to shred the expedition docs, bury 'em in the snow. We could try and sell it as a cover plan if it was found but it might be better just to avoid it altogether. Selling the philanthropic piece will be tough enough,' she said, flashing him a condescending smile.

Becker gave Connie the phone, beaming approval. 'Thank you, Connie. This means a lot…hey, I knew you cared,' he said, still grinning widely, putting his hand on her shoulder and squeezing it gently, thinking he might just extract himself from this disaster yet.

'I'm protecting myself…then Joe, then Quincy, then you. Yes I care…you great big oaf.'

Connie had devised the cover story soon after she realised what the object was. She'd been struck by the devastating feeling of failure from the outset, but the meteor had really taken care of it. If it wasn't the rock from space it would've been some other unknown, because there were just too many poorly machined pieces in the puzzle. Becker knew it and ignored it, she understood it, respected it, Murphy's Law wasn't just an eponymous theory, it was L-A-W. Only fools ignored it.

Stumbling wearily into the tunnel, Connie hit Call on the Motorola. That idiot Weems would get with the program if he wanted even a dime out of this debacle, she was sure of that if nothing else. Connie knew what was ahead of them now, there was no going topside, at least not now. What they had to do was clear, it felt right, logical. To truly live the lie they needed to coax something from the enigmatic object. Maybe if they were vaguely fluent with it, if that was even possible, they might convince the UN that they were here on some genuinely altruistic expedition. If there was some sort of meaning or faculty locked inside, and they could jimmy the door open just a tiny bit, the planet would be too gob-smacked to give a rat's ass about the hows and whys of discovery.

Even if they were deemed guilty of trespass, violating the Madrid Protocol, gifting the most momentous news in the history of, uh…she searched for the right word, deciding that it would sit right at the top…make them global superstars. They would be beyond the reach of any Court of law, world Government or the pious clowns from the UN. Of course, there was a massive human assumption built into it, Connie knew, and it was a total, unabridged mystery. Was the imperative of the artefact good or bad or was it imprecise, maybe somewhere in between, or nothing resembling intelligence at all? That was the kicker. Delivering no news or bad news simply wouldn't do the job.

9. Numbers

"Nothing is more frightening than a fear you cannot name."
~ *Cornelia Funke*

They'd thrown it around for a solid hour, hammered out the details, identified the primary deficiencies, and in their minds, the alibi was as good as fact. Weems was now acutely aware of his pivotal role in executing the ruse. Becker had doubled his payment, rounding it up to five million bucks so he was fully onboard. If he failed, he got dick, so to say he was highly motivated was somewhat restrained.

The Portaloo was sitting proudly near the western wall of the chamber, bright blue against the lighter blue of the cave wall, a garish testament to human biology and its need for regular ablutions. Connie gazed around at the material contrasts in the chamber and thought they were comical if not a little embarrassing, the mysterious object on one side and the portable dunny on the other. Connie smothered a nervous laugh, imagining the likely technical disconnect that might exist…but surely, they'd need similar conveniences, if they were still biological of course. Joe reckoned they might have discarded their organics in favour of a more resilient silicon vessel. And by resilient he meant immortal, pretty sure they'd only have to be slightly advanced on humanity, bullish that intelligence and eternal life were connected at the genetic level, the former literally programmed to strive for the latter. In his words, the cerebral cortex was an immortality chaser and with another five hundred years, humanity would be at the precipice of eternal life, he enthused, eyes sparkling, bouncing foot to foot, but slowly becoming still, disheartened that he wouldn't be part of it. Missed it by that much, he moaned to himself, the pain carved in the lines on his face.

Cracking open some army-style rations, Becker gazed miserably at the dirty cans, guessing they were at least a hundred years old. 'It says Insalata di Riso but it smells, Jesus…it tastes like cat food,' he said, sticking out his tongue, mimicking a hearty retch.

Connie turned to him, smirking, 'you familiar with cat food Becker?' she said, winking cheekily. 'I'd have expected more from a man of your means, hope you're buying a premium brand, none of that funky fish guts stuff.'

'You're laughing with me, right?' Becker said, looking hurt. 'It's disgusting is what I mean…have a look, check this stuff out.' He held up his spoon and chunks of odorous slime obediently slid onto his plate.

Joe and Quincy watched the good-natured sparring with interest. Becker and Connie had played the old-married-couple thing almost non-stop since Joe had known them, initially believing it was some sort of pre-mating ritual. But a decade later he knew better, the same tomfoolery was still happening with not the slightest hint of anything more intimate. Despite Connie's bitter asides, she seemed to love Becker in her own way and Joe knew damn well Becker couldn't live without Connie. They were puzzling indeed, but if nothing else, it was entertaining and helped cut though the nightmare of Becker's Antarctic addiction. He had to suppress an outburst of laughter at where they were standing, their own personal Insanitarium Mission de rhodium. Buried under claustrophobically thick ice at the arse-end of the planet and now eyeballing some extra-terrestrial artefact they'd quite reasonably mistaken for a richly mineralised deposit of the world's rarest metal. I mean, seriously, Joe could only shake his head dumbly as he conceded the cockeyed situation they'd managed to stumble headlong into.

***

It was time to enact the final piece of their plan. As overwhelming as it was, to avoid wrath from above, they needed to engage the object physically, to see if it would respond in any way. That was the reason they were in Antarctica, that was the alibi, the new thinking, the mission. Everyone

68

had committed it to memory, tried like hell to forget rhodium and anything related to it. The drilling rig and spectroscope were there solely to test the surrounds of the artefact, to extract cores for carbon dating and ice core chemistry. Becker was confident the ruse would work because as long as they believed it, so would the Government types…he hoped.

Quincy joined the others who were standing directly over the small hemisphere, peering intently at it, as one might scrutinize a microbe through a microscope.

'This actually has a purpose, right?' Becker asked, 'I mean it's not just a beacon or a galactic buoy of some sort?'

Connie sized him up searchingly, breathing an affronted sigh. 'We've already been through the pros and cons,' she said tersely, 'for the sake of the exercise, we assume it has a purpose, we focus on how we might activate it, trigger it or whatever word you want to use.'

'Are we sure we want to muck around with it, to try and, uh…get it going, activate it or whatever?' Joe asked tentatively, 'because if we do, there may be no going back…turning it off I mean.'

'Jesus,' Connie said sharply, 'we've been through this Joe…we all agreed.'

He raised his hands in the air, 'okay, just thinking out loud is all.'

'Well don't,' Connie said, flapping a hand at him.

'You say this is an alien artefact,' Quincy said, 'have you considered an Earthly origin?'

'Yes, we have, it's not human,' Joe said firmly. 'No way it's human, not under here.'

Quincy wasn't so sure. He touched his forehead, picking at dry skin, 'so what about an ancient civilisation, they achieved some crazy things, many we probably don't even know about. You've heard of Angkor Watt, Teotihuacan…Ziggurats? What about Vimanas, the Indian— '

'Have you lost your frigging mind?' Becker interrupted, shaking his head impatiently. 'I know you're into that crap but this metal ain't your hardware store variety, and that,' he jabbed at the mote of light, 'it's not the work of a bunch of Indians or Chinese or whoever.'

Quincy glanced fleetingly at the imperious light, lowering his head. 'You're probably right,' he said weakly. 'But I don't think anything should be ruled out until we know definitively, reliably to the contrary. Oh, and remember Roswell? Makes you think doesn't it.'

'Oh Jesus,' Becker moaned, 'I'm surrounded by nutters and UFO junkies, what is going on?' He looked mortified, all knotted eyebrows, criss-crossing lines, protruding eyeballs.

'Look, this object is here and if it's what we think it is then they have been here. Fact,' Connie stated unceremoniously, punching Becker with an icy stare.

'For God's sake!' He roared. 'We're on a non-existent time line, can we focus brain power on that?' He glanced over at the light and squinted, 'and not on some mythical mumbo jumbo.'

'Okay,' Joe said, 'let's get on with it then.' He paused and maneuvered his thoughts. 'So in terms of skill sets we've got a geophysicist with a bit of theoretical physics – that's me, a code writer, programmer,' he glanced at Quincy, 'and a geologist with a background in astronomy – that's you Connie,' he offered, smiling warmly at her.

'Don't forget a Masters in acidity, oh, and a minor in bullshitting,' Becker said, lifting an amused eyebrow, looking rather chuffed with his sense of timing.

She turned slowly to face him, 'and you Becker, what do you bring to this rather studious group? Let me have a go…um, ego, impatience, self-interest and a buffalo-sized helping of ignorance. Did I miss anything?' She said firmly, glaring but unable to hold it, breaking into a smirk that quickly faded.

'How about dependable, loyal, maybe trustworthy?' Becker said, looking into her eyes.

'You describing my dog?' She said, whistling and rubbing two fingers together in a "come here boy" motion. Actually, she hadn't expected such a sober response from him but predictably, it was fleeting.

'Can I have a proper shot at you?' Becker said upbeat. 'Okay, uh…annoying, tactless, unfunny are the highlights…no offense, you know, in the spirit of fairness and such.'

'Good work,' she said, 'a word smith you ain't.'

Joe let out a loud breath. 'Have you two finished?'

'Yep, completely.' Connie said, shooting Becker a sour look, turning toward the large object, wondering whether he really meant it. Apart from his fragile body image, the jerk had a hide thicker than a rhino but her sensitivity ran deep, even though she tried to bury it. Screw him, she thought, he was a tactless fool with little more than hair and a gob full of gold fillings upstairs.

Becker said, 'apparently I'm the dunce of the group, so who's taking the lead on this?' Their eyes spun back and forth, all of them ending up peering at Joe. 'Oh Christ,' he murmured, getting slowly off the rig and ambling over to the object. 'Fine,' he said, surveying the surface of the small hemisphere, one hand scratching his mouth, muscles in his jaw and neck tight with a mix of intent and anxiety. 'So, um…if we look at this rationally, from a human standpoint, then the small hemisphere is probably the one to start with,' he said tentatively. 'I'm going to touch it – any dissenters?'

'No,' they all said in unison. 'Just bloody do it,' Becker urged from the rear, face flushed despite the cold.

'Here goes nothing then,' Joe groaned uneasily, imagining what sort of apocalypse might be invited by his clumsy intrusions. Human flesh, his human flesh, was about to caress the unknown outworking of an alien mind, the moment wasn't lost on any of them, they knew this was as historic as it came. It made Joe feel like losing his army rations, the pain in his gut swelling into an acid reflux nightmare.

Bending down, his vision swam as he cupped his hand over the black hemisphere and held it there. Fuck he screamed to himself as the small object immediately responded by turning boldly white. Joe yanked his hand away, inspecting his palm, half expecting to see burnt flesh and exposed bone.

'Shit!' he barked.

'What?' Becker blurted, edging closer to the group, staring fixedly at the small object that was now strangely snow white. Joe's breath was coming in frazzled gasps as his heart pumped painfully near his Adam's apple.

'Okay, other ideas?' Becker said lamely, knowing he had none. 'Like you said, it probably needs some other— ' He stopped talking midway through the sentence, distracted by the large hemisphere, seeing its behaviour change, becoming a little more animated, the vague patterns moving faster, the light stronger. Becker screwed his eyes up, bringing his hands to his forehead to block out the glare.

The object was now pulsing in regular bursts, like a lighthouse, the difference being that the flashes were punctuated by colour - blue, white, black - various sequences coming and going as they watched, sometimes white would follow blue, other times the same colour would flash repeatedly. Each of them lasted about a second, occasionally interrupted or maybe separated by black, which lasted several seconds longer than the others…meaningless but intriguing.

Becker watched the colours reflect in Connie's huge brown eyes, every part of her eyeball exposed, mesmerised by the strangely hypnotic light, stammering something incomprehensible under her breath, overwhelmed by its beauty and strangeness.

'Touch it again,' Becker said without looking away from the light, scratching the back of his head impatiently.

Joe wasn't sold but he bent down anyway, placing a hand over it, realising Becker would elbow him out of the way and do it himself soon enough. Maybe the display of intelligence for this thing is simply finding it, Joe thought, revisiting the idea.

This time, nothing happened. He placed both hands on it then pulled them away, the rhythmic pulsing remaining the same. So much for the easy activation theory Joe thought, easy to turn on, way more difficult to extract something was his best guess. 'Who knows what the makers had in mind,' he said a little shakily, 'and speaking of mind, well, we have no idea on that one…could be like snails and dolphins right? Maybe this is all it does, a pretty lightshow to thrill the savages.'

'Relax,' Connie said, throwing her hands up, 'you'll go nuts if you keep trying to think so fast, medical help is a world away, remember that.'

'Yeah,' he returned quietly, inhaling deeply several times, doing his best to slow his breathing and calm his pulse, fighting the adrenaline pumping in his brain and body.

Becker inched closer to the large hemisphere. 'This thing looks like it's got a proper surface sometimes but other times it's, y'know, gas-like.' He lifted his arms high, then rubbed a fist across his face, 'I mean can something, like, um…pass through it? He said, gazing at Connie with focus.

She stopped and mulled it over, conceding it wasn't entirely stupid. Go figure she thought, supressing a callow snort, studying it more closely, squinting to see detail that simply wasn't there.

Quincy joined her, beady eyed as he zeroed in on it, saying, 'so if something can pass through it, then…pass through it to what?' His eyebrows were almost lost under his hairline as he wrestled with images he was struggling to define; slivers, slices of colour, burning brightness, flashing behind his eyes. He started shuffling around in short steps, touching his hand to his chin, watching the light for minutes at a time. Finally tearing his gaze away, he made to speak but closed his mouth again, lowering one eyebrow, looking deeply puzzled. 'I reckon it might be a simple, um…algorithm of some sort, the pulsing, I've been tracking the colour sequences, there seems to be structure, I think maybe it's math…numbers.'

Becker gazed at Quincy bewildered. 'What the hell has math got to do with it?' He eyed him suspiciously, hating it - it was the bait that attracted nerds and geeks and probably more to the point, Becker admitted he didn't understand a goddamn thing about it. He paid accountants six figures to run his numbers at tax time, four-eyed weasels the lot of 'em. Boring as bat shit.

Connie was certain he had some sort of science-based dementia. 'I've told you about this how many times? Mainly when you've had a few, you damn soak.' She touched an outstretched finger to her forehead. 'Math is probably the only way to exchange information with something that's evolved independently…like on a different planet. I mean, evolution is seriously random, it's only by the most spurious means and a lot of time and luck that we're here to debate it. Most everything about us is subjective, based on a whim, so math is the only way…based on stuff that's the same everywhere.'

Becker cocked an eyebrow, shaking his head doubtfully, mainly to piss her off. He was still struggling with the whole, math might be involved, thing.

'Oh for the love of God,' Connie said, raising an arm as if to strike him, 'are you just playing dumb or are you actually that dumb?' Connie nodded pityingly. 'So let's just say if we wanted to base it on philosophy then we'd be fucked forever 'cause there'd be endless variables that would lead to a big fat, permanent silence.'

'Yep, if it's not math we have no hope,' Joe agreed, looking out of breath, almost like he was going to vomit, the colour almost completely drained from his tanned face. 'Like Connie said, it's gotta be based on something consistent.'

While the trio had been exchanging ideas and a few insults, Quincy was watching the colours flash across the hemisphere, processing sums in his mind. 'Does anyone have anything to write with?' He asked thoughtfully, trying to firm up his suspicions.

Becker grabbed a pen from the top pocket of his parka and handed it to him.

'Paper?' He quizzed, 'something to write on…doesn't matter what.' He looked around at the blank faces. Connie strode over and ripped the Blu-John sign off the Portaloo, handing it to Quincy.

'Go your hardest,' she said with a subtle wink.'

'So, uh…I think the pattern is repeating,' Quincy murmured, opening his eyes wide. 'Everyone quiet,' he said. 'I gotta concentrate.'

Connie's heart ached under her breast so she closed her eyes, focussing on the joy of getting the fuck out of Antarctica. She was bathing in a euphoric feeling, seeing the Globemaster soaring into the air, getting a final contemptuous glimpse of the ice, raising a middle finger, not looking back. Fuck you Antarctica.

After several minutes of furious scribbling, Quincy stopped and looked up, smiling broadly as though he'd just penned a description of dark matter right there on the dunny label. 'The pattern is repeating,' he said, 'there is information, data of some sort.'

Becker was scowling. 'Well that's just great but does it mean anything...does your precious math tell you anything we can use to impress the suits upstairs?'

'Oh please,' Connie growled, smacking her forehead. She tilted her head back and looked up momentarily. 'Seriously, is it getting dumber in here?' She felt like slapping him or forcibly dragging him further away where he couldn't be heard, maybe lock him in the loo. 'This is going to take time, probably more time than we've got and that's assuming we ever get anywhere with it. Just stand over there in the corner and shut it.' Becker was intimidating but she didn't care nought about his overbearing, larger than life bullshit, giving him as good as she got, in fact she gave better.

'Okay I've seen enough,' Quincy said evenly, 'now pay attention.' He looked at Becker and nodded slightly.

'Hey, I'm listening...go.'

'Don't just listen, concentrate,' Connie said abruptly, 'engage the mushy thing between your ears.'

'You'll keep Connie, Quincy, go.'

'There are six colour patterns as far as I can see and each lasts about a second except black, which lasts for around five seconds. I think black signals the end of a pattern and the beginning of another.' He paused, glancing down at the figures on the paper, making a low humming sound under his breath.

'You know, it's pretty funny,' Becker said, grinning from ear to ear, 'that you're trying to decrypt an alien message on the back of a label from a Portaloo crapper.'

Quincy hesitated then smiled disarmingly, thinking about it, realising how grade-A bonkers it was. The loo label was their own cognitive initiative, even if it was just ripping a brand label off a dunny to assist in the process.

Quincy's forehead was a mass of interlacing lines as he made feverish notations, the others sitting uncomfortably on the hard, damp surface, watching him intently. Most of the condensed water had drained away through the incisions, confirming that they were more than just a surface rendering or a shallow cut. They were sure they had to extend downward a fair distance, Becker suggesting they might go all the way to the Earth's core, prompting derisive retorts from Connie around his level of schooling, orientation of his desk in class, things like that.

'Can we help you with this Quincy?' Joe offered, 'Connie and I should be— '

'You're lucky you've got someone who knows math down here,' Quincy interrupted, 'because you'd never get this stuff on your own.'

'You're a star Quincy,' Becker piped, 'you're killing me.' He started to slowly clap. 'Just give us what you've got, remember, time is a luxury we don't have.'

'Leave him alone,' Connie snapped. 'Quincy, do you have something?'

He looked up at her, barely conscious of Becker's droning in the background. 'Binary,' he said simply. 'I think it's pulsing numbers...Base Two, you know, ones and zeroes, assigned values.'

Connie's eyes brightened, surveying him cautiously. 'You sure?'

'Well, pretty sure,' he said, giving a half shrug. 'I assigned blue to zero, white to one, black to a reset. That didn't seem to give anything so I reversed it - blue to one, white to zero.' Quincy's eyes seemed to glow and grew wider as he spoke, wired on the numbers thing, making it clear he was as comfortable with Fortran and COBOL source code as he was, in his words "with English and cursing". Binary files used to be his thing as a programmer and compiler at Microsoft before Becker recruited him with his supersized chequebook.

Connie saw Quincy's eyes glaze over as he chewed on the Portaloo scribble, drifting off into distant contemplation. 'Well?' she prompted hopefully.'

'…er, right, well the first number was six white pulses, two blue pulses followed by black. So if we use my second colour assignment that gives the number three.'

Becker gazed at him silently for a few seconds, screwing his face up, buzzing his lips. Great stuff, that's it, you've solved it. Three. Thank God, I was getting worried we mightn't get anywhere.' He shrugged mockingly. 'Shit, I'm not paying you to dodge and weave down here. We don't need the detail— '

'Shut it!' Connie yelled in an avalanche of echoing that made all of them flinch. She'd had enough. 'For God's sake just shut up. Count your toes or fingers or something. 'Quincy, keep going.' She shot a venomous glare at Becker, suffused with dire warning.

'So if I'm right about this,' he continued, 'the six are three, one, four, one, five and nine which is, well, astonishing, but uh…probably not unexpected I suppose.' Quincy felt a little wobbly as he considered the import of what were quite special numbers. Moreover, he weighed on what creature, entity, thing had taken the time to engineer what they were so arbitrarily fiddling with under the ice. And not just engineer, that wasn't it at all, but to go to pains to place it so surreptitiously on the human planet.

Joe recognised the pattern of numbers straight away, completely bowled over. 'Pi,' he said softly, 'the numbers are Pi, right?' He looked at Quincy who was once again a million miles away.

'Uh, yes…they are indeed,' he breathed in a voice coloured with incredulity. 'Isn't it amazing? They are talking math to us, like we thought, like we hoped.' He was staring blankly, mouth open, yellowing teeth just visible.

Becker walked forward, bemused. 'Excuse my ignorance,' he cocked an eyebrow at Connie, 'but in what universe are pie and math related?'

Her eyes flashed at Becker with undisguised disdain, 'you're not serious?' She asked, taking a step in his direction. 'Tell me you're not seriously talking about pie with an e?'

He grinned boyishly at her, 'of course not but I had you right?' His grin grew into a face splitting smile.

'Okay then, explain it to us,' Connie demanded sternly.

Becker's face melted into a thoughtful frown. 'Oh, er, well I know of it, not actually it,' he admitted. 'It's something to do with a circle?'

'Archimedes, you ain't, but yes, circles. Joe do you want explain it to him?'

'I thought you were the expert Con,' Becker goaded, 'you talk yourself up…walk the walk for me, come on…Pi is what?'

'Joe is all over this stuff so I'll, uh, defer to him,' Connie said without much conviction.

'Yeah, okay, sure.' Becker mocked, staring pointedly at her.

'Piss off, you're the bonehead here, don't try and make it what it isn't.' She looked over at Joe, nodding.

'Okay, if you're done. So, Pi is the ratio of a circle's circumference to its diameter, roughly three point one four.' Joe looked over at Becker and summoned a bland half- smile, 'Pi never ends and as far as we know, it never settles into any sort of pattern. Not sure if you saw the reports a few years back?' Joe paused and saw a forest of wood, 'well anyway, the Australian cloud computer crunched it to sixty trillion decimal places…and still just random numbers spiralling toward infinity.'

Becker was watching, listening intently, finding it all quite irritating. 'So this thing is flashing Pi – so what?' He said glibly. 'Does it mean anything, other than they understand what a circle is? I mean, bully for them, right?'

Connie rolled her eyes, called him a twat and demanded he keep his bloody-minded sarcasm to himself, Becker returning with a look-away middle finger.

The patterns continued to cycle without change, the first six decimals of Pi were on some sort of loop, never going any further, making them ponder any special significance they had over the uncountable decimals that lay in their shadow. They didn't think so, agreeing that it was likely a welcome of sorts without deeper meaning, a greeting in a language that we could recognise as definitively intelligent. Hello, we hear you.

Joe stepped up, walking closer to the large hemisphere. 'So we know what the sequence is, maybe we need to show it that we understand, you know, that we get what it's saying,' he said tentatively, 'if that's what it's, uh…doing of course.

Becker's Walkie buzzed a couple of times, an alert from Weems to call him, sent by the topside inferometer that bounced static off the walls of the tunnel, into the chamber. 'I hope that idiot Weems is playing the game up there,' Becker said, crossing his arms loudly, trudging into the tunnel, dreading what might be going on up top, mashing the Call button. Weems picked up, sounding like he'd just sprinted around the perimeter of basecamp. 'Jesus,' he puffed, 'the UNEP Team just landed in a fucking Super Puma…we've got eyes on them right now,' he wheezed, taking a long, shaking breath, 'they look like they've got paramilitary with them – there's twelve that we can see.' Becker could still hear him gasping, 'and they're packing semi-automatics, God knows what else.'

'Relax Peter,' Becker soothed, searching the floor. 'You remember what Connie told you right…the story?'

'Yep, got it, but…but they look ready to start a bloody war down here.'

'Don't worry, stick to the plan, we're here for humanity not for rhodium. Do not mention the fucking R-word! Anyway, there's no rhodium so the second part is solid gold truth.'

'Okay, okay…they're almost at the front gate, and, um…they don't look happy. Gotta go.'

'I'm relying on you down here Weems. Remember your paycheck relies on your acting ability. Get it done.' Becker terminated the call, mulling anxiously over the next few minutes topside. He was a good man but was he a good actor…under pressure? He didn't think so but time would tell, probably never win an Oscar, Becker mused darkly, having the distinct feeling they were all screwed…they just didn't know it yet.

***

'Maybe we could plug some more digits of Pi in,' Joe suggested. 'It's given us Pi so let's return the favour, show that we get it.'

Connie looked at him blankly. 'That's brilliant,' she said with a sharp exhalation, 'but how do we plug them in?' She stared at Joe, sucking her lips in.

'What, no keyboard?' Becker said. 'That's gonna make it hard. What about telepathy or wait, maybe just speak to it,' he smirked sourly, 'in case you've forgotten, we need to hurry!'

'You're not funny. Unless you've got something meaningful to contribute just—'

'Like a billion dollars isn't a contribution?'

'Money means shit down here,' Connie said, stiffening her posture. 'Anyway it's your goddamn money that got us into this mess.'

'Into the most impactful moment in history, is that the mess you mean?' He bit his bottom lip, looking at her quizzically before grinning shamelessly.

Opening her mouth, she yelled right at him, 'you seriously have a— '

'Focus!' Quincy boomed, scowling at each of them. 'We need to stow the bullshit and get on with it,' he said in a more even tone. 'This object has to do something more than produce a few slices of Pi.' He glanced at Becker who smiled obligingly back, 'so let's get about finding out how.' He bent down, touched the small black object and when skin hit surface the lights suddenly went out.

'Shit,' Connie bleated, 'what'd you do?'

Only the rig was lighting the chamber with a dim ghostly glow, the bright object in the centre of the great circle simply shutting down, now so black it almost seemed to have disappeared into itself.

'Did it turn on or off?' Connie said in a murmur. She assumed black meant off but chided herself for assuming anything.

'Well, we haven't done anything to show capability yet,' Quincy said cautiously, 'so maybe it's in some sort of, um…stasis mode, uh…waiting for us to do something.' He had no idea, venting whatever came into his mind.

'Sounds reasonable,' Becker said. 'So do something else, see what you— '

'What would you suggest?' Connie snapped.

'Jesus, you're the geniuses,' he said, throwing his hands at her, 'come up with something. We've got Weems up there battling a fucking army. We need to get something from this thing, get our arses topside and table it. Any minor wrongdoing will be forgotten…forest and trees, right Connie?'

'So you have nothing, that's what I thought, you have nothing,' Connie said. 'We understand the plan Becker, it's mine remember, it's how we do it that's the issue. That's the game right now.'

We'll see, Quincy thought. It sounded fine in theory but none of them had a clue if that's the way it would play out.

***

Quincy had been rolling Pi around in his head for ten minutes now, stewing over the best approach, dazed by an avalanche of tangled thoughts. If it were us on the other end, what would we consider to be a show of intelligence? The object itself had initiated circular math so that seemed to be an obvious route to travel. Maybe a certain sequence of Pi was needed until a critical mass was reached, proving we had a decent serving of higher brainpower, which might tip it into a more insightful mode. Of course the question of how they would input a sequence of numbers was anyone's guess and maybe that was part of the test, if indeed it was a test, trial or whatever. He was aghast at the irony of someone being down here who actually knew a decent stretch of early Pi decimals. The capricious nature of everything was bugging him, because seriously…what were the chances?

Not bothering to engage the others, Quincy bent down, cupped the small hemisphere twice, one second apart for each. Two was the seventh decimal of Pi and the next one in line following the six the object had so kindly delivered. He didn't reckon using binary was right because they'd already proven their grip on base two stuff. That test had been passed or so he assumed and they could always go back if they needed to.

'Damn it,' he said under his breath, lowering his head. Quincy wouldn't be denied, so he caressed the small hemisphere six times, then five but it still remained indifferent, each time he pulled his hand away he felt a slight static charge tickle his palm, his mind spinning, heart thudding high in his chest. Now that it was dark it looked like nothing was there but clearly there was. It had electrical, maybe magnetic properties of some sort, prickling and gently pulling at his skin like an electric current.

If it were composed of silica glass, polycarbonate or anything humans were remotely familiar with, Quincy figured there would be some reflection from the lights in the chamber but there was none. Lights from the mining helmets and the rig weren't reflected by either the large or the small hemisphere and he couldn't think of anything manufactured on Earth that was transparent and didn't reflect light, at least a little bit. Did that insight their technology, did it mean there was no actual surface to these things? He knew he was touching something so it made no immediate sense. Quincy imagined shaving a piece off and chucking it under an ST Microscope, seeing what manner of stuff it was, mind blowing no doubt, if it was stuff at all.

'Maybe we need to change tack,' Joe said, slowly pinching the loose skin on his throat. 'This clearly isn't working, so maybe we do need to use binaries,' he conceded, mulling over what other type of math they could try if this ended up a bust.

Becker had the harrowing feeling they were going to be down here forever trying to give this interminable thing the kiss of life. 'What if this object just is and has nothing else to give,' he said gruffly, scowling at Joe, 'and don't tell me that's not a possibility.' He shifted his glare to Connie, hearing the tick-tock of time vanishing into the chamber as they screwed around with semi-random shots in the dark, getting nowhere.

'Anything's possible,' Connie said, shrugging hesitantly. 'Like I said, we're using our humanity in every decision we make so the solution could be completely different, as in opposite to what we think.' She turned to Quincy, asking him if he agreed.

'Completely, but we have to keep going, at least for now, it's all we've got. If we start going counter-intuitive already we could end up— '

'Time,' Becker snapped irritably, holding his hand straight up like a basketball ref. 'We need to move on this or abort. Weems is probably under armed guard and if he cracks and the true story comes out, well it's not gonna be good for anyone…mainly me.'

'Of course, mainly you Becker.'

'Oh Christ, you know what I mean, we're all relying on Weems and trust me, that's not how we want it.'

This time Quincy was the one with his arms up, both of them, as though heartily waving a touchdown. 'Let's keep going then,' he said, thinking again that those two should just trade punches, have sex or something, defuse the tension, get it the hell over with.

Quincy knelt down, visualising the early decimal sequence of Pi. He'd once memorised a hundred decimals through a simple mnemonic system, adding consonants to the numbers to create short words, but no way he could go that far now. The next three numbers he knew were three, five, eight. After that he had no idea, but he did know the circumference and diameter of a circle they'd used in College. With that and a simple equation, $c=\pi d$, it'd be a piece of piss he thought, grinning, feeling it dissolve as quickly as it came, realising they couldn't possibly be accurate enough. They might be right but the error factor would be unacceptably high, and putting wrong numerals in might be very bad indeed. They could radio Weems to get more from Iridium but he'd rather avoid even thinking about topside, cringing at the likely ordeal playing out up there.

Quincy palmed the hemisphere three times and waited, following with five, eight, nine, swearing to himself and glaring at it blindly, wondering again if binaries might hold the key. He pulled himself slowly to his feet, groaning and stepping back, hearing a heavy, ground-shaking thud somewhere deep beneath his feet, like it was emanating from the bowels of the Earth itself.

10. Journey

"there ain't no journey what don't change you some."
~ David Mitchell

Connie heard it start growling behind her, spitting and fizzing, growing in strength like a gathering cyclone or an A380 engine powering into full rotation. She yelped, spinning around, stumbling back drunkenly, darting eyes from Becker to Joe, then fixing steadily on Quincy.

'J-Joe?' Becker shouted, seeing the object transform the chamber into a hellish discothèque of beating light and sound. It was quickly becoming unbearable. Blood was pounding under his scalp, he couldn't think, almost sinking to the ground in sensory overload.

The large hemisphere had broken into a maelstrom of swirling crimsons and blues, rotating so fast it was lost in a super rotational blur, with a visual rhythm almost hypnotic, certainly seductive. Connie found it hard to look away, drawn to it as though a primal yearning was drawing her to connect with it.

'This is insane,' Joe yelled, battling to be heard over the clamour while struggling to tear his eyes off it.

'Becker...no!' Connie barked, taken aback. 'That's a bad idea, you're gonna piss it off.'

'Bullshit,' Becker said with a curt nod.

'You might take us back where we started, it might turn off and never turn back on.'

'We need to start pushing the envelope or we'll be down here for the next decade,' he said, pacing back and forth, staring at the light. With rock hammer in hand he advanced on the hemisphere as one might stalk a deer in the woods, treading lightly, avoiding any sound despite the deafening noise in the chamber. As he closed on it he felt like it was studying him, assessing the threat as he approached. Coming within about two metres of the light, the turbine-like roar stopped, leaving only the uninterrupted light show. Becker froze, wondering if it had marked him as a threat? His heart was beating so loudly he was sure everyone could hear it in the silence.

Connie fevered over the sudden absence of sound...did Becker and his size fourteen's cause it to dial down, the same as approaching a cricket in full song? She turned to Quincy, voice faint with disbelief, 'uh...wh-what happened?'

'Everything has a meaning, that's what I think,' Quincy said firmly.

Becker rolled his eyes theatrically. 'Okay...so any ideas then? You're big on the obvious, less large on the whys.' He surveyed him intently, lifting an eyebrow, coaxing an opinion, an out and out guess would do, he just wanted to hear something...from anyone.

'Not sure if you're awake,' Connie snarled, 'but we're dealing with a machine created by something with a far greater intellect than that lonely kink of grey matter in your head.' She stabbed a finger at his temple, wiggling it. 'Until it does something we can understand or shows us the way, we might as well be trying to rework relativity down here.'

Becker peered at her, pursing his lips impatiently. 'Well this idiot is engaging affirmative action.' Becker strode forward, arm extended, raising the rockhammer close to the light.

'No!' came raucous shouts, reverberating off the ice in a thunderous echo.

Becker spun his head around and glared at them. He hadn't got filthy rich by listening to the cautions of a bunch of wieners, pushing the sharp end of the hammer into the tendrils of colour flaring from its surface. The rockhammer was instantly gripped, then ripped from Becker's grasp, disappearing into the light storm. Becker howled, looking down at his hand fearfully.

'We did say no, you idiot,' Connie said, concerned and enraged. 'What the hell were you thinking?'

'I was thinking we needed to find out what this thing is, stop screwing around and do something. Like you said, everything's guesswork, so actually doing rather than saying might be the way to go.' Becker stretched his arms above his head, nodding, seemingly pleased with his succinct assessment of their plan.

'Balls out, right?' She sneered the words at him. 'Let's just charge in, no passing, no dodge and weave, nothing…just barrel straight through like a fucking line backer who has no idea on forward strategy. Seriously, you are such a jerk sometimes.' She maintained an icy stare. 'No offence.'

'Oh, none taken, got off pretty easy I reckon. But you know what? Sounds like you were worried about me…the whole hammer thing,' he said, lowering his head, shooting her with puppy dog eyes.

'Piss off,' she spat, looking over at the anomaly, hating it when he read her like that with his stupid lopsided grin. Connie so wanted to slap him in the moosh.

'Strange thing,' Becker said curiously, 'it only pulled at the hammer…not at me. Pretty sure it could've yanked me in without much effort.' His face grew serious, rearing back ever so slightly, saying in a gasp, 'wonder where it went?'

'It's not too late,' Connie shot back, 'stick your hand in and fish around for it, you might get lucky.' She grinned at him coyly, index finger pointed upward, rubbing the side of her nose in a clear gesture.

'We need to think first, maybe even discuss it as a group, then act,' Joe said, taking a half-glance toward him. 'This is a group effort so no more glory shots. If this thing turns off it may stay that way which means we go topside with squat.'

'And we'll all be cooked,' Quincy added. 'You'll be the Burning Man for real,' he said, breaking into a hesitant grin, knowing his affection for the Ten Principles.

'Thanks Quincy, appreciate it,' Becker said, smiling vaguely, wondering what the hell they should do now.

'So, um…what if this really is a test?' Connie said, raising her eyebrows shakily at Quincy. Her mouth stayed slightly open while she chewed on the implications of that. They'd spoken about it but mostly as an aside, not seriously. 'Sounds nuts right, but can we rule it out…anything out?''

Quincy slowly nodded, 'that's why we think, we plan, we act to make sure we move in a logical way. If we fuck up at least we've chosen a considered way forward.' He glared at Becker who put both hands up defensively, stepping away.

'Okay, okay…I'm on board,' he said, 'but we're running out of time.' He looked exasperated, 'and by the way,' he said in a muted whisper, 'seriously, where do you think my hammer went?' He steepled both hands over his nose and mouth, conceding the endless possibilities.

'Maybe it's gone wherever, uh…they come from,' Joe offered, drawing his eyebrows together. 'I mean this thing could be some sort of transit system, right?'

Connie snapped her head toward it, taking a sharp intake of breath. 'What, like a wormhole…a Lorentzian thingy?'

'Yes, wormhole, Einstein-Rosen bridge, you know,' Joe said, intrigued by the notion.

Quincy looked stung. 'Come on,' he questioned doubtfully. 'They're mathematical relics from relativity…we're talking billions of gees, singularities, zero dimensions buried in black holes…event horizons and so on.'

'Yeah but maybe we're looking at a solution to it, maybe this is a working model,' Joe breathed, his vision sparking with light. 'Perhaps they're commonplace on their worlds, you know, suitcase wormholes.' His mind reeled with images of shortcuts in the vacuum, gravity-driven doorways through the entropy of spacetime.

'Maybe we're supposed to enter it, now that it's activated, go where my rockhammer went.'

'You volunteering?' Connie asked, throwing him a whimsical look.

'Well…er…no, but what do you think?'

'I think you're an idiot for suggesting it.

'Well, someone's gotta say something, you geniuses have come up with the grand total of jack so far.'

'Well step right up Becker,' Connie said, gesturing him toward the anomaly, 'send us a postcard from Betelgeuse, it's kinda' hot there this time of year…don't forget the sun cream.'

'There's more unknowns than we can possibly imagine,' Quincy said ominously, 'if it is a doorway of sorts, maybe it leads into orbit somewhere…you want to exit into vacuum?' He asked quite seriously. 'I don't think so.'

Becker suddenly looked ill.

Connie was studying the swirling patterns when it abruptly changed, a rhythmic centrifugal rotation melding into a sort of inward spiral, like water flowing down a drain. She felt her heart skip a beat, struck by an uneasy thought that might have given substance to what Becker had said. 'So, what does that look like?' Connie said anxiously, thinking it was pretty damn obvious.

'Uh…an invitation,' Becker said, shocked by the change, 'sort of like c'mon in…maybe.'

Quincy was angling his head around to take it all in. 'Strange that you spoke about entering and the motion changed from angular to, er…inbound,' he said in a thoughtful hush. Quincy cautiously stepped a little closer to the light, slowly extending an arm. As he thought, the hairs on his hand and arm bristled in response to some sort of energy field.

'Maybe we should enter more digits of Pi?' Becker suggested in desperation.

Joe and Quincy shook their heads in unison. 'We don't know any more digits,' Joe said, 'and we don't have the equipment to work them out accurately enough down here.'

'And I'm not guessing from memory 'cause if we get it wrong, well, we can't know the consequences,' Quincy said evenly. 'It could be bad,' his lowered eyes, adding grim emphasis.

'Asking Weems to look them up isn't an option either,' Becker said. 'God knows what those military jerks would make of it.'

Bomb was Connie's recurring thought, the idea bouncing around interminably inside her skull, unable to shake the feeling its agenda was nasty somehow, even though it had demonstrated none of that. It was the fragile nature of sentient life she told herself for the umpteenth time. From a basic instinct to not die came the most powerful survival advantage of all – sentience, intuition, self-awareness. And of course, a whole bunch of crazy emotions that screwed you over daily, made you bonkers and not infrequently led to judgments you really didn't understand, just like Connie was doing now. She reckoned the human brain was becoming overcooked to the point where decisions and logic were being blurred by its very complexity. She even had fears that it might ultimately be the thing that brings down the species. Forget comets or meteors, nanotech or cosmic diseases, it would be Cognitive Armageddon where people basically went nuts en masse…due simply to the march of time, the tick-tock of evolution that was so acutely, fatally angled toward complexification.

***

Battle-scarred and patently dead, the planetoid looked like it had been through a centuries long nuclear war, but wounds of warfare they weren't, rather the misfortune of lacking an atmosphere to blunt the relentless impacts from space. Meteors, asteroids, giant comets had struck its surface for Eons, forging a hellscape of craters, battered mountains and rocky basaltic ridges. It was sheathed by only the most tenuous helium froth, barely clinging to its meagre gravity.

An observer on this world would have been mesmerised by what they were seeing only a few hundred kilometres away in space. Objects clearly unnatural were crystallising from nothing more than the vacuum itself, emerging through sparking, flickering grids of light until they were there in all their eurythmic, axiomatic beauty – flawless, astonishingly unexpected. Visitors.

In an arc of light, they grew from nothing to kilometric in diameter, perfect spheres, vitreous and gorgeous in the reflected starlight, departing the sparking, fizzing energy that allowed them egress, dying behind them like brief magnesium flares.

79

In perfect sync, they started rotating on their axes, all of them sharing identical angular momentum and only a slight tilt from the perpendicular. At the same time, they started to move in a highly elongated free-fall around the moon, following each other in single file, maintaining precise spatial separation. With an obvious choreography of spin and speed, the spheres presented like electrons orbiting a tremendous, battered nucleus.

The Moon had acquired fifteen new companions and when its phase was conjunctive, they could be seen clearly with the naked eye from Earth, girdling its equator like a sparkling diamond necklace.

* * *

Becker swore and flung his head back, hearing static blare from his radiophone again. It was bad news every time and the ache in his gut told him this wouldn't be any different. They were getting nowhere down here but he knew with grim certainty things would be progressing rapidly topside. Ripping the phone from its holster he swept toward the tunnel to bridge the connection.

'Becker,' he answered flatly, clenching his toes in anticipation, feeling moisture pimple his brow.

'It's Peter, uh…obviously…look, we've got a situation up here,' Weems said nervously, 'er…well, more of a situation that is. The UNEP team has just received contact from JPL in California. Their GRACE satellite picked up…irregularities they called them…around the Moon, anomalies they said, fifteen of them…they just appeared, like from nowhere.' He paused abruptly and Becker could hear muffled voices in the background. 'They uh, reckon whatever you've got down there is part of it. ESA's GOCE bird has confirmed the reports so there's no doubt it's real.'

'Jesus Christ,' Becker heaved, looking back at the light and the monstrous shadows playing on the walls of the chamber. 'What sort of anomalies?' His mind was churning with scenarios, pondering the whole sorry journey, convinced everything was a fucking anomaly.

'No idea,' Weems said. 'I asked but they won't tell me. This isn't a friendly crowd up here and, oh, I should have said…they're listening to us now - they're on the line too. They want me to tell you and your team to take no further action. They're shutting you down, this is now a military op domained under DoD.'

Becker's face collapsed and he took a quick, sharp breath. 'The hell it is!' He said, gripping the phone hard enough to make it creak, 'DoD? How the hell does the US claim jurisdiction down here? Tell 'em to fuck off.'

'…uh, you just did.'

'Good, they're overzealous pricks,' he said, bringing the phone closer to his mouth. 'I dealt with them on a mining tenement in Arizona near an army base, idiots thought we were there to steal their stupid military secrets.'

'I don't think you're helping…just relax, breathe. We don't need more enemies up here. The US Navy owns Byrd Station, which is the closest territorial claim. Remember, this place is no man's land, no one gave a shit about it, until now. Now everyone and their dog wants it.'

'So what next?' Becker said tensely, 'what have the egg-heads said?'

'The Secretary of Defence has briefed POTUS - an order for full militarisation has been made. The Pentagon and UNEP have authorised a team to fly to basecamp to take control. Apparently, there's a NASA SETI team coming as well, some post-detection task group or the like.'

'Looking for little green men I suppose?' Becker said acidly. 'Goddamn suits.'

'They want an undertaking that you'll come out of the tunnel immediately,' Weems said. 'I've got four armed military guys sitting on top of me so a yes would be nice. If they're happy I'm happy, what do you say?'

'Where do we sit if we come out?' Becker quizzed, wondering if they'd swallowed the humanitarian horseshit they'd concocted. It sounded reasonable at the time but whether it would fly with enforcement knobs schooled in bullshit alibis, well who knew? Becker held his breath. If they baulked at it then in short order it would lead to the nulling of his financial empire, not to mention his personal freedom, oh and that of his closest friends. Fuck, he thought, horrified all over again.

'No problems,' Weems said, 'they understand our motives were in the global interest but now that things have taken an, er…unusual turn, they want full control, also in the global interest, eminent domain, that sort of thing.'

Becker slumped a bit and let out a loud breath, staring at the ground. They actually swallowed their story, but then he hesitated, frowning. Was there a huge dose of DoD spin here, a counter-ploy to get them back to basecamp so they could be manacled arm and leg and frog-marched off the ice like disobedient penguins? He realised the only way they'd find out was by doing it, walking out, hoping like hell the suits were telling the truth. Becker doubted they were but options were seriously limited, as in zero.

'Okay Peter, we agree. Hello out there, we agree, so back off!'

'Go and tell the others Becker, get them out of there, this is the DoD's gig now.'

'Okay, got it, see you soon buddy,' Becker said, lying. He wanted the Feds to think he was rolling over and maybe he was, but they needed to think it through before they jumped.

Becker disconnected the surface line and strode back into the chamber, eyeing the anomaly, stopping on a dime. He blinked at it, struggling to make sense of the bizarre scene in front of him. When he left to talk to Weems the hemisphere was radiating light, but now it was frozen stiff as though someone had pressed a pause button. First the noise had gone and now the motion had gone with it. Becker saw that the other three weren't even looking at it, instead they were staring headlong at the small hemisphere, oddly inert, expressionless like human popsicles. Becker was gasping for breath, his pulse thwacking high in his throat, maybe whatever was affecting the machine was effecting them as well.

'Hey!' Becker shouted at them. No response. He edged closer and bellowed at the top of his voice, the echo bringing it back at least half a dozen times. Quincy slowly turned, Connie followed suit, Joe as well. When Connie stumbled away a few steps he could see white figures scooting across the surface of the smaller hemisphere, rows of them like data across a computer screen. Moving closer, Becker counted twelve lines of tiny figures streaming left to right.

'What the hell is going on?' He demanded, waving his arm toward them. 'We've got a shitload of trouble topside, DoD are shutting us down, militarising the project. If we go up we can walk, no questions asked, free to go apparently.'

'They bought the story?' Joe said, nodding doubtfully.

'Well they said they did but what are the chances they're just trying to coax us out of this hole?' Becker said. 'So, they can arrest our arses and evac us to Gitmo. I think they're telling the truth though, so does Weems I think.'

Connie studied Becker narrowly, rubbing her forehead with two fingers in a circular motion. 'C'mon, no bloody way they'll let us walk,' she said. 'They won't want this getting out, that's why they're shutting us down, so they can manage whatever it is. I mean, this might be proof of other life for fuck's sake, another intelligence, something beyond our planet. Can you seriously imagine them letting intel like that hit the streets?' She frowned then raised her eyes. 'This'll cause a fair chunk of the population to lose their lunch in panic, and you reckon they're going to let us waltz on out, catch the first plane to Sydney?' She looked wholly stupefied, stifling a belly laugh as she weighed up what they would say when they hoofed it off the plane. She looked squarely at him, tilting her head defiantly, imagining her response when she was asked about the "trip". *Oh just fab thanks, the surf and Sun, unbelievable, great food, new friends…oh and we found an alien artefact,*

'Best case scenario is they'll detain us on site and let us go when they've done what they need to do which may be months away…perhaps never.' Connie's mouth stayed open well after she'd finished speaking, not believing that Becker could be so gullible. If the DoD were telling the truth with this "come hither and you'll be fine" bullshit, then it'd be the first time in history she reckoned, knowing they were all self-serving arseholes that couldn't be trusted, like ever. They'd say anything, promise anything, sell their first born to achieve their security mandate, and that's what was happening here, Connie thought emphatically.

Becker scowled at Connie and gave a silent whatever. 'Oh and Weems mentioned some sort of irregularities, anomalies they called them, around the Moon…just appeared apparently,' he added matter of factly, 'but he had no other detail. That's all the gun-toting Berets would tell him.'

Connie clutched her neck with thumb and forefinger. 'A-Anomalies….and that's all they would say, no detail…just anomalies?' Her mouth was hanging open loosely as she tried to think of something to say. 'What the hell?' She managed.

'Well he did say they thought that we'd caused them by tinkering with this thing,' Becker said, eyeing the now immobile light source.

'Shit,' Connie murmured, 'it can't be a coincidence…can it?'

'No way, they have to be related,' Quincy agreed, tapping his temple with a finger.

'There's fifteen of them,' Becker continued, 'they think our machine thingy here is responsible and they want to know why.' He pulled a brief, sour grin. 'The best bit is that if conditions are right, these things are easy to spot with the naked eye. Joe Public on Earth can see them just fine when the Moon is in the right, uh…phase.' Becker puffed his cheeks out, weighing the probable disquiet on the streets back home. 'DoD can do all they like but there's no keeping this quiet.' He grinned like a school kid who'd stuck thumbtacks on the teacher's chair and gotten away with it. Fuckers, he thought maliciously.

'No wonder they're so eager to get their people all over it,' Connie said, 'they'll have whole populations terrified, demanding answers, wanting comfort from the Government, NASA, the UN—

'There'll be panic,' Joe said, nodding at Connie, 'visual anomalies in the night sky…around the Moon? The sky is meant to be static, that's human expectation. Anything out there changes, well that'll terrify most on the planet. Do you know how many medical events Halley's comet causes?' Joe said with a heavy sigh, knowing the psychosis and stress related ailments these rare cosmic objects brought with them. 'None of the Government agencies would tell you but trust me it's there, even in '86 when it was totally underwhelming.' He shut his eyes and opened them heavily. 'The religious lunatics, anyone wanting an excuse will be out there, if not on the streets they'll be on their cellphones, flooding social media, email servers, it'll be mayhem.' Joe's eyes were wide and unfocussed, gazing idly into the distance.

'Whatever,' Becker said, 'I've thought it through, we need to pack our gear, get our arses topside. Weems needs rescuing and like it or not, we need to take a chance on the DoD and their, uh…polite invitation.'

'Weems can look after himself,' Connie said bluntly. 'We need more time with this thing.' Her eyebrows rose. 'You haven't seen what it's doing have you? Come. It's amazing.'

Becker followed Connie, walking the few steps to the small hemisphere, intrigued but still impatient to get the hell out of this hole.

'As soon as the large object froze, the smaller one dimmed and then these numbers started,' Connie said, slowly inhaling a lungful of cold air, breathing out a pendulous column of white vapour, voice sinking to an awestruck whisper. 'Becker, these are our numbers, not binary, these are human decimals.' She stared at him with eyes seemingly half way out of their sockets as she grappled with the implications of what seemed on first sight a nonsense. What the fuck were our numbers doing on an alien artefact?

Becker grimaced and threw his head to the side slightly. 'How can that, uh…how would they know our numbers?' He scratched the thick stubble on his chin, screwing his face up. 'If this thing is as old as you say, how could they, like, know before they were, uh…invented? Becker stood as still as a basement dummy, vacantly stewing over the madness.

'You've got it Becker,' Connie said, nodding briefly, 'how could they? We threw it around when you were onto Weems and it's, um…well it's perplexing no matter which way you cut it up. We figured binaries might be explainable because the zero's a circle and a one is a vertical line. That could be coincidence but decimals, nuh-uh, no way, not possible, chances are invisibly small…zero pretty much.'

'Like we said before, maybe it isn't off-world at all, maybe it's from here,' Becker offered uncertainly. 'I can't see how that could be but— '

'No,' Joe said firmly. 'If it was anywhere but here, maybe, but this place is a natural timer. The damn thing has to be thirty million years old…at least.'

Quincy nodded. 'I mean, we're fishing big time but maybe it updated itself after we turned it on,' he said, glancing doubtfully at Joe, shrugging, 'you know, had a system update, something like that.' He smiled tight-lipped but then reflected, initially thinking it was nuts, but conceding it could just be possible. The insane was now the plausible, crazy the new norm it seemed, down here anyway.

'Whatever though,' Joe weighed in, 'we think this thing is now cycling decimals of Pi. We're not totally sure but they seem to be random enough. But you're right,' he said, touching his chin thoughtfully. 'The really screwed up thing is that they're using English numbers. I mean, seriously? His expression had a note of amusement, suggesting that things were indeed ridiculous.

Connie listened intently to Joe, a deep worry line growing above the bridge of her nose. 'You're so right…why not Greek or Russian? This is our language…ones that we in this chamber understand…more coincidence?' She shook her head woodenly, plodding over the absurd puzzle.

'Hey, I agree, but seriously, who knows?' Joe said, tilting his head this way then the other.

'It's unbelievable,' Connie breathed in a low rush. Conspiracy dropped into her mind but she didn't exactly know why. It was a good word though…had the right feel to it.

'Well maybe it scanned us, you know like a barcode and it knows what we understand,' Quincy said in jest, wiggling his eyebrows, breathing in shallow spurts. 'I mean it's pointless using a foreign language.' The last part was definitely right he figured, they might as well use alien symbols as Greek or French or any language they weren't familiar with.

'I think we need to focus less on the why and more on the what, or we'll be down here forever,' Joe said, glancing at Becker, moving closer to the small hemisphere.

Becker nodded at Joe impatiently, agreeing the answers were beyond their grasp - also knowing time was way beyond short. Soon enough the DoD would send an armed force rappelling down the tunnel to haul them out kicking and screaming, or maybe they'd just blow up the tunnel, pretend like it never happened. Pretty hard with the pearl necklace around the Moon, but he was sure they'd come up with some half-arsed subterfuge to explain it. He knew how the military worked. If they killed Kennedy to prop up the economy with a war chest they sure as hell wouldn't bat an eyelid at killing everyone in the tunnel. And whoever pulled the trigger wouldn't lose a night's sleep 'cause it was all in the national fucking interest!

'Well I for one am not going topside until we get some answers,' Connie said, hands on hips, glaring at Becker, daring him to come at her. She was tired, irritated and ready to annihilate him where he stood if he started prattling on about "poor old Weems".

Becker swallowed, lowered his chin and met her gaze head on, setting lines in his forehead like Martian canali. The open disdain in her eyes bordered on frightening, making him soften a bit. She was ready to blow and when she did, he didn't want to be anywhere near ground zero.

'They'll arrest us, probably hold us in some godforsaken bunker,' Becker said, 'you've heard of Gitmo, I know you have, it ain't no beach strip in Cuba, we have to take them by their word…I don't like it any more than you do.'

Connie kept staring at him, steely eyed, holding her tongue because he was speaking so bloody quietly. Man up for God's sake, just give me an excuse she told herself, clenching her jaw.

Becker continued calmly, watching her like a hawk, 'they've got a SETI team, a UNEP crew and a shitload of paramilitary. It'll be standing room only in here soon enough, and make no mistake, we'll be the centre of attention.'

She'd heard enough. 'Even if we walk out of here they'll arrest us, or worse, be sure of that,' she said, pacing around irritably. 'Use your brain! For God's sake, we know way too much for them to let us fly off into the sunset. Either way we're screwed. Go, don't go, same deal.'

'We need bargaining power!' Quincy boomed, 'we need to give them something they don't know so they need us. That's our ticket...that's our protection, make ourselves indispensable, you know, subject matter experts, the only ones there are.'

Joe cupped a hand to his mouth, grunting under his breath. 'Agreed,' he finally said, 'but we've been down here for hours and everything we know, which is about this big,' he held his thumb and forefinger almost together, 'is running across this surface here.' He jabbed at the small hemisphere that was indeed very busy.

Quincy knelt next to it, placing his palm on top of the object, gripping it tightly as though he were trying to lift it out of some invisible sheath. 'I can feel it pulling at my flesh,' he whispered, glancing up wide-eyed. To his surprise it was stronger now, wondering with some unease why it had gathered strength. Quincy kneaded his forehead with fingers from both hands, trying to stem the flow of questions, and the ache behind his eyes. Placing his hand back on the object the numbers reacted instantly by becoming a blur, the numerals now formless lines, a dozen of them.

'Do it again,' Becker said, bouncing foot to foot, 'hold it for longer, mix it up, do anything that comes into that crazy Quincy mind of yours.' He urged him on, flourishing his arms with a go.

'Becker, please,' Connie snarled. 'This is science, not digging in the dirt for old bottles.' She didn't look at him, didn't want to, didn't need to. For the head of a global corporation he was excruciatingly erratic and unscientific, basically a grunt with a shitload of luck and money. Actually, the thinking that hit her was involuntarily and an oft thought one, that Becker was a likeable fuckwit with an ego complex that was utterly unrivalled. Oh...no offence she thought, supressing a giggle.

'In this case there's not much difference is there?' Becker said, 'we're chasing something, information, we think might be in there but we're not quite sure? Sounds like old bottles to me.'

'Oh Christ,' Connie moaned, placing her head in her hands, 'how did I end up in this nuthouse?'

'We still need to think each step through,' Joe said seriously, 'who knows what we might set off if we just start wrestling with the damn thing.'

Quincy was still hunched uncomfortably over the small object, mulling over Joe's words, wondering if he or any of them should be screwing around like this. Their actions were based on nothing more than unfettered guesswork. They had a go at Becker for suggesting they try anything but the reality was that they were doing little better. He felt like ripping out what little hair he had because it was either do what they were doing or pack up and bug out with almost zero to show for it. Quincy was pretty sure they'd end up trying any crackpot idea eventually. They needed to gather something of interest, hopefully to effort its purpose for being here on this windswept rock at the end of the bloody world.

Joe was chewing uneasily on what they were doing, meddling with this thing on behalf of the whole planet without the flimsiest mandate from a single soul, seven billion people on the planet and they were snubbing the lot of them. He felt like hanging his head in shame. They had some useful skill-sets but the population of Earth had hardly given them the green light to go forth and tinker.

'Er, maybe we should let the SETI team lead this,' Joe said uncertainly. 'I mean they're trained for this stuff, right?'

Connie sized him up, rolling her neck slightly. 'Do you honestly believe that?' She sneered, 'no one is trained for this stuff. They're schooled in hair-brained theory, textbook guesswork...it means squat down here. They'd screw around for weeks taking notes and measurement before they did a damn thing, then they'd need a line of approvals right up to the President before they'd do anything more than extract a few ice cores. Being careful is one thing but no one's got time for that.'

'Well maybe it's the right approach,' Joe said. 'We don't know anything about this object so maybe pragmatism is the best way forward.' Looking at Becker he hoped for some sign of understanding or approval. There was a suggestion of sharp pain in his stomach, a murderous glare.

'Let's vote,' Connie suggested.

'Do it,' Becker said sharply.

'Okay, Joe said softly, 'so who wants to keep going with this, the trial and error, the invite your own extinction stuff?'

'Yep,' Becker said without hesitation.

'Definitely,' Quincy said, 'it's that or we're done.'

'Yes,' Connie said uncertainly, grimacing a little as the words rolled out.

'Christ almighty,' Joe said, screwing his face up, wondering how four people could vote for the entire human race. It felt wrong but he was out-voted by his peers so some of the guilt flushed away. He'd be sure to note himself as a conscientious objector.

Placing his hand on the object, Joe withdrew it, repeating the movement three times in total. Why? Because he thought it was a good number, no more, no less. It was the first number of Pi, all quite random but he could honestly think of nothing else - his mind was blank, his body a hive of vascular pumping. They didn't know any more Pi decimals and had no time and zero strategy. All they got for certain was the object's glib response to the axiomatic numbers buried in Euclidean math.

The small hemisphere did what it did before under human pressure, a more rapid flow of white, flashing across the surface as quasi-solid lines. Then it would slow down again and revert to its original tempo when pressure was removed. Joe kept massaging the object for several minutes nonstop when something happened behind him.

Turning expectantly from his seated position on the ground, he watched shadows melt across the walls, hearing the dizzying tumult rising again, an echoing avalanche of concussive noise. For an advanced race they were bloody loud, Becker thought instinctively, fighting to block the noise out with his fingers.

'Whoa!' Joe bellowed, the prickling energy hitting every nerve ending in his body.

The noise diminished a bit and was interrupted by two different, deeper clunks that sounded like metal on metal off to the side somewhere. The curious source of the "double clunk" became obvious because sitting motionless on the surface in front of them, lying there was Becker's hammer with its metal T-bar glistening in the light.

'Jesus mother,' Becker exclaimed, not believing his eyes, 'it's back!'

'Your h-hammer,' Connie said, squinting at it. Her eyes opened wide like dollops of ice cream as she sized up the intriguing object. They should've strapped a GoPro to it she mused idly, feeling a tingling shiver run head to toe.

'The hemisphere looks like it should be sucking things in, not spitting them out,' Quincy said, 'I mean, the motion…the pattern suggests inward not outward, um…right?' Was their logic completely wrong or was the counter-intuitive visual trying to tell them something? Left means right, up means down? Nup, too simple. Maybe it was playing them, testing their steel, measuring their reactions to stimuli maybe. Humans and lab mice, Quincy thought suddenly, stewing over the chances grimly.

Tentatively, they inched up to what was basically a regular tool, seeing if it was the same hammer so ingloriously ripped from Becker's grasp. They knew it was, but still, to see it come back like returned mail was off-putting to say the least.

'Hang on,' Becker said hesitantly, looking closely at it, nudging it with his foot as though testing road-kill for signs of life. 'That sort of looks like mine but it's…what happened to it?' Becker picked it up carefully. Turning it over, it was his all right; the CB initials were stamped on the end of the wooden handle.

'What do you mean?' Joe quizzed, 'different how?'

Connie saw it immediately. Becker's rockhammer never came out of its wooden case - the last thing he'd ever do was spend energy when he could pay some other poor sap to do it for him.

Becker's brow furrowed as he inspected it, turning it through a full circle, 'it looks so bloody old,' he murmured, 'the wood is discoloured, look at the grain, it's split…Jesus.' Becker peered up from the hammer, ogling Connie incredulously. 'The head is oxidised with, um, well…age I guess.' His jaw dropped open, then snapped shut as he contemplated where it might have been. What had it witnessed, what might have touched it? Whoa, he thought to himself, a shock of energy running straight through him. What if they had picked it up…then sent it back?'

'All that in an hour?' Joe asked doubtfully, the buzz in his brain growing into a full-blown adrenaline rush, something sour burning the back of his throat.

Quincy stepped back to the small hemisphere, applying pressure, faster and faster, seemingly in desperation, repeating it, applying more pressure each time, daring it to remain inert.

'Go Quincy,' Becker urged, thanking God for some hurried action, convinced they wouldn't get a result by standing around mooning at the damn thing.

Joe looked at him, starting to panic, 'stop Quincy, we haven't agreed to this, you could seriously make— '

'Shut it Joe,' Becker shouted, throwing his arms up, fists balled, 'we have no time.' He waved him away with a flick of his hand.

Connie was silent, her frown deepening. She had no idea what was wrong or right, realising one or both might not even exist. Maybe it was just action that stimulated it, despite what Joe said about needing a considered display of intelligence. Road testing it with circular ratios initially seemed encouraging but had come to a brick wall pretty quick. Connie couldn't decide whether she wanted Quincy to stop or keep going. None of them had anything, so it was either stop altogether, spend precious time deliberating, or just hammer it and see what happened.

Quincy was sweating profusely, hands working harder and harder, each one cupping the hemisphere then letting go, changing pressure, time of compression continually. He eventually stopped, crawling back a few metres, puffing to catch his breath, wiping the moisture from his forehead with the back of his hand.

'Goddamnit,' Quincy puffed, trying to slow his breathing. 'Ideas…anything?' He wheezed between intakes of breath.

Becker's face was sagging, head lowered. 'Look,' he said heavily, 'we've tried to get something from this thing, to give them a reason to keep us here but we need to call it, we're done, there's nothing left to do.'

Quincy nodded his head reluctantly, agreeing with Becker. They were almost out of food, water, were exhausted and mentally fatigued. He knew their judgements might be off as a result. None of them, despite what they said, were sure their decisions were in the best interests of anyone, and bottom line, it was time.

'So hang on here for a minute,' Connie said, 'we go topside and what then?' Both her hands were raised, 'I'll tell you what then, we get arrested and spend the rest of our born naturals in some military style lockup.' Have you completely lost — '

Connie's ranting was drowned out by an echoing growl, so low pitched the vibrations prickled the soles of their feet, rumbling through them as though the metal plate was shaking…or cracking into pieces. Connie instinctively stepped backward, watching the object churning out light and pulsing almost organically, looking disturbingly alive. More troubling was the thermal radiation it was now producing, like an open fireplace suddenly stoked into life. Despite being surrounded by kilometres of ice, they were already uncomfortably warm, dressed as they were in parkas, polar mittens and polyester-lined waterproofs. Ice and heat Joe brooded, realising the simple chemical reaction they could expect, and the dire implications of the phase change should it continue. Fuck was his brain scream.

Connie peered around, breathing faster, already bathed in sweat, trickles of moisture running down the small of her back. She could see ice starting to melt, drops of water accreting into streams, falling to the ground in waves and disappearing into the incisions, giving the impression their whole world was starting to liquefy.

'Jesus,' Quincy said, twisting his gloved hands together, gazing straight up. 'There's a frozen ocean up there!' Staring blankly at Joe, he frantically contemplated motivation. Is this the way it ends? His mind was racing, searching for answers. Maybe there was a certain window of opportunity to unlock this thing and if you screwed up or took too long, some apocalyptic auto-sequence locked into place and started ticking toward a pretty rotten outcome - in this case melting a few billion tonnes of ice and flushing them all to hell.

Joe's eyes visibly widened in their sockets, fessing up to fear that he reckoned was as bad as it could possibly get. Did this alien bastardry actually want them dead, heating up the ice and melting it, giving them absolutely no hope of escape? It would simply end in a watery grave for all of them, and maybe that was precisely what it had in mind. Swim my pretties...

'We're screwed if this keeps up,' Joe said, turning in a slow, sloshing circle, horrified by the sight of water streaming off every surface around him. 'Is that the reason it's here…I mean, what the fuck right?' He shouted so they could hear him over the swell. The colossal racket and reverb was so loud and so bass-filled it felt like they were part of some crazy carny ride.

The clamour from the object increased as its angular momentum grew, the rotating heart of the great circle now a richly painted blur of extraordinary complexity. Adding to the panic was an unbalancing inertia, growing stronger, like they were pulling extra Gas in the direction of the hemisphere. Something baffling was happening, punching them in the pit of the gut, gripping them physically, like an endless b-double slamming past in the street.

Ice was thawing so rapidly the water was no longer disappearing into the incisions in the metal - it was pooling everywhere, gradually rising up the dirty blue walls. They stood together, human mannequins, nowhere to go, powerless to help themselves as water sheeted around them, even bubbling up under them. Waterfalls cascaded from every surface, beating drums, an irresistible tide, unnerving to the senses.

'We're going to fucking die down here,' Quincy whined, watching terrified as water lapped his knee, wrestling with the perversity of it all. Oceans, lakes, rivers, bathtubs - he hated water.

It was a good lesson, Connie thought distantly, short though it might be, because nothing was off limits. This object didn't conform to any predictable set of behaviours, they assumed it would be benevolent, enlightening, perhaps even welcoming, a glorious testament to cognitive altruism. Well fuck that, Connie told herself harshly, never assume, never apply homespun logic to something that might be mega-parsecs beyond it.

Icy walls were being gradually liquefied into a surging sea, pushing water above their thighs, deepening rapidly as they peered around desperately. 'Get in the bloody car!' Connie yelled, throwing a hand desperately toward it. She had a sudden, wrenching thought, what if this thing kept getting hotter, would it eventually melt the entire icecap, leaving a naked continent? Connie imagined a nuclear furnace gone mad under the ice, flooded islands, inundated lowlands across the world, visions of devastation, courtesy of Becker and his little band of polar marauders.

Sloshing toward the tunnel, it was difficult to get traction on the metallic floor and predictably, Becker skidded and slipped, falling headlong into the water like an uncoordinated bear, legs and arms everywhere.

'Shii-it!' He yelled, followed by a yelp of panic.' Becker soon realised that the water wasn't freezing cold or even cool, in fact it was generously warm. All of them were insulated from the water by their Gore-Tek waterproofs but when it hit his face he was stunned, bracing himself for freezing needles to claw into him, but it didn't happen.

'Christ, it's warm,' he spluttered, scrambling to his feet in the deepening water. 'The water's bloody warm.'

Connie ripped off her outer glove, running her cut off inner mitten through the water, opening her eyes wider, 'like mother's milk…wait, but it's meltwater…meltwater is cold…has to be cold.' Connie stared blankly at it, hanging onto Joe. 'There's so much ice…it shouldn't be more than a few degrees C.' No one had an answer, it quite literally defied logic.

With everyone aboard, Joe thumped the Start button, powering it up so he could lean on the Reverse lever that would get them motoring up the tunnel, not quickly but with no heavy equipment aboard, he figured they could outrun the rising tide.

Joe's face went still as stone as he realised there was no noise. The starter engine should have been instantaneous but there was only the sound from the bubbling rapids around them. Peering down at the engine, the pain and anguish was stamped on his face as he caught sight of the compartment door hanging open, exposed circuitry visible through the meltwater. 'Oh God,' he murmured helplessly, turning to Connie, pointing briefly, lifting his eyes to hers, 'it's full of fucking water.' She rarely heard him swear, knowing immediately it was bad. It was like something didn't want them to leave because no way it was loose before. Connie shouted, "drilling rig" but Becker howled at her, reminding them it could only go down the tracks, the godless machine didn't have the power to ascend the steep incline. Its journey had been stamped one way before they'd left.

'Get to the tunnel,' Joe yelled, it was futile but it was their only connection to the surface.

'It's a forty-five-degree incline,' Becker roared back, 'how do you plan to get up it…with fucking ice boots and cleats? We can't climb that sort of slope…not like this.'

'No other option,' Joe croaked, feeling his voice almost give out. 'The Inclinator tracks…we might be able to inch our way up, stay above the water.' He knew it was unlikely but he had to offer something to himself as much as anyone, be it hope or just empty words,. He didn't think the pitch of the tunnel was acute enough for them to simply float up. And they had nothing inflatable for buoyancy if they could, he thought bleakly, chewing on the non-existent traction they'd have at forty-five degrees on ice and slippery tracks, being chased by rising water. It was hopeless, he was sure of it.

The water was above their waist, rising way too quick to keep above it. Connie was breathing in primal gasps, picturing this rotten place becoming her grave. They'd uncovered an astonishing alien something and unless things changed quickly, they were going to die because of it.

Wading further into the dark tunnel through hip deep water they searched blindly for the tracks that ran along the bottom of the ice. Half swimming, half standing, Connie could just make out the gradual pitch of the roof as it increased to a ridiculous incline a hundred metres or so ahead, letting out an uncontrollable whimper. She stopped dead still in the tunnel, conceding that the tunnel was a useless lifeline to the surface. Connie tried to find a foothold, fighting panic and shortness of breath that made her clumsy and slow. Becker was in the lead, Quincy and Connie were coming up behind him, Joe was grumbling at the rear, all of them gasping from exertion as the tunnel pitched up to its full slope. It was almost totally dark with only their harrowingly dim helmet lights for illumination, showing the water as foreboding as ancient sump oil, the swirling waves catching the flicker from fading batteries.

'We're not gonna make it,' Becker wheezed, taking short, quick gasps.

'If we can just get up the incline a bit, uh…the water level might start to level off, uh…shit it might even start dropping,' Quincy puffed desperately, willing it to be so but doubting it before he'd said it. If the object stopped radiating heat they had a chance but if it didn't they were fucked.

Joe stared unfocussed at the water, racking his panic thickened mind. 'Why is it warm…I mean how?' Even in the dim light Connie could see the fear and disbelief in his eyes as he struggled to stay upright. 'It has to be ice cold,' he splurted again, mystified. 'And how did that cover loosen on the electrics? Something's not right,' he said faintly, between breaths.

'Nothing's right,' Connie said through rising dizziness, hearing something behind her, tensing her body like a steel rod. It sounded like waves crashing onto rocks, breakers on a reef.

Becker barked something incoherent as he glanced over his shoulder at the barest glow of the chamber entrance. It was about forty-five metres away. Everyone followed his gaze, eyeing the source of the chilling sound.

'Oh God no,' Connie moaned, jerking back, the horror of drowning now visibly real.

Quincy whimpered, trying to back away, up the tunnel, but slipping, having no foothold.

Becker saw the end of his life laid out like a terrifying watercolour behind him, the end of existence surging through the chamber entrance. He turned away, steeling himself to take it like a man but feeling like a little boy, mouth trembling and about to lose control.

Raging through the tunnel was a ceiling high wall of foaming water that was on them in seconds, sending them catapulting through the tepid water. Almost as soon as it hit them an irresistible rip began dragging them backward, a vicious tide with an inescapable grip.

Now, with about a foot of air separating an icy ceiling from the rising water, Connie panicked uncontrollably, struggling to get a breath, bobbing above, then below the water. She dragged in air every time she popped out below the frozen roof and with a final rush of blood freezing terror, she knew soon there'd be no room to breathe, the coffin lid would slam shut.

The tide was pulling them back toward the deeps of the chamber and despite her panic, impossible was Connie's first thought as she rounded the bend, getting a first glimpse of the fearsome sight within. In an instant of proper reckoning she knew it had been a mistake to activate it, they should've backed off, let the Feds handle it, they should've fucking run.

Connie was being pulled under the water, barely under the icy roof now, seeing it sparkle and glimmer in the light from the brilliant object beneath. She was suddenly ripped below the surface, kaleidoscopic colour everywhere.

They hit the horizon of the object almost at the same time, the water now so crazy transparent they could see it wasn't a hemisphere at all – it was a perfect sphere although only half of it was sitting above the metallic sheath it sat in, now no more than a tenuous silvery veil shimmering at the bottom of the shallow sea. All of them were bunched together, struggling against the tide, running the gauntlet toward some strange oblivion. Connie screamed with the last scraps of breath left in her lungs, feeling herself coming apart as she made contact, all of them vanishing from the chamber.

The Sphere slowed its manic rotation, coming to a halt in a few short seconds, any semblance of heat already gone.

11. Luna

**"A blade of grass is commonplace on Earth; it would be a miracle on Mars...
and if a blade of grass is priceless, what is the value of a human being?"** *~ Carl Sagan*

Vic stole a glance at Harry, then back through the shuttle's fore window panel, squinting warily at the jewels sparkling in the distance. 'Incredible,' he said, raising a thin eyebrow, 'a little threatening but seriously amazing.' Vic's eyes were deeply intelligent, alive with wonder, poring over the possibilities.

'Yup,' Harry offered languidly, stifling a yawn. 'Not sure about the threatening bit, but incredible, yeah.' He angled his head forward, grinning wryly, 'hope you're not getting cold feet, pretty sure there's no Death Star running around up there,' he said 'well…hopefully not, right?'

Vic gave him a wink, 'until we get up close and personal who knows, it's a big Universe.'

'Okay, so Death Star it is then, done,' he said with a choke of laughter, pulling at his moth-eaten beard and peering down.

'Forget the fantasy crap but we do need to be open to anything,' Vic said more seriously, 'this is a fact-finding mission…pretty sure our report to NASA will be a little more mundane.'

'You're the boss Vic…wait, hang on, no I'm the boss. I say Death Star.' Harry flashed a coy grin, shrugging lightly. Humour, such as it was, was Harry's thing, all that separated him from going stir-crazy on extended missions with only Vic for company.

Six hours earlier the shuttle executed a de-orbit burn and trans-lunar injection, coasting toward the Moon on a carefully calculated parabolic free-fall. About forty-five metres long, the ship was like a slightly gaunt Series 3 Space Shuttle but the similarities were barely skin deep because this was no normal spacecraft. It was a dual-prop Gen2 Raptor - a rapid transit vehicle able to reach lunar descent orbit in less than eight hours. Compared to the old STS clunkers this was Lamborghini versus Volkswagen.

Everyone at NASA could see that Harry and Vic were pretty much polar opposites, but it seemed to work well because after a dozen super successful flights they were charged with the sole Raptor in the fleet. Harry Bowden was a NASA veteran, occupying the big chair for more than fifteen years. Vic Gervais was a brilliant space scientist NASA had identified, coerced, then shunted into the astronaut program years before, growing him into their best and brightest, a pin up boy for a generation of space nuts.

As a team, they were the first to test the new generation SLS technology that combined noble gasses, rare-earth magnets and ion cyclotrons into a stunningly dynamic, low stress propulsion system. It might have been an electric engine built around a simple microwave arcjet but it genuinely kicked arse.

Eighteen months earlier they were front and centre when the Raptor ushered in a new age for space travel in the broader solar system. If things continued to go well, a mission to Mars was scheduled to deploy from Space Platform Eridanus in less than twenty-four months, a manned mission no less…finally. The third occupant of SLS Sagan was Skylar Powell, joint head of SETI's Post Detection Task Group who was shifting uneasily in her seat, trying like mad to relive the dreams she'd had about them, but they'd lost favour, because up here, well…things weren't going so well. Since they'd lifted off from Kennedy her heart didn't seem to be in the right place, pounding in her neck and banging painfully on her soft palette like a kettledrum. Back home on Earth, her dreams were inspiring, exhilarating and she wanted into orbit like an addiction, but now she was here, Sky wasn't sure she liked space at all.

NASA was heading a mission toward Luna to eyeball the anomalies that were found free falling around it in a stable, highly elliptical orbit. At one end, they swung within seven hundred kilometres of the battered surface but at the other they were more than five thousand clicks away.

Space agencies on Earth soon realised that whoever or whatever had placed these things near the Moon had a very detailed grip on the mechanics of a stable lunar orbit. It was a topic of great interest and heated debate on Earth, no longer the who but more the how, because it posed a clear and captivating question. Had they visited our neighbourhood before, calculated a stable Newtonian orbit and taken it back with them, or did their intellectual grunt simply allow them to know…easy as squashing bugs?

***

Earth had taken as much as it could from the Hubble, GOCE and LISA remote orbiters, now they needed to see if proximity gifted a deeper understanding.

Every country on the planet was desperate for information, billions of people plugging into the media 24/7 to follow what was expected to be the story of the millennium, possibly the greatest game in history.

Decent chunks of the human race were spooked, saturating mass and social media with every crackpot theory imaginable. Where did the anomalies come from, was it genuine first contact or were they simply machined automata, self-birthing Von Neumann probes or maybe something totally beyond humanity's frame of reference? The globe was salivating for anything, mainly some comfort that what they took for granted today was going to be around tomorrow.

It was generally accepted that the objects weren't natural because no one could come up with a plausible explanation, at least one that didn't simultaneously shatter the laws of physics and sanity. A few caught the wider imagination, claiming it might be dark matter made observable through an unknown and steeply exotic process. The initial stupidity of the idea was countered by surprising results, the objects exhibiting gravitational gradients far in excess of what they should, based on their calculated mass and acceleration, meaning they weren't composed of regular stuff. That's all some needed, leading to barking mad theories of quark nuggets or strangelets, maybe even naked singularities arriving on our doorstep, anything apocalyptic or annihilative would do the job, forget the science. Ludicrous and screwy, but hey, they sold newspapers, drew people to websites, cranked over advertising revenue.

***

The sight through Sagan's forward window panel looked more like an artist's futuristic rendering than any reality they knew of. It wasn't the Moon anymore, the visual was profoundly alien - this was surely the satellite of some far distant planet, a different galaxy, not Earth's little soldier. No way. The unmistakable impression was that these objects had no right being there, the second impression was perhaps even clearer. An intelligent hand had designed them, created them and decided that this was where they needed to be.

'LOI,' Vic said evenly, confirming lunar insertion, 'we're right on it, no course corrections needed,' he added, extending his arm and pressing the MECO switch, eyeing MEDS and satisfied they were orbitally in the slot.

'Okay,' Harry replied, 'oxidiser valves open, periapsis four hundred and sixty clicks.' He peered at the head-up screen, confirming their closest orbital altitude above the lunar surface. 'Pitch two, yaw one,' he said quietly, painting a picture of their orientation in space.

Skylar inhaled deeply through her nose, watching with a weighted chest as the duo engaged RCS to execute a braking procedure, dipping them into the new lunar corridor. Gravity would take hold of the craft and grip it in a synchronous orbit only fifty clicks above the free-fall arc of the anomalies. Damn, they were close, Vic said to himself uneasily, gaping at the sight through the window panel.

'Both burns were by the book,' Vic said lightly. 'What do you say Harry?'

'I say we're squared away…nice job,' Harry offered, picking at his beard with two fingers, checking out the imperious view.

91

Skylar watched Harry closely, unable to lose the thud of dread every time she cast a glance at him. Shaking her head minutely she studied him, wondering again if he had the smarts to command anything, let alone a shuttle mission. Harry had a kick ass reputation as an astronaut, technician and leader, she'd been told endlessly, but the proof was in the eating and, well…she hadn't eaten yet, at least not enough to get a decent taste. Relying on sight was simply unnerving. Best shuttle commander maybe, but Harry looked like a bum, maxed on cheap grog, maybe someone spending his days pawing over trashcans for spent fags. It was the physical aspect of Harry Bowden that filled her with something bordering on panic, mixed with the slightest sweep of comedy, a prickling feeling that he was about to kill them all, and do it with nary a change in his breviloquent demeanour.

Harry had a beard that never seemed to grow, knots of grey, bits of black summing to a patchy, moth-eaten mess. She was sure he combed his hair with a fork, all of it made worse by permanently red-rimmed eyes, and, well…that was Harry. Sky was struggling mightily to reconcile the intelligence and technical brilliance she was assured he possessed…with that. Vic was the complete right shoe - puriously kempt, slick and shrewd, the stereotype for NASA's astronaut training programme. Clean cut, NASA proud, Vic was a first-rate scientist, scooping first prize in the Dillinger Award only twelve months earlier.

'Unbelievable,' Skylar muttered under her breath, looking from one to the other with a slow, deliberate wag of her head, gazing beyond Harry and through the window panel at the bow of the craft. Sky felt something catch in her throat as she glimpsed a glistening pearl emerging over the heavily cratered highlands of the Moon. She pushed her toes as far into her boots as she could and massaged the back of her neck with a slightly trembling hand. 'So b-beautiful,' she said owlishly as it slid toward them, punched by her racing pulse.

'That's why we're here,' Vic said, smiling eagerly. 'And I'll bet they're perfect spheres too,' he added, 'chuck a laser micrometre on 'em and I bet they'd be exact to any scale you wanna throw at them.'

Sky steeled herself by focussing on their sheer eurythmic beauty but blood was roaring in her ears, her mind swimming with bright, swirling dots. She gripped the sides of her seat a little tighter. Was it nerves, mild panic…fuck she thought bleakly, what was wrong with her?

'Yep, they're just terrific,' Harry said coolly. 'Vic, are we go for manual burn?'

'On your mark, RCS…fifty-five percent.'

'That'll get us on the tail of the one in front of us,' Harry said, studying Sky a little closer, curious about her odd behaviour. He could see she was a little off.

The Sphere was getting visibly larger as they watched it, growing from a tiny orbital chunk into a mirror-like ball of light a few hundred kilometres behind them.

Skylar was hypnotised, not just by its visual beauty and symmetry but by what it might be, tiny hairs standing proudly at attention on the back of her neck as she fought back a shudder. Sure as shit it wasn't the physical response she was hoping for, Goddamnit she thought, struggling to catch her breath, admitting she wasn't properly in control and hadn't been since they'd dusted off from Kennedy so hastily, with zero think time. During simulations, the eggheads at Johnson said it was normal to be apprehensive at takeoff, but once you're up there…you'll be fine! What a crock she thought miserably because when she "got up there" the tremors, the panic started peeling her away, and now it was dismantling her bit by bit. Something was off. It was space.

On Earth, it was mind-blowing, inspiring, a wonderland of incredible scientific and cerebral possibilities. The greater Universe was her world, work or play, every hour, every day, but up here, Jesus, it was just plain frightening. Sky desperately wanted to suck it up, be resilient, show the assurance of her station. She was part of NASA for Christ sake.

Harry was parked laconically in the Commander's seat, Vic busily scanning head up displays in the Pilot's seat next to him, and Skylar as Mission Specialist, occupied one of two large rear seats. The forward area of the Raptor was crammed with the best tech the planet could offer and the sight was never lost on Harry, reckoning it was fucking awesome, an Aladdin's cave of state-of-the-art techtronics. It filled him with a humbling sense of pride to be human and with a personal life in freefall this was where he wanted to be, pretty much his home, the only place he felt comfortable.

Surrounding the pilots in a semi-circle was a daunting assemblage of real-time, integrated flight enabling technology that was one of a kind. Sagan was a multifunction beast, able to take off from Kennedy or Edwards, fly like a jetliner in the atmosphere and when needed, crack Earth's gravity, de-orbit and head through the inner solar system, going, landing wherever it saw fit.

Closest to Vic were large pushbutton shunt switches to choose Hydrazine or Magneto propulsion. Regular or rocking Harry had so eloquently dubbed it. Vic also had the brake and rudder pedals, the rendezvous and docking controls while to Harry's left were the payload operation controls and joystick for the remote manipulator.

To the layman it was an asylum of unintelligible SLS technology but to Vic and Harry it had the smell and look of caramelised onions, a roast dinner, a nice full-bodied glass of red. They knew every bit of it and loved it, perhaps a little unhealthily at times, Harry figured, but hey, it was all he had.

The Sphere was massive now, clearly moving faster than they were. Skylar could see another one rise above the Birkhoff crater below, starting to crawl toward them like a sparkling micro-moon.

'...3, 2...mark.' Harry said, glancing sharply at Vic.

Vic twisted the rotational hand controller, taking it slightly beyond the dead-zone, initiating an RCS burn, mixing and igniting nitro and hydrazine in the fore mounted pods. They felt inertia as the craft yawed and pitched, gradually increasing velocity to align its speed with the incoming object. Plasma surged from the RCS nozzles that were gimballed fore and aft to give the three-axis dynamics Sagan needed. Vic punched the forward thrusters to trim the shuttle's attitude so it increased its moonward yaw and upward pitch to centre the Sphere with the shuttle's window panel. They were Harry's instructions...to eyeball the fucker. The apparent motion of the Sphere increased as their speed reduced below six hundred metres a second, allowing it to slowly bridge the gap.

'Am-aaaazing,' Vic said, stunned by the object front and centre beyond the shuttle window. He knew seeing was all they had, but he posed the imponderable anyway, whispering, 'what...is it?' His mouth barely moved wider than a pencil line, feeling instinctively threatened by what was so casually hanging outside. It was made worse by the fourteen others just like it, because if they were unfriendly in some way, they were fucked in fifteen ways.

Despite the familiar mathematical contours, it looked clinical and cold, but still, the reality was that it was simply a sphere. Everything else was just emotional icing frosted around it by a juvenile intelligence that understood dick about off-planet cultures or extra-world mindsets. Deserved or not, it made Vic feel things he was struggling to define, an unpleasant pressure, that's really all he could tell, like a premonition of disaster based on nothing more than a melting snowflake.

Sky rocked slightly in her seat, fighting dizziness, 'uh...extraordinary,' she said brokenly, trying to sound awed to paper over her anxiety.

'Looks like a marble I used to own,' Harry said with a wandering gaze, 'an Aggie...all the kids wanted it, could never beat me, never got it. Suckers.' He grinned at Skylar, wiggling an eyebrow, 'just temper those nerves kid because we haven't even started yet.' Harry offered as he slowly got out of his seat and walked on the textured flooring to the window panel. 'Let's go with the study protocol, before this thing starts doing whatever the hell it's here to do.' Standing still, he stared at it blankly, wondering what these objects had in mind...analysis, rub elbows with the locals, colonise, exterminate, maybe a bit of one, a bit of another. Fuck knows he thought, freely conceding it didn't have to be anything positive, after all where was the welcoming party? As far as he could see there was no forward handshake detail or reassuring messages of hello anywhere to be seen. He shook his head, adding up all the pieces, that's the first thing we'd do, it was an absolute given, so what the hell did that say?

93

Skylar tilted her head toward the window, not trusting herself to speak. Like Harry, she was bemused by the absence of even the most perfunctory hello. As he had so neatly summarised, it was a waiting game, biding time, twiddling thumbs until the objects did their business. Maybe it was to unload a population of galactic travellers or maybe just their leaders, or perhaps something none of the scientific knuckleheads on Earth had even considered.

*****

Harry surveilled the equipment they'd shifted to the airlock, and was bent over, rubbing his back with his thumbs surreptitiously, feeling it aching, hurting. Even without the effect of gravity, his back was still dodgy - it was the flexing and twisting, not the weight that did it. He wouldn't let on though, anything suggesting he was less physically capable than the rest of them was to be avoided at all costs. Older he might have been but he was just as goddamn able. Even without a bad back, walking was slow by design aboard Sagan so no one was the wiser. To overcome some of the feeling and inconvenience of weightlessness they were wearing the new NASA Velcran© suits and boots. These beauties boasted multi-layered, specially designed "keyhole" Velcro to attach them to the ribbed surfaces of the shuttle, extending to their flight suits that would stabilise them on walls, seats or whatever they chose to make contact with. It allowed them to move quite "freely" by landing the foot straight down and gently sliding it forward to release. Initially it was awkward but after a while it felt sort of okay, although the lack of gravity still made it difficult to keep the upper and lower body in synch. Harry felt the pain in his upper thighs and lower back as he engaged those muscles most to maintain a rigid posture, allowing a reasonable forward motion. Good old Vic he thought, feeling a flush in his cheeks. Wonder boy had developed Velcran in his spare time, patented it and NASA bought it from him for a tidy sum and then fuck me if he hadn't won the Dillinger prize for it. Pete Conrad would be spinning in his grave, he said silently…astronauts just fly, right? What a load of unholy bullshit.

All the equipment was assembled in a semi-tidy heap outside the airlock, the array of tech designed to analyse the EMAR spectrum as well as gravimetrics from their spherical companion. When they were up and running, a live stream would be sent to JPL in Pasadena, hopefully for some rapid analytics and insight. Frequencies and wavelengths would hopefully allow them to fingerprint some of the atoms and chemical structures in the outer skeleton. They'd already identified Auroral Kilometric Radiation using the Interball 2 spacecraft, which was thrilling the scientific masses from Max-Planck to Laboratoire d'Astrophysique de Marseille. Detection of AKR was intriguing because it meant emissions were intensely structured and propagating in all directions at high frequencies in several wave types. It was scientific mumbo-jumbo to most but it revealed an underlying layering that was winding up the nerds like never before.

Scientists from almost every branch of study were frothing at the mouth, desperate to get their hands on some hard data to paw over, maybe something definitive and incredible could be added to what they already knew, which on a Big Data level was pretty much squat.

Everything was activated and good to go, sitting in the payload bay, self-test routines run, blue lights noted on all tech. There was something there for everyone. The Short-Range Reconnaissance Imager to study different wavelengths, the multicom MEMO detector for more on AKR, radio experiments for temperature and pressure, the teddy bear shaped multispectral array for sub-surface mapping and several accelerometers for radiation, gravity waves and heavy magnetics. It was a decent chunk of cutting edge technology NASA reckoned would give them at least something. Consensus was that if it was there to find, they were well positioned.

The final piece of analytics was in the form of BAE's Argus Camera, a one-point-eight gigapixel lens that delivered the world's finest picture. This was attached to a drone and would be piloted toward the Sphere by Skylar, once again with a live feed being streamed to JPL and Sagan. They wanted quality resolution of the Sphere's surface and then they would pause, take a collective breath, then reach out with Viper and touch the object. In a manner of speaking it would be first contact, courtesy of their tiny, unmanned one-eyed robot.

Supporting Viper was Sagan's altazimuth telescope, programmed to track the drone all the way to its target, providing a video diary of its short journey, beamed directly to the head-up screen in front of Vic.

Sky had been trained to use the remote piloting system but it was pretty much automated, requiring only a few propulsive and nulling inputs. Orbital coordinates were already loaded into the drone's navigation system, Skylar would simply control the speed of approach using a throttle up and down controller with gas brakes that worked much like an aerosol can full of inert gas. The question she kept replaying in her mind was always the same and each time it came, so did a churning wave of nausea. It was the inside, that's what unnerved her, the endless, numbing possibilities. Sky was of course assuming there was an inside, and they weren't just solid all the way through like jumbo-sized ball bearings. Hardly likely she figured, although it would eliminate a lot of the troubling thoughts bubbling in her mind.

All the experiments seemed to be running okay so far, Harry confirming the high def data was being received by Pasadena in perfect order.

'Okay Sky, power up your bird,' Harry said calmly. 'See what this Aggie really is.' He smiled his mercurial smile, splitting his bird's nest beard asunder. Skylar's heart was pounding, perversely seeing Harry was having the time of his life, wired by the need to know, staring intently at the screen as though it were the last seconds of NBA extra time with the Celtics a few points behind.

Viper was sitting in the airlock located on mid-deck and with depressurisation complete, the outer hatch popped and the drone was good to go on Skylar's command. She muttered something, cupping her hand over her mouth, peering at the small group of controls in front of her. It was go-time and she felt like collapsing, squeezing her thigh muscles hard to stifle the trembling…but it just made it worse. She was intimate with everything about the remote system but right now it was as foreign as a Soyuz flight panel with Russian pushbuttons. Skylar had done endless conditioning tests at Dryden and passed them all, even acing the so-called vomit comet, notorious for sorting the "men" from the rest. Her physical reaction to spaceflight was never the problem, it was above the neck. Things were happening to her mind she didn't understand, and hated. Sky pushed herself gently back in her seat and pressed her toes hard down, battling dizziness, pleading with herself to get the fuck on with it.

Punching the Activate toggle woke Viper's primary propellant and navigation systems, bumping it out of standby mode. Skylar gripped the joystick with a sweaty palm, pushing it forward shakily to lift Viper off the polyceramic floor of the airlock. Deflecting the Impulse controller, she initiated a spray of gas, propelling the drone away into space.

'Vision is good,' Vic said, watching the CCTV feed on the screen in front of him.

Harry blinked at it, lifting his chin, smirking, 'wish it was in 4K,' he said, 'we've got the best bloody camera on the planet and we're watching it in 1080. Vic, remind me to complain to JD when we get back, give the bastard something to do.'

Sky laughed nervously, catching a glimpse of their tiny explorer from the side window panel, silhouetted by the Sphere, like a planet transiting its parent star Sky thought. 'Throttling up,' she said, slowly rotating the joystick to the left, pinpricks of moisture rising above her top lip. They watched the gas escape into space behind Viper as it closed on its prey. Sky had the hand controller in a death-grip, white-knuckling it, trying to null the tremors in her fingers.

The craft would gradually come to a standstill two hundred metres from the Sphere through its collision avoidance software, activated by automation at contact minus ten kilometres. At least that was the plan.

'Fifteen clicks,' Skylar whispered, barely audible, 'five to auto-sequence.' She felt her heart take an erratic beat, waiting for something to go horribly pear-shaped, tasting a sharp metallic taste on the back of her tongue. Damn it she thought, pulling her free hand through her tangled hair, drawing a deep, steadying breath.

Viper gradually stole the distance to its target, shrinking until it was barely a smudge near the middle of the Sphere. Telescope feed showed it in crisp detail, dark and distinct, the sparkling orb just to its right. Vision from the on-board Argus imaging system showed a brilliant white circle with the double shadow of Viper cast on it by light from the Moon and the Sun, both now behind them. The shadow of the diminutive craft grew as they watched the live feed, seeing it gain foreboding distinction as it approached, an earthly darkness swelling on a profoundly alien curvature.

'One click,' Skylar said vaguely, fighting to maintain composure, and above all else, not fainting. That would be the final ignominy, an unambiguous, debasing nod to personal failure.

All of them were picturing it in their own minds, their machine reaching out, sampling the alien curiosity with its human metals. Vic grimaced, mulling over what it might touch - something wildly exotic, unexplainable, or would it be just like regular stuff back home? Frypan metal. And if indeed it was the creation of an intelligent hand, which seemed a no-brainer, then this synthesis between Viper and Sphere was a singularly profound moment for the human species.

Sky gazed dumbly at the distance indicator, watching it dwindle to two hundred and fifty metres. Her heart squirmed, making breathing difficult. 'Auto-sequence…er, stop,' she managed tentatively, turning to Vic with cow-eyes that screamed get me the fuck out of here.

'Override,' Vic said loudly, 'keep going.'

Harry nodded affirmatively.

'O-Overridden,' Skylar said brokenly. Vic saw her trembling fingers hit the Purge button on the joystick. Christ, she thought despairingly, further unsettled by a growing warmth in her loins. Vic's eyes were all over her. Sprung.

As the drone loomed large toward its target, the Sphere seemed to pulse, sort of like a brief but violent shiver, hitting it everywhere at once. Then its surface broke like an ocean suddenly under tempest, rippling, swirling tessellations rising across it, the entire surface breaking into distinct parallel waves as though a king tide was being drawn by an unseen mass beyond.

'You're seeing this right?' Harry said, gesturing briefly with a hand, eyes fixed on the Argus vision. 'It's, uh, reacting to the drone…right?'

'Who knows,' Vic murmured, pushing his eyes wide, keeping them fixed on the activity, 'I'm with you though…I reckon it just responded.'

'By texturing up?' Harry said, grinning impishly, 'like it's got a boner for the drone?' He slapped his head softly with his palm, rolling his eyes.

Sky shook her head humourlessly, looking at the ground, then up at Vic. 'Jesus Harry,' she muttered uneasily.

'I think we woke it up,' Vic said, pondering the strange new dynamic. If it was asleep before and awake now…did that mean it was about to do whatever it was here to do? He swallowed nervously, figuring action was probably imminent.

Skylar was straining to control her breathing, grinding her teeth, watching what they'd apparently provoked. Counting down the distance she took a long, deep breath, fighting to slow her heart. 'Uh, twenty…ten metres…f-five...' Her voice trailed off as distance melted into single digits. They could see the flurry getting more manic by the wavelengths steepening around its surface.

'H-Holding at two metres,' Sky said in a gasp, staring vacantly at the CGI image, displaying the axial orientation of Viper.

'Why?' Harry said, throwing his hands up. 'For God's sake just get it in there…touch the fucker.' His head jerked forward, eyes slitted, urging her on.

'Have a look at it,' she said, motioning him with the tip of her head, 'I'd say it's, well…angry. Maybe we should get Houston's buy in on this. I don't know that we should make— '

'Bullshit,' Harry said roughly. 'They'll debate non-issues for hours. Decision's ours so send it in, we need answers.' His eyes flashed angrily between mounds of crinkled flesh and hairy eyebrows.

Pragmatism and patience were never Bowden strong points, which was why he and Vic were joined at the hip as shuttle combatants. Collectively they made a terrific crew- separately Harry would struggle to get a gig on a fishing skip.

'I agree with Harry,' Vic said to Sky, nodding gently. 'We're here for insight, Mission knows that. It's a remote vehicle, that's as risk averse as it gets up here.'

'Ok-kay, fuck it,' Skylar said nervously, aiming for emphatic but getting nowhere near it.

Vic raked his head around, appraising her curiously because she almost never used profanity, in fact he'd never heard her use the f-bomb.

Sky blinked slowly, as though her eyelids had turned into heavy metal. Vic eyed her vulnerable expression, worried about her ability to cope if things started to get hairy.

They continued to split their view between the two screens, the video feed from Viper and the telescoped view from Sagan, the latter giving a perfect third person view of the drone's progress toward the Sphere. Viper kissed the surface of the Sphere, gently striking a propagating wave. They stared wordlessly at the images, holding their breath, knowing the next second or so could be impactful on a level they could barely guess at. The drone did something they knew was a possibility, but seeing it actually happen, watching it up close, well…that was a whole other thing.

'Motherfucker,' Harry gasped, raising reddened eyes from the head-up screen to the window panel.

Skylar sagged into her chair, moaning quietly, glancing skittishly at Vic.

Vic's eyes were frozen on the Argus screen. 'Uh…h-horizon,' he finally said, putting a hand to his chest, seemingly stopping his heart from exploding.

The three of them had seen Viper slide into the Sphere and disappear in a burst of ripples that spread rapidly outward, like a stone thrown into a still pond. Almost in unison Harry and Skylar joined Vic, gazing toward the blank Argus screen, Lost Transmission floating at the bottom of the screen in bold white letters.

'Holy sweet—, 'Harry said with fingers in his beard, pulling it gently. 'Replay the vision…last sixty seconds,' he said, looking eagerly at Sky, urging her with a raised hand, dancing fingers.

'Don't think we got anything after it hit ground zero, but sure,' Sky returned, feeling her head swim in waves of broken light.

'I saw a flash before it went off-line,' Vic said. 'It was there, then not, subliminal almost, colour…blue I think.'

'Whoa,' Harry said quietly, chewing over Vic's words. 'Sky, do it.' His eyes were massive now, criss-crossed with tiny red capillaries, bruises beneath, growing darker with each heartbeat.

Engaging playback she directed the drive to the last pieces of feed, watching intently as the replay showed the drone approaching the Sphere, gradually meeting up with its two shadows, then making contact. Dazzling brightness became instantaneous darkness. There was a flash of colour then the transmission dissolved. Contact.

'Son of a bitch,' Harry exclaimed, 'there is something there, did you see it? He bent his head this way and that, nodding spastically. 'There was a flash, interference maybe, pause it on that piece,' he said, heart going nuts in his chest, loud in his ears. He knew there was something there, a glimpse, a hint of something just like Vic said.

Skylar tracked the video back frame by frame until "Lost Transmission" started to break up and disappear. The image was grainy and incomplete but it was pretty damn clear what they were looking at.

Harry froze, finally tilting his head at the screen, like a dog focussed on a sound. 'Oh for the love of…fuck me,' he said incredulously, staring dummy-like at the image on the screen. 'Wh-

what?' He peered unseeingly at the others, pushing his head even closer. He repeated his question over and over. Wh-what?

When Vic's mind finally started registering, it came hard. Stone cold perspiration stood out on his skin and looking at Sky he saw her mouth gaping, coin-like eyes. In front of them was the coarse form of a planet and without doubt it was alive in every sense of the textbook definition – though grainy and coarse, they could see clouds and landscape, mahogany and oceans verdant green, the image of a biological Eden running over with the stuff of life, visually at least.

Sky's voice was barely a whisper in the back of her throat, 'is, um…that where they come from?' Her mouth was almost shut tight as she locked her eyes back onto Harry, studying him, lifting her eyebrows as high as they could go.

'Forget that,' Harry said, 'Jesus, you're missing the point, what the hell is this Sphere? I mean, the drone went through it, winked out, and it's like…reappeared somewhere else. He wagged his head disbelievingly, staring at the image. 'Is that it…is that what happened?' His eyes darted around, resting on each of them for a time, then back at the image, gobsmacked.

A sudden movement pushed them firmly against the side of their seats, sending Sky stumbling sideways, just managing to stay upright, finishing up sprawled against the bulkhead wall.

'Hey,' she said, startled, groaning as she regained her standing position, looking at Vic, wondering if he'd tripped the RCS or Vernier.

'We seem to be, uh…moving,' Harry said, looking straight ahead,

Vic raised both arms back at him, 'hey not me,' he said defensively, 'but we are moving…four, wait, five metres a second.' He scanned the instrumentation around him. Sagan was completely off-grid, zero prop, DAP nominal so whatever the cause of their motion, it wasn't coming from them.

'Sagan this is Houston Flight, are you reading movement?' Mission was clearly seeing motion and Harry could sense urgency in Jack Raines' voice.

'Flight, we have unidentified movement toward the bogey,' Vic said, a deepening frown of incomprehension clouding his face. 'All prop is off-line.'

Skylar was breathing in shallow spurts, rocking ever so slightly in her seat. 'Jesus, we're being pulled in…the object, the Sphere is pulling us—' Her eyes were massive, watching ripples and other complex tides on the Sphere's surface, ebbing and flowing as though it were alive. Oh God she prayed, not like this, she wasn't ready, there's no way she'd ever be ready for it. Spatial break, she repeated Harry's words in her head, feeling sick and faint, hot blood pumping everywhere.

Harry gazed at the Sphere through the starboard window, seeing it in a new light. 'Strap in Skylar.' Harry yelled. 'What's the range…Vic?'

'Twenty-eight clicks, closing at nine hundred a second. We're accelerating toward it.'

'How long?'

'Uh, estimated time to contact…five minutes if acceleration remains nominal,' Vic said, feeling sweat dripping down the small of his back.

'Sagan, Houston Flight – report status.'

'Flight, we're initiating a high-grade burn.'

'Copy.'

Harry's frown vacated. 'You know, maybe we shouldn't resist,' he said uncertainly, 'surely whoever placed these things here doesn't mean us harm. I mean, we have to call bullshit on that…right?' He looked at Vic, raising an eyebrow curiously.

'Define harm,' Skylar said, leaning forward against her restraints. 'Maybe their idea of harm is way different than ours. We can't go into that thing…what if we can't get back?'

Harry paused. Shit, he thought suddenly, 'that hadn't even occurred to him and it damn well should have. Maybe he was losing it like Sky, he just didn't know it yet.

Vic nodded at Harry, then at Skylar, coughing to clear a tickle in his throat. If they didn't find a way right now they were, well, he wasn't sure, it was down the rabbit hole come what may.

'Full OMS burn port side,' Harry shouted. 'Leave nothing in the tank.'

'Copy,' Vic said, game-face stiffening his expression as he studied the panel in front of him. 'ADI switches are good, ENG to ARM.' Vic punched the pushbutton and it dutifully illuminated in yellow, then he did the same with vector control. 'APU pre-start, vent doors— '

'Just gun it Vic, no time for a fucking narrative,' Harry snapped, jabbing him with a finger.

Vic pressed the EXEC key.

They felt the rumble from the powerful orbital manoeuvring engines as they fought to halt their movement in space. Vic was glued to the Star Tracker as it sent pulses of radio waves at the Sphere, speaking to him about distance and rate of approach, all the things that were bad.

'No change, we're still accelerating.'

'Goddamnit!' Harry yelled.

'Sagan, Flight, velocity still increasing,' Jack said, a little shrill over the S-Band.

'No shit,' Harry grumbled, 'Vic, main engines, full burn.'

'Copy,' Vic said. It was the only way.

Vic actuated a forty-five-degree starboard yaw by gimballing the aft and portside RCS and initiating a delicate left then right pod burn to position the main engines head on to the bogey. Vic peered at the ADI Screen, the "eight ball" that was modelling their position in space.

'Come on you fucker,' Harry said, spitting the words, watching the realignment happening too slowly.

Skylar was watching everything from her mission specialist seat to the rear of Vic and Harry, unable to do anything but sit in white-knuckle terror, waiting for her fate to play out, listening to her heart thud dully in her chest. The thought of being dragged to some insanely distant moiety of the Universe, not being able to return, ever, was mortifying. She clutched her throat and stifled a scream, all she could think about was Alysha, her daughter back on Earth who was waiting for her to roll through the door like she always did, promising her with a hug and a kiss, with complete confidence she'd do exactly that. "Of course I'll be safe honey, we're talking NASA for goodness sake! They sent men to the Moon and they came back just fine". Now Sky had to deliberately blank her mind to avoid crying like a baby.

'Helium levels look good,' Vic said. Pre-burners at temperature, hydro-manifold pressures are green, oxidiser valves open, MEC's on— '

'For Christ fucking sake Vic do it!' Harry said, swatting at the air, irritated with his "by the book" crap. The kid needed to grow his hair, miss a shave or two, eat a fucking donut, and loosen the hell up.

Vic immediately looked at his FCS. 'Main engine burn.' He punched three yellow lights to his right, one after the other and the programmed burn jumped in. It was a 105% burn, which sounded nuts, but that's what a full burn was in Sagan. Good old NASA he couldn't help thinking, screw you mathematical convention!

The craft was facing directly away from the Sphere, its conventional liquid-fuel cryo engines ripping it at maximum, giving over a million pounds of vacuum thrust. Sagan was shaking, straining to counter the force of whatever had them in its grip.

'Talk to me,' Harry growled impatiently.

'Wait,' Vic said, holding up a palm, staring at the RRS.

Skylar watched blankly, unable to move or think as the engines fought to slow their progress. 'Are we going to…make it?' She said, gasping and praying irrationally. 'Are we slowing?' Sky wasn't religious by any means, but suddenly regretted not making the effort to take her family to church. If only the pastor wasn't such a tool and a pervert maybe she would have.

Vic looked directly at her, shaking his head minutely. 'Whatever's got us is too strong,' he said. 'We're not making any headway against it.'

'Contact time?' Harry asked.

'Three minutes,' Vic said, mitred to the ranging radar.

'Goddamnit,' Harry said, tossing his arms out in despair.

'Shutdown,' Vic said as he mashed the MECO button, cutting off main engines, conceding they were useless against whatever had them. The Magnetoplasma drive was a graduating propulsion, offering no hope of doing any better so Sagan was stuck like an insect in a web, embedded in some odd unbreakable field. Jesus, Harry brooded, thinking it made the Twilight Zone look like midday in Manhattan.

'Thirty seconds,' Vic said, his face settling into blank acceptance, idly wondering if destination was potluck or by design…whether the environment inside the Sphere was even survivable. Watching it reach out to them, he felt a pall of inevitability settle over him, figuring answers were only seconds away…or death. He guessed they were the options. Answers or death. Maybe both.

'I don't want to, you know…die,' Skylar said, trying to smother a sob. 'I c-can't die. I promised her I'd come home.' She gazed pitiably at Vic, shaking her head softly and dabbing at her nose. 'Do something,' she begged, feeling moisture welling behind her eyes. Vic shrugged lamely, holding her gaze as contact came. Sky was gripping the sides of her seat so tightly her knuckles were bone white, every muscle clenched, ready to cramp. Harry and Vic stared unblinkingly forward at the golden tempest that filled their entire view, a perfect curvature, so chaotic.

Sagan was almost entirely within the Sphere; its pendulous main engines the only part remaining in solar space. The rest was, well…somewhere else entirely.

The last voice was Skylar's, hoarse and filled with foreboding. 'My God…the galaxies…'

12. The Other Side

"There are varieties of life unknown to you. Their whole identity is: you can't find out."
~ Dan Chiasson

Luminescent blue light slowly resolved into a dull glow, warmth and wetness, like they were bodysurfing on a bubbling wave of water that was rapidly retreating. Beneath them was a harsh metallic surface, all of them sprawled over it like kelp left behind by a dwindling tide.

Becker awkwardly pulled himself into a sitting position. Joe and Quincy groaned as they got to their feet, none of them looking particularly the worse for wear.

'Uh, everyone okay?' Becker croaked, giving them a quick once over, surveying himself and satisfied all was in order. 'Seriously…the fucker dragged us in, spat us out, delivered us …here?' He peered around nervously, 'but where is here?' he said, squinting blindly into the distance. Connie let out a loud breath, doing her best to organise her jumbled thoughts, struggling to believe she was still alive, in the last seconds death appeared to be a certainty.

'It's as hot as a bitch I know that much,' Becker said, wiping sweat from his forehead and neck with the back of his hand. '…tropical nightmare,' he grumbled to no one in particular, still bobbing his head around, thinking South America, central Africa maybe, equatorial for sure.

Behind them was an analogue of the hemisphere they left back in Antarctica, complete with the small hemisphere, which at least in part seemed to control the larger one. Connie glanced at the black object, then at Becker who was sweat covered from the heat and humidity, already flushed and flustered.

'We need to get out of these clothes,' Becker said, gasping loudly, 'feels like we're in fucking Ecuador.'

'You seriously want us to go naked? No way I'm defrocking around you pervy,' Connie said humourlessly, staring him down.

'Seriously, is that what you think? You got nothing I ain't seen girl.'

She peered deliberately at him, a fleeting grin crossing her face, 'you sure about that?'

'Oh Christ…we all have linen undergarments under our polar gear, right?' Everyone except Quincy nodded. 'So let's strip down, leave the rest here. Quincy, underwear yes?

'Jocks and singlet,' he said, 'Christ that'll be the look,' he said, grimacing self-consciously.

'You'll be fine,' Connie offered, 'Becker's no prize fighter, trust me.'

Becker shot her a wounded look, quickly becoming serious, wondering where the hell they'd been sent.

'…some sort of transit system,' Connie said, gazing at the Sphere, reeling at the physics and how the prosaic object did what it did.

'Er, teleporter?' Joe said, looking blankly at her, shrugging doubtfully.

Quincy narrowed his eyes, 'oh Christ…beam me up, right?' He said with a brief lip curl.

'I'm onboard,' Becker boomed from the background. 'Sounds reasonable to me and hey, I've still got my soul,' he said, grinning mischievously.

'You mean you had one to start with?' Connie twisted her mouth down, 'oh…arsehole, right? Sorry, I must've heard you wrong.' She flashed a grin at Joe.

'Okay, I guess if you two weren't going at it, we'd truly be in a strange place,' Quincy said, guessing the machine was probably all of those things and in all probability, way more. Looking around, the evidence of its spatial abilities was staring him square in the face and he was thankful they were alive, ecstatic to be out from under the bloody ice, but like Becker said, where was this?

For the first time they looked seriously at the horizon, scrutinising their new home. 'Oh Je-Jesus,' Connie said unsteadily, staring goose eggs at what was around them, as in all around them.

'What is this? Becker muttered, taking a few paces forward, letting his arms drop limply to his side. Joe and Quincy tried to process the inexplicable landscape ahead of them, lacking any frame of reference to explain it. Everything around them was so surreal, like an artist's impression gone horribly wrong, as though it had oxidised over time into a bohemian rendering of a steeply tropical landscape.

Surrounding them in a complete circle was a luxurious rainforest dense with vines, ferns and storied vegetation, growing right to the edge of the metallic plate they were standing on and extending far beyond. The silvery dish was gigantic this time, at least a kilometre in diameter.

It wasn't just the forest that was unexpected - it was the goddamn colour. The forest was bright blue with a few browns thrown in, but there was no green, or even the slightest scrap of anything close to it on the artist's palette. The overall impression was a dazzling wall of sapphire rainforest encompassing them like an inviolable barrier, to the human mind, looking wrong on every scale imaginable. Connie's mind was wrestling with purple elephants and red lions, same damn thing she reckoned, raising a hand to cover her mouth, rubbing her cheek at the same time, clawing over the improbability.

'What the hell is this place?' Becker said, studying the strangely pigmented plant life, trolling his head around, grunting a strange melody.

'Jesus, you need to work on your game,' Connie snarled, 'that's the same bloody question, seriously…how many times?'

'Answer it and I'll stop asking.

Connie had to suppress a belly laugh. In his white jump suit, face red as a beet, pot belly like ET, it was all quite hilarious. No one could take that seriously nor get too angry she guessed. 'Okay Becker,' she said, snorting ever so slightly. 'Blue leaves, they're beautiful no doubt, but I don't think anyone has an answer for that right now.'

'Screw that,' Becker said, 'where are we…Joe?'

'No idea, we honestly could be anywhere,' he offered, turning full circle to take it in, head moving skittishly like a hawk, scanning for movement between the foliage. 'We're obviously nowhere near home.'

'Oh, brilliant,' Becker said caustically. 'Thanks, I'll jot that down.'

'Maybe we should try and get some height,' Joe suggested, 'so we can get some perspective, the night sky might help too, see if any star groups look familiar.'

Connie saw that Becker was wet through despite losing the heavy clothing. 'Well at least you're safely out of the Feds jurisdiction I guess,' she said ruefully, shaking her head softly at the insanity of the idea.

'Yeah, but how far out,' he said. 'I'd rather face the boys from DMV than, um…what might be in there.' Becker's eyebrows drew together as he squinted apprehensively at the forest, pointing briefly, heart pounding like a bastard.

'You scared?' She said, nodding her head, 'just stay close…you'll be fine,' Connie taunted, hiding her own dread with sarcasm. 'Seriously, you're such a wiener.' She was doing her best to corral her nerves, picturing some of the local wildlife that might call this pretty blue world home.

'Thanks hero,' Becker said, managing a thin smile and a half-hearted shrug. Why was there no sound though…did that mean no animals? He bloody hoped that was the case, maybe the forest was barren although that made no sense but he guessed it had to be a possibility.

'Obvious question,' Joe said, 'but is there something here for us or is this just some random rock we've ended up on?' He raised a hand and rubbed his wiry moustache, realising what a bullshit imponderable it was.

'Into the forest, right?' She whispered uneasily, eyes shifting from one to the other, weighing up the reaction. Odd plants probably meant odd animals she reckoned, finding it increasingly difficult to breathe.

'Why, is there no sound?' Becker said haltingly, likening it to what he'd expect on Earth, which definitely wasn't this.

Joe regarded him curiously. 'There's sound … listen.' He lifted a finger into the air.

Becker cocked his head, glancing sidelong at Connie, frowning. 'All I can hear— '

'Shit, are you kidding…you can't hear that? Turn up the hearing aid pops,' she said with a finger wiggling in her ear.

Becker shrugged, 'I can hear wind,' he offered meekly, still straining mightily.

'There is no wind, like no wind,' Quincy said. 'That whooshing is coming from the forest.'

Becker turned his head the other way, moving it this way and that, his features going blank. 'Shit, yes,' he said slowly, 'I hear it.' Becker grimly acknowledged there was something in there.

'It's harder to breathe,' Quincy said, emphasising the point by puffing loudly, 'either we're at high altitude which I don't think so, or the air has less oxygen.'

'Agreed,' Joe said, breathing deeply, wrinkling his brow. 'I reckon we need to breathe more of this stuff to get the O2 we need.' He gazed up at the very Earthly looking clouds curiously.

Connie clenched her hands tightly, wondering if they actually got their predicament. She was all over it and if they had half a brain they should've been too. She sighed sharply, guessing it let Becker off the hook, eyeing them sceptically. 'You do realise we have no water, no food, no protection…like, nothing to survive on?' She sized them up, cocking her head and shaking it. 'We're on our own here, isolated…no idea if we can last even a few days. I haven't even factored in what might be waiting in there,' she said, stabbing nervously at the blue visage, 'predators and the like.'

Becker swallowed hard, battling to hide his fear, to act normally and put the thought of the forest out of his mind. He'd probably regret this but hey, what the hell, he did say act normal. He looked coyly at Connie with his best hangdog expression. 'Aww, Con, just you relax and take a load off,' he drawled in his best southern twang. Becker had to concede he felt a bit lightheaded, probably from the thin atmosphere and wasn't really sure why he'd come out with it. Sounded lame, very unfunny, but too late, it was out.

Connie studied him disdainfully, like one might line up an insect right before you squashed it. 'When your arse is nearly dead from exposure and you're begging for help, I'll ask you the same damn question,' Connie said, drawing her lips in tight, 'And I will say I told you so.'

'Whatever,' he said, 'we'll find something to keep us going.'

'Famous last words,' she barked impatiently. 'Can you see the foliage out there? It's blue, so I doubt there'll be anything edible…anything that won't kill us I mean.' Connie's brow jack-knifed into a serious scowl. God, he was such an insufferable oaf.

Quincy eyed both of them, lifting his chin and nodding. 'Connie's spot on,' he said bluntly, 'we need to work together or we're in deeper shit than we are already know…we're screwed without water, calories and the like. You get that, right?'

Becker rolled his eyes, groaning, 'I was just having some fun, I get it, of course I get it.'

'We'll see,' Connie muttered doubtfully, catching Becker's gaze, seeing a red flush run up his stupid neck into his face.

'Fun Nazi,' he murmured sourly under his breath, just loud enough for her to hear it.

Quincy cut them off, 'look, let's find higher ground, everything's pretty flat out there, so hills, if there are any, might be a bit of a walk.' Hell of a walk he really meant to say, which in this atmosphere was going to be a major bummer, not to mention the unknowns of the forest. He reckoned there was a lot hidden from view because the horizon was short, so this world or moon was diminutive, the steep curvature and massive canopy veiling any potentially higher ground.

'Maybe we should go back, not forward,' Joe offered, turning around, making a noise in his throat. 'Or not,' he said biting a lip in dismay. Both hemispheres, large and small, were black. Joe palmed the small one as he'd done under the ice in Antarctica, but it remained impassive.

'Well okay then…seems like it's forward,' Becker said huskily, hypnotised by the colossal wall of demented vegetation that ringed them full compass.

Quincy was frustrated by the unnecessary indecision, watching perspiration dripping from his chin and spotting the metal ground with moisture. Getting up, he started moving slowly, plodding toward the forest, looking at the others while he moved. 'C'mon,' he urged. 'Walking, exercise…healthy body, healthy mind, right?'

Becker felt sure low oxygen was hitting him as well because that sounded out of character for Mr all-business, humdrum Quincy.

Connie was stuck in a loop, spooked by the objects behaviour and why it was so hell-bent on getting them to this weird place. In her mind it had deliberately flooded the chamber, sucking them into some netherworld and spitting them onto this peculiar planet of blue foliage and oxygen-poor air. It was another world, another star system they felt sure, but was there a more fulsome significance to this rock they weren't aware of? Maybe not but maybe yes, perhaps it had massive meaning and they just didn't get it, hadn't found whatever it was they were supposed to find…yet. There was no obvious sustenance so the trip had to be a short one, Connie hoped, admitting it was nothing more than a wishful crock because the Sphere makers had no insight about what it meant to be human, or didn't give a shit. She'd once kept ants in a jar when she was a little girl in junior primary but forgot to punch holes in the lid. Oooops! Next day she'd gone to check on her little prisoners and they were all dead, little legs sticking up in the air like tiny wooden sticks. She'd felt no guilt at all - just irritation…so she flushed them out under the tap and got a new lot, even put holes in the lid for 'em. Stupid ants, she remembered thinking as they washed from the jar down the drain to insect oblivion. The relevance was terrifying, the questions in her head like sand grains in an hourglass, coming in way quicker than they were going out. In fact they weren't going out at all. Moving forward felt right to Connie, even though what lay within or beyond the sapphire forest had possibilities as numerous as there were stars in the Universe. Stupid humans, she pondered grimly.

'Can you hear it?' Connie said, snapping her head around to catch the drifting sound, eyes wide-open, heart smacking her breastbone. It wasn't distinct but it was definitely louder, a background of amorphous something like a distant ocean, gently breaking waves, a warbling, whispering alien-ness.

'I can't make it out though, like individual sounds I mean,' Quincy said, tugging his ear repeatedly. 'There's no birds in the sky but that…over there, it's definitely moving and it ain't wind.' He pointed an index finger firmly at the forest ahead. 'See the top story, shapes…moving…see?'

Joe could see things, barely visible, moving slowly, scampering high up in the canopy, silhouetted by backlight, things.

'I don't like it,' Becker said with a slightly quavering voice. 'We might end up on the menu…we're talking predators, and prey, aren't we?' He lowered his voice, 'why would it be any different than back home?'

'Damn sure they won't be all vegans,' Joe said soberly, knowing how the grim scenario would play out on Earth. There'd be those that ate fruit and berries and those that ate them. That was the web of life – as far as he knew, there was only one way it could work and that was it. Meat eaters eat the plant eaters who eat the plants. Scavengers scavenge, insects clean up the crap. Without it, the food chain dissolves into mass extinctions, and it's all over.

'So what do we do?' Becker said, brushing moisture off his nose. 'We can't just go traipsing into the jungle like we own the place, right?' His eyes were huge, face blank as stone as he weighed up the possible perils that might be in there. 'We wouldn't last five fucking minutes.'

Connie glared briefly, her features softening because she silently conceded the same fear, the one they all had. She frowned, thinking it through. 'I don't reckon we'd be brought here just to end up on some predator's dinner plate. That can't be it. They went to pains to get us here so, I use this word advisedly, logically, we have to trust that we can go in there, you know, safely.'

Becker snapped his head around. 'Trust?' He blurted, driving his head forward in the direction of the forest. 'I really don't think so, I'll give you a big fat "I told you so" when you're hanging out of some alien lizard's gob, how'd that be for trust?'

'For God's sake use your… oh hang on, I was going to say brain but for you it's some-'

'Jesus,' Quincy blurted. A flush of exasperation glowed on his cheekbones, 'Connie's right, it makes no sense,' he said, a little more composed, 'we'll be fine, maybe it's a test of some sort…y'know, see if we make the right decisions.' He sighed loudly through his nose, lifting his head up, gazing at the sky thoughtfully.

'Logic?' Becker said scornfully. 'My logic is to sit my arse right here…wait and see what happens, maybe our transport will arrive.' He gave her a rueful grin, shaking his head in frustration.

'You'll end up a sad skeleton if you do that,' Connie offered glibly. 'And if what you say is right then those things out there will sniff you out, eventually they'll come looking…trust that.'

Becker looked up as that dismal realisation crossed his mind. He got to his feet, grunting all the way. 'Christ, whatever…let's go, but don't say I didn't warn you.'

'Noted,' Connie said brusquely, waving dismissively, slowly moving forward, all of them harbouring the same feelings of dread, waiting for something with a meal on its mind to explode from the undergrowth, and if it did, they had no shelter, no weapons. All of them, including Becker, pinned their hopes on Connie's half-arsed belief that they weren't brought here to feed the animals. Cold comfort to be sure, Becker told himself with a heavy stomach.

About five minutes into their slow, sweaty journey they could see real detail of the forest ahead. It was so incredibly unworldly, almost phosphorescent, and had a dizzying effect on the senses. Murmuring nervously, Becker said they'd get used to it eventually but Connie just cut him off, saying they wouldn't be here long enough to worry about it, but the tingling in her limbs told her all she needed to know, the Sphere was dead so where the hell was the egress point?

Connie looked briefly at the star in the sky and could see it was approaching what would have been mid-afternoon on Earth. With a furrowing brow, she debated whether its position was due to the inclination of the planet or the star's transit through the sky so she'd keep an eye on it, seeing which way it went. Back in her hometown, the Sun changed from overhead to quite low in the sky based on seasonality. Connie winced, realising surviving was the priority, not sciencing the sky.

'We need to find cover,' she offered quickly, 'it might be cool when the star sets.'

'Into the jungle?' Becker said like a gunshot.

'Haven't we already hammered that out?'

'You have, doesn't mean I agreed, I just— '

Connie was staring at him deadpan, pinching her nose. 'What do you suggest? Dig under it, fly over it? We're surrounded by jungle.' She rubbed an eyebrow slowly. 'Look around you and do the math. Going forward means into the bloody jungle…through the damn thing.'

He was about to have a crack back when Joe prodded the air with a finger, 'we should head left, over there, looks like the ground gets a little higher. If we can see what's around us we might get a clue why we're here…maybe there's something we need to find.'

'Yeah, get us off this rock,' Connie murmured, eyes fixed on the unsettling shadows in the forest. 'Maybe there's another Sphere somewhere, you know, the one behind us was entry…maybe another might be the exit.'

'Brilliant,' Becker said, smacking his forehead lightly, 'or maybe we'll find a fuelled-up starship so we can get off this piece of shit whatever-it-is.'

'Maybe we will, but if we don't go into the forest we'll never know,' Connie said, spitting the last few words at him, sweat and all. She was plagued by fears of being permanently marooned, it was a beautiful place but looks were likely skin deep. That was top of her mind.

Moving closer, the noise gradually resolved into more distinct and chilling sounds. Becker stopped, freezing like a snowman in underwear, hearing a tremendous trumpeting sound thundering from somewhere inside the forest proper.

'Jesus fuck,' he barked, tensing, ready to run like hell, 'and you still think going in there is a good idea?' He frowned skittishly at Connie, arms out from his body, eyebrows on the verge of splitting. 'Surely you can't be— '

'It's the only way,' she said roughly. 'I'll say it again, I don't think we'd be sent here to be eaten by the frigging wildlife.' Connie spoke the words by rote now, half believing them, half not. She didn't want to go in anymore than he did.

Becker listened to the dissonant caterwauling, most disturbing, a manic wheezing Becker equated to something with a colossal fur ball stuck in its throat. They could see motion in the vegetation, shadows moving around high and low but nothing came at them or close enough to be seen, all remaining conveniently veiled behind the curtain of blue and brown. Quincy expected to see at least something if only by the cacophony of sound, the heavy ground-thumping footfalls of something brutish lurching its way through the overgrowth, but vision was zero, just shadows, glimpses of colour. Becker's mouth hung open as he gazed terrified ahead. Shit, he thought, clenching his fists, trying to keep his heartbeat in check by deliberately slowing his breathing but he was stonewalled by fearful images of jagged teeth, devouring gobs, ugly death in the midst of so much astonishing colour.

The four of them stepped cautiously off the inferred safety of the metal slab and onto the lightly vegetated rim of the forest. Their feet were standing squarely on something resembling coarse sky-blue grass with a concentric growth pattern, much like the cross section of a tree with its annual growth rings on display.

In front of them was an overwhelming world of colour, a primary tropical rainforest…but what a fucking rainforest! Almost nothing looked familiar as they inched their way forward over dark soil that was soft underfoot. It was highly organic if looks meant anything, littered with bunches of small purple domes, a little like fungi, radiating spurts of crimson particles every now and again, almost as though they were on a timer. Finding a way through without touching anything would soon be impossible, ahead was lush and dense foliage, not far away looking thoroughly impenetrable.

'…what are these things?' Connie whispered, dipping her head around pigeon-like, searching for similarities but to no avail. She thought there might have been a trace of "Earthliness" but it was subtle. Everything was deformed, misshapen and just plain perverse.

Tree-like things were everywhere but their trunks were not trunks…no way, Connie thought, peering upward at the monstrosities. They were more like upright slabs of cavernous woody material, some maybe ten metres tall, separated, or was that joined she wondered, by densely knitted cobwebs, the colour of a gorgeous tropical ocean. It gave the odd impression that a colossal spider had hollowed out a tree trunk, whittled it into a finely detailed sculpture then spun a vivid web inside it. At numerous points in the "trunk" the interlaced webs spread out about five metres into narrow plate-like masses, meeting up with other similar "trees" around it. The bright blue plates looked a bit like finely woven Frisbees, the intricate "not trees" jabbing through them like mighty spears. Hanging from the webs were threatening hook-like structures, thick one end, tapering to a sharp looking point at the other, almost like they were waiting to catch some unsuspecting beast that might stumble by. On the ground all around them, sticking to the trunks like ornaments were heavily veined mushroomesque things with numerous gaping mouths with the same red particles puffing out like garish talcum powder. The bright substance coated the floor of the forest in a gorgeous crimson carpet, the overarching visual like a land of endless, vibrant colour with masses of delicate cotton candy sticking everything together into a tessellated aquamarine wonderland.

'This place is nuts,' Becker said warily, between gasps of warm, wet atmosphere, eyes darting, hoping to keep tabs on anything creeping up on them from behind, the side, in front, above.

'Something out of a children's storybook,' Connie murmured, awestruck and dizzy from a racing pulse. '…it's so pretty.'

Joe caught something in the corner of his eye, snapping his head up, double taking, grabbing onto Connie. 'L-Look,' he stammered, pointing with his eyes and a panicked thrust of his head, the rest of him stuck to the spot like a marble sculpture.

'Uh…contact,' Quincy said faintly, averting his gaze.

'Sweet Mother—' Becker spat, suppressing his voice almost immediately, swaying backward, then inching the same way until he was hard up against one of the not-trees. Clutching carefully onto a hook in the blue webbing just above them was a brilliant crimson creature, large wings heavily ribbed, extending in a fearful V-shape. It was glaring at them, bright yellow pupils and sharp, stained teeth lining a massive, oddly asymmetrical beak. By the look of the wings it was ready to take flight, possibly to slip into attack mode.

'Oh shiiiittt' Joe whispered under his breath, eyes wide enough to showcase the entire workings of the human organ. By the look of the teeth it was a predator, worse, it seemed to be taking a very serious interest in them. The lemon-centred eyes stared at them unrelentingly, flitting from one to the other, head perfectly still, a slight rustle in its feathers.

'Over there,' Connie whispered with a sudden rush of air, directing them with her eyes and turning slowly, they saw another dozen creatures of the same ilk. Other things had seemingly dawdled in for a look too. Fuck, it'd be standing room only if this kept up, Becker thought seriously. Gawking at Connie, he didn't think a "told you so" was in order right now, seeing her face pinched with terror, watching Quincy and Joe shuffling, inching behind a not-tree but still exposed on three flanks.

Only a few metres away, black sluggy things about a metre long sat in a group of five or so, resembling slick worms with pendulous soft antenna lining their spine. The loathsome creatures left a trail of bright sticky goo behind them that tiny crab-like things were gorging on. A bit further on there was a bunch of crazy looking yellow blobs with feline ears and four vibrating limbs they were using to drive themselves clumsily around, bumping into one another. Triangular things were all over the place too, blue like the forest with four short bony chicken legs and ridiculous bright red lips, well, they looked like lips, Connie wasn't sure. Above them were three huge oval eyes, bright and white like the light from a torch. Wherever they looked, the eyes of these odd creatures lit up the dim, understory locale as though hundreds of beams were criss-crossing across the blue landscape.

It was as though the forest dwellers had suddenly decided to come and see the strange new arrivals, ending in a madhouse of astonishing strangeness. Evolution clearly had some left-field ideas on this world, she thought, chiding herself immediately, guessing it was simply a matter of perspective, maybe we of the pink skin were the truly odd ones. Becker had two words for what he could see. Butt ugly. The whole godforsaken lot of them.

'Um…slowly,' Connie said, puffing, certain they were about to be attacked, maybe eaten by these presumably predatory winged things. That couldn't be their plan, she repeated weakly, but looking at the avian horror, her confidence was flat-lining, her conviction, like her faith in logic, crumbling. She stared down at the dark, loose soil, blood loud in her ears. Connie's brain lurched in another direction. Maybe what they'd assumed was illogical and impossible was the exact reason they found themselves on this world. She stared at the wildlife, heart pumping in her chest painfully as she strained to get enough breath. Maybe these fuckers are short on food or certain nutrients and we were part of the solution, maybe one of who knew how many "food-drops" to follow, giving take-out a ghastly new meaning. If she wasn't so petrified Connie would've laughed out loud, maybe slapped her thigh, that thought was plain crazy because this place looked like it was running over with food and anything else you could possibly need to survive.

Moving slowly away, as stealthily as they could manage, they slid deeper into the forest, taking mincing steps, stopping every few metres, peering cautiously behind every piece of alien shrubbery before moving on. None of the creatures seemed to be shadowing them, as far as they could tell. The critters were curious but made no move that seemed aggressive, they just looked, sniffed, crept, slithered, flew or ran off, quickly losing interest. Quincy was struck by the odd behaviour, it was different to what he'd expect back home, but maybe they were just reading it wrong.

A shrill whining gathered momentum high up in the forest, growing until it was deafening, drowning out all other noise in the forest. 'Motherfucker,' Quincy splurted as it reached a crescendo, spinning his head upward, narrowing his eyes at the canopy that was now shaking violently, raining turquoise bit-and-pieces freed from the upper storey, making a sound like heavy rain.

Becker squatted on his haunches, joining the others, searching fearfully upward toward the wall of sound. Hundreds, maybe thousands of purple-orange creatures were screaming through the upper storey of the forest. They couldn't make out individual animals but they were everywhere in a cacophonous flow of variegated colour and in a minute, they were gone.

'Monkeys?' Becker offered tentatively, noting the similarity in behaviour.

'Doubt it,' Joe said, 'nothing will be like Earth, I think that much is pretty clear.'

'Only one monkey on this planet,' Connie muttered, looking outward into the forest, grinning thinly, surprised her remark got passed the knot in her throat.

Becker nodded in surrender, wiping sweat off his forehead, sighing wearily. 'Yep, had that coming,' he said, too edgy to indulge her with a counter-strike.

'Keep moving,' Quincy said urgently. 'The ground is starting to rise, we need height and, well…maybe it'll thin out the higher we get.' Human logic again, but screw it, options were naught.

Becker yelled something incoherent, more a panicked grunt than words, then fell silent. At the head of the group, he was tracking a path, but now with both arms extended behind him, body stock still, Becker was ever so slightly muddling backward. He was mumbling something with an urgency that was chilling, suggesting a very serious problem indeed.

As he slowly drew backward they could see why he'd stopped. Connie was sure her heart stopped for a few beats, admitting her human expectation was an utter falsehood, a load of homespun hope. Silent explications came instantly, foretelling bloody death.

In front of Becker was a creature defying any human language. Becker's *butt ugly* comment was an ill-conceived understatement. Connie gulped sharply, her mind swimming in waves as she eyed its insane contours. Their first instinct was run. The feeling was so powerful it was almost irresistible but it was countered by a complete lack of motor capacity. Wheezing and puffing as quietly as they could in the anaemic air, they shifted their gaze, desperately trying to disappear among the foliage. Connie was certain the creature could hear the thudding of her heart, it was deafening in her ears, equally sure it was making her breasts tremble it was so manic. She could feel blood draining from her face, then the shivering in her feet started, moving to her thighs until both legs were shaking violently. They were dead, Connie knew it, if not this creature then the next, they'd been in the forest half an hour and already they were staring death in the face.

In front of them was a something, two metres tall, thick muscled arms, four talons on the end of each that sparkled like scimitars, standing erect on massive legs, heavily veined with claws set into them at various spots. Connie wondered idly if they for climbing, hopefully not for eviscerating…gutting. The head was the killer, basically one horrible funnel, ringed with dirty triangular teeth, not unlike a shark she thought, unable to shift her eyes. Its skin was primeval, criss-crossed with oozing sores, pierced by pencil thick hairs and eyes, soulless and spider-like, six of them, fearsome and grey, set in two juxtaposed lines. The thing was a spectacular red colour, yellow stripes flashing across its bulging stomach and legs, the most repulsive, fearsome thing any of them had ever seen, be it dream, nightmare or screwball work of fiction.

Connie was barely breathing, not moving a muscle.

'Run,' Becker whispered without moving his mouth. He wasn't scared of much but he was scared of this monstrous alien fuck, feeling a disconcerting looseness in his bowels as he gazed at the insect-like eyes.

'Hold your ground,' Quincy breathed. '…stay still…don't move.'

The creature started moving toward them slowly, steadily advancing, staring with six unblinking eyes.

'Oh God, oh shit,' Connie moaned under her breath. She was going to collapse she knew it, her legs were still shaking and she could feel her cheeks and mouth twitching. Every hair on her body was sticking up - sweat dripping to the ground in pools. Connie saw it making a beeline for her and tried to inch her way to the side but it followed. She stopped, looked away but it was on her and she could smell it, rotten meat, sulphurous, sour, making her want to retch. She clenched her teeth, didn't want to breathe or look.

'…still…stay still,' Quincy repeated as firmly as he could without moving anything. The beast spun its head toward him and roared an inhuman burst that smashed through the foliage in explosive waves, then instantly twisted back to Connie.

She swayed back without moving her lower body, squeezing her eyes shut, sobbing, small mewing sounds escaping as she breathed in cat-like gasps. She could hear it raking in breaths in front of her, could smell the rotten remnants of its last meal. Connie pushed her eyes into slits but wished she hadn't. Bile flooded her throat, panic like she'd never known welled in her throat, needing to scream to let it out. Coming even closer it seemed to sniff her, a deep guttural slash of air held for long seconds before an equally loud exhalation of acrid breath. Connie edged back, dragging her feet through the organic soil, waiting to die. Lights started flashing behind her eyelids, huge tears falling from her eyes, rolling onto the alien ground, blending with the bright blue grass.

Squaring its ragged shoulders, the cavernous jaws dropped open wider, exposing several rows of banged-up teeth, then suddenly it roared again, sending sputum flying through the air. Whatever this thing was, jumped metres into the air, ran straight up one of the not-trees and disappeared instantly among the blue foliage.

No one spoke for more than a minute as they waited, still as stone, for it to return with a dozen of its ugly mates for an all-in.

Connie finally collapsed to the ground, holding her head in her hands, wiping moisture from her eyes, sheets of sweat from her forehead. 'Jesus,' she muttered, eyes roaming the forest. 'Fuck, shit, I'm…we're still alive.' She wiped more tears away with the back of her hand, all of them seeing how certain she was of a brutal death.

'We need to be as quiet as we can,' Quincy breathed, 'Christ knows how many, uh…others…are out there.'

'What was that fucking thing?' Becker wheezed, 'and why the hell did it leave us alone, I mean it was a predator, it had us on toast, yet it just up and left? Was the ugly prick just full…or maybe didn't like what it smelt?' He glanced at Connie, lifting an eyebrow, 'I mean it had a good old sniff…you forget the Eau de parfum Con?' He grinned disarmingly at her.

'I think it smelt you Becker, even a hyena would find you objectionable.'

'Ouch,' he returned, scrunching his nose up.

Joe rolled his eyes slowly up to the sky. 'Okay, let's keep moving,' he said, 'you can spar later. Everyone…slowly, quietly. Watch what you step on.' He had both hands out, gesturing slowly.

Moving cautiously on, they stepped between thick foliage, scanning intently, watching for movement or colour, praying for no more close encounters, holding little hope it would turn out the same next time. Fuck human logic, Connie said to herself, anything was possible. Becker didn't have to say I told you so, she told herself so.

The incline started to steepen as they weaved around masses of strange plants, colourful growths and not-trees, all stuck together by sheaths of cotton candy as fine as gossamer.

***

They ambled along for over an hour, terrified some hideous beast would unfold itself out of every hidey-hole they passed. A variety of brightly coloured animals passed overhead, eeking, clicking and grumphing in the foliage around them. Some sounded a little like Earth but others were indescribably strange, the most disconcerting was a whining, barking sound like a sick leopard seal that just went on and on, modulating in pitch as it went on. But they were alive, and apart from serious hunger and thirst, they were okay, so far.

Quincy's expression grew curious as he walked in step with the others. 'Do you get the feeling the forest critters are avoiding us?' He lifted a shoulder, wrinkling his brow. 'We can hear noises, these things are in the forest, it's their home but we've only seen a few, only really encountered two. And even those ignored us after a sniff or two.'

'Jesus, and you're complaining?' Becker said, eyebrows hoisted like flags. 'We should be downright bloody thankful.'

'Well yes…but it's odd is all,' Quincy replied lightly, 'but then we have no idea how this place works I guess, we assume it's like Earth, you know ecosystem and all but I reckon it's way different here.' He paused, glancing at Connie thoughtfully. 'These, um…creatures wouldn't know we're from another planet, we're definitely something new but should that mean they ignore us?' He scratched his chin, pondering the reverse scenario on Earth. Joe beat him to it.

'What if it was Earth and little green men set down on an African savannah…I bet lions, crocs and the like would treat them as a free meal, until they decided they didn't like the taste.' He looked around the group quizzically, 'I know they wouldn't just smell, they'd tear off a chunk or at least take a decent bite.'

Connie gave a shaky smile, 'thanks for the confidence boost.'

'I'm saying it appears to be different here, though nothing's guaranteed to last I suppose.'

'Okay Joe, stop talking now,' Connie said, scowling at him, holding a finger to her lips.

Something ahead was different and moving by stealth through the foliage they heard it grow louder until it was everywhere around them. Becker trudged toward the noise having a pretty good idea what it was, getting a little excited as he dodged a spray of crimson-tipped pods and pushed heavily through a broken line of sapphire fronds. Becker threw an arm up, yelling 'stop,' stepping slowly backward, staring forward. 'Come,' he said quickly, poking with a finger. 'Water,' he said eagerly through a huge smile. 'Thank God.'

'You bet your arse thank God,' Quincy said, ticking one survival requirement off in his head. Things were looking up he told himself with the slightest sweep of optimism.

Below them was a small stream, almost hidden by thick overhanging plants, a bit like garden-variety ivy but brilliant, iridescent blue. It was about five metres below them and seemed relatively easy to get to. On the other side of the river the incline of the forest floor went up dramatically.

Connie hoped like hell the water was potable…or at least not lethal.

'Wait,' Quincy shouted, throwing an arm in the direction of the stream, where it rounded a bend into an ox-bow. They saw it immediately, drinking from the stream.

Becker squashed his nose up, studying it closely with slitted eyes. 'That is one ugly some-bitch,' he said curling his lip, hoping like hell it didn't see them. His face collapsed further as he studied it, tongue almost hanging from his mouth.

'What is up with evolution in this place?' Connie said exasperated, straining to see some sense in its ridiculous appearance.

'Evolution doesn't think, it just does,' Joe said, feeling uncertain as he gazed at the critter.

'Sounds like you Becker,' she said, raising her eyes. 'No thinking, just doing. See money, chase money. That's you, right there, all tied up in a box with a nice ribbon on it.'

Becker stared at her woodenly. He had nothing to fire back, needing water and food way more than argument.

Quincy ignored her, glancing over at Joe, 'I can't see much of a survival advantage in all that. Whatever nature was trying to do, it's wheeled out the ugly stick…big time.'

'Two from two Becker,' Connie said, grinning, 'someone's on a roll.' She gave him a mischievous wink.

The creature was standing near the water, presenting like a stick insect on steroids, maybe a jigsaw put together wrong, pieced together by a blind person, more in hope. It was standing, well, it was sort of upright, two crab-like arms articulating up and out as though striking a strange bodybuilding pose. Its head was lizardish, topped with two large orange antennae sticking up like bright, sturdy chopsticks. The abdomen was alarmingly narrow and rested on the ground, slightly coiled like a snake, four slender legs boxed around it, holding it up like a napkin stand. It looked equally terrifying and ridiculous as it breathed in spurts, periodically sticking out a narrow tongue. Suddenly it stiffened, lifted itself and darted off into the jungle in a manic ballet of scrabbling skeletal limbs, displaying unexpected agility and speed. Holy sweet shit, Quincy thought, shocked at the nonsensical design, weighing the bizarre nature of life on this asylum world.

After a few minutes Becker started down the slope to the water, watching everything closely as he went, making sure nothing was lurking in the vicinity. Quincy glanced suspiciously at the water, conceding that it looked friendly enough. 'How do we know it isn't full of alien bacteria,' he said warily, instantly realising what a nonsensical statement it was. 'Well, of course it is, right?' He snorted, at his own stupidity. By definition it had to be full of bacteria and of course alien.

'If we don't drink it, we die,' Connie said matter of factly. Bacteria, lethal, whatever.' She scooped some water up in her palm, downing some of it, spilling most of it over her face.

'Jesus Con,' Becker squawked, do you have a bloody— '

'Relax…it tastes fine…salty for river water but fine all the same,' she said, smiling coyly at them, scooping water into her mouth ravenously, loving the sensual feeling of tasting liquid again.

'Taste has bugger all to do with it,' Quincy said seriously, 'it may be running over with deadly this and lethal that. Bugs don't have taste.' He drew his mouth in and glared at her accusingly. 'This planet has a completely unfathomable process of cellular evolution so we have no— '

'Oh fuck it,' Becker spat. 'Shut up Quincy, he said abruptly, squatting and using both hands to drink from, like a cup. Quincy and Joe looked at each other, silently agreeing that doing it, not doing it, the end game was probably the same. Quick death, slow death…still death. If the water was fatally tainted they were fucked…so what else was new?

Starting up the side of the bluish hill they went in search of a decent elevated view to hopefully get a better understanding of where they were and what might be anything worthy of investigation. The gradient gave them hope their direction of travel would eventually do them some favours. Quincy felt an overpowering sense of surrealism everywhere he looked and as he trudged up the hill, puffing and wheezing, he wondered if they'd ever get used to the wacky colours.

Connie sensed the light dimming and instinctively looked up, shading her eyes with a cupped palm, glimpsing the star, quickly looking away, seeing it wasn't due to set for a while yet.

'Wh-what is it?' Becker spluttered, wincing and shielding his eyes, seeing something but not sure what, also noticing the loss of light. He expected some colossal clawed bird-thing to be screaming toward them with an evening meal on its mind. He was now conditioned to dying.

'A moon…transiting…uh, an eclipse I think,' Quincy said, stammering, holding his hands over his nose and forehead like binoculars. 'But hey…what a moon, right?'

Above them, an elongated and noticeably angular moon was racing across the face of the star, blocking maybe half of it as it went, the whole thing over in a few seconds.

'Man, that thing is moving,' Becker said, flicking his eyes on and then away from the star, seeing its odd, craggy shape quite clearly.

'Or it's in low orbit,' Joe said, moving his head as he followed it with his eyes.

'Low orbit it is,' Quincy said. 'I can still see it, wow it's really motoring…almost no curvature,' he continued curiously, 'captured asteroid?'

Connie peered at Quincy. 'Thanks Professor,' she said, nodding and pushing her chin out, grinning thinly.

'So you're starting on me now?' Quincy slumped his shoulders in mock pain.

'Let her go,' Becker said, 'she'll run out of oxygen pretty quick, especially in this place.' He puffed deliberately and poked his tongue out just a little bit and wiggled it.

Becker if I had the strength I would come—' Connie stopped mid-sentence, casting a nervous glance at the forest and at Becker as a snarling roar thundered up at them from the land of the not-trees below.

'Move!' Joe yelled. 'Go for fuck's sake.'

'Go where?' Becker said urgently. 'Up? But what if it goes on for miles?' He looked mortified by the prospect of more trekking through the jungle without food, especially uphill. They were already on the verge of collapse from simple want of calories.

Quincy glared, 'unless you wanna stay here with whatever made that noise, yes…up.'

Becker glanced back at the forest, giving a tense nod.

Quincy started moving and suddenly stopped, holding an arm up with a single digit raised. 'Ssshh…do you hear that?' He queried, trying to resolve the noise that was getting louder.

Connie's heart jumped as she scanned the near distance nervously, expecting anything.

'Uh…flapping,' Joe said, frowning nervously, 'wings maybe…birds?'

'I don't like it,' Becker growled, shaking his head.

'Nothing here is to like,' Connie said, regarding him with distaste. It was like he expected candy-canes and Christmas crackers to magically appear.. Didn't he get it? This was hell!

Joe caught movement in the sky. 'Get down!' He said, arms waving them frantically to the ground. Dashing to the nearest thatch of shrub-things, they squashed themselves as low as possible. Something large was approaching beneath the forest canopy, they could see it, flying between the lowest story of vegetation.

'Oh…whoa,' Quincy whispered, wagging his head numbly at the sight. There's two…a pair…of um—' He was bug-eyed, following their progress. Connie shivered in revulsion as she watched the transparent abdomens fly toward them, pulsing with bright discharges and vivid fluids surrounding what looked like strange internal organs. The wings buzzed like a fly but there was a second and third set of wings that were motionless like grey canvass sacks, intricately folded and crimped inside. Multiple eyes formed a semi-circle on their hairy craniums and passing overhead, they disappeared without incident into the greater forest.

Quincy stood up quickly and motioned them on. 'Go,' he said quietly. They got to their feet stiffly, moving as fast as they could, keeping noise to a minimum, keen to find the edge of the forest, hopefully the end of the crazy wildlife park.

Joe scratched an eyebrow in a sawing motion as he dodged pieces of the forest. 'Is anything going to make sense?' He said, nonplused, glancing around searchingly. 'I mean, the size of the creepy crawlies on this world is nuts.'

Quincy glanced at him, puzzled. 'Earth had big buggers too,' he said, '…when dinosaurs were around, mozzies the size of seagulls, you should know that, Earth science guru…your words.'

'No, well yes, that's my point,' Joe said, 'we had colossal insects when oxygen levels were high but when it dropped, the big ones died out and tiny ones took their place, you know, because they could tolerate less oxygen.'

'This is riveting,' Becker said, sighing heavily, so not wanting another bullshit science lesson. 'I should care because?'

'Jesus,' Connie snapped, 'no one cares if you don't care. She slashed the air with an outstretched arm. 'Look at all the pretty plants over there.' She sighed heavily, 'Joe, continue.'

'Insects don't have lungs, I'm not sure of the finer details but I think they get oxygen through their bodies…so when oxygen is high, well they grow big, less oxygen, smaller.'

Quincy's face went serious, 'so…it's the other way around in this place?'

'Yep,' Joe said, nodding. 'There's less oxygen but these things are giants, so like, go figure. It's the reverse of Earth, totally counter-intuitive.' He shrugged curiously, 'is there something in that for us, that everything so far is so wacko?'

'Well maybe they have lungs,' Becker offered lightly.

'And maybe they don't,' Joe replied, staring vacantly into the air, puzzled.

Glancing at one another wordlessly, they batted around the idea, realising it meant dick, except that the world they were stranded on was illogical, unpredictable and in a nutshell, deranged.

***

112

'I think we must be near the top,' Connie wheezed, wiping her forehead with a swish of her hand. It was a little cooler than before but still damned uncomfortable.

'Great, then what Captain?' Becker puffed, his breathing and heart rate pretty much maxed.

'Then you get to shut up and stop grizzling about climbing,' she said sharply, stifling a curse. The walking did nothing for her mood but at least she didn't continually whine about it.

Muddling through the rapidly thinning undergrowth they stumbled onto a relatively flat expanse almost completely free of foliage. The strata was dark and marbled like cap rock, basalt maybe, with deep green inclusions of something striking, olivine maybe, but the geology was forgotten because as soon as they escaped the forest and stood on the flat they saw what it really was.

'Jesus nailed to a cross,' Becker said, mouth dropping open like a drawbridge, the vein in the middle of his forehead swelling and popping out. What the fuck?

'So much for the top of the hill.' Connie said breathlessly.

They gazed at a sight that defied imagining, straining their eyes to see into the distance.

'Not the top of the, um…what did you call it…hill?' Becker croaked, raising his chin, staring upward and offering a few timely expletives, shielding his eyes with a hand.

Connie was bewildered by the scale of things around her, wondering how they could possibly have missed all this from the edge of the forest. The flat surface they'd stumbled onto was simply a ledge on a stupendous volcano that stretched onward and upward, lost in the mists of distance above. The view was numbing, the sapphire and brown forest, the sparkling cerulean seas and the tremendous volcanoes forming islands of tapering rock, piercing the rusty clouds above.

Quincy's eyes were bulging, ogling the horizon as though hypnotised. 'Man this planet is small, the volcanoes are crazy big but this rock is way smaller than Earth.'

Narrowing her eyes, Connie variously shook and nodded her head as she chucked it around, totally conflicted. 'But, uh…why didn't we see this, um…from the metal plate?' She paused while she replayed events uneasily in her mind. 'You know when we were looking at the forest.' She scratched her chin, then the bridge of her nose, sizing up the madness of the view.

'They must be kilometres high…so the curve of the planet couldn't be it,' Quincy said doubtfully, 'could it?' He was second-guessing himself, pulling at loose skin on the side of his face with a thumb and forefinger. 'The hazy atmosphere maybe?' His voice was guarded.

'Something's wrong with this place on just about every level,' Joe said, mentally counting the ways, 'and by wrong, I mean, like, controlled, stage-managed…you know.' His eyes grew wide.

'It's not Earth so things are different, that's it…simple,' Becker said.

'Spoken like a true non-scientist,' Connie said acidly, 'or should that just be oaf?'

'Look, I'm too hungry to give a toss what you think, we need food, we're all starving, if we don't get it we're done.' Becker glanced painfully at each of them in turn. 'And by done, I mean dead.' He glared at Connie who lifted a shoulder and blew a kiss. Becker grimaced, adding, 'thought I'd qualify it, being an oaf and all.'

Quincy had to agree with Becker. A plan was needed or they were indeed done. No food meant death within days, simple as that. 'We can use this place as a base,' he said, surveying their little rocky alcove, guessing it would do the job.

'Shelter fine, but we need food!' Becker boomed loudly, hand on stomach, patting gently.

Connie had been thinking about their options on the way up and pretty much knew what they needed to do. It was far from ideal but in this place, palatable options seemed to be zero. 'Well I reckon we've got a couple of choices,' she said, 'we catch some of those small yellow critters or we take a chance on the pods and berries we passed on the way up here. This place is full of them, they sort of looked edible,' she said, peering at them with a gaze that was bouncing around.

'You try 'em first Con…if you live, we'll follow,' Becker said, supressing a lemon-tart grin. 'Start frothing at the mouth, we're back to the walking canaries.'

Connie clenched her toes, ignoring Becker's ill-timed mirth and again pondered the left-wing nature of these others that had led them to this alien place, and whether they were taunting them deliberately, a trail of anger blazing across her face. 'Why?' Connie said sharply. 'Why here…why this place?' She stared at Joe who shrugged, licking his lips nervously.

Becker groaned, 'give it a rest, like we already said, who knows how they think. They might be getting their jollies off…send the savages to a strange planet, see how they fare— '

Connie ignored him, raising both arms in a ballet of emphasis, 'why would they lead us to this glorified fucking asteroid.' She paused, taking a calming breath. 'It's total nonsense. Gotta be a test, a trial, an experiment, call it what you like.' She ended up looking exhausted, out of breath, most of all confused.

'Like I said, it's their version of— '

'Shut up, for God's sake put a sock in it,' Connie said abruptly. 'Enough of the horseshit claptrap…think before you open that cakehole of yours.' Connie scowled, pulling her mouth tight. Becker held up his hands in a show of mock surrender. Christ, he thought, she seriously needs to eat.

Joe barely heard a word, he was so focussed on eating something all his other senses were dialled back to almost zero. His stomach was begging for anything, even his sister's "medley of hell" would do, her bile inducing combo of sweet meats and indeterminate offal that was gastronomically horrific. The aching and primal desire from his survival and pleasure centres was chewing him up. 'I think it'd be safer to trap one of those yellow things,' he said hesitantly. 'They're everywhere down there, they seem innocuous enough.' Joe swallowed visibly, raising a skittish hand to his throat. 'We saw bunches of them on the way up here.'

'Agreed.' Quincy said firmly, 'I'd risk a protein more than a berry or a pod. We've got things like that back home that'll kill you where you stand…maybe these are similar…worse.'

'Okay.' Connie said, eyeing them in turn. 'Quincy and Becker, you're the hunting party. Joe and I'll collect some of the broken trunk pieces, maybe some of the webbed stuff to make a fire, hopefully it'll burn in this atmosphere. If you can't catch anything we go with the berries and the pod things. One way or another we fucking eat,' she said, dragging fingernails down her cheek, leaving blush red marks.

'We need to move,' Quincy said urgently. 'The star's gonna set in a few hours.' He glanced sheepishly at Connie, then down at his spartan underwear, 'food or no food we'll need a fire.'

Connie nodded and with Joe set off down the hill, Becker and Quincy coming in behind them. No, food wasn't an option, she said silently, trying to put aside the pain and the weakness.

Becker and Quincy hadn't hunted anything in their life but oddly enough found themselves crouched behind a spray of fibrous palm-things, waiting for something manageable to waddle by. By manageable they meant small and defenceless. Killers they most definitely weren't but here they were, sinfully poised to knock something off - yet another entry in the growing list of things that felt perversely wrong.

Becker didn't give a rat's ass, he was so hungry he would've butchered the last furry-faced member of an endangered species, ripped out its beating heart and eaten it whole in front of anyone who cared to watch. Extreme hunger did strange things to the psyche, although most would agree Becker was left of centre even on a gutful of food.

'I don't like this,' Quincy said nervously under his breath. 'What if we end up as the prey? We know shit about these things. They've been disinterested so far but that could change pretty quick…right? Especially if we start trying to beat one to death with a stick.'

Becker met Quincy's gaze, nodding and thinking furiously. 'They might have, defences we have no idea about so we go easy, y'know, carefully.'

Quincy eyed him. 'We're going to kill them so how do we go easy with that?'

Good question Becker conceded. Killing something with a sharpened stick was hardly going to be gentle or quiet, let alone predictable. They might look helpless but who knew how an alien being might work, how it might react, what deadly weapons it might be packing?

Looking at Quincy he could barely stifle a burst of laughter. Both of them were huddled untidily in their underwear in the bushes, waiting for an alien creature to happen by, looking docile and mellow enough to slaughter. It was utter madness but no way he was backpedalling. Hunger was overwhelming. God what he would've given for a few lost chooks to come clucking past.

Quincy tied several palm fronds together using some cobweb material as stitching. If they actually managed to trap anything, they could carry it back to camp inside his makeshift bag. Wishful thinking, counting his chickens, he thought wistfully, clutching at his neck nervously.

Quincy gawked guiltily at what they held in their hands, wondering if it was really the best they could do. A hundred thousand years of cognitive evolution and this simplistic nonsense was the best they could come up with . Crouching behind a bush with a piece of not-tree whittled into a semi-sharp point was all they could think of, hardly a showcase of humanity's ingenuity - still, they'd never hunted before so they would have to go with what they had, deal with the indignity later.

Quincy saw three of the yellow creatures come waddling along on their ridiculous thimble-like legs. How evolution came up with those he had no idea because they looked so damn inefficient. Wasn't it supposed to angle toward a reproductive and survival advantage? How these things qualified as either he couldn't even hazard a guess. Focus, he screamed at himself. Looking at Becker he gave the go sign with his eyes. It was now or never…he said never, his stomach said now.

Becker initially shook his head thinking maybe they should wait for a single animal, but it was pretty much life or death so he lunged forward, stabbing each one before they had a chance to move, the animals making a horrible clicking noise like crickets, worse, they spread bony yellow wings they didn't even know they had, presumably in fright. Now though, they were motionless and bleeding hideously into the soft soil of the forest.

'Oh shit, oh crap,' Becker moaned, cringing and recoiling, revolted by what he'd done. Peering down, he felt like heaving but had nothing to bring up, ending up dry retching in the dark soil. The birds were bleeding thick arterial blood but appallingly, it looked like something from a candy store.

'It's blood, but Jesus…it's pink…yuck,' Quincy stammered, pulling back, trying to make sense of the marshmallow fluid staining their yellow feathers. He put his finger in it, bringing it up to his nose. 'Doesn't smell like blood but it does smell sort of minerally.'

Looking closely at it he turned his finger to catch the light, stewing on the aberrant colour, wondering why? 'Maybe it's based on…well, cobalt or manganese? I'm going cobalt.' he sucked in a quick breath and felt his skin tingle. 'Amazing, isn't it?'

'Just fucking great,' Becker said, wincing, sickened by the gruesome sight but feeling not shame or sadness but joy because he sensed food, such as it was, wasn't far away. His ravenous gut was rumbling like a Mangala ore-train, his mind craving the sensory input of anything with calories.

Quincy hastily wrapped up the birds and started back toward camp, leaving a trail of bright pink blood in their wake as they wearily ascended the slope. Daylight was retreating as the alien sun started to colour up on its journey toward the horizon of this strange little reverse world.

***

Becker strode onto the ledge with Quincy, feeling a little proud of the booty they'd managed to gather…murder that is. There was still a sense of guilt but that was fading as the delightful prospect of eating drew nearer.

Connie and Joe had fashioned a rough circle of rocks around fragments of trunk and wads of knotted web. Questions were front of mind; would this stuff even burn…would the birds be edible…non-lethal? Becker knew the proof would be in the eating and he couldn't wait to indulge, leaving the confab on risks to the nerds, he didn't give a stuff.

Connie yelped in fright, looking at the lipstick pink fluid dripping from the birds. 'Is that like…blood?' She said, holding the back of her hand against her nose, staring in disbelief at the macabre scene.

'Er, yes, pink blood,' Becker said casually, glancing at Quincy, 'something to do with cobalt or the like he thinks…you know, instead of iron.'

'Disgusting,' Connie said under her breath, squashing her nose up and leaning away.

'You're a Barbie fan Connie, thought you'd be up for it. ' His mouth twitched with amusement.

'No. It's hideous. And you're not funny Becker,' she said, jerking her chin up angrily. Anything remotely related to blood or gore made her sick. Even low-grade medical shows were too much. Connie peeked at the birds, not sure if she could stomach it, mulling grimly over the hellish nightmare she'd managed to drop headlong into.

Joe had the irrational sensation that his stomach was a black hole without any spatial dimension at all, such was the implosive pain in his gut. 'Let's get this show on the road…anyone know how to light a fire? He said, looking glumly at the ground. 'Friction, sticks, y'know.'

Becker smirked wryly, grabbing at a waist pocket in his undergarments. 'Try this,' he said, pulling his hand out, throwing Connie a gas lighter. 'Backup in case the pilot failed on the rig. You know, the battery warmer. While I'd really love to see you fumble around with a stick and a rock for an hour or so, but eating is more important. Even more than laughing at your expense.' He grinned shamelessly at Connie who returned with the standard fare, a raised middle finger, killer glare.

'…and rotate,' she added. No smile.

Quincy unrolled the birds from their makeshift carry-bag, laying them gently on the rocks in a neat row, knowing it wasn't ducks lined up but it was as good as it got in this place.

'God…what are they?' She said, goggling at them. 'Are they feathers…so they're birds?' The bewilderment was splashed on her face, she thought they were ground dwellers, maybe mammals or marsupials, rodents even, but clearly not.

Quincy was rubbing the back of his neck, 'well they have wings and feathers, so I guess they are birds…maybe they just can't fly…like emus.'

Joe felt like throwing up. He closed his eyes and reopened them, battling with fearful images of gutting them. 'Er, um…so who's gonna clean these things?' He shook his head, tasting sourness, 'you can count me out...nuh uh, no way.'

Quincy looked away. Connie glared straight at Becker.

'Well?' She asked firmly, tapping her foot ever so slightly.

'So, I caught them and I have to do the plucking?'

'You're the man, you've said it yourself enough times.'

Holding her gaze vacantly, he knew arguing was pointless. No way she was going to do it with her weak stomach and Quincy was no good, Joe, even worse. 'God…fine,' he said, half smiling, half grimacing, peering at the dead animals coolly. 'I've got a stick and a rock with a blunt cutting edge,' he said unimpressed, 'don't expect haute cuisine, in fact, Jesus, it's gonna be rough.' With that, Becker grabbed the birds and took them to the edge of the forest, hoping they were really dead. They sure looked dead, there was definitely no heartbeat but who knew how these things worked. Maybe they were hibernating or playing dead, or immersed in some unknowable stasis that may well scare the living shit out of him when they popped their eyes open.

Pulling at the feathers they came away easily, revealing primrose flesh beneath that resembled corn-fed chicken. Had to be a good sign he figured, anything with an earthly feel got a massive tick in his book. Cutting the head off seemed right but there was no neck so he moved on to the gut area where he made ragged incisions to get rid of the digestive innards, seeing knots of pink and blue veins, arteries, solid masses like no organs he'd ever seen, feeling an irresistible urge to hurl. 'shit,' he groaned, turning away, taking a few long, deep breaths to steady his swimming mind. Fuck, he said to himself, trying to breathe through his mouth to avoid the repulsive metallic scent.

He understood enough about anatomy to know that these things were nothing like critters back on Earth, there wasn't a heart or kidneys, a liver, anything that looked remotely like home. Becker ripped all the crap out, running his hand around the inside of the tough internal cavity to clean it up. Standing up, he stumbled back like a drunken artist, admiring his work. Could do without the head and eyes though, that gave him chills. It'd probably drop Connie where she stood he thought, grinning maliciously and chuckling. Half an hour later Becker was done, returning to camp with four pretty decent looking birds.

*****

Connie was hypnotised by the bizarre creatures Becker had hanging from his stick like hunting trophies, averting her eyes and pinching her bottom lip with her teeth, conflicted by an equal serving of hunger-lust and revulsion.

'Pretty good fire you got going there,' Becker said, 'that stuff seems to burn good.'

'Strange thing is,' Quincy said, rubbing his mouth, 'is that the fire burns at all, thought the lack of oxygen would make it tough but it started just like that.' He snapped his fingers in front of his face. 'Almost as though there was more oxygen. Go figure, right?'

'Maybe it's the stuff we're burning,' Connie said, puckering her lips.

Quincy gave an exasperated huff, ruminating on the oddness that showed no signs of relenting. 'I don't know, that gas lighter burnt pretty good.'

Becker laid the birds on the raised stones between the flames and stood back quizzically. 'Okay, anyone got a recipe?' He said with a wink. 'Oven roasted canaries, uh…of the alien kind…sound good? Becker scratched his chin stubble, smirking, '…so what's that, close encounters of the, uh, fourth kind is getting intimate…maybe this is the fifth kind…eating the fuckers?' He threw his head back and laughed but there were no smiles, just unbroken stares at the cooking birds. Becker could see how much of an acute survival instinct hunger was, even trumping his irresistible humour, he thought with a brief snort.

Connie prayed to God that these things tasted okay. With the bright pink blood, lack of Earthly organs, she had serious doubts, and what if they tasted like shit, were repulsively vomit inducing, or worse, were toxic? Death had to be a possibility. They had already discussed the likelihood of diseases and microbes existing to which they had zero immunity but it was all meaningless banter because there was nothing they could do about it. Connie pushed her thoughts aside, licking her lips and joining the others gaze, willing the birds to cook quickly, sweating on them being something they could at least keep down and if they couldn't, well they were probably finished.

After ten minutes on the hot rocks the smell from the cooking birds was lip smacking as they crackled and popped, delivering a delicious, alluring aroma, different certainly, slightly sweet maybe, but beguiling to the point of being an addicts drug of choice.

'You gonna crack a nice red with that Con?' Becker said, chuckling quietly.

She glanced at him, pursing her mouth, 'I'll crack you.'

'Feisty,' he said, rearing back.

'Hungry is what,' she said with a flicker of a grin, walking over and sitting with the group, staring at the fire, listening to the thumping and whooping from the forest below.

*****

Connie felt the guilt of killing an alien life form, conceding that it was hardly the textbook gesture of first contact. Their death was on them but the simple fact was, it was kill, eat or die.

The meat was nothing like corn-fed chicken because once it was cooked it became dark and dense, a little like venison Becker reckoned, slightly red and very fibrous. It didn't look like it was going to kill them, but Joe lectured them about invisible bugs, that maybe it was crammed full of an alien version of salmonella or listeria, or quite probably way worse, but none of them cocked an eyebrow. Mangiari! Becker declared loudly, to him meaning food, eat, now!

Connie was unsure because she was so hungry she would've eaten almost anything, but knew the first bite was still going to be hellishly confronting. It was an alien animal for Christ's sake, pink blood, no neck, strange internals, concealed wings. She had to physically avert her thinking because the thought of chowing down made the muscles in her stomach clench and almost cramp.

Pulling small pieces of the aromatic meat from the carcasses, they tentatively lifted it to their noses, chewing tiny pieces, assessing as they went. They couldn't help lamenting what they had in their gobs, the peculiar biology of a distant planet that clearly had very different rules to Earth.

Becker closed his eyes as he put the meat in his mouth, finally about to savour food again. Adrenaline coursed through his body, saliva filling his mouth as pleasure centres melted into orgasmic expectation, as though he hadn't eaten in...well, forever. His contented smile was junked by surprise that soon turned to confusion, then utter bewilderment. 'Hey...what the hell?' He snapped, gently rolling the meat from side to side in his mouth, frowning, narrowing his eyes into disbelieving slits.

Joe looked straight at Becker with the same vexed look on his face. 'H-How...is this possible?' He said slowly, tentatively swallowing what was left in his mouth. Connie eyed the birds suspiciously as she chewed on it minutely.

'This has no taste...at all,' Becker said, touching his lips, staring at Connie with slumped shoulders. 'What is going on?' He moaned, 'are we like, being played?' He looked around, half expecting some YouTuber arsehole to emerge from the bushes with a geeky grin.

'This really is the end,' Quincy said nervily, 'it's so—, ' he paused and rolled the meat around in his mouth, '...so contrary.' He put his hand on his throat again, 'I mean, it smells like meat, looks like meat, is meat...but has zero taste. Like you said Becker, it's got nothing. There's those fucking words again,' he said bitterly, '...it doesn't make sense, right?'

'Yeah, it's not like pass the salt 'cause it's under seasoned,' Becker said, still eyeballing the meat poutily, confusion gradually swelling into anger.

Connie surveyed every fibre of the meat, blinking at it, like she was ogling an abstract painting, trying to recognise something that made a grain of sense. Did different planets, different sources of life and protein mean what they took for granted didn't apply? Connie felt a tremor run along her temple, punctuating the wrongness of it all. Maybe if it's not DNA then taste buds are locked out. That made a molecule of sense but overwhelmingly it sounded mad. Glancing around she saw their tortured expressions as they ate meat that wasn't just bland but had the taste of fresh air.

'This is crap,' Becker said, maddened at not being able to relish the taste of his daring and hard work. 'But eat it all,' he said abruptly, 'we need the nutrients. Leave nothing. Suck 'em clean.'

They ate the lot with little gusto until there was nothing left but fearfully misshapen skeletons and scattered bones. They just hoped against hope that what they'd thrust down their gobs didn't kill them during the night. Viruses, bacteria, any number of nasties could decide their fate and if it was bad, it might get very ugly indeed.

***

The fire had died down and the night sky was star filled and beautiful. Noise from the jungle had intensified to a point where it was almost aching to the ear, definitely unnerving. Yet nothing came at them despite the lingering heat and flickering light from the fire. Not an insect, a crawler or a climber. It seemed crazy odd because back on Earth they would have been besieged by mozzies, gnats, moths and a bunch of other infuriating pests. The indigenous life was being most respectful, mystifyingly so.

'Recognise anything up there?' Quincy said, tilting his head up, having already looked and not seen anything remotely familiar. Knowing Joe was an astro-nut he'd be the one to recognise something if it was there.

'Sirius, Canopus, Vega...none of them are there,' Joe said quietly without breaking his skyward gaze. 'I mean there's bright stars but none where they should be. Means we're a damn long way from home...not surprising I guess but maybe— '

118

He stopped talking abruptly and stood up, staring intently at the horizon, pressing his hands out for quiet. Joe peered in silence for almost a minute, grunting, jerking his head forward then back a few times, his brow dipping into a deep frown. 'Jesus Christ,' he suddenly said, eyes still locked on the horizon, face softening into something like incredulity, then hardening again into something unreadable. Drawing in a deep breath he shoehorned his gaze over to Quincy who watched him blink slowly, puzzling over something.

'What?' Quincy said sharply, watching his forehead crimp, then flatten, then crimp again. He felt his heartbeat rise in his chest. Whatever Joe was seeing, he was struggling to process it.

'Say something for God's sake,' Becker blurted loudly, gesturing with both arms in the air.

Joe swallowed, then licked his lips nervously and started talking in hushed tones, barely more than a rattle in the back of his throat. 'Can you see the light about ten degrees above the horizon…there?' He pointed with a finger that was trembling ever so slightly.

'The slightly bluish one, right?' Connie said softly, starting to feel anxious.

'Yes,' Joe breathed.

'What do you think it is?' Quincy said quickly, 'is it Vega, that's a blue star?'

'It's not Vega.' He said flatly.

'Um, Rigel?' Connie said. 'Are we playing guessing games here Joe because let me—'

'It's not Rigel. It's not any star.'

'Okay so let us in on the secret,' Connie said, feeling apprehension rising further in her chest as though her heart was somewhere it shouldn't be.

Falling silent again, Joe returned to deep contemplation. 'Fuck,' he said under his breath, shaking his head numbly. 'Um…this is well, I don't know how to say it really…it's nuts pretty much.' Joe was breathing in shallow mouthfuls, feeling like something was lodged in his throat sideways. 'I might be wrong but I don't think I am. I know I'm not.' He glanced at them, eyes like silver coins in the dying light from the campfire. 'Okay, I'm just going to come out with it. That light, the bluish one, is Earth.' Turning back to the horizon he didn't need to look, he knew that'd get 'em.

The sentence didn't register or align with any reasonable idea or concept they had access to in their minds. Connie's expression faded into nothing as Joe's words rolled around in her brain trying to find somewhere to go. It was madness because if that was Earth, well, the question was obvious…where the motherfuck were they?

'Have you lost your goddamn mind?' Connie asked seriously, pushing her eyebrows down as one would to a naughty child. 'Which of our planets has this wigged-out biology Joe? Hello?'

'You are out of your mind,' Becker told him straight, 'Connie's right, look around you smart guy, does this look like one of ours?' Becker stared squarely at him, expecting a retraction, at least some backpedalling, uncertainty maybe.

Quincy shook his head. 'Like you said, all the stars we're familiar with, are missing so there's no bloody way you can— '

'Oh for the love of…shut up!' Joe shouted, closing his eyes with the force of the words, making Connie recoil, a little stunned by his sudden show of irritation and probably more so by his conviction. He absolutely had their attention now. 'Look…okay, listen,' he said, walking over to the glowing embers, peering almost straight up into the brilliantly painted sky. 'I can't believe it either but facts are facts…it is what it is.' Joe hesitated, glancing back at the fire. The realisation was stripping gears in his mind as it ran up an ever-steepening logistical ravine, realising it was unexplainable and implausible but knowing that the math summed perfectly. All the pieces locked into place, creating a picture that was bone chilling. There it was, up in the sky, he said to himself, the image, evidence of something beyond the most drug-fuelled psychosis. Turning back to them he gazed wordlessly, looking harrowed.

'For Christ sake Joe, , you think that's Earth because it's blue? Surely you can't just— '

'Leave him be,' Connie said, her eyes hardening, 'he's the only one who understands this stuff, the sky, that sort of thing.'

'Fine but just tell us. Are you building the tension…or are you not sure? What's the problem?' Becker's heart was racing, he wanted it over with.

'Jesus, stop the alpha male horseshit,' Connie snapped, eyeballing him, ready to knuckle him on the shoulder if he kept it up.

'You know what Carson, screw you,' Joe said quietly. I'm not here to make stuff up. I can tell you the truth or I can just lick your arse and ignore it so you don't flip out.' He glanced at Connie who winked and smiled at him. Holy shit, she said silently, this was the first time in…forever he'd stood up so stoically to him and she frigging loved it.

'Okay then, here it is,' Joe said firmly, pointing toward the horizon above the ocean. 'Up there is Jupiter and Saturn, see the bright ones at ten and eleven o'clock in the west? They don't twinkle because they're planets, you know…closer.'

Becker looked up. 'That could be anything,' he said doubtfully.

'Trust him Becker, this is his world,' Connie shot back.

'Everything adds up,' Joe said with a heavy sigh.

'That picture taken by the Mars Rover of Earth, you remember the one…it went around the world? Front page of a lot of papers.'

'Must have missed it,' Becker said glibly. 'Slow news day, right?'

Joe looked passed Becker, talking over Connie's sarcastic profanity, 'it was the first shot of Earth from Mars and showed both it and the Moon just above the horizon. Gorgeous photo.'

Connie looked confused but Quincy's face had transformed into a look of pure wonder, mouth open, eyes wide, tongue slightly exposed. The story Joe was peddling was gradually dawning on him and it was a fucking killer.

'That's Earth over there but there's no Moon, it's not visible like it was in the Rover's pictures.' He looked at Becker and Connie, rocking slightly. 'Don't you get it?' Joe looked dazed, shrugging disbelievingly. 'My God come on…we're on Mars! This planet,' he raised both arms in chilling emphasis, 'is Mars.'

Quincy studied him intently. 'Yes it is…it's incredible…astonishing,' he said unsteadily, knowing it was coming and when it did it still blew his mind.

Connie gasped, her breasts rising and falling as she laboured to breathe, wrestling with Joe's words, struggling to find sense. Becker rubbed his forehead, then the back of his neck, squinting blindly at the sky, massaging the idea into something a little more rational. He gave up and shook his head, 'hang on, so you think this is, um…the red planet?' His words were slow and deliberate, contempt etched on his face. 'I just ain't feeling it, look around you buddy…this ain't bloody Mars…where's the fucking red in red planet?'

Joe gritted his teeth, 'listen, when the Earth was young, the Moon was ten times closer to Earth, the two were damn near touching. That's why we see only one light in the sky, that bluish one there is Earth and the Moon, they're so close there's no distinction from here.' He watched him, waiting for the penny to drop, which he knew it wouldn't…not for Becker not yet.

Becker was grappling with the raw insanity of Joe's theory, to him like rocks in a blender, simply unable to be processed. After all, they were on a vibrant planet with blue foliage for Christ's sake, not to mention a planet load of incredibly complex wildlife. Mars? 'No, no…it can't be,' Becker said, pausing for a moment while he pushed it around a bit more, his face eventually softening, 'are y-you sure?' He was unsure what to think, who to believe. Joe was smart, that was a given and he couldn't remember when he'd gotten anything wrong, especially something he was so damn certain of. This stuff, this double-talk technobabble was so far beyond his skill set there were no words.

'I'm positive…remember the potato shaped moon we saw before, that was Phobos, you've heard of it right?'

He nodded hesitantly, having no idea what he was talking about.

Connie was still studying Joe closely with a brain full of half-questions, feeling flushed and woozy. Taking a quick breath, her eyelids seemed to peel open as she was punched by sudden comprehension. 'G-God, 'she said haltingly. 'We're on Mars but not Mars Mars…the dust, the deserts,' she hesitated, punting the barmy idea around, 'this is past Mars, ancient Mars, right?' Hardly a flash of brilliance she knew, it was obvious, but the madness of it. Strange shapes billowed behind her eyes like errant sparks. Humans were nowhere near evolving on Earth, even fucking dinosaurs were billions of years away if Joe was right. And she knew he was because the other planets were out there, he'd said that as well. Christ, everyone she knew, had ever known, hadn't even been born, wouldn't be for…fuck me, she thought grimly, how many billions of years? The entire species hadn't even started. Grasping her temples, she massaged vigorously in diminishing circles, hoping her thoughts might resolve into something she could deal with, god forbid, understand. How the hell could this be reconciled with the reality she knew on Earth? It couldn't be, was her definitive on it.

'So, what…the Sphere sent us back to a time when Mars was lush and plentiful, so okay, fair enough,' Becker said brokenly, trying to keep it together without much luck. 'Uh…why?'

'You can ask as many questions as you like,' Joe said, 'there's no answers and unless they decide to give us some, there may never be any.' He eyed Becker then shifted his gaze to the sky, 'I mean, shit, we might die here knowing only that we're billions of years in the past, nothing more.'

'Fuck me,' Quincy spluttered. 'Could you dial the reality back a bit, I mean seriously, it's hardly a morale booster.'

'It is what it is. We need to confront it if we're going to do anything about it. Know your enemy…Art of War and all that.'

Quincy gave him a quick, disgusted snort, 'might as well use the hard-bound edition as a weapon for all the good it'll do us here,' he said. 'We know nothing about anything, apart from what you've so nicely laid out for us.'

'Okay then,' Becker said drolly, 'a final one, genius-with-no-answers. If all this is here, all the plants, the screwed-up wildlife out there, why haven't we found even one rotten fossil on Mars? All the rovers, the landers found dick…just a barren desert, right?' Raising his eyebrows he moved his head forward, opening his eyes wide, daring him to fob it off. 'Or is it all a conspiracy by the US Government…the DoD just hid everything from us?'

Joe nodded knowingly, 'now that right there is an excellent question, and I've been wondering about it. Forget the conspiracy crap though, I've seen enough live feed to know that doesn't wash but the other part, the where is it part doesn't fly.'

Connie had the unsettling feeling of being out of her body, looking down on herself. It was too much to digest. 'Time travel,' she gasped, staring at Joe owlishly, blinking slowly and heavily.

'Hard to believe, but there's no other explanation,' Joe said. 'These Spheres are amazing.'

'Fair fucking understatement,' Becker said quietly, glancing around, baffled.

'Pretty scary,' Quincy said. 'If they can do that, what's on the "can't do list"?'

'Nothing,' Connie said distantly, staring at the piercing blue light that had suddenly assumed a brand new, spine chilling aspect. It was their home planet before anything more complex than a bloody germ had begun to stir.

Joe stood up and shuffled over to the barely glowing embers. 'So Mars was once like Earth, different obviously but…plentiful and alive. The question is,' he paused momentarily, 'sorry, I mean one question is, what happened to kill this place off?'

Connie thought about it, 'well, asteroid, comet…maybe one of those in the forest evolved, became intelligent, went and screwed everything up, like humans'll probably do eventually,' she said a bit dejectedly, 'but then we'd have found evidence of that. A lost civilisation…ruins and such.'

Quincy kneaded his forehead with a thumb, brow heavily knotted. 'All guesswork,' he said cautiously. 'And continuing on the theme of having a stab, I've got a theory about those animals out there.'

'Oh Christ, here we go,' Becker spurted, 'more scientific blather…brilliant.' He looked petulantly at Connie and then down at the ground. Goddamn nerds, he said to himself bitterly, dreaming of a whisky or bourbon, even a fucking light beer, anything to take the edge off.

'Just listen carefully, you might surprise yourself,' Connie said, raising a hand to her ear, 'we all know you're science-simple.' Retarded she was going to say but decided to cut him a break.

Becker narrowed his eyes, 'just because I haven't wasted half my goddamn life wedged in a text book doesn't mean— '

Quincy held his palm up toward Becker. 'Anyway, I was adding up the events on this planet and we all agree that they're odd, really odd. The fact that the predators all pretty much ignored us…that therapod having a sniff then moving on and so forth.'

'I thought I explained that,' Becker quipped, glancing at Connie with a sarcastic wink.

Connie muttered "dickhead" under her breath, offering a stiffly pointed tongue. 'Wanna know why it didn't want a piece of you?' She said, scowling at him, 'fat content, not enough protein or iron.' She turned away roughly, the barest of grins on her face.

Quincy sighed in exasperation, tiring of playing referee in this irritating bout of one upmanship. 'So then there's the meat from those birds, absolutely no taste and I don't know about you but I only felt full for a few minutes, and my hunger's come back worse than before.'

They nodded agreement, increasingly nervous about where it might be leading, wondering whether they'd ingested something lethal and didn't know it yet.

'Well, I think the genetics of life on this junkyard world must be different to ours. The broader structure is probably around the mark but I think a little contrary in the detail, well a lot actually…mirror image aminos, stuff like that.'

Joe murmured something, cocking his head, shoving the idea around in his brain. It's possible…makes some sense but seriously, would that mean we couldn't taste the meat?' He massaged his temple with a busy knuckle, 'I guess our experience might be proof, but, I don't know… it's a long bow.' He lowered his eyebrows, gnawing on the intriguing idea.

Becker looked blankly at Joe and Quincy, staying silent and pretending to focus on what they were saying. He'd learnt a tiny bit of Latin between goofing off at school and it sounded disturbingly like the crap on offer here, with barely a quark of meaning. White noise at best. What he did know was that these idiots needed to get a fucking life.

Quincy watched Becker's star-crossed expression with interest, already figuring he wouldn't get any part of it. He'd explain it to them once, understand, not understand, whatever. 'Okay Becker, pucker up,' he said. 'So our DNA molecule twists to the right,' Quincy explained, slowly twirling a finger to add emphasis, 'and is made from proteins twisting the other way. I reckon everything around here might be in reverse, which would make them a square peg for our round hole.' He paused, smiling faintly. 'Well, that sounds a little off…but you get the gist, right?'

Becker was hesitant to make himself look more of a goose but bugger it he thought, in for a penny. 'So, uh…you mean like a lion humping a tiger, hoping for young'uns…ain't gonna happen, is that the deal?'

'Yeah, well, that's sort of around the mark. We can't extract nutrients when we eat them and same for this mob. I reckon they sensed it on some basic level, which is why they didn't bother with us. I mean, it mightn't be based on DNA at all. Whatever though, they just didn't see us as prey, I don't think we smelt like food to them. There not gonna waste energy on killing something for no gain. We looked like food no doubt, which sparked the interest, but well, thankfully I guess, we lacked that final piece of sensory validation.' He paused and nodded with a slow smile. 'Of course it could have been because we were totally unfamiliar, it might be that simple, but the lack of taste in that canary thing is the clincher…for me that's it.'

'Pretty incredible,' Connie pondered out loud. 'I mean, two separate life events in the same solar system. The Universe has to be running over with it, life has to be everywhere, like everywhere!' Connie was blinking rapidly then stared cow eyes at the sapphire light in the sky, bathing in the knowledge of what had to be a genuinely plentiful cosmos. The Fermi paradox sprung to mind, now seeming way more paradoxical in the face of what all this seemed to be saying.

Becker was frowning openly at Quincy, increasingly vexed by their ignorance of the bigger picture. 'Well fuck me, am I the only one that gets it? He was scowling now, rolling his shoulders irritably. 'You lot might know science but what about sheer bloody survival? The upshot of all your mumbo jumbo is that we're in some seriously deep shit. There's no food, and if you're right we can gorge on meat, berries and whatever the hell else we can find until we heave…and still die of starvation…is that how it is?' He loomed over Joe who reared backward and stepped away.

Quincy nodded awkwardly. 'Yeah that's right. Eating won't save us.'

Becker was grinding his front teeth together, fighting to overcome a lifetime of thinking he knew what food looked like, of having a grip on what he was. He winced as he visualised a meat and cheeseburger served up from the curious biology of this perverse little world, him digging in and tasting fucking spring water. It sounded bonkers but it was agonisingly clear that death on this world existed in the genetic detail.

'So what do we do?' Connie said to no one in particular. I've still got *'why'* in front of my eyes like a bloody thumbtack dug in to the hilt. If we were brought here deliberately, which seems probable, what the hell? Whoever brought us here must know we can't survive here. I keep coming back to the idea that it's a test…some screwed up challenge. Maybe we need to prove our mental prowess…overcome.' Connie's voice was rough, laboured, the lack of nutrients a looming problem.

Becker smiled faintly. 'If that's the case we're in a world of pain, I mean, seriously, killing the wildlife with sharp sticks, nearly getting eaten by some crazed fuck and now on our haunches from starvation…do I need to spell it out? No way that's a pass mark in my book.' He rolled his eyes upward, if he had the energy he would've belted out a raucous guffaw.

'If we somehow dialled up the destination on the small hemisphere back in Antarctica then I guess it makes a little more sense,' Connie said, 'because that means we've come here by chance, you know by our own doing. But if it's deliberate, if we've been brought here — '

'We should be efforting a solution,' Joe said, pacing back and forth. 'Asking questions is a waste of time, there's no answers here. Like I said, it is what it is. I think our only option is to find our way back to the Sphere, hope like hell we can get it working…get off this piece of shit rock.'

Their faces sunk at the idea of renegotiating the jungle and dealing with the left-handed freaks for a second time. But if Quincy was right they should be okay because as prey, they were useless to the food chain, about as enticing as waxwork dummies. They might hunt and sniff but they shouldn't eat. Mind you, if he was wrong by just a little bit then they might all die in a rather unsatisfactory fashion.

'So it's back through the forest?' Becker said in little more than a whisper. 'Crap,' he added, feeling his heart jump as he recalled the harrowing nature of their first crossing.

'It's the only option,' Joe said evenly. 'I don't think we're going to find a way out in this direction and if we don't in the next few days, well…it's game over. We need to play the odds, it's the only way.'

'Okay then, we go, 'Quincy said firmly. 'If we keep this up I agree with Joe and we're done.' All of them, grudgingly nodded, agreeing their only path of redemption lay on the other side of the forest.

13. Through the Sphere

"Man has gone out to explore other worlds and other civilizations without having explored his own labyrinth of dark passages and secret chambers, and without finding what lies behind doorways that he himself has sealed."~ *Stanisław Led*

They slipped inside the Sphere as easy as diving through a pool of water. Their first glimpse was an endless visage of monochromatic radiance. Viper's Argus camera had revealed none of it. All they could see beyond the window panels were tiny black and white dots flicking on and off with staggering speed. Black became white then white became black like a pulsating three-dimensional chessboard on acid. Regular "space" was gone, replaced by whatever this was. Sagan was engulfed by it, coursing through a never-ending ocean of highly ordered flashing and switching.

'W-what is this place?' Skylar whispered, looking through her fingers at the crazy black and white landscape outside. 'Are we still…inside the Sphere?' she said, 'or is this outside…like, in space?' She had her hands firmly over her face, confused by the unfathomable whatever it was outside, not sure what she was saying or even thinking.

Harry was craning his neck around, grunting and groaning as his mind searched for something familiar. 'Well I reckon we're still in the Sphere but hey, who knows?' He was bereft of ideas, bereft of anything. 'Otherwise we're in a very strange part of the Cosmos,' he said, pulling at a bushy eyebrow, studying the pulsating vista.

Vic had absolutely no idea what it was, what it meant, what they should do. The black and white switching formed a solid mass, a collective that was everywhere, but the dots or points that made it up were changing constantly, individually and in grids everywhere they looked. Vic asked himself if they were particles, dots, pixels maybe? He had no idea except to say they were everywhere…they were space, seemingly comprising the vacuum itself.

Skylar was blinking fast, breathing even faster, 'is this supposed to mean something to us? It pulled us in, so…is this stuff for us?'

'Well it doesn't mean much to me,' Harry growled, stifling a yawn. 'Black, white, totally bewildering, that's about it. Maybe they think we're smarter than we are.' He looked at Vic through narrowed eyes, scratching his beard, mulling it over briefly, having nothing.

'The first image from Argus was the planet,' Vic said curiously, 'there was no static or dead feed first…so if it went through this stuff we would've seen it.' He looked at Harry quizzically.

Before Harry could respond, Sagan started crawling out of the monotone envelope, returning to what they knew as normal space. Watching his HUD, Harry saw the Sphere shining in brilliant amber, looking like a small star gradually receding behind them into the cosmic deeps.

Sky felt her heartbeat slow a bit, her mind start to uncoil as she spied familiar space ahead. But that was wrong, she knew immediately, looking to the far right, it was black and without the crazy masses of switching dots but it couldn't have been any more abnormal.

'A planet…the planet,' she said, slashing the air with a single jab, feeling the pressure in her stomach return. They recognised it as the planet Argus spied before it went off-line, but where in space was this planet and why were they here, distinctly against their will? There was no courtesy or propriety, no invite to the party, they had been taken by force, effectively handcuffed, manacled and dragged like street thugs.

'It's b-beautiful,' Sky said, biting the inside of her cheek until it hurt, 'different to Earth but just as amazing, just as stunning.' She was trying to convince herself, focussing on the beauty.

Vic's eyes roamed the world beyond, figuring that questions were academic because short of landing and looking, it was anyone's guess…but was it where they came from?

Despite fighting it back, Sky's mind kept wrenching itself back to her ill-gotten role in the mission, her palms moist and cold, seemingly running the gauntlet between anxiety and a full-blown panic attack. With the undeniable prospect of first contact, she was terrified almost beyond respiration, certainly beyond any higher brain function. Lifting her chin she shook her head softly, picturing herself searching for some way to connect with them, to find a basic level of understanding, all while gazing at what she was sure would be blood curdling contours. These grand fucking ideas were fine and dandy within the terrestrial confines of the General Assembly, but she could barely remember her name up here. Sky grimaced painfully certain of only one thing, that her hope of coping with it, even surviving it, were upward of eight out of ten a week ago, but up here it was barely measured in fractions. Sky admitted in a soul crushing rush that she wasn't the person she thought she was, not up here, space wasn't an inspiration and a glorious dream… it, and she, sucked.

Surveying the small part of the planet that was in darkness, Sky couldn't see any lights, yet the glow of a civilisation should be evident if not in your face from up here, although maybe once darkness spread across the globe they would come into view. Perhaps it was a massive area of wilderness down there, maybe the inhabitants live underground, leaving the surface untouched.

'Do you really think they're down there?' Skylar said, exposing her innermost fear, snaking her eyes over to Vic. He shrugged, watching Harry unstrap and walk to the portside window for a better view.

'Oh…fuck me,' he said in a drawn-out growl. 'I don't think they're down there Sky,' Harry added, his voice sunken and raspy. 'Come…take a look.' He pointed at something beyond, eyeing them with an expression that was unclear. Nothing much fazed Harry so whatever he was seeing outside had to be big.

Joining him they followed his finger which was still resting on the window, seeing a striking grey moon similar to Earth's but less scarred and with signs of active volcanoes, they could see the glow of red hot lava pouring onto the surface in two places near the horizon.

'Well? Vic said, 'we're not blind, we can see it.'

Harry stared at him as though he'd grown another leg. 'Are you actually serious? I thought better of you, you're NASAs wonder boy for Christ's sake!' He cocked his head and looked up briefly. 'They must run cooking classes at Johnson because that my friends is our moon…as in the Moon. You know, Luna.'

The words were so unexpected and took a few seconds to filter in, to translate into meaning, well, unmeaning mainly. Vic did a double take, bemused by Harry's reckless statement because this was an active moon. Our Moon was dead; inert, expired, stone cold from surface to core.

Skylar blurted, 'there's active volcanoes, way less craters than there should— '

'Come on,' Vic interjected, 'what are you on buddy?' He reached out to touch Harry's shoulder and he reared away.

'Jesus H Christ!' He roared, flicking a hand up roughly, paying animated homage to his reputation for suffering fools badly. 'You people are so dumb.' The whites of Harry's eyes were bugging out. 'Okay, back to school it is. Strap yourselves in, it might get a bit bumpy.' He paused, glancing outside. 'See that large crater in the south down there, the curving chain of smaller craters inside it…can you see them gradually get bigger as you move your eyes to the east?' He hoisted an eyebrow at Vic. 'Well that's Clavius, absolutely unmistakeable for any old Moon-dog,' he said, grinning smugly.

Vic drew his lips into an amused pucker, studying him, seeing if there was some Harry leg pulling going on. He was a notorious practical joker but normally in the visual, not with anything as understated as mere words. His pegmatite expression returned. Harry was deadly serious and Vic was suddenly tingling head to toe as he stared uneasily at this odd moon, struggling to think straight in the face of Harry's dogmatic outburst. 'But, where are the ray craters and what about the, active volcano there?' He said thickly. Harry had to be tripping, his imagination had always been way too elastic, but there was something in his expression. Vic felt like a prickle was lodged in his brain, chip-chipping away at him as he turned his gaze to the world-dominating continent on the blue world beneath them. Gazing again at this satellite of the blue world, he could see it was in such a snug orbit the ocean visibly bowed toward it, the tides had to be enormous, kilometres in places, he guessed.

After a few seconds, his brain had assembled the bits and pieces and it gradually came in a flush that was both chilling and unsettlingly warm. Harry was right, he was always bloody right.

Sky snapped her head around, looking at him with a knowing so dreadful it scared her in a way she never knew existed. 'We've gone back haven't we…in time?' She mewed pitifully, exchanging half-glances, listening to her own words, instinctively questioning her sanity. 'That's what you're saying, the Sphere was some pathway through space and time right?' She shifted her eyes to the floor, composing herself, clenching her fists to steady her mind. Sky wondered not where they were this time, but when they were.

'Yep,' Harry said easily. 'That's the Moon and that's dear old Earth. The Sphere pulled us in and for whatever reason sent us back…a long way. The question is, how far?' Harry felt a wave of light-headedness roll through him as he struggled with warring emotions. 'All I know is that we're not talking thousands or millions of years …we're talking maybe a billion or more.' Having said it, Harry wobbled just a little bit, more affected than he cared to admit. Sitting in the Commander's seat he scrutinised the bewilderingly youthful and active Moon that was sitting just a few thousand clicks in front of them.

Vic knew time travel didn't break any physical laws he just always thought there'd be something to stop it, some subtle quirk that would block its path. Time distortion at high speed or near intense gravity, no problem, he could happily run with that because it made perfect sense, relativity said so. But the screwy Grandfather paradox convinced him that instantaneous time travel had to be bunkum. Any Universe where you could pop back in time and mow down your own parents, well, he wanted none of that. Surely, no universe could be built like that, it was just theoretical, whiteboard claptrap. And now we have this he lamented with an ironic sigh, these enigmatic Spheres that apparently bashed down the door and cracked the backbone of space and time apart like a splayed walnut. Vic reckoned these others would probably regard straight-line travel as we view the concrete wheel, guessing it was no more than where you were on your evolutionary timeline, anything even slightly beyond your own understanding seemed impossible, akin to wizardry, but not so. The differences created gods and savages but it was no more than simple relativity…just time.

***

Skylar searched for the Sphere, it should have been bright in the light from the Sun behind them but it wasn't, it was nowhere to be seen. Begging silently, she was seared by images of her baby girl back on Earth, alone and terrified when she didn't come through the door like she'd promised. And here she was, lost somewhere in the ghostly corridors of time, never to be seen or heard from again. The ultimate fucking castaway, she thought grimly.

Vic peered through the window panels at the front of the shuttle.

'…we're stuck here,' Sky gasped, feeling the walls push in, short of breath. 'Sphere's gone,' she said in a rush, closing her eyes, feeling her face run cold, blood draining away.

Harry was doing the math, carrying the one and coming up with horseshit and nonsense. 'There's no going back now so I guess we need to figure out why we're here,.'

'Maybe there isn't a reason,' Vic said. 'We might be sort of…just here.'

'Maybe you're right,' Harry agreed, 'but if you ain't then we need to look, see if we can find something.'

'Copy that,' Vic said. 'You're right of course.'

'Of course,' Harry said, nodding slowly, grinning faintly.

'Go for low orbit, uh…Earth, that is,' Harry said, 'but watch out for our friend here, man it's close.' He was sure Apollo could have gotten to it between lunch and dinner if it had been like this in '69.

126

'The tides it's pulling—, ' Vic said in a voice flush with awe, watching the bulge of water moving east to west as the Moon ambled along its line of orbital free fall around this ancient paradise.

'Enough sightseeing…move,' Harry said sternly.

Vic made a few finger movements with the aerojet DAP input, grabbing the rotational hand controller to his right, rousing the transducers by deflecting it to give a line of sight rotation for the shuttle around three axes. He carefully placed his thumb near the trim switch. 'DAP armed, APUs, Active Controller on,' he said, pushing his head down at the GC, 'RCS roll and yaw active, pitch set to auto.' He pushed back in his seat, 'OMS burn in 3, 2...' They all felt the inertial thump as the conventional propellant punched them toward the strange blue rock.

'Whoa big fella,' Harry barked, 'easy does it. If you break it, we're a long way, er…a long time from home.'

'Relax,' Vic sighed, looking at Harry with his best game face. 'If I break it, I'll buy it.' He said dourly, 'DOI in twenty minutes.'

***

They heard the rumble of the OMS engines cutting out and the fore RCS thrusters sparking to life to yaw the craft and null momentum, easing them into the desired orbital perigee.

'DOI,' Vic said. 'Twelve hundred kilometres at ten-point-two clicks.'

Harry unstrapped himself and walked over to the window panels with the others following in step. Skylar's heart felt like a mallet punching her chest as she peered at the familiar but terrifying world below.

'So, when, uh…are we?' Vic said out loud to no one in particular, surveying the colossal continent below, stretching like an African desert over both north and south horizons.

'Two ways of working that out I reckon,' Harry said, '…won't be accurate but it'll give us a clue.'

Skylar stared at the haggard astronaut, urging him on with her eyes. She still couldn't get past the visual, he looked so desperately in need of a shower, shave and a decent bloody stylist. Harry closed his eyes, drawing his lips in so they disappeared behind his woolly beard.

'Well?' Vic prompted. 'Tell us what you think…how far back?'

He opened his eyes, having apparently come to an answer. 'Okay, so I know a bit about the Gemini and Apollo landing sites, I was a spotter back in the day for NASA you know.' He paused, sizing them up, shaking his head slightly. 'If we had to rely on you lot we'd be clueless…no offense.'

'Oh, none taken,' Vic said loudly, 'now speak. Yes, you're a legend, you happy?'

Harry grinned widely through his beard, thanking him for the overdue nod. 'So, the Rheita crater is one I know about. It ain't there and I know that was dated to around nine hundred million years…so we're further back than that.'

Skylar groaned hard, pins and needles prickling her body with tiny electric shocks. 'A billion years...a billion…years? Her legs were wobbling, the desire to run hitting her again - the urge was so ridiculous it was beyond comical.

'At least that far back, and the landmass must be one of those old mega-continents,' Harry said uncertainly. 'Vic, you've done a bit of digging around in the dirt, what do you reckon, nerd?' He winked at him playfully.

'There's only one nerd here,' Vic said.

'Yeah I know,' Harry said, looking right at him. 'So…what do you think?'

'Oh for God's sake you two,' Skylar weighed in, 'is it Gondwana something? I've heard of that.'

Vic gazed through the silica window panel. 'I think it's older than that. I can't remember what it's called but a billion years ago that monster landmass down there, from what I can recall, seems to make sense.' His voice trailed off as he kicked it around. There were no animals on the land, bugger all in the oceans as well. A bit of algae, a few simple swimmers…oh, and a consciousness in

127

orbit that had returned from the future. Shit, he thought feverishly, the whole thing was seriously fucked up.

'How can –' Sky said with the tiniest whisper, stopping suddenly and gripping her hands together in a white-knuckle embrace. 'How can we be here?' She shifted her hands, grabbing the side of the seat to steady herself.

'Well, physics makes it possible,' Vic said softly. He articulated what he'd thought through before, 'no law forbids time travel, I guess it's just a matter of working out how to do it.' He stared at her, lifting an eyebrow.

As the Earth turned beneath them the scope of the supercontinent became obvious, covering Earth mainly south but extending north, looking like a deeply alien world. But they could make out bits and pieces that were familiar although all of them were jumbled up like misplaced pieces in a jigsaw. Vic was aghast that even a billion or so years ago some of the present-day continents could be recognised from orbit. The northern part of Australia was there, Antarctica, a chunk of North America...

Continental drift would soon start the gargantuan process of cracking the continent apart like tempered chocolate, shuffling them around at a snail's pace over Eons, eventually amounting to hundreds and eventually thousands of kilometres. Then they would all come back together again and it would be a complete do-over until their familiar modern-day world emerged in a few hundred million centuries. It was tectonic Groundhog Day on the most monumental scale imaginable.

'Sort of like Mars,' Skylar said, surveying the rusty visage, 'so dry looking...the whole thing is like a huge desert.' She was gazing at Vic when the flight deck suddenly lit up, filling his eyes with light from whatever was shining behind her.

Vic shoved his head forward, squinting at it, his first thought a question, what was this thing doing on such a primitive world?

'If that's Earth,' Harry said, 'I mean it is Earth...but no way that should be there.' That thing is...I have no idea what that is.'

Vic was still bent forward, 'is there something down there capable of building it or—'

'Just park it and wait,' Harry said, despising questions without hope of answer. Ideas, theories were fine, stupid questions, not fine.

Skylar was making odd little noises in the back of her throat, watching the thing on the horizon inch its way toward them as their headway in orbit brought them closer. To Vic it looked as unlikely as a lunar pioneer stumbling over a nuclear reactor on the far side of the Moon.

Coming toward them was a piece of landscape that looked like it had been copied in native metal, reflecting light from the Sun in blinding bursts as it moved beneath them. Erupting from its centre was a rod of light, shooting straight up for several kilometres. It didn't reduce in intensity, then peter out, it just stopped as though it were a laser hitting an invisible electrode somewhere in mid-air.

'That's where we need to go,' Harry said, pointing his hand like a cocked gun at the imperious light. 'Vic – make it so.'

'Maybe we should wait a bit,' Skylar said urgently, 'not make rash decisions, I mean, we have no idea of their intentions, right?' She shook her head so hard it was more like a neck spasm.

'That's exactly the point Sky, we have absolutely no idea, so my decision is based on what feels right, sounds logical, because that's all we have.'

'What if there's no place to land? Sky said pleadingly, 'I mean you said we've got all-terrain tyres, but we won't know what it looks like till we get there, right?' She looked intently at Harry, hoping to see some sign of pragmatism in his eyes.

'Look, if there's no place to set down we return to orbit,' he said, letting out a loud breath, 'we've got plenty of prop so don't stress, put your feet up, enjoy the ride.' He nodded firmly at Vic but reckoned Sky was losing it.

'What if it's a warning or a keep out and not an invitation at all?' Sky said. 'We have no idea what it is…what it might be…could be. Jesus, this is ridiculous Harry.' She crossed her arms loudly and pulled her arms tight.

Harry grunted something at Sky and turned back to the window. 'So they've brought us here to warn us off as soon as we arrive?' He said, grunting again. 'Vic, enough of this, execute the transfer by the book, do the checks, we need to get this right.'

Vic didn't look convinced but did as Harry ordered, gazing at the panel in front of him, going through the mental list for de-orbit. Last thing they wanted was a screwed-up entry angle. He scanned the avionics panel, engaging, then punching instructions into the digital autopilot. 'Re-entry corridor set,' he said, studying it closely, 'OMS helium levels are green, de-orbit program enabled.' He depressed three pushbutton yellow lights on the avionics panel, moded MEDS Descent to Normal and breathed in heavily. 'Strap in Sky…TIG in thirty seconds. Entry interface software is on.'

Sagan started to dip from orbit tail first, reorienting itself with an RCS steering burn so its nose was pitched up at forty degrees.

'OMS burn in five,' Vic pushed down on the control stick, sending them slicing into the atmosphere, enveloping them in a cometary fireball of superheated plasma. After several turbulent minutes they were beyond the thermosphere. 'Glide slope looks good, RCS roll jets off, S-Turns commenced,' Vic said, visibly sweating, fighting to burn off speed to bring the craft to subsonic.

Flying among patchy Cirrus, Sagan was burning through the atmosphere of this incredibly young Earth, all of them pondering their fate, fearing the unknown technology that had taken root on the surface. At least their craft could be relied on. If they needed to, the powerful engines, lighter frame and aerodynamic delta-5 wings on Sagan could shoot them back into orbit, unlike the old STS Shuttle, they were no longer a "dead weight gliding" once they dropped into the atmosphere. These SLS shuttles were a powerful, highly effective, dual-fuel aerospace vehicle.

'Landing should be, uh, okay…I think,' Vic said, surveying everything he could below, tossing his head around, determined not to miss anything. He reckoned it was just thin soil over bedrock and there were country sized acreages to choose from. The well of light was about a hundred clicks away, front and centre on their line of approach.

'If we get in trouble on contact, throttle up,' Harry said, pushing his eyebrows toward his hairline, 'we'll try somewhere else.'

Sky made a clicking noise with her tongue. 'Are you…Jesus are you serious?' She snapped from behind, 'listen to you. If the wheels drop into thick sand, there's no getting out of it, there's no throttling up…were done, dead. The wheels'll stick like ants in a glue trap.'

Vic could see her cock-eyed expression reflected in the window panel. She was killing his confidence but he needed to hang tough. 'It's not just sand, there's hard strata between the topsoil…look,' he said pointing with a bent finger, 'I'm trained to identify emergency landing areas. You need to trust that.'

'I'd trust that on Earth, our Earth but this place is, well, who knows,' she said, scanning his face gravely. 'I think we should return to orbit and stay there.' Skylar was certain it was going to end in an apocalyptic fireball

'Two thousand metres, four hundred knots, five-point-five degrees,' Vic said, every muscle in his body tensed, knowing it could get ugly quickly, 'speed brakes deployed.'

'Just take it in as easy you can,' Harry said, eyes mortared on the looming landscape, 'pick the right spot…for God's sake pick the right spot,' he said louder, with a slight note of pleading.

Skylar was staring at the floor, she couldn't look at the burnt landscape in the window any longer. Bunching her fists as tight as she could, eyes pulled closed, she waited for the thump of the wheels. Hopefully it was a thump and not a meteoric detonation. 'Oh shit,' she screamed, as the orbiter pulled up suddenly, making her stomach heave.

Vic pulled the nose of Sagan up to slow their rate of descent, both feet planted firmly on the rudder pedals, making fine adjustments to their yaw rotation as they approached. If they didn't land wings-level they were screwed, Vic was sure, because this terrain looked hard enough to rip off one of the delta's with a single strike.

'Five hundred metres...one-point-five degrees,' Vic said, depressing a blue pushbutton switch on the panel to his right. 'Main landing gear, nose gear down,' he said, hearing a loud whir, then clunk as the wheels locked into place. The tyres were treadless, nitrogen filled and made of carbon graphene, strong enough to land on just about anything at a high punch rate.

'You're doing good...nose up, reduce speed.' Harry injected.

'Pitching up,' Vic said sharply, pulling the stick up.

Harry spun his head around 'we're drifting.'

'...drag from this bloody atmosphere,' Vic yelled, 'ailerons one-point-five.' He looked at the eight ball, saw the roll even the wings up. 'Okay,' he puffed, 'okay...good.' He stayed frosty, eyes glued to critical instrumentation. The shuttle's rear wheels descended on cue, kissing rock and coarse soil, spraying sand and grey smoke across the ancient land.

Skylar stayed frozen in the last few moments of descent, then flinched violently when she felt the wheels thud onto rock, waiting for them to descend dune-deep into sand, leaving her burning alive in freed hydrazine.

'Wheels down,' Vic barked, punching reverse thrust and hyper-extending the wing spoilers to slow the craft. Vic's forehead was covered with perspiration as he fought to keep their world in a straight line on the slippery sand. Fore-mounted retros continued rattling through the craft but it was a struggle to keep her on the ground as it raced across the rock-hard surface, blowing away shallow sweepings of coarse brown sand. Sagan eventually rolled to a halt about fifty metres from the edge of the metallic plate, a perfect circle of silver and grey encompassing the strange arrow of light.

Harry was puffing. 'Grade A landing, seriously good work,' he said, giving a smile that took a while to get going, laughing shakily.

'Piece of cake,' Vic said, flopping back in his seat, 'a little like Kennedy really, ground was hard like concrete, more of a slip factor but not too bad.' He glanced at Harry, making the sign of the cross, grinning. 'Let's power her down. APUs, purge, vent, drain. VDU on.' Vic turned to Sky, smiling broadly with his boyish good looks, a fact not wasted, despite her mental state and genuine shock to still be alive.

'Yeah, um...sorry I doubted you,' she said, thinking it was more dumb luck than good execution but hey, they were still here. She squinted at Vic, wondering *what now*, knowing there was no plan apart from risking their lives ... land, look around. Brilliant strategy, she mused sullenly.

'I know you disagree...but maybe we were being warned not to land.' Sky said as evenly as she could, not much above a whisper, respectful, but firm.

'Nah,' Harry replied with a subtle wink, 'if it was a warning it would've been in red, not white.' He smirked at Sky who peered at him wondering why he was being such an arsehole, surely there was logic in her argument. She looked contemptuously at him, seeing an ageing relic from the Mercury days, the boys club, the gung-ho, huevos style of men-only crap that made her sick.

'Seriously, is everything a joke to you?'

'Yeah, well, it is what it is, so you need to deal with it. See that seat, it says Commander so I make the decisions.' He gazed at her pokerfaced.

'Get real Harry, it's not an autocracy, we're in this together.' She tried to say it with authority but her voice came out shrill and uncertain. 'I say we vote on decisions, go with majority rules, this isn't your ordinary by the book NASA mission. You need every idea, opinion, buy-in, not just yours.' She spat the last word at him, looking away quickly, feeling justified but apprehensive.

'Bah,' Harry snarled dismissively. 'Vic, what do you say?'

He turned away from the avionics panel toward Harry, nodding. 'I'm with Sky. Majority rules,' he said matter of factly.

'Oh…so it's mutiny is it?' He tilted his head up, then down, looking directly at Sky who returned his gaze skittishly. 'Okay then, the majority has decided that…majority rules.' Harry got up, walked to the rear of the flight deck, muttering something too faint to hear.

'What's the strategy then, in your view?' Vic asked Harry, loud enough so he could hear.

He walked back toward them, scratching and pulling at his beard, 'I think we should investigate the light, see what we can find out, but God forbid I should sway you two, you need to have your say, what was that you said Sky, your buy-in?' Harry ended with an overblown exhalation of breath and a pointed shrug, looking from one to the other.

Skylar felt like tearing some of Harry's beard out. 'Jesus, you're a piece of work.' She spun away and then sharply back at him. 'We each bring something to this mission so it's a no-brainer we all contribute,' Sky said, scowling at him but it thinned rapidly. She said the words because in theory they were spot on, but she wasn't sure she brought a damn thing to the mission.

'What I think is irrelevant but—' He stopped mid-sentence, checking himself. 'Okay, look, fine, yes I do see that,' Harry conceded abruptly. 'I'm just having some fun,' he said, lying. 'Lighten up, we're not dead yet.'

'Thank you,' she said, almost tearing up, tightening her hands into claws, desperately wanting to feel part of the group again. 'So, okay, before we exit the craft I have a question about what's outside, as in you know…temperature, oxygen. Does anyone have any idea…Vic?'

Vic went blank then suddenly turned his head, gaping through the window panel. 'Shit,' he spat like a gunshot. He scraped his chin, genuinely concerned, thinking furiously. 'You're right, this is Earth but not our Earth.' He pushed his gaze to Harry, searching for facts he'd learned a long time ago that were mostly lost in the rumples of his mind. 'We could use EVA suits but they'd be hopelessly awkward in this gravity,' he said, recalling the back-breaking simulations they'd done in Nevada which were pretty much like having a full-grown person in piggy-back.

'It looks okay out there,' Harry said uncertainly, 'but hey, so does Mars when the wind ain't blowing.'

'Okay,' Vic said, 'so if we're right and this is Earth minus a billion years or so then the atmosphere would be way different. Temperature should be warm, humid, equatorial-style I think. I remember O2 levels fluctuated a lot so it's a guess but I think it's low…the oxygen I mean.'

'Thank you Professor,' Harry growled, 'how low is what we need to know…like is it breathable, can we survive out there?'

'Maybe five or so percent…at best that's less than half the current level. The pressure should be okay, I guess it'd be like breathing at high altitude…how high we can't know until,' Vic stopped talking as Harry started ambling toward the equipment locker.

'I'll get in the airlock with the EMU, let the air in from, um…out there.' Harry's mind was working overtime. 'I'll flip the visor, see if I turn green.' He gave a casual snort but looked a little uneasy, dancing a slow jig with his feet.

'You sure?' Vic questioned, knowing it was a risky move. 'If the O2 is close to zero you'll be in trouble.'

'I'll be fine, I've climbed the Bishorn in Switzerland, I know what it's like.' He gave a nervous half laugh.

'That's barely more than a hill, it'll take eight minutes for the airlock to re-pressurise, you could be in a world of hurt, confusion, hypoxia, you know the drill. After two minutes you should be able to breathe okay though.'

'There you go, walk in the park,' Harry said, 'decision's made…majority rules, right?'

***

Harry was decked out in the EMU shell, standing in the shuttle's airlock like a pale grey crustacean. Hitting the Cycle Airlock pushbutton it turned red and started flashing, adding a

131

cautionary emphasis to what he was doing. The Abort button was also illuminated which would immediately reverse the airflow if he punched it. Harry watched the pressure as it dropped from nineteen PSI, gradually inching its way downward on the circular gauge until it stopped on sixteen PSI. The pressure detectors told him that pressure outside was only slightly lower than Sagan's internal atmosphere.

With partial depress complete, Harry saw the light turn a solid green, then the outer door popped open automatically, showing him a world strangely similar to Mars, up close it was even more obvious. It just lacked the dunes but it sure as hell had the colour. 'Whoaaa,' he murmured inside his suit.

'Everything okay?' came the voice in Harry's intercom.

'Hatch opened at sixteen PSI, I'm standing in it, about to crack the visor,' he said with a slight croak in his voice.

'If it's no good,' Vic warned, 'hit Emergency Pressure right away, don't wait, punch it.

'Copy,' Harry said lightly. Thanks Dad he thought. Good old Vic.

It was time to stop talking and start doing. Pushing back the cover on his suit controller with one hand, he pushed Visor Release that would gently blow the helmet seal if not overridden in ten seconds. Hearing the gentle click and swoosh of venting gas, Harry pushed his visor up slowly, deliberately. HIs eyes bulged as he took a tentative breath. Then he took a deeper breath, trying his best to breathe normally in the young atmosphere.

'Harry, report,' Vic asked anxiously. 'You okay? Report!'

They could hear a straining, choking sound at the other end.

'Jesus Christ!' Vic screamed. 'Punch the fucking button Harry!' Skylar's face twisted with horror as she listened to the ghastly noise. He was dying.

'Punch it!' Vic shouted again, wondering what the hell they'd gone and done.

'Relax astronauts,' came the voice. 'Just playing you…atmo seems fine, it's Earth, not sure how that's possible but, well…it is.'

Vic looked at Skylar shaking his head furiously. 'You rotten prick,' Vic snarled. Skylar thought of the Mercury macho bullshit again. This guy was off the charts.

Vic stowed the angst pretty quick, damn glad his oddball friend was okay. Knowing him better than anyone, he should've expected it. 'Good one,' he said, trying to defuse the situation, mainly for Sky who looked ready to kill him, or collapse. Vic met her gaze, shrugging soothingly. With Harry, you got the lot, intelligence, technical brilliance and a complete horseshit attitude that was unpredictable at best.

'Come on down,' Harry crowed, 'let's take a look around. This place is amazing.'.

'Maybe there's too much oxygen,' Skylar whispered, 'Sounds like he's on happy gas.'

'You know I can hear you right?' He said, static filling the intercom. 'I'll try and be more downcast, apologies for the momentary lapse.'

Skylar saw Vic smirking and stifled any response.

'Funny guy,' Vic said, raising his eyes.

They walked to the equipment locker and grabbed their survival kits and backpacks.

'Ladder's good to go Sky,' Harry grinned, awkwardly removing his EMU. 'What about the O2?' Harry queried, 'man you were way off 'cause it feels just fine out here…temp, pressure, all like home.'

Vic looked around awestruck, pondering the paradox of being on an Earth that was anything but home. 'Yeah, not sure,' Vic said, 'my brain tells me oxygen wasn't like this for a long time, but they're only best guesses I suppose.' Vic knew that was crap as soon as he gave it air. Studies were based on palaeogeology that simply didn't lie. Sulphate concentrations in ancient rocks provided empirical evidence, so how was it so off the mark? He didn't get it and it grated on him painfully, pinching in the pit of his stomach, barking at him that things were wrong in ways he had no hope of ever knowing.

Descending the ladder in single file, they stood together on the rusty, sand encrusted surface. Vic pictured their location, pretty much central to a colossal landmass that battled ocean tides that see-sawed more than two kilometres up and down its gargantuan beaches. Incredible he told himself. The Moon was overwhelming in the sky, so bright, so different from their diminutive Luna, Harry reckoning it was six or seven times the size of the one back home. It was slightly golden, not far from full as it climbed slowly into the sky, looking more like a fully-fledged planet than a moon, seemingly only arm's length away.

'Forget that, look at this,' Skylar said, gazing doe-like at the cylinder of light arcing skyward from the bulls-eye of the monolithic dish.

'Well, I'll go both of those and raise you that,' Vic said, gawking over his shoulder at the shuttle. 'Now that is a sight to see,' he said, glancing back at them, dazzled by the stark panorama of machine and desert.

The sight was inexplicably strange, Sagan an image to behold, the pinnacle of Earth's modern space launch technology with state of the art Magnetoplasma engines, sitting dispassionately on the surface of a largely lifeless Earth. It had absolutely no right being there, paradoxically designed by a species whose forbears wouldn't part from their Orangutan ancestors for more than a billion years. Crazy much? Harry mused, feeling bewildered but oddly proud.

'Not something you see every day.' Harry said, grinning broadly enough to split his haggard beard.

'Crazy,' Skylar agreed, 'but amazing.' The gleaming NASA emblazoned shuttle in the foreground, the youthful landscape everywhere was irresistibly compelling, strangely emotional.
They were about ten metres from the metal surface when the vertical explosion of energy stopped. There was no winding down or slowing, it just turned off like a blown bulb.

'Shit,' Harry blurted, startled. 'What...where'd it go?' He looked around manically, searching for what, he had no idea.

'Did we do that?' Vic asked uneasily, 'did it see us coming and...turn itself off?' Looking at the centre of the metal plate all that remained was a black hemisphere, looking distinctly dead.

Skylar felt a need to return to the craft, like fucking run because if it was an invite, which she seriously doubted, had the welcome mat just been withdrawn? 'Do we k-keep going?' She asked, rolling her shoulders.

'You're the ones who voted for democracy,' Harry said, 'you decide. I say yes we do...no point going back now.'

'God this is so screwed up,' Skylar laboured. 'I feel sick, tired, it's a struggle just to move. You sure this atmosphere is okay to breathe?'

'I feel fine...Vic, how about you?'

'No problem, good.'

'Just you Sky,' Harry said coolly. 'Probably nerves, anxiety...I mean we're trained for the unusual, not like this madhouse, but we're trained all the same. You're a civvy and well, you're doing fine...decent breaths...try and relax.'

'Oh, real comforting Harry,' Skylar said sourly, rejecting his insipid platitudes, irritated at being treated like an emotional cripple, no matter how much she might agree with the sentiment.

Harry ignored her, starting forward with a tentative first step on the metal circle. He yelped, startled by sudden animation beneath him, hastily withdrawing his foot. 'Did I do that?' He exclaimed, glancing back at them and then at the plate. 'It's um, the whole thing is...alive.'

Soon as Harry's foot caressed metal, the parallel grooves, incisions or whatever they were, began pulsing. Like Antarctica, the bullseye in front of them was enclosed by concentric incisions and they were pulsing with an obvious pattern. The outermost circle would break into white light penetrating no further than the next contour, then that would null and the next one further in would brighten and so on for all of them, each illumination lasting only about a second. The light show formed an inward pulsing, starting at the outside and ending at the hemisphere, bang in the middle.

'Well this is interesting,' Harry said, quirking an eyebrow. 'Is it just me or did the invitation just get more explicit? Like it's beckoning us forward…showing us the way if you like.' He looked at Vic, pulse quickening, pretty certain things were escalating.

'Yep it does,' he said. 'Absolutely.'

'To a human mind,' Skylar said. 'But seriously, it could mean something else entirely.'

'Too true,' Harry concurred. 'So what does the democratic country of Skylar think we should do about it?'

'How about back to Sagan, into orbit and hope like hell the Sphere reappears so we can get out of here.'

'Okay forward we go then,' Harry said, ignoring Skylar's blather.

'Fine,' she whined softly, toeing up to Vic. Sky didn't have the strength to argue with Harry anymore. She felt drained and really just wanted to curl into a ball and close her eyes, hopefully wake up far, far away from this godforsaken nightmare.

They stopped behind the outermost circumference, watching the light creep inward - from edge to middle it took about eight seconds.

'I'm really not sure about this,' Skylar said, edging back a bit. 'If we step over them or on them when they illuminate, well…what are the odds?' Her face was like fired clay, fear evident in her tight expression.

Harry walked straight ahead, over the first, then over the second, seeing it light up beneath him. 'All good,' he yelled back. 'Not even par-fried,' Harry added, holding his arms out, walking slowly toward the hemisphere where he assumed the rather banal animation was leading them. Harry stopped and stared at the Sphere for a long moment, rubbing his mouth and chin, wondering if he was reading the signs right. He felt like he needed to exude an air of authority but the question remained like a beating drum. Simple it might have seemed but were they right in their thinking…even in the right ballpark…the right Universe.

14. Unreason

"What is called a reason for living is also an excellent reason for dying."
~ Albert Camus

Why won't this prick stay on? Becker said, clenching his fists so hard they were shaking, wanting to hurt it, quite irrationally, wanting to kill it. 'Fucking useless piece of shit.' He was hungry, exhausted, pissed off.

'Like swearing will help,' Connie hissed.

'It helps me!' He fumed. 'If we don't eat soon…well, you know,' he said in a voice which was dulled with fatigue. 'I've had this nightmare up to here.' Becker lifted a fist over his head. 'I mean, seriously, what do these arseholes want?' He was ranting and cursing with every negative emotion rolled up into one hateful mind-set.

Becker's mood was soured further by what he'd stumbled across on their journey back through the forest, the proverbial straw that killed his mood for good. Crossing back over the small stream in a slightly different spot, they'd happened upon a group of what could best be described as "cow serpents". Becker was appalled, then briefly amused, thinking they looked a little comical, like a cow-snake combo with scaly, slimy bodies and perfect cow legs, albeit six of them. But it was the heads that were killer. Instead of cute moon eyes and a kindly face he was agog at their cobra-like noggins and depthless black eyes, pronouncing the place Neverland for the butt ugly.

After they moved off into the deeper forest, his torment started to truly take shape. He thought they'd been feeding on banana coloured flowers, but as he moved he saw arcs of light sparkling as he moved, almost like it was reflecting off something synthetic…glass maybe. Walking from the group, he gingerly approached, making sure he was alone, stopping dead in his tracks and taking in the view of the small river canyon, only partially concealed by weeping blue foliage. Becker bent down and retrieved one of the yellow "flowers", rolling it around in his palm, stumbling back a step, stammering almost incoherently, 'g-gold? He struggled to focus, his mind swimming. Rasping for breath he blinked slowly several times, bringing the centimetre square specimen closer, aghast at its almost perfectly crystallised form, blocks of gold crystals, flawless octahedrons, a goddamn Mars nugget! He inched over to the exposed strata in the cliff face, mouthing expletives to himself as he studied the formation. Was this a deliberate ploy to appeal to him, to exploration, shit, no that was wrong…to discovery? Staring back at him was a dirty white quartz pipe a metre or so across crammed with what looked like almost solid gold. Weathering and erosion on this ancient planet had broken thousands of nuggets free, and they were everywhere, like golden toffee, littered over the blue crab grass of the tiny Martian floodplain.

'Hey!' Becker yelled to the group, 'wait up!' He said, blood pounding in his neck, making him unsteady.

Connie put her finger to her lips, hitting him with a killer glare.

'Oh yeah right.' Shit he thought. The creatures. For Christ's sake move your arses he wanted to scream again, waving them over wildly with flailing arms. Becker was still fevering over the nuggets, strewn all over... some small, some the size of a fist, a few the size of footballs.

Well, what have we here?' Quincy said after arriving, seeing gold scattered around like common beach pebbles.

'Seems like you finally got your deposit Becker,' Connie teased, surveying the pieces of yellow metal. 'How big are your pockets?' She pressed her lips together, feeling a ripple of mirth run through her, knowing full well what was going on in that stupid Becker mind of his.

His expression stalled, melting into frustration as the realisation sunk in. Fuck, he thought, instantly horrified.

'We need to go,' Joe said. 'We can't eat this stuff, it's useless.'

'But…b-but…Mars gold,' Becker bleated. 'It's the discovery of a…it's impossible. Look at it. Mars gold,' he repeated pitifully, peering around desperately, knowing his plight was way beyond screwed.

Connie should have expected it, but was still dumbfounded by his childish behaviour, so wanting to whack him back to reality. 'So, you reckon you can take it with you?' Connie sneered, 'just like Antarctica…dig it up, load it aboard right? Or maybe bring a backpack full of nuggets home?' She curled her lip a little steeper daring him to say the wrong thing.

'We're going,' Quincy said, throwing Becker a fuck you look. 'You can stay here and guard your gold against the cow things if that's what you want…good luck with that.'

'Like the dragon and the Golden Fleece, right? You crack me up,' Connie said, turning roughly, raising an arm sharply and legging it toward the forest proper.

Becker stood there pouting, looking from the exposed lode of gold to the nuggets and then to the group retreating up the hill, feeling a need to scream. He was sure there was some dark force playing him for a fool because to someone with his unique personality, this was an exquisite agony. 'For fuck's fucking sake,' he spat fiercely, the vexing irony ripping his heart out and shredding it in front of him. Becker started shuffling reluctantly in the direction of the group, glancing over his shoulder as he retreated from the astonishing geological hideaway, aching inside but weighing whether any of this, or anything period, mattered a dram.

***

'It's not going to work,' Quincy said. 'As soon as I take my palm away it turns black…shits itself instantly.'

Joe had even jerry-rigged a palm leaf wrapped around a rock, placing it on top of the small hemisphere…but the object could clearly detect living tissue, refusing to react to any of the inanimate bits and pieces they'd tried to fool it with. They'd even trapped a creature resembling a giant blue leaf with five compound legs and placed it unhappily on the small hemisphere like a bizarre alien sacrifice. Again, nothing, before it scrabbled off with its strange, bony legs, both objects remaining black and profusely dead. So far it reacted only to their human touch. And they had to maintain contact with it to sustain the yellow aura that they took to mean the damn thing was on, that would hopefully shunt them back to Antarctica, or just anywhere other than this rotten rock.

'So, the plan is what?' Connie said, flicking moisture from her forehead. They hadn't eaten in what felt like a month, the weakness, the hunger, the fear had been building steadily since they got here. Her stomach was going to eat itself, the time was nigh to get the fuck out of this place.

Connie grabbed a fistful of moist hair, 'I'll, uh…keep it open while you go through,' Connie said softly, hearing the awful words escape, echoing like a death sentence. She didn't want to do it but something had to give, otherwise the whole lot of them would die at the foot of this ugly black piece of alien machinery.

'We've already discussed it, we all go or no one goes,' Becker said dismissively, waving her away. 'We agreed on it, no one gets left behind.'

'Well that was before we'd exhausted every angle,' Joe offered wearily. 'The facts are that this thing reacts only to us, dies when we lose contact, which is what's going to happen to us.' Joe gazed at Becker, shaking his head in submission, conceding that they had no choice than to yield to the inevitable.

'This pernicious fuck is forcing it on us,' Quincy said, bearing his yellowing teeth, 'making us do it…leave someone behind.'

Reflecting on Quincy's words, they reluctantly accepted that he was right. As horrible as it seemed, they had to confront the reality of one of them staying behind to die amid the oddness.

136

Becker's face was reddening violently, now almost purple as he fought with himself and this contemptuous place. Tormenting Mars gold was fresh in his mind and now this, the final debasement of their little group, being forced to offer up one of their own. 'Can this seriously be what they want?' He said, rubbing his temple hard enough to hurt, outrage souring his stomach. 'Can it be that stupid-simple, like some screwed up game, you know, find a way to all get out…or one of us pays the price?' He was out of breath, almost out of mind, and patience definitely.

'Christ I bet SETI didn't see this coming,' Connie said, lifting an eyebrow, still finding it hard to process.

'Thought they'd find a sneeze of radio waves from some kindly race of benefactors…not some bastards with torture and misery on their minds.' They glanced at each other, nodding silent consensus, also acknowledging that the transit system could be operating as an automata. But then someone must have pieced it together and they sure as hell would have known the implications if the savages got their paws on them, and God forbid, revved 'em up.

Joe looked Quincy full in the eye, exhaustion, and the pain of hunger etched into lines on his face. 'This is such an unknown, all of it, I mean, it might return us home, but it might take us somewhere else.' His voice sank to a whisper, 'somewhere even worse than this place.' Joe cleared his throat nervously, 'somewhen else maybe. Better the devil you know.' His eyes narrowed as he mulled over what might confront them if their luck turned to shit. Maybe torture was their M.O., just the way they did things. The way they rolled. If that was how it was then they were in the deepest pickle imaginable because maybe this loathsome place was just the beginning, he winced thinking about it, and maybe this planet was the best of the lot.

Quincy had finished crunching the numbers, clenching his fists, banging them on his hips, opening his mouth and pausing before finding his voice. 'I'll stay behind and get it done.'

Joe turned his head, 'we've already decided that no—'

'I said I will stay behind and get it done,' Quincy said, throwing his arms out. 'Go!' He shouted. 'Otherwise we're all gone.' He implored Connie with his eyes to set the example and go. Quincy urged them on. 'I'll be fine, I'll figure something out.'

Connie already felt the moisture of tears welling behind her eyes. She knew someone had to do it, hunching her shoulders, sinfully grateful that no one took up her barely audible offer. Connie didn't mince words with herself, she was sure he had no hope, none of them did, there'd be no reprieve on this capriciously fertile, barren world.

'Hurry!' Quincy yelled, 'before I change my fucking mind.' Slivers of light flashed around him as it filtered into his consciousness. Crap he spat silently, fighting with a shrill voice that questioned whether backing out and recanting his offer was an option.

Connie touched Quincy's shoulder, kissing him gently. 'Thank you Quincy,' she said, dropping tears on his shoulder.

'Fucking go!' He screamed this time, an ear-rattling shriek from deep in his chest.

The three of them spun around and moved toward the half sphere that was alive and alight with eerily warring currents. Its topmost point was about three metres above the ground so Joe and Connie simply walked in, disappearing from Quincy's Universe. Becker loped up and stopped, close enough so the syrupy tendrils were licking at him, sensing its allure as it physically dragged him forward ever so slightly. Turning back, he glanced at Quincy, then lengthened his gaze into the forest, pondering the likelihood of ever getting back to this nut house, admitting with a humph that it was stone-cold zero. It was nothing to do with any monetary value, that didn't mean squat, it was what it was…gold on Mars! Another thing on this world that seemed bitingly wrong, dead-set cruel.

'Fucking move it!' Quincy yelled, one hand on the hemisphere and one gesturing crudely at Becker. 'Go, now or I'll change my mind you prick.'

Becker snapped back, sizing up the poor soul. Four-billion-year-old Mars. Fuck me was his final lament as he burst into the Sphere.

Quincy watched him vanish into the machine, letting go once he was through and sliding down next to it, staring at the dark, dead curvature. As he considered his next move he had a disturbing thought, half wishing he'd considered it earlier, half wishing he hadn't thought of it at all. But it could be the answer, if he had the stones to go through with it. Quincy wasn't sure but something sour was spreading in his stomach as he brooded over how he might do it, figuring if it could save him he'd have to suck it up and find a way. The mental image was a killer, blood, guts, searing pain, probably losing consciousness, bleeding to death maybe. The idea was to cut his hand off and place it atop the hemisphere, a human trophy of sorts, Quincy gulped, a five-finger testament to their will to live. The words, the thinking, the feeling of what he had to do was horrible. Somehow he'd have to hack it off, stem the bleeding with a piece of clothing and then, if it worked, if he stayed conscious, race through the Sphere and pray like hell he ended up with the rest of the group. Or at least somewhere he could get medical help.

Peering around, Quincy searched for anything remotely sharp, then he wondered whether a single finger would do it? So, he placed a digit on the small hemisphere and bingo, it came to life. 'Okay,' he whispered under his breath, trembling, weighing again if severing it from his body would screw things up? Whatever, he was shit out of options so he stood up and started walking hesitantly toward the forest to search for something he could fashion into a tool…a stick maybe, like the one Becker used to slice up the alien birds. He reckoned that would do it, and it was only a finger, *pffft*, he said anxiously, telling himself he wouldn't even miss it. Just a finger, he repeated out loud. It wouldn't be so bad, a pinkie for escape, maybe life, sounded reasonable, a trade anyone would make…right? Pay the piper Quincy said to himself, flinching as something around him changed.

The Sun was still high in the sky but twilight had fallen across the landscape… there were no clouds anywhere. He assumed it was Phobos making its way across the Sun, but shielding his eyes there was no shadow.

Quincy froze as he gazed at the heavily forested horizon, watching darkness loom. It wasn't just darkness though, he could tell that much straight away, the visual was like nothing he'd seen before. An expanse of lightless nothing was expanding grid-like in every direction at the same time; up, down, away from him, toward him. Whatever it was, it was de-colouring the sky, melting the blueness into an absence of…well, just an absence he thought, seeing it moving everywhere in crab-like bursts.

'*Whaaat?*' He said slowly to himself, admitting it looked sort of supernatural, that was the only thing that stuck. Whatever it touched, chunks of the landscape vanished, while next to it without any graduation at all was, um, he frowned dumbly, what word should he use, reality he supposed, trees, plants, dirt, sky. The forest all around him was disappearing block by block. The sky was almost gone, the Sun no more, the forest just a memory. In a minute all that remained was the plate he was perched on, surrounded by space…just him, the metal slab and a dim radiance visible within.

Quincy was without the slightest notion of what was happening to him as he watched his surroundings slough away like an etch-a-sketch landscape, and felt the sepulchral beats from his heart, the hits from his jugular overpowering. He was having trouble breathing from terror…was this thing eating the air as well?

The blackness slid slowly onto the metal dish. Quincy could see it approach from all sides in symmetrical, ordered stutters that soon had it reaching out for him. He genuinely thought he might have been able to get off the rock but there was no hope for him now, and anyway, now there wasn't any rock to get off. Beyond the silvery surface there was only darkness, as though the vacuum of space was overwhelming everything, an irresistible tide that was almost on him.

Slumping down, he peered at his feet, thinking about his son, his girl back on Earth, torn by memories, resigned to dying. Quincy saw that the plate was dimly lit and a little translucent, watching disturbing apparitions below, sparks of light, spider-webs of interlacing energy like chemically saturated neurons tipping on and off in some mighty brain. Quincy's thoughts were thin and distant, images of his kids hitting him hard, the life they'd loved together. Precious would never know what happened to Dad, stranded a hundred million kilometres away, oh…and four billion years in the past! He would be lost forever in the most profound way imaginable.

Quincy was struck by curiosity, picturing the little rover stumbling over a human bone in the sediments of Mt Sharp. Maybe there'd be enough DNA lurking in his bones to let them know it was him. The visual in his mind was darkly, horribly ironic.

His heart took another disconcerting thud as he considered the screwy paradox. If he died millions of centuries before he lived his "other" life on Earth, how in the name of all things sacred could that work? It was pure card-carrying insanity, abjectly failing any test he could think of. Decoherence and superposition were one thing, even Schrödinger's fucking cat, all of them seemed relevant, but this was real life, the macro world, not a convoluted subatomic study book.

He'd travelled back in time, he sort of got that, but if his remains were left where he sat, and he'd also lived on Earth way in the future, how could he have existed in both states, albeit one of them dead while he was alive on Earth? It meant that every moment of his future life…living, loving, working, playing…had been spent while his bones were fossilising on Mars. He felt his mind jerk steeply to the left as he delved deeper. Quincy broke it off, shaking his head hard, looking up just as it struck and consumed him. Now there was nothing left, no blue planet, no forest, no crazy animals, no reverse DNA or super volcanoes. All of it, including the dimensions of spacetime it existed in were gone, evaporated like a drop of methanol at room temperature.

15. Visitors

**"People are supposed to fear the unknown, but ignorance is bliss when knowledge
is so damn frightening." ~ *Laurell K. Hamilton***

Harry saw the change in the object first, shuffling back a little, squinting at the yellow radiance that was suddenly a brilliant ball of light, visible above and below the slightly translucent metal surface. The object was a complete sphere, half above, half below what seemed ground level.

'Let's keep going,' Harry said, 'I mean, can this be anything but a…you know, come on down, we've got something for you?'

Sky exhaled shakily, 'inviting or luring?' She said weakly, feeling her legs grow unsteady. 'No way Harry.' She wasn't going into that godforsaken thing again, once was enough…too much…never again. Transit system, techno-fucking-wonder it might be but the unknowable roadmap buried inside was the harrowing twist. Majority rule could screw itself she thought. They'd have to drag her in kicking and screaming, and good luck if they tried.

Harry stopped suddenly and with one arm waved them back. Skylar and Vic were about three metres behind him, still as stone on the hard, silvery surface that continued its animated pulsing.

What?' Vic barked under his breath.

'Ssshh,' he whispered, poking a finger at the object about thirty metres distant. The light was brighter now, there was a different tinge to it, more orange, a deeper hue. 'Uh…shadows…can you see shadows?' Harry said in a hushed murmur, apparently worried they might be heard. 'Look,' he added with gravity, 'something's … in there...moving.' He felt a suffocating wedge in his throat as he watched the darkness gather solidity.

Skylar felt a sudden ache near her temple, an alarming ringing in her ears, then abruptly sticking her arms out tried to steady herself on nothing more than thin air. 'What do you mean, something?' She saw darkness amid the light, shapes, fuzzy, indistinct, disturbing.

Harry turned around, blinking nervously, 'they, uh, well…look alive I guess,' he bumbled almost incoherently, noticing the spidery, spastic movements.

'Sweet God,' Skylar gurgled, rearing back. Alive? Wild animal spurts came from her mouth as she wound herself up with visions of what might unfold itself from the depths of the object. Maybe it was one of them, or perhaps a forward scout, a Von Neumann here to do some preliminaries. She was horrified by the prospect of an encounter, knowing she wasn't ready, would never be ready, for Christ's sake she could barely remember what SETI was…the pressure in her brain was brutal. Wringing her hands together, she strained to recall the Article of Faith championed by the Post Detection Team, even though she'd penned most of the damned thing herself. She hated herself right now, everything about her screamed weakness, frailty, disappointment.

Harry watched the shadows, his mind telling him he could see limbs, possibly heads, 'whatever's in is comin' out,' he muttered, inching his way backward as he spoke, heart pounding on his ribs as one of several entities scrabbled untidily from the light onto the ancient landmass.

***

Harry snorted, feeling an iron block fall off his shoulders, looking back at Vic blankly, then at the strange new arrivals 'We expected…uh…you're human…right?' His brain was surging, surveying them hastily up and down, relieved but confused.

'Who are you?' Vic said, comforted to see a friendly form as he tapped his fingers nervously against his lips, a little light headed at seeing something so familiar.

Becker's eyes flitted around the group wildly, trying to connect his thoughts. 'We, um…found an object under the ice, apparently ended up—'

Harry could tell he didn't like this guy already, mainly by the look of him and the sound of his voice. He interrupted Becker sharply, 'and then the Sphere's appeared around the Moon,' he said, screwing his face up accusingly. 'So you're the ones that did that?'

'Well, yeah, apparently we were the ones,' Becker conceded more calmly, 'If we did, it was accidental.'

Connie struggled to her feet, grunting with exhaustion, leaving Joe sitting on the ground. 'Look, I'm sorry but do you have food?' She said, a wavering note of desperation in her voice. 'We haven't eaten in maybe three days. Connie could feel the desire, ready to beg if needed, get on her hands and knees, whatever it took. Her whole body was trembling, every strand of DNA screaming for nourishment, anything would do, just nutrients, taste was irrelevant. Connie was so frantic she would've eaten damn near anything, just adios, down the hatch.

Harry wondered where the hell they'd been for that long without food. Locked in a cage maybe, at the behest of some off-world gaoler? They didn't look in any condition to answer questions but it was mighty intriguing. After they ate he figured. 'We have food on the shuttle…come.'

Becker's face went wooden, a slight tic under his eye the only sign of life. 'The what…shuttle you say?' He repeated, snapping his head back, glancing at Connie who looked equally shovel smacked. He turned around, searching and spying in the distance. He was awestruck, seeing it gleaming like a silvery phantasm in the heat haze of a noonday Sun, also clearly reading USA and NASA on the tail section and belly. It was amazing he thought, turning slowly in a full circle. 'What the hell is this place?' He said, lifting a hand to his forehead that felt cold to the touch despite the warm atmosphere.

'You mean when the hell is this place,' Harry said with a wry smile, his beard piling up on his cheeks.

Oh Christ, not again Connie thought dismally, comforted by the appearance of the shuttle but the monster in the sky shattered her hopes to dust, her mouth slack as she touched Becker lightly on the shoulder, pointing upward a bit to her right. 'Uh…Becker,' she croaked, the words barely a murmur under her breath.

'Whoa!' He howled instantly, losing his eyebrows under his knotted fringe.

'Yep, apparently,' Harry said casually, 'minus a few craters but it is her indeed.'

Having just fled a rather peculiar Mars, Becker scanned the landscape and even he made the connection pretty quickly.

Connie squinted at the Moon, it looked different, bigger obviously, but with less of the iconic dark and lighter regions she was familiar with. Her neck was starting to cramp, '…so this is Earth how long ago?' She said, fatigued, her belly gurgling, limbs continuing to shake, waiting for the answer she knew would blow the rest of her mind away.

'About a billion,' Skylar said from the rear of the group. This was no time for scientific dissertations. 'Let's go,' she said, happy for an excuse to get themselves back on the shuttle. Sky tilted her head up at the clouds, hearing a dull roar like distant thunder, then wind hit them from nowhere and with-it rain, but what bloody rain!

Pendulous drops of warm water poured from the sky although the clouds seemed little more than springtime cumulus. Back on Earth, his Earth that is, he'd barely expect more than a sprinkle.

Becker yelped as he was buffeted by wind and drenched rotten by the sudden pluvial downpour that was turning the sand into mud as they watched, the whole place beyond the plate rapidly becoming a quagmire.

Shuttle…now!' Harry bawled, just able to be heard over the rain pounding on the metallic slab, sounding like tonnes of shellgrit hitting a tin fence at speed. They were about two hundred metres from the ship.

Connie turned to where she thought Joe was but he wasn't there. She spun the other way and saw him, still idle next to the dark hemisphere maybe three hundred metres away. Whacking Becker on the shoulder, she said, 'look,' shouting as loudly as she could, 'he's still out there!' Connie started waving at him, realising he wouldn't be able to hear her over the hammering rain, doing slow motion star jumps with energy she didn't have.

'Oh, for God's sake,' Becker muttered, hoisting his arms in the air, waving him back. 'Joe!' He bellowed, loud enough to wake the dead but he was lost in his surveillance of the object, finally snapping his head around as he caught Becker's booming voice.

Joe was beyond hunger, beyond caring about rain, more curious to know why touching the small object did nothing while the Martian analogue sprung to life immediately. He was pretty sure they weren't just machines that ran on pre-cognitive code, he felt sure they planned, calculated and were probably executing some thoughtful, clandestine plan none of them had a clue about. *Todos es posible,* his Dad used to say in a perfect Spanish accent and Joe was certain this little pearl of wisdom drummed into him years ago was more multifarious and relevant than even he realised. Joe had gobbled up his belief with gusto, believing that we all needed to pare back our logic, to really open our minds to the never gonna' happen stuff. People across the world needed to concede things that "normal folk" would consider more at home in the local nuthouse. The problem with believing "normality" is everywhere, he said, was as simple as size. The Great Wide Open was expanding faster than the speed of light in the outer 'burbs and getting so colossal and unwieldy that eventually Nature's playground will see every possibility emerge, somewhere. Every manner of creature, every possible mindset, every physical form is written in the math. Picture your most horrific phobia driven nightmare, his dad would say, terrifying him half to death, and hold onto your hat because one day it'll have life breathed into it by an endless, escalating game of dice throwing. Joe remembered it well, being scared witless, listening for noises outside his window, it was hardly an upbeat bedtime story, pleasant dreams and all, but it raised him with a massively broader view than most.

Most folk had zero notion and even less interest in what might be milling around only a stone's throw from their workaday world. Go to work, come home, cook dinner, feed the mutt, go to bed, repeat the process day after day until you dropped off the twig with nary a thought for anything beyond the blue sky of home.

***

The rain and wind abruptly came to a halt, Sol bursting through the remaining clouds, transforming the metallic surface into a mirror of sparkling light.

Becker bent his head forward, finding it a little far-fetched that gale force winds and a massive downpour could stop pretty much instantaneously.

'Odd,' Connie said, gazing around at the perfectly dry surface of the dish.

'C'mon Joe,' Becker roared at him again, 'time to go buddy.' He watched him finally start ambling toward them, noticing for the first time a strange dim spot further out, like a chunk of obsidian made prominent by the brightness around it, a single busted pixel on a colossal liquid screen. 'Huh?' He said, closing and re-opening his eyes. The square was swelling into a larger block as he watched. 'Connie…uh,' he paused, craning his neck forward, 'what is that…see, near the edge of the forest?' He directed her with his index finger.

She raised her eyes quizzically. 'It's, er—,' she hesitated, turning to the group behind her, shrugging at them.

Harry's eyes widened as he followed its erratic behaviour, his mind thickening, watching it spread organically, but moving way too quick to be anything of the sort.

Connie could see the darkness accelerating its growth, part of the jungle behind the plate was now black and structureless, the spread almost half way to where Joe was. The realisation struck them pretty much at once, whatever this thing was - it was going to kill them.

'Joe run!' Connie and Becker screamed in unison, 'run, run!' Connie poked at the air over Joe's head and turning awkwardly, he saw.

He turned almost instantly, running for his life, pumping his arms, desperately sprinting away from whatever the hell was sweeping up behind him.

'Get to the shuttle,' Harry yelled as he too started running for all he was worth. 'We'll leave the hatch open—'

They were inside Sagan within a minute but Joe was still a few hundred metres away, running as hard as he could, the darkness spreading crab-like behind him, lurching unpredictably in every direction, including up.

Vic depressed a pushbutton that glowed bright yellow, hands flashing everywhere, on the panel, punching the keyboard, the APUs, gripping the RHCs, glancing feverishly at Harry. 'GPC valves…MPS prop, uh, pressurised,' he puffed, still not seeing Joe, heart jamming in his throat. He continued to check everything off, resigned to this being a once only take off attempt. 'Hydrogen feed,' he tapped the VDU, '…yep, thrust vector control on, isolation A, B switches…enabled.' He jerked his head around, still no Joe. 'Find something to hold on to,' he yelled, 'this is gonna be rough.'

Connie was fixed to the side window panel, still not seeing him. 'Fucking run! She screamed at the window, seeing the darkness divide over and over again into more grid-like tentacles, accelerating its irregular, spastic motion, only fifty metres behind him, closing. Whatever it was, she could see that when it touched something, bang…it ceased to exist.

Harry likened it to space somehow forcing its way in, bleeding into the atmosphere as if the barometric pressure was no longer able to keep it out. Ridiculous he knew, but there it was.

'Main engines on-line, good to go,' he said, gasping, 'flaps full, roll spoilers maxed.' Vic looked at Harry pensively, waiting for the sign, praying Joe would come running up the stairs. 'TOD is one click Harry, if we're not off the ground by then well—'

'Wait,' Connie pleaded, her voice a broken croak in the back of her throat. 'No, no, fucking no,' she wailed, tears spilling down her cheek. She knew Joe wasn't going to make it, seeing the speed of the spread behind him, the distance he had left. Connie wanted to stop watching but she couldn't, feeling ill, waiting for her heart to explode in her chest. He was running, every now and then looking back over his shoulder, a hundred and fifty metres to go, the nothingness almost licking at his heels. It almost seemed to be playing with him, accelerating toward him, almost touching him, then retreating sideways and returning for another go. Connie saw him slow down and come to a halt, bending over with his arms resting on his thighs, staring right at it, shaking his head slowly, disbelievingly. 'Joe…no…don't stop…Joe…no.' She had her nose almost touching the fused silica of the window panel, burning tears heavy behind her eyelids.

'Hatch close,' Harry said, the hydraulic whir, followed by a dull thump as Joe's entryway to the craft was withdrawn.

Connie felt blood retreat from her face as she gazed pleadingly at Becker who shrugged sadly, placing a hand on Connie's shoulder, squeezing it gently, turning her away from the window.

Joe turned around and eyeballed the darkness. '…come get me you fucker,' he snarled, watching it flash toward him, hitting him noiselessly and continuing on toward the shuttle, reducing everything to *something* unexplainable, or was that *nothing* unexplainable, Vic pondered distantly, seeing Joe simply overtaken by the darkness.

'Joe's gone,' Becker said, seeing tears trailing down her cheeks. She bit her lip, trying to hold them back but no way it was going to happen, she clenched her jaw to suppress a scream, her shoulders quaking as she tried to blink them away. 'I'm so sorry Connie,' Becker said in a soft whisper, putting his arm protectively around her shoulder. 'M-Me too,' she said in a hollow stammer, staring up at him with huge, limpid eyes.

'Go!' Harry said, throwing both hands at Vic. 'Main engines…get us off this fucking rock.'

MPS exploded in a hail of superheated plasma, punching the craft forward but Sagan was already slipping sideways on the muddy surface. The rain had turned the sand into a greasy nightmare, the ship going sideways and forward at the same time, land speed growing way too slow.

Skylar watched the darkness claw toward them, already the sky was midnight, much of the landscape pitch black like thick crude. 'We need to get out of here,' she howled, gripping her head tightly, 'it's fucking on us.' Her hands shifted to the side of her seat, holding on desperately, every muscle hard as she saw her future in Joe, whimpering quietly.

All eyes were on Vic as he wrestled with the craft, their fate resting with his ability to pilot Sagan in the most extreme conditions. Even with the main landing lights burning bright they could only see a few hundred metres in front of them. If there was a rocky outcrop or anything else the tyres couldn't deal with, they were dead. The only option was to get Sagan off the muddy ground as fast as possible. Vic had pre-planned the takeoff route and hoped he was following the correct vector but in the darkness he wasn't so sure. DAP said they were and he hoped to hell it was right.

'Max thrust,' Harry barked, knowing Vic was already gunning the three GE-130 main engine cores, he could feel the power making the shuttle vibrate wildly.

Vic glanced at his ASI, pleading for it to tick over to one-fifty, watching it like a hawk, praying, looking away and praying again. Normally he wouldn't consider pulling back on the control stick until it cracked one-eighty but he was sure the air density was higher here, but if he was wrong, engaged rotation too early they would go up then come down in a fiery heap.

Glancing back down, finally it was there. One fifty-three. He held his breath, tensing every muscle he had. 'V1 rotate,' he barked and the vessel obliged by lifting its beautiful blunt nose into the sky, soaring above the planet that was inexplicably blackened as though something had taken ragged bites from it. Becker had seen the human rigours of polar exploration, dead tissue imposing on living tissue and he reckoned the view below was uncomfortably similar.

'Incline vector to max,' Harry said with feverish eyes. 'Positive rate.'

'Copy,' Vic said, 'climb vector V2 confirmed on VSI. Gear up, flaps back,' he confirmed as nose wheels and main gear retracted into their housing with a thud.

'What's happening down there?' Vic said with forced calm, one eye on the window panel, one on the avionics, sweating, not entirely sure he wanted to know.

'Not good,' Skylar whispered, turning away from the window, her pupils crazy dilated, expecting death at any time.

They watched transfixed as the planet below them was gradually dismantled by the blackness that Vic couldn't help thinking of as a disease, some sort of cancer. Since takeoff, the spread had enveloped half the supercontinent. Their home was Earth way in the future yet this ancient Earth was seemingly decaying before their eyes, the paradox, the disconnect as unfathomable as anything else they'd encountered so far.

***

Harry thought he'd try and break Sky's mood, tipping his head and catching her attention, smiling warmly through his patchwork beard, 'can you, uh…fetch a box of the irradiated beef, maybe the dried fruit?' The way Becker and Connie looked, their twitching, harrowed faces, he honestly thought they might die in front of him, maybe drop into a famine-induced coma. 'Make it the big boxes Sky,' he said, nodding at Connie who blinked at him woodenly. 'And flight suits, the lock and key type, we'll show 'em how to use them.' He looked over at Vic, nodding - he invented the damn things, he could do the bloody training.

Despite the situation they were in, Joe dead, the planet seemingly being undone beneath them, Connie and Becker still felt a primal urge to eat, watching the entrance to the equipment bay intently. Skylar returned with a backpack full of vacuum-sealed containers. 'Ionised beef and dried apricots,' she said, screwing her nose up, 'no expense spared I guess, courtesy of the white hats at NASA.'

NASA has chefs? Connie mused curiously, strangely amused by the concept. Whatever though, bring it, her eyes said, licking her lips, digging in, brooding over the horror of Joe.

'Orbital interface,' Vic said, sounding a little surprised they'd actually made it.

'Okay,' Harry said, 'maintain ten-point-one.'

'Copy,' Vic said, fighting to pull his heart back, slowing Sagan with a puff of fore RCS propellant to stabilise its equatorial orbit above what was left of the deeply damaged planet below.

Connie reckoned around half of it was gone, the dividing line between planet and darkness looking incredibly precise, a line cutting the world in half. It looked like night and day, but with a sudden pained expression, she could see two stars twinkling…where Earth should have been!

'Orbital vector says it's all still there,' Harry said, frowning, 'we're in regulation free-fall at ten clicks per second, same old same old. The blackness may have done whatever its done but all the stuff is still down there…somewhere,' he said, picking at his beard, knowing if it wasn't, the lost mass would result in vastly different orbital alignments.

'That's bullshit Harry, that stuff was—'

'Easy Connie, 'Becker soothed, 'just stay calm, we don't—'

'Stay calm?' Connie said in a rush, feeling herself flush. 'That stuff down there is more than just colour, it's amniotic death, you saw what it did to Joe, he came apart at the seams, vanished into it, dissolved like fucking…I don't know…just gone.'

'That food has brought you back Con,' Becker said, shooting her a smirk and subtle wink.

'Careful,' she said, clenching her teeth and pushing her head toward him.

'Okay, okay,' he raised his hands, stepping back with a cautious grin on his face. 'Plucky,' he added under his breath.

'I'm talking about Joe and you're grinning like an idiot, making jokes…are you serious?' Her lip crimped down in disgust. 'God you're such an arsehole.' She sized him up disdainfully.'

'I didn't mean disrespect,' Becker offered, sighing and looking down at his feet, 'he was my friend too, you reckon I don't feel it?'

'Goddamn it,' she said in a rush, squinting at him, 'Joe was terrified of you, you treated him like you owned him, like a fucking trinket…a possession.' Her voice had lost its edge, she swallowed hard, biting back tears. 'You never had a good word for him…take, that's all you did, he would've done anything for you but all you did was play him.' Her voice ended flat and dull, she turned away sharply. 'You're a son of a bitch.'

'Connie, I never—'

'Just leave it,', her eyes grew large, the pooling moisture reaching critical mass.

Sky walked over and offered a sympathetic sigh, nodding weightily, turning slightly to Harry and Vic, keeping Connie in view, saying the first thing that came into her head. 'Do you, um…reckon this might be the classic termite scenario?' She was hoping to divert her thinking from Joe for a moment, pondering the grim choice of subject, but continuing anyway. 'You know, as in, um...why would sentient beings bother to go out of their way to destroy a nest of insects.' Sky gazed at them with a growing ruefulness. '…ever zap a bug under a magnifying glass?' Connie stared at her vacantly, taking slightly more interest in what she was saying. 'And did you feel any empathy for the poor little sod, crackling and bursting like popcorn?' Sky's mouth stayed open, it was all making a little too much sense, she needed to stop.

'You can theorise all you like,' Harry said, shifting restlessly in his seat, 'all day, all night for the next decade and you'll get about as far as that bulkhead there,' he pointed with a thrust of his forehead. 'Unless our buddies tell us, show us or whatever, we'll never know shit. And that presupposes that they even want to tell us anything in the first place. So, let's give the questions a rest, start thinking about our next move. Maybe you've overlooked it but we're stranded up here. No biggie, but we need to come up with some ideas on that.' He turned to the avionics panel, tapping his heel on the base of his seat.

'Okay then Haz, smart guy, where to from here?' Becker said, with acid in his tone, irritated by this know-all who looked like he'd just fallen out of bed, not to mention off the fucking wagon. The similarities to a down and out wino were unnerving.

He eyeballed Becker. 'It's Harry, you best remember that.'

'Hey, no offence, just trying to be friendly,' Becker shot back, turning away dismissively.

Harry shrugged, twisting his mouth aggressively, watching him from the corner of his eye.

Connie glared at Becker, pissed off with his macho bullshit approach, 'can't help yourself can you,' she said, feeling her temperature rising. 'Just try and get along with the big kids.'

'Rich coming from you, human relations a strong point?' He said coldly, forgetting the Joe softly-softly stuff. Tough love was all he had.

'…such an arsehole,' Connie repeated, walking away to the deployment bay, needing time away from Becker, away from Harry for that matter. He was almost as pig headed and exasperating as Becker. She swore to herself, realising she was surrounded by them, it was a goddamn nightmare and worse, there was absolutely no escape. Connie surveyed the irrational scene aboard the shuttle, imagining how an alien mind might interpret the dysfunctional human interactions, nervously admitting that they might be watching them right now. Maybe they were about to slash Mr Red through the page, maybe that was the motive behind this sorry adventure, see how the savages progress, keep 'em, get rid of 'em, well, let's wait and see if they get it first. If that was the case, given what they'd gleaned so far, which was the grand total of squat, Connie was sure they were screwed in the most explicit sense.

Skylar was bemused by all the inconsequential blather, she wanted home, so they needed some concrete ideas on how that might happen. Loudly, she said, 'Can we get serious and start—'

'Quiet!' Harry yelled suddenly,' bringing instant silence to the flight deck. He was pointing dead ahead, watching an object growing in space.

Looming over the horizon of partial Earth was an object bright in the light from the Sun, occupying a slightly higher orbit than Sagan, rolling around Earth like a gigantic, reflective marble.

'Vic, take us into complimentary, holding at twenty clicks,' Harry said, without looking away from the object.

Vic deflected the RHC slightly, engaging RCS and gently thrusting Sagan faster and higher. Vic then slowed her down ever so slightly with barely a kiss of fore prop to null her into the same vector as the Sphere.

'You're an artist,' Harry said, with a grin and a wink, knowing he made complex orbital manoeuvres look crazy easy, having tickled the primary TVC gimbal ring to change up their pitch, yaw and velocity with the deft skill of a piano savant.

The group was assembled at the back of the cabin to decide a way forward. 'Everyone gets a say if they want one,' Harry said, 'for mine it's pretty clear, there's no option. We either wait for something to happen which may be never or we ask Vic to take us in, take our medicine, get it over with. You know, dial up the chocolate wheel, if that's how this bloody thing works. My vote is Sphere.' He glanced over at Skylar.

'Agreed,' she said nervously, desperately wanting out of this cosmic nut house. If there was a chance to get home, no matter how slim, she'd take it, no questions asked.

Connie fidgeted, 'Jesus, of course we go, staying here is bullshit, let's do it.'

Harry saw Vic lift a shoulder and wag his head. 'Let's stay in orbit a while, see what happens, we don't have to make a decision right now, maybe the decision will be made for us.'

'Oh God,' Connie murmured, touching her throat, fingers spread wide. 'Seriously Vic, shall we break out the fucking knitting while we wait.'

'Everyone gets a say,' Harry reminded her. 'Plug it.'

Crap, Becker thought, good luck with that strategy. He held his breath.

Connie fought to stay quiet, so wanting to put this idiot in his place.

'Damn, that's impressive…you ready to explode yet?' Becker said, smirking behind his hand, knowing he shouldn't bait her but lacking the steel not to. He could see she was moving into eruption mode. Mt. Constantine he mused with a whimsical snort.

'You are such a…seriously Becker.' She scowled at him furiously but she held her tongue.

Harry glanced at Becker, hoisting an eyebrow, waiting for his decision.

'We go.' Becker said.

'Four to one in favour,' Harry said, 'Vic make it so.'

Vic shuffled in his seat, prickly with the verdict, not seeing the need for a hasty decision, gently throwing his hands in the air. 'I just…look, we don't have the slightest clue where we'll go,' he said, 'look what's already happened…two dead, only dumb luck we got away in one piece. Christ, that's probably not a way home, it might be a ticket to hell.' He turned away sharply, staring blankly at his head-up display. 'Think long and hard because once we're in, we're in, there's no way back until they say so.' Which may be never he said in his mind.

Vic was right and wrong, they all were, but if they didn't take a chance then they could be screwing around forever trying to decision a "prudent" call. It was gambling in the truest sense, having no idea what cock-eyed rules the house was playing by. Every conceivable, inconceivable outcome existed and they had voted to flip the lid and see what it dealt them. Vic knew it was a return to Schrödinger and his infuriating cat. Probability collapse could well be fatal.

Vic was the first to see it and was a little numbed as he struggled to reconcile it. 'Oh you have to be—,' he said trailing off into silence. His expression darkened as he studied its behaviour.

Light streamed onto the flight deck, particles surging through space in a glowing molecular cloud made brilliant by the Sun. Not far below them it accreted into a single point, diffusing again when it touched the atmosphere, swathing the decimated world in a radiant cocoon. The piece of Earth killed off by the darkness gradually grew until the planet was as it had been before – blue, white, beautiful, not the slightest hint of battle scars, and in Harry's words "good as a bought one", Becker having no idea what the fool meant, cursing under his breath.

'What uh, just happened?' Sky said timidly, 'I mean, I saw what happened but—' She looked at the others for help, an opinion, an idea, anything. They looked at her blankly, headshakes, shrugs, furtive glances, a Becker grunt. Not a clue.

'So, what? The Sphere is on our side now?' Connie said, not sure what to think. 'What was that stuff…the particles?'

Harry winced at the inane question, growing his trademark lopsided smirk. 'Maybe we're smack bang in the middle of some galactic battle…you know, good versus evil, light versus dark,' he chuckled quietly, looking disturbingly like a bum on metho. 'Let's do it Vic, take us in, we have a mandate from these lovely people, so do it.'

'I'm sorry,' Connie said, raising her hands to her forehead and scraping them down her face, 'but did all this, uh…shit really happen a billion or so years ago or is this some charade for our benefit?' She eyed them sceptically. 'We've been sent here, but um…is this genuine history?' She walked slowly to the shuttle window.

Oh fuck me, Harry felt like screaming, now she thinks she's the bloody Eye of Providence. He gaped at her. 'Do you honestly think we have an answer to that?'

'Well, no but what do you think?'

'I think we shouldn't ask everything that just, you know, pops into our head,' Harry said, tapping the middle of his forehead.

'Taking up your valuable time, is that it?

'Don't ask what there's no hope of knowing,' he snapped, looking back at the window.

'So we just ignore everything, ask nothing…is that how you want it?'

'Yes…well no, but put forward an idea, a theory, not just mindless questions. How's that?'

'Yeah, okay Harry. You're an arrogant, insufferable oaf…that's a statement, not a theory or even a question. How's that?'

Harry rolled his shoulders, giving an inflated sigh, the slightest trace of a smile on his face. She was good, very good he thought, not to mention funny, sexy and pretty damn smart. Connie had it all going on but it was wrapped in such an infuriating, bloody-minded package. Big downside, but no one's perfect he guessed.

Becker watched on, it was good to be out of the firing line for a while. Bowden didn't seem to mind it, in fact his somewhat amused expression suggested he might be enjoying it. A twinge of unease prickled the back of his neck.

***

Sagan was in the same corridor so it was a simple matter of increasing speed to catch up with it, but not so much speed that they pushed into a higher orbit. Vic grabbed the hand controller to execute an RCS X-jet translation manoeuverer to boost Sagan from six-point-four to the calculated eight clicks per second they would need to run it down in about ten minutes.

'Contact minus nine point two.' Vic said. 'When we enter this thing you need to be secured...it might be rough.' Vic had programmed the system to monitor the approach of the Sphere and count down the time to entry. When he looked at the TTC his first thought was that he'd screwed up the programming, but he checked it and it was correct. The numbers were counting up - not down.

Harry saw Vic's pinched brow. 'You okay?' He said, feeling his pulse increase a notch.

Vic gazed back at him deadpan, one eyebrow cocked. 'Um, the numbers are going up,' he said, 'the Sphere is moving away...increasing velocity.' He inspected the TTC again, looking up suspiciously, weighing the evasive behaviour.

'So it dragged us in and now it's playing what, hard to get? Skylar said, combing roughly though her hair with her fingers.

'Increase speed Vic,' Harry said evenly, 'ten-point-five.'

'Copy. Ten-point-five. That's maxed Harry, any higher, we transfer orbit.'

They felt the pull from the aft OMS pod as it executed a Vernier burn. The Sphere still wasn't coming closer, strangely it seemed to be getting further away, now dipping below the curve of the Earth ahead of them.

'Oh for the love of—,' Vic said loudly, gripping the hand controller so hard his fingertips were white. The PAR or precision approach radar was telling him the Sphere had an orbital velocity of thirteen kilometres per second.' His mind was trying to connect the dots and find a reasonable answer, one that physics allowed anyway. Taking a few steadying breaths, Vic tried to think but there was nothing to think about. It was like he'd been dropped into some fictional sideshow where laws and age-old constants didn't apply anymore.

'Harry?' Vic murmured, not moving his eyes from the readout.

'What?' He said, snapping his chin up. Harry wanted into the Sphere but it was snubbing them...his mind was clawing over reasons why.

'It's retreating faster than escape velocity,' Vic said, freeing his stare, peering toward Harry. If he looked confused before, he was completely baffled now. 'But it's not breaking orbit...it's still on an identical vector to us.'

Connie watched the Sphere dip behind the massive continent below, 'that's not right, um...even possible is it?' Newtonian Law right, says it will move higher, away from the centre of gravity?' She knew her physics and equally understood Vic's consternation with this increasingly metaphysical whatever it was.

'So what...the object isn't obeying physics?' Harry said, puckering his lips and squashing his beard, 'or maybe it has some ability to maintain orbit above escape velocity. I'd go with the latter, maybe there's an anti-gravity drive or dark energy motor hidden under the hood.' He grinned mischievously, 'or hey, maybe one of them new-fangled quark-gluon generators?' Harry smacked the side of his head gently.

148

Vic gave a shaky smile, acknowledging Harry's humour, but still more fixed on the muddling orbital incongruence.

I'm serious,' Harry said, losing his smile, 'this thing probably has capabilities we can't possibly imagine.'

'Oh God, whatever,' Connie said, giving a melodramatic eye roll that lingered on the roof of the shuttle. 'That aside, what's the plan?'

'You tell me, you're the one with the mouth,' Harry returned with equal sarcasm.

'Whoaaa!' Becker yelled suddenly, stabbing with a finger, 'we need to slow down!' Ahead of them the Sphere was growing visibly larger, looming, clearly on an intercept manoeuvre.

'Speed is still ten-point-one right?' Harry said, nodding once.

'Yep, nominal.'

'It's coming fast,' Becker said, shifting in his seat.

'No, we're coming fast,' Connie said, leaning back, 'the damn thing's slowed down.'

Harry opened his mouth, holding it for a second, 'I um, well it seems to want us to enter at a particular spot…maybe a specific time. It dragged us in last time, this time it held us off. Whatever this thing is, it seems to be thinking very hard about when we do and don't go in.'

'Contact four minutes.' Vic said, flicking his eyes over at Harry. 'Secure yourselves,' he added, turning back to the glass cockpit. There was a flurry of activity as they strapped themselves into their seats or found a bulkhead corner to wedge themselves against.

Skylar's heart was vibrating on her spine and breastbone at the same time, feeling arrhythmic or at best a little off.

Becker was mesmerised by the approaching Sphere, acknowledging how awesome to the eye it was, sensing a truckload of dread mixed in, like arsenic with a side of béarnaise he reckoned with a grunt. He wondered if his existence was about to come to a screeching halt.

'One minute,' Vic said, barely audible, a flicker in his cheek a tell sign of steep uncertainty.

'Hang on,' Harry yelled, 'it might be smooth like last time…or not.' Being thrown around inside the craft was the least of their problems he was sure. The real issue was being thrown into another nightmare scenario, the rest was incidental. Vapour atop the flames of hades.

'Thirty seconds.'

The Sphere was massive in front of them – rippling, boiling, distressingly clear in front of the silica glass. Concentric waves pulsed their way inward, the same funnelling pattern they saw on the object beneath the ice in Antarctica. She didn't know what it meant up here but it'd meant get in or else, down there. They held their breath as the golden storm engulfed them, Sagan sliding beneath the surface of the mathematically pure object like passing into the atmosphere of a tiny gas world.

16. Shut Down

"Impossible is Nothing." ~ *Sumit Gavel*

Eyes took time to adjust to the darkness and when they did, beyond the panelled window, the view was unnerving, mystifying certainly.

Sky wondered out loud where they were, stumbling over her words, straining to work out what Sagan was coursing through, fixating on the profuseness of it all. It wasn't the switching black and white, she knew that much, not sure whether different was good or bad. No one bothered to answer, knowing the eerie netherworld was beyond human resolve right now.

'Are we, uh…still inside the Sphere?' Vic said, pushing forward on his seat restraints, maintaining his rigid forward stare.

'The ripples we saw on the Sphere,' Harry said, 'can you see the, um…silhouette?' He rammed his index finger at the still visible patterning outside the window. 'They're vague, like a heat haze…small swells, waves…see?'

'So we're inside?' Connie said, blinking rapidly, feeling trapped but looking beyond the Sphere, thought it might be for the best, at least right now.

'Yep,' Harry said distractedly, still studying the surface patterning.

'So what do we do?' Becker said, glancing at the others.

'There's nothing we can do.' Harry said abruptly. 'Until this thing spits us out, we wait, we watch.' He curled his mouth, raising his eyes at Becker. He assumed the object would excrete them at some point, wondering in the back of his mind, what if it didn't? They'd eventually have to throw caution to the wind, burn the OMS, even the MPS…burn themselves to a crisp maybe.

Becker inched closer to the window panel, frowning, scratching at his forehead. Harry would be pissed but screw it, the prick deserved everything he got. 'So what are we looking at…seems to be speeding up…right?' He kept his head still, looking straight out.

Harry bit his cheek hard. 'You'll keep,' he drawled ominously, knowing they had bigger fish to fry than his meathead attitude.

***

The sight made little sense. Space was jammed full of light from uncountable stars, packed so close together in the centre they merged into one monumental core of light. Around it was a gradually rarefying halo stretching outward, meeting up with incalculable galaxies that were all visibly rushing inward. The whole vista was interlaced with masses of swirling pink and blue gas, glowing molecular clouds being sucked toward the centre mass that was condensing and brightening discernibly.

The scale looked all-wrong because observing such a colossal expanse of space in such granular detail should have been impossible. No way that could happen, Vic told himself, feeling increasingly bewildered and troubled. Harry was massaging both temples with his forefingers, gazing hushed at the squashed and distorted stuff that was now everywhere, so wrong and seemingly compressed for their own viewing pleasure.

Connie had no clue what was happening, all she could think about was the pounding of her heart, the clamouring of blood in her ears, the unsettling thud of her jugular. Things were accelerating past them, defying belief…stars, enormous galactic arms, nebulae dotted with every type of sun, all colours, sizes, singles, doubles, triples, more. Plumes of white hot matter were spiralling into black holes, being consumed and digested right in front of them. Pulsars like spinning lighthouses, gaseous supernovae remnants, clouds of everything imaginable, masses of planets and rock all went hurtling past them seemingly at arms-length. Everything the Cosmos had to offer was flashing past their eyes in an accelerating parade of matter and energy. The centre of their forward view was now a coalescing leviathan growing visibly more luminous as they gawped at it.

None of them moved or spoke, unsure what they were witnessing but pretty certain something was off, because it was unfolding so absurdly fast. The question of where they were was a stone-dead puzzle. Vic had surveyed the cabin and dismissed group delusion, leaving several dozen other possibilities that were equally nuts.

Connie finally found her voice. 'Uh...some of this stuff must be passing through us,' she said, pointing with a shaky thrust of her head, tasting hot acid, '...because it's appearing right...there.' Her finger sliced the air. 'How...I mean, what does that say?' Connie's eyebrows drew tightly together, staring like a startled gibbon.

'Um, that we're not actually here?' Becker offered, 'is that it?' He wasn't really sure what he meant, but it felt about right.

'Looks pretty damn real to me,' Vic said, feeling like his mind was winding down, somehow self-protecting itself as he gazed at the inexplicable rush of matter that flouted reason.

Sky felt like she'd been inserted into a movie as a post-production character, such was the troubling feeling of unreality. Everything was fuzzy and dream-like. She thought about pinching herself but managed to stifle the urge, longing to just curl up, close her eyes and sleep until whatever it was went away.

***

The whole lot seemed to be speeding up, a three-hundred-and-sixty-degree deluge of undifferentiated cosmic matter racing past them, through them, around them at ludicrous speed. Suddenly, the mass at the centre winked out but everything continued raining down, streaming into the blackness from all points of the compass. Harry had the distinct impression they were watching an event not in real time but over many millions or even billions of years squashed into a few inexplicable minutes.

Connie finally moved, splurting and almost choking, coughing violently, raising a finger toward something. The downpour of matter was slowing and at the periphery of their field of view was a mysterious glow, now everywhere. Looking up, down, fore and aft, it was far distant, but distinct against the nearer darkness of space.

Sky, you okay?' Harry asked gently, seeing her strewn untidily on the floor, sobbing ever so quietly, breathing in shallow gasps, lips trembling as she rhythmically clenched and unclenched her fists.

'No,' was her groaning reply, shaking her head slowly, rocking back and forth a little.

'Whatever this is, we're in it together...we'll be fine,' Harry soothed, thoroughly unsure. 'Sky, look at me, close your eyes...relax,' he said stiffly, knowing his mechanical attempts at reassurance were cheesy at best. Relax? He repeated ruefully to himself...Jesus, great strategy. Emotions, especially of the female kind, were an alien landscape, a bridge he'd never successfully crossed, or even known how to approach.

Connie was dumbfounded but not surprised, so far the guy was a jerk. 'Are you serious...relax? That's a joke right? Not sure if you're keeping up with events, but it looks like the Universe is about to shit itself out there.'

No one bothered with Connie's question, bringing only an irritated grunt from Harry. Vic was puzzling over it, he knew space was dark because in the bigger scheme of things, matter was scarce and volume large so there just wasn't enough stuff to reflect the light, so what was the answer for the glow? He placed his brain in neutral, waiting for something more.

The baffling brightness rose everywhere around them as darkness diminished into a pitch-black sphere, amid the expanse of ghostly light. It held there for a second or two, stable and ink-like, then it was gone, leaving Sagan in a void resembling an alpine whiteout. There were no contrasts or patterns, just light overtaking dark... the familiar ebony of space now just a memory.

151

Skylar looked up at Harry, glassy eyed, mewing incoherently, a mute whisper in the back of her throat, no words.

'Close your eyes Sky, there's nothing to see up here.' He meant it, there was literally nothing to see. Amorphous white light like an endless cloud of cirrus, that was the sum total of what remained around them.

Connie padded over to Harry, her voice faint, 'so we're outside the Universe and in some sort of—' She stopped abruptly and deadpanned him, having no ideas, not even guesses.

'Outside the Universe?' Vic repeated, throwing his hands in the air, grinning ironically. 'Are you…that's bullshit…the Universe is all there is, all there ever will be, if it's gone then so—'

'Look Einstein,' Connie said, gesturing with her arms expansively. 'Everything that was the Universe just motored past us on the way to oblivion…it doesn't fucking exist anymore.'

'This is horseshit,' Harry said, raising his voice. 'This has to be some sort of vision, projection…we're still inside the Sphere so it might be concocting all this.' He shrugged, feeling heavy in the gut. 'Maybe they've given us a glimpse of the far future.' Harry didn't have the slightest clue if it was right or wrong, just a pitiable shot in the dark at best.

'Jesus,' Becker blurted suddenly, snapping his neck forward, seeing the Sphere raining a stream of something toward the spot where the darkness had winked out, lighting it up with colour. But what a fucking colour! Becker narrowed his eyes in the glare, squinting blindly, feeling his mind start to unravel a bit. He found himself unable to name it, describe it or even vaguely define it, it wasn't an unusual combination of colours, a different tint, maybe a shade of a common colour because he would've recognised it, could have described it with ease. It was a visual entirely beyond his experience, eating into his mind with a chemical savagery, more than anything else screaming impossible, and for Becker, a reason to curse.

Connie turned to him then spun back to what was outside. 'Oh please,' she shrilled beside him. They looked at each other, attesting to the lunacy of what was screaming through space.

Vic scratched his neck, leaving crimson tracks, muddling through colours in his head, comparing them, feeling giddy as his mind dredged around, searching for something to appease his headache. He had nothing, there were literally no words to define it. Can a colour be made he asked himself absently…white light only had so many components…so what the hell was this?

Harry looked just as vexed, variously pulling and picking at his knotted beard, 'a new colour…seriously, is that what this is? It's bullshit, no way.' He shook his head. Was this colour like regular matter was to dark matter, sort of similar but different on the most fundamental level? Was it dark energy or dark matter made visible to the human eye, shown to them in some grand revelation of physical mastery? Whatever the hell it was, these others needed to footnote it because we weren't clued in enough to get it. Guess wildly maybe, but not get it, no way.

'Maybe it's like animals that hear frequencies we can't,' Connie said. 'This could be some sort of, um, fringe colour, right?' She looked up, meeting Vic's gaze, lifting a shoulder.

'The only thing fringe here is you,' Becker leered tensely. 'Do you seriously think it's—'

'Least she's having a crack,' Harry said, ignoring his own "have a theory" bullshit. 'Better than shovelling out mindless drivel one bucket load at a time.' He eyed him directly, curling his mouth sourly, the implication clear. I'm the fucking boss, he may as well have yelled.

'You know what Harry, I'll tell you what—' He was stopped dead in his tracks by a sudden smothering darkness so total they couldn't see hands in front of their faces, every trace of light vanishing, including all the internal illumination.

Skylar cried out behind them, moaning uncontrollably, clamping a hand over her mouth, banging her feet gently on the textured floor of the shuttle, too scared to move.

From nowhere, a stupendous, noiseless detonation flooded the flight deck with brilliance unsurpassed, a perfect sphere of blinding light soundlessly igniting in front of them, right where the big crunch had seemingly crushed everything into nothing. It flashed over them but they felt nothing but a gentle rocking beneath their feet. Sagan slid slowly out of the Sphere.

17. Clues

**"There is always pleasure in unravelling a mystery, in catching at the gossamer
clue which will guide to certainty." ~ *Elizabeth Gaskell***

Flight Director Raines and SLS Project Engineer Pete Harper were in serious conversation, a fist slamming onto the table as they came to terms with the futility of Sagan's plight. They were surrounded by dozens of flat panel console screens and massive visual displays, bannering the head of the war room. Behind them were TITAN and Atlas super consoles where PROP and FDO controllers were sweating over alternate trajectories and optimal sequences for escape manoeuvring. Other operators on telemetry, tech consoles and ops stations occupied a dozen rows, each of them stretching wall to wall, crammed with mission specialists, flight officers, aerospace technicians and controllers, all of them bustling around with intent. Noise in the Security Zone was an amorphous blend of hundreds of anxious, concerned voices, the White Room, now the MCC-21 in Building 30-S had been free of such unruly tumult since STS-107 burnt up on re-entry.

Jack had finished his final transmission to Sagan, if they couldn't break away, well it was clear what was waiting for them, although their fate was utterly unknown…good, bad, whatever.

'Quiet!' Jack screamed across the FCR, noise hushing instantly, leaving only the harried sound of breathing. Everyone feared the wrath of Jack. He was not to be messed with. 'Fuck me,' he said, rubbing the bridge of his nose. 'How long?' He flicked his gaze to the vision from Hubble.

'Forty seconds,' Pete said, eyes visibly widening, a sense of impotence was overpowering.

'Jesus Christ,' Jack murmured, glaring at Flight Dynamics, snapping, 'Robbie, status?'

'Negative Flight, MPS burn was, a no-go. Main engines are done. Velocity still increasing.'

'Goddamn it,' Jack said, surveying the dozens of flight officers.

'Options?' He shouted, lowering his eyebrows so they hooded his eyes ominously.

Pete looked at him squarely, shaking his head. 'Zero,' he said. 'We've tried everything. If MPS doesn't work, RCS, OMS, Mag…all useless.' He paused for a moment, 'maybe they could get out and push,' he offered with a derisive grin.

Jack clenched his teeth hard. 'Shit Pete, you're better than that…but no that will not be necessary,' he replied glibly, frowning at his old mate. 'They're not getting away from that thing.'

Every eye in the room was plastered on the VDUs, showing 3D renderings of Sagan and the Sphere, the proximity between the two closing toward zero

'Contact five seconds Flight,' Pete reported, holding Jack's gaze for a second, then peering back at his screen, wondering what unfathomable event was unravelling up there.

The entire MCC team had ground to a halt, the Flight Control Room now silent, eyes mortared to the Hubble feed as the craft made contact, then simply slid beneath the surface of the bogey. Images from Hubble showed ripples left on the surface after Sagan dived into its soft belly, crests sparkling in the light from the Sun.

The remaining sound was bleeding from the air conditioners, which had just kicked on, everyone was staring blindly at the Hubble image front and centre… now a perfectly stilled Sphere. New and barely discernible ripples were rising, gathering momentum and depth of amplitude.

'Uh…something's happening Flight,' Pete called out, spinning around to look at him. 'Same, uh, pattern,' he said curiously, eyeing the familiar motion on its surface.

Jack studied the image nervously, blinking to focus, puzzling over the turbulence that suggested something might be pushing at it from the inside. Was it some inscrutable game of swap-and-share where we supply a ship full of ours for a ship full of theirs? He wiped sweat off his top lip, as he gaped at the vision from Hubble's main wide screen scope. The blunt nose and midriff of the

Shuttle was poking from the belly of the Sphere in some cosmic mimicry of a birthing process, Sagan falling from the object in the same place it entered, although its direction of travel was reversed.

Jack breathed out in a rush of air, not even realising he'd been holding it. 'Well…damn, that was quick,' he said, unfurling his fists and relaxing his shoulders. 'Sagan, Houston Flight, copy?' Jack threw a sidelong glance at Pete, wondering what the in and out meant.

Static

'Vic this is Flight, do you copy?' Jack's jaw tightened as he tried to guess what was playing out up there, running some numbers in his mind, feeling his pulse hammering in his throat.

****

Harry asked Connie to help Sky who was still out cold, keeping one eye on what was happening outside. Pulling her gently back to a seated position, Connie balanced Sky against the bulkhead and the equipment port, feeling her pulse a little slow and thready but she seemed okay. By the paleness of her skin, Connie thought she might have carked it, succumbed to terror, literally scared herself to death. She'd never seen anyone so unhinged in her life and she was from SETI for Christ's sake! Go figure she said to herself disbelievingly. Picked the wrong one there, need to up the psyche assessments before they hit send on the letter of offer next time.

Becker saw space that looked familiar, but he realised it mightn't mean much because by familiar he meant black and not emblazoned with drugged up colours that meant nothing to any of them. 'We're back, right?' Becker said hesitantly, a smile ruffling his mouth, searching for a positive.

'Well by the look of the Moon, I reckon so,' Harry said upbeat.

'You sure we're not on another, uh…tour?' Becker said, raising an eyebrow nervously.

Harry eyed him square. 'Earth-Moon distance looks about right, all the majors are there, no new craters, I can see no big ones anyway.'

'Is that it?' Connie quizzed, feeling a disconcerting fluttering in her chest, hoping Harry had something a tad more ironclad to back up his statement.

Look…there,' he said abruptly, a little miffed, pointing down. 'That shadow is the Antares lander from Apollo 14…now there's no Moon cities or satellite grids up here so I'd say we're not far back or very far forward.' He winked at Connie, 'Anything on S-band?' Harry said, glancing at Vic.

'Shit,' Connie thought pensively, that didn't convince her one bit, it was nebulous at best. Even a hundred years either way would completely screw them up, didn't this guy get that?

'Only static but it's showing off-line,' Vic said.

'Run the self-diagnostic, get it up!' Harry said sharply.

'Already on it,' Vic said, 'here it comes.' He watched the green bands light up, '…sixty…eighty…system's nominal.'

Radio transmission started immediately, they got the backend of something from Houston. '…you copy?'

Harry bounced back to his seat, punching the PTT button. 'Well fuck me Jack, you're a voice…you sound fantastic.' He grinned widely at Vic. Yes, he mouthed to Skylar who'd finally come around, smiling weakly through swollen, red eyes. 'Thank you God,' she whimpered silently, taking a slow, deep breath. Tears pooled in her eyes, overflowing and floating away.

'Copy that!' Jack said loudly, punching a fist in the air. 'Great to have you back buddy.' Good old Harry, he mused, NASA's biggest cowboy, best goddamn shuttle commander.

'What've we missed Flight?' Vic asked, tensing his body, hoping nothing had escalated since they'd been kidnapped from orbit all those days ago. His heart was in his mouth as he braced for rotten news. Everything looked okay, by Jack's voice it sounded okay, but was there something they hadn't told them? The Spheres were still in lunar orbit, looking exactly as he remembered, a string of pearls hugging the grey talcum in the near distance.

Jack puckered his mouth, pressing a hand to his forehead, wondering what the hell he was talking about. "What?" He mouthed to Pete who looked equally mystified.

'Houston, I say again, what did we miss?' Vic repeated, getting increasingly nervous at Flight's silence. Looking at Harry he shook his head almost imperceptibly. S-Band was fine, four green bars.

Jack said, 'ah, Sagan, you've been gone about two minutes…what did you miss?' He said, tilting his head. 'What was inside the Sphere Harry?' Jack held his breath again, waiting for something mind-blowing because brief it might have been, but there was still time for something to have happened…an encounter…was contact out of the question? Maybe a brief hello we see you, an even quicker goodbye. Jack's heart was drumming as he waited for the crew to respond.

Everyone aboard Sagan peered at Harry. 'What the hell?' He mumbled, lost for words.

'He said five minutes,' Connie blurted, taking a sharp breath.

'No he said two minutes,' Harry corrected.

'What is he talking about…we all remember what happened out there…right?' Connie said, staring uncertainly at Vic, taken aback by the unexpected words.

Becker stared at her blankly, trying to think, 'we were gone at least five days…five days, not a few stupid minutes. What the hell is he banging on about? He looked almost bug-eyed as he fumbled with the nonsense.

'Flight, you said two minutes…we were out of contact two minutes, copy?' Harry asked evenly, having heard clearly, but doing the NASA thing. 'Flight, repeat out of contact time?'

'Two minutes, a few seconds.'

Vic assumed there was a symmetry break buried inside the object, perhaps collapsing, opening or unfolding spacetime into something they had no understanding of. It felt like they were there for a lifetime but time was relative, Vic got that…not like Einstein, but as well as anyone alive.

'Er, yeah okay, copy Flight.' Harry disengaged the comms system by flipping the PTT switch on the avionics panel and thumping the XPNDR button.

Harry's skin paled as he searched for meaning amid the steep contradiction. 'So…okay, we were gone two minutes their time but we experienced the best part of what…a week out there? We didn't imagine all that…?' He glanced rapidly around the group, 'no…of course not.' Becker and Connie were bordering on starvation when they were picked up, Harry knew there was no way a hunger like that was built in a few minutes. There was a very serious, real disconnect here.

'Do we tell Houston?' Skylar muttered, groaning as she got to her feet. 'They'll think we've cracked…I don't think I'd believe it to be honest. If someone blurted that, um…stuff…no way, I'd call bullshit on it.'

Vic had been typing away on his remote Citrix terminal for a while, his face melding through various shades of confusion and puzzlement as he went, like he was working on a math problem that was really jerking him around. Connie had been watching him on and off for five minutes, his countenance had her intrigued.

'What's going on with you?' She finally quizzed, watching him tapping frenetically on the keyboard. Glancing up, he lowered his brow and focused.

'I've been trying to figure out why we were taken to these places, these times…you know, find a clue, some insight, God forbid some meaning.' He scratched an eyebrow roughly with two fingers. 'Were they random places or was there some cryptic meaning we needed to pick up on…maybe some alien whimsy spiriting us to these long-gone places for reasons unknown.' Vic's eyes were burning as he tap-tapped his fingers next to the keyboard impatiently. 'We need to catch a break or we're gonna be in the dark forever.'

'Well, you're gonna blow a valve if you keep it up,' Connie said with a sigh. 'There's no way we'll ever know unless they bob up from somewhere and tell us.'

'Or give us some clues we can work with,' Harry offered seriously.

Vic looked at his console quizzically, frowning, fidgeting. 'Well there's actually a few problems with our experience,' he said cautiously, 'that make no sense…and just maybe that's where the sense is.' Vic's eyes were glazed, lost in thought, his voice rifling a bit on the last few words.

'Problems?' Harry probed, 'how so? I know you think you're a physicist but seriously, some of the left-field crap you come up with is—'

'I've confirmed it on the web Harry, from various sources actually,' he said, looking at Harry with slitted eyes. 'If we apply what we know of science then things are a bit, well…askew.' 'Oh, on the web, shit why didn't you say,' Harry snorted, rolling his eyes slowly upward, '…that's never been wrong. Jesus Christ, are you serious? My good wife, and I say that advisedly, diagnosed herself on WebMD, raced out and bought a big-arsed life policy for something that turned out to be a fucking insect bite. Your all-knowing Internet diagnosed her with metastatic melanoma…down there. And this is where you got your intel?' Harry stared at him stiffly.

'Relax, these sources are impeccable, Stanford, Cambridge and the like. Give me some credit,' Vic said, irritated by his insulting rhetoric. 'It's not bloody Wikipedia.'

'Whatever, just spill it,' he said crankily.

Becker surveyed Harry closely, feeling heat flush through him. 'You're a piece of work Bowden,' he said abruptly, 'at least he's thinking, not just bad-mouthing for the sake of it.' Becker was sick and tired of Harry's bullshit, steeling a glance at Connie, freely conceding that he himself could be a prick but this guy took it to another level.

'So, what have you got?' Becker asked lightly, throwing a final scowl at Harry who was now focussed on the fore window panel, ignoring everyone.

'Well, two things and a third that's, uh…probably not so important.' Vic was screwing his face up thoughtfully. 'They make no sense if we apply our own thought process but the bottom line is that we experienced them and quite unreasonably, survived them with no ill effects. I have zero in terms of explanation but the simple fact is that the math doesn't work. I've thought about it every which way but I can't explain it…well, unless it's our science that's screwed.' He paused momentarily, glancing at the screen. 'Which it isn't…in my view.' Vic looked up, watching them absently for a bit, chomping on the inside of his cheek.

Connie shifted her hand roughly to her hip. 'Okay, give it to us Vic, ignore your mate over there and tell us what you've got.' Glancing at Harry sideways she pressed her finger to her lips. She would seriously go-him if he interrupted.

'Okay,' Vic started, steepling his fingers. 'Connie you told us about the blue foliage on Mars.' She nodded perfunctorily. 'Well blue is wrong…red perhaps, even black, and of course green. The most unlikely colour for anything trying to rip energy from a star like the Sun is blue, so how…why was it blue?' His eyes widened a little, then narrowed. 'Evolution is haphazard at best but it will always head down the most advantageous path, eventually, and we're not talking some mutant blue weeds on a hilltop here.' He squinted knowingly at Connie and Becker, 'it was a bloody rainforest enveloping the planet like a blanket right?' Vic was straining, fighting for control as his mind sprinted ahead, searching for answers.

Harry was looking at Vic disdainfully. While he respected, even loved Vic in his own way, he wouldn't be shown up by his younger comrade, he was the flawed genius on this tugboat. 'No,' Harry said abruptly, 'evolution will do crazy things on different worlds, be sure of it. What is senseless to us, probably makes sense elsewhere, different conditions and so on. Evolution is relative, driven by local circumstance.' Harry was pretty sure he nailed it. Put simply, a wider perspective was needed, not just a one-planet view because one size most definitely didn't fit all.

Vic wagged his head, almost laughing out loud but held it in, in deference to his commander and friend. 'Harry, blue light has the most energy so leaves, plants, biology will want it…they won't reflect what is the tastiest, it makes no sense. It doesn't matter if you're on Earth, Mars or somewhere in the Sombrero Galaxy.'

'Anything can happen,' Harry said firmly, staring him down.

'Blue plants are impossible,' Vic said loudly, jerking his chin up, 'Earth, alien, uh…whatever,' he added slightly more calmly.

Harry flinched when Vic raised his voice, realising how edgy he was and how serious Vic was with this colour crap.

'Ninety nine percent of all species that have drawn breath are now extinct, that says something pretty damn important,' Vic said firmly, eyeballing him.

'Yeah…evolution is stupid,' Harry muttered, having heard enough, feeling a little unappreciated. He knew he was being petulant but was too tired to give a shit.

'It came up with you Bowden so I'm onboard with that,' Becker trumpeted. Harry flashed him a middle finger, looking back at Vic churlishly.

'Oh Christ Becker, don't. You'll never win,' Connie cautioned with veiled contempt.

'What are you saying?' Becker shrugged disarmingly, scrunching his mouth up sarcastically, looking wounded.

'Don't try and compare brain pans is all I'm saying. It won't end well.'

Harry flashed a beard splitting grin at her. Connie was a beaut, sticking up for him, making him feel slightly more valued.

'Okay,' Vic said, 'let's all take a breath here, there's nothing personal in all this, just my opinions…which um, happen to be right.' Vic smiled at Harry who returned the favour, nodding dryly. 'So there's no way evolution is going to spit out a planet-load of blue plants…maybe a few short-lived ones but not that lavish forest, no way, nu uh.'

'Okay fair enough,' Harry offered, sneering slightly, 'what's the second pearl of wisdom you've got hiding in there?' Harry's response was dripping with sarcasm, something his NASA counsellor referred to as "inaffection auto-pilot". Load of double talk mumbo jumbo he reckoned.

'Oh God, pull your head in,' Connie snapped, 'are you so dumb you don't realize this might be important? None of us have any idea what this is about, so listen and play nice.'

'Nice? Harry shot back, chuckling under his breath. 'Is it do as I say not as I do? Is that how it is, I mean seriously, that's a joke right?' He was trying to work her out, suddenly aware that he had no idea at all. She was a mystery, inconsistent, unpredictable, surly as hell.

'Screw you Bowman,' she spat back, turning away roughly.

'Okay, okay,' Becker said, holding up a palm. 'Let's see where he's going with this.' He only half understood the first bit but at least it was an advance on what they had before.

Vic looked at Harry ominously, 'how old did you say the Earth was…roughly?'

'A billion years, give or take,' he said. 'The Moon, continents, I reckon that's about right.'

Vic recalled the young Earth they'd travelled to, his memories already like spun gossamer drifting in the breeze, lacking any sweep of cognitive inertia at all. The bricks that supported his life felt like they'd been pried loose, the footings wobbling on friable clay, waiting for the slightest zephyr to finish the job.

'At the risk of alarming you,' Vic said softly, 'oxygen levels, by every paleoclimatic report, were around four percent, possibly less. You and I'll pass out at ten and die quickly at five...cerebral hypoxia, aneurism, foaming at the bloody mouth, death.' He glanced at them suspiciously. 'The conditions on Earth should have been way beyond Everest…yet somehow they weren't.'

'So we should've died out there?' Connie said, squishing her eyebrows together as she batted around the unsettling nonsense.

'That's pretty much it in a nut shell,' Vic said, 'should be dead but aren't. In deference to Harry I won't ask why, because who the hell knows right?'

Harry nodded, giving him a quick salute of thanks.

'Goddamn it,' Becker groaned, 'okay, so what's the third one, the um, less important one.' He was starting to feel something sharp gnawing at him. Conspiracy came to mind but in what form he had no idea, the word just appeared from the depths of his mind, much like the effects of an Indian Tindaloo on his gut. It came with little warning and was quite overpowering.

'This isn't much,' Vic said in a murmur, 'but there was no ozone layer so we were right in the firing line, UV rays would've monstered our DNA, slowly but seriously…permanently.'

Becker was losing the small slice of patience he had to start with. Metaphysical bullshit, the lot of it, he thought and based on what, the scientific fancy of some overblown geek with a microscope and rock hammer. 'So if none of this was actually possible, what's the answer? I say we don't know enough about it to know how it was. The nerds and pencil necks got it wrong, I think we've proven it by the simple fact that our ugly mugs are still here. We're alive right…hello?' He looked himself up and down, glancing at Connie with a boyish grin.

'Mentally or physically?' She asked without missing a beat. 'Your heart's pumping but on the former I think the jury's out. Lights are on but—'

'For God's sake,' Vic bellowed, 'palaeo-fucking-sulphate evidence doesn't lie, it's written into the planet like hieroglyphics.' Vic looked like he was trying to swallow something big but couldn't quite get it down, scratching his forehead with a single finger. 'For Christ's sake…blue plants, almost no oxygen or ozone and some black whatever that digested half the planet.' He finished a little out of breath, still tossing it around, gobsmacked. 'Then the Sphere apparently undoes the bloody lot and then fuck me if the Universe doesn't end in what for all money looked like a big crunch.' Vic pressed the side of his palm into his brow and raked hard. 'Can anyone read anything into this stuff, does it mean something as a collective, individually, sideways maybe, a theme, a clue…like anything?' He paced back and forth slowly, surveying them solemnly, searching their eyes, seeing that nothing was forthcoming as he expected. This stuff was so rarefied, so off-script it was beyond anything reasonably imaginable. They were a smart group but this was beyond the pale.

Opinions, speculations were wall-to-wall but no one wanted to give the questions life, if only to avoid Harry's ire, because sure as shit there were no answers. Was it just some messed up alien self-gratuity, a cat and mouse game, the rules and the end-game a total mystery? That was top of mind because all things considered, everything pointed toward a less than satisfactory outcome. There wasn't a single shred of positivity in any of it, leading Connie to the only answer she reckoned she had a grip on - they were fucked.

***

A sudden lurching sensation sent Becker, Connie and Skylar sprawling forward toward the nose of the craft, only managing to stay upright with the help of their lock and key footwear.

'Again?' Sky barked. 'Seriously…again…already?' She said in a guttural rush. 'Vic engage the—' Skylar tapered off mid-sentence, knowing resistance was useless.

'I don't…um, shit,' Connie moaned, meeting Sky's gaze, shaking her head grimly. 'I've had it with this.' She gazed vacantly into thin air, pain glittered in her eyes. Connie was breaking like the rest of them but Sky was the worst off by a fair margin.

Harry and Vic agreed that stirring the Magneto engines, even if they withdrew the graduation controls, would be as fruitless as conventional tet-hyrdrazine. There was no busting away from this thing. If they'd learned anything that was it, the Sphere's death grip was implacable.

'Sagan, you copying?' Jack's voice was loud and shrill on the S-band.

Vic threw his head set on. 'Go Flight,' he returned, looking stoically at Harry. 'Yes we're moving, no, we're not initiating it,' he said sharply, guessing what Jack's first words would be.

'MPS, full burn.' Jack said quickly, demanding main engines.

'Negative Flight,' he said dismissively, seeing main engines still at fifty-five per cent liquid propellant. 'This thing has us…there's no getting away from it.' Harry nodded and shrugged reluctant agreement.

'You need to try, for God's sake you can't just give up. Try RCS full gimbal for a lateral burn, FIDO thinks that might break it, or fore OMS full—'

Vic terminated comms, discarding his headset.

'They just don't get it,' Harry said. 'Jugheads,' he added tersely.

158

'Here we go again,' Connie said unsteadily, seeing their destination ahead of them like a big fat helium balloon, coming straight at them.

Skylar's limbs were shaking. She tried to pare back her breathing by focussing on her daughter, imagining her face, the lop-sided dimple in her cheek when she smiled, but her mind refused to yield. It swept back to end-time delivered by a civilisation that cared nought for the things humans held precious. Sky tried to focus on carefully reasoned logic, that these others wouldn't harm another intelligence. Bollocks she decided bitterly,, because the bastards had slaughtered Quincy and Joe without a backward step. She swore under her breath, grabbed her head firmly with both hands and pressed it hard, praying to any God who might be looking her way.

***

The Sphere loomed at them once more but this time it was the fleshy colour of a deep-sea salmon and its surface patterning was way off. It was more of a geometric lattice setup made of tiny elemental points, variably switching between lighter and darker orange.

Vic reckoned they could have passed as intricately laid dominoes collapsing in all directions, then remaking themselves to repeat the process all over again, in a different drop pattern.

Harry drew his lips in and sucked on his beard, chewing like a cow gently nibbling on its cud. 'Here we go ladies and gentlemen, first floor…careful of the first step, it's a fucking killer.'

'Here we go,' Vic said uneasily, debating Harry's state of mind, quickly conceding that humour was his defensive M O. He just wasn't very good at it.

Connie inhaled deeply through her nose and held it as the shuttle hit the Sphere. Sky's plaintive stare was clouded with swelling tears, slowly falling away into the cabin, spreading like a shower of tiny, glistening meteors.

***

Gazing at the planet it was like beholding death itself, a vision more repellent and sadder than anything they'd seen. Earth from close orbit was a sapphire jewel, speaking to victory over incalculable odds. Below them though, it was distressing in the most acute way imaginable.

'Well we really fucked things up didn't we?' Connie said, trying to reconcile the planetary debacle below.

'It's a goddamn wasteland…there's nothing left,' Harry said, sighing dejectedly. 'Well, humanity's gone,' he added, looking like he'd been struck in the face with something heavy.

Below them was a planet that had clearly seen the fires of Hades pass across it, the atmosphere an anorexically thin haze drifting only a few kilometres above the burnt surface. The oceans were gone, the continents lifeless charcoal silhouettes with long gone fluvial systems cutting the landscape into intricate filigrees of devastation. The only sign of life was the mid-oceanic ridges, still chugging along, glowing in molten crimson, magma still forcing its way to the surface and pushing relentlessly at the lifeless continents. The most confronting part of the world was a chunk that was quite simply gone, like a massive asteroid strike but way too symmetrical. Stranger still, where the piece was missing there was no sign of subsurface structure at all, the guts of the planet was just forebodingly black, no texture, it was like looking at a hunk of outer space, inside Earth.

Becker's face was plastered to the window panel, searching for something he recognised, or remotely understood. 'So, like…when is this?' He said in a hollow whisper, 'this is the future?' He stared poker-faced, tossing around why they'd been brought to this awful, godless place.

'Well done Becker,' Harry said, nodding cynically. 'What gave it away?'

'Okay smart arse, stow it.' Brainpans, he hadn't forgotten.

Giving an exaggerated sigh, Connie said, 'does anyone have a clue because if we can work out when, maybe we get an idea why.' She looked at Harry who was staring blindly at the planet below.

159

'Look I'm sick of asking stupid questions,' Vic said awkwardly, but seriously, why show us this…the remnants of our home, the cradle of us…why shove it in our face?' He paused for a moment, rubbing his brow with a knuckle, stewing on the ounce of Intel they thought they had. 'Whoever, whatever we're dealing with, well…if we didn't know it before we absolutely know it now.' Vic was pacing around, tapping his mouth. 'There is something seriously off about this…cold-blooded, inhuman…call it what you like but make no mistake, something is way off-plan here.'

Harry gazed at the pitiable rock below, then at the Moon, scanning the depths of space in front of them, peering emptily. 'I remember when the Moon was the dead one…I liked that more,' he sighed, continuing to stare for a full minute in contemplative silence, taking everything in, trying manfully to process it. 'Do you wanna know what I reckon?' Harry finally said, surveying the group.

'No,' Becker said flatly, followed by a single exasperated profanity from Connie who thrust her jaw sharply at him.

Harry raised his eyes then lowered them. 'I don't want to tread on any precious toes or delicate majority-rules sensibilities,' he said pointedly, glancing at Connie then Sky woodenly.

Connie instantly rued having shut Becker up. 'You know Bowden, you and I have a real problem,' she said, clenching a fist as hard as she could by her side.

'Maybe,' Harry said brusquely, 'but we're in a sardine can so we probably need to find a way around that. Murder in space is bad.' He blew his cheeks out and gave a bleak, thin-lipped smile, adding to the niggle.

Connie closed her mouth, the tightness in her chest and rush of heat in her core telling her how close to murdering him she was. Her mind's eye view was sweet, marching up to him, maybe kneeing him in the balls, bringing him down like an African heifer. Displaying his irritating moosh on the wall of her Bondi cabin would suit her fine.

Becker saw her jerky head movements and jumped in. 'Bowden, finish what you were saying,' he prodded hastily. 'We've shifted forward, we get that, how far?' He was hoping to see her unwind a bit but her almond-shaped eyes were still boring into Harry, daring him to push her just once more. She was perched cat-like, waiting for a prod, one more smart-arse jibe and she'd reach down and rip 'em off, figuratively at least. They could adorn the cabin wall along with his melon.

Becker nudged Connie and made eye contact, lowering his eyebrows to warn her off. She nodded almost imperceptibly, indicating she'd play along for the moment.

'Let's not get too sciency,' Vic said to Harry, smiling. 'You're the space guru, I'm the physics dropout right? So don't make me feel too much like a lesser species.'

'But you are lesser,' same species, definitely lesser,' Harry smirked. You, uh…know I don't really mean that right? He could feel Connie's eyes burning into him, quite aware she was the punch first, ask questions later type…plus she was right behind him.

'Just go, speak,' Vic said impatiently.

He took a loud breath, 'okay, so you probably know what the raised pieces of land down there are…the sad bits of burnt toast.' He drooped an eyelid at them, nodding, 'the oceans are gone but I don't think they've been gone long, you can still see stains from the waterlines on the continental shelves,' he said matter of factly, pointing through the fused glass.

'Jesus,' Connie groaned, sounding like she was in serious pain, 'what happened to them…the creeks, rivers, er…oceans? It's so dead…horrible.' She turned away, looking at Becker expressionless, not knowing what to make of it, real, not real? It sure as hell looked the genuine deal.

Harry ignored her, 'you can still make out Antarctica above Australia, Africa with Asia, South America next to it. See Florida there, Cape York? He said, jabbing the air, glancing back at the others to see if they were following him. 'It's a continental jig-saw gone completely off the rails.'

'Hell, if there were oceans,' Becker murmured obscurely, 'no need for boats, right?'

'Yup,' Harry agreed, playing ball, 'just one giant chunk of real estate.'

They craned their heads forward as they flew directly over the ominous dark hole, seeming more and more like empty space the closer they got.

It's not like any impact crater I've ever seen,' Sky said haltingly, turning from the window panel to Harry, eyes still swollen from crying.

'Agreed, it's like nothing I've ever seen, maybe that's where the, er…accident happened that junked everything.'

'How far?' Becker asked impatiently, 'you know…in the future? Humans are gone so, how long have we got?' He cupped his mouth and placed the other arm across his chest nervously.

'Oh Christ,' Harry replied crankily, 'we could have blown ourselves up a day, a year, a century after we left, no one can answer that. But seeing South America pushed up against Africa is interesting. I know the plates move a couple of centimetres a year, but they may have been stuck together like this for, well…who knows? I mean, there's nowhere for them to go unless they split apart again.' He wiped perspiration from his forehead with a flourish. A headache was looming, he could feel it behind his eyes, way too much thinking.

'So what do you reckon then?' Connie asked quickly. 'Enough of the posturing, just spill it, tell us what you think…guess.'

'Two or three billion,' he said, 'give or take a lot.'

Becker let out a huge exhalation of air. His brain tried to get hold of it but it was a flapping cod in a bucket of oil. Everything was rattling around, condensing into nothing more substantial than a cotton wafer.

Sky was trembling and squirming, sitting herself slowly on the floor, ramping her knees up to her chest as she wobbled ever so slightly, wringing her hands. 'So we're the last humans, um…left?'

'Not so sure about that,' Harry trailed off.

'You mean there's still life down there…like some of us?' Connie quizzed doubtfully, surveying the dark part of the planet below for the tell-signs of a civilisation. The thought of anything alive on the dead husk seemed ridiculous, it looked deader than dead, especially with the ragged bite taken out of it.

'Nah – Earth looks cooked,' Harry said, curling his lip down, 'there might be something alive but nothing more than bacteria.'

'So what the hell are—'?

'Look far right then left, 'Harry interrupted. 'You've been so focussed on that down there you haven't noticed. What do you see…look closely at what's out there?' He studied each of them curiously, wondering if they'd get it.

'There's two blue lights out there, I mean really blue…like s-sapphires in the darkness,' Connie stammered. Was that good or bad, she had no idea.

'That's gotta be Venus and Mars,' Harry spruiked, 'meaning they've been terraformed and by the look of them they're probably richly atmospheric with the good stuff, you know, running over with life.'

'So we've moved planets…left Earth?' Connie asked, sounding confused. It didn't make sense - why leave when they had the power to terraform?

'Seems so,' Harry said, 'although it could be anyone or anything out there.

Skylar suddenly looked up, meeting his eyes unsteadily, 'if it's us, that would put humans beyond a Type Four, um…on the Kardashev scale.' She visibly swallowed, looking nervous. 'At SETI we use it to model likely contact scenarios. We're a Type Zero but after so many billions of years, if that's really us out there, Jesus, we should be immortal, technically, well…omnipotent. Of course it's just a theory,' she said, shifting her gaze back to the floor.

'Omnipotent…what, like Gods?' Connie breathed with a shaky laugh.' It sounded comical, but at the same time her mind was battling with broken images of such ludicrous advancement.

'Well…Gods might be underselling it a bit actually,' Sky said with a glint in her eyes, straightening herself a bit, pleased to be able to add something a little insightful. 'We should be able to slice open spacetime, be able to transport ourselves wherever we liked, pick open time, dark matter, take the energy from every piece of matter in the Universe, even be able to fiddle with entropy. Basically there'd be few, maybe no limits.' Sky got awkwardly to her feet, a little unsteady on the way up. 'Sounds, um…nuts I know, it's sort of like an intellectual equation that says a shitload of time will exponentially expand the collective IQ of a species, assuming it didn't destroy itself along the way. Eventually it would allow mastery of things we can barely imagine.' She sucked in a sharp breath as she finished, gazing from one blue light to the other, weighing up the likelihood and despite herself, feeling a little awestruck.

Harry was sceptical because he didn't think humanity would last another hundred years let alone billions. What about the wars, the sectarian bullshit, the racial, social disorders, global terrorism, population explosions in the east, food shortages, nanotech gone mad…fucking asteroids. You name it, it was either snowballing on Earth or coming at them from space. There was a thousand ways we could be brought down, Murphy's Law was irresistible and Mother Nature was a surly, malevolent bitch with extinction on her mind. It could be one, two of them, or a combo that did the job, reckoning some crazy fuck would eventually nuke New York and start everything tick-tocking toward a rather grisly end.

The direction they were heading in seemed pretty much terminal to him but then, go figure he thought, nothing was done till it was done. Listening to Skylar and apart from Becker, they all recognised the new possibilities the blue lights might represent.

So the whole sorry tale might be fundamentally different from what they'd initially thought, Vic mused, still deeply vexed and uneasy. They used the term *others,* threw it around like rock candy, but maybe that was the wrong word entirely.

Connie was the first one to give it oxygen, hesitating, then speaking in a flood of words, 'we all get it right? This Type Four thing I mean, what we've seen inside the Spheres, the time-shifts and—' She stopped talking and seemed to pan a new idea from the muddle in her brain.

Becker turned his gaze to Connie, dragging his eyes from space. 'So those two planets…I mean, we've spread through the Galaxy…the Universe?'

'If it's Type 4, we're talking everywhere,' Skylar said, 'assuming it's human occupation.'

Connie looked up suddenly, 'hang on, you mean Earth might have been given—'

'I mean, Earth might have been wiped out by visitors who moved on and made themselves at home on Mars and Venus,' Sky said, wrestling with the horror of such a hostile takeover.

Surely not, Connie thought it wasn't possible but she knew it was as soon as the words were out. If these events taught them anything about space it was just that, what they considered impossible was now undeniably possible.

Vic had heard enough bullshit, time to cut to the chase. 'So we're saying there's a chance these so-called *others*…that they might be us in the future? That there's no aliens, only humans with a technology congruent with magic…like gods?' He looked dumbstruck, almost like he'd dropped into a hypnotic trance, shaking his head sharply to recover himself a bit. 'So maybe these Spheres and all the rest of it were engineered by what…post-humans?' Vic said, wearing a condescending smile, not buying it for a second. 'Come on for Christ's sake,' he exclaimed, eyeballing them one by one. Anything might have been possible he reminded himself, but seriously, that?

Connie initially saw some sense in it, but was acutely uncertain because if it was true then it seemed to make even less sense. If they were human then their logic should be like ours, at least vaguely. So why all the crap that made absolutely no sense, starting with the remote envoys…the artefact under the ice? Of course there was the small issue of what billions of years of evolution might do to the brain. That was a big *fuck knows* she thought, not bothering to even weigh in on it.

'Yes,' Sky eventually said, looking like she might cry again, wiping a tear into the air. 'It could be us.' If that was right it was a concept even bigger than they thought.

'So what happened to Earth?' Vic said, struggling to believe it, 'why the hell are Venus and Mars terraformed and Earth left behind like a discarded meat tray?' He peered at Harry, raising a thinly haired eyebrow.

No one could offer anything meaningful, the best theory suggested by Harry was that humanity terraformed Mars before whatever killed off Earth started in earnest. Then they high-tailed the best and brightest to Mars and after that made a home of Venus. And then continued the rise to technical providence, spreading beyond the solar system into the heart of the Galaxy. And maybe nothing could be written off.

'So why the hell terraform Venus and not rebuild Earth?' Becker asked, 'it was closer, had to be a little—'

Harry was getting impatient with the never-ending Q&A sessions that seemed to be dominating their entire existence. 'Look, who knows, maybe Earth was screwed on some fundamental level, there must have been a good reason but we'll never know it.'

Becker disengaged, not in the mood for a fight, peering down, feeling despair sweep through him, even though none of them were sure how real any of it was. Real, unreal, it was still achingly sad to see their cradle of life so horribly scorched, devoid of water, air, life, a planetary corpse of the most disturbing kind.

Becker caught movement from the corner of his eye, spinning his head toward it, closing his eyes and quickly reopening them. There was definitely something moving. 'There!' He said, sweeping his arm down, gesturing them over. 'Look,' Becker urged, still jabbing vigorously at something on the surface. 'The hole, um…something moved, the whole damn thing moved I think.' He was staring at it fixedly, willing it to become clearer.

'Oh Jesus,' Connie muttered, peering at him disdainfully like he was high on something. They could see Earth was as dead as dead, no bloody way there was anything alive down there, it was a depressing crematorium.

Despite that, Skylar picked it up too, joining Becker, staring straight at it. 'Yes…there,' she said, finger tracing it uncertainly, 'it's moving…doing something, the edge is, uh…unstable, like it's caving in maybe.'

'No, I think it's vibrating…well sort of,' Connie said, not really having a clue what she was seeing, the sight unlike anything within her frame of reference. It looked to her as though a gargantuan coal mine was being gradually consumed by flying soot and coal dust, like there'd been a monumental collapse deep within that was forcing uncountable tonnes of blackness to the surface.

Harry looked closer, 'It's getting smaller…uh, closing on itself.' He squinted through slits, 'wait, shit, is it repairing itself?' He uttered, struggling to get a grip, it was a question, he knew, but at least it was qualified. The tremendous bite mark seemed to be reforming from the inside out, like a healing flesh wound set to rapid fast-forward.

'Definitely repairing.' Vic agreed, 'but how?'

Harry clenched his jaw, wagging his head. 'Oh right, sorry,' he pushed his shoulders up, shooting him a smirk. 'Old habits.'

***

They stood at the window of the shuttle, seeing the Sphere rise over the top of the Moon on a congruent orbit to Sagan. It was definitely approaching, doing so slowly, almost stealthily, cat and mouse like, Connie thought uneasily.

'Time to go,' Harry assumed.

'Apparently,' Vic agreed, solemnly.

Connie hadn't taken her eyes off what was happening below, death and regeneration seemed to be a repeating theme because Earth was mending itself before their eyes, like a movie playing in reverse, effect before cause. The colossal hole was gone, the mighty ocean returning around the globe, atmospheric eddies visibly thickening and white clouds condensing around a swiftly ripening world. Transforming from charcoal to mahogany, the landmass was now swathed in vivid greens of majestic forests, the whites of snow on the peaks of active mountain ranges. Complex

163

fluvial systems were returning to fill dead furrows, rivers and streams, lakes were everywhere beneath them. Everything brought with it a mudslide of questions that were torturously out of reach.

'Why are they showing us this?' Connie said, voicing a most blatant imponderable.

Harry groaned. How dumb were these people? He glared briefly at Connie, not saying a word, wary of her spiteful tongue. 'How long Vic?'

'Couple of minutes max,' he said, looking at the phased array radar data.

'Try and get away from it,' Harry said, 'see what the prick does.' Vic looked at him doubtfully, then grinned. Yeah, fuck 'em he thought, let's give these arseholes a run for their money.

'OMS gimbal test CRT,' he said. 'Complete, nominal.'

Skylar warned them against it but they shut her down. She didn't think pissing these creatures off, be they human or otherwise was a particularly well thought through plan.

'Going for a dual OMS burn, fore pods,' Vic said, referring to a parallel thrust vector. 'TVC yaw, pitch program in five seconds—'

The ship lurched backward as the conventional hydrazine boosters at the front of Sagan roared to life, lighting up space with burning plasma.

'What are you trying to do? Connie protested, 'tick them off? You can't be serious.' She peered uncertainly at Harry, then scowled, 'great strategy Bowden…piss off the race with the fucking death ray.'

'Five clicks…increasing,' Vic reported, stifling a snort.

'Velocity of bogey?'

'Increasing, maintaining three plus clicks, slightly higher than previous.'

'Okay, douse 'em. They want us inside on their time-line, like we thought.' Harry sighted the RRS. 'One minute.'

Earth had gone from a dark corpse to a living, breathing world in less than five incredible minutes. Everything that was inside them, that made them human, said it couldn't be done but the proof was in the eating and they had eaten like profligate pigs, roundly agreeing the madness appeared to be the real deal.

'Harry, block those Spock ears of yours,' Connie said with a derisive smirk. He turned his head, shaking it disarmingly, knowing what was coming.

'With you lot I knew there was no hope,' he said, wincing and faking pain. 'You know, with all this going on what do we have apart from asking questions. I mean, I get that…why, why, why right?' He repeated the words with growing irritation.

Connie was annoyed by his ridiculous preoccupation with what amounted to anti-curiosity. What a prick, she thought, he actually made Becker look caring and god forbid, almost thoughtful. 'Okay,' she blurted, 'but why don't—'

'I mean it,' he shouted, shutting Connie down. 'I don't think any of us are stupid, in fact as a group we're probably damn smart if it comes right down to it. Yet, none of this,' he raised his arms straight up, 'makes a goddamn lick of sense to you, you, you, or me.' He stabbed his finger at each of them, eyes steely.

'Maybe it's not meant to make sense,' Sky offered, seeing the torment on Harry's face. He looked like he was ready to blow an artery and keel over, maybe die in front of them. 'Um, perhaps it'll make sense later…maybe we'll find clues, insights at some point…you know, stumble over them.' Skylar spoke the words but doubted it, the whole frigging lot was so senseless it would probably stay that way forever.

Sagan was overrun by the Sphere, falling into it and vanishing high above the thick atmosphere of a perfectly refreshed Earth.

18. Lawless

**'As far as the laws of mathematics refer to reality, they are not certain;
and as far as they are certain, they do not refer to reality.'** ~ *Albert Einstein*

Skylar had been to the galley and retrieved a bunch of prepared meals that they were snacking on, some eagerly, others less so. Becker almost purred over the tortillas and ionised beef, eating with such gusto there were crumbs everywhere, on his lips, chin, and in a cloud of pieces around him. Connie winced at each bite, likening it to something having wriggled its way up from the recycling plant.

'Pew…sterilised beef…seriously?' Connie groaned, surveying the green Badura label on the plastic pouch. 'Tastes like something you'd feed a dog.'

'You had experience with that Con?' Becker chortled, not moving his eyes an iota from the meal he reckoned was as good as a thousand-dollar Fleur Burger.

'You seem to be inhaling that stuff so I'd say you're the one with the dog love.'

'Hurtful,' he said, pursing his lips and lowering his eyes as though mortally wounded.

'Just truthful big guy…now finish your food, there's a good boy.' She poked at him.

'Well if this is dog food, I'm in for a pound,' Becker said, smiling proudly.

Connie smirked, handing Becker a brown bag that looked like a doggy-doo pouch. 'Here you go, chew carefully fella…might be bones,' Connie, giggled, realising he was making up for lost time, eating like a bear in the woods with not the slightest regard to appearances. Classic Becker.

'We're motoring,' Harry drawled, trying to work out why there was no sense of weight when the object started moving. Harry fought to disengage his brain but it was way too hard. Everywhere he looked there were bizarre visuals that kept him worrying, thinking, forever analysing, doubting. He'd keep his questions inside though, until or if, he ever managed to effort the slightest breath of insight. Relax, don't think, he implored himself, repeating it punitively several times, muttering into his beard, under his breath, darting his eyes around and wondering if he was finally going nuts.

The Moon was a distant memory but they were coming upon a blue light that was rapidly resolving into Mars, approaching it as though a telescope was flipping rapidly to higher and higher magnification.

Skylar focussed, her nerves forgotten for a moment as the stunning world took form. 'God the snow…the poles. It's so beautiful,' she trailed off, peering dumbly at the Eden-like world, heart pounding, thinking about life on the surface. The idea was disorienting in its scope and it brought the breathtaking anxiety crashing back.

'Green continents?' Becker said, opening his mouth to continue but closing it, struggling to find the right words. He wondered how many guises this crazy planet had. It had seen more script changes than a fucking Broadway show, he chuckled, feeling a sinking feeling in his gut.

Connie splurted something, a hand to her breast, '…blue and lush to blush and dead, then…um, Earthly green.' The astonishing paradox stared back at them, impossible to reconcile with the planet they'd visited not so long ago. She chided herself, not long ago was actually billions of years. The concept was completely lost in the ridiculous, having no sense of reality and zero mental traction. They were just words that skimmed off her cortex like stones bouncing off a pond.

'So, where are the inhabitants…the terraformers?' Connie said, seeing no signs of life, not even on the dark side that was approaching over the horizon. 'Shouldn't it be humming with the commerce of life? Shouldn't they be everywhere, cities, towns, ring systems, satellite networks and so on?'

'If they're as advanced as Sky thinks,' Vic said, 'maybe they've all left…gone off system.'

'Or maybe they don't leave a biological or EMAR footprint at all,' Harry offered glibly, 'unlike us dirty savages who slash and burn and leave their crap everywhere. Not to mention they probably don't belch their radiation into space. An advanced race may have no waste products at all, be a flat out zero on the environmental intrusion register.'

Nodding gently, thinking it through properly, they realised it made a little sense, an untouched wilderness didn't mean it wasn't populated.

Connie was at the side window panel, straining to make out any detail suggestive of life but there was nothing. She'd love to prove the jackass wrong but it wasn't happening, the dark side was just that, dark and the daylight side looked like virgin country. The planet looked untouched, it was beautiful, lush and alive but eerily empty. Harry actually made some sense and God forbid he might even be right.

Harry watched Mars vanish behind them, their breakneck speed moving them rapidly into the deeper solar system. Jupiter came and went in seconds and they came upon a bizarre gas giant no one had a clue about. It was stippled with beautiful concentric rings of colour but looked foreign to the solar system - had they somehow acquired a new planet? Connie had no idea, Harry nodded his head almost imperceptibly, staring at it. Wow, he thought. 'Saturn,' he said as they whipped past it on a course taking them below the solar plain, beyond the narrow ecliptic of the planets.

'Saturn?' Becker puzzled. 'But…oh…lost its rings, right?'

'Yep, sucked into the planet eons ago I reckon,' Harry said. 'Looks naked without 'em.'

Sky was still bum down on the floor of the shuttle, holding her head, agonising over their destination, knowing they wouldn't be able to predict it in a thousand lifetimes. Her daughter's innocent, pixyish face was everywhere in her mind. The concept of family, loved ones and the baffling events they were facing up here…it seemed like the most massive disconnect conceivable. Sky felt her sense of self slipping, brooding over how many ratchet-stops she had left until there were none left to save her from freefalling into the inky abyss.

***

'Um…you're seeing this right?' Connie asked, straining to keep her voice level, flitting her eyes around with a just-slapped look on her face. Harry tried to ignore it but the show outside was way too compelling. Eyebrows squashed into a single bushy line, he was struggling to equate it with something that added up in his mind, waiting for the click that was probably never coming.

'What does it mean?' Skylar mewed uneasily, 'is it real, or something else...maybe a lensing effect?' She had no idea but it was fearfully unbalancing.

Harry gritted his teeth, trying to block his ears with sheer will. Skylar was like a human question mark. Asking fine, but keep it inside or have a bloody theory about it at least.

Outside the Sphere, space had once again morphed into something quite implausible. Instead of darkness with various points of bright and not so bright light, there was now complete darkness to the sides of the shuttle. Literally no light, just the blackest black, extending as far back as they could see through the small side window panels. Connie had one eye on a tremendous blurry blue *something* ahead of them, the other on Vic to see what his take was. Being the level headed one, his body language was a pretty good gauge. The thing ahead was an almost solid mass of light that became gradually diffuse at the edges, fading and merging into the surrounding darkness of space.

'Safe to say we're going fast,' Harry said, perplexed by the bizarre visual outside. 'Relativistic effects I guess. Vic, you know this stuff, you're the pilot, the physics guy, what do you reckon?' He flourished a hand in his direction, wiggling a quizzical eyebrow at him.

Vic made several attempts to speak but no words came out. He tried to swallow the knot in his throat while he stared at *it* wildly, pushing deeper into his chair, scrutinising the view. 'Well, I think we're travelling, you know…close to the speed of light.' He glanced furtively at Harry who nodded gently. 'Doppler seems to be squashing everything together, but, shit, hang on…wait—'

'Motherfucker,' Connie splurted like a whip crack. 'Where'd it all go?' She jerked her head around in every direction, finally looking skittishly at Vic, unblinking.

The blueness ahead was gone and as it disappeared, a tremendous disc lit up like a glorious floodlight across their entire view of space, dazzling white this time.

Skylar cried out, no way she was looking outside now. That was it. She kept replaying the question in her mind, agonising over how she ended up on this ghastly carnival ride, fevering over why they were being forcibly exposed to things that meant absolutely dick to them.

Vic was battling to recall his Uni astrophysics. Chuck Boyden was his undergrad lecturer, he remembered the ridiculous comic detail, his wiry thinning hair, classic mad bastard features. What he'd taught him though, he was struggling to remember. Boyden loved aberration. Strange shit that could never happen because there were rules that forbade it. He was always looking at ways to bend the laws to make impossible things happen. 'Shit,' he cursed under his breath. Then he remembered EMAR reversal and the penny dropped like a steel block. 'Oh…w-wow,' Vic spluttered, swallowing thickly, 'this is worn out, I get that, but that…out there…um, is stone motherless impossible.' His cheeks looked like they were full of air as he puffed them out and released it with a drawn-out sigh.

'Okay, lay it down Vic.' Harry studied his tense expression. The boy wasn't prone to exaggeration and that worried him because something clearly had by him the balls. If it was a mystery to him, it was squarely fringe. Whether this was genuine or not he wasn't certain but it had every hallmark of being the genuine article. If it looked real and felt real…it was real. It passed the shit test.

Vic's eyes were open so wide it looked like he'd been shot full of adrenaline. 'Right or wrong I have no idea but the light from all the bits and pieces in front of us has been shifted to invisible wavelengths…X-rays and so on. And you've heard of the Cosmic Microwave Background…the left overs from the Big Bang that's all around in infra-red?' He nodded at them and they returned the gesture, Becker looking sheepishly to the floor, trying to remain inconspicuous, irritated by the geek-speak that made him look like a dill.

Connie glanced at him, stifling a full-blown laugh. Becker was trying to look serious, scholarly even and it just wasn't cutting it. He frowned at her, urging her back to Vic with his eyes. Bitch he thought sourly, outing him like that.

'So, all the infra-red has been shifted into light we can see, that's what the massive headlight out there is? Incredibly, it's the CMB…like now you see me. And everything previously visible has gone to X-ray so we can't see it.'

Becker's eyes lit up, 'so it's reverse-world,' he said, lifting his eyes, 'that's all you had to say…reverse world.'

'Struggling with the grown-up's language much? Connie said, lifting a mocking eyebrow.

He gestured to her in a most unsavoury fashion. 'Geek 101 you mean? If I ever become fluent, take me out and fucking shoot me,' he said with a bitter smile.

'Count on it.'

'Well, that's actually an apt description because reversal is precisely what it's about,' Vic said, nodding positively at Becker who broke into an arrogant grin. Take that, he thought, thrusting his chest out. He mightn't have both oars in the water when it came to science but he had his own brand of logic which he reckoned served him okay.

'Look,' Vic continued loudly, 'this stuff is only theory, I mean some things are meant to stay on a physicist's whiteboard because laws stop it happening for real.' He paused and rubbed his tired eyes with bent thumbs. 'Sorry but, uh…any takers on how this is happening?' No one had anything, Harry stared into thin air, sighing emphatically.

'Building the suspense?' Harry said, making no eye contact, patting his beard.

'We are definitely travelling faster than light,' he said evenly, hiding his bewilderment by squeezing his eyes into slits.

Harry smiled at him strangely. 'Okay then…anyone else. What about Albert and his glorious book? He weighed the idea briefly, knowing it was nuts, also knowing it was true.

'You might want to listen to him Harry,' she said, 'he's pretty much the smartest guy at NASA.' She gestured at Vic with a raised palm, 'how certain are you?'

'I'm right,' he said dramatically, 'It's the only thing that'll shift visible light to invisible and vice versa…Becker's reverse world. There's no other reasonable explanation.' He gaped, opening and closing his mouth, 'if you call it, um…reasonable.'

Harry glanced over his shoulder at Vic. Like he said it was impossible and there it was again, that fucking throw away. He'd quickly grown to despise it, seriously needing to expunge the word from his vocabulary, burn it at the stake…forget it as a concept. 'Fuck a duck,' Harry said under his breath. It felt like his reality had switched to a completely different frequency. Something was happening that was so much bigger than humans and their distant address, the outer 'burbs of the Milky Way on some wispy spiral arm known as Orion. Whatever this was, it was massive, he felt it deep within, bowel churning, disorienting and aching.

'I agree,' Vic said as firmly as he could muster. 'Einstein's work has been validated how many times? Near Earth, beyond Earth, distant reaches of the Universe by Hubble, Tyco and radio, it's there wherever we look. So how can we be going FTL? And yes, it's a question Harry and screw you, it needs to be out there.'

Harry nodded, half smiled. He almost got it.

While they were debating the unlikelihood of what they were seeing, space started to return to its friendlier disposition and Vic watched as the blue cone of light reappeared then vanished and the cosmos they knew emerged from the distortion and weirdness. Vic was happy to see the lingering radiation from the big bang returning to its familiar clandestine wavelengths. Not seeing it felt good he admitted. 'I was wondering if maybe we'd be stuck in FTL forever,' Vic said suddenly.

Connie's head shot forward. 'You honestly thought that?' Jesus, she said to herself, that hadn't even entered her mind.

'Not sure anything's off limits,' Vic said with a small nod, fatigue shadowing his face, making his voice husky. 'Where this is heading, none of us can know.'

'It's utter bullshit. How's that?' Connie offered glibly, enough she felt like screaming.

'You're doing fine,' Harry chipped in. 'Bottom line is that it also seems to be F-A-C-T. Impossible, nuts is the new black, right?' Harry chuckled under his breath, hiding a fathomless dread.

***

The Sphere started slowly rotating, bringing a different part of space into view through the shuttle windows. They soon realised that this time at least, they'd been brought here for a reason.

Sky gushed a series of expletives as her visual brain glimpsed it for the first time, cold sweat rising on her skin as she gaped at the grandeur and the awfulness of the construct in front of them. She dropped slowly to the floor.

Directly in front of Sagan, maybe a few thousand kilometres away was a Sphere similar to the one they were in…oh apart from the size! It was difficult to gauge its absolute dimensions but Harry thought it might be the size of the Moon, give or take a bit. Becker's barely audible words were "ape shit huge", the familiar checkerboarding conspicuous on its surface, squares switching with speed, in patterns careening around its surface like an almighty tide.

Sky mooned up from her untidy position on the floor, glancing timidly like a shrew at Harry then Vic. 'I want to go home,' she whimpered, feeling her legs shaking. 'I can't do this anymore. I'm done Vic, finished, over,' she shrilled the words unsteadily.

Vic could see what a mess she was but couldn't relent. 'It's not our choice, it's not like we're here voluntarily, we go home when they say we can, um, if they do.' Crap, he scolded himself, the last bit was out before he could pull back. Sky's haunted expression told him all he needed to know. He'd poked her good and there was no taking it back now.

'Christ is that what you think, that this time…that's it?' She looked around, eyes wild like an antelope in the moments between capture and the death bite.

'Uh, look…no one knows. We just need to hang tough, assume we'll get back, find what we can while we're here,' he said weakly, offering the feeblest of grins, knowing there was no way to backpedal from this shipwreck.

Sky murmured something, placing her head back in her hands, staring at the floor again, mumbling something and giving a fine impression of a lifer at a state sanitarium. Harry was up to here, and felt like shaking her until she snapped out of her crippling melancholia or whatever the hell it was. They were all in the same rotten boat, every one of them had to suck it up because options were as short as they got. All they had was whoever was standing next to them and if they didn't pull together they were done. So far they were doing a piss poor job of it he reckoned, antagonism, arguing, bitching. Harry knew he was part of the problem but yielding to Becker or for that matter, Connie, was beyond him. They'd have to find common ground somewhere, a shaky truce, a collective understanding. Maybe they were screwed anyway but it would make finding a way out so much harder he figured, gazing at the group miserably, sensing a feeling of fate already decided.

*****

Sky's mental state had been declining for days and was close to terminal collapse, one look was enough. She was shaking her head in tiny movements that were more like a convulsion or paroxysm. 'I need to get back,' she mewed again, 'the world I know, out of this…this nightmare.' Her voice was choked with emotion, tears flowing in a thickening stream. 'I need Alysha, she n-needs me.' Her shoulders were shaking, then heaving as she bit down on her lower lip, battling to hold back the sobbing.

Vic kept it quiet but knew their journey at impossible speed, if taken literally, meant that thousands of years might have slipped by on Earth, and everyone they'd ever known were, well…gone. All their families, their kids, even their kid's kids and their kids would be long dead. In fact, everything that was alive when they left, down to animals, plants and bacteria would be replaced by entire new generations. But equally, Vic had the feeling it might not be like that. He was suspicious of everything he saw, guarded at best. Sceptical? You bet your arse.

Sky was no fool and understood time dilation at relativistic speeds only too well. She squeezed it to the back of her mind, but she could feel the thoughts, black and heavy behind her eyes, swelling into something horrible, wedged sideways in her mind, making her think things, want to do things she never thought she would.

'Sky I'm so sorry,' Connie said softly, 'this is no place for anyone with a young family, although what this place is, well…its anyone's guess. It just might turn out okay though.' There was a chance, of course there was she told herself, but a fat one she reckoned, fessing up.

Peering up blearily at Connie she was going to say thank you but the words caught in her throat and she nearly choked on them. Sky coughed weakly several times, lowering her head without speaking, fighting to vacate her tangled mind. There was a scream in her lungs and a guttural desire to give it flight but she was terrified, because once it started, she was finished. It wouldn't be a release, it would be acknowledgement and a dark, one-way descent from her sense of self.

Connie watched Sky and felt like crying herself. She was such a wretched soul, slumped on the floor like a pile of ragged clothes. All of them were so acutely detached from loved ones, the pain was torturous and inescapable. And what if they did get home? Earth might be as good as alien, people, politics and ideologies utterly unfamiliar to them…if Earth was there at all.

*****

The object completely dwarfed them, Sagan so close now it presented as a planet completely swamping their horizon. The sheer bloody magnitude of the thing made their heads spin, and then there was the small issue of what might be waiting inside.

They were transiting directly toward one of its poles, near a permanent marking on the surface, so the question of inside would probably be solved soon enough Vic guessed, the skin drawing tight around his eyes as he probed their approach. It seemed to be the only aberration on the surface, a slightly darker patch of gunmetal grey, different from the greater Sphere, which was a silvery colour like antimony or platinum with a mildly radiant quality to it.

Harry opened his mouth and said nothing, words were irrelevant - they were at the whim of unknowable motivations, possibly so alien it rendered any form of contemplation moot. Harry was a veteran of space but this was out of his league, the events, the journey, made him feel permanently punch-drunk. Everything was dreamlike, blurred around the edges, a little off-centre, like reality had been tinkered with, tilted so you were always fighting to stay upright.

The small Sphere slid into its gargantuan equivalent right where the darker blemish was, like a pimple on a flawless face. Sagan immediately entered a boundless space dusted with light, not unexpected but it was still incredible as they passed into what appeared to be an endless interior.

The scope of the internal space, the sheer flat looking walls seemed to stretch to infinity, losing themselves in the mists of distance. Central to their view, in every direction were millions, maybe billions of things lined up end-to-end and side-to-side, parallel rows and columns in perfect geometric pattern. The individual structures swept up and out in every direction as Sagan motored down a narrow channel. On each side the stacked objects glistened in the soft twilight.

Connie whispered the obvious question, asking what the hell this place was. Individually they didn't look like much, but the astonishing number of them was completely overwhelming.

Surprisingly, Skylar hacked out some words, reckoning the whole thing looked like something she called an Amsler grid, which meant nothing to any of them. She explained it as tightly bunched horizontal and vertical lines opticians used to test for macular degeneration. Only difference Harry thought, was that this one was in three dimensions and the size of a fucking world!

'They sort of look like telescopes,' Becker said, hearing the words echo ominously around them. He looked knowingly at Connie, 'like the one in your office, but without the knobs and twirly things…just cylindrical er, somethings.'

'Jesus, spoken like a true scholar,' Connie said, twisting her lip down.'

'Yup,' Harry added, 'fat telescopes is what they look like,' he said, pushing his chin up, peering, 'but Jesus, the number.'

'So fluent in language, both of you, I'm impressed…where'd you go to School Harry?'

'Didn't,' he said wryly, 'oh wait, no, Brethren Reform School, you know for wayward kids, swearing, smoking and such.' His mouth curved with amusement.

Connie returned the smile, surprising herself.

'If you've finished,' Becker said impatiently, 'why so many?' He waited for Harry's reaction with interest.

Harry didn't engage, Becker was just like his question, moot and deeply vexing. He snorted in his direction, looking up, down, left, right, fighting to work out maybe a molecule of what they might be dealing with.

The cylinders were dull black, each about a metre long, half that wide, connected to ones above, below and on either side by something with the aspect of a human hair. They could see it because it shimmered in the dim light, stretching out with the cylinders in a cobweb arrangement.

Connie pressed her hands to her face, 'I would've thought they'd be facing in all directions, not pointing the same way. Are they receivers or transmitters, some sort of communications centre?'

'Doubt it,' Harry grunted, waiting for a throng of feckless questions to follow. 'Look we can stand here like wood ducks and guess for the rest of our lives but I guarantee we'll never get close. Familiar shape maybe, but that's where it ends.'

Connie turned to him, smirking, 'quite the enquiring mind aren't you?'

'No point pondering the imponderable…waste of air,' he said, deliberately avoiding eye contact. He remembered his pipe dream of working together, knowing that's exactly what it was, a pipe dream. He was Harry and they were so fucking irritating, it made his blood boil.

Connie glared at the side of his unkempt beard, dumbfounded by his bloody-minded arrogance. 'Hey, if I've got a question I'm gonna ask it, and you're dumber than I thought if you think I won't.'

Harry grimaced, clenching everything to stifle a full-blown assault on this infuriating woman. 'Whatever,' he said flippantly, maintaining an uneasy stare through the window panel.

'Screw you,' Connie said, jabbing a finger at him, thinking quite seriously that his arrogance was more suited to some totalitarian egomaniac. Stalin she reckoned, that was it, the old "one death is a tragedy, a million is a stat". That was Harry right there, reducing people to numbers. She conceded he wasn't really that bad, but the general drift was about right.

Harry glared at her, his pounding heart a blatant tell-sign that he was going to lose it on this perfumed steamroller if he was interrupted again.

Becker snapped his head up and swore, 'uh, something flashed, up there, a reflection maybe,' he said, scanning the near distance.

'I saw it too,' Skylar murmured, 'corner of my eye…like a photo flash.'

'Someone taking pictures?' Becker said, his heart suddenly pumping hard.

Connie watched Becker's half-arsed attempt to focus and giggled despite her fear. 'You reckon you're hot shit Becker so maybe it is,' Connie said with a lopsided grin.

'Man, if this is some twisted Big Brother scenario—'Harry smiled a toothy grin through his beard, forgetting his nerves momentarily, 'I think we're safe Becker although I did say anything was possible…so nothing's off the table.' He rolled his eyes upward, a little nonplused at the chuckles of amusement, given where they were, what might be on offer. Humanity, he told himself, it was a means of coping, he understood it, part of the conscious brain's survival mode.

Well I'm happy to be evicted from the house right now,' Sky said humourlessly, scared shitless, staring at Harry miserably. 'Fucking bring it.'

***

Vic was looking through Sagan's telescope, searching for any hidden details on the things they'd mundanely dubbed cylinders, while listening to the mildly agreeable exchanges behind him. If not for Becker's intrusion, he was sure it would've ended in tears, or more likely a black eye for Harry. Glancing over his shoulder at Connie he surveyed her a little closer. She was dangerous he could see that, opinionated, smart and damn sexy, watching her hands slide gracefully over her hips as she spoke to Becker. Vic shook his head forcefully, refreshing his mind, returning his eye to the telescope, ignoring the rising blood.

On the lowest magnification he had a close-up view of the surface of one of the objects, noticing it wasn't completely blemish free. He attempted to resolve the image further but the digital control seemed to have a frustrating mind of its own.

'Anything?' Harry asked impatiently, thankful Connie had shifted her attention to what was outside.

'Hang on,' Vic muttered, 'I'm getting this thing set right.' He was struggling with it, seeing the image gain focus then lose it, sighing irritably.

'Hurry up,' Harry grumbled, pounding a fist against his leg.

'Jesus, chill. What's the goddamn—' He was going to say hurry, but stopped mid-sentence, bringing both hands gently to the eyepiece to steady it.

Harry's eyes narrowed. 'What?' He rushed, blinking rapidly a few times. Vic pulled his face away from the eyepiece on the Takahashi, mouthing something unintelligible under his breath.

171

'My God,' Vic said louder, moving his eye back to the 'scope, looking intently at whatever was looking back at him from the other end.

'Talk to us,' Becker shouted, 'for God's sake, speak.' He was almost dancing on the spot. Don't be bad, he prayed. Sky was numb, her heart sinking and tears welling behind her eyelids for no particular reason. Her emotional reaction to almost anything made her furious to the point of wanting to bash her head on something, knock some sense into herself.

Vic turned around to them and they could see fire within, his eyes were shining as they moved squarely onto Harry. 'Numbers,' he said, gasping a little, 'they've all got numbers on them…frigging numbers.' He was staring at Harry woodenly, trying desperately to put it all together.

'What sort of numbers? Harry blurted, bounding over to the altazimuth mount, spinning it around so he could check it out himself.

'Each one has two lines,' Vic said hesitantly, 'the first, um…is numbers, not sure what the second line is. The first one has twenty-nine characters, the second I don't recognise…gibberish.'

Harry peered expectantly and saw, the first line was inexplicably familiar but the second was like Vic said, a complete mystery.

'Binary,' Vic whispered with bulging eyes.' Staring at Harry, he paused, then slowly read out all the zeroes and ones that meant nothing to any of them, apart from being zeroes and ones. When he finished he said, 'did you get that Harry?'

'Er, no, should I recite them from memory?' He jibed quizzically, eyeing him blankly.

'Jesus, write them down will you.' Vic repeated them and Harry scrawled them on the whiteboard above the bulkhead near the pilot's seat.

The black numbers stood out boldly against the whiteness. Everyone stared at them in various states of puzzlement, realising the conundrum that was before them.

11110001001001010111101011010101

Oh just great Becker thought, more fucking numbers. Strap yourself in, he told himself, clenching his jaw. 'What about the second line?' Becker said. 'Can't you geniuses work it out? he added wryly, staring at the board full of scribbled numbers.

Connie stared at Becker indignantly, giving a drawn-out breath. She looked approvingly at Vic, nodding, urging him on.

'So, they're symbols I've never seen before. I mean, lines, vertical, horizontal, criss-crossing, oblique dashes, dots of various sizes, stuff like that. We can forget finding meaning in that for now. But the binary stuff is pretty easy, if it's binary, if it's just a number.'

'That number is easy?' Becker groaned, tipping his head up and to the side, 'Jesus, look at it…in what world is that easy?

'It's just Base-2 math, positional values, power of two…very basic.'

Becker stared at Vic unblinking. 'So, when does the easy part start?' He asked vacantly, with a touch of dark amusement sweeping across his face.

'C'mon brains,' Connie said, elbowing Becker lightly, 'Just let him do his work.'

Like Harry, Vic had been gobsmacked since he'd seen them. 'If it's binary this is human numbering. I mean it's based on math, which is great, but the one and zero as we write it? That's not coincidence…it can't be, can it?' He rubbed his chin, sizing up the shocking development, trying to work out what words to use. 'H-How?' He said, looking sheepishly at Harry.

'Shall I answer that? Harry growled. 'Fuck knows.'

Connie looked knowingly at Vic, raising a pensive shoulder. 'These are the same numbers we found on the thing under the ice in Antarctica,' she said.

Harry eyed her curiously, folding his arms. 'Did you think maybe we should have known about that a little earlier?' He said, flapping a hand at her.

'Just remembered it,' Connie said sharply. 'It pulsed decimals of Pi using binary. Joe worked it out. He plugged some back in and wallah, it seemed to like it, just started up…and well, the rest is history I guess.'

'Yeah well, good work on that,' Harry said, shooting Becker with a killer glare.

Vic nodded, agreeing it was a gut-wrenching development…a rather backward numbering system used on such a massive scale by a presumably savant technology.

'So, all this was built by humans?' Becker asked boldly, posing the question they all had boxed inside their heads. Harry turned to him, snorting at yet another inane interrogatory, knowing he may as well converse with his avionics panel. The guy was a loose cannon, myopic, disengaged and painfully unscientific. And yes, he, Harry Bowden, was perfect came the droll reply from the voice in his head that asked, "and you?"

Harry exhaled heartily, steadying himself. 'Look, park the questions, focus on the numbers. Humans, aliens…maybe we'll find out, but it sure as hell won't be now unless they pop out and tell us.' He looked around, wondering if he was right or wrong, as his heart had dropped into his stomach.

Vic was punching his calculator, working out powers of two from right to left. He had it done in a few seconds, knowing it would be a whopping number but this was seriously fucking big.

'Well?' Harry said, tapping a foot. 'Is it good or bad…a post code, IP address…what?' He pulled his top lip under the bottom, sucking on his beard and making a disgusting slurping sound.

'Funny Harry…expressed as a decimal it's slightly more than four billion.' Vic tried to talk and swallow at the same time and nearly managed to choke, giving a piercing cough as he wrestled with the big arse binary. 'So, all of them are numbered,' Vic said thoughtfully, 'and they're not sequential either, they're all over the place. I saw some in the millions next to one in the billions next to one in the hundreds of millions. Their order, if that actually has any meaning, seems unusually random, as far as our thinking goes.'

Skylar was engaged in a rather painful inter-bodily war, her face twisting interminably, jaw tensing and grinding. She opened her mouth, shut it, opened it again, clearly unsure whether to speak or not. 'So if they are Type 4,' she managed, 'why would they need to number things like children? Wouldn't they be beyond base 2, developed a more efficient system?' She turned her head down but her eyes were darting everywhere.

Vic looked thoughtful, his initial feeling being an emphatic yes but he wasn't sure. 'Well, we don't know what we're dealing with firstly. But if they were a T4 the finer details could be anything. Certain things we do now as a Type Zero might never be outgrown, however steep the ascent is.' As soon as he'd said it he had doubts. After all, Type 4 were gods according to Sky so everything could be optimised, presumably down to the quantum state. Uncertainty principle, delete, superposition, delete. Hermitian conjugate, delete. Vic grunted, mulling over the immodesty of comparing humans with gods.

Jesus Christ, Harry thought, pinching his lips together. The amount of speculation, wasted oxygen, squandered energy in this place was incalculable. 'Bottom line is we're clueless,' he said, frowning heavily, 'totally in the dark, without even a bare-arsed idea that's probably within a galactic radius of being right. But hey, we do have plenty of bullshit questions, so bully for us right?' He glared at Becker, then eyed the rest of them.

'Speak for yourself,' Connie said, feeling her hands grip into fists.

'No, I was speaking for you madam,' He said, looking squarely at her, in the mood to brawl, even though he knew he should back off.

'Madam…what the hell does that mean?' Connie said, furiously, 'I am not a fucking madam you arsehole. Where do you get—'

'Oh for God's sake, quiet you two!' Becker yelled. 'Nice as it is to see you giving someone else both barrels, just dial it back, we're in this nuthouse together, we've got nowhere to go.'

As Becker spoke, they sensed movement. The Sphere they were cocooned in started to retrace its steps, gliding gently back toward the edge of the chamber. Time to go they assumed.

***

Far enough away now, they could see the entire Sphere, intrigued to know it was jam packed with the oddly prosaic cylinders that appeared so benign and out of synch with what they assumed was a stupendously advanced intelligence. Of course what was inside them might have been something they wouldn't even recognise as technology, even on the most elemental level. Vic felt a sense of impotence, almost certain they were appraising something beyond human imagination, perhaps as an insect might blindly eye a printed circuit board.

Harry spelled it out again, couldn't help himself, did it quite matter-of-factly. He wasn't trying to cause trouble, just venting to relieve some of the pressure in his brain. It was all quite unnecessary but there they were, a flood of words echoing around the flight deck, tidings of doom, and for Sky a fate worse than death. Harry droned on about their time-like travel, reckoning tens or maybe hundreds of generations of loved ones back on Earth could've been born and died while they were up here. Sky tried to shut him out but couldn't and wasn't able hold it in any more.

She finally snapped her head up, glaring at him violently. 'Screw you, you don't know that…you don't know shit,' she said, eyes wild and hard as flint. 'You think you know everything but you don't…it's all just dumb guesswork. We've seen some crazy stuff up here but we've always returned to the same space, the same time so why should this be any different?' Sky watched him wag his stupid head. 'Don't fucking shake your head,' she screamed, looking directly at him with a face flushed red. Harry was quickly understanding his folly, chastising himself for being such an insensitive jerk. Female emotions. Fuck it, he spat silently, annoyed at his lack of intuition.

'I was just venting, letting off steam,' he said gently, '...you're spot on, none of it might be right.' He smiled awkwardly.

She nodded, smiling vaguely through tears and a heartbroken expression. 'Alysha, she's only five years old,' Sky gasped, breathing in squirts, short of breath. 'My daughter's gone, I know it, as we sit here, she's gone.' Sky collapsed into uncontrollable heaving, tears falling from her eyes.

How much can one person cry? Harry mused, puzzling over how much water was stored up there, watching her grief play out, clueless how to help.

Everyone turned to Vic who responded with a 'nuh uh' under his breath and a melodramatic eye roll. Him, the university failure in human relations, almost as bad as Harry. You cannot be serious, he said to himself, clamping his mouth shut but planning his attack, guessing he had to give it a go. Sky's descent was driving them nuts so he'd just have to wing it.

'I'm not so sure,' he said, building slowly, adding to what she'd said earlier. 'Remember the first Sphere that took us to Mars? The time we were in there summed to nothing on Earth, so it might balance out the same this time.' He nodded his head, smiling warmly, feeling like it was forced and tight. 'So there's a chance Sky, we need to keep the faith, it's all we have.'

She peered at Vic like a frightened kitten, nodding, wiping tears from her eyes and cheeks with the back of her hand. 'You're right, there has to be hope,' she croaked in a feeble whisper.

Connie knew damn well that mass and energy shared an unavoidable juncture, Einstein's theory had been proven a million times and its grip on anything with mass accelerating through the cosmos was inescapable. So, if what they saw was how it was, she wondered, what was the answer?

Harry wore a frown that was digging parallel lines right across his forehead. 'So they've smashed physics somehow.' He glanced down for a moment, laughing in a burst, pulling at his beard near his ear. 'I thought impossible was absolute but maybe it doesn't exist at all…maybe it's relative. Impossible to one, possible to another with a superior technology.' He rubbed his wrinkled up nose, 'but I don't care how advanced you are, you close on light speed travelling in a straight line, mass grows, keeps growing exponentially so you can't ever get over the line. You can get near it but not on it or over it, $E=MC^2$ says so with a big fat fucking exclamation point!'

'Vic?' Connie said softly from the window panel, 'so…what do you figure's going on?'

'Not possible.' He said firmly and evenly. 'I don't have an answer because there is no answer. Harry's spot on though, mass and energy are unforgiving, Higgs says so.'

'So that's it then,' Harry said, flicking his chin up, 'no answers, just more questions…situation normal.' He walked back to his seat, sat down, strapped in and watched the retreating Sphere that looked so much like the Moon, minus every one of its surface imperfections.

Vic was giving them a run down on the Higgs Field, how it filled all of space like air in a balloon, bequeathing mass to all the familiar particles that filled the physics books. Some pushed through easy like photons and were massless, others had to push harder like squeezing through gelatine. 'That's why superluminal travel is a no-go,' he said, musing over the defiling concept again.

Harry tapped his temple, thinking how much his brain hurt, watching Becker yawning, sighting movement and light from the corner of his eye. The giant Sphere was glowing, not everywhere, but around its edge as though a mighty object was shining behind it.

Harry shouted, drawing their attention to it.

'Christ,' Becker said, shielding his eyes with a palm. 'What is this?'

Brilliant needles of light formed a pinwheel of radiance as though a sparkling ocean of light surrounded the Sphere, and then it simply slid into it, disappearing from view, from space.

'Holy mother…uh, Jesus,' Becker gasped slowly. 'What is it doing?'

'Um…leaving I guess,' Vic said, studying the strange visual, his heart pounding as he fought with the scale of the event.

'Leaving…to where?' Connie whispered, glancing sidelong at Vic.

'Oh Christ,' Harry fumed, raising an arm. 'Seriously?'

19. Passage

"One cannot answer for his courage when he has never been in danger."
~ François de La Rochefoucauld

'Sagan, this is Houston Flight, you copy?

Nothing.

'Vic, this is Flight, copy back,' Jack repeated more urgently.

Pete and Jack watched the shuttle from the Flight Control Room in Houston as it repeated its previous manoeuvre, dipping into the Sphere, then exiting at pretty much the same time, from the same spot. Jack released his pent up breath, grateful they were out and determined to keep them the hell out because if this kept up, he reckoned they'd eventually go for good. Not on his watch he reminded himself. No way he was losing another goddamn shuttle. No way, never again.

The TITAN controller confirmed zero telemetry.

'What is going on up there?' Jack said anxiously, baffled by the silence.

'All systems nominal,' Atlas confirmed. 'Zero outages.'

'Okay then, let's give 'em a minute to get sorted,' Jack said with growing concern.

***

Sky was seated on the cabin floor facing away from the window panels, readying herself for the worst. For the rest of them, the sight was breathtaking and completely unexpected. To the side of them was the Moon, on the other side, in the distance was Earth. And just ahead of them was Viper, their little camera-carrying friend who was apparently spat out in pretty much the same orbit as Sagan. The question of when rose in their minds, it all looked great but—

'Sagan, this is Houston Flight, you copy?

'Oh God yes, yes!' Connie squealed, flinging her arms out and whooping with delight.

'Jesus Sky,' get over here,' Vic yelled. 'You'll want to see this.' Vic looked like he'd been clocked with a hammer, genuinely stunned that the story he'd peddled to Sky was true, he thought it was a complete boner at the time, but there you go he mused happily.

'Sagan, Flight, copy back,' Jack said again, more urgently than the last.

'Acknowledge him Vic.' Harry said, 'poor bugger sounds twitchy.'

'Not till she gets her arse up here…Skylar for God's sake come on.' There was still no response as she sat motionless, eyes closed, arms extended over her knees, having completely turned the key on the outside world.

'Hey!' Harry snapped like a gunshot. She spun her head up at him in shock, tripped from whatever zone-out she'd been locked in.

'Shit, what…you scared me,' she wheezed, fighting to catch her breath.

'Please come here,' he said, waving her up with his arm, keeping his expression stilled, not wanting to give it away quite yet. Her heart started beating faster as she shakily pulled herself to her feet. Sky saw the view from both the left and right window panels and spied Viper only a few hundred metres away. The intake of breath was dramatic and she held it in, eyes widening until they had nowhere else to go.

'Oh God…please tell me this is our Earth…not some other, uh…one.' Sky looked stricken, unhinged by the possible answer. Shivers ran across her face and she put her arms out awkwardly to steady herself, staring at Vic, searching for confirmation in his eyes, pleading for good news. She knew the next five seconds would determine the rest of her life…if she had a life.

Vic grinned, waiting, knowing it was coming. 'Sagan, Houston Flight, read over.'

At the sound of Mission's voice, Sky hastily grabbed the back of the pilot's seat. 'Oh, dear God…we're home,' she whimpered, dazed by the notion of finally being back. 'Thank you…thank you,' Sky moaned, sobbing uncontrollably in a rush of relief and elation. She finally had the answer to the nightmare she'd been living for what seemed like forever. Maybe these others weren't the bastard race they'd assumed, Sky thought, gazing out at beautiful blue Earth, bracing herself. Not yet, these creatures, their possible nature…way too early to call.

'Houston, this is Sagan, we copy you loud and clear. Great to hear your voice.'

Jack spun his head around to Pete, throwing a clenched fist in the air. 'We thought you might be in a spot of bother up there,' he shot back, flopping into his chair, seriously relieved.

'No, all's good with us,' Vic chirped, looking at Sky, cocking a cheerful eyebrow.

'Another rapid exit, what's the report?' Jack said.

Vic peered at Harry, releasing the PTT button. 'We need to tell them what's going on, this is not ours to keep.'

'Yup, agree,' Harry replied. 'I'll fill 'em in, not the details, not yet…just the general drift.'

'Do it,' Vic said.

Skylar had zoned out of the conversation, staring through the window at Earth, overwhelmed to be back but terrified that things might unhinge at any moment. There was a sense of comfort in the fact that twice they'd been reeled in and twice they'd been sent back home to their own space and time. Third time unlucky she pondered grimly, feeling the black dog rise, growling.

'Flight, Sagan, do you have me?' Harry wasn't sure where he'd start or what he'd say but he wanted to keep it short, to the point. Detail could come later.

'Copy Sagan, what do you say Harry?'

'Jack, um…our entry and egress from these bogies is not what you think. These things seem to er, well…I guess they carry their own space and time along with them. What you see as instantaneous ain't how it is. For us it's days.' That'd hit him where it hurt, Harry knew. Jack was a no bullshit, facts type of guy. This would sound like storybook horseshit to him, he'd think they'd downed the medicinal alcohol, were stoned, worse maybe.

There was extended silence, he heard several muffled voices over the S-band, sounds of scrambled sentences, arguing maybe, probably calling hogwash on Harry's words.

'So…is there a punch line coming, um...Vic, did you put him up to this?' Jack's voice was part uncertainty, part amusement.

'This is straight up Jack, no crap. Space and time are disconnected inside these objects. Our time and its time are not the same. As soon as you break the surface…well, it's a goddamn madhouse really.'

Jack was frozen, staring blankly at Pete who raised a hesitant shoulder, returning his bland expression. 'Jesus, we'd ask you if you were sure but we won't. So, okay, where've you been all that time?' He wasn't sure he believed it, but he'd known Harry for more than a decade and felt compelled to accept it. Bowden was a stone cold veteran, prone only to truth and fact. He was wired that way so his seemingly whimsical story gave him great pause.

'That's not important,' Harry said roughly, 'just know that we've been to places that make no sense, sort of like sight-seeing between the pages of physics, no itinerary, no guarantee of return.' He glanced over at Becker and Connie. 'Oh and Jack, we're heavy two civilians.'

There was an even longer silence this time, Jack's elevated breathing all they could hear. 'Um, repeat, last sentence,' Jack said between breaths.'

'We picked up two civilians.

Jack was sprinting over broken thoughts, ending up with a colossal line of zeroes.

'What…how…er, picked up…where?' For the first time in his career, as CAPCOM or NASA Flight Director, he didn't have a clue what to say, he wanted to swear but held it in. How the hell do you pick people up in a space shuttle? Jack was exasperated, muddling over the strange visual in his head. What…they just floated by…hey, you out there, come on in, join the party? His world was suddenly askew.

'Yeah it's nuts, I'll tell you but no questions right?' Harry demanded. 'It's seriously screwed up. They were apparently dispatched through the artefact in Antarctica, ended up on Mars so they say. Not our Mars Jack, the red planet billions of years ago when it was blue, alive, crammed with plant and animal life. We picked 'em up on one of our sojourns and well, here they are.' Harry stiffened and went still, wondering how whacked out Jack might think they were. Having proffered the words, it sounded laughable, at best fictional, at worst like a load of midnight delusion.

Silence persisted for so long they thought they'd lost comms again. Harry pictured the MCC back at Johnson, barely able to imagine the commotion, unable to stifle a gurgle of humour as he imagined the reaction of stoic JSC controllers to claims of time travel, life   on Mars, blue plants for fuck sakes...it would be pure gold. Several were involved with the Martian Rovers and Odyssey, obsessing day and night about finding a molecule of fossilised life on Mars. They dreamed of stumbling over the tiniest microscopic imprint or cast that could be proven to be a different life event from Earth. For if life was indeed not some sort of miracle, could be confirmed twice in the same solar system, then it was doubtlessly everywhere through the cosmos. They just needed to find it.

So how would they go when told that Becker and co. had witnessed first-hand a planet straining under the weight of an ecosystem replete with rainforests, wacky animal life and bent out of shape DNA? Harry knew they'd be reduced to childlike disbelief, no doubt simply disregarding it, putting it down to some devastating delusion aboard SLS-11.

'You there Flight?' Harry finally said.

'You said no questions,' Jack replied stiffly, 'I have no idea how to respond to that without questions. I guess you must be fucking joking would do as a starting point. That's not a question I guess, more of a declaration.' He paused momentarily to catch his breath. 'A lot of people have a lot of, er…queries, a few have statements that are um, let's just say they're less than kind.'

'That's what I expected Jack,' Harry said upbeat, 'and trust me that's only a small part of it because there's detail to go with it that would really blow your mind.'

Another pause settled over the MCC. He assumed Jack was trying to think of something that wasn't a question, clearly struggling with it.

Jack finally came back on line, the urgency in his voice replaced by a faltering uncertainty. 'Sagan, uh, news from Mauna Kea and Pan-STARRS…are you seeing this Harry…Vic? Hubble feed is confirming movement, the Spheres are moving.'

'We're aware of that Flight,' Vic said, raising an eyebrow at Harry, nodding curiously.

'No,' Jack snapped, 'moving laterally, not orbital, they're moving away from the Moon.'

They shifted their eyes to the panelled window, seeing what Jack was alluding to. All fifteen Spheres were executing a collective de-orbit manoeuvre that had them moving directly away from the Moon, casting ominous shadows on the lunar surface as they went. Everything about them cried symmetry and rhythm, from their harmonic rotation, distance of separation, the motional spin of the collective, which was right now changing up its strategy.

'Flight, they might be heading your way,' Vic said, mulling on the Earth vector.

'How many? We can see maybe five or six through Hubble.'

'Uh…all of them Jack. They're all coming.'

'Jesus,' he barked after a brief silence. There were heated voices in the MCC, they heard Jack say *quiet*, after which a single voice could be heard talking, something they couldn't pick up. 'Um, okay, we need to enact the RSOE Protocol,' Jack said, clearly having just been told. Any threat NASA identified that met the criteria for "Actionable Intel" required immediate application of Section 20 Defence Protocols. Jack continued after a brief pause. 'That'll feed real-time data to DoD, the Joint Chiefs, UNSC and NORAD.' There was more background chatter from the same voice, sounding strained and grave. Jack acknowledged several times with a couple of grunts and "okays", someone shuffling paper, seemingly reading something to him. 'Um, so we'll also be copying in

HomeSec, US Strategic Command, NES, NSC, and, uh…NATO Allied Command Ops. Pete, where the hell is Pete?' They heard Jack ask impatiently. 'Vic, you're the only ones with insight, you've been through them right…any ideas? Could this be something pre-emptive?'

Oh fuck Harry scoffed silently, almost laughing out loud at Jack's words. They had no more idea than Houston did. The summary was that they had squat, the insight Jack demanded, zero. Their entire experience had given them little, none of it seemed logical or sensible in any way they could identify. None of it could be pieced together into a meaningful picture. All they got a handle on was that these others were aberrant…deeply dissimilar to their expectation of an advanced technical species. The objects were spatial disconnects, some sort of decoherent, temporal rifts in spacetime, that was the size of their so-called insight. Whatever else they might have been, their true intentions, they had zilch, zero…an absolute goose egg. Insight? Harry snorted again, louder, bobbing his head in exasperation. Chuck that word in with impossible he thought, space 'em both.

'We don't know,' Vic said honestly. 'You'll have to wait and—'

'Vic, they've stopped,' Jack interrupted, speaking slowly, trying to understand what was happening as he spoke, scopes from Hawaii to WISE to MIT and Hubble studying their every move.

Becker could see they were still moving…just differently.

'What're you seeing?' Harry shot at him.

'I'm not sure, they seem to be…um, reorganising, shifting around.'

Skylar walked nervously to the middle window panel, seeing their transit toward Earth had indeed stopped and they'd lost all signs of angular momentum. Now they were swapping positions, seemingly moving to particular coordinates then holding there quite abruptly. Once they'd shifted, rotation began again, in acute symmetry, steeply angular waves rising around line curvatures.

Skylar murmured, 'wow,' under her breath, eyes wide open and staring, sensing a palpable intelligence. There was a discrete alertness, a simpatico in the way they all moved, individually and as a group, an intangible connection extending between all of them. She edged backward, watching each Sphere form a tell-point in a monumental sphere that stretched for hundreds of kilometres.

'Sagan, Flight…you copying these images?'

'Copying, uh…things are happening quick, the President's acted, he's got us at DEFCON 2, we haven't been there for fifty years. Heavies from NORAD, DoD and the Joint Chiefs are on route, plus HomeSec and even fucking FEMA. All of 'em will be on the doorstep in a few minutes. POTUS doesn't want a live feed to these jerks, they want direct comms with you from here.'

'Shit,' Harry hissed, 'goddamn pencil-necks.' His face twisted and a vein punched out in his neck. 'You know you're screwed when these clowns get involved.'

'We've also got some top scientists coming,' Jack added, 'some Laucasian Professor of Math and a couple of top-notch astrophysics types from NASA. Apart from the ISS, you're the only bird up there so we're running the show from Johnson.'

'Okay, so no pressure right?' Harry said, winking at Vic.

'Yep, no pressure,' he said quietly. 'Take a close look at those things,' Jack said. 'You're the only ones with proximity, anything will be invaluable because down here we've got nada…and we need something. These Government pricks will be here soon enough and they'll want intel, be it qualified, a hunch or just a goddamn finger in the air.'

Vic grimaced, knowing facts were absent, contemplating where the hell they should start. 'You heard the man, we need to effort something up here,' he said seriously. 'These things have de-orbited and well, I hate myself for asking this Harry, but we need to find out why?'

'Like asking the question will make it happen.'

'Nearly every country is working on them,' Jack said, 'searching for anything - Russia, China, Japan, Australia, but what do you analyse when there's so little data? Everything we thought would give us insight has led nowhere. We've got you and you have proximity so you're the game.'

Pandemonium seemed to hit the MCC in a rush of noise. 'Harry we'll need to go off comms for a bit, we've got some, arrivals here at Johnson. You won't be blind, if you need us, squawk.'

***

'Sagan, Jack, you copy?'

'Been waiting,' Harry said lightly.

'We have Professor Nate Davis with us, Laucasian, uh…guy from Cambridge University.' He looked at Nate contritely. 'We've also got Tara Burns and Yoshihara Yasunari from NASA, pretty much the best astrophysicists on the planet. Oh and courtesy of the US Government my FCR is full of DoD people with guns and uniforms…stuff like that.'

'Are we on a closed line? Harry said gruffly.

'We are, but the General is breathing down my neck, he wants us on open mic. Harry, it's getting real down here. These guys are deadly serious. They think we're goddamn magicians, that we can just flip a few switches and tell them exactly what these things are.'

'Fuckers, the lot of them. I've dealt with them before. Okay,' Harry inhaled and let out a gush of air, 'switch to open mic.'

'Done,' he confirmed.

Harry and Vic heard a different voice, some background static. 'Can they hear me?' Someone asked with a gravelly voice.

'Yes, fire away sir,' came Jack's voice.

'This is General Will Ballard, commander of NORAD/NORTHCOM. I've got a direct line to the Secretary of Defence who has the army, navy, air-force and Joint Chiefs on standby.'

Christ, Harry thought, were they on a frigging war footing? 'Good to meet you General,' Harry said laconically, lying.

'Jack tells me you claim to have seen some strange things up there. We need you to focus on finding out what these things are, what threat they pose. Can you and your team do that for us?'

Harry glared at Vic, mouthing claimed? Who was this fool? Vic saw the flush sweep across Harry's face so he took over. Swearing at the commander of NORAD, creating an incident would be bad form…at least so early.

'Sir this is shuttle pilot Vic Gervais here—'

'Hang on,' Harry interrupted, 'what do you mean claimed?'

Vic ran his hand across his neck but Harry's eyes were fixed, expression like alpine granite. He didn't tolerate idiots or Government puppets and didn't see much separation between the two.

'Let's focus on the now, apologies if I found the story a bit fanciful.' The General said in his softest tone. He knew Harry and the crew needed to be kept on side but playing the sensitive card wasn't the NORAD chief's strong suit.

'It is fanciful,' Vic whispered to Harry, trying to get him to chill. After a few seconds Harry's eyes uncoiled a bit, his fists relaxing and unfurling.

'Okay, fine. Jack, what's the plan? We go in for a closer look, see if it brings a response?'

'That would be the idea,' Jack said. 'Nate and Yoshi reckon it could be a test of some kind, that we need to demonstrate certain solutions to geometry and the like.' Jack looked at Nate, nodding vigorously, 'before you ask, they don't know why that would be, but it might be important. Who knows is the upshot but they reckon we might control our destiny with our higher brains.'

'So it's a fucking IQ test?' Harry said sourly, 'that's what they think?'

'Well…yeah, pretty much,' Jack said hesitantly, looking at Nate again who shrugged, 'but it's all a guess at this stage…obviously.'

'Everyone's got the same questions,' Pete broke in, 'why did they stop and why did they start moving in the first place? Their conclusion is that these objects are waiting for something.'

Fuck me, Harry thought. 'Something from us right?' It was the only reasonable conclusion.

'Yep, that's what they think.'

While they were talking to Houston, space outside the shuttle was flooding with surges of light, illuminating the cabin like bursts from a lighthouse.

'You getting that Jack?' Vic blurted, squinting at the light, shielding his eyes with a palm.

'Getting it on Hubble. Well, if it wasn't clear before…seems our friends want to help us out,' Jack said slowly.

Now there was one Sphere rotating rapidly in the very centre, thirteen marking out the coordinates of a sphere that was about a hundred clicks through the middle and further out was a single orphan Sphere scooting around the primary structure rapidly. Piercing circles of light in latitudinal and longitudinal lines it joined the thirteen Spheres to fill in the blanks, in case you weren't smart enough to realise it was a sphere. Der, Harry thought, feeling a little miffed, any idiot civilisation would have got it.

Jack suggested it might be a remedial chemistry lesson for dummies, maybe it was page one of Der Chemica Universe, to upskill the savages, or how to build a bomb and blow yourself up.

'Hydrogen atom,' Vic murmured, confirming what most of them already realised. Becker nodded his head, suggesting he got it, which he didn't. Masking his lack of science was all he had, nodding seriously, doing it badly, to Connie's ongoing amusement.

'That's just great,' Ballard snapped sarcastically. 'What does Science think about it?' He glared over at Nate and his team.

'Er…well it means nothing sir. It's probably just issuing a signature of intelligence, which we don't think was necessary given what's gone before. We think it's a positive sign.'

'Yeah, we'll see,' Ballard growled. 'Better a chemical element than a death ray I guess.'

Nate stared at him vacantly, not sure how to respond, wondering if he really meant what he said. This guy was hard-core military so he probably did. Ascending the ranks of commissioned officers was still a leave your brain at the door exercise, he got that with absolute surety. All you needed was a ballistic ego and the habits of a serial killer, minimal thinking required, just a string of yes sir strategists. And of course, you had to know the words to the Star Spangled Banner by rote. Ballard had the first few in spades, probably the last as well.

'They're on the move again,' Vic barked urgently, casting his hand forward at the vanishing rods of light. The depiction of the hydrogen atom dissolved as the Spheres gracefully re-shuffled themselves and returned to their former disposition.

***

Ballard had just terminated a phone call to the Secretary of Defence and was walking with intent back to the Atlas console where Jack and Pete were seated, in animated conversation.

'We need action,' he said from five metres away, gesturing with a pudgy half-closed fist, scowling at Jack savagely.

'We're on wait and see General, activity is being monitored, our next move is being considered.'

Ballard's face was ruddy and fissured with uncountable lines. 'No time to wait, get your boys in there to take a closer look.'

'Maybe we should wait and see what happens,' Jack said, returning Ballard's iron gaze, holding it, barely. 'Ideally we base a decision on an actionable event, let's see if it does anything—'

'Decision's made, make it happen.'

Jack looked at Pete who rolled a shoulder, nodding weakly. 'You know what General, that's our stick up there and we're entitled to—'

'It's ours now Raines, this is military, DoD are calling the shots and we expect you NASA boys to fall in line.'

Jesus Christ, Jack thought ruefully, great way of on-siding us, but knowing the way the military worked, pushing back was a waste of time and energy.

***

The Pentagon wanted Sagan to get a closer look at the Spheres, eyeball them, see if they reacted. It was one thing being dragged into the things kicking and screaming, but what if they approached under their own momentum? Would it result in a No Vacancy sign being posted, or perhaps something more aggressive? Ballard and his five-star cronies from The Pentagon, Fort Bragg, Chesapeake and dozens of other installations were happy to roll the dice on that one.

POTUS wanted something to give to the people, something awesome and inspiring to lift the spirits of a terrified nation, and by extension the wider world, but that was just collateral, there were no votes in it. The President's non-negotiable was decisive intel and he ordered the Secretary of State, and Defence to marshal the troops, get the hell out there and make it happen. The time for bullshit politicking was done, he demanded positive, definitive action starting yesterday. There was no time for elongated debating sessions in Congress, seeking consensus from the UN or from other NATO countries - that was just pissing in the wind. Sagan was America's bird and they had jurisdiction or at least that's the position POTUS took. He would update UNOOSA, the UN's outer space affairs division but no way he'd take orders from them or anyone else. If he affronted the Soviets or the Chinese, the Japanese - tough shit, he was front-footing this thing come what may. Walton's popularity and presidency was hanging by a thread, less than one percent, if it was called for, it was time to be capricious, not prudent.

'Vic, this is Flight,' Jack said slowly, 'are you reading?

'Copy, we have you,' Vic replied calmly.

'We want you to take a closer look, recommendation to approach on a nominal trajectory toward the central Spheres, report everything that happens. How do you copy?' He went to pains to be polite so he didn't piss Harry off. He asked them, he didn't "fucking order them" as Ballard had barked at them so crudely.

Harry raised an eyebrow slightly, nodding to Vic. What other options were there? Sit here for eternity, wait for something to happen? He didn't think so. Harry had already made the decision before the question was asked, it was time to be proactive, not sit around like dummies, waiting to be hauled in like a flapping fish in a trawler net. His thoughts shifted to Sky and he swallowed heavily, she was such a bloody nightmare, this wasn't going to be pretty.

'Copy that,' Vic replied. He turned the Flight Control switch to on, waited for APU and hydrazine pre-start. When the three LED's turned blue he had manual control over all three axes of Sagan with prop good to go. Vic rotated the translational hand controller for a longitudinal RCS burn, pitching and yawing them slowly toward the bogies. As directed, Vic was propelling them toward the two spheres at the very centre of the fifteen objects. Both of them were rotating around each other like tiny binary stars, albeit with no energy output, or none they could detect anyway.

'Hey, what's happening here?' Vic said, scowling at his GPS and gyroscope data. 'I'm seeing drift.'

'They're moving again,' Harry said, eyes pasted on the forward view. Vic followed his gaze, seeing the Spheres gradually moving beyond the window panels. The shuttle was pointed toward empty space. The RCS altitude burn was tracking the GPS coordinates correctly but the objects had bolted.

Vic engaged the Digital Auto-Pilot and re-targeted the central Sphere, causing the RCS thrusters on the OMS pods to lock on and burn oxidiser so the craft yawed right and pitched downward.

'Jack, you copying motion?' Vic asked Houston.

'Copy motion. Earth transit, same heading.'

Vic was nervously, picking at his chin. 'The question is why are they coming?'

They heard Jack cough and clear his throat over the S-band. 'We've got a room full of military chiefs who are efforting that right now. Of course they don't have a clue, never will, but the perfunctories have started. It's up to you more or less.'

'Once again, no pressure?' Vic offered lightly, raising his eyes at Harry.
'Just the fate of the world buddy…maybe.'

***

Ballard was in animated discussion with the DoD. The Joint Chiefs of Staff Combatant Commands were being mobilised in the Pacific, Central, European and Southern regions. Pentagon Force Protection and Agencies for Defence Intelligence, Threat Reduction and the NSA were all on high alert. The National Guard and HomeSec were already on a pre-war footing. FEMA and NES were in a state of readiness for what might be to come although none of them had a clue what any of them could do should an off-planet crisis eventuate. That said, the United States was activating every division of its security and defence forces to White Status in the presence of what they arbitrarily determined to be clear and present danger. The facts were, they didn't have a clue if these things were a threat but the assumption was taken that they weren't popping in as part of a goodwill mission.

The way of the military was to identify, prepare and mitigate, with the first of them generally being a semi-qualified guess, the rest of them meaning get ready to kill, then kill. The scenario presenting itself in space seemed little different. This would be a military show, SETI or NASA or some other benevolent UN puppet-show would play no role in directing first response. As far as The Pentagon was concerned, the visitors had done no service to themselves through what was, by human standards, highly inflammatory behaviour. No hello or beg pardon, just barge on in elbows out, inflaming a bunch of natives on the way through. Hardly the way to garner favour.

***

Sagan was slowly closing in on what Vic pictured as two quantum particles falling around one another in perfect symphony, identical angular momentum drawing matching patterns on each.

The shuttle eased its way forward and as it did, the two Spheres visibly slowed their rate of rotation, both orbitally and rotationally. It was as if the objects were sensing their approach, waiting to see what the white beast might do next. There was zero movement now, just two Spheres sessile next to each other like identical twins. Malevolent fucking eyes

'Take it slow Vic,' Jack said. 'If you think you need to back off, do it.'

'I honestly don't think these objects mean us harm,' Vic said, his eyes wide, belying the erudite but still wishful words. 'We have no idea, but I think we'll be okay.'

Famous last fucking words, Harry thought silently. Had he forgotten the deaths these bastard objects had caused, not directly perhaps but certainly as a result of the destinations they'd dished out. Hardly benign outcomes.

'Well what is this then?' Harry said abruptly. 'Shit,' he said, slapping his thigh, rebuking himself for calling out an empty question. He was trying to set the example for these people and he'd screwed it up already.

'Sagan this is Jack, you okay up there?'

'We have eyes on unidentified light…variable output. Coming from the central objects, all other bogeys are nominal.'

'We've got the science crew on it Harry,' Jack said, 'we'll report when we have something.'

Really? Harry thought acidly. When they have something? 'They're deluding themselves if they think they're gonna strike something down there,' he sighed. 'Fuckers,' he grunted as though he hadn't quite made his point.

'So what, they just sit in limbo, do nothing, is that it?' Connie mocked. 'Wait for us to do everything…not allowed to ask questions either?' She gave a disgusted snort. 'Seriously, are you hearing what comes out of that hairy gob of yours?' Connie's eyes were like pavement cracks, squashed by her protruding brow. He really did have a messiah complex, both Becker and Harry were cut from the same piece of infuriating cloth, no wonder they hated the sight of each other.

'I'm just saying they've got no hope, they're too far away,' Harry said, backpedalling, seeing the murderous look on her dial. He wasn't in the mood to argue, she fought like a street dog over a mutton bone no matter how trivial it was. No matter what, Connie would hang off the tendons and gristle with her teeth, snarling.

'You're not the only one with a brain,' she sighed irritably. 'We need input from as many sources as possible, different perspectives is the only way we're gonna get the job done.'

'She's right Harry,' Vic said. 'If they come up with something we don't, then we execute it up here, you know, road test it.'

Harry shrugged, surveying Connie closely. 'Why the hell do I feel like the odd one out?' He asked with a momentary grin. 'I'm just telling it like it is, if it turns out different then great, I'll be the first to say well done, how's that?'

'Better,' Vic said, with a slight tilt of the head.

Connie looked away and took a protracted breath, making a point of her exasperation. Vic was brilliant and a great guy but he was such a goddamn pussy. 'It's bullshit is what it is.'

Harry glared at the console, his heart rate maxing, the need to vent going up another notch. Know-it-all bitch, he barked to himself, feeling the beginnings of a pounding headache.

The two central objects were moving laterally through space with the rest of the Spheres but were no longer orbiting one another. Side by side now, they were emitting timed bursts of light, not unlike a lighthouse whose five thousand watt globe was on the way out, flickering and dancing until it went dark for good.

'Maybe it's trying to communicate with Morse code,' Becker said grinning sideways at her, 'hey, we need to consider everything, pretty sure I heard that.'

'Jesus, we're not that bloody primitive and how the hell would they know it, it's not based on anything objective like math. I'm fairly certain it's just word based.' She glanced at Vic who nodded distractedly. He wasn't sure because of the Earthly numbers they'd seen earlier, it brought everything into question.

'Just spit-balling Con,' Becker said defensively.

'Well whatever it is, the egg-heads in the science team might be able to work it out,' Harry said, hoping that might buy him some brownie points with her majesty in the corner. 'Maybe it means nothing…just lighting up the way,' he said, pushing his haggard beard apart with his lips.

'Everything means something,' Skylar said. 'Make no mistake, the light means something.'

'Welcome back Sky…thought you'd gone for good,' Harry said with a theatrical wink.

'Just deep in thought is all.'

'Yeah,' Harry said gently.

Connie picked at her fingernails with a thumb, watching the lights power up, then down, pretty sure she knew what was going on. 'Uh…what about binary,' she said, raising her hands and spreading her fingers quizzically. 'Like at the Pole.' She glanced at Becker. 'It spelt out Pi using the same method.' Everyone was staring right at her. 'You know, bright for one, dull for zero or maybe the other way around.' She suddenly recoiled with horror, remembering the meltwater, the ungodly noise. Connie was grappling with the memory, shaken by a lurching sensation that sent her stumbling backward. The shuttle was vibrating and shook violently a few times as though some beast had the craft in its mouth and was trying to break it into bite-sized pieces. Sagan was now transiting directly toward the central Spheres.

'Christ, it's happening again,' Vic said, peering down at avionics and confirming what he already knew.

Sky's knees jellied and almost buckled under her despite zero-g, howling something from the depths of her lungs, not words, just a jarring moan that echoed unnervingly around the cabin.

Sagan, Houston, 'Nate is pretty sure the pulses are binary.' He heard the pitiful moaning and ignored it.

'We worked that out too. Get 'em working on it,' Harry boomed, 'it might be a…well, who knows, it might be something. Maybe it's in the binary, why they're here, why they're screwing with us.' Harry's eyes flashed and narrowed furiously, he tried his best to imagine humans doing this as a pre-emptive step in first contact. It was lunacy, these others couldn't be human, no way, no how. Harry figured after millions of years their mind-set would be more rounded, a holistically inclusive race respecting different social orders, on and off-planet. Otherwise there's no way they would have survived even another millennia. So was this screwed up scenario their considered protocol when they located other civilisations? Send in the crazy spacetime drones to piss them off, kill a few and then—?' Fuck, Harry spat to himself, stopping abruptly. Nothing made the slightest sweep of sense.

'Good luck crew,' Jack said reluctantly, peering at the Hubble feed, seeing the distance between the two objects gradually dwindle to single figures.

***

The Flight Control Room watched on in silence as Sagan collided forcelessly with the Sphere. Ballard was mesmerised, watching it penetrate the golden round, disappearing like a ship beneath muddied water.

'Keep watching General…for us it's an almost instantaneous return but for them, well, it can be days or longer spent in there.'

'Christ,' he gaped, lines of worry digging into a steeply furrowed brow. 'Sounds like frog shit to me, but if you say so.' He blinked heavily, slitting his eyes, concentrating hard on the visual.

They waited, nothing happened. The Sphere's surface quietened as it always did but this time it didn't change. Nary a sneeze of movement could be seen. Jack's breath was shortening, his throat dry, opening and closing his mouth, licking his lips nervously. Why hadn't they come out…that was the deal with these things wasn't it? Jack thought about it uselessly, rubbing his chin with a fist. 'This ain't right,' he said hastily, straining to find a damn thing on the surface. 'Fuck.' He snapped his head up at Ballard who was glaring back at him, features like cured concrete, breathing loudly through his nose. Jack raised a shoulder, lifting a shaky eyebrow, not sure what to do or say. This was a first and not in a good way, he was pretty sure Sagan needed to get the hell out right now or it was game over.

Jack could hear Ballard wheezing behind him, shoes tapping out an impatient beat on the ceramic tiles.

'Where are they?' He said bluntly, tired of waiting for him to speak. 'You said they'd be straight out so where are they Raines, is this going pear-shaped already?' He bent his head toward him, arching both eyebrows and screwing his nose into a crinkled mess, face flushed with blood.

Jack was mortified. Should he be honest or feed this guy some NASA bravado…stall him for a bit and hope like hell? Screw it he decided. 'I think we um, well, we may have lost the crew General,' thinking this can't be happening. Harry and Vic were the Agency's best and brightest, then there was Sky and the other two. What a colossal fuck up. Now they might have no one up there, just distant eyes on the ground, robotic eyes in orbit – no way that was enough.

'We need another shuttle up there, two if possible, find the best heads to take 'em up,' Ballard demanded. 'What are you doing about it Raines?' He was short but he loomed large on Jack, breathing stale garlic all over him. 'It should have happened already. Lucky the bloody Russians aren't up there front and centre and trust me, they wouldn't share zip if they found something.'

Jack edged back a few steps. 'Okay General, on your first point we are between shuttle programmes, as you know. The Gen-1 shuttles have been mothballed, we only have one of the Gen-2 Raptors functional, that's, uh…the one inside the Sphere. We've been refitting Endeavour since all this started but it's a week away from being launch ready.'

'Jesus Christ,' Ballard groaned, 'can't we just send it up…like it is?'

Jack stared blankly at him. 'Are you seriously asking that question General?'

'No, I suppose not but Jesus, this stinks… everything.' The General looked down at the floor, exhaling and tilting his shoulders one way then the other. 'So we've got nothing up there and no prospect of getting anything up there. We spend three hundred billion dollars on a crewed orbital launch capability and what do we have?' He scowled at Jack murderously. 'Fucking squat, that's what we've got…I mean, can this get any worse?'

Jack ignored his blustering. 'On the second point, the Russians are also between programmes until they get their PPTS up and running. But they are up there.'

Ballard's eyes widened from slits to finely rumpled crescents. 'What do you mean, where are they…what craft?' He looked genuinely stunned.

Jack was amazed this guy knew so little about the Russian Federal Space Agency. He was the commander of NORAD/NORTHCOM and knew shit about Soviet movements in space. What a monumental confidence builder that was, serving to deepen Jack's sense of doom. He guessed, hoped, he had more pressing domestic concerns. 'There's a Soyuz TMA-M docked at the ISS,' Jack said with a ghost of an eye roll, 'it's an emergency vehicle for the space station, fuelled up, ready to go. There's three Russians aboard the ISS but for whatever reason the ship is still there…still docked.'

'Why haven't they tried to use it to get some intel for themselves? Surely they get the gist of what might be going on?' He lifted his eyes. Stupid fucks, Ballard thought glibly, wondering what the commies were thinking, why they weren't thinking. He would've expected the Kremlin to be all over it, to try and beat the US to the punch or to try and protect themselves at least.

'POTUS put it to Putin, he refused to answer, saying they were still collecting information, analysing carefully before acting,' Jack said, 'I mean go figure, the overlords of jumping in prematurely and he comes out with that cheese.'

Ballard was aghast, he definitely would've expected Putin to be up to his eyeballs in it. Collecting information? Analysing – it was comical. 'If they really wanted to analyse something they'd undock the bloody Soyuz and motor it over to the bogies,' Ballard fumed, smelling a fat black rat. 'You know insider trading's legal over there, can you believe that shit? What a way to run a country, it's a fucking madhouse.'

Jack switched off the S-band, looking squarely at Ballard and Pete. 'So, what do we do?' He turned his head, glaring at the Flight Control Room. 'Do we rely on the guys with the guns and those three whiz kids over there?' He rubbed the back of his hand across his mouth, peering at the tiled floor, wondering what the hell their next move should be.

'Easy, those three whiz kids are some of our best scientific minds.' He waved them over.

'Well they better be,' Jack said, praying. Savants was his hope.

Nate was an absolutely brilliant mathematician and astrophysicist. Few were better positioned to extract meaning from a message as long as there actually was a message based on something we could comprehend, namely math and physics. If it was anything to do with unified field theory, the glorious GUT that no one had cracked, then they were done.

'So what's the go?' Jack asked expectantly, Nate stared back at him dumbly. 'Any results?' He said, re-stating it, forgetting these genius types were actually idiots in the real world. Great start, he thought, seeing Nate's puzzled mug.

'Er, well, it's a series of basic base two binaries that has no repeating pattern so far. It may even be machine code but we honestly don't know without a, um…fulcrum of some sort, a key but we don't have that…yet,' Nate said almost sheepishly, sorry he didn't have more to offer.

Jack glanced at Ballard and saw colour thicken under his skin. 'Okay Nate, that's great, but can you simplify it a bit for the General.' He was going to say dumb it down but thought better of it. The General grunted, looking back at Nate expectantly.

'Right, okay,' Nate said, blinking nervously, 'so machine code is the most basic computer programming.' He glanced at Jack quizzically and he urged him on, nodding as inconspicuously as he could. 'It's made of ones and zeroes, is executed, processed directly by a computer's brain, the CPU…very specific task based instructions.' He paused, 'you, ah…with me?'

'Yep,' Jack nodded, looking at Ballard who was sweating, still ruddy as he concentrated hard. The General was a relic of the bow and arrow days, still living in the world of ledger cards and glorified radars. He had hundreds of agents and staff to do the tech stuff, at least that was the excuse.

'Machine code is a primitive language that's basically extinct,' Nate said, trying to simplify it to Ballard's level of comprehension. 'We use text-based stuff now, executable algorithms.'

'But you don't know what it is? Jack asked flatly.

'No we don't,' Nate said, scratching an eyebrow. 'There's no repetition, nothing mathematically significant in it, nothing that resonates with human stuff. Converting it to decimal reveals nothing, no prime sequences or successions of Pi. And in the interests of formality, and pardon me General, there's no cyclic quadrilaterals, Secant tangents, alternate segments or any other transcendental or circle based Euclidian geometry in it.'

Ballard looked like he'd been slapped. 'Okay son, good work, I think, um…Jack?'

'Keep digging Nate, if you need to engage others, tell the General and he'll get 'em here on a helo or a plane ASAP, just ask.'

Nate looked a little miffed and glibly agreed to consult if the need arose. Fuck off he really wanted to say, then slap his résumé in front of them, dropping it with a desk punching crack. Newton and Hawking had held the same Chair as he did and Nate briefly considered throwing it out there, conceding Ballard would probably grunt and ask "who"?

The objects, their motional behaviour, the streams of basic numerals, all of it lacked any deeper meaning which surprised no one. It was primitive, uninformative and try as he might, Nate found it infuriating that they would give humans something science based that he couldn't unravel. He was a decorated, post-doctorate math virtuoso but he had nothing. It could be machine code but they had to be dealing with a highly evolved species so why the hell would they serve that facile crap up? Nate's immediate retort was they believed we were genuinely primitive so they began with something akin to tic-tac-toe, something the barbarians could get their heads around.

He assumed they'd chosen the moment of acquisition of AI technology as the time they wanted to connect. That seemed fair enough. Nate knew they'd moved a long way beyond simple binaries and machine code but it was only around fifty years since they'd graduated to it, then beyond it, less than a heartbeat in the bigger scheme of things. Nate had wrestled constantly about the entities behind the Spheres, debating their nature, their lifespans, guessing they could well be measured in millennia, might even be immortal through a flesh for silicon trade, or some other yet to be discovered biological amaranthine.

Putting all that aside, Nate concluded that having gifted their intriguing machine to what would slowly become an ice-trapped continent, they or at least their proxies were back, now that we'd shouted out our binary-based technology. Was that really it though…could it possibly be that simple? The twist in the tale for Nate and the world was why? Based on what Jack had told him, nothing seemed particularly friendly or aimed at assuaging our fears and anxieties, the encounter had all the hallmarks of a less than munificent approach. Dread for humanity was an overriding emotion.

***

Everything was dark beyond the shuttle's window panels as though the silica glass had been sealed with thick black paint. They thought their eyes were still getting accustomed to the low light but nothing appeared in the darkness, no stars, galaxies or light of any kind.

'Douse the cabin lights Vic,' Harry said quickly, hearing the doof-doof of his heart thudding in his ears. With the flight deck lights off they couldn't see their hands in front of their face, reminding him of caving, kilometres underground, without a light.

Skylar's heart was hammering worse than Harry's, in her throat, her chest, even her mouth was getting a work over. 'Where are w-we? She whispered in a hollow voice, almost incoherent.

Connie and Becker were staring at the inky vista, weighing the same thing, this was completely different from anything they had seen before.

Zero visual stimuli,' Vic breathed, his own brand of anxiety rising in his chest, a feeling of hopelessness enveloping him like quicksand.

'This is bullshit,' Harry hissed, scowling at Vic blindly in the dark. 'Drag us in, spit us out. I mean, did they haul us in last time because we approached it or was it going to happen anyway? Questions waste oxygen and I'm breaking my own golden rule, but do we have any control?' Harry was muttering negatives, expletives, flapping his hand in the darkness, suspicious and bitter. 'Do our actions even matter, do these creatures decide when and where we get hijacked, and…what the hell determines where we end up?' His mouth was pulled tight as he paused momentarily, still seeing nothing, adding, 'we've spoken about it I know but does each one have a single destination or is it some crazy carny game of chance…like spin up the wheel, see where you land?' Harry shook his head in bewilderment, surveying the absence of anything outside. Damn it, he thought. That's a shitload of empty questions right there. Cabin lights on Vic.'

Vic punched the pushbutton to illuminate the cabin. 'We're still in the Sphere,' he pointed to a barely visible haze of patterning, appearing here and there beyond the shuttle's main window.

Harry got out of his seat and walked up to the small viewing recess, peering out, searching for anything, 'is there anywhere that could look like this?' Another dumb question, he hastily noted, pretty sure he was losing his grip.

'Only one that comes to mind.' Vic said, glancing back at Harry who looked seriously conflicted, scratching the front of his neck, leaving it glowing red.

'Well? You gonna keep it a secret or what?'

'Just an idea, can't think of much else.'

'Just throw it out there,' Becker hollered. 'Forget the palatable crap, we're all grown-ups here, we can take it.'

Sky bit her lip doubtfully, she was a grown-up but her mind felt like an egg on its end, balancing above a concrete path, waiting for the slightest zephyr to send it tumbling to a grisly fate.

Vic hauled himself out of the pilot's seat and walked over to Harry. 'I thought maybe we were in a black hole, beyond the event horizon but that can't be,' he murmured, trailing off.

'If you think I'm jumping in with an answer, forget it pal. It sounds fair enough to me.'

'Wrong,' he snapped back. 'Light can come in but not get out so that can't be it. We'd still be able to see the Universe, just not talk to it.'

Harry gestured at him with a flourish. 'This isn't a fucking game show Vic.'

Skylar would've put fingers in her ears to block it out but didn't want to look like a complete twat, already acutely embarrassed by her butchering of the role she was so kindly handed, confronting the extraordinary, should it be out there. The only thing she'd confronted was her own feeble personality and catastrophic weakness of mind.

'So,' Vic started gravely, 'and while I don't necessarily believe it, we may be so far in the future, everything's been lost beyond the particle horizon.' He paused, glancing at the deadpan expressions, except Becker who was gazing cloudily at the blackness outside. 'Maybe everything is so far away that only islands of matter remain that are totally disconnected…skies in between that are, well…black like this. Perhaps we're between islands, you know, complete spatial detachment.' Vic saw all of them tuned in now, suggesting that they might be trillions of years in the future. Vic didn't believe it but it was all he had and like just about everything else, it was a possibility.

Harry watched the now visible interior of the Sphere move off them as though it were falling away like a worn out husk. Skylar yelped something indeterminate, looking fixedly past Vic at something behind him. 'Oh shit,' her eyes widened and hands rushed to cover her mouth.

Becker saw the thing approaching and could literally smell the iron-rich scent of his own demise, shuffling back as far as he could, ending hard up against the back of Vic's seat. Part of the coppery Sphere had somehow clawed its way into the shuttle's interior, coming straight toward them like a gelid gas. Avoiding it wasn't an option, there was nowhere to go.

'It can't be in here Vic...it's not...it doesn't make sense,' Connie whimpered.

Fucking der, Harry thought, having not the slightest idea what to do.

'It doesn't seem to be effecting the shuttle,' Vic soothed with eyes that said otherwise. 'We should be okay,' he repeated, breathing in bursts, feeling unnerved by something so unexpected, not in his wildest dreams contemplating coming face to face with the stuff of the Sphere, unprotected. He hadn't anticipated his physical response either, which was pure panic...to run.

'But we're made of living bloody tissue Vic, not metal or plastic,' Skylar mewed, watching owl-like as the horrible wall of whatever-it-was loomed, covering her face and tensing every muscle in her body until she was cramping. It struck every pore of Sky's body despite the thick suit she was wearing, like being gently sand blasted with static electricity. It wasn't unpleasant, in fact Sky conceded it was mildly pleasurable, like a massage from a million tiny fingers. Then it was gone.

Vic's relief became sudden concern as he ran his hands from his waist up to his shoulders, checking everything was still there, face melding into incredulity. 'I don't, I mean...it can't have come through the aluminium...titanium of the hull, the joints are fluor-siloxane rubber with a bit of cadmium mixed in, so that can't be the answer either...I mean, Harry, can it?'

'It's airtight, everything tight...it's a fucking spacecraft,' Harry said, nodding brusquely. 'The thing is...if it's come through the shuttle then it's gone straight through us as well.'

Sky was peering intently at him, still feeling the tiny pin pricks under her suit, worrying about what this stuff might have done on the way through. Had it taken a bit of them with it, maybe neurochemistry, biology, or had it left something behind, in them? Sky winced as she paced back and forth in tiny steps, a thump of dread kicking her in the gut.

Each of them looked more closely at the other to see if there was anything strange going on. 'Uh...does everyone feel okay?' Connie said, glancing about. Apart from Sky, everyone indicated in the positive, nodding, still sizing each other up. Sky wasn't sure, she'd been nauseous since they'd broken from Kennedy, pretty certain it was just anxiety. She'd have sold her soul for a few Xanax.

'Okay then,' Harry waved his hands around assertively, 'we all seem fine, no ill effects.'

'Let's give it some time before we start on the motherhood statements. If you grow another melon in your sleep we'll know for sure Harry.' She taunted testily then looked away.

'Long as it's me and not you, cause if you end up with twice the attitude I'm through the airlock, swimming to interface.' He threw a stupid grin and a thumbs-up at the back of her head.

Connie looked back and put her hand under her chin and shoved it straight out, giving him clear instructions to go forth and multiply.

***

Pete kept one eye on the vision at the head of the FCR, still hoping, but it continued to confirm the worst. What he'd seen on the Hubble feed was nothing less than terrifying, watching Sagan swallowed and digested right in front of them. Jack was next to him, Ballard to his right, staring heavily at the central visual, waiting for the ripples of an exiting vehicle.

Like all of them, Jack held grave fears but he admonished himself for assuming the worst, he wouldn't concede it yet, despite what he'd said in haste before. 'There's gotta be hope,' Jack said, crossing himself, well aware he owed them belief and support, in public at least.

One of the Atlas controllers yelled Pete's name, frantically gesturing him over. 'Christ,' he whispered, glancing at Jack, hustling over in a dozen quick steps. Jack watched him look intently at the visual on the screen, then point at something and step back with his hands up defensively. He walked back slowly, repeatedly rubbing his face. Jack didn't want to know but could see it was coming, he looked like he had something wedged in his throat.

189

'Well okeydokey then,' Pete said, pausing for a moment, gathering his thoughts. 'Um, the objects are accelerating.' He coughed, smoothing the rumples on his jacket. 'They're a hundred and eighty thousand k's away and they were inbound at five clicks, but now they're coming at ten, increasing at almost a click a minute. They're on a direct heading for Earth, 90 degrees south, zero degrees west.' Pete raised his eyes for a moment, sighing, mulling over the aggressive behaviour.

Jack looked at him nonplussed, Pete returned his stare likewise. 'Which is where?' Jack asked impatiently, debating whether Pete thought he was a mind reader or maybe a human GPS.

'West Antarctica. Marie Byrd Land,' he said, recognising the steep irony.

'Jesus,' Jack murmured as it sunk in, 'of course it is…the site of the original bogey. Does Nate know?'

'He's all over it,' Pete said, 'Science is getting everything before we do.'

Ballard came steaming up from the back of the FCR, looking ready to declare war, have a stroke or suffer some other medical malediction. Massive jowls of loose flesh hung around his neck, everything about him was the colour of fresh blood, squirming beneath layers of jiggling skin.

Taking a few deep breaths he spoke in semi-measured gasps, telling them what they already knew. 'We have an escalating, clear and present danger, to the US…to the world.'

Jack looked at him sceptically. '…and we didn't before?' He blurted out the words before he could swallow them.

Ballard's blood pressure flashed brighter, the poor prick was glowing like a tropical sunset. 'Bogies are coming in harder, we need to prepare, priority is White Status, no exceptions.'

'Prepare?' Jack questioned, examining the General closely, battling to understand what was going on inside that shiny balding dome of his.

Ballard eventually softened his expression. 'Look, whether we can do anything, we have no idea but we can prepare.' He took a massive breath, coughing with the grating hack of a heavy smoker. 'We're almost on pre-war status for Christ's sake, against an enemy we can't possibly fight.'

Fuck me, Jack thought, feeling an empty space open in his mind. 'So what's the plan General?' He was trying to get him to the gravy stroke if there was one. Ballard was a perfect fit for NORAD, but his staging was over the top, coming off way too melodramatic. Poor bastard, Jack said to himself drolly, the guy was so military, such a stiff Army caricature it was hard to take him seriously. Ballard was all formality, suit, tie, impeccably dressed, perfectly pressed, voice guttural and Hollywood. Shortish and pudgy with the countenance of a brick wall, he had it covered every which way, the bearing and demeanour, the look of a bulldog.

'The whole goddamn tribe is coming to Houston,' he said, gripping his hands together briefly. 'The Secretary of Defence and two of his senior execs from DoD, three from the National Security Council, Chair of the Joint Chiefs, CIA Director Knowles, deputy CEO of HomeSec, Chief Administrator of FEMA and the Exec Director of the National Guard. They'll report through the Defence Secretary to the President.' He raised his eyes briefly, staring at Jack gravely for a moment. 'This is now a war room, National security…international security is on the line.' Maintaining his glare, Ballard was as serious as it got. 'We don't know what these things want, what they are, but they're being treated as a threat, until we learn different that's the way it stays.'

Jack thought it sounded like typical conspiracy horseshit. He agreed they needed to be ready for anything but should it be an overt war footing? Hell no, and anyway they had no orbital capability for battle, so any supposed offensive was a load of bollocks. The best it could ever be was a show of intent and unity, but did we really want to be seen as hostile when we had less than zero to back it up? It was talking the talk without the faintest hope of walking the walk. They were wedged in the deepest end of the twilight zone with no primary plan, no back-up plan and no actionable understanding of what was approaching from space. If Ballard and his cronies were right about their intentions and we pissed them off even more, the numbers added up to something a four year old could work out. Great fucking strategy General he felt like screaming into his flushed, pug face.

'There's two hundred security agents coming from Langley,' Ballard said, 'they'll be blanketing Building 30 so don't plan on leaving anytime soon. All you NASA boys are in for the duration.' He grinned spitefully.

Pete looked at Jack and gulped uncomfortably. 'Uh, so…pizza delivery?' Pete said to Ballard lightly. 'We need to eat.'

'You don't have a goddamn canteen here at NASA son?' He said, staring him down with an implacable glare, saying don't waste my fucking time. 'We pay you boys thirty billion a year, you got to have a place to get a dog and sauce right?'

Shit Pete thought. It was just a throwaway. 'Er, canteen yes, fine.' He said with a visible swallow, lowering his gaze.

Damn, so much for Charlie's birthday Jack thought, hearing a vague thumping in the distance, growing rapidly into full-blown thunder. 'They're here already?' Jack said, guessing it underlined the planet-critical nature of what was going down.

Ballard gazed through the sweeping windows of Building 30, watching as the Sea Kings and White Hawks slapped their way in, slowly coming to rest on the bitumen and lawn, sending a billowing cloud of dust and leaves flying in all directions, shrouding the west wall of the Johnson Space Centre. Jack felt his body tense, peering at Government agents pouring out, shadowed by dignitaries who were carefully ushered away in the direction of the MCC. He wasn't religious in the true sense, but he offered a prayer for the crew, hoping they were still out there somewhere, and if they were, they'd find a way home. If they were dead or stranded, he wasn't sure what they'd do down here. No eyes in space, no Harry or Vic, the parlous thought made him feel like dry retching into his wastepaper bin.

***

Sky was going to voice her darkest fears with the crew because it was no longer negotiable, if it stayed bottled inside she was sure there'd be a detonation of blood and skull bone. Sharing might decompress her a bit, but as she took a heavy swallow to launch, the Sphere was suddenly back, emerging from nowhere in front of them, bobbing up like a deep-sea Bathysphere, bursting from the depths of the ocean. Now it sat in front of them in all its simple, primal beauty. She was thankful there was something out there apart from nothing but reckoned assigning positives of any sort might be inviting the worst. She quietly suggested it could be very bad news indeed, they just didn't know it yet. Listening to her endless negative spin, Connie felt her face flush, she could understand it up to a point, but the never-ending stream of fatalistic bullshit was infuriating. She distantly admitted that anger management might not be her strong point.

'Jesus, give it a break,' Connie said, finishing with a heavy exhalation, 'just stow the death crap for five minutes, focus on something else, like getting home.' She shot her an indignant glare.

'Oh, and you seriously think we have control over that…give me a break.'

'Whatever,' Connie returned in typical dismissive style, 'just think it don't say it. I'm with Harry on that, we're all sick of your crap.'

'Think it, say it, sing it, scream it…what's the difference?' She said weakly, 'won't change a thing, it is what it is right? We're screwed or we're not. Just don't think we have any say in it because we don't. We're being played, poked, managed by something,' Sky said, shifting her eyes down, not willing to engage Connie further.

Connie felt twitchy as she regarded her, about to jump in but stopping dead when she saw her sniffing softly and wiping at her nose. Sky's chin was trembling and she'd slumped even lower to the ground, moisture welling in her eyes, the corners of her lips about as low as they go.

'Jesus…fuck!' Harry yelled suddenly, lurching against his chair restraints as a wave of energy hammered the shuttle, causing it to rock slightly. Harry unbuckled and shuffled over to the window with Connie and Becker, leaving Sky cross-legged on the floor, facing the payload bay doors. Her eyes were shut tightly, fists clenched like mallets on her lap.

191

The Sphere was boiling white, visibly convulsing, radiating rivers of shining particles, or at least something in every direction. The streams of Sphere stuff stretched as far as they could see, lighting up the darkness like a beautiful, diminutive but incredibly potent star. All of a sudden it shut off again, dying like a spent phosphorus flare. The light had come and gone but it had definitely not been for nought.

Becker splurted a string of expletives, finishing with a typically cogent summary, 'whoa, it's full of…er, well, everything you'd expect I guess.'

Vic blinked blindly, shot full of adrenaline, it was hard to control his breathing, eyes straining forward, numbed by the surreal canvass of light, colour and energy invading the blackness.

Vic recalled some of the freaky stuff he'd seen along the way but this was a leap beyond even that. If what he reckoned had happened, had actually happened, then the implications would challenge the very faculty of the humble human processor called brain. It made Vic consider whether these others had any insight into the human condition at all or maybe it was just the peculiar way of the cosmos - no one had a decent handle on their neighbour's state of mind, it was all just an abstract mystery and just maybe, cerebral divergence was the norm. Vic screwed his face up, not knowing what to think, kicking around the enigmatic little non-law coined evolution that was barely an ant's dick above unqualified chaos. Even Darwin shunned the word, throwing it in as a footnote in the last line of his epic Origin of Species, but ironically the noun stuck fast and was widely misread, a concept the great man came to despise. Transmutation was his poison, the other spoke too much of good, better, best and some grand, pebble-bricked road to perfection that spoke to some grand Designer. The thing was, life on Earth swung wildly through dystopia and perdition on its circuitous journey. Ninety nine percent of every remarkable species that drew breath on Earth was now gone. The evolution of the word evolution, Vic knew, was way off kilter. He was with Darwin. Evolution was an outlaw on the lam with a million bucks in her kick and a billion hideaways spread across the globe. The choices to pursue were endless, and sure they were tapered broadly toward survival advantage but that was the start and the finish. If by some miracle, intelligence found its feet, everything was up for grabs, the way a species interpreted things, its value systems, culture, definitions of pleasure, of right and wrong, they could be anything and maybe proof of concept was staring them in the face.

Beyond the shuttle, in every direction, a normal cosmos had emerged from the emptiness. Space was brimming with stars, galaxies, colourful noble gasses and gorgeous nebulas crammed with dazzling stars. Some were dimmer, flickering on and off, slowly becoming steady like they'd just gathered the mass to spark nuclear burning. Quite impossibly, light from nearby and distant stars was everywhere around them, space was suddenly rich with evolved mass and energy.

Skylar turned around but was still sitting on the floor like a dutiful young school kid at assembly. Seeing the stars and everything else through the shuttle window she wondered if it was all a con. Visual effects like this would be child's play for an advanced civilisation.

Harry realised how absurd it was from a simple physics point of view, peering at Vic, assuming he would have got it straight away.

Vic nodded at him, 'go on, say it,' he said knowingly.

'Say what?'

'It.'

'It what?' Harry was playing him now.

'Fucking it,' Vic said a little too harshly. 'The bloody E and the C of course.'

'Oh Christ, okay,' he relented grudgingly. 'All the light takes centuries, millennia or more to span the distance. I mean a light year's called a light year for a reason.' He looked at Vic deliberately, 'it cuts through every natural law you can rattle off.'

'A mighty paradox it is,' Vic said curiously, having no answer to it, unless it was some inexplicable set up, like Sky said. It was real, his higher brain was convinced, it was only his grip on what was logical and reasonable that rebelled against it.

Skylar watched them closely, wondering how these borderline geniuses could have so little imagination. Harry had gotten part way there. She continued to eye them quizzically, 'have you not concluded that this is just some mock up and not real at all? I mean, you can't break the laws of physics, you know it better than I do.' She twisted her brow into an affronted frown. 'I know the whole fake imagery idea doesn't make a lot of sense either but the question has to be asked, is it their intent to make no sense?' Her eyes were unblinking, battling with the disagreeable possibility.

Vic raised a slightly mocking eyebrow. 'Makes um,' he searched for another word but couldn't find one, 'no sense.'

'To the human mind it doesn't,' Harry said, 'but maybe Sky's right. It might be just the way they are, you know, their MO as a species.'

'Sounds nuts,' Becker weighed in. 'What about friendly old E.T…the plucky little fellow with the big eyes, swollen finger, that's how it's supposed to be.' He concealed a smirk with his hand.

'Oh for God's sake,' Connie said, 'that's just flowery crap peddled by film makers to rip away your hard earned.'

Becker looked offended. 'How dare you, I'll have you know that ET was held in high—'

Connie let out a breath that morphed into a groan. 'Funny,' she said with amusement. 'But let's face it, it's a huge Universe…lots of room for every possible outcome, every possible mindset,' she looked at Becker, 'and idiot. Now you can look offended. Comprendè el dancer?'

The Sphere had more or less returned to its previous state, now very deliberately approaching them and clearly brighter than it had been before. Vic studied the object as it edged closer, seeing the light from stars reflecting crisply off its perfect curvature. And then it hit him, causing his breath to catch in his throat. He thrust his neck forward to make sure he was getting the whole picture. It felt like he'd been cracked in the head with something hard.

'What the hell?' Why wasn't this thing reflecting the shuttle? He gulped unconsciously, narrowing his eyes to focus, all things being equal, Sagan should have been front and centre in the middle of the object with its cabin lights right in their face. Everything was there on its inscrutable curvature except them. Somehow it was excluding their image, or was it proof that this was just some bullshit sham? Pins and needles ran over his body, pushing the hair up on his shoulders as the Sphere kissed the nose of the shuttle.

***

Jack surveyed the sea of suits and if it wasn't so damn serious he would've laid his head back and laughed at the surreal scene. It looked more like the incident room at The Pentagon he reckoned, scanning the grim expressions around him. Mission Control had never seen such a throng of Government and military types, certainly not at the same time, even shuttle disasters and Moon landings were less chaotic. Earl Griffin, the Secretary of Defence was calling the shots, right now in heated debate with Ballard and others from DoD, NSC and a bunch of other defensive organisations. Even the bloody CDC was there in case these things seeded the Earth with some horrific, world ending disease. When Jack heard that, he did a double take, wondering bleakly if that was a possibility, conceding it had to be, along with anything else anyone cared to imagine. Every combatant commander was now on standing alert, readying for some obscure battle even though they would never, ever be ready for it, if it came.

Ballard waved Jack over with a desultory air slash, inducing an involuntary swallow that hurt. Fucking great, he said to himself, getting up and ambling toward the daunting throng of suits and officialdom, all looking harried and decidedly unwelcoming. He couldn't help feeling ticked off that they'd so easily annexed his turf, briefly considering what might happen if he told them to back off, or better yet, get the fuck off his patch, pointing the way with a stiff one fingered salute. Marched out at gunpoint he assumed. In his mind's eye he saw a comical vision of being unceremoniously thrown into a Nighthawk for dispatch to Gitmo as a prescribed enemy of the state. These guys were largely bluster but they were seriously off-putting and jumpy enough to be genuinely scary.

193

Ballard looked ready to burst, venting abruptly at the science team, 'so you're getting what from this binary stuff?' Nate and the others looked over at him timidly, not ready to report because they had zero to report. 'Yoshihara, summarise what you have, in English.' Ballard's face was lined like deeply eroded granite, eyes steely, not in the mood for bullshit.

Yoshi was hopelessly overawed, staring at Jack with his chocolate eyes screaming for help. Glancing down at his sneakers he tried desperately to slow his breathing, to get some moisture into his mouth. 'Er, uh…sir, please call me Yoshi. Only my mum calls me Yoshihara, when she's angry mostly.' He squirted out a brief chuckle, just serving to deepen the lines in Ballard's already furious expression. Christ, Yoshi gulped, who is this maniac? 'Uh, anyway,' Yoshi continued, 'collectively we are fluent in all major branches of math. One of my specialities is 3-Spheres, higher dimensional analogues of normal Euclidean math, four dimensional manifolds, Hope hyperspheres and the like, as well as regular stuff.' He pulled at the collar of his jacket nervously.

'Oh well that's just great,' Ballard said acidly, hacking out a coal miner's cough, glaring even harder at him, silently cautioning him on the words he was using, eyes slitted. 'So, okay,' Yoshi murmured, 'we know math inside-out but I think we need a code builder, a programmer to cut up the code, if it's source-based, which is a possibility. We know it's potentially CPU feedstock so there's a chance it's something to do with AI.'

Griffin grabbed his cell, phoning Pentagon DI, telling them to get him the best AI programmer and get him on a fucking helo an hour ago. He spat profanity at them endlessly, demanding they kidnap the bastard at gunpoint if they had to. It was DEFCON 2, Status White, maybe the dawn of a fucking interstellar war, so just get it done.

Ballard turned to Pete and blew his cheeks out. 'Status report… distance, velocity?' He lowered his face toward Pete until he was so close the hairs in Ballard's nose were disturbingly obvious.

Pete gawped at the Atlas console, watching time rapidly peel away. If these things were indeed a threat to Earth then zero time was coming quick. Should direction and velocity remain unchanged they would reach atmospheric interface in little over an hour. And what then, that was the kicker for humanity, Pete guessed, what the hell then? He shook his head hard, re-focussing.

'Sixty-nine thousand clicks sir, ten point eight per second. Time to impact sixty-six minutes.

'Fuck in a frog bag,' Ballard spluttered in a cloud of spittle. 'Earl, do you have a minute.' The Defence Secretary broke off from the NSC exec, striding over.

'Jesus, 'we've got an hour…one goddamn hour,' the NORAD boss said quietly, struggling to keep his voice even.

Griffin glared at Ballard, finger tapping his thigh impatiently. 'No one has any useful intel, none of 'em, not a zac, MIT, Caltech, Johns Hopkins, Texas A&M. These things aren't Soviets or some fucking two-bit terrorist cell.' He paused, closing his eyes and rubbing the middle of his forehead, realising there wasn't a single pro to grab hold of and hack their way through the tangle of cons. 'We've got no basis for strategy, nothing to build tactics on, no background, no actionable intel, not a goddamn iota of insight.' His eyes were barely open, rimmed by dark lines and baggy wrinkles, some of them red like marbled beef. Griffin was in brand new territory, he had access to global best practice everything but he had zero detail, zero Intel and he fucking hated it.

'War footing is all we have…mobilising troops, assets, weaponry,' Ballard offered gravely, 'maximum readiness is the only go-to.'

Griffin spoke directly to the Secretary of the Air Force, giving the "go" he was waiting on to scramble warplanes. Shock and awe in numbers only was the strategy, after that, no one knew. It would depend on "events" as they unfolded. The Secretary asked what they should send up, suggesting F4 Phantoms, Tomcats, Strike Eagles but was cut off mid-sentence by a mighty intake of breath. 'Are you serious Dale?' Griffin fairly screamed, 'for fuck's sake man, send everything!' He was shaking his cell violently, it was all Jack could do not to laugh. 'Follow the plan, send the lot up, recycle 'em, refuel 'em in mid-air, whatever. Just fill the bloody sky.' He hung up abruptly, holstering his cell roughly. 'God damnit,' he wheezed. 'Send up what, did you hear him? Gee Dale let me think, a couple of bi-planes and a fucking Lancaster. Christ Almighty.' He was puffing, fighting to catch his breath, lamenting the twat that was running the US Airforce.

Jack couldn't question the Defence Secretary but seriously, scaring them, shock and awe, was that a joke? With the likely technology these others possessed, did they honestly think warplanes would do the job, psychologically or physically? We weren't the slightest bit space capable and these jets, mighty impressive to us, quite likely had less shock value than an insect buzzing around an elephant's arse. The fate of the world was in the hands of some short-sighted, politically motivated aggressors that knew dick about space, or anything remotely off world. They had their scientific advisors but the meatheads from Washington still decided when the trigger was pulled.

'So, what's going up?' Jack asked despondently, knowing the "everything" strategy was absurd, no more than a waste of jet fuel. It might even kill us all, he considered idly. Piss them off, maybe the hammer falls.

'Damn near everything son, F-35s, Raptors, Eagles, Falcons, things like that. The Russians and Chinese are deploying too so it's gonna be grid lock up there.'

Pete was listening to Griffin, mightily unimpressed. 'So, you're thinking these objects might actually enter the atmosphere…like land somewhere?' It was possible he thought but unlikely surely, although the Trojan horse scenario did give him pause.

Griffin looked at Ballard who nodded vigorously. 'We're planning for that scenario,' he conceded. 'We won't engage unless we're threatened but we need to be mobilised, ready for whatever comes. The US is where it's at gentlemen, no one else can be relied on.'

Oh dear God, was Jack's first thought, this guy was seriously narcissistic, not to mention clinically nationalistic. No doubt he thought the borders of the US sign-posted the end of the world, beyond that, well, you just fell off. 'You're aware of Sagan's experience with these things right?' Jack said as respectfully as he could, avoiding the urge to tell him to pull his fucking head in.

Griffin and Ballard locked eyes again, this time without expression, silently sharing their derision over the Sagan report. 'We're aware of the claims,' Griffin said, 'and that's part of why we're mobilising at White Status. He steepled his fingers, resting them on his mouth and chin. Jack stared back blankly. 'Anyway, if these things land,' Griffin said, 'who's to say an army of who knows what won't pour out and overrun us poor bastards?' He eyeballed Jack ominously, nodding. 'Sounds crazy but until we know definitively to the contrary we can't rule it out.' He finished by drawing a raking breath through his nose, blowing out an impatient sigh. 'Nothing's off the table until it's empirical, confirmed, proven.'

Jack shrugged at Pete, agreeing that whilst this guy would fumble anything that wasn't military, he was partially right in theory. Nothing was off the table – fact.

On the face of it, presenting an aggressive front to these objects seemed wrong but Jack wasn't sure there was any other way. If they had decent intel maybe it might be different, but all they had so far were hostile actions mixed in with some very pretentious, threatening behaviour. All things considered, could a world dominated by egocentric, sectarian militaries just sit on their haunches and watch these off-world objects approach without mobilising? It would beggar belief if it happened. The options in this sorry scenario were crystal clear, either every nation found the collective will to sit on their hands and count sheep, or some or all of them cranked up their militaries.

Jack chewed uncomfortably on Ballard's words and didn't bother to counter them but if the NORAD chief reckoned Tridents, Sparrows and Minutemen would rattle these visitors he had his hand firmly stroking his nether regions.

'Forty-five minutes,' Pete barked, 'ten point eight per second.' He wiped sweat from his upper lip with a steeply angled palm.

Four figures burst through the doors of the FCR with a reverberating crash of metal hitting hard wall. Three of them were clearly Government agents, the fourth a dishevelled young male looking agitated and to put it mildly, pissed at his current condition. He was being hurried forward, almost carried over to Griffin who stuck his hand out.

'Earl Griffin, Secretary of Defence, you are?'

'I know who you are, I thought you'd know who I am. You asked for me by name apparently.' He glared at each of them, then back at Griffin, 'your goons weren't too forthcoming with information.' He raised his arms over his head, stretching as they released him. 'Hardly a frigging welcoming committee.'

'I didn't ask for you, I asked for the best AI programmer in the country and I guess you're it son.'

The lead agent glanced up at Griffin. 'Actually, the best programmer was MIA sir, so we got this guy, recommended by Stanford, youngest professor ever apparently.'

'Oh, so second best, nice to know,' he said, pushing hair out of his eyes. 'Arseholes,' he repeated out loud this time.

'This is Max Keller,' the agent said. 'Research Professor at Texas A & M, holds some College of Engineering Chair in Computer Science. Almost the best we have.' The agent grinned sourly at Max.

'Well if you put it like that,' Max said, 'how can I refuse?' He swept his hair off his face again, sneering at all of them. 'So, are you going to tell me why I've been kidnapped by NASA and dragged to the Johnson Space Centre?' He was staring scornfully at Griffin who glared back in kind. 'Something kinda big has happened with these Spheres of yours I assume…grown teeth right?'

They brought Max up to speed with everything, Griffin taking unexpected pleasure in his stunned expression. Initially Max scoffed, staring widely at them, but surrounded by the jungle of pokerfaced suits, he winced and sucked it up.

'Unbelievable,' he breathed in a voice barely audible above the background noise. 'That is some mind-fuck,' he added skittishly, gazing down. Yoshi was standing next to him and as soon as he could he grabbed him, leading him over to the science team and introducing him. They'd managed to glean nothing from the binary numbers – the same vexing result achieved by dozens of other specialist teams fevering over the "data" in the US and overseas. UNOOSA and UNGI were coordinating information for every G20, but to date it amounted to fourth fifths of very little. The UN Outer Space Affairs and Group Intelligence departments were in twice daily contact with every nation contributing to the effort and based on the last briefing an hour ago, the frustrating status-quo remained. Either humanity was incapable of unravelling the depths of the message, if there was one, or worse, countries were concealing intel for their own use, considered unlikely because global security, even continuity was at stake. But it couldn't be entirely ruled out. Some countries had agendas nothing short of unfathomable, so hey, Griffin spruiked bitterly, the pricks in the east are on their own, knowing in himself that everyone on the planet was in it, had everything on the line.

Pete suddenly jumped up from the Atlas console, sending his chair rolling back and hitting the wall with a sharp crack. His eyes stayed rooted on the console. 'Jack, come here…take a look…the numbers.' He sounded half excited, half scared, though the latter seemed to be preponderating.

Jack hurried over to Pete who was poking at the screen. 'It's slowing down,' he said, hushed. 'Look at the numbers, uh…it was stable at ten point eight but it's down to six-point-four and…still declining.' His eyes were gaping as he pored over the data. 'It's forty-two thousand clicks away…and shit, now it's down to six-point one.'

'Good!' Griffin spluttered, 'that's great,' he said, pacing over to Laurence Ashcroft, Head of the NSC, barking at him to send the data to the Pentagon and Joint Chiefs of Staff Director, James Hillier. 'Move the intel Ashcroft,' he snapped loud enough to make him backpedal a step. 'Kent, get over here,' he said. Kent Morgan was an executive with DoD, a trusted confidante of Griffin's. 'You're only job is to convey everything from Atlas through the Joint Chiefs to the Secretary of State then on to the President. Make sure they all get it. Watch Ashcroft, it's on you Kent.' He emphasised the point by jabbing his forehead at him.

'Got it,' he said, walking off hurriedly, heart pounding, sweat already standing above his brow like he'd just pounded out a few laps.

'One-point-two clicks,' Pete said. 'Jack…they're stopping…zero-point-seven…zero-point-three.' Fuck me, he said hoarsely, watching the Doppler radar count the radial velocity all the way down to nothing. 'Velocity is uh, zero…motion nulled.' Pete jerked his head back. 'The Spheres are stationary,' he said, gawking blankly at Jack, eyes burning with one question…why?

'Distance?' Jack asked.

'RRS says thirty-five thousand seven hundred and eighty-six clicks plus change. I'm analysing the orbit,' Pete said distractedly as he worked on the keypad, pretty much already knowing the result based simply on distance.

'Let me know if anything changes,' Griffin ordered, sizing up each of them with blood shot eyes, twisting his mouth grimly.

Pete looked up from the console. 'The Spheres are in a synchronous orbit,' he said, glancing at Griffin, then Ballard who both stared back at him vacuously. 'It means they're orbiting at the same speed as the Earth's rotation. We do that when we want a bird to stay over the same piece of real estate. You're Airforce pals will know all about that.'

Jack didn't need to ask, but he did anyway. 'So which piece of real estate is the Sphere so interested in?'

'Well I'll give you a coupla' guesses Jack but you're only going to need one.'

Ballard threw him a murderous glare, silently telling Pete to fucking stow the horseplay.

'It's directly above Antarctica.'

'Above the original anomaly,' Jack murmured, fully expecting it, but equally questioning how the hell an orbit could be stable at that latitude.

Pete was of the same mind, his brows almost knitted above his eyes as he tossed it around. 'A stationary orbit is centred above the Earth's core, as in the equator…not the poles. All things being equal, which they're obviously not, the bogey is stationary from a free-fall perspective but it ain't orbiting at the same angular speed as Earth.' He shook his head gently, glancing at Jack for an answer.

'Christ,' Ballard puffed, exasperated, 'speak English, what are you trying to say, what's the fucking problem here?'

'Just that they should be falling into the atmosphere but they're not, the collective is stable in deep orbit but it shouldn't be, Newtonian physics says it can't be. The object must be producing some forcible resistance to remain where it is. No biggie really but it is interesting.'

One of the Atlas controllers gestured urgently to Pete to come back to the console. Looking at the VDU he could clearly see the individual Spheres winding up their rotation again, like they had nearer the Moon. It looked like a bunch of cogwheels slowly spinning up to speed inside some grand cosmic machine.

Pete was eyeing the Hubble visual, wondering again who was orchestrating these movements, the astonishing angular harmonics.

The Spheres approached Earth as a sessile framework that came in head on. But now it was spinning around a point of axis designated by the two central Spheres, themselves orbiting each other, rotating in synch with the individual Spheres and the greater structure. It was a complex celestial ballet, exquisitely choreographed, playing out high above the frozen ice fields of the South Pole.

***

An eruption of noise rifled through Mission Control. Everyone not already looking, turned and gazed at the wide-field Hubble view running on the massive projection screen at the head of the FCR. The field of view took in all fifteen Spheres and plenty of space besides.

'Yes, yes…goddamn yes!' Jack cried, spouting joyously, almost falling to his knees. 'Finally, goddamn it, some good news.'

197

There was elation on the faces of Pete and all the MCC flight controllers. Ballard slapped Griffin on the back, shooting Jack a tired grin. Griffin snapped his head around, ready to drop Ballard where he stood but eventually drew his lips into a tight smile. For Griffin, smiling made his features look malformed, more like an outgassing of gastric wind than a display of pleasure.

In the dead centre of the Hubble field of view was SLS Sagan, bone white and shining in the light from the Sun, reflecting the radiance from the Spheres in arcs of dazzling light. Apparently the shuttle had been ejected from one of the axial objects, now sitting proudly in Earth orbit, gently tumbling away as though hawked up like an inhaled fly.

Jack sat down quickly at the console, thumping the S-band Press to Talk button. 'Sagan, Flight, do you copy?' There was no response but the green light suggested there was open mic on the craft. Silence and a minor interplay of acoustic static played in the background.

Sagan, Houston Flight, copy? Jack repeated louder, more urgently. He looked over at Pete, eyes staring fixedly, holding his breath, waiting for some proof of life aboard Sagan.

They heard a grating noise like tape being ripped off fabric, then a voice. 'Great to hear your voice Jack,' came Vic clearly, 'we most definitely copy. How're you guys doing down there?'

Jack grinned broadly and said, 'fine Vic, we're heavy on Government types but all is well down here. Um…what's your shape?' He crossed and uncrossed his arms.

'Physically good, mentally …well, I'm not so sure,' he said, flicking his eyes across the group. 'The things we've seen Jack, we're being seriously tested up here. We don't feel like we're in physical danger but everything is nuts, it's taking its toll.'

Not in physical danger? Sky felt like grabbing his ear and screaming in it until he got it, heat suffusing her face. She felt depressed and alone, her life so different from that back on Earth, which seemed like it had played out a million years ago. It was as though space had changed her DNA somehow, altered her so fundamentally as a person that she'd lost almost all the positive behaviours that made her who she was.

'Okay Vic,' Jack started, 'like I said, we've got an FCR full of military and Government bods, as well as a bunch of leading science-types trying to make sense of the limited data we have.' He glanced uncertainly from Ballard to Griffin who stared back expectantly. His heartbeat rose a notch, tapping alarmingly near the front of his throat. 'Our science team needs a download of everything you've seen, they'll feed it to the UNGI for global distribution. Every detail Vic, they can decide what's important.' The Defence Secretary nodded his head effusively, mouthing the words with thin lips, every fucking detail.

'Copy that, but if recent history is a guide we may be shifting again…possibly soon. These things seem to get impatient with us hanging around up here for too long.' Vic paused, his voice dropping a fraction lower, 'you know, maybe they want to test us…see how much of this we can handle before we break. Maybe see if we can work out what they're doing, why they're doing it, decipher their messed-up game plan, that sort of thing.' Vic reckoned it was almost laughable, almost he chided, seeing Sky still laid out untidily on the floor of the shuttle like human wreckage. 'Most of us just want off this bloody merry-go-round,' he said, steeling his voice, 'Sky's ready to jump into the EMU and freestyle it over to the ISS, and Jack, I mean that.' She glanced up, grimacing and offering a slow, painful head nod. The thought of spacing herself from the airlock was starting to take on a weird attraction. The idea of never hugging her daughter again was repugnant but the agony of just existing was something she never thought she'd experience. If she lost her daughter, that was it for her, she'd end it in space, somehow.

Ballard and Griffin resembled two Howdy Doody bobble dolls as they shook their heads in perfect unison, Griffin mouthing the word stay in no, tilting his neck forward aggressively.

'Copy stay Sagan,' Jack said uncertainly, knowing it was more statement than question. They wanted out but equally understood there was a higher priority at play right now.

'Yep, copy stay,' Vic replied softly, ruefully. Shit he thought, hearing Sky start to moan incoherently, cradling her head again, swaying slowly back and forth. 'Oh Christ,' she murmured twice under her breath, the last a sunken gasp. The blood in her veins felt heavy like congealing concrete. No thoughts came to her except that her fate was sealed, and she had no say in it.

Sky seriously doubted she'd survive another journey, mentally or physically, but mainly mentally because her thinking was aberrant, dark. And they'd all heard Vic's comms with Mission where he'd graciously spoken for the crew, freely committing them to more torment. Thank you so much Vic. Fuck you very much Vic. They had to stay put, keep an eye out for anything worth anything, squashed together in this sardine can until they were either dead or Houston removed the No Entry signs, allowing them atmospheric egress. Peering at the floor she tried to corral her breathing, which was shallow and way too rapid. Her family, her girl, Jesus, they were deciding whether she'd ever see any of them again, like ever. Despite the bleakness though, there was enough of her left to concede that priorities had to rule. The greater good had to win because this might be a world's end scenario, orbiting above the pole like Damocles sword. The deeper part of her brain still flipped the bird though, love of family would overcome damn near anything, even the end of existence. Getting back was a biological urge no less primal than the need to eat, drink…or procreate. The priority stuff was in there, understood, but fizzing in the background like thermal interference.

'Vic,' she said, lifting a desperate shoulder, 'take me home.' Sky looked him full in the eye, tears forming reflective pools that were about to escape into the cabin.

'Sky, we can't,' Vic said softly, glancing at Harry, seeing a shadow of grief cross his face. He normally wore a Hazmat suit over his emotions but his face was briefly filled with pain as he gazed at her. It flashed tenderly beneath his tumbleweed beard.

'I need my little girl, I do,' she whimpered, tears breaking free into the air, tiny, glistening rounds of moisture. Sky pulled her knees up, grabbing them with both hands remaining steadfastly on the floor, head tipped back. In an instant of clarity she knew her sanity was cracking like an over-cooked meringue and pretty soon Sky saw the whole lot falling apart, spewing pieces everywhere.

'Sky, it's not our decision. We're the only craft up here, 'Vic said coolly. 'I wish it was our call but we have orders from pretty much the highest authority on the planet. When it's over we go home but the US President has asked us to stay. I mean…does anyone here wanna say no?'

***

The science team occupied their own makeshift home near the head of the FCR, directly in front of the Hubble feed that was projected above them on a mighty 4k Mercury screen. They had sequestered a bank of computer terminals and were huddled together in animated conversation.

Tara was still muddling over the so-called information being pulsed by the central Spheres, feeling a little overwhelmed, and crestfallen. Jack and Pete had been called over so they could give them what they had, which in Nate's words was a big hill of mung beans.

They were a brilliant quartet of minds, no argument there but they still hadn't found anything in the data, leading them to wonder if the light show was anything cognitive at all. Maybe it was set up as an exercise in futility, see how long it took them to realise their search was nothing more than a castle in the sky. They saw an irony in that because it would fit nicely with everything they'd heard about to date. They had theories, but an empirical result, true insight, not even close.

'And you've gotten what so far?' Jack said, lowering his head, knowing.

Nate looked at Max, then uneasily at Tara and Yoshi. No one was keen to speak, to own up to what could only be described as consummate failure. Still, if it wasn't there, it wasn't there, Nate told himself, still unconvinced.

'Hello?' Jack prompted, looking from one blank face to the other. Jesus, some of the world's best thinkers and they couldn't look him in the eye let alone proffer something of interest. He couldn't help questioning if this rag-tag bunch of misfits was the best the country could offer.

Tara finally met Jack's gaze, shaking her head softly. 'It's nothing more than random numbers, we can't identify any patterns, configurations, meanings. We've used automated pattern

199

recognition and got nothing. It's not Pi, primes, Fibonacci, Euler Rotation, Zipf's, Gamma or Merten's…or anything Euclidean or even non-Euclidean that we can identify. Nothing is all we get, no matter what we try and match it up with, how off-script or left-field we take it.' She raised her eyes hopefully at Max. 'That's the math side of things, not much help I know,' Tara said sheepishly, angling her chin down.

You got that right, Jack thought ruefully, probably the only damn thing they got right so far. This was going nowhere fast. Like them, he was questioning whether there was anything in the numbers. Maybe they were just flashing on and off for no particular reason, something to make us dance like a fucking cockatoo on a perch. Jack felt like laughing out loud, the whole thing was so absurdly empty of substance.

Max curled his lip down, 'as a programmer, this stuff is meaningless. You mentioned machine code, well if it is, we can't know what it's supposed to do…and why the hell would it be that?' He hoisted his eyebrows, offering an irritated lift of a shoulder. 'I can't come up with any possible reason. No one uses it in its raw form. We use tools to sequence it into operational blocks, but seriously, machine code or assembly code? I'm sorry,' he said with a heavy release of breath, 'but this is all quite ridiculous. Why would they even send us anything in such a naff format? Maybe they've assumed this is all we can understand and if so, then they're not too fucken smart either.' He grinned wickedly. 'I mean, we're designing quantum computers, a quantum meganet, atoms instead of circuits, superposition, uncertainty, probability, using qubits…and they send us this remedial bullshit?' He pushed his head to the side angrily. 'What a bloody wank-fest,' he said, swatting at the air in front of his face. If this is a program, it'd be like trying to decode DNA one molecule at a time.' Max was flabbergasted he was even called into this chickenshit group. 'This'd be like us finding an advanced race,' he paused momentarily, grinning contemptuously, '…and trying to communicate with grunts and whistles.' Max had zero time for the Government and this debacle wasn't helping his attitude one bit.

Strike two, Pete thought. No math, no AI program, or at least none they could identify. As far as he knew, that was it. If there was meaning in the binaries then it was likely going to stay hidden until these, whoever-they-were, lent us a hand, or at least gave a bloody clue one of these so-called geniuses could get a grip on. Game over, he figured.

Ballard came barrelling up holding his cellphone like a pistol, demanding an update from Jack, ignoring the science crew and their endless, irritating drivel.

'Wait,' they're starting again.' Tara said, jumping in front of the middle terminal, already pushing the zero and one keys to get 'em down. If the sequencing was wrong, substituting zero for one and one for zero should correct it…if they were binaries. Her fingers ached already, sinister images filling her mind as she tapped out an off-key tune on the keyboard.

Jack's cellphone rang to the tune of Nirvana's Lithium.

It was Steve O'Donnell from JPL in Pasadena, sounding strangely out of breath. Jack paused briefly, 'haven't spoken to you in years Steve, your birds dropped out of the sky?' He chuckled briefly, stopping abruptly as he considered the reason for his call. If it was good news he'd drop dead where he stood. Had to be bad, he decided uneasily, frowning at his cell.

'You idiot,' Steve said dryly. 'We've picked up some interesting data on our accelerometers and microwave set-up.'

Jack was immediately intrigued. 'Steve, I'll put you on speaker so you can talk to the team. He placed his cell in the dock. 'You got us?'

'All good,' Steve confirmed.

'Whatta you got?' Jack felt his heart rate change up as he contemplated what Steve's babies might have seen from their high orbit.

'GRACE has found, uh, gravity gradients radiating from the objects,' Steve said, sounding jittery. 'The gradients are crazy, seriously nuts…never seen anything like it before. They're narrow, incredibly well defined, sort of like channels in the vacuum.' He paused momentarily, gathering his thoughts. Lowering his voice he said, 'but the most astonishing thing is that each object is only propagating one ripple. They can't be gravity waves because the objects aren't moving and most definitely don't seem to be energetic enough. And like I said there's only one ripple…there's no everywhere radiation, so go figure right?' Steve was breathing in short, fast grabs, 'I'm getting a false colour image rendered as we speak so you can see what I'm talking about.' He hesitated again, longer this time, reflecting on his next words. 'Jack, we're pretty sure these things aren't complying with relativity,' he murmured, openly staring at his cell. What he meant to say was that these Spheres were doing things that rewrote the text book on physics.

'And that's possible how? Jack asked, recalling some of the weirdness reported by Sagan.

'It's not,' Steve said wistfully, 'it's not possible. Producing unidirectional gravity waves from a stationary object, well…unless they've got some crazy servo-device that's capable of generating the waves, it's anyone's guess.'

'Okay…you said they had different, er, connections?' Nate said quizzically, seeing Ballard equally bemused, struggling mightily with the science but figuring something big was up.

'Thirteen of the Spheres are transmitting the ripples found by GRACE, the, um…central Spheres are dark.' Steve said. 'They seem to be like bridges, connecting each of the thirteen to different things.' His voice lost speed and trended into awe, stopping abruptly, leaving them floundering with O'Donnell's words.

It was amazing and frightening Tara thought - single linear ripples in spacetime – forget the how because it was impossible, like why, what did it mean, connected to what? Scenarios flashed in front of her, broken visions, disturbing images, gates of hell stuff.

'I've got the image you sent,' Nate said, opening it on the screen, scanning the colourful image that looked like a busy geological map with contours, mountainous elevations and the like. Jack and Pete variously snorted and gasped in unison, seeing bright crimson tendrils extending from every one of the thirteen bogies. One was hitting the western edge of Antarctica while all the others went off-planet to destinations unknown. The first question Jack thought of was whether the endpoints were in-system, out of system, maybe off-galaxy?

'You still there?' Steve asked, peering at the mystifying ripples.

'Yep,' Jack said distantly. 'Just looking at your colourful map here…quite incredible.' He moved closer to the image, squinting. 'Any idea where the other gravity waves, er, ripples go…the ones heading away from Earth?'

'They're false colour so don't get excited Jack. We only know where two of 'em go. We've calculated the declination and right ascension of a distant point along a linear projection of the ripple. If they continue in a straight line, and of course they should, but hey, anything's possible, right? Anyway, if they do then there's one hitting Mare Insularum on the Moon, one striking Jupiter on an equatorial hot spot. The rest are targeting beyond our solar system.'

'At what?' Tara said, scratching her jaw, utterly at a loss.

'Dunno.' Steve said. 'We're efforting that, we'll let you know when we do.'

'Okay,' Jack said, feeling a hollow sensation in his gut. Steve killed the call, retrieving his phone and pocketing it. Jack raced back to the Atlas console, throwing his headset back on. 'Vic, this is Flight, you copying?'

After a few seconds Vic came back and Jack updated them on what was invisible to them but disturbingly real and deeply entangled in spacetime, radiating like prison bars around them.

'Just stay where you are, you'll be fine. The anomalies only extend from the outer Spheres, your position near the core of the structure is clear.'

'Uh, copy,' Vic said warily, wondering not for the first time if they were telling them the whole story. Gravity waves ordinarily generate from tremendous velocity or cataclysm…seriously, it sounded fucked up.

Tara felt like crying out in elation. She now had an hour's worth of data and was sure she recognised pattern repetition, which might mean they had the entire sequence. Tara couldn't be entirely sure but more than anything else she sensed familiarity with the numbers she was punching into the laptop. Opening her Binary Analysis Tool, she copied and pasted the whole lot straight in, crossing everything that could be crossed, desperately wanting to identify something coherent within the mathematical miasma. Adding so little value was soul destroying given the stakes at play, and she saw the bitterness in the others' eyes, none of them wanted to bomb out on this one. They were the science virtuosos brought in specially to crack the code, but so far it was a total bust.

'Jack, over here,' she shouted, waving him back to the head of the Flight Control Room. Jack headed toward her praying for something positive, anything that wasn't nothing, something to feed Ballard and Griffin, get 'em off his arse for a while. 'These numbers cycle every hundred and twenty characters on a sort of loop that keeps repeating. That's the good news,.' Tara sighed

Jack winced, feeling the deflation hit him like a physical blow. And now the bad new he thought gloomily.

'We still don't know what it's saying but at least we've got a parcel of characters to work with,' Tara said, smiling cautiously, relieved to have something positive to offer.

'That's true,' Max weighed in, 'we've got a definitive cluster of information…to analyse, get our teeth into.' Max's insides jangled with anticipation as he studied Tara's screen. It was far too short to be anything related to CPU script. Peering blankly at Tara he bit a fingernail down to the quick as he contemplated the surprisingly short series of numbers.

Max suddenly stiffened a bit, eyes narrowing, jaw grinding so hard Jack reckoned he was going to bust a molar. 'Je-sus,' Max said, slowly enunciating the word, glancing purposely at Tara, clearly taken aback. His face was vacant, confused, definitely surprised. 'It can't be …I mean why not just tell us in English.' His eyes were darting around like a hawk as he chewed on the peculiarity.

'Speak,' Jack said, knocking on the table impatiently. Waving Ballard and Griffin over with a sharp flourish, he said loudly, 'Max here has something to say.' He glanced at Max, lowering an eyebrow, 'you do have something to say, yes?'

'Er, uh…yeah I do,' he murmured, peeking a look at the double doors that led outside. Shit, he thought, it's only the Defence Secretary and the fucking NORAD Chief, no pressure. Max coughed nervously, why he didn't test his idea before saying anything he had no idea, feeling the heat from their gaze boring into him, his mouth running dry, features almost frozen stiff. Oh well, screw it he thought, here goes nothing. 'Ass-key,' he forced out in a dull croak, shuffling back a step.

Ballard's eyes visibly bugged. 'What the hell?' He said, barking it at Max, face as tough as a brick wall. 'Are you trying to be funny son because let me assure you I will dispatch you from this base if you are.' He was fuming, mouth only inches from Max's face.

Max was horrified, edging away from Ballard's unnerving proximity and foul breath. He drew in a deep rasp of air and steeled himself. 'Happy to leave at any time,' he said quietly, tensing his mouth, mincing back another step. 'Then you can work all this shit out on your own,' he added without thinking. Max wasn't sure where it came from but Ballard looked like he was going to physically attack him.

'Do not test me boy, I will— '

'Just let me finish,' Max said in a more affable voice. 'Ass-key is spelt A-S-C-I-I, it's a standard method of information exchange.' Max watched Ballard's ruddy face squash up as he concentrated. 'English characters are encoded in seven bits.' It lost him entirely, he may as well have spoken in Hebrew.

'Are you shitting me,' Ballard exploded. 'Just speak like regular folk…who do you think you're talking to?'

'Don't!' Jack said sharply, pointing with a stiff finger, seeing Max about to fire an answer back to what was clearly a rhetorical question. Calling him an oaf or a mental midget with or without expletives was bad form no matter what the circumstances.

Max closed his mouth and smiled thinly at Jack, clinically explaining it. 'Each letter and decimal number has a Base-2 digit assigned to it. How's that?'

'Uh, well, a bit better I guess,' Ballard said uncertainly, face still flushed but slightly softened, from a pegmatite granite to a more gossanous limonite.

Max turned to Tara, 'open your browser, search binary to ASCII converter and copy in the sequence.'

'a-s-c-i-i, right? She asked.

Max nodded, frowning. Jesus, who were these fools? He wondered, minutely shaking his head, hoping she knew about it and was just checking the spelling.

Tara clicked on the first result and a two-way converter opened. She dumped the tranche of digits into the window on the left.

00101101001101010011011100110001001101000011000100110010001100000110001 0011001100110111001101000001100011

Then she hit Convert. A series of numbers appeared. They'd expected nothing, perhaps letters, maybe words but to Ballard's horror, they got numbers and a fucking minus sign.

-571412013743

'Oh for God's sake,' Griffin moaned, 'what is that now?' He glared at Max, then Jack. 'Like you said, why not just give it to us in English. Whoever these arseholes are clearly know our numbers, no doubt our language.' Griffin was panting, at a loss. 'This stuff isn't alien gibberish, it's our stuff. What sort of game is being played here?' His glare descended into a hateful scowl.

'We've been putting everything together,' Nate said, pulling hair near his temple, 'it has to be a test, it's the only conclusion that makes sense.' He looked at the Secretary of Defence. 'If it was simply contact and information exchange they were after then this could've been made a lot easier.'

'Putting it mildly,' Griffin growled. 'Maybe it's a fucking pop quiz.'

Nate stared at him with a glazed look, unsure how to respond.

'So here we are again, trying to figure out what the numbers mean,' Ballard said exasperated. 'Have we actually achieved a damn thing here? I mean, is this gonna be never ending, stumbling from one pile of horseshit to another?' Ballard looked fractious as he studied Nate.

Jack cleared his throat deliberately. 'I, uh…think I know what it means,' he said quietly.

'What…already?' Ballard spluttered. 'Jesus Christ, are you sure?' His eyes were normally slitted like a reptile but now they were peeled open.

Jack grinned broadly. 'I used to be a trajectory programmer in the bow and arrow days at JPL so this stuff is pretty familiar. Heard of FIDO? Well that was me, one of the last Flight Dynamics Officers to grace the old Apollo MOCR-2.'

Everyone was gaping at him, hoping he hadn't gone barking mad. Nate was at the back of the group feeling impotent as the guy who was supposedly a math guru, but who'd actually contributed the grand total of a breakfast egg. Yet Jack had apparently identified the numbers with no trouble at all...like shelling peas, just by looking at them. Damn it, he thought, sneering at Jack, outdone by a goddamn NASA grunt.

'I think they're spatial coordinates,' Jack said evenly. The first six would be declination, similar to latitude, the last six, right ascension…like longitude.' He grinned wryly, 'who woulda thought hey? 'Let's plug 'em into the plotter, see if I'm right.' Jack's eyes were goggling with expectation, at the same time feeling a prickle of unease stir the hairs on the back of his neck. Where the hell was this place, another star system, another galaxy, where they were from? The answer was limitless indeed, sending a flush of adrenaline tingling through his body.

They were being directed to a piece of space for a reason, but it was the why's that were so intriguing. Jack closed his eyes and when he'd regained his train of thought, slowly reopened them. Christ, he thought, this might be it. And by it, he meant the answer to everything.

Under Pete's direction, Tara had the NASA/AMES 3D plotter on the screen in seconds and dropped in the numbers. She held her stomach and gnawed on a lip, tensing for the answer. Tara clicked Calculate and in a few seconds a colourful animation of the inner solar system appeared.

'Shit, it's local,' Jack called out, seeing the general location was proximal to the Sun, watching unblinkingly, waiting for it to red-spot the position on the screen. 'Come on,' Jack murmured with intent, willing it into action with his eyes.

The program clicked and a red dot with a circle appeared not far from Earth in a direct line with the Sun, carrying the narration 'L1, blinking on and off, seemingly emphasising its import.

L1, Nate said to himself, it sounded familiar but he couldn't quite place it, almost like it was in there but lost in the misty corridors of his mind.

'Lagrange,' Yoshi offered quickly, 'that's the first Lagrangian orbit from Earth.'

Jack could hear Ballard's feet as he shuffled back and forth on the tiles in a maddening arrhythmia that was turning into a staccato dance. Yoshi heard it too, peering at him vacantly, pondering what manner of military sawdust filled his head. 'It's an orbit kept stable by the effect, er, that is gravity from both Earth and the Sun.' He lifted an eyebrow at Ballard. 'It's around two million clicks away, something like that.'

'Why the hell would it be directing us there?' Ballard said bluntly, frowning.

'You tell us,' Jack said with a thread of sarcasm, 'because you've got as much idea as we have and that's saying something General.' He shot Ballard a short-lived grin.

'Careful,' Ballard returned, grimacing.

Jack's expression hardened. 'We need to get the ball rolling on this.' He spun around to Pete. 'We need Jackson on the phone from Flight Ops at Goddard, get Griffin to authorise moving Hubble's Wide Field 3 to the coordinates. We need a visual on it.' He waved a hand and gave a hollow chuckle. 'Of course, there may be nothing there, and the way things are going, hey…maybe it's fucking Elvis.'

Ballard guffawed involuntarily, quickly checking himself, straightening his tie and patting down his suit jacket.

'You got an Elvis thing going on General?' Max said lightly, Ballard gritting his teeth, averting his gaze.

'No judgement,' Max said softly, grinning at him, then at Jack who was gently shaking his head, holding his hands up, concealing a smile.

Jack replaced his headset. 'Sagan, Flight, copy?'

'Yup,' Harry said, 'how goes it down there?'

'We need you to check something out,' Jack said in a way to keep it conversational. 'Is the shuttle in good order Harry?'

'Sagan is great,' prop's at seventy-four percent for Magneto, forty-four for hydrazine so we're good to go.' Jack filled them in on the ASCII decryption and they agreed with Mission, puzzling as to why encoded text was chosen to effort communication. They'd clearly elected to use it quite specifically, which was curious. The fact that it was so offbeat meant it simply had to be of import Vic figured. It must have meaning beyond the data it was conveying although he could be reading way too much into it. He was thinking frantically, asking questions, answering them, disagreeing with himself, then choosing a different line, even telling himself to fuck off a few times. It was an irritating, tiring mental loop, without hope of resolution.

'Wait on our call,' Jack said. 'Once we have the data from Hubble we'll send it up on the Ku-band.' He paused and deliberated, feeling his pulse rise in his neck. 'Maybe it's nothing but we've been given hard coordinates so we have to assume it's something kinda big. Flight out.'

***

The Hubble feed was projecting on the screen at the head of the FCR. It was still blurry and dark as the gyroscopes and reaction wheels steered the scope in the right direction, searching for the coordinates coded into its directional hard-drive. The fine guidance sensors would soon kick in, using Hubble's selected guide stars to gradually move the wide field lens and multi-object spectrometer onto the precise target coordinates, one-point-four-nine million kilometres from Earth in a direct compass line with the Sun. Hubble was about to get up close and personal with a piece of space specially selected by their faceless protagonists.

After forty-five minutes the picture started cleaning up, gaining focus, revealing something in the vacuum. An indistinct, blurry brightness dominated the middle of the screen, distinctly blue, like Earth viewed from a great distance. It could have been anything, an out of focus galaxy, a star, even a gas nebula but they knew better. The address was local, barely a stone's throw from Earth where space should be dead empty apart from a couple of human robots, a few hydrogen atoms, some fizzing particles and the tiniest sweep of dark matter. These robot travellers from Earth were held there eternally by the interplay of gravity from Earth and the Sun, although nothing was forever.

Hubble's focus was moving forward and they could see the thing slowly becoming clear, and suddenly it was front and centre, distinct but…indistinct…utterly bewildering.

Ballard's mouth dropped open but nothing came out except a strange gurgling sound. He was never caught short of a word but the thing on the screen had him by the balls and left him speechless. It bore not the slightest resemblance to anything he'd ever seen before, and he'd seen some weird shit in his time. All he knew, and his thudding heart was pressing the point, was that it looked bloody terrifying.

'Holy Mother in Heaven,' Tara muttered almost soundlessly, gobsmacked by the thing swamping the front wall of the FCR. 'God it's…uh, actually gorgeous,' she added, gazing at it, head tilted to the side, battling to make sense of its baffling shape, extraordinary colour, its utter majesty.

Jack peered solidly at it, weighing up what the strange contours might be. It was like nothing he'd seen, nothing in space looked like this, until now, he figured.

'What do you reckon Jack?' Ballard said in a wavering voice. His comb-over slipping, making him look harrowed and anxious.

Jack's frown dipped deeper as he pored over the chilling image. 'No idea,' he said, showing his palms, 'and I mean that in the true Dictionary sense. This is something er, new, like never seen before…that's what we do know.'

'So, this is where they're pointing us with their numbers?' Tara said in a whisper, feeling her hands go clammy. 'I gotta say…this, uh…thing means zero.'

Ballard shook his head in dismay. 'I agree with all that, but you're the goddamn geniuses here, don't you have any ideas…an educated guess?' He darted his eyes over all of them, sighing.

Jack did the same, sizing up Pete and the rest of the group, looking for the slightest spark of insight, seeing only dull, wooden faces. They turned almost as one to Hubble, really studying the anomaly it had captured so beautifully. The thing gave the impression of animation as it visibly convulsed with some sort of vivid energy.

Connie, all of them, agreed its beauty bordered on the supernatural, stunning on a level provoking almost every human emotion that had a name. Even hard as nails Ballard was mesmerised by it, staring impassively, moving his head minutely side to side. But it was more than just its appearance, as crazy as it was, it was more about what it might be, what might lie within that made the blurry visual extraordinarily overpowering.

According to the scale on the screen, the object was around ninety kilometres long, maybe ten wide and was radiating something into space, as though an ocean of blue meltwater was pouring through from behind. It had the aspect of a titanic gash, edged with pendulous filaments like brightly painted eyelashes. Jack tried to avoid thinking in clichés but he kept coming back to it, he couldn't shake it loose. The contours, the silhouette had taken root in his mind, generating its own reasoning.

'Guesses General? That's all you'll get,' Jack said, feigning a smile, feeling his breathing quicken. 'Until we get closer to it, take some measurements, analyse the radiation, well…it could be anything. And by anything, that's exactly what I mean, so until we get some intel from Johns Hopkins in Maryland, empty guesses are as good as it gets.' He'd about had enough of Ballard's bullshit demands, twisting his mouth into a sneer. Hubble was busy analysing the anomaly with its four eagle-eye and decoding instruments, which would slice up every part of the spectrum and see how hard it was shining and in what wavelength.

'Maybe it's a big fucking eye looking for its next meal,' Jack said abruptly, turning away from Ballard roughly, knowing he'd probably poked the bear but he cared nought, he was frustrated, tired and bloody hungry. The dog and sauce Ballard had so condescendingly referred to would go down just fine he thought, picturing it in his mind, feeling it sliding down, no bite marks.

Surprisingly, Ballard remained expressionless, pausing momentarily, then turning on his heels and walking swiftly back to where Griffin was standing with his DoD and HomeSec buddies.

'Reckon he's going to dob me in to the boss,' Jack said, glancing at Pete dryly. 'Have a look at him over there, he can't be that sensitive…right?' The suits were talking earnestly about something.

'Detained by the DoD for disrespecting the stars…not a good look for NASA Jack,' Pete chuckled, grinning widely and nodding.

'Fuck 'em,' he said, smirking, picturing the dog and sauce again.

***

'Punch system Vasya, let's see what these things are.' He gave a quick salute to his comrade. 'Six months on ISS, I wanna go home but Kremlin calls, we fucking answer okay?'

Yveginy nodded effusively, scanning the instruments in front of him. 'Attitude Control System is on line, Soyuz is—, ' he paused, punching a flashing red light, 'good to go.' He glanced around the tiny crew module, splitting his whiskers with a toothy smile, loving what he saw. 'TMAM is kick arse vehicle,' he said, tensing, waiting for gravity to smash him.

'Yes, Vasya, definitely. Asymmetric dimethylhydrazine is kick arse, not like Americans with their nitrogen-tet bullshit,' he said, grinning briefly at his pilot, shifting his head back to the luminous green avionics panel, satisfied all was in order. 'Punch it Vasya, let's go and maybe we finally become heroes to Soviet country.'

The spacecraft formed a perfect letter T with its fully deployed solar array, having the aspect of a delicate insect in flight. Tiny compared to the shuttle, it was certainly less attractive to the eye with its spheroidal crew module that looked disturbingly like a fly's head.

Yveginy cycled the KURS hard-dock and briefly fired the main SKD engines to break away from ISS. Twenty-four hydrogen peroxide thrusters lit up and gimballed, executing a programmed manoeuvre to rendezvous with one of the Spheres sitting near the extremity of the group. The Russian President had determined their destination for no other reason than a vodka driven toss at a dartboard, praying for communist glory, licking and lifting a finger to the Americans.

***

Ballard's eyes almost disappeared beneath the mounds of flesh thrown down by his scowl. He punched his cellphone to terminate the call. 'Fuck me Jack, it's gone,' he snapped, staring blindly at him, baring his teeth. 'The goddamn Soyuz is gone. The Soviets said they were waiting to gather data before they moved. My arse, they were waiting. Planning, scheming more like it.' He threw his hands in the air, snorting derisively. 'And so much for informing us if they decided to move, not that they had to, but that's what the pricks said. Goddamn it,' he wheezed, peeved that the Soviets were doing what they always did, say one thing, do another…in short, fucking lie! We tell 'em everything, what do we get in return… bullshit propaganda.' His expression was a mix of loathing and disbelief.

'So, is the Soyuz inside…like inside one of the Spheres?' Jack asked tentatively.

'US Strategic Command and the SSN picked up its departure from ISS forty minutes ago. It disappeared ten minutes ago, radar image vanished so you do the math, it's not in space so it's inside the Sphere, there's no other place it could be.'

206

'Sagan didn't see it?'

'They reported no sighting,' Ballard said, raising his voice.

'Must have been on blind transit behind the Earth when it happened I guess.'

Ballard nodded vacantly. 'So now we've got two cosmonauts, God knows where, and the commies refusing to talk. POTUS has told, that is asked, the Kremlin to share any insight if they happen upon it, but like that's gonna happen.' He pushed his shoulders up, speaking through his teeth with forced restraint, 'according to them they're not even up there, seriously, what is it with them? They know we know, but still they duck and weave, playing mind games.' Ballard paced in small circles. 'Even with the possibility of project doomsday on our doorstep they're still peddling out the horseshit.' Staring at Jack, he closed his eyes, flapped his head a few times and exhaled irritably. 'Fuck me,' he grunted, giving a throat clearing cough, 'what a goddamn cock up.'

20. LaGrangian 1

"Strangeness is a necessary ingredient of beauty." ~ *Charles Baudelaire*

Jack wasn't sure he wanted to send them but he had no options, because Sagan was the only viable go-to. There was one Magneto Shuttle in the fleet and that was her, perfect for the voyage that equalled five trips from the Earth to the Moon. The other four shuttles were powered by conventional hydrazine, slow-haulers NASA called 'em derisively, taking almost seven times longer to span the million or so clicks. Although the entire STS programme had been junked, Endeavour and Discovery were being retrofitted, prepped for space but were still ten days away from being launch ready. Like it or not, Sagan was NASA's, and now the planet's eyes in space, the ones to accept the oddly encrypted invite on behalf of their species.

'Vic, this is Flight, you copy?'

'Yep, got you Jack,' Vic said, blinking as he spoke.

Harry joined open mic. 'You got the visuals from Hubble?' He said impatiently, keen to know what jackass mission Houston was sending them on. It didn't bother him one way or the other, his concern was for Skylar whose mental state was decaying pretty much before their eyes. Another journey into hell wasn't gonna help any. He shifted in his seat, feeling restless, realising there was bugger all any of them could do. Despite his below average personal skills and similar privation of empathy, that was the pretty sorry wrap from his last Dryden psyche report, Harry felt some of her grief. He tried to resist it, but it hit him where he lived. An errant tree branch had killed his boy when he was ten thousand kilometres away in deep Earth orbit. NASA didn't tell him until the Chaplain from the Kennedy Space Centre met him at the bottom of the shuttle stairs, grim faced, arms raised toward him like a fucking field umpire. At that instant, time stopped for him, Harry's heart was ripped from his body, his brain re-wired and set forever in work mode. He'd never been the same again, his emotions freezing like crystallising silica, his wife eventually walking out on him, friends drifting away as his personality soured. So Harry did what he had to, threw himself into work every minute of every day, all the time knowing he'd never recover. He didn't want to recover and was at peace with that. This was the first time he'd felt something approaching a genuine emotional sensation since the day he'd gotten the news that destroyed his life.

'We have the visuals,' Jack confirmed, slightly out of breath. 'There's some sort of object, er…anomaly,' he said in a murmur of palpable understatement. 'We'll upload the coordinates including those to get you out of the Sphere without running into trouble. We'll send some data files through Ku-band.' He placed a hand on his cheek as he considered the update he'd received from STSCI in Maryland. 'PJ from HST says there's no emissions in any other spectrum, apart from visible light. No UV, IR or anything in between…just what we can see with our eyes.'

'But how is that— '

'No one has an answer Harry, there's a hundred and fifty PhDs working on it at JHU, but all we're getting are frowns and fucking head shakes.'

Harry's mind churned with splintered images as he mulled over what might be waiting for them at this special crossroads in space. 'So, uh…what do you know about it?' He said directly, 'I mean, the close ups, any indication if it's natural, artificial, stuff like that?'

There was something Jack knew, based on a lost satellite but he wasn't sure he should squawk on that one. 'We don't know what it is,' he said, glancing at Pete, 'what we see is unclear…it looks like a small…nebula type structure but it's impossible to say, there's insufficient detail in the image,' he lied. 'We need you to get up close, measure radiant qualities, have a close look,' he said with a note of apology. 'One thing we do know is that it wasn't here yesterday,' Jack said hesitantly, clearing his throat. 'Our SHOAL satellite was orbiting at L1 so we checked its imaging records.

Yesterday there was nothing, today, um…well, something. This thing seems to be brand new,' Jack said, he needed fresh eyes on this thing, see it for what it was without his fatuous preconception.

Vic narrowed his eyes, rolling the word around. 'You said was orbiting…should we read anything into that Jack?' He stared at the comms unit waiting, hearing only uneasy silence.

Shit, Jack chastised himself, realising his folly. Oh fuck it, there was no going back now. He took a long breath. 'It's gone,' he said abruptly. 'We don't know— '

'Gone where?' Vic said, raising his voice.

'Uh, none of its last moments were captured because it was in software update,' Jack said icily. 'It's well… just not there anymore. Hubble imaged its last coordinates and there's just empty space, and, um…the new arrival.'

Vic glanced over his shoulder at Skylar. He knew he had to keep this quiet. They were on PTT mode so no one could hear what Jack was saying. She'd be a one person mutineer if she got wind of this, all arms, legs and tears, he saw it clearly and stifled a snort. The Tassie Devil was an amusing aside from his childhood, a cartoon favourite, all arms and legs…manic, cyclonic motion.

'So, this anomaly has, um, taken it, is that what you're saying?' Vic whispered.

'That's what we think,' Jack said, seeing no point in trying to sweeten the deal now.

Vic turned to the bank of avionics and hand controllers, away from the group. 'So that's our fate, rendezvous then sayo-fucking-nara? Jesus, we need to keep it between us, not everyone's of like mind up here.'

'Yes of course…copy,' he said, keeping his voice low, 'won't breathe a word.'

Vic could see the group from the corner of his eye, all of them watching him curiously. 'Sagan out,' he said evenly, trying to look and sound as though nothing was up. If Sky found out that SHOAL had been gobbled up, he knew they could look forward to a hellish journey, irrespective of what they found at L1. It was the getting there that might lead him to commit murder along the way. Taking a peek at Sky he said, 'fuck it' under his breath, deciding on the Band-Aid approach, rip it off, get it the hell over with.

***

Vic took another deep breath, fighting the urge to yell, maybe swear or maybe find somewhere to hide. The airlock would be nice, disable it from the inside. Totally soundproof. He'd used a forced measure of calm in reasoning with her, it lasted shy of thirty seconds. 'Sky, we have to go, they're not asking us, they're telling us, it's not our decision.' His voice was unnaturally shrill as he tried to keep it together. 'The position of this thing, whatever it is, was spelt out by the Sphere. Logically, it must be something important, decisive…critical maybe.'

'Logically?' she quizzed, spitting the word at him. 'Jesus Christ, look, oh whatever…I mean, just do what you like.' Skylar knew arguing was useless, their journey was as good as fact. She put her head back in her hands, shoulders drooping with bleak resignation.

'It might be the way we save ourselves,' Vic said, focussing on the pros, 'if we need saving it might be a step toward making sure we have something to return home to.' He'd shuffled the cards, dealt the daughter card with the deft timing of a QB pass. Sky peered up at him, opening her eyes wide, hesitating, seeing the possible prize at the end of it, which of course was all about her and hers. She nodded slightly, unable to get any words out. Vic had dangled the bait, Sky had swallowed it, how long it would last, he had no idea.

***

Harry had the image of the anomaly Houston uploaded and was turning it slowly through a full circle. 'You know it really does look like a half-opened eye. The Hubble photos of deep space never saw anything like this beauty.' He was blown away by its incredible weirdness. 'Connie,' what do you reckon? Harry asked, seeing her chocolate brown eyes open like an owl as she inspected it.

'What do I think? I think I don't like it,' she said warily, handing the image to Vic.

209

'It is odd looking,' Harry agreed.

'Yeah well that's part of it…but why has it suddenly appeared? That's the thing,' Connie muttered, 'it just emerges, swallows a satellite, then we're given oddly coded marching orders to go introduce ourselves? Christ, is it just me or is this seriously messed up?'

'Just you Connie,' Harry spruiked, 'sounds fine to me.' He crinkled his face, chuckling. She cursed under her breath, looking away. Such a dick, she thought.

Skylar was appalled by it, she had no clue what it was but it looked evil and plain wrong, like stumbling over a cubic planet or a flock of seagulls flying past the shuttle's window panel. Everything was off - colour, shape, the strings of gas or energy or whatever it was that was radiating from it. She wanted none of it, nowhere near it, the baffling object was death, Sky was convinced.

'Coordinates are being fed into MEDS,' Vic said, watching the numbers on the multifunction display subsystem. 'Good to go in four.'

'Lock and load.' Harry said, smiling at Sky who was sitting with Connie near the rear of the cabin. He got nothing but bleak vacancy, no sign that she'd even heard him, few signs of life at all really. Both Connie and Sky presented like felons, counting the seconds to a group hanging.

'Strap in,' Vic said firmly, 'egress two minutes.' He motioned Connie and Skylar to the two Mission Specialist seats. 'Becker, wedge yourself behind the back of the seat there. The burn will start with low grade RCS then OMS, then the XPT engines so you should be okay. Just hang on tight.'

Vic held the translational hand controller, flicking an altitudinal switch on the avionics panel in front of him. 'F4 depressed, CSS manoeuvre enabled. RCS pitch and roll in 3, 2— '
The aft thrusters pushed them forward and they felt the craft roll to the left and pitch up a bit. After a minute, the conventional engines ramped them up to around five clicks per second.

'Magneto XPT nine seconds,' Vic said as he eyed the glass cockpit. 'It's a graduating propellant, so pull will be minimal.'

The dynamic EMAR engines slowly roused themselves, xenon propellant started to ionise and heat, resonating with radio waves, compressed by the electromag cyclotron and thrust violently through the electrothermal arcjets. This pushed the craft forward, eventually reaching close to a hundred clicks per second. Vic doused the hydrazine engines leaving Sagan cruising on electro only.

'Get comfortable guys, eat, drink, next stop is L1, ETA eight hours twenty-six minutes.'

Shit, Sky said silently, mouthing the word to Connie who nodded fulsome agreement. Eight hours to linger over it, scare yourself half to death, knowing whatever you thought you were on your way to meet would wrong. Sky'd have dealt with the devil to feel Earth under her feet, would've signed the contract in a furore of ink on paper without the slightest give a shit about the fine print.

'Let's eat,' Becker said, grinning at Connie, exhaling noisily.

'Last meal,' she said forlornly without breaking her bleak countenance.

No one spoke as they raced onward, seemingly making no progress at all toward the tiny colourful blur in the distance.

***

It dominated space like a horrifying celestial beast. Brilliant sapphire light spewed into space from a carapace that Becker thought was shaped like an evil grin,. Vic and Harry were busy trying to reconcile the flush of energy, they couldn't work out where it was coming from. It certainly didn't have the mass to sustain anything close to nuclear burning so they were stumped because it was plainly radiating a whopping amount of electromagnetic radiation.

'Um, I don't believe it but what about a white hole?' Connie said, deeply uncertain, 'you know, where the wormhole thingy connects back into normal space. Not sure why it'd be blue though, uh…a blue hole?' She flashed a half-grin, knowing the concept was a throwaway.

'Oh brilliant,' Becker said with amusement, 'blue hole…really? And I'm the dunce?'

'Better than your bonehead evil-grin comment.' She was goading him to come get some.

210

Connie's retort burnt on his lips but he kept it in. Now wasn't the time. He turned his attention to Vic, 'well, you're the science guy, what've you got?'

'What you've got,' he snapped, glancing at Connie to include her in the response, 'nought.'

'Yup,' Harry said, adding agreement.

'Flight, this is Sagan, you copying?' Vic said, waiting the ten seconds but there was no comeback. Being four light seconds from Earth, that should have been long enough but there was just background whine of static.

'Flight, you there?' Harry said louder, as though volume was the problem. Vic reached over the comms panel, switching from open mic to PTT mode. 'Flight, Sagan, copy?' He repeated more urgently, shaking his head, swearing under his breath.

'Go ahead Vic,' Jack replied.

'We're on Press to Talk, open mic has shit itself.

'Right, okay, copy,' Jack said matter of factly.

'So how close do you want us to get to this thing? We're holding at a thousand clicks, still not picking up any EMAR, we're only getting a visible. Other than that, silence across the spectrum.'

'Confirm no non-visible EMAR,' Jack said ominously.

'Confirmed.'

'Copy,' Jack said. 'Keep moving toward it; if things change, abort, your call to make.'

'Got it,' Vic said, glancing at Harry quizzically, deflecting the rotational hand thruster slightly. The aft OMS burn brought them up to a closing speed of four clicks per second. 'Arming forward RCS pods for abort manoeuvre…uh, if we need it.' Vic felt himself paling, certain if it was needed they were cooked. If they wanted you…they got you. Period.

After a few minutes they were almost on it, close enough to see why they weren't detecting the expected emissions. This thing wasn't active at all, at least in the sense they thought it was.

Vic spluttered and paused, pulling in a rapid breath. 'Are y-you seeing this?' He kept his eyes mortared ahead, hoping his heart didn't rip through his rib cage.

'Is that good or, uh, bad?' Becker faltered, not understanding the strange condition of the object. It wasn't what any of them expected, from a distance it looked dynamic and energetic like a star, but closer, well it just wasn't. He thought, with no confidence, that it might be for the better.

Vic knew immediately it wasn't natural, hardly a shock he admitted.

'This object is…it's like crystallised or something,' Harry said, fist firmly against his lips. 'Like, boiled sugar, cooled, hardened.' The streams of "energy" were actually set hard like camphor ice. 'Jesus Christ,' he gasped, his head almost touching the window panel. 'Can you see?' He pointed, goggling, 'like it's thrust its way through, then exploded into the vacuum, and, just frozen there.'

'Thrust its way through from where?' Vic stared at Harry who shook his head slowly.

'Astonishing,' Vic finally said, 'there's movement…a pulsing, but no output. It's dark from a radiant point of view but visually, well, take a bloody look at it!' He said, bending forward as he wrestled with the paradox. 'The light is blue, you can see it right?'

They nodded. 'Of course,' Becker said. 'Blue.'

'So visible light means there's EMAR but we're getting nothing else, just visible stuff. I mean, look at that thing, our high-gain antenna should be swamped with IR and UV, but we're not getting a zac. Vic shrugged and wound down to an exasperated sigh.

'Take it in as close as you can Vic, let's check it out, then we get the hell out of here,' Harry said, patting his beard nervously.

Vic inched the shuttle toward the centre of the object with a few spurts from one RCS jet, mulling further over their summons to this odd place. What were the odds of something genuinely life changing happening out here…why would they be gifted coordinates to something inert and meaningless? Beautiful it was, intriguing no doubt, but what did it want from them, or just as disturbingly, what did it have for them? His heart was tommy knocking on his ribs, pounding in his ears as his mind pitchforked off-road, wondering.

21. Us

"Travellers aren't found. They're called." ~ *Chess Desalls*

'Jack, Sagan.' Vic said, gazing fixedly at the comms unit.

'We're here Sagan.'

'We're at a hundred and eighty metres, closing at point oh-five. The solid structures we called "eyelashes" are crystalline, extending from all sides of this thing.' He followed them with his eyes. 'They're towering around us, it's pretty awesome. Are you getting the video stream?'

'Yep,' he said, sounding a little breathless, 'it's a bit grainy, drops out now and then but it's incredible.' Jack's tone had drifted into agitation as he paced mindlessly back and forth.

Harry yelled abruptly. 'There!' He pointed to the left of centre through the window panel, jerking his head back and waving them over. 'A shadow,' he said, 'I saw…I thought I did, a darkness…inside.' He stared rigidly ahead, searching for movement.

On hearing Harry's words, Sky froze into something like Munch's Scream, slowly backing away, mincing her way to the rear of the cabin where she ever so slowly sunk to the floor, back facing the window. Sky stared deadpan at the wall, chin trembling pitiably.

Vic studied the elongated object carefully, sweeping his eyes over the central "mouth" where the bright crystalline stuff seemed to have set hard between dark jagged "lips" that defined the anomaly proper. Giving a sudden yelp, he was startled by movement at the periphery of his vision. 'What the hell,' he snapped, turning to catch it, forced off balance by his pulse suddenly exploding at the base of his throat. It was a definite shadow and it grew as he watched it, darkening, lengthening, like something was approaching from the other side…beneath the sapphire gristle. There was no mistaking it. The sharpening shadow, like the darkest part of an eclipse, suggested an approaching…Vic hit a brick wall… he had nothing but an empty space in his mind.

Starting as a blemish deep within, it quickly resolved into something visible, the murky crystalline substance had gone, or altered, now it was transparent like lead crystal, hitting them with a numbing visual passage.

Vic's head wrenched back, hands flying to his mouth. 'Um…ah…oh,' he said haltingly, in slow motion, ending with a burbling sound, his mind failing to register a molecule of sense.

The first glimpse of the exposed object reached in and blunted brain tissue, replacing higher thinking with a primal instinct. The first thought that dribbled through was mirror, but that immediately melted away as wrong. Vic's second thought was aberration, that maybe he was having the mother of all medical episodes, perhaps a breakdown, but glancing at the others, he dismissed it.

Connie had paled alarmingly and took two stumbling steps backward, seeing nothing but a hail of sparks as she fought to absorb the image. She stared at Vic, lids peeled back like orange rind, as though a flash-bang grenade had detonated inside, stunning every one of her corpuscles.

All of them peered fixedly forward, then at each other, then back at the thing lying stationary below the surface of the frozen pond. It was close. They were almost on top of it.

Vic asked himself what the fuck several times. He'd never fainted in his life, didn't even know what it felt like, but he was certain the flush of hot blood surging up his spine into his neck and face was the beginning of a dead faint. He tightened his muscles, desperately trying to steady himself.

Harry was the first to thump back to reality, conceding that breaking laws and fracturing physics seemed incidental in the face of this fucked up thing in front of them. He supposed probably nothing actually broke the laws of physics here but it was sure as hell bending them square.

Facing them about a hundred metres away was a spacecraft identical to theirs. It wasn't similar or sort of like their ship, it was their fucking ship, Harry accepted, peering dumbfounded at the words "Sagan" stuck smack-bang on its mid-section above the letters USA and below the ultramarine NASA emblem. And most troubling of all, they could see five curious beings standing behind the fore window panel, gawking at them, just as they were doing to them.

Connie's amniotic stare continued, her throat swollen and cramped by her pounding heart which seemed to be everywhere. Pressing the heel of her palms into her eyes, she rubbed them hard. 'What is that?' She finally said. 'Is that another Universe, dimension?' Gazing at Vic, her eyes were trembling in their sockets, pleading for an answer, to explain what was hanging outside the shuttle.

Becker was unmoving as he tried manfully to think. 'That's like, uh…us over there…I mean not us but there's five people we can see. We're four, five including Sky and the shuttle is only made for three so that's a fair—

'Of course it's fucking us,' Vic said sharply, scraping a hand down his face, 'Jesus, they've sent us out here to meet, er…us.' He stiffened his posture, peering sightlessly into the air, 'how in the name of Jimmy fucking Hoffa?' He was bereft of reason as the blood surged from his fingertips to his toes. 'So, we unravel coordinates and find this, uh… us, staring back from some quantum rabbit hole.' Vic felt like he was going nuts, a river of noise rushing to and fro in his ears.

Harry was still staring through the window panel, bringing his arm up, pointing with an index finger that was trembling. 'So…you know…right?' He chuckled oddly, lowering his arm back down slowly. Harry didn't wait for a response. 'That's me, I can see myself standing in the window looking back. It's me looking back at me. Jesus…shit!' He groaned, like he'd cracked his head on a brick wall. Placing both hands on his forehead he massaged his scalp as one would knead fresh dough.

'Sky,' Vic said gently, 'you need to come up here.' He motioned her up but needn't have bothered. She had fingers in her ears, pinkies hard over her eyes, fighting to keep the outside world just that…out. Sky wanted none of it because she knew it'd nudge her off what she was so precariously balancing on. She had three fingers clutching a wad of crab grass and once it went, it was into the pit and then it was good night. Harry gestured to Connie to do her best to bring her over. There was no hiding from what was outside, for any of them.

Vic was on the Takahashi, guiding it onto the other craft when he turned and saw Skylar slumped on the floor in an untidy heap, held fast by her key-lock suit. 'Get her into a seat, buckle her up,' Vic said coldly. It was like having a child aboard and it was starting to piss him off. He muffled a grunt, picturing a Baby on Board sign hanging over the NASA badge on the Magneto.

After another minute of groaning and sighing Vic took his eye away and stared at Connie, opening and closing his mouth, searching for words. 'I um, honestly don't know what to say. It's us…all of us.' He looked borderline ill, pale. 'But we're, um…not in synch.' Vic's eyes were wide open in surprise, struggling under the weight of the visuals. 'The Skylar over there is looking right at us, wide-eyed, seemingly curious at the whole she-bang. Ours is a bloody train wreck, I mean, seriously, look at her.' He drew a long, rasping breath. 'They're like us in every detail down to weight and age but they're doing their own thing, acting, reacting to things in their own uh…world. They don't look surprised to see us…curious but not like us…calmer I think, a level of expectation.'

Becker looked up. 'So why would they send us here?' He said as Harry started to groan, to which Becker raised a defiant hand, looking right at him. 'Now that we've seen these er, other-us, what now, what's the purpose?' He squinted at the craft, brooding over WTF. 'We're separated by whatever that stuff is between us, so are we supposed to find a way through it…like escape into whatever nuthouse is on the other side…is that the deal? Tap-tap-crack…then whizz through with Sagan, come what may?' He puffed his cheeks out and moaned dismally.

'Maybe,' Vic murmured, having nothing to offer. 'That's as good a reason as any although perhaps they are supposed to…you know, come to us.'

Damn it, Harry thought, mulling over the unmeaning. 'Look, we have no idea on the why, but I reckon if we wait just a little bit, well, we might,' he said, shrugging uncertainly. 'We were summoned by personal invitation so we're here for something, make no mistake.'

A few things flashed through Vic's mind that made a little sense, but they were from the subatomic world, not here in macro land where things were orderly and predictable. Well, used to be he checked himself. Quantum strangeness, decoherence, the detail was hazy but he knew the basics, some of the more intriguing notions but the minutiae, no. One of those he did remember was the Many Worlds idea, that all possible histories and futures are real, meaning there might be universes out there that contain every conceivable outcome from every possible action and reaction. Sounded nuts but surprisingly the idea had a bit of street cred with a few eminent physicists. So, the time Vic's ex-fiancé told him to fuck off and go marry NASA, well maybe in some other universe they were married, even had kids. Maybe she wasn't a rotten, money hungry bitch either, he smirked, knowing that was pushing it a bit. The decoherence bit said that none of the worlds can ever talk to each other but maybe that part didn't apply here, maybe it had unravelled for some reason, been deliberately tinkered with…maybe undone like a sailor's knot. Or maybe the crystalline slash in front of the shuttle gave them a glimpse of one of these sliding door universes, much like a quantum peephole. He was pretty sure all of it was wrong but at least it was a half theory, better than no theory at all.

Vic watched curiously as the other-them started waving their arms around, glancing from one to the other then back at Sagan. Vic2 had something in both hands and placed them on the narrow ledge in front of the window panel, facing out toward them. Peering through the 'scope, he could see they were the shuttle torches. Son of a bitch, he thought suspiciously. What were they planning? One was the small airlock torch, the other a large halogen payload bay illuminator. Vic edged closer to the window, gazing with focus. 'What are you doing? He repeated to himself.

'Torches…facing toward us,' Vic said, casting a sceptical eye.

'To signal us?' Connie suggested.

'We're already here, why the hell would they need to signal? We can see each other.'

Connie looked at Becker vacantly. 'Thanks for the news flash. Obviously, they know we're here but maybe they want to tell us something you jerk.'

'Oh, okay. That makes sense I guess,' he said, 'text messages a no-go, right?'

Connie sighed, 'email and Facebook too Becker,' she said, without looking at him.

The two torches convinced Harry the infuriating status quo was going to continue. 'I'm guessing this mob wants to message us the same way as the, um, others…same as the Sphere.'

'Binaries?' Connie asked, taken aback. 'What is it with that, why can't they just write it down…you know, like words?' That would be way more reasonable so she assumed it wouldn't be the way it went. It was too simple, out of step with everything about the convoluted journey so far. If it could be made more complex and more circuitous, then that was the way it went, senseless, frustrating, torturous, absurd - they were the only expectations in this enigmatic whatever it was.

'If that's the case it's ironic, or maybe suspicious is a better word,' Harry said. 'Same as the Spheres, like you said Vic, what's the relationship? They look like us but use the same bullshit as the Spheres. Or what we've taken as bullshit anyway.' Harry's eyes were steely, carrying a strong suggestion of mistrust and doubt over everything he was seeing. 'It's way too strange up here.'

'Take a deep breath,' Connie said, irritably. 'Not everything's a conspiracy.'

'Horseshit,' Harry exclaimed after a moment's reflection, 'open your eyes. If they start flashing those tubes, which they will, this is a clue, be sure of it.'

'He's right,' Vic said, sitting up straighter. 'They've got a telescope so wouldn't they think we'd use ours to read anything they jot down on a piece of paper? Just write it down…easy as that!'

'Maybe they don't speak our language,' Connie said, 'or maybe they're just images, robots, you know…proxies to serve whatever godforsaken purpose the Sphere people have.' She cast a sharp eye at Harry. 'One thing I know is we have no idea what's going on out there.'

'Well maybe you're right,' Harry said, ignoring Connie's rant. 'Using radio wouldn't work I guess because they're behind whatever that stuff is.' It was transparent but they saw currents, twisting like a heat haze in front of them. 'Personally, I don't think they're even in our Universe.'

'Agreed,' Vic said. 'We're looking into a different—,' he paused, well, who the hell knows, what. It's all speculation, and it's probably more than we can imagine; that, I reckon, is spot on.'

Connie regarded him curiously, giving a barely perceptible nod.

Skylar regained consciousness but was frozen like a human Popsicle. Her unblinking eyes were stretched open, mouth ajar, appearing comatose but awake, seemingly waiting for death to tap her on the shoulder. Harry felt an irresistible urge to grab her and shake her violently, but if he did, Connie would probably attack him like a bandicoot or kick him where it hurt, probably both.

Something was happening outside and he knew damn well what it was before he bothered to turn his head. It was an alternate bright and dim light flashing arrhythmically. 'Surprise me,' he snapped under his breath.

'Same old,' Vic said, watching Harry raise his arms in mock surrender. 'If someone is trying to piss us off they're doing a five-star job,' he added, arching his brows until they were tangled together in a single bushy bar above his eyes.

'No time to think buddy, let's get the n numbers down, see what these clowns have to say.'

'Uh, those clowns are us Harry,' Vic said dryly, smirking.

Harry grinned, touching his forehead, 'shit, you're right,' he said, 'hey Becker, maybe you're a genius in that world.' He chuckled to himself, louder than he'd meant to.

'Easy,' Connie said, 'breaking physics is one thing, that there is quite another.' She threw her old sparring partner a broad smile.

Becker hung his head, holding a hand up to ward off the assault. 'Happy to be a source of amusement,' he said agreeably. Mongrels, he thought without malice, accepting it with grace, wondering if maybe he was mellowing up here in space.

'Pen and paper, Connie, grab it from equip bay,' Vic said, 'we'll take 'em down.'

'You want me to take dictation junior?' Harry said, quirking his mouth into a vague sneer.

'Yeah, I need your eye for detail. I'll use bright as one, dim as zero… you're the other.'

'Well yes sir!' Harry piped, equally impressed and irritated.

Connie handed them square-lined paper and a pen each. 'And I ain't no secretary either,' she said with a thin smile, 'so don't ask.'

'Wouldn't have given it a thought,' Harry said, 'you're more of a thinker, right?

'Focus,' Vic said, 'they're dark, he said firmly, 'They might be about to start for real.'

'What do you reckon they're thinking?' Connie said wistfully, focussing on her other self who was standing immobile at the window of Sagan2, not more than a few hundred metres away. 'That's…us,' she added dreamily, more to herself than the others, 'flesh, blood, I guess DNA as well.' She studied herself closely, admitting she looked pretty good, but couldn't help thinking the other Connie was a bit slimmer, had slightly bigger breasts. Bitch, she said to herself.

'They're probably different in mind,' Harry guessed, a frown crossing his face. 'We, uh…think we're the originals, don't we?'

'Well yeah I guess we do,' Connie said a little uncertainly. The concept was so dark she couldn't believe she was giving it airtime.

Harry came straight out with it, a flood of Bowden delirium. 'So, what if they're the originals and we're just copies…or what if there's millions or billions of "us" and every other person on Earth? And we're all spread through a multiverse with only circumstance being different?' It was as though the Universe had somehow come undone, revealing things that should be hidden behind laws that were inviolable. It all seemed to have a grave wrongness to it.

'So where do you reckon they come from?' Connie said without much enthusiasm. 'If I had one question that'd be it.' She ogled the other shuttle anxiously, 'both Sagan's look the same so everything else is probably the same…Earth, the Sun, the whole box and dice, right?' Every person she knew was probably on Connie2's planet as well, perhaps doing different things but looking roughly the same, sharing the same genes, family tree. But maybe they had different partners, more money, a better job, maybe dead people were still kicking around in Connie2's world. The car that lined them up, the cancer that nailed them just didn't, and so on multiplied by a fucking billion. 'Jesus Christ, she thought grimly, feeling a persistent ache near her temple. The concept was way, way left of crazy, it had the feeling of storybook fantasy, and, maybe it was.

22. Message

"Your message means less than the way the message is delivered, because in actuality, the way the message is delivered, is the message." ~ *Bryant McGill*

Connie saw lights start up from the other craft, conceding that the whole scene through the front panel of the shuttle was plumb impossible. Everywhere she looked was sapphire blueness except in front of her where it was transparent, punctuated by a single white craft, identical to theirs in every detail they could see. Connie idly imagined her mind digesting its own neurons as she struggled vainly to filter reason from nothing more tangible than the vacuum itself.

The bright light had been shining steadily for thirty seconds, then went off, followed by a semi-rapid pulsing of strong, weak light combinations.

Harry and Vic were visibly straining, slamming down sequences of ones and zeroes that went on uninterrupted for about four minutes. Then it went dark, followed by another four minutes of manic pen on paper. Then the lights went off and stayed off. The other Sagan turned its cabin lights back on, confirming, they guessed, that the game of big light, little light was done.

Vic appraised the scrawl on his page, agreeing with Harry that both sets seemed at first glance, identical. 'Maybe a redundancy in case we screwed one of them up,' Vic said, entering the second set of binaries into the ASCII converter he had open, figuring the final set would be the one to use. It took a little while to get your eye in with this sort of thing. Vic entered the hundred and sixty digits and without "fucking around", hit Text.

Harry was frozen solid, watching converted letters appear on the left-hand side of the app. They were letters but it was a meaningless jumble. 'You got the short sheet, junior,' he said.

Vic turned to him sourly. 'Sit here smart mouth, put your bloody numbers in.' They both assumed Vic had the incorrect assignment, the ones and zeroes reversed and meaningless. 'They'll probably spell out Harry's an arsehole,' Vic said nodding agreeably at Connie, smirking softly.

'We don't need any heads up on that, let alone a written message,' Connie said, looking at Harry blankly, then cocking a curious eyebrow.

'Oh, so it's like that is it?' Harry said without acrimony as he got out of his seat.

'Just plug 'em in,' Becker barked from the rear of the flight deck. He was impatiently pacing up and down, wanting answers so they could exit this insane asylum.

Harry punched his numbers in and without pausing hit Text. They stared for several seconds as the results rattled around in their brains. 'Okaaaay,' he whispered under his breath, 'it's incomplete, right?' He frowned, shaking his head slowly, looking at the others. It was truncated, but he knew he got it all, when he was focussed he never missed a thing, just let anyone say different.

'You sure you got it all?' Vic said, staring at Harry doubtfully.

Harry raised his arms toward him defensively. 'I know I got the last digits down. I missed nothing, trust me, I got it all.' Harry gazed up from the converter, scowling at Vic.

'Okay, fine, you got it all. Put the first series of numbers in Harry, if you didn't miss anything then the message will still be incomplete.'

Harry punched them in, converted the numbers, got exactly the same result. The message still remained painfully incomplete.

'There you go,' Harry said smugly. Fuckers, he thought sourly.

'Alright then,' Vic said upbeat, 'it's not the whole message so I guess we'll have to try and complete it ourselves…shouldn't be too hard.'

Harry called everyone to the terminal. Sky didn't move, was unable to move, peering with eyes frozen like a night owl staring at the Moon. He looked at her until she returned his gaze. She didn't budge. He snapped his fingers once, twice. 'Hey, Sky, come over here please,' he said as gently as he could. 'Come and see.' He gestured her forward with a gentle wave. Eventually she blinked and hoisted herself gingerly off the floor, slowly inching over to the pilot's seat. They looked curiously at the message, the original in binary at the top, the converted ASCII text boldly below it.

0110000101101110011101000110000101110010011000110111010001101001
01100011   011011110110001001101010011001010110001101110100
01101101011101010111001101110100 0110001001100101 0111001101110100
Antarctic object must be st …

Surprisingly, Sky spoke first. 'Is that it…all those digits and that's what we get? And it's not complete.' That last word is "stopped", right? The object must be stopped.' She stared at Vic, still wide-eyed.

'Maybe started,' Harry offered, 'but…er, yes, stopped seems more likely I guess.'

'Anyone else? Vic said, seeing them frown almost in unison, racking their brains.

'Why don't we just ask them to give us the message again,' Connie said, irritated, 'and we'll all take it down so there'll be no chance of screwing it up…twice.' She flipped her eyes up at Harry and winked woodenly.

'I got it all,' he insisted, 'I'm telling you I missed nothing.'

'Yeah well, we can confirm that you didn't make a hash of it, how's that?' Connie said, believing him but not giving him the satisfaction of knowing.

Harry crossed his arms deliberately. 'Maybe as the secretary you should've volunteered to do it.' Becker couldn't believe anyone could be so stupid, holding his breath expectantly. Oh shit, he thought, good luck taking the female stereotype angle.

Connie's face was hard as flint, gaze swivelling like a nest of mortars, gun sighting him. 'Look you misogynist fuck, if you had half a brain in—'

'Stop!' Vic yelled, raising a stiff palm in the air, 'let's just cut through this, write our message down, ask them what the final word is, and if there's any more to the message. You two need to stow the shit, there's no way off this tin can till we get this done.'

'Fine,' Harry said, 'There's a hundred questions we could ask, right down to where the hell do you come from? Maybe we could chuck some of those in as well, see what we get back.'

Vic grabbed paper and pen. 'Okay, we'll get the questions down, place it in front of the window panel, illuminate it with the Maglite torch, see what happens.' They nodded anxiously.

Vic wrote the message they'd decoded in bold print. Below it he added a bullet point, seeking confirmation of the last word and if there was more to the message. Then he queried why they were using text coded binary to communicate, followed by the kicker. Why do you look like us?

'Okay, other ideas?' Vic said, 'we may as well get all of them down, as many as we can fit on the page anyway.'

Connie watched Becker tense every muscle in his face from jaw to brow, clearly trying to come up with something but by the look of it, pretty much failing to register a decent thought.

'Careful,' she teased, 'you might have a stroke and bleed out. Best leave it to the adults Becker, you just stand there, look pretty.' She smirked, winking lightly.

'Y'know the last piece of the message, maybe the st is for stuffed as in get stuffed,' he growled back.

Connie was about to insult Becker's piss poor attempt at humour, but stopped, seeing the light from outside start to wane. Shuffling closer to the front of the shuttle she watched the vista change. 'Hey, it's, um…shrinking, I think,' Connie said, craning her head forward, studying the retreating contours of the object. 'Vic?'

To him it exuded the curious impression of healing. At its extremities, the vacuum surrounding the glowing interior was sort of pulling itself together like a zip lock, repairing itself from either end, sort of mending its way inward. Space was gradually falling in from both ends until only the very centre of the anomaly remained, the other-Sagan only partially visible, and then in an instant it was gone. All that remained were the crystalline columns, towering around them like tremendous corrugated prisms of copper sulphate. Except now they were protruding from nothing more than regular space, remnants of something they had few words to describe.

Connie ran through everything in her mind, rubbing her neck suspiciously, 'you know, pretty much as soon as we mentioned communicating with those others, bang, they're gone.'

Harry looked at her vacantly, agreeing that it seemed odd, puzzling certainly.

'Curious,' Vic said slowly, 'think someone's listening?' His face went as blank as Harry's. Vic grabbed his headset. 'Mission, Sagan, you copying?'

Static.

Flight, Sagan…Jack you there?'

Silence. There wasn't even static this time. He'd tried before and it was a similar result. Vic assumed the anomaly was interfering with radio transmissions but the strange manifestation was no more. Looking outside at the crystal things he wondered if they were to blame for the EM silence. 'Shit,' he said, feeling uneasy with the lack of connection to Mission.

Skylar peeped her eyes up at Vic timidly,' let's go, we're done here, it's time to leave.' She watched him like a hawk, waiting for him to grab the hand thrusters and give them a good tweak.

Vic sought Harry's cue and he obligingly nodded his head. 'Yep, time to go. Mission's off-line, the anomaly's gone, there's nothing to keep us here. I'm calling it.' Harry continued nodding minutely, gazing at the centre of his electronic display system, 'Prop and charge are good…MEDS and DAPS say we're good to go. She's yours Vic. Main engines, electro-transfer on your call.'

Connie turned her body, crying out in surprise as a flash passed across the shuttle window like a massive blue fizzle stick. A slight thump and lurching sensation followed as they felt something strike the ship.

'Damn it, there's debris,' Vic yelled, his voice stone cold as he searched space outside, shifting his eyes to the instrumentation for clues.

Becker had been staring outside when it happened, seeing it up close. 'The columns are breaking up,' he said, stabbing the air manically with his ring finger, 'see, they're, well…Jesus, move it Vic, get us out of here!' He roared, waving his arms wildly.

'Fucking well move,' Skylar roared in a rare moment of animation, pressing fists either side of her head. 'Gogogogogo,' she blurted, continuing to groan in the background.

Vic had hold of the RHC, ready to fire the OMS but before he could do anything the shuttle was rocked by something else, something much more substantial. It was a thunderous collision of matter on metal, creating a clamorous noise inside Sagan that was explosively loud.

Vic tensed every muscle he had, waiting for death screams as they were sucked violently into the void. A wail of klaxons and disorienting light from the emergency strobes went nuts around them, turning the cabin into a hellish discotheque.

Harry watched his MEDS display flashing Hull Integrity and immediately thanked it for the fucking news flash. His heart took one almighty beat, realising life support was open to the vacuum, taking a steadying breath, game face fully on.

Vic was screaming, 'into your pressure suits now!' He moved as quickly as he could toward the equipment bay, grabbed all the suits and part walked, part swam back to the flight deck. Fuck, he yelled to himself…Becker and Connie! Vic could feel the loss of pressure between his ears, there wasn't much time, maybe minutes before they were unconscious, then dead soon after that. There was no time to fit Connie in the AX-8 hard shell because it took two people ten minutes to suit the prick up. That would doom them all.

Harry saw the problem immediately. 'Suit up Vic, I'll get 'em in the AVP, get 'em off craft. We can pick them up with the GPS once we've fixed what we need to fix.'

'What about the airlock?' Vic shouted.

'Jesus, just do it, the airlock might be damaged, if it is there's no time to get them in the AVP. Do it…now!' Harry waved him away.

'Skylar, put it on,' Vic said, throwing the pressure suit toward her. 'Becker, Connie, go with Harry!' The noise, the flashing lights were dizzying, adding to the terror of the intruding vacuum. Sky could see her daughter's face, as she zipped up her personal life support, pretty sure her heart was about to detonate.

The AVP was a space-only Abort Vehicle Pod able to be tracked by the shuttle, carrying life support for three astronauts for around forty-eight hours. It had gyroscopic thrusters and carried about a hundred kilos of conventional liquid oxygen propellant.

Harry was pulling up his suit as he pushed himself awkwardly toward the payload bay, knowing if he passed out they were screwed beyond redemption. Thumping the AVP toggle, the twin doors slammed back with a thud, liberating an odorous smell of stale air. He thrust them both inside, harnessing them up with skilled, frenzied hands.

Connie looked at him, holding back a whimper, 'why c-can't you just leave us here in the ship,' she said, totally freaked out. 'There's no need to deploy…this is pressurised, right?' Her pretty heart-shaped face had tremors everywhere, lips, cheeks, eyes. Becker looked almost comatose, Harry wasn't even sure he was breathing. If he had time he would've

'This won't fully pressurise until it's off-craft, it's designed that way…it's an abort vehicle. Talk to the fucking engineers,' Harry yelled, exposing a yellowing line of teeth. If they stayed put they'd be relying on atmosphere from the shuttle. Harry closed the hatch, pulled the abort lever up, rotated the yoke clockwise until it clicked, then thumped it until it locked with a clunk. He felt the rumble from the LOX thrusters as it backed away from the shuttle, peering at it through the windowed doors. Harry could feel himself puffing in the thinning air as he finished fastening the suit. The warning lights abruptly turned off and the infuriating noise went with it. 'That's good, that's good,' he said quietly, realising Vic had manually terminated the emergency protocol. Fully in his suit, his breathing was rasping in his ears. Harry hoped to God at least one of their propulsion systems was undamaged. Being stranded out here would be terminal for all of them, they'd have to wait weeks for an old STS clunker to get into space and then span the distance to L1. And resources aside, he knew spending that long with Sky would end up with all of them wanting to slit their throats. 'Jesus fuck,' he said inside his helmet, what an unmitigated balls up.

Vic was looming over MEDS, studying the breaches in the superstructure displayed on the VDU. It showed a graphic red triangle in the payload bay on the side bulkhead wall, about three centimetres in diameter, small, but enough to completely de-gas the shuttle in ten minutes, evidenced by the almost complete vacuum they were standing in. Harry had the resin pads in hand, making his way to the deployment bay where he sighted the rip in the hull, ominously seeing a couple of stars, like a set of eyes through the hole.

Harry cursed silently, frowning at it. The hole looked was only a few finger widths across, but still black and terrifying, even to an old space dog like him. His hands shook a bit as he went to work, making him fumble, but the impenetrable seal was strong as the rest of the carbon nano-hull. Harry ambled back to the cabin, joining Vic at the avionics panel, a little shocked to be alive.

'Pressure's at sixty,' Vic said as he started ripping away the Velcro lashes.

Skylar was all eyeballs and monobrow behind her visor, her porcelain face, stiff like a Halloween pumpkin. He'd hoped to see her expression uncoil a bit after he plugged the hole but her eyes remained classic bovine surprise. Vic was still struggling with her almost vertical descent into what seemed like clinical depression and worse, her almost complete forfeiture of critical mental capabilities. For someone near the head of something as fringe as SETI he'd expected more. She was basically useless to the mission and quite frankly a fucking liability and a massive pain in the arse.

MEDS was telling them that the airlock was indeed damaged. The internal structure was okay but the external docking mechanism was inoperative, the capture yoke fractured, possibly by whatever ruptured the hull of Sagan or maybe by the first hit they took.

'We've got the AVP,' Vic said, pointing to the GPS visual, realising the nasty truth as soon as he got the updated specs on the airlock. Gaping at Harry forebodingly he had a clear message on his face. 'But, uh...they can't dock...we've got no way to onboard them.' A sensation like seasickness made him woozy as he confronted the harrowing reality, to which he had no solution.

'Jesus Christ,' Harry muttered, his voice hollow, picking out the meaning in Vic's words. 'There's portable 02 cylinders in the AVP. We could get them, like really close, and they could fire themselves into the airlock with air-pressure from the AVP...you know, breathe with the canisters.' He was chomping on his own words as he spoke...was it survivable or even recoverable? The idea of executing such a deadly exercise in space, unprotected, was truly dawning on him. Shot through the vacuum like a champagne cork, 'fuck me' he groaned, staggering under a shiver of dread that fish hooked up his spine.

Vic knocked his fist on his forehead, thinking through the unthinkable. Exposed to the vacuum even for ten or twenty seconds, what would that do to a person? He understood it a little and just rolling it around in his head scared the bejesus out of him. It was the temperature, the profound absence of pressure that were killers. Bodily fluids turning to vapour, swelling them like the skin of a balloon, flesh burning, oxygen torn from their blood, their entire vascular system dissolving, turning them cadaver blue. Eyes and mouth, anything with fluid would freeze or boil, blood pressure zero out, and if you made the fatal mistake of taking a breath before you got shot out, well good luck with that. Explosive decompression, a prick of a way to go. If by some miracle, they happened to live, recovery would be a bitch. Twenty, maybe thirty seconds was survivable if it was done right, but he knew they'd never win any beauty contests afterward...like ever.

'Hang on,' Harry said, 'aren't there pressure suits aboard?' He couldn't remember and neither he nor Vic were ever appraised of the inventory audits. They were just assured that all was in order. Whether that meant yes or no, they had no idea.

'They might have elasto-fabrics but they're for oxygen loss, not zero pressure EVA,' Harry said, sighing. 'Might as well be fucking naked,' he grunted. 'How much life support do they have?'

'Two days, another on the cylinders and re-breathers.' Vic said. 'There's no hope of fixing the ring and yoke, you've seen the feed from the docking camera...it's cracked and most of it's gone.'

Sky was out of her pressure suit, peeking at the distant lights from the AVP. The diminutive little craft was about eight hundred metres away. So close she thought, watching it curiously. 'Why are they just sitting there like that...shouldn't they be coming back?'

'They wouldn't know how to operate it,' Vic said. 'Sure, they'll work it out, well Connie will. The plan was for us to get as close as we could, guide them in, instructing them as we go. But, well...it's moot now. Short of propelling themselves through three metres of vacuum into a depressurised airlock, they're stuck on that thing, and I can't get them on comms. They'll figure that one out soon enough too...although they'll wished they hadn't.' Vic lifted a shoulder, dreading the conversation, feeling an ache in his temples.

'Why aren't there EMUs aboard?' Sky muttered, staring at the floor, looking gaunt and pale. She was blinking fast, eyes cupped by dark circles, breathing in shallow sucks of air. A classic image of a woman on the edge, a frigging knife-edge. Vic reckoned she looked dead-set barmy.

'There's no room, it's an abort vehicle pure and simple, designed for rapid exit and re-dock with another vessel. That's it. No shells.'

'Piss poor foresight,' she said, making no eye contact.

'We'll be sure to bring it up with the engineers Sky.'

'*Not*,' he mouthed to Harry, flicking his eyes up.

'What the hell is wrong with comms?' Harry said, wanting to punch the piece of shit. 'The anomaly's gone so what's up?' Were they being deliberately blocked, because he couldn't come up with any reason for it.

'Not sure about Houston,' Vic said, 'but I reckon Connie and Becker still don't know how to use the radio, they need to activate PTT or VOX but they probably have no idea on either.'

Maybe that was it, Harry conceded, putting aside his conspiracy idea for the moment. 'It's not bloody advanced engineering,' he snapped impatiently, 'it's press to talk or open mic, and just bloody speak!'

'Who knows what's going on?' Sky said miserably. 'The only thing I know for certain is that we need to get home, they may need us.'

Harry almost did a double take at Sky, glancing sharply at Vic, silently exchanging a single thought. They knew she was desperate to get home would do anything to get the job done.

'We're not leaving them behind,' Vic said coldly. 'We all go or none of us go, they're the rules up here, you know that.' He wasn't a hundred percent sure, but it was their fall-back position until something changed.

Harry nodded emphatically at Sky who abruptly turned on her heels and walked off the flight deck toward the deployment bay, muttering something unpleasant.

'Fuck you both,' Skylar fumed under her breath, feeling a sense of isolation and separation seeping deeper into her mind.

***

Becker and Connie had finally worked out the thrusting system for the AVP, comprising small flexible thrusters fore and aft that provided a high degree of manoeuvrability.

Their attention was now on the comms system. Connie pressed the PWR switch, which brought the unit humming to life, also pressing a small black pushbutton called VOX. They were in zero-g with no textured surface assist, so remaining still while trying to figure out the systems was doubly difficult.

'Vic, this is Connie, are you reading?' She held her breath, her heartbeat thick in her ears.

They heard an indistinct profanity followed by static, then Vic's voice came on strong. 'Shit,' he said loudly. 'Yes, uh…Connie, well done, copy. What's your status?' He said urgently.

'Status? Well we've worked out how to get this bucket moving and now the comms is working so hey, things are looking up. Are we coming to you or are you coming to us?' Connie's voice was upbeat. There was a long silence as they waited for Vic to come back. 'Hello?' Connie prodded, suddenly uneasy and heavy in the chest. Her eyes plastered on the comms unit, waiting, tapping a finger against the joystick.

'Um, we have a problem,' Vic said gently. Skylar felt sick, staring at nothing, waiting for him to say the words. She so wanted to go home but this was horrible, heartbreaking, inhuman. There didn't seem to be any reasonable outcomes because whichever way it went, it was going to be ugly.

Connie turned to Becker, lifting her eyebrows. 'Um, p-problem?' She asked shakily, feeling her mind start to spiral.

Vic just came out with it. He told them the docking cylinder was cactus and there was no way to hard dock the AVP to the shuttle. Take that.

Connie seized the horror instantly, and if not for zero-g would have collapsed on legs turned to mush. Becker frowned deeply, at her, then at comms, assuming there was a workaround, a backup plan, some NASA contingency that would simply lock into place like a cogwheel.

'What do we do?' Becker said to Connie, feeling a shaft of pain sweep through his bowels.

'We fucking die. That's what we do…we, uh…run out of air.' He stared at her and continued staring, slitting his eyes, searching her for something that suggested overreaction.

'Sweet shit,' he eventually said, darting his eyes around the cabin.

'Connie, you still there?' Vic asked as calmly as he could.

'B-Barely,' she gurgled, seeing her mortality splayed in front of her. How had her life led to this gruesome juncture…in space of all places, with a seemingly inescapable death sentence?

'We're going to come to you, line up the AVP hatch with our airlock—'

As Vic was talking, Connie was suddenly overwhelmed by dizziness, nausea, faintness, the irrepressible desire to run…to hide. Even though there was no weight on them, her legs trembled

221

violently under her, she wanted to retch, face ashen, cold perspiration pooling in the small of her back. Connie was so confused she could barely remember her name. Just thinking about floating unprotected in space was hideous to the point of cognitive shutdown. She couldn't do it, knowing if push came to shove the final step would never come. The notion of the hard vacuum on her flesh was genuinely worse than death. She saw Becker shaking his head disbelievingly, visualising what might be in front of them. They'd tuned out, neither of them listening to Vic as he described the indescribable.

'Becker, you oaf, they're asking us to swim through the vacuum into the open fucking airlock. We use this,' she gestured around her with an open hand, 'to propel us in, then they close it, pressurise it…come see what's left.'

Becker continued his blank stare. 'Oh d-damn,' he stammered. 'Can we, you know…survive?' He sighed with a long exhalation of built up breath.

'We can…we might, but in what form, well—,' she stopped talking, tasting a growing sourness in her mouth.

'What if we, like…miss the airlock?'

Her face shocked forward, eyes bulging out. 'Shit Becker, don't even—'

'Connie, you still copying?' Vic said, raising his voice.

'Sorry, we were just talking this through…trying to decide…thinking…you know.'

'Sure,' Vic said softly.

Harry had heard enough of this gently-gently horseshit. 'Connie this is Harry. Look, there's nothing to decide, if you don't do this your gone. If you want to die by oxygen starvation, slowly, badly, then by all means just stay where you are, keep the doors locked, draw the blinds. Breathing will do the rest for you because once the air's gone well—'

'Harry, we're just trying to—'

'Just tell us!' Harry roared, hating himself for doing it, but it was time to get this over with. 'If we're wasting our fucking time here, tell us and we'll leave, because Earth might need us. If you don't want saving then we'll focus somewhere that does.'

Christ Vic thought, it was good cop, rotten cop up here. Gently as he could, Vic said, 'guys, we want you back here with us and this is the only way. There is no other way. We have medical equipment, defibrillators, ventilation, resuscitation, adrenaline, plenty of plasma, we can bring you back. This is it, live … die… right now, you need to make the call.'

Connie cried out like a wounded animal, making a shrill noise that sounded inhuman. She wouldn't do it, couldn't do it, no way. The problem was she knew too much about the horrors of vacuum exposure. Maybe if she didn't her decision might be different, but she did, and there was no forgetting it.

'Are you shitting me?' Becker said, shoving out a hand. 'So, we just wait here till we run out of air? You're a bloody coward,' he said, stabbing a finger right at her, 'look at me…aren't you?'

'Fuck you Becker you arsehole.' Her eyes were moist, the warmth behind her eyes telling her all she needed to know. She was going to lose it.

Becker's blood was boiling so he gritted his teeth, fighting to remain calm. If he started yelling she'd win, that's how it always played out. This wasn't office politics though, it was life and death so he needed to be cool and reasonable, hardly his strong suit he admitted. 'Let's just get the job done,' he said as coolly as he could, 'let's make the decision together, let's live…it might be bad but at least we'll be around to talk about it, something to bore the grand-kids with, right?' He made strong eye contact with her and held it. 'The day we spaced ourselves…and lived! Now that's a keeper.' He softened his gaze, smiling as warmly as he could. 'Hey, if you don't do this, you'll never have those kids you wanted, pigeon pair, right?' It was all or nothing, he had to play every card he had in his deck and bag of tricks..

Oh, fuck she thought desperately, holding her head in her hands and murmuring jumbled syllables. Connie's expression suddenly broke completely, tears flowing into the air, tiny spheres of shining, salty desolation. 'Oh God, I'm so sorry,' she said, peering up with reddened, sorrowful eyes.

He grabbed her hand. Time for some tough love. 'Well you know what, I'm doing it. You stay here but I'm going home.'

'Vic?' Becker said loudly, 'come get me, I'm coming in so fire up that airlock, prep the med centre. Code fucking Black.'

Connie's head was shaking softly as she watched him go, still sobbing and feeling utterly conflicted. Go, don't go, live, die. It would be a grisly way to go no matter which path she chose. It was just that one of them was so much worse than the other, or so the tortured voice in her head kept telling her.

Vic and Harry knew it was all over unless Becker could convince Connie to take this rather gruesome leap of faith. Vic told them that once the atmo from the AVP was dumped, driving Becker into the airlock, that was it. There were no atmosphere generators aboard. Connie would only have one 02 canister and a couple of re-breathers, giving her maybe a couple of hours. And if she changed her mind there would be nothing to flush her into the airlock, she'd have to use the pitiable pressure from the gas canister to push her, and one wrong squirt, it was death in the vacuum. Best case, Connie would be in space for maybe a minute, not seconds.

'Connie, you can fly this thing, right? Becker said hopefully.

'Um, yes, pretty much,' she said, looking haunted.

He felt so sorry for his lifetime mate. Becker wasn't going to leave her behind, he'd forcibly take her with him, he was just trying to work out how that might happen. For the moment he'd play along, still hopeful she might snap out of it. Connie was pig-headed like he was but she was always sensible, logical, the prudent one, until now. The drop-dead terror of swimming through the void, effectively in her birthday suit, had killed everything inside her, including surviving.

Connie was fevering over options, struggling with decisions, chewing on the future, life, death…and resetting back to zero each time she needed to decide.

'You'll need to strap yourself in tightly,' Becker said soberly, 'then line the hatch up with Sagan's airlock and hold the position. I'll take one 02 canister, everything else is for you. Should give you a few hours hopefully—'

Connie broke from Becker's gaze and looked down at the floor, face collapsing again, heaving as she tried to stifle the emotion but simply couldn't, the pressure and pain were too much. Tears flew from her eyes like a spreading shockwave of tiny meteors, hands opening and closing rhythmically, seemingly seeking a solution to the conflict but knowing every option was torture…as bad or worse than death.

'Okay,' she whispered, terrified, 'I'll go with Becker but we go together. If we hold each other tightly enough maybe we'll be okay. She swore repeatedly to herself, terrified by what was in front of her, what she'd chiselled in stone and set in history. The awfulness just hadn't happened yet.

Becker smiled, sighing gratefully, gazing at the forlorn figure in front of him. 'Okay, let's get it done.'

She was still wiping the last of her tears away when the AVP pitched and rolled, inertia sending them straight into the comms and navigation unit, which they had to fend off with their hands.

23. Scourge

"Evil might not prevail in the end, but it certainly doesn't fail to devastate in its time."
~ Richelle E. Goodrich

Connie was hard up against the navigation unit and spun back to Becker who was pushing himself toward her, gripping onto the narrow ledge that stuck out below the bottom of the silica glass window panel. 'W-What?' She blurted wildly, wondering if the pod had been struck by something…same as Sagan.

Becker let go of the window, propelling himself over to the Nav screen, seeing that they were moving in the opposite direction. They had been moving nominally toward the shuttle but now they were edging away from it at maybe a click or so.

'Connie, we're going the wrong way,' Becker said, eyeing the shuttle and seeing it becoming gradually dimmer, '…we burning fuel?' He asked, knowing otherwise.

Connie looked at the small display unit, seeing that power to LOX was set to LKD.

'It's not us,' she said ominously. 'And we weren't hit by anything either.' They peered at each other, then at the shuttle that was now a distant light, slowly retreating into the deeper cosmos.

Becker rubbed his eyes with his thumbs, putting his face right up against the glass, certain he could see something. At first he wasn't sure, then he was sure. There were two bright stars above his vision line, a vaguely glowing smudge just below it, indistinct but it was there. Becker felt his pulse increase, pushing back a bit from the window, acknowledging there was something out there.

Connie gawked at the Nav panel, frantically weighing up what to do. Should she try and counter their movement, attempt to send them back toward the shuttle, it hadn't worked before, why would it now? Especially with this tinpot propulsion system that barely amounted to a single Vernier on Sagan.

'Speed's increasing,' Connie said, looking up sharply. 'one point four…one point six…wherever we're going, headway's increasing.' Her brow was almost under her hairline as she gasped for air.

Becker pointed to the aft window, she turned and saw nothing but the blackness of space. 'Where?' She said, raising her arms, sensing doom but seeing nothing.

'Get to the window, it's dim, blurry but there is—'

An ocean of light poured into the pod, washing out his words and everything else in a perfect spectral aura. Shielding their eyes with their hands it seemed to be similar to the anomaly but this time it wasn't blue, it was pure unalloyed white.

Connie shook her head in denial, clutching her throat, knowing the awful truth, the thing was reeling them in, same as the Spheres. That meant they were going in or through and there wasn't a damn thing they could do about it. The Spheres, the blue anomaly, both were hair-raising but this thing looked like it promised a whole new world of hurt.

'Vic…you getting this?' Connie almost screamed, terror twisting her face into a rumpled mess. There was only silence. 'Vic, Harry…do you read? She stared at the comms, waiting, praying for noise.

'Comms are dead.' Becker noted studiously.

'No shit,' Connie said, eyeing Becker nervously. 'Screw this.' Grabbing the joystick, she flipped off the safety, pressed the aft LOX lever and thumbed the throttle all the way to the end. They both felt the thump from the igniting propellant, seeing the Nav panel light up like a Christmas tree, confirming a one hundred percent burn, but sensing no inertia.

'Come on you prick,' Connie yelled, steeling herself, knowing it was their final play. They studied the GPS terminal, pleading for their motion to slow but still they felt no weight from the burn.

'Two clicks,' Connie said, grimly shouting out their rate of travel, gaping at the chilling numbers on the readout. 'Prop nineteen percent.' Despite what was waiting for them, Connie wanted back to Sagan. 'Motherfucking piece of shit, let us go!'

She pushed herself over to the window panel, facing the dimming lights of their only possible saviour, almost gone from view and little different to the other points of light in the sky. There would be no rescue, they grasped it with depressing clarity. Their future, if they had any, was inside the thing that looked like some misbegotten left over from the beginning of time.

Connie rasped, 'shutting down. Velocity two point two clicks. We're not getting away from this thing.'

'How long?'

'A minute, maybe two.' Connie flitted her eyes around for something, anything, but knew their destiny was written, done.

Connie grabbed Becker's hand, squeezing it tight, so tight it almost cut off his circulation. He gripped it back, a little startled.

'Gym work's been good to you Con, Christ you got a grip.'

Connie squeezed even harder. 'I'm scared.'

'Yeah,' Becker sighed, 'you know what, I won't accept it…no way…this can't be the end.' He peered into Connie's eyes, seeing his reflection, hearing his hollow words and wondering if this was really was the end.

Connie hid her face with the other hand as the light outside became everything, dazzling, sparkling arrows of energy everywhere. 'Here we go,' she murmured hazily, still gazing at Becker with luminous eyes, reflecting everything he didn't want to see.

As they spiralled inward they saw the familiar columns, white this time, slashing into space like serrated blades. Then they were falling, seeing monochromatic brilliance for a full five minutes without detail or contrast before something else assumed its place.

In part it carried the feeling of childhood awe, peeping into a storefront window, gawking at a lolly shop full of dazzling treats. It was a transient sensation because as they clawed their way back into what seemed like normal space, sitting not far ahead of them was an object profoundly incomprehensible.

Connie couldn't reconcile it with anything remotely within her experience. Off-planet, off-script, off-grid, an emphatic yes to all of them. Thankfully they were weightless because her mind finally yielded, had tripped a breaker and switched her prefrontal cortex to standby. Connie fainted and floated beside Becker like a river corpse as he stared blindly at the monstrosity that blocked space in front of them.

Surveying it closely, Becker felt reduced to zero, a barely-able-to-stand Hominid humping in the mud, staring impassively at an approaching starship, hammering home just how low on the pecking order we might be. The object ahead of them looked like a kilometres wide ball of yarn composed of tightly wound strands, forming an intricate dome and valley landscape. But that was only part of it because surrounding it were incredible acicular needles, spreading kilometres into space, seemingly protecting the entire incredible curvature.

24. Failure

"Now, I am become Death, the destroyer of worlds." ~ *J. Robert Oppenheimer*

"Unlimited power in the hands of limited people always leads to cruelty."
~ Aleksandr Solzhenitsyn

Vic and Harry watched helplessly as the AVP descended into the wrinkle, disappearing as though swallowed, digested...absorbed. They'd seen it open, engorge with light and then slam shut on itself like a massive clamshell, vanishing like a drop of water might evaporate on a desert rock.

Vic saw what happened clearly enough but was struggling to get why, intent, that was it. 'First blue and apparently solid...now white and it's...some opening to—' Vic's voice slowed, coming to a grinding halt, realising he had no idea what he was going to say.

'Same as the Spheres,' Harry said. 'Transit … temporal system, way less curvature, more in your face, right?' He wore a strange grin that melted away as he grappled with their next move. He thought Becker was a dead-set tool, Connie a hot-headed pain in the arse, but in their own way they'd assumed a sense of family, and who the hell liked their family? Damn sure he didn't, goddamn assholes, the lot of them. Still, you looked out for 'em, they were the rules.

Sky came ambling up with a face burning with colour, eyebrows squeezed so tight there was a single wrinkle in her forehead like a dark ravine. It couldn't be kept caged up any longer, if it was, she was sure the bony confines of her mind would yield in an inglorious implosion.

'We need to go...now,' she said, glaring first at Vic then pushing a finger at Harry. 'We could go the same way you know, once we're caught there's no getting away, you're done for...gone...fucked.' She raised her eyes, waiting, praying for a molecule of affirmation. After a few seconds, she lowered her eyes, knowing it wasn't coming, supressing the need to scream, instead covering her pallid face with a hand and gently sobbing.

Vic studied her closely, seeing the true depth of her mania, which was worse than he thought, and he already thought it was pretty bad. He spoke as soothingly as he could, trying like hell to shut out the irritation. 'What if they eventually come back? I mean, we can't just sail off without them, leave them stranded until they run out of atmosphere. That's not what you really want right?' He eyed her quizzically, pondering the twisted mind games going on inside her mad-hatter head.

'Vic's right,' Harry agreed, 'we need to stick around for a bit.'

'Oh Christ, 'Skylar moaned, realising she had no hope. 'Okay, how long? An hour, two hours, a week?' She had a shaky hand on her hip, wiping tears away with the other hand.

'When it feels right, we go,' Vic said, a little less generously. 'I get your need to go home but we can't abandon them, not yet. Not until we know they're not coming back.'

'God, you're making me out to be an arsehole,' she cried. 'I don't want to abandon them but my point is that we may become the next object of affection for that whatever out there.'

'We'll be fine.' Vic smiled, lying.

Sky's cheeks were burning red now. 'You sure you're keeping up with what's going on out there?' She swallowed heavily, looking directly away from them.

Arms folded tightly across her chest, Sky looked like a petulant child, pissed with the world because she couldn't get her way.

***

Flight Control at Houston lost contact with Sagan hours ago, not long after it started to close on the anomaly, but they hadn't lost the Hubble feed although to be honest they sort of wished they had. It provided witness to everything, albeit from a distance with a rather grainy view.

Jack watched Sagan sitting in space, weighing up whether it had prop issues, technical problems or if it was just busted and dead. Atmospheric loss shouldn't be it because there were firm protocols for dealing with it and he knew Harry and Vic well enough to pretty much rule it out, unless the puncture was massive and they had no time. Still, he didn't think so. The AVP had escaped so if they had time to prep it, then air loss couldn't have been catastrophic. Jack tugged at an ear until it was red. What if all of them were aboard the AVP? He guessed it would explain why the shuttle was drifting on the cosmic tide like a stranded conch shell. He stood up and squinted at the Hubble images, thinking the whole goddamn lot was bullshit. Answers, he pleaded silently.

Ten minutes later Jack and Pete were dealing with Ballard's insufferable bluster next to the Flight Director's Atlas console. Griffin, Morgan and Hillier were bickering like schoolyard toughs on the other side of the room near the comms and trajectory console. Picton-King was by the far wall on his cell and Jess Trevise had just joined them from US Strategic Command. The Science team was milling around aimlessly near the front of the high security area, still chucking reckless theories and guesses around, little different from everyone else in the United States and around the world.

'Why are they just sitting there like that?' Jack asked impatiently for the second time. Pete looked at him, not bothering to speak. He knew Jack would answer his own question in time. 'They've got dual prop, surely both can't be off-line. They're independent…everything is separated…mixing, burning, emission.'

'Yep,' Pete concurred, a little amused.

'But still there's no comms, no prop, unless they're waiting for the AVP?' Pete smiled at him knowingly.

Jack sat up in his seat, looking at Pete. 'Jesus, they think it might come back, they're waiting for it.' He knew he was under pressure, maxed on stress but he also reckoned he should have got that, like straight away. He thought of Kurt again, pondering his enigmatic third element.

'I told you ten minutes ago,' Pete crowed. Jack gazed at him, lifting an eyebrow and twisting his lips into a pucker. Eighteen hours without sleep he said to himself, idly watching Morgan grab his cellphone and answer it. He was about to apologise to Pete for his lack of mind when he saw every drop of colour drain from Morgan's face and distinctly heard him utter what like a whipcrack. Jack's first reaction was to freeze, a curious tingling sensation sweeping up his spine as he watched him, seeing him spin hastily to Griffin and mouth a few choice words. Griffin's face fairly melted before him, eyes bulging and head tilting back oddly as though he'd suffered some serious cervical injury. None of them had seen Griffin's teeth because he never smiled but by God they were out now, courtesy of a violent grimace. Jack felt his body tensing, muscles tightening as he watched their reactions play out. These guys had resilience and ballistic toughness that was barely measurable against regular folk. His heart was pounding, running the numbers, deciding it had to be Sagan.

Both men turned abruptly and looked furiously at Jack, striding in his direction with faces he wanted to run from. They were veined, lined, set hard as pig iron. Jack instinctively took a couple of steps backward. Shit, he shouted silently, feeling like scrambling for the nearest door.

Hillier threw his cell in the dock. 'Tyson, can you hear me?' He asked harshly, looking deathly pale.

'I can hear you,' he said in a voice faint with disbelief.

'Just give me a minute,' Hillier said, looking gravely at Jack. Hillier was a senior exec with DoD and like most of his peers, took shit from no one, apart from Griffin. 'I've got Tyson Alavanos, Director of the GSSAP surveillance satellites…they sit in geosynch orbit. They've imaged something that's already news around the world.' He sighed, shaking his bearish head irritably, 'how this got out so quickly we have no idea. The sheer bloody scope meant it would get out, but already?' Glaring at them one by one he added a sense of drama by narrowing his eyes and blowing out his cheeks. Whatever it was, he was struggling with it and the rest of the suits didn't seem to be faring any better.

'Oh for fuck's sake Hillier, just tell 'em,' Griffin roared. 'No time for showboating.'

Hillier felt his blood boil, turning back to his cell, 'Tyson, repeat what you told us.'

'Okay, sure…GSSAP3 was surveilling the Spheres when one of them disappeared, the one with the connection to Antarctica. It just, well…winked out, gone. There's only fourteen there now.'

Hillier was pacing and grunting, feeling the heat from Griffin's stare. 'Get to it,' he fumed, looking daggers at the phone.

'When the Sphere vanished,' Tyson continued, sounding deeply ill at ease, 'um, well, the ice in Antarctica went with it.' The words briefly hung in the air.

The whole group stared at Jack mutely, Tyson's words bouncing around their brains like Incan symbology, Jack receiving it, rejecting it, eventually hooking onto a low hanging branch. 'W-Wait…what?' He breathed the words raggedly, 'it…melted the ice, is that what you're saying? Repeat…please.' His mouth was slack, his voice halting and shaky. Images of devastated coastlines hit him, islands being inundated, general global carnage they would have no way of stopping. Disorientation, detachment was overwhelming him.

'No,' Tyson said, raising his voice abruptly. You're not getting it. Not melted, gone. No water, no vapour cloud…just gone…vanished. Like out of there.'

'Jesus Christ,' Jack said, springing his hands off his forehead into the air. By human standards it was absurd, sounded like gibberish, beyond possibility, yet apparently it was fact.

'I've checked the facts,' Tyson said, 'fourteen million square kilometres of ice, ninety percent of the planet's fresh water just up and gone…in a heartbeat.' Pausing momentarily, Tyson hacked something from his throat, 'um, gents, we now have an ice-free continent at the South Pole…not even a snowball.'

'Three thousand people presumed dead,' Ballard growled, 'and a shitload of penguins. This is an attack, a declaration of war but we, the, uh…Pentagon, the White House, the United States can't fight it.' His features were furrowed by frustration and indecision, punctuated by a massive exhalation through his nose. 'The prospect of a hostile encounter has already been considered by the Situation Room so we know our position. We can be at DEFCON1 and White Status for as long as we damn well like but it doesn't change a thing, we have zero off-planet capability for battle. No country on Earth, the United States included, can do anything from here or take weaponry into space and have it do the slightest bit of good.

Having a look, fine – offense, defence - stone cold nothing.' His deeply set eyes were vacant, flat, almost resigned.

Griffin nodded bitterly. 'Unless these bogeys go atmospheric we can only watch and hope. We can buzz around down here like fucking mosquitoes at a blood-fest but the reality is that we're in the deepest shit imaginable if they,' he paused and grunted sharply, 'are genuinely unfriendly.'

'Fucking wood-ducks at a redneck carnival,' Ballard said with venomously.

If they're unfriendly? Jack thought incredulously. Did he think they're actions were generous, benign, misunderstood perhaps? For the love of God, he thought, but he was a little gratified by the words, that the hammer hadn't fallen completely on what their intentions might be. He was certain that firing AMRAAMS or minutemen nukes at these things would end very badly for the planet. 'We need to get a grip on what these things want,' Jack said, thinking he might as well throw in the fucking sky is blue too, knowing he was labouring the obvious. 'Fighting can't be the answer. Knowledge is key, has to be the focus, that's gotta be our battle plan.' Glancing at Griffin he got a death stare in return. 'Find out who is controlling these things, see what they want from us.'

'How do we know they want anything?' Hillier snapped. 'They may be doing all this just because they can.'

Jack said, 'I don't care how goddamn different they are, they want something, even if it's to see us squirming down here, be sure of it. Whatever this is, it's part of a plan.' He was less convinced now that he'd said it, recognition slowly dawning on his face as he rolled it around, really gave it some gum. Maybe this was part of something bigger, something way bigger than just us. Jack knew if the Spheres came into the atmosphere and push came to shove, the military wouldn't be able to control itself. One look at Griffin, Ballard and Company. was enough to know they were basically automata, slaves to inflexible, defensive protocol and blind nationalism. It'd be a slaughterhouse. Humans would have no hope, a cursory peek at Antarctica provided a prophetic insight.

Griffin stepped forward, pinching the bridge of his nose and pulling his fingers over his mouth and chin. 'The UNGA is holding an emergency session in New York, the Security Council is introducing resolutions around a global response.' He paused, sighing almost in self-defeat. 'But it's just, well…it's no more than window dressing, showing that we're not back on our haunches, that we're out there doing something,' he said, giving a laconic shrug. 'You know, that we don't think we're fucked. The UN can authorise military action, probably will, but like I said, we don't have an enemy to engage. It's just a display, a show, no more, no less.' He paced back and forth. 'Ever heard of that stupid bird…wards off predators by copying noises made by bigger birds? Well that's us in a goddamn clamshell, whooping it up, acting tough, talking the talk…with shit to back it up.'

Jesus, thanks for the rev up, Jack thought grimly. If the military were thinking like this maybe we should just roll up the bloody footpaths up and let whatever happen… happen.

They each surveyed the other in rapid fire, wondering if extinction was at stake? Was that where this sorry story was leading, game over without explanation or answer?

Jack was gazing loosely at the screen which still had Sagan front and centre, motionless in space. He hoped to Christ the shuttle wasn't a dead stick because if they were going to learn anything, get anywhere, Sagan was critical if only by sheer juxtaposition. They were the ones up there amongst it, eyeballing it.

***

Skylar was pacing around the rear of the flight deck like a caged lion in slow motion. She'd spent forty-five minutes in the payload bay, cursing under her breath, prowling around, head down, eyes glued to the floor. Now she was back, glaring at Vic and Harry, waiting for the go to depart. There was no way Connie and Becker were coming back, she knew it beyond doubt, was sure Harry and Vic did too. Sky felt guilty as hell, but justified it by knowing in herself she was smack bang right…whatever godless pit they were in, they were in there for keeps.

'That's an hour and a half,' Harry said wearily, peering at his wristwatch. Skylar glanced up, spinning her head around, feeling her muscles tighten with anticipation. Now we get to go home, she fevered, her pleading eyes lasered on Vic, waiting for the words.

'Goddamn it,' Vic said, sighing dejectedly. He spat the words, pushing air out long and loud, ending up staring blankly at Harry, feeling a sting of regret as he pondered their next move. 'Goddamnit,' he repeated angrily.

'Fire it up,' Harry said. 'Skylar, strap in, were going home.'

She tried to act casual but it was hard. She turned away, smiling, securing herself in the Mission Specialist's seat. 'Good to go,' Sky said quickly, trying to look serious, but not succeeding.

'Straight to Magneto,' Harry said loudly. Fucking go, Skylar silently screamed, panicked by her mind's-eye image of the anomaly reaching out with invisible fingers, grasping Sagan in a final, implacable death-grip. Come on, she begged silently, her body rigid, waiting for the glorious inertia of forward momentum.

'Compression APUs armed,' Vic said as he depressed two yellow switches, moving his fingers to the bottom of the MPD panel. 'Cyclotron pre-start, electrogmag, arcjet, cold plasma is in the green Harry, MPD on-line…I say we're good to go.'

Well go then, Sky bellowed to herself, now ramrod straight in her seat, feeling like her spine was ready to crack.

Electrical currents were rebounding off condensing xenon in the bowels of the shuttle, ionising and melding into rich thermo-cold plasma, soon to be propelled through the engine by the self-propagating magnetic field. They were pushed gently back in their seats as they slowly accelerated toward their target of fifty clicks a second. Thank you Vic, she thought, repeating it several times, closing her eyes, thinking of home.

229

Vic scanned the instrument panel, 'eight hours to DOI,' he said, curiously studying Sky's newfound expression. Lines of dread and worry had melted into a relaxed, almost tranquil countenance that softened her face. He could see the old Sky, the one he'd met at KSC a week ago – calm, attractive and without speaking a word, deeply intelligent.

Sky gazed dreamily through the window panel, wanting to bounce around the cabin like a five-year-old, but didn't, knowing that would be rather bad form. Avoiding elation was impossible, the feeling was everywhere inside her, she was glad the AVP hadn't come back - there she'd said it! And she meant it, fighting to side step the self-loathing.

A few seconds of static abruptly resolved into Jack's voice, slightly higher in tone than normal.

'…the hell is going on up there?' They heard him say impatiently, presumably talking to someone in the FCR, probably Pete, Vic guessed.

'We have you Jack,' Vic said, raising a fist and gently shaking it, 'not sure what happened to comms but all seems fine now, five bars.'

There was a slight pause. 'Good to have you back,' he said, sounding a little subdued. 'What's your, uh, status?'

'…fine up here, crew and craft.'

'Great, that's…great,' Jack said hesitantly. Vic looked at Harry, his eyes flattening, detecting an unusual note in his voice – worry, anxiety maybe – strange because it continued after he received their status update.

'So, what did we miss?' Vic said, feeling a snap of energy run up his spine, idly checking the GPS to confirm they were on heading and everything looked good - MPD systems, Star Tracker, trajectory were nominal. 'You there Flight?'

Jack cleared his throat. 'Um…well you have missed a few things. You need to get back as soon as possible. We'll brief you when you get nearer to Earth.'

Harry and Vic picked up the ominous tone and evasive posturing, pretty sure what it meant, anxiously throwing around how bad it was going to be.

'Why not brief us now?' Harry said, 'we've got nothing else pressing…nowhere else we need to be.' He winked at Vic but looked restless, scratching his beard, shifting in his chair.

Jack finally relented, relaying the devastating events at the southern end of the planet. For everyone aboard Sagan, the scope of the happening was initially impossible to grasp. Vic couldn't reconcile the bleak implications, the sheer magnitude of what they'd done – it was incomprehensible - thirty thousand cubic kilometres of ice gone without a trace. NASA's Suomi-NPP satellite had swung its VIIRS instrument onto Antarctica and couldn't find a single flake of ice, a drop of meltwater, an eddy of vapour left on the continent. The incredible exactness of what they'd done was astonishing. All the ice had gone but the landscape, at least from the VIIRS close-ups, was entirely untouched. Even the glacial striations were still there, underlining the surgical precision of what was quite simply an assault on the planet.

Fuck me, Harry brooded, what might be next, another of the gravity connectors swinging itself onto Earth like a colossal artillery turret, redoubling the warning? It might not be the icy patina from a largely unoccupied continent but maybe a city like Beijing or Washington, or a continent like Australia…an ocean like the Pacific or perhaps the whole goddamn lot.

Jack said, 'Vic, we've got think-tanks here at JPL, at AMES, the Pentagon, Texas A&M, Cambridge and a dozen other places trying to figure out what the hell all this means. We need something, anything, a basic framework to effort some sort—,' he trailed away, pausing to find the right word. 'I don't know…I mean, maybe we're screwed and the whole lot is way beyond…' He came to a grinding halt again, Vic could hear his accelerated breathing. 'But if we have a chance then we need to find something, an answer, a solution, clues, insights, whatever. If there's something to find, we damn well need to find it.'

'There is no answer,' Skylar said, jerking her head around, ending up staring squarely at Vic, arms like planks by her side. 'Don't you get it, wake up, this is extinction by a thousand cuts. These whatever-they-are will never let us go, no matter what we do. They'll keep this going until we break…all of us.'

Vic had heard enough. 'Bullshit,' he shot back. 'If they're as advanced as we think they are then I don't buy the cruel mindset crap. Is it possible? Yes, likely, no, no and no. I don't accept it. We're missing something…a lot.' He glared at Sky, staring her down, making it clear the conversation was over. She shook her head slightly, shifting her gaze to the wall of the shuttle, appalled by his ignorant, myopic view. She knew Vic was straight down the line, believing the acquisition of intelligence was magically shackled to some grand rise in munificence and altruism. For some it might be true but why should it be one size fits all? It was a childish, blinkered view based on nothing more than precious human sensibilities. Sky drew in a grating breath, wondering whether Earth was just shit out of luck by scoring contact with a very unsociable, nasty race of belligerent fucks. Looking at Vic's sanctimonious expression, she felt like screaming at him to wake up and smell the roses. Because they might not be roses at all, they might be flowering hemlock waiting patiently to strike you dead. Sky stayed still, said nothing, stared out into space, pondering the odds.

***

'You're our hope,' Jack said gravely. 'If we come up with something you're the ones in the hot seat, to do the prac work.'

'Sure…okay Jack, copy.

Harry looked at Vic and mouthed, 'the message?'

Shit, Vic thought, wondering what the hell was wrong with him. 'Jack?' Vic said hastily, 'did you get a visual on the inside of the anomaly after we arrived?' He knew they didn't because Jack would've called it straight away. He would've been falling over himself to confirm that Mission wasn't suffering some folie à trois…group madness.

'No,' Jack replied, sensing something in Vic's voice. He paused, followed by a pregnant silence. 'So, uh, what was inside?'

Vic glanced at Harry, shrugging. He knew this was going to rip Mission's mind into tiny pieces. It was going to sound like the biggest pile of steaming horseshit in the history of NASA, so he just came out with it, ripped off the bandage, hair and all.

'We were inside Jack…other people, humans that looked like us, were us, staring back from the other side. Same shuttle, same crew…identical in every detail down to clothing, weight and anything else you'd care to think of.'

Well not quite Sky thought, glancing at the floor, remembering what Connie had whispered to her with a veiled smirk.

Vic stopped talking, leaving a pin-drop silence, visualising their frog-like stares as they weighed up what strain of near space psychosis had afflicted the group. Vic could almost hear them batting the words around, pretty much striking out on all of them.

Jack took a long while before he summoned the composure to speak. 'So, you're, uh…serious?' He was almost incoherent, waiting for someone to break into a chuckle, a muffled snigger perhaps.

Vic gave Jack and the rest of the FCR details of the encounter, hearing not a peep from them for almost a minute after he stopped.

'Ok-kay,' Jack voiced delicately, brokenly, 'so what was the message?'

'We think it was incomplete, by intention or just the way we took it down, we're not sure.' Vic could feel Harry's gaze burning into him. 'It said Antarctic object must be stopped. The last word was clipped at "s-t" but we think it was going to say "stopped". No other words seem right, but anyway…get the message to your "think tanks" okay? Get 'em on it.'

231

'Got it,' Jack said, feeling a little giddy. 'There's general agreement that Becker's object was a syntype, the primary device, machine or such, like that conveyed our, readiness to whatever is running the show.'

'Get 'em down there,' Harry barked, frustrated with all the bullshit banter.

'…get who where?' Jack said uncertainly.

'Jesus,' Harry implored, 'get a team back to this syntype in Antarctica, see if we can switch it off. That's where it started, maybe that's where it finishes…the message is pretty clear.' Harry rubbed the middle of his forehead, wondering where IQs had gone. The message referred to the southern continent by name so it seemed a no-brainer to get back there.

Vic pondered the likelihood. 'Maybe they removed the ice to make it easier for us to execute the message.' He wrinkled his nose and thumbed an ear. Were these infuriating creatures assaulting us but also helping us…or were they some broken Kardashev riddlers who got their jollies by teasing and torturing, lighting the insects on fire as it were? Whatever it was, it was just beyond, Vic thought, closing his eyes, resting his head on the back of the leather seat.

Harry's brow was in constant motion, squashing up and releasing as he lingered over the endless possibilities. 'So, hang on, they give us a message in binary, a partial one mind, then strip the ice off a continent so we can go and have a look?' He had one hand on the back of his head, raking it around his neck. 'I'm trying not to say it, but,' he paused and raised his eyes, 'oh fuck it, turn it up…why? There has to be a reason but as usual we're just sitting here whistling fucking Dixie like brainless twats.' Harry spat the words, pounding a fist into his palm. 'They're setting us up, giving us false hope…fuckers.' Harry slammed his mouth shut and closed his eyes, groaning, puzzling over the unknowable motives of this very peculiar species.

'Let's get a team down there,' Vic said firmly. 'It's the only way.'

'Better than posturing and guessing,' Harry said roughly, curling his lip into a sneer.

Griffin was nodding so quickly he seemed at risk of slipping a disc. 'Do it, do it now,' he said, looking venomously at his deputies. 'We should've done this earlier,' Griffin said, throwing daggers at Hillier whose face was pulled into a bullish frown.

'Your team Nate,' Jack said instantly, 'you're the ones.' He glanced urgently at Griffin. 'We'll need air transport, military escorts, a base camp on site.' He didn't believe he would ever say this but what the hell he thought, it was the new normal. 'Remember, there's no ice down there but it'll still be cold…freezing.' He turned his head to Griffin, scratching at an eyelid, global warming was one thing, ice-sheet thinning another…but this? It was off the scale, worse, it was true.

Griffin was on his cell, berating someone at the Pentagon, some poor sucker from DoD, barking his demands one by one, then repeating them as though lecturing a wayward child. He wanted Sea Knights for personnel and equipment transfers, the best logistics experts, engineers, mine-site designers, military techs…now! Griffin told them what, how much and where, and told them to make it fucking happen. He stormed off but they could still hear him barking demands from fifty feet away. After a few minutes he returned, red-faced but apparently satisfied.

Staring at Nate he fairly growled, all bulging eyebrows, ruddy flesh. 'You four, be ready for relocation in two hours. You'll be taken by an MV-22 and escorted to the site of the original bogey. Logistics, living supplies will follow, base camp will come a few hours later.'

Tara glanced at Nate with huge cow eyes. 'What's an MV-22?' She asked nervously. He shook his head and lifted his shoulders uncertainly.

'Oh Jesus,' Griffin said, rubbing his jaw, 'it's a big fucking chopper.'

25. Vexed

"Why should things be easy to understand?" ~ *Thomas Pynchon*

Sagan had entered a descent orbit around Earth an hour ago, only a few hundred clicks from the alien structure that was geostationary in its most unusual polar orbit.

'Um, Vic, what's happening?' Sky said uncertainly without looking away from the window, feeling goose pimples rise across her shoulders.

Before Vic and Harry got to the window, they could see it. Movement. 'There's six, wait, no seven objects on the move,' Vic shouted.

Harry was going to ask why but caught the question before it escaped his mouth. 'It's a de-orbit move,' he said instead.

'No doubt atmospheric trajectory,' Vic conceded with forced calm. If they were heading that way, into the envelope of life, what sort of welcome would the world's military have for them? Vic cursed under his breath, would Griffin and POTUS, the Joint Chiefs, DOD, unleash their ludicrous shock and awe strategy, and if they did, how would the Spheres react? Every molecule of his body sounded jangling alarm bells at the same time. Military intelligence was a monumental oxymoron.

The greater Sphere was slowly shedding its building blocks, half of them breaking free and transiting in the direction of Earth, the other seven remaining as guide pieces, gently edging closer to conserve the integrity of the round.

Vic was about to punch telemetry when Jack's voice rifled at him.

'Sagan, Flight, you there?'

'Right on cue, are you scanning radial motion?'

'Yep, JT from Strategic Command got a call from the Space Surveillance boys. They have eyes on multiple bogies, some are going northern hemisphere, some south but all will reach particle interface inside an hour if velocities stay nominal.'

'Christ,' Vic said, his mind reeling. 'The military need to hold and monitor. Tell me they're not going to try their shock and awe bullshit.'

'I'd like to tell you that but I honestly don't know,' Jack said. 'The whole Exec team, Griffin, Ballard, Hillier and Kent, even Picton-King have commandeered a break-out room and it's like a fucking hen house…it's a screaming match in there.'

Harry couldn't see any other outcome apart from abject disaster, pulling at his beard hard enough to hurt. 'I mean is there any other possibility here?' His features suddenly lightened, wiggling an eyebrow, 'oh wait, hang on…maybe they'll glide on in, settle down gentle as a baby's kiss on the White House lawns all friendly like.' He gave a loud, derisive snort. 'Seriously Jack, add it up, no way it equals a benign outcome.' Given the events down south, Vic wondered if maybe they'd unfurl some absurdly powerful neutron weapon to erase everything, then stick their godforsaken flag of conquest in the ground, staking their claim to the planet formerly known as Earth.

'Given what's happened so far, I agree,' Jack shot back ruefully.

'Yep, if they're friendly they've got a screwed-up way of showing it.'

Vic heard Jack's cellphone ring. 'Hang on,' Jack said. Through the intercom Vic could hear a few muffled words, raised voices, then extended silence followed by a clipped goodbye to whoever was on the other end. Jack came back on line, grunting, short of breath.

'Oooo-kay,' Jack started ominously, 'SST is tracking incoming on phased array…five are going north, two south, all higher and lower latitudes by the look, nothing equatorial. Inbound at twenty clicks, Karman line will be breached in around twenty minutes.'

Vic's brain was scrabbling over the possibilities. 'Report if anything changes,' he said cautiously, unsure what to do or say. They could talk all day but intent would only be known once these things did whatever the hell they were on their way to do. Predicting, contemplating, guessing…all useless.

'Copy that. US Strat Command have 'em on radar so if something changes… when we know, you'll know.'

Vic terminated comms with Houston. 'Holy Mother of God,' he breathed heavily, watching the Spheres motor beyond their field of view, sparkling in the sunlight. As Jack pointed out, their trajectories seemed clearly divergent, as they appeared to be journeying toward their own piece of real estate on the planet. He didn't give the question of where any air-time because it was just another elusive pain in the arse, but he couldn't avoid asking himself, it was inside his brain, swelling like a hot air balloon. Why were seven alien sacs heading to different parts of the planet, all apparently chosen ahead of time?

***

Four hundred and fifty clicks north of the Arctic Circle, an isolated sweep of tundra stretched as far as the eye could see. No trees and barely an undulation spoilt the sheer desolation of the frozen landscape, leaving it mostly free of any permanent population, held sway by roughnecks who slugged it out on the oilrigs offshore. Run by the multinationals, this place had scored the geological equivalent of a dozen lotto wins in a row. Favoured by ancient humidity and massive organic decay, blessed with perfect cap rock, it had given up tens of billions of barrels of West Texas Intermediate, and there was a shitload left in the tank.

On the red and white rig anchored closest to land in Prudhoe Bay, three Helos were arcing away with two more gunning their props on the helipad, workers manically shoving their way in. Lifeboats dropped into the ocean from every corner of the rig, men dropping through escape chutes in their dozens, reaching out, desperately clinging to overcrowded and listing craft. A pack of hundreds jostled around the perimeter of the helipad, fingers stabbing the air in the direction of the sky that was deeply bronzed and seemed to be literally dropping toward them.

The North Slope nightmare that was Deadhorse sat on the edge of nowhere and looming at it, that is, descending toward it was something beyond language. The leviathan came to a soundless halt about a thousand metres above the oil rich bay and as it stopped, the gravity driven tides disappeared, the great curvature smoothing itself and instantly reflecting everything below it in a perfect mimicking of reality. Although bleak, isolated and home to less than fifty permanents, the Sphere had chosen Deadhorse Alaska.

***

After an hour locked in the breakout, Griffin, Ballard and the rest of them swept purposefully into the FCR sporting brutal expressions. Pete glanced sideways at Jack and didn't need to say a thing, rubbing and twisting his hands. Griffin's face was creased with worry, Ballard looked as though he'd been shot several times without sustaining a mortal wound.

Griffin sounded like he'd been gargling gravel, at best severely hung over. 'They've moved POTUS from the White House Sit Room to the PEOC bunker with his exec team and NSC Advisor. He'd been East Winged because these things, right now they're in high and low lats, but who knows when that might change. PEOC can take a nuclear strike but is that enough?' He scowled at Jack narrowly, posing the unknowable question, peering down at his cell and satisfied there were no messages, re-pocketed it. 'They might be moved to the NMCC at the Pentagon but it's suck and see. The Sit Room's getting real time data from the SSN and Director of National Intelligence, that'll feed to the President in the War Room and to me. The Morning Book will be updated two hourly and you'll be privy to everything. You and Pete now have SCI Intelligence Clearance.' He looked at them

234

murderously, pulling at his tie. 'If you repeat shit beyond these walls, send anything in any form you'll go straight to the Bay and I'll fly the fucking helo myself, are we clear?'

They both nodded effusively. 'Yes, clear,' Jack confirmed hesitantly, thinking the warning was rhetorical but by Griffin's expression, realising he was on the level. Military and focussed was one thing but Griffin, in fact all of the Agency leaders, presented as bloody-minded lunatics.

'You boys know what SPACETRACK is?' Griffin said, raising his voice. They continued nodding like morons. 'Well AMOS, that's the Maui Optical Station, tracked the bogies trajectories on the way in.'

Ballard looked at Griffin, 'No entry tracks right?' He'd already read the comms.

Griffin eyed him suspiciously, 'yeah, no entry tracks...you know what that means?' He looked squarely at Jack with deeply shadowed eyes.

'Frictionless entry?' Jack said, immediately blurting no way to himself.

'That's right, they entered without slowing down and didn't heat up. Temperature gradients stayed nominal, thermal signatures were like they were swanning though deep space...that was the quote from Alavanos.' Griffin raised his eyes to the ceiling. 'Fuck!' He said with enormous force.

Jack rocked back a bit, watching Griffin bare his teeth and rub his eyes, leaving them brown in the middle and bloodshot everywhere else. 'So, they entered at what, ten thousand clicks and there was no aerodynamic loading at all...no heat, no fireball?' Jack's eyes widened, glowing with disbelief. 'What the hell are they made of?' He asked abstractly, chewing on his lip, seeing his vision spotting like confetti. 'Well, uh...pretty impossible, right?'

'Sure as hell not metal or anything we know about,' Griffin said blandly.

Jack suddenly realised how close the Spheres were, for whatever reason, half of them had taken up residence in their own backyard. He held his breath, looking through the massive MCC window, then squarely at Griffin. 'The army, navy, they're not taking pot shots, are they?' Jack's face paled because if they had, the engagement would surely have been depressingly short and they wouldn't be here pondering it now.

'Relax Jack, the President is accepting directions from the UN, and like all nations, has enforced a watch and wait protocol,' Griffin said, a little downcast. 'Any plans by any country to engage with a first strike pre-emptive play have been shelved, so decreed across the globe by the UN's OMA advisors,' Griffin scowled. 'Not that anyone normally listens to those dickless dolts from Turtle Island, but hey, that's the decision and it's holding,' he said contemptuously.

Well shit in a shoebox, Jack thought with a measured exhalation. The military, the world's military had actually come down on the side of prudence and pragmatism. I'll be damned he said to himself. 'Smart strategy sir,' Jack offered agreeably.

Griffin's cell rang again and he peered blindly at the number, then motioned Ballard to the wall of the FCR.

Jack watched them amble over to the massive whitewashed wall and was about to speak to Pete when they both turned abruptly and came barrelling back. Griffin fairly smashed his phone into the speaker dock again. 'An interesting, um...development,' he said curiously. 'Stefan, you there?'

'Got you loud and clear,' the deep voice said.

'I have Jack Raines and Pete Harper from JSC. Gentlemen, this is Stefan Walsh, National Security Advisor to the President. He's currently in the White House Situation Room. He's just received an update from SpaceCom which is part of the SSN...anyway Stefan, go.'

'So, right, like Earl said, this is the latest info from the Space Surveillance Network. Our ODS arrays are tracking these objects and they've all stopped, all seven of them. We think that wherever they're going...they've arrived.'

There was a long pause, allowing them time to look warily at each other and roll the words around. 'So where is there?' Griffin demanded tersely. Does he think we're going to fucking guess? His face was split like alpine granite, winding up to scream at the phone when Walsh continued.

'It makes no sense. We've kicked it around the Sit Room with the Watch Team and sent it straight to PEOC for the President and his teams. No one can make anything of it. I've forwarded emails with map attachments to each science centre including yours at Johnson, direct to you.'

Jack opened the email, printed the attachment and handed them out. It was a little map of the world showing seven large green dots with accompanying text in small blue-bordered boxes.

If they had to guess where they might be going they would have assumed major capitals…population centres although they could probably thank Hollywood for that. Jack would've guessed New York, Moscow, Beijing, but the objects were in the sky above wild backcountry, away from populated areas, basically the antipathy of expectation.

'Explain it Stefan, I dare you,' Griffin said impatiently. 'Why have they taken up residence in redneck country?'

'That's your voting area Earl, thought maybe you'd know.'

Griffin maintained an icy stare at his cell, saying nothing. Jack was sure he saw smoke wafting from his ears.

'Let's go through the locations to get some perspective on what we're talking about,' Stefan offered. 'All the objects are stationary and we've measured them using the SAR antenna on the TerraSAR-X satellite and they are at exactly one thousand metres elevation. You can imagine the sight from the ground…well, actually you won't need to because CNN and Fox and every other news network are on their way to the nearest bogey. Just tune in and you'll get a front seat view.' He had a slight tone of amusement, which caused Griffin to glare savagely at the dock. '…these things are half a click through the middle so they're mind boggling close up as you can—'

'Fine, location now!' Griffin wailed, 'focus for Christ sake. We can't control the fucking news, as much as we'd like to.' He surveyed the group, flaring his nostrils. 'Shit, social media will be in meltdown. Good luck to HomeSec and NSC,' he sneered.

'Okay,' Stefan said lightly, hold onto your hats or your rugs. Uh…no offence Earl,' he said, grinning cautiously at the phone.

'You got a mirror?' Griffin snapped with no trace of humour.

'Er, well I was—'

'Oh Christ,' Griffin interrupted fiercely. 'You're as clean as a cue ball Walsh, get on with it.' Nodding self-consciously, Stefan knew things were bad but could this jerk just chill a little?

Stefan continued with a clearing cough, 'so we have bogies above the following, communities - Deadhorse Alaska, Oulu in Northern Ostrobonthia…that's Finland, glorious Dikson in Krasnoyarsk…that's Russia, the middle of the Weddell Sea in the Southern Ocean, Alert in way northern Canada, the Greenland Sea and lastly, most unsurprising I suppose, Marie Byrd in Antarctica. So, tie me down if they haven't chosen some of the saddest places on the face of the planet.' He stared at the ground for a few seconds, chuckling faintly. 'Go figure, right?'

'What are these places,' Jack murmured suspiciously. 'I mean is there anything special about them, a thread, a lead, a commonality…anything?'

'Hah,' Stefan chortled. 'What you mean like the middle of a frozen ocean, some tin-pot settlement in Alaska or the most northerly human outpost on the planet…and the South Pole? These places are nothings. We've asked the question of our research teams but if you ask me it just beggars belief…rack up another nonsense.'

'What about the names of these places or the lat and longitude,' Jack implored.

'Again, our research and science teams are efforting research as we speak,' Walsh said. 'Maybe the locations mean nothing,' he said in a lower voice, 'perhaps they're random, selected at whim, make us fever over them for no reason, waste time, send ourselves around the twist looking for nothing.' He lowered his voice doubtfully. 'Maybe to distract us from something else.'

'Be that as it may,' Jack replied testily, 'when we come up with nothing we'll consider it further, till then, hammer the shit out of it.'

'And don't come up for air Walsh, until it's done,' Griffin added sharply, thinking bald fucker as he disconnected.

Jack looked over at the Johnson based science team, seeing them in deep conversation, poring over the maps. Nate was pounding feverishly on the keyboard with a face comically like a woodchuck as he focussed on his work.

***

Nate and his team had been working non-stop for hours on the enigmatic outposts the sacs had seemingly gone to pains to find. Griffin halted the team's relocation to the Pole reluctantly, realising he needed every geek he could lay his hands on to effort some sort of insight into the latest shambolic events.

The names of the towns or oceans had been analysed every which way, but wait, he bemoaned, massive fucking surprise - they had zero. He touched his hand to his forehead, shaking his head lamentably. They checked elevations, geologic structures, lithography, graphed the variances between locations, cut and diced everything in every way they could think of. The answers they got were meaningless. They'd even looked for geomorphic similarities, ocean depths, tides and speeds, direction, temperatures, Koppen climatic zones, human population numbers. Nothing seemed to clue them in to anything of note. Just worthless crap was Nate's considered conclusion.

Tara leant toward latitude and longitude, or maybe one or the other by itself. She had all the GPS numbers printed on a sheet and stuck up on the whiteboard with a piece of ragged white tape. Sitting around it they gazed fretfully, searching for patterns in the chaos. Tara was reminded of the message the Sagan crew had decrypted earlier, wondering if that might be the way forward. Nate had thrown the numbers into the converter and tried binary and its more compact forms, Hex and Oct and even Decimal but came up with zip. Nothing it spat out resembled anything useful.

'You keep saying useful,' Tara said, glancing at Nate. 'By that you mean something within our sphere of knowledge…something we get. But what if the clues, if that's what these even are, what if they're simply beyond us…I mean, what then?'

'Then we're fucked,' Max barked roughly from the background, giving an affronted snort. 'That's an easy one,' he added, 'royally screwed is what.' He glanced back down, continuing to fiddle with his phone, resuming his disdainful expression.

'It's possible,' Nate offered honestly, 'but I don't buy it. If all this is here for us to actually do something with, then I think we should be able to at least partially sort it out. Could I be wrong, shit yes,' he conceded with a thoughtful shrug. 'But even if we didn't fully understand, we should be able to recognise the science in it…I'm pretty s-sure of that.' His last words stuttered into uncertainty. 'If these whoevers handed us a stapled thesis on quantum gravity…would we get it? Maybe, maybe not, but we'd see the science and the consistency in it, we'd get bits and pieces of it, see the intelligence in the data.' Apart from Max they eventually nodded, agreeing that to the human mind at least, what he said made sense. The big arsed *'but'* was whether it reflected the reality of where they were.

The ASCII language was used by computers to code characters as text so naturally they assumed that Max, the computing guru, knew something about it. Trouble was, his attitude sucked so much, he was virtually useless, still pissed at being treated like a prisoner, no matter if it was for the greater good, like saving the frigging world maybe. But that was just Max, all he could focus on was his deep-seated hatred for Griffin and the motherfucking Government who could apparently kidnap scientists at will. Max reckoned he was aptly named, he'd learned about the Griffin at school, some ugly piece of shit creature in myth with the head of an eagle, body of a lion. Perfect, he mused, powerful, bold, and a fucking ugly freak.

Worst of all, the Griffin in mythology was a death omen.

Yoshi had printed off the ASCII Chart and stuck it up next to the GPS data that spelt out the terrestrial location of the seven Spheres. Kneeling next to Max he was speaking pointedly to him, massaging him in the direction of the whiteboard, explaining that they were probably sunk without his help, fighting to pique his competitive spirit, telling him that Harvard, MIT, Princeton and Stanford were working on the exact same problem and the first one to crack it, won. Max straightened in his seat and narrowed his eyes, face hardening. His close Harvard connections left him with a deep disdain for Princeton and there was no way he wanted those Ivy League pricks feeling any more superior than they already did. Max's eyes probed for a common theme, a thread of some sort, ping-ponging his gaze across the data on the whiteboard. Standing up he walked closer, studying the ASCII alphabet, the GPS coordinates, mentally manoeuvring an intersection between the two. He stopped moving and stood up straight, oh so slowly shaking his head in poorly concealed disbelief. Were these idiots just dragged off the street at random?

'Have you even looked at this…I mean really looked?' He pointed at it briefly and snapped his fingers. For the love of fuck, he thought incredulously.

'Um, we've only just put them together but we've used the converter and we only got random stuff…meaningless characters.'

'There's no way those New Jersey fucks won't get this, if they haven't already,' Max said tersely. 'Forget longitude but look at the lat data…portion it up, see what looks right to ASCII.'

Nate, Yoshi and Tara walked closer, examining the pieces of paper stuck on the whiteboard.

'Okay,' Max exhaled impatiently, twisting his mouth to the side. If he waited for these plodders to get it, the game would be over before they got their hands above their waist. 'Plug the numbers individually into the ASCII converter,' he said, figuring whatever it was had to be big. 'We're going to take the first two lat coordinates from each piece of real estate and type them into the ASCII converter…got it?' Max's face was tight, a little uneasy about what might be coming.

Nate said, 'okay fine, go.' Arsehole he felt like yelling.

'I'll give you each of the numbers, you hit "Decimal Convert" for each one of them.' Max eyed him firmly. 'Write down the text results for each set of lats.' He actually had a pretty good idea what it was, he'd done the sums in his head, one of the few who could.

'I got it.' Nate said, rolling his eyes, pissed off by his condescending tone. 'Good to go.' Arsehole, he repeated silently, feeling warmth cross his cheeks.

Max wrote the numbers on a piece of paper. 'Sixty-nine, sixty-five, seventy-three, seventy-six, seventy, eighty-two, eighty-five.' These were the first two numbers of the eight digit GPS lat coordinates for each of the intruders. Max scrutinised the piece of paper in front of him, his eyes burning bright. Holy shit he said to himself eagerly, waiting for confirmation of something pretty fucking amazing…and bad.

'Don't fuck it up,' Max said crudely. 'Use capitals, they have to be capitals.' He handed the numbers to Nate who started typing digits into the app, pausing to write in pen strokes below the numbers Max had given him. Finishing, he stood up, stuck the paper on the whiteboard with a tiny bit of tape to hold it there and gawked at the cryptic letters. Nate couldn't make head or tail of it, staring blankly, tilting his head this way and that, like a confused canine. 'I have no idea what that is,' he said in a whisper, pushing his head forward and squinting at the jumble.

E A I L F R U

Yoshi breathed the word faintly, reckoning it sounded like some mispronounced Australian marsupial. 'Is that some word in their language, you know, phonetically maybe?'

'Oh, for God's sake,' Max snapped. 'The letters aren't in order, we chose them randomly, simply by the order we punched 'em in.' There was a flash of anger in his face. 'Can you not see the word in there?' He urged them with deeply rounded eyebrows, thrusting his neck forward. 'Look, it's a simple Word Find,' he said, scowling at them in turn, seriously doubting whether these people were half as smart as he'd been told.

Yoshi's expression softened as he got it and called it out, to Max's grunting contempt. The first instinct was to question the possible motivation for sending such a miserable message. The distressing, gnawing sensation deepened into muscle tightening anxiety as the word prickled its way into their consciousness. Max grabbed a marker pen and wrote the word on the whiteboard loudly and squeakily in large black letters, underlining it with an inelegant flourish.

FAILURE

Nate shifted his eyes uneasily to Max, then Tara, then over his shoulder at Yoshi. 'Failure,' he said, taken aback. His eyes darkened as he studied the simple little word on the board. 'They sent us that…is it meant to sound the way it does? I mean it's pretty explicit, there's no doubt or ambiguity, no uncertainty about what they're putting out there.' Nate looked mortified as he searched for something more than just a cutting insult.

Max scraped a thumb across his cheek, thinking through a thickening swell in his brain. He'd known what it was for a while but seeing it in black and white, seriously…why would they send it?

Nate rubbed his nose, then his forehead, finishing with two fingers and a restless thumb on his chin. 'Is it directed to us…like as a species? Or maybe it's about our half-arsed attempts to decrypt their bloody battle plan. Whatever, it's hardly a welcome to the boys club is it? Holy shit, what am I missing here?'

'Nothing,' Max said, 'you're missing nothing. This is the message. The bigger question is why they would go to so much trouble to tell us, to insult us…in all probability to piss us off?' He got to his feet and inched closer to the whiteboard. 'Why send a fleet of automata into the atmosphere to convey it in puzzle form?' A slow, bitter smile built on his face that drew into a heavy frown. 'We don't know how their minds are wired but come on, gimme a break, this is what…its madness surely.'

'Damn right,' Yoshi said, feeling his heart thudding, 'travel a billion light years to abuse us…thanks, terrific.'

'Well they went to a shitload of trouble to do it, no doubt,' Max said solemnly, 'I think we need to take notice. No one goes to all this effort to extend half-truths, motherhood statements and the like.'

If they're rebuking us like you say, is there a, uh…punishment? Nate said warily, bouncing the question around in his brain and was horrified for the planet, then outraged. What gave them the right to cast any form of judgement on us? Nate debated it, feeling increasingly irate and uneasy.

26. Ice

"Don't ascribe to evil what can be attributed to well-intentioned stupidity."
~ James A. Owen

'Vic, you copy?'

'Here Jack.'

'Okay, we've got a team for relocation due to leave in a couple of hours. We'll have three-way field comms in place. They'll have a microwave Ku-band so they can talk to us and to you at the same time. It'll support uplink for images and video. Nate will set up a real-time feed so we can see what's happening, see what they're doing, view any results first hand, stuff like that.' Nate nodded his head obligingly. 'They're going to see if they can effort some sort of control over it...power it down hopefully, if that's even possible. We'll take damn near anything but the status quo really.'

Yoshi and Tara glanced at Max, then at each other, failure, it hardly filled them with hope but it did fill them with every negative emotion, rolled into a feeling of almost psychedelic terror.

Harry swore to himself as he revisited Griffin's words about the extraction fleet on route to Houston. It'd normally take an eternity to decision a military mission to the Pole, thinking it amazing and a little amusing to see what an annihilative threat to national security can do to a Government's thinking. He smirked, debating how long such an op would take in less desperate times, a month, maybe two or three...a year.

***

Griffin's cell rang and he almost punched it, immediately striding toward the rear of the MCC to escape the incessant wall of chatter. Ballard and Hillier followed like lap dogs, a few paces behind. As he listened to the shrill voice, Griffin's left arm flopped lifelessly to his side with a thwump and his cellphone slipped from his hand, hitting the Chilton tiles with a sharp clunk. It came to rest near the wall face down, his face twisted and frozen like a garish Paper Mache mask.

After a few seconds, he bent down awkwardly and retrieved his phone. Pausing for a few seconds he stared blindly, taking a visibly cavernous breath. He then walked slowly back toward Jack, speaking to his two comrades in small verbal jabs as he approached. They seemed to be firing back at the same time, all three looking ashen, avoiding eye contact. Jack's heart started pounding and his neck seemed suddenly unable to support his head, which seemed to weigh a tonne. Griffin and Ballard looked like they'd just gotten wind of a hundred nukes inbound from North Korea, one minute to detonation. Jack watched Hillier's face, corrugated and withered as he loomed closer.

'Alright, that's it,' Griffin growled maliciously. 'Jesus Christ Almighty,' he said, gasping for breath to feed his booming voice. 'The President is moving to the NMCC war-room in the Pentagon. Jerry wanted us there as well but we need to hook into Hubble and Sagan so we're staying put...for now.' After a few more steadying breaths he stood erect, and shut his eyes tightly. He abruptly re-opened them, ogling Jack and the rest of them who stared back rigidly, convinced that whatever it was had to be a showstopper. This guy had seen damn near everything, including the Antarctic event and he hadn't reacted like this, he was a mess, seemingly on the verge of collapse, seizure or some other godforsaken medical event.

'Are y-you okay Earl?' Jack asked, studying him closely.

Griffin peered over at Jack, eyes glassy, half closed. 'No I am fucking not okay,' he snarled. Opening his mouth, he hesitated again, choosing his words carefully. 'Okay, okay,' he steeled himself. 'Shit,' he said. 'The Administrator of NASA phoned me, you know, Matt Jenson, he's a good guy. NORAD-NORTHCOM through GSSAP-5 he reported only six Spheres are in orbit, another one has just up and vanished on us.' He tightened his lips, expelling the last bit of blood.

Jack held his breath - he had an inkling of where this might be going. Jesus, he screamed silently. No one moved or spoke, just heartbeats, waiting, sprinting over possibilities, all of them bad.

'The Sphere with the lunar intersection's gone,' Griffin said solemnly. It dropped out earlier this morning. Just gone, like poof, no more.' He unfurled a fist in front of his face for emphasis.

'Oh God, Jack thought. As soon as the words were spoken he felt the veins in his temples start to beat wildly, the rush of blood enough to make his head swim. Bile clawed its way into his throat and he tried to clear it with a cough that only made it worse. He was now in a fit of coughing and splurting that he managed to swallow down. Feeling the heat from Griffin's glare he sipped some water, seeing him clench his eyebrows into a vicious V-formation.

Griffin looked away from Jack, back at Hillier. 'The Moon's gone,' he said quietly, puckering his lips. The words sounded absurd, a little funny, full of whimsy…horrifying.

Everyone stared at him in various states of stupor, straining to attach some veracity to the idea, the notion was so preposterous it almost had no meaning. But in the same breath they knew it was true because of Antarctica. That was surely impossible yet it was visible for all to see.

The Earth and Moon were born as twins, one not long after the other and while their relationship had distanced over time, one of them had now flown the coop for good. The Moon had simply vanished from the vacuum.

Jack tried hard to steady his breathing but the air around him seemed suddenly thick, difficult to pull into his lungs. His next thought was searing, scorching the length of his brain…what the fuck was going next? Was Earth on some godforsaken list, and if it was, where was it…like how far down? He grabbed the sides of his head feeling a relentless aching. Earth didn't intersect with any of the linear waves but that was hardly a guarantee, nothing was certain anymore.

'Keck in Hawaii and AAT in Australia have confirmed it,' Griffin said bleakly. The Moon ain't there…not anywhere. According to NASA, deep-water buoys in the Pacific are relaying a single tidal bulge from the Sun. The Moon…its gravity…effect on tides…no more.' He couldn't believe the sanatorial words falling from his mouth as rock hard fact. It had the flavour of fantasy…madness.

What unthinkable, soulless power would do this? Griffin thought, taking a moment to disconnect from the group. They were removing things so colossal, seemingly erasing things with a simple strike of a pen. There was nothing resembling explosive power or residue whatsoever, no clouds of dirt and rock, no detonations, no suggestion of weaponry. Surgical was the word and what hope did they have if they turned their attention squarely to Earth? That was the easiest question of all Griffin conceded, they finally had a fucking answer to something. Absolutely, categorically no hope. We'd be here one second, gone the next, with nothing left behind to show that humans or the planet had ever existed. Not even a ring of planet and people particles, just an absence of all. Humanity would disappear like the ice in Antarctica, solid and real, then gone. Extinction. Worse.

CNN was broadcasting on a huge wall mounted flat-screen in the corner of the Flight Control Room, the developments in space being reported 24/7 to a world now coming to grips with the gravest of situations. Jack could see POTUS addressing Americans from the Whitehouse, wondering what he was going to say. What could he say, that they had no ability to fight or avoid what was coming? That they had zero intel about the enemy and were, in the truest sense of the words, sitting ducks watching, waiting for whatever it was that might be approaching from the stars.

Willard did what good Presidents do in times of chaos – lie through his teeth, downplay the risks, emphasise their awareness and readiness to deal with the threat. He declared "forthrightly" that the country and the world were carefully assessing events, weighing up the threats, determining a way forward, decisioning a response that would secure their safety. Analysis and planning were underway with a dedicated team in space, one en-route to Antarctica, supported by a hundred think-tanks and the best minds in the nation, all striving for a solution. And make no mistake, he avowed with a clenched fist and a steely resolve, a solution would be found. Griffin knew it was no more than a mound of camel dung, lip service to stave off unrest, anarchy in the streets.

Hopefully, something would come of it, Jack thought ruefully. He hoped some smart-ass savant whizz kid could work something out and they could plan some sort of way out…if it existed.

'So now we know,' Jack murmured to the group. Those gravitational creases, the ones GRACE detected, show us the asset at risk, right? When a Sphere goes, so does the anomaly including whatever poor sod happens to be tangled up with it.' They were executing this for a reason, but it was the purpose of the show that remained an unutterable mystery. Jack just wished the codeine would kick in, he felt like shit.

'There's thirteen Spheres left,' Nate said, 'seven atmospheric, six in polar orbit. One of them connects to Jupiter, the remaining twelve are aimed out of system to locations unknown.'

'Well, thank God they're out of system,' Tara sighed, 'small mercies, right?'

'Take nothing for granted,' Griffin said more sedately. 'NASA is working on defining the targets using GRACE and ESA's GOCE satellite, but it's going to take a while.' His jowls were slap-slapping as he shook his head vigorously, incredulous that any of this shit could happen outside the illusory pages of a graphic novel. Griffin looked Jack in the eyes, drawing his hand nervously across his brow, 'Jesus, what a fucking nightmare.' He sat down, grunting all the way, peering at Nate this time. 'The Osprey will be here in forty-five. You'll be briefed en-route but that's more for the environment, there's no ice but it's still damn cold down there. Now listen,' he said, moving his head closer, 'no one can give you much advice on what to do down there, not yet anyway. You know the detail on what Becker and his crew did, so you'll use that and your scientific wisdom,' Griffin sneered, raising an eyebrow at them, giving the tiniest hint of sarcasm. 'Try to disable it or whatever you think is the right approach. You know as much as anyone does, you're science smart, you're our ground zero team, what you do there may be critical to all of us.' His demeanour was deadly serious.

'You'll be plugged into us, to Sagan, to genius workshops everywhere,' Jack added, 'so you'll have a ton of support. we've got Sagan in space, you're our ground crew at the Pole.'

'Okay, sounds good,' Nate said weakly, a little dazed by the uncertainties, the responsibility of the task ahead. Were they even up to this? He honestly didn't have a clue but they'd have an answer in a few days he guessed. He was semi-thankful for the so-called support but when would they get some value from these overhyped think tanks? The power of their brainpans was so immense, surely they'd be able to provide a molecule or two of insight? Never far away from Nate's thinking was the real tickler, if there was nothing to actually get then it didn't matter how much IQ was thrown at it. He visualised locking Kasparov, Hawking and Rosner in a room for a decade and their look of consternation never changing, because there was no solution or even an ant's dick of a hint to start with. The grandest hunt of them all, the Theory of Everything, had logic and meaning, it was just the physics and math that were elusive. At least the pursuit had form and purpose but this glorious, enigmatic, intellectual cowpat had none of that and it settled heavily in his gut…were they really trying to solve something that had no answer?

They were just starting to sense the guttural thumping of the VM-22 Ospreys slashing at the air as they descended toward the Johnston Space Centre, just southeast of downtown Houston.

'Twenty minutes early,' Griffin said, checking his wristwatch, 'impressive. Pentagon boys are getting it done,' he added upbeat. Fuck me, he thought, something's actually gone right today.

As the thunderous noise grew overhead, the trio scheduled for extraction felt the first serious wave of anxiety. Five military monsters were now punching them with sepulchral waves of bass that spoke to the drama of what was about to unfold. Unnerving wasn't a sufficient description but it was way too late to say no.

***

Earth was in chaos in every sense of the noun's definition. While the full story of what the Government knew hadn't been revealed, there was no hiding the Spheres or the fact that the Moon, and the entire goddamn ice shelf of Antarctica were no more. They were both consigned to history, like ancient civilisations, the Aztecs, the Mayans, they were there…then not.

The Governments of every country tried to blunt the unrest that was swelling into outright rebellion, and in some places into regional anarchy. The UN trod a similar path on a global scale, the Secretary General showcasing an ill-founded but wholly necessary confidence that they would soon understand the motives for events unfolding in space and on Earth.

As far as most were concerned it was an alien pre-emptive heading in one direction, the end of humanity. No one on Earth understood why it was happening or had the remotest clue why things they'd taken for granted forever were being taken from them.

The Moonless sky was a source of alarm across the globe, not because they hadn't seen it before, everyone had seen a New Moon when it was in conjunction with the Sun, but it was the knowing that it was gone for good that ate into the human psyche like a cancer. It ain't coming back Jack. The nights were now permanently dark around the globe, save for the dim glow from the Milky Way Galaxy.

Governments and the UN were streaming commentaries around the clock, bullish on their odds of success, talking up countermeasures being implemented and already well in play. The science team was at the South Pole, SLS Sagan in near Earth orbit, efforts were progressing, an understanding was in the offing, but patience was required while data was gathered and assessments made, a forward move determined. The reality was chillingly different and most had a sense of it. Everyone in the know realised if they didn't uncover something soon there might be nothing left to save.

The general populace had no idea about the gravitational entanglements or the strangeness at L1, or the disappearance of Carson Becker and his COO. Every tentacle of mass and social media was smothered by an avalanche of hellish commentaries, the upshot being that humankind had little hope, many assuming that Earth would simply wink out of existence like the Moon…it was just a matter of time.

The civilised protocols on Earth were fading as populations lost the motivation of tomorrow. Vicious riots were global, Marshall Law entrenched in thirty-three countries, some with inhuman brutality, highlighting the darkest side of the human psyche, drawn out by a complete loss of hope. Hostility and disorder were snowballing, chain reactions of panic and terror seemed unstoppable as it spread across the planet like a deadly, swelling blast zone.

A fair proportion of the global labour force had simply walked out, and kept walking, staying home with family, living on their own terms before existence wound down to zero. A little more of the social fabric seemed to drain away each day, the justice system had gone, stock exchanges were closed around the globe, Universities, Schools, sports, commercial activities almost in-toto had terminated their businesses, most farmers locking up and shooting anyone who approached. If next week didn't exist where was the incentive, few gave a shit, only today had meaning, staying with family, friends, keeping the hell off the streets, eschewing a violent death.

The world economy had ground to a halt in the face of the inscrutable threat from space. Tens of trillions of dollars had been shed and hundreds of trillions would follow if they couldn't find a way to understand, solve or somehow diminish the hellish fulmination from space. No one in Government or anywhere else had the barest inkling or insight, maybe the Spheres would just motor away at some point and things would gradually return to normal. Or perhaps it would continue to escalate, eventually ending with lights out for seven billion residents of planet Earth.

27. Strange Land

"Not only is the Universe stranger than we think, it is stranger than we can think."
~ Werner Heisenberg

Four Ospreys' flew a standard military V-formation two thousand metres above the ocean, hacking through the southern skies with serious intent. Not far from the 60th parallel, they were only a few hundred clicks from the formerly wild, west coast of Antarctica.

Nate could see a dark smudge on the horizon, taking it to be the edge of the newly exposed southern landmass, all of them struggling mightily, realising they would be the first to set foot on the newly naked South Pole. The concept, the mental images it brought with it, like the first lunar explorers, they'd be standing on a surface never seen before, let alone touched by humankind. It had been thirty-five million years since the warm, humid climes had been replaced by a gradual deep freeze, courtesy of a snail's pace process of hot rock liquefication. The whole lot eventually degraded into an icy hell, the last creatures roaming the Antarctic plains, the mammals, the amphibians and a sprinkling of reptiles, all wiped out by the cold.

Tara couldn't hold it inside anymore. 'Losing the ice, okay…but the Moon? That's pretty much a cap on us surviving, I mean, smaller tides aren't a huge deal but the tilt of the planet, that's kept stable by the Moon right?'

Yoshi nodded, 'yep, it'll end up like Mars, all over the shop, wobbling and shit…sayonara stable climates I guess, and the jury's out on whether it effects magma flows, like beneath the surface I mean. If it does then the shit gets way deeper. The mag-field will shut down, atmosphere will erode, we'll be irradiated like shelf stable prawns. No cellphones…hey major hair loss right?' His sombre expression softened into a thin smile.

'Anyway,' Nate voiced impatiently, 'let's fix on finding a way to shut this thing down.'

Hear fucking hear! Max said to himself irritably, totally nonplussed by the pseudo-scientific bullshit echoing around the cabin. He felt a pain in the pit of his stomach and wondered if the aircraft had a toilet. He started looking for one, the pain and the urge getting worse.

Looking through the Osprey's huge front window, they took in a sight that bordered on the incomprehensible, and it wasn't just the unnerving view, it was what they knew it to be, Antarctica the continent as it would have looked tens of millions of years ago. It was like unveiling a time capsule maintained in perfect stasis for a period of time almost half way back to the dinosaurs.

Tara felt like she was in some nebulous dream-state, like she was laying eyes on a distant alien planet for the first time. It was dauntingly dark, composed of crazy looking mountains, deeply incised valleys and bizarre asymmetrical landforms, jagged on one side, smooth on the other. She was mesmerised as the iceless continent grew larger beneath her, without any signs of ice or even a suggestion of whiteness, as though nothing had fallen on it since the glaciers had been cleaved away.

Nate was gobsmacked. 'Like nothing you could imagine,' he breathed in awe, staring at the chocolate and nougat landscape, its primal essence baring itself in front of him.

It may have been newly de-iced but it looked anything but new, carrying stark wounds and deep incisions. It was so surreal to look down on the formerly ivory plated continent, utterly devoid of anything but brown and grey, no life, no soil, no interruption to the colours of Earth.

There were troughs and steep gorges, clear evidence of ancient rivers that had meandered across it before it was snap frozen so long ago. And every part of it was scarred by dark lines that transected the continent like thousands of aimless, primeval train tracks.

'Not a drop of water,' Tara said, looking slackly at Nate, 'all that ice and not a frozen lake, an icy pond or any sign of anything.' She heard Max groaning behind her and turned, shocked to see him hunched over, peering down at the Osprey floor, breathing hard. 'Jesus Max…what the hell?'

Max slowly pulled his head up and was so pale it looked like every corpuscle of blood had been squeezed from his face. 'I um, feel like shit,' he groaned back. 'Get me a bucket…something, I'm gonna hurl. Motion sickness I guess…Jesus, it's bad.' He clamped a fist over his mouth.

Tara emptied a tattered plastic bag of its contents, handing it to Max.

'Really?' He said looking at it, holding his stomach.'

'It'll have to do,' Tara said, 'this isn't a commercial flight.'

'Keep your eyes open, watch the ground below, it'll help,' Yoshi said keenly.

Nate ignored his moaning, turning his head back toward Tara and Yoshi. 'Y'know, now that we're here it's even more messed up,' he said, gawping through the cockpit glass like a whale spotter. 'How the hell do you remove billions of tonnes of ice without leaving something behind?' He screwed his nose up, tapping fingers on the side of his seat. 'Shit, if we could answer that it'd be a step forward, maybe insight into their technology.' Nate's mouth pulled into a sour grin, knowing an answer to the puzzle was as likely as finding a penguin waddling around on the rocks.

They were flying just east of the sprawling mountains of the Vinson Massif, a brutal barrier between Ellsworth Land and the massive Ronne Ice Shelf to the north. Once the MV's hauled themselves over the top of the peaks their destination should be obvious as they got a first look into the yawning valley of Marie Byrd. That was where the anomaly was and armed with its precise GPS coordinates they expected to find it in short order.

'Here we go,' Nate said as the Osprey thundered over the final craggy ledge of Mt Tyree and started to gradually drop into the deep valley below.

'Oh whoooaaa,' Tara breathed, awestruck, as she eyed the sweeping valley of rock that extended to the distant, dim horizon, her voice faint as she watched blinding arrows of light reflect off something in the mid-distance.

Yoshi looked away sharply to give his eyes a rest from the almost star-like glare. 'Is that it?' He said softly.

Nate studied him deliberately, cocking an eyebrow. 'Gee, wait, ummm.' His voice petered out as he broke into a broad grin, giving him a playful nudge. 'That my friend, is most definitely it…and it's pretty damn amazing.'

As they flew closer, the reflection dimmed, allowing them to get a good look at what they were approaching. The visual looked insanely out of place atop the desolate landscape that was made entirely from ancient Proterozoic rock without even a suggestion of soil or even anything loose. The picture below them already looked alien, a different planet in a different star system but add the object in for good measure and it took it to a whole new, troubling level of unfamiliarity.

They sensed the craft slowing dramatically, punched in the gut by the feeling it was losing power and simply coasting to a stop in mid-air. The pitch of the engines deepened as the prop nacelles pivoted upward, at the same time the thumping of the triple blades grew louder and even more dissonant. This fucker was loud Nate thought, feeling a little dazed as the Osprey converted from jet mode to chopper mode by articulating its rotors until they were above their heads, all over in seconds.

About five clicks in front of them was a gigantic metal plate, perfectly circular in plan, sitting like a fried egg on the chestnut landscape. To Nate the object looked the colour of bismuth, deep, silver-grey with a slightly vitreous lustre. Dead centre at the great circle was the hemisphere and they knew from talking to Jack that this was their focus, the nerve centre of whatever this thing was, together with the small hemisphere that Becker's team had so indiscreetly fiddled with, apparently activating the machine, if it was a machine at all.

'So out of place,' Tara said, watching Yoshi who was staring like a snowman, frozen at the sight now almost directly beneath them.

They set down with a three-wheeled thud on hard rock about fifty metres from the edge of the plate, waiting for the pilots to signal before they made a move. After a few minutes, the roar and rotation of the rotors came to a stop and an eerie silence descended across the landscape. The co-pilot finally stuck his index finger up and twirled it around like a little chopper blade, telling them they could unstrap their safety harnesses. The pilot ripped open the starboard door, punching them with freezing air as he motioned them onto a flat moraine. With safety clothing secured, goggles on, it was sort of okay, although they wondered what shape they'd be in after an hour or so.

Tara almost tripped over a massive machine gun on the way out, mounted on some sort of retractable ramp. She swallowed hard, peering at the grimly dark hemisphere in the near distance, the sight made her blood run cold. It looked overwhelmingly alien, malevolent in a way she found impossible to quantify, a big, ugly doomsday button for some giant being to reach down from the sky and give a good whack. She broke away deliberately, gazing at the beautiful mountains, the dim sky, the pinks and yellows of the gorgeous pseudo-sunset beside a towering range of mountains.

Max had finally regained some colour and made his way a little unsteadily toward the open hatch, still not feeling quite right.

Military people were swarming everywhere, carrying crates, boxes and large bags from the rear hatches of all the 22s. Jason Haigh was a big swarthy bear of a man, employed as camp coordinator and he stood pointing a pudgy finger at their destination. Two others who seemed to be the military equivalent of Sherpas shadowed him and were literally swaddled with bags and massive backpacks. Haigh himself carried a large rucksack with all sorts of odd-shaped things poking out, looking like an ageing tennis pro with a bag full of racquets and cans sticking out at odd angles.

'Let's go,' he said firmly. 'The video unit's broken…in pieces actually, but we'll get field comms and tech up while these guys organise camp. Then it's up to you gentlemen, and er…lady.' He glanced at Tara, giving a small clearing cough. 'Jack wants you to check in ASAP, then maintain hourly contact.' He eyeballed Nate, waiting on confirmation.

'Yeah, got it.' Nate said haltingly. Jesus, he thought, we're at the Pole…chill dude.

Haigh shook his head. 'So you copy right?'

'Oh, yeah right, copy, yes.' He kicked himself for forgetting the conventions they'd talked about. Guy thinks I'm a dick. Great way to start, Nate groaned silently, as he ambled toward the plate's edge, goggling at scene in front of him. One thought hit him as he narrowed his eyes, digging a vertical wrinkle between his eyebrows. What the fuck have we gotten ourselves into?

The four of them stepped tentatively onto the metal-like substance for the first time, Nate feeling like he'd stepped onto some massive reef of malleable native metal, half expecting to look back and see footprints embedded in the surface. Shiny expanses of polished silver were everywhere. He came to a halt, bent down on his haunches and poked at it curiously, like he thought, it was slightly yielding and when he went to pull his finger away it was like something had a gentle grip on it.

'Hey!' he spouted, surprised by the unexpected pull. The others glanced over their shoulders at him quizzically.

Haigh's eyes were burning. 'Move it,' he demanded curtly. 'No delays, they're the orders from HQ, you know … CIA, DOD, not people to trifle with friend.'

'But this stuff, it's like it's magnetic or something.'

'You got a plate in your head boy?' Haigh questioned sharply. 'Magnets need metal…ain't you a scientist?'

'Well yeah, of course, but that's what makes it so interesting.' Nate grabbed his phone from his waist pocket and held it loosely in his fingers, lowering it gently onto the surface, then slowly pulling it away. There was no pull, it came away freely. 'It doesn't pull at the metal of my cell but it pulls at my skin.' He stared at nothing for a long moment, pondering.

'Fuck me,' Haigh said in exasperation, 'science lessons later, right now my brief is to get you lot set up and started safely. No delays. Move it, I mean it son, get up, move your arse.'

Nate saw the intent in his eyes and started moving. 'Biomagnetic maybe,' he murmured,

As they got closer, the hemisphere looked like a stark black egg-yolk sitting in the centre of mountains of silvery albumen. A smaller, radiant yolk sat near it, pulsing with animation. Nate's brain was whirling in tightening circles as he peered at strange figures scooting across its surface, like a computer, processing reams of endless code.

'We'll set up here,' Haigh said, wheezing and dropping their bags near the smaller object, proceeding to remove the heavy Army backpacks. In twenty minutes they had everything in place, including a simple cyclone-proof canopy, a prosaic metal table with the comms unit and several chairs. The Skype unit that was supposed to feed video direct to Houston was junk, destroyed en-route, smashed by means unknown. The comms unit was operational so that would have to do.

Nate had been wondering about the climate down here since he'd first seen the pristine continent from the air. He turned to Tara. 'Do you notice something strange about this place? I mean apart from the bleeding obvious of course.'

Tara looked at Yoshi, sharing a puzzled look. 'Um…do we get a clue?'

'No clue,' he smirked. 'There's no ice crystals anywhere down here, not on the mountains, not on the plains, it's like blizzards have ceased since the event. It looked the same from the air but I thought once we landed there'd be at least a few grains of ice hanging about.'

'Yeah…you're right,' Yoshi said. 'It snows down here a lot I guess.'

'Pretty much every day but not snow - rock hard ice crystals that can draw blood, knock you unconscious, stuff like that.'

'So what's changed? Tara posed. 'Did the event effect something…the climate, wind, ocean currents maybe?'

Nate rubbed his chin with a thumb and forefinger, speculating on this strange new land, suddenly stripped of several of its "world's worst" personalities.

Nate got Jack on SatCom, reported in per standing orders, then turned his attention to the small hemisphere, seeing a stream of figures forming a distinct vertical pattern in twelve tightly bunched parallel lines.

'So strategy one, input individual numbers of Pi, one at a time, pausing to assess status after each. If there's no change, we proceed to the next number and so on,' Nate said, nodding hesitantly, thinking it sounded a little aimless. Frigging unimaginative now that he'd spoken it out loud. Surely there was more they could do, throw the net wider, be a hell of a lot more creative. He was determined to get something from this thing to prove their worth as a team. 'So let's get 'em up Yoshi, see if we can coax something out of this baby,' he said, rather excitedly.'

Tara's eyes flew to Nate. 'You mean try and shut it down right? That's our brief down here, to shut it down, nothing more. We're not here to play games with this thing, to try and extract science…we're here to deactivate…to kill? You get that …

'… idea what we're doing so one might lead to the other or the other might lead to, well…something positive maybe,' Nate fidgeted a bit, 'We're flying blind, unless of course you have ideas, maybe a solution you'd like to share?'

Tara crossed her arms. 'No, I don't, just keep Griffin's words high in mind.'

'Sure, whatever you say, turn it off, we got it, right Yoshi…Max? Nate looked at Yoshi who nodded vigorously at Tara who now felt doubly anxious. Was their focus really set right, they said so but she wasn't convinced. It was starting to feel like a boy's club.

Max was sitting on the ground, still not looking too flash.

'You okay?' Nate asked, seeing his grey pallor which seemed to be getting worse.

Max eventually willed his head up, forcing a few words out. 'Dunno…feel like I've got the mother of all hangovers. Just give me some time, I'll come good.' His lips had a disconcerting colourless edge to them.

'Probably just air sickness,' Yoshi offered, frowning at his deathly countenance. 'That was a hell of a trip in those things, surprised we didn't all succumb really.'

'You're the closest thing to an ice-sheet here Max,' Tara giggled playfully.

He looked at her and rolled his eyes, coughing a frigid white exhalation that rapidly disappeared into the polar air. Max hauled himself up and stopped where he stood, looking away from them. Walking over to the equipment bay he started rifling through one of the backpacks.

'That's a good sign, hunger,' Nate said to Yoshi gratefully. He was sure he'd be fine.

'I've got ten thousand decimals of Pi,' Yoshi beamed, fanning a mighty wad of paper in the gentle breeze, showing a shining set of teeth. 'Reckon that'll be enough?' He said, grinning even wider at Nate who looked past him, peering down, planning his next move. Approaching the small object, he cupped his hand as he was told to do.

'Stop!' came a booming voice from behind him.

'What the' Nate spun around, and saw Max bolt upright about three metres away. There was clearly something wrong with him and it wasn't just a dose of airsickness. 'Jesus Christ…what are you doing?' Nate said, rearing back, his heart taking an almighty thud against his ribs. Yoshi and Tara were slack-jawed, eyeing what was in his hand, bewildered, stammering broken words.

'M-Max, w-why are you holding that?' Yoshi finally stuttered, goggling at the hunting pistol in his hand, edging back, inching closer to Tara.

Nate now understood what Max had been searching for in the backpack and it sure as hell wasn't food. Part of their armoury down here was two Smith and Wesson 500 pistols, insurance was all they were, for leopard seals that sometimes got a hankering for the odd, unsuspecting explorer. Max had one of the silver guns in his left hand, holding it arm extended toward the ground, held stiffly against his leg. But the gun in his hand wasn't the only surprise, it was his eyes, no longer brown with flecks of grey, they were sparkling blue like azure marbles. Nate could see they were way too bright straight away, the damn things looked like they had a power pack of fissionable material behind them, firing them in some unknowable way.

'What the h-hell?' Nate whispered, having no idea what influence he was acting under, studying him awkwardly, gulping…was he a criminal or some juiced up junkie? They had no time for background checks before they grabbed him off the street, but for Christ's sake, he occupied an eminency at Texas A&M. Nothing was adding up.

Max spoke suddenly, almost without moving his mouth or jaw and more strangely, his voice was way off, Max, still Max, just, way less animation, less movement in his face. And the way he looked, his lips were blue as pack ice, his skin the pallor of a long dead river corpse. This couldn't be their Max, just about everything about him was wrong and they fucking well knew it.

Max lifted his chin and his eyes glowed brighter as words somehow clawed their way from his almost closed mouth. '…you believe you are intelligent,' Max said with the slightest kiss of belligerence, pausing momentarily, surveying their faces before moving on. 'You think your science is strong, but it is not as it seems.' His mouth cornered up slightly into an odd, disagreeable expression. Nate wondered again what was standing in front of them. He felt his hands start to shake, tremors in his fingers and cheeks, spots before his eyes, fainting now a real possibility. Max broke the harrowing silence. 'I cannot determine how all this is possible,' he said, raising his free hand and gesturing outward, 'how you are possible, so frivolous, poorly focussed, how your failures are possible.' A twisted half-smile flashed across his face, quickly replaced by stony vacancy. With that Max lifted his other arm, aiming the gun directly at Nate's head, cocking the firing pin into a killing position. His face was still blank but his eyes shone and convulsed wildly.

'Max no!' Nate screamed, raising his arms over his face in a vain effort to protect himself. Collapsing down next to the small hemisphere, he curled himself into a ball and waited to die, his heart pounding so hard it had become erratic, leg muscles cramping under him, waiting for the bullet that would end it.

'Put it down!' Tara shrieked, looking around desperately for cover. 'She clapped her hands as loudly as she could, trying to snap him out of whatever delusional trance he was in, but his face remained impassive, the gun still pointing ramrod straight.

Yoshi made to run at him but Max whipped the gun barrel onto him, raising it to eye-level. He froze and put both hands up, retreating slowly backward. 'Okay, okay, Max…easy.' Max raised the gun slowly and deliberately to his temple in what Nate took to be some strange, symbolic gesture. Without pausing, he squeezed the trigger, followed by an almighty blast, exploding from the muzzle and almost severing his head from his body. The bullet drove through Max's prefrontal cortex, blowing a horrible exit wound in the side of his head, spewing cerebrospinal fluid and chunks of white bone over the ancient rocks in a dreadful human parody of a sudden icefall.

Haigh and a bunch of soldiers were already running toward them, hearing the crack from the Smith and Wesson.

Tara held her hand tight against her mouth, trying to process the idea of Max killing himself in front of them. None of it made the slightest speck of sense, the words, the eyes…fuck, the gun.

Nate was still looking at the horror of Max. For the love of God, he thought, tensing, doing a double take on the whole gory mess. 'Oh, this is…what is this?' He mouthed the words disbelievingly, pinging his eyes around, surveying what could only be described as a macabre crime scene. 'Um, uh guys…there's something wrong here.'

'Everything's wrong,' Yoshi blurted, 'the eyes, the gun. I mean what the hell right? He felt like vomiting where he stood, tasting bile in his throat.

'No, I mean yes, but…I'm talking about that.' Nate pointed at the pieces of Max's skull and tissue blown over the rocks like road kill. He looked back at them and they could see his mouth hanging open. 'Where's the blood?' He said searchingly, 'there's no blood.' Nate felt like gagging, forcing himself to inch up to the carnage and analyse it…there was everything expected from a catastrophic head injury apart from pools of blood. There wasn't a drop anywhere. The ground should be covered by dark red cerebral blood it but it was strewn with bone and tissue and that was it.

Haigh and his contingent came barrelling up and saw Max lying on the ground with the hunting pistol not far away. Two of the soldiers had M16's trained on Nate and his crew, looking distinctly twitchy.

'Jesus…what the mother fuck happened here?' Haigh puffed and wheezed as he tried to catch his breath, staring uncomprehendingly at the scene confronting him. 'How…how did this happen?' He said, gripping his neck and scratching hard with one finger, eyeing what had been Max. Haigh shook his head in horror. 'Jesus,' he said again, holding the back of his hand against his nose.

'Shot himself,' Nate said, breathing in spurts. 'Started prattling on about something, then waved the gun around…fired the damn thing point-blank, just like that.' He saw Haigh staring at the remains of Max's skull and the ground around him. 'No blood, right?' Nate said, guessing that's what he was puzzling over.

'I can see that,' he murmured in a slightly higher vocal pitch. 'So, we have a body but…no blood.' He rubbed his forehead, squinting distastefully at the body, rolling the madness around in his head, picking at one of his chins. 'So how, I mean…how was this dude even alive? Seriously,' he said, eyeballing Nate squarely, 'how was he alive?' He moved back a few steps and slumped a bit, then stood tall and rolled his shoulders, battling to compose himself. Haigh eyeballed his men gravely. 'Bag him up, get him back to Main Ops. Get 'em to see what's going on with this fellow.'

Tara took a rattling breath. 'We needed Max, we're down a very critical component.'

'No, you're not,' Haigh said, 'just get on with the op, we'll take care of it. I'll talk to Jack. The mission remains go until you hear different.' He didn't want to look, but he rolled his eyes back to Max's broken body. 'Holy fuck, this shit is so far beyond my pay grade.' Looking gravely at Nate, Haigh gingerly picked up the gun with two fingers and marched off across the metal landscape.

Within ten minutes two of the soldiers returned with a grey body bag with USAF stencilled clinically on the side. The corpse formerly known as Max was zipped up and on its way to be loaded into an Osprey for immediate evac to Houston for an urgent forensic autopsy.

None of them could ignore what happened, or forget it, so Nate figured they may as well just push on through, try and get the job done, put the unnerving visuals aside, as far as they could. Tormenting images of his head half blown off were etched on their minds, and there was the small detail of his body being devoid of blood, a riddle of epic troubling proportions.

'We just keep going…it's the only way,' Nate repeated solemnly, still feeling physically ill, certain his stomach would need another washroom trip sooner than later.

'He said that word,' Tara muttered, raising her eyes, 'failure.'

Nate nodded uneasily, 'yeah I noticed that.'

'Coincidence?' Yoshi said, widening his eyes.

'Nate scoffed, 'no way,' he said firmly.

Tara turned to look more directly at Nate. 'So, whatever was driving him was one of them?'

'Yep, that's what I think. Max was a proxy - they used him, then killed him, Nate said, sighing disbelievingly.

Yoshi's face sagged. 'Jesus,' he sighed, 'they have n-nothing, no respect…for us, for life…intelligent life.' He took a sharp intake of breath as it sunk in. 'That's a clue…an insight we…probably could've done without.'

***

Nate didn't hesitate. He knelt down, palmed the top of the object five times, then stood up, stepped back, counted to ten.

Tara urged him on, 'go again,' she said, rushing her words.

He repeated it again with three, five, eight and nine. The numbers kept spinning along without change. He stood above it, pondering a change in strategy, something apart from throwing random chunks of Pi at it. Scratching the next six decimals on the back of his hand he knelt and shifted his weight uncomfortably to the other knee, palming the device seven times, then nine times, then three times, pausing after each. Nate suddenly ripped his head back, shuffling sideways a little from his crouching position on the metal. 'Shit!' He barked, bobbing to his feet. Tara and Yoshi looked up abruptly. 'It's stopped,' he said, goggling at the bold figures now static on its slick surface.

'That's good, right?' Yoshi said effusively, not having a clue but hoping like hell. 'That's what we wanted?' He eyed Nate for confirmation.

'Let's tell Jack, see what GRACE is saying, maybe something's changed.'

'You mean like it might be off?' Yoshi said under his breath.

'Doubt it, but I hope so because this is– '

Tara nudged Nate with her elbow while he was rabbiting on. 'Look,' she whispered, 'It's going again!' Tara bent over, moving her head closer to the action, fearful they'd tripped some sequence they really shouldn't have.

The numbers were racing across the screen, seemingly speeding up, blurring into a fat white line bereft of detail. They seemed to have given it pause briefly, but now it was seriously making up for lost time.

'Yoshi, tell Jack what's happening. Ask him if we keep working it with numbers, my recommendation is yes but ask him.'

Before Yoshi could take more than a few strides the landscape seemed to explode with light, like a shock of cold lightning flashing across the moraine. The large hemisphere had broken into a swirling, gyrating ball of light, the other half of the "hemisphere" now visible beneath the metallic surface, full of eddying, churning currents that were mesmerising and oddly alluring.

'Oh crap,' Nate shouted, seriously doubting whether this could be a turn for the better, seeing Yoshi motionless and shaded by the light behind him. 'Tell Jack!' He roared, brandishing his arms wildly to get him moving. Rather than stop it, the demeanour of the small object looked more manic, and now the large Sphere had kicked in as well, suggesting that they might have sparked a rather ominous state of affairs. Great work team he thought bitterly, idly weighing their spurious role in the downfall of humanity. Go to the Pole, use your judgement, turn it off, he mused humourlessly. Jesus what a fuck up. The Old French word hit back at him heavily. Failure.

Haigh and three military types were back again, sprinting from camp when they saw the starburst light up the sky. 'You guys okay? He puffed, glancing from one to the other, down on his haunches again, spitting on the metal. 'Christ I, ah…might as well take up camp here.' His chest was heaving. 'Fucked if I'm running the gauntlet every time you get in trouble.'

'Whatever,' Nate said. 'We're fine, but not sure about those things.' He pointed toward the objects. 'Yoshi, you got Jack yet?'

'No reply,' he yelled back, line's dead, off-line or something.'

'Shit,' Haigh said, muttering something unkind under his breath as he strode over to the comms unit to check the intercom. He took one look at it and scowled at Yoshi, placing a fist on his forehead, tapping. 'I'm not sure where they got you boys from but attention to detail is something you should have in fucking spades. PTT means Press to Talk, we showed you how to use it.'

Yoshi sighed uncomfortably. 'Yeah right, oops.' He'd activated the Sat-line after putting the headset on, expecting it to "just" work.

'Oops?' Haigh repeated quizzically, closing his eyes. 'Are you fucking—'?

'Hey!' the military guy interrupted, directing him with a jabbing bunt of his head.

Haigh looked and was lost for words, finally finding his voice. 'What is she doing…for the love of God!' He said, chucking his hands in the air, 'another one?'

Tara was walking slowly, taking mechanical steps in the direction of the Sphere. Eyes, it was the eyes again. Nate could see them, wide, unblinking, mortared to the object like she was under a spell, light from the Sphere flaring in her eyes, adding to the strangeness.

'Is she…like hypnotised?' Haigh asked unsteadily, 'she sure as hell looks like it.'

Tara was like an automata, walking reflexively with her head pushed forward on a neck that looked as stiff as an iron rod.

'Shit she's not stopping!' Nate screamed. Haigh was closest to her and he sprinted, lunging, but she was like a bloody freight train on rails. He bounced off, ending up half in, half out of the orange tinted light. When Tara hit the Sphere, the parts of her body that penetrated first, her arms and one leg, melted into something else, it was ill defined. As soon as she'd vanished within it, the radiance stopped dead. One second it was dazzling and turbulent, the next, as dark as a kilometres deep coal seam. The colour change was accompanied by a strange, unsettling slurping sound.

Nate's legs first wobbled, then he almost collapsed to the ground. 'Oh Christ, oh shit,' he wailed, wanting to but unable to tear his eyes away from the hideous scene. 'No,' he said thickly, repeating it louder, then screaming it. This place was turning into a fucking killing field. He tasted vomit, trying to swallow it down, only partially succeeding, coughing explosively.

Yoshi was still sitting in the chair with his headset on, mouth hanging open, the same look of revulsion and smashed in the face look he had with Max. The military trio were similarly mitred to the spot, staring blindly, not believing what they were seeing.

Nate gave in to the rancid tide in his throat and threw up where he stood, bending over a few seconds later to repeat the process properly. Eventually finding the will to stand up, he wiped his mouth with the back of his hand and slowly, reluctantly gazed back at the Sphere. 'Oh fuck me,' he muttered breathlessly. 'This is…oh fuck me.'

Haigh was left half in and half out of the Sphere when it deactivated after Tara passed through. The object had apparently re-formed into something solid, slicing him in half along the line of his torso, leaving the horrible, bloodied stump of his body protruding from their end of the Sphere like some fearful leftover from a violent battle. The rest of him, the head end they guessed, ended up wherever Tara was. Nate felt like puking again, mainly from the smell of his own vomit.

This time there was nothing but blood, dark almost black fluid pooling over the metal and around the small hemisphere, leaving it looking like a bizarre blood encircled island. There were litres of it, dreadful acrid blood smelling minerally and metallic, like a bag of wet coins.

Yoshi finally summoned the strength to get up and inch over to Nate. The soldiers walked over and gently grabbed the half-Haigh and pulled him away from the Sphere, freeing a new wave of blood to add to the lake of crimson-black lapping at their feet. The smell was beyond potent and this time Yoshi lost the lot, canned corn and all. Fucking nice, Nate brooded, appalled and feeling his stomach bubbling upward for the third time.

Once again the soldiers had the grisly job of transporting the dead, grabbing a leg each and hauling the remains of Haigh toward the camp, presumably to bag it up and ready it for evac along with poor old Max. Unlucky bastard, Yoshi thought bleakly. What a rotten, screwed up way to go although he guessed it was quick enough. He didn't subscribe to that oft-used bullshit though. Haigh was still dead and he sensed a growing bitterness in his gut.

Yoshi ambled over to Nate who was staring at the Sphere. 'Tara's gone,' he said in a barely audible whisper, 'but the question is, where in the name of Jesus and Mary did she go?' His mind was hazy as he chewed over the ridiculous possibilities. 'Shit, this is so nuts, you know it could be us next right?' He exhaled roughly, venting a white haze of breath. 'Yoshi, get Jack on the line, let me know when you have him.'

'First Max...Haigh, now Tara,' Yoshi said dismally. 'We're dropping like fucking flies out here.' He could feel himself sweating under his polar outfit. '…and soon there'll be none.'

'Er, Jack this is Antarctic base, do you, uh…copy? He sounded drained like it was a struggle just to push air through his larynx.

Jack's voice came back almost immediately. He must have been sitting on top of the damn thing. He could hear the anguish grating in Yoshi's voice, taking it for very bad news.

Yoshi gestured Nate over with a rapid sweep of his arm. 'I'll let Nate explain it, you better sit down Jack.' Yoshi got out of the way, letting him slide in. As he did, movement caught his eye.

'Hey Jack, it's Nate, I think we're going to need some—'

Yoshi was looking at the anomaly, at the same time nudging Nate with his trailing arm, pointing frantically, knifing the air.

'Yoshi, Jesus, wait till I'm done here—'

Nate stopped mid-sentence, glaring at Yoshi who was staring at something behind him. Nate instinctively turned his head. Good God, he thought instantly, feeling his heart stand still, then take a decent thud and start woodpeckering his Adam's apple. 'What the—?' He hissed, seeing something staggering from the Sphere, a creature walking out real casual like, now standing on the metallic sheath, not moving, peering around.

Yoshi was speechless. Nate gasped, squinting to resolve it.

'What is it?' Yoshi breathed, all white eyes and frigid breath streaming into the air.

It was humanoid, they could tell that much, maybe a person but none they'd ever laid eyes on before.

'Uh…Jack,' Nate said shakily, 'we'll um, need to get back to you, uh…something's come out of the Sphere.' Nate could hear Jack almost frothing at the mouth as he terminated the line. 'Sloowwly,' Nate whispered, gesturing Yoshi with a gently swimming palm to follow him cautiously for a closer look.

'You sure?' He asked unsteadily, falling into step behind Nate anyway.

'How much worse can it get?'

Yoshi flinched and sized up the words, vexed because he was damn sure it could get worse.

The being that exited the anomaly was slowly, stiffly looking around and not surprisingly, seemed totally unfamiliar with its surroundings. Finally spotting Nate and Yoshi, it stuck its head forward as though struggling damnably to focus.

'What…I mean, who the hell is that?' Nate said, slowly inching their way forward on the silvery metal. It was clear that it was human, or human looking, an old woman, maybe ninety years he reckoned, possibly more.

'Oh Christ,' Nate warbled thinly, 'have they sent us, Jesus, I don't know… uh, one of their elders?' He narrowed his eyes, puzzled by the wrinkled thing that looked equally bemused.

She smiled weakly at them, hobbling forward on what appeared to be arthritic limbs, stopping suddenly and peering down. She raised an arm, inspected it, then did the same with the other, gazing at them from about ten metres away. The smile died as quickly as it came, fading into a glazed look of despair, mixed with regret maybe, expelling a wailing sound and slowly sagging to the ground. Her chest was heaving, tears fell to the alien surface from catastrophically wrinkled eyes.

Human she most definitely was and Nate sensed the heaviness in his chest recede a bit, his heartbeat slowing to almost normal. His nightmare inspired visions, images of something grotesquely inhuman unfolding itself from the Sphere like a Meccano set monster, receded for a moment

Nate stepped up to her warily, taking in every detail, his first thought ancient, like this chook was seriously old. He looked at her, fighting to stifle the revulsion. He'd never been good around aberrance whether it was deformity or dwarfism, Downs, whatever, anything remotely odd triggered an embarrassing shiver of panic. While he wasn't happy about it, that's how he was wired, and she looked so damn old as to appear already dead.

Taking a deep breath of bitingly cold air, Nate braced his muscles and forced himself to speak. 'Um, so, where did you come from, who are you?' He said, seeing no response or any indication she knew they were even there.

Yoshi poked him gently with a finger and turning to him, Nate was startled. His eyebrows were so high they'd almost retreated behind his perfectly black hairline. Nate smirked instinctively, thinking in the first instant that he no longer even looked Japanese, his eyes were pulled so wide. Yoshi was pointing a trembling finger and hissing under his breath, 'the p-pendant.'

Nate ogled the shiny object that was hanging around the wizened turkey flesh of her neck. 'Oh...for the love of...fuck,' he said quietly but forcefully, gawking closer at it, hair prickling on the nape of his neck as he did. Nate didn't know what to think and had to forcibly look away to collect himself. 'Fuck,' he whispered. Yoshi was bewildered, suddenly unsure what day it was, where they were. Nate grabbed his shoulder and walked him back a few steps, feeling his body tremble.

'H-how long was she in there?' Nate said haltingly, screwing up his forehead as he raced over the possibilities. Both of them recognised Tara's heart-shaped pendant her fiancée Jules had given her a year before, a one of a kind piece as definitive as a retinal scan. And then there was the small matter of the heart shaped tattoo on the underside of her wrist which although faded and crinkled was a classic Tara giveaway.

Nate gasped, keeping his voice low, 'no wonder she's fucking beside herself. She's been in and out of that thing in a few minutes and aged...Christ, half a century...more maybe?'

Yoshi turned to her and felt like crying himself. She was so pitiable, so wretched. '...reverse fountain of youth,' Yoshi said distantly with a sad smile, feeling physically ill at the prospect of such a short trip that ripped away most of your life. Damn it, he thought, was there anything worse? Death was surely more humane.

Tara was unrecognisable save for the pendant and the tattoo. Her gorgeous auburn hair and delicate porcelain features had been ravaged, stringy white hair hanging in untidy clumps half way down her back, everything about her unkempt and haggard. Perversely, her polar clothing looked clean and new, like she'd just stepped off the Osprey. Go figure, Nate thought, totally baffled. Everything was without explanation down here, he guessed nothing should come as a shock.

'Tara...Tara, look at me,' Nate said, looking down on her thatch of spiderweb hair, searching for the right words. 'What happened in there, do you remember why you, um, did it...why you went in?' She ignored him for a long while, then slowly turned her head toward them, causing Nate to flinch and inch back a step. This was Tara but it'd take time to reconcile this dishevelled old woman with the vibrant young girl they knew, like less than an hour ago. Her face was an Arizona arroyo, eyes hiding behind deeply weathered flesh...but she was in there. Miserable, sad and a virtual centurion this was the new, old Tara.

She peered up, her head shaking ever so slightly. 'My son was in there so I went to get him,' she said in a tone that carried all the earmarks of old age. 'I had to save him but I don't even know why I thought he was in danger.'

Yoshi studied her hard, scratching the back of his head, idly twirling a lock of hair, 'but you, uh…don't have a son,' he said cautiously, wondering if she'd simply lost it due to age. It could be anything he thought, dementia, senility, delusion, or simple human decay.

She eventually summoned the composure to continue. 'Of course I know I had no child, but I was convinced I did,' she said absently. 'I can still see his chestnut eyes, little smile…in my soul I knew he was mine.' Moisture was welling in her eyes. 'It wasn't until I was inside that I realised it was a ruse of some sort. But it wasn't that simple.' She stopped, drawing in a rattling breath, wiping moisture from a weeping eye. 'Jesus, the emotion was crippling, like nothing I'd felt before. It was like death would be a relief if I couldn't get to him.' Tara gasped and the breath seemed to catch in her throat. Her grey stigmatised stare was pregnant with regret, vivid in her eyes.

Nate felt the wind pick up so he pulled Tara gently to her feet, helping her slowly to the covered comms area, sitting her down gently. Wind was whistling through the broad weave of the tarpaulin, juxtaposed as it was on the three sides exposed to the katabatic winds.

Tara was still peering at her skin, poking it, hating it, agonising over what she'd done to deserve such an obtuse death sentence. Nate started to get an inkling of the problem. Tara had never seen herself until now, until she came back through the Sphere.

'So, how long—,' he paused, grossed out by the random pigments spotting her eyes, 'uh…were you in there?' He managed to finish, admitting shamefully that he was repelled by his friend, resembling pictures of his Nona from Pescara in Italy who was really old…pushing a hundred he was sure. Dark, heavy emotions wrestled inside him, the most pressing one being the paralysing dread of this happening to him.

'I don't know,' she said finally, with a wheeze and an old person's cough, 'maybe a few hours.' Tara closed her eyes tightly as a new wave of tears fell from her eyes.

A few hours? Nate pondered incredulously. He realised there could be any number of reasons, including that she'd just plain forgotten, had a chronic case of Alzheimer's or that she was just plain off her fucking rocker. Maybe a kiss of all three, he conceded sadly.

Whatever time displacement Tara had bumped up against was utterly counter to Sagan's experience because according to Mission, they'd gone in and come out almost at the same time, even though they'd spent maybe a week on the other side. The horror story playing out here was totally contrary, a few hours in the Sphere by her account had ripped away more than half her life.

Like Nate, Yoshi was struggling to look at her, but not because she was old, because she was still Tara. The Tara he knew, because this gentrified old bugger wasn't her anymore, just not. Despite the reality of who she was, the conviction that this person was a stranger had become a banging drum in his head.

Nate saw sweat standing out on her sallow skin as she battled to think, or maybe the memories were too painful. Whatever it was, she was clenching her teeth, the wrinkles in her forehead now deep corrugations.

Tara opened her mouth to speak but was interrupted by a thunderous roar that struck from nowhere. The Osprey's mighty blades drove the craft vertically into the air as it slashed with dissonant punches, clearing the U-shaped valley in under a minute. They assumed it was repatriating the bodies of Max and Haigh, the bloodless corpse of the former, the residual "chunk" of the latter that had fallen so ungraciously on their side of the Sphere.

Tara wobbled her head up and regarded Nate morosely, the look of human hope gone was hard to stomach because they knew it could just as easily have been them.

'My fiancé Jules,' she breathed hard, 'I'm as old as his fucking grandmother, my mum…Jesus I'm so much older than even my poor old mum.' Her head was in her hands as she murmured the words, looking for all the world like a mortally wounded animal. 'Why would they be so cruel?' She puffed, feeling anger rise between the desperation.

'So, uh…what did you see in there? Nate said, aghast as he glanced at her skeletal hands that were discoloured by dark, crisscrossing veins, and swollen knuckles that were holding tightly to the sides of the chair as she struggled to push her voice out. 'I entered into a room. I thought I'd been taken somewhere on Earth but adding everything together, I really don't think I was, um…at all.' She paused and swallowed slowly, loose flesh around her neck jiggling like barely set jelly. Shifting heavily on the chair, Tara recovered herself with an effort, her eyes almost closed as she combed her mind for detail. 'The room was big with high ceilings and three large curtained windows on each side. I remember daylight streaming in on one side but on the other was darkness. The floor was, um…something like ceramic tiles, black and white, patterned I think.' She paused for a moment to allow her breathing to slow. Yoshi fetched a plastic cup of water, placing it on the table next to her.

'We need to brief Jack,' Yoshi said soberly.

'Later, we need to get Tara's story. Continue,' Nate said, smiling at her as softly as he could manage, hiding the distaste, nodding his head in encouragement. 'Please.'

'There were chairs at the far end of the room, a lot of them,' she said shakily, 'and there was, um…one person seated, looking right at me.' She took a heavy swallow, clearly uneasy with the memory. 'He gestured me over with a wave of his hand so I approached and sat down, facing him.' She took another sip of water, then another. Jesus come on, Nate screamed silently, hanging on every word but she just sat there like a fucking stone, panting and staring into thin air. She was maddening, but he chided himself, it was Tara, and closed his eyes, told himself squarely to settle.

'Who was it?' Nate asked a bit too loudly, 'who asked you to sit down?' His face was hawk-like as he waited.

Tara snapped her head up abruptly, the only move he'd seen that could in any way be described as nimble. 'Why it was a boy, a human boy maybe fifteen years old with the most remarkable blue eyes…that gave him a sense of, well…great intelligence, but strangely, he never smiled, never frowned…well not really.' Tara forked her fingers through her scaly hair, lingering over memories. 'He oozed seriousness and I got the disturbing feeling he was dangerous.'

Nate reared back slightly. 'Dangerous?' He repeated.

'I wasn't sure because he hadn't uttered a word but I got the clear, unsettling sensation that the kid had untold power…and not in a good way, I can't explain it.'

Yoshi had been staring fixedly at Nate since Tara spoke of the blue eyes, jig-sawing the pieces together, quickly deciding it couldn't be a coincidence, no way, no chance. Tara may as well have been describing Max with those crazy sapphire eyes that appeared just before he'd suffered some sort of terminal meltdown. Nate caught the same thing, his heart squirming high in his chest.

Tara was taking small ragged breaths, raising her eyes and breaking the short silence. 'Kid-thing spoke to me in a mature and, well…quite manly voice that sounded like a well-schooled westerner, uh… clipped English you know, every word full of meaning, no wasted language. What he told me made little sense and it seemed like he wasn't only talking to me…but maybe through me…to a larger collective perhaps…you know, us.' She lowered her head, drooping her shoulders and Nate heard her start weeping again. 'Why did they send me back like this?' She said pleadingly. 'I think they were unhappy with me, unhappy with us. There was no favour in him…nothing but thinly veiled hatred I think.'

Nate recalled the shocking words that Max had started shouting and the assumed connection between the two became a fucking hard-dock. 'You mean similar to Max right?'

Her eyes glazed as she glanced up at him. 'I er…don't remember that, should I?'

'Well you probably should because it was only—' He stopped suddenly, knowing full well it was minutes for them but God knows how long for her. She said hours but in this case, looks may not have been deceiving. It could've been a lot longer than that…maybe she simply didn't remember.

'So how do you know he was unhappy?' Nate said, intrigued with the unfolding riddle, his chest fluttering a little.

'He said so…the boy told me.'

'Told you what exactly?

'He threatened me,' Tara said, finishing her sentence in a barely audible murmur.

Nate was sweating over what these others might have done to her on a deeper level, his mind corkscrewing as he imagined the screwed-up expressions on some of those exobiology scholars right now. The unique moment in time when contact happened was generally expected to bring with it an avalanche of altruistic learnings and cultural expansion of a like that overwhelmed the entire history of the planet. Yeah, well fuck that, Nate thought because the supposed munificence had instead delivered death, destruction and bewilderment, and now add torture as well.

'Just settle Tara, relax and breathe, tell me what he said. It might be important, go as slowly as you need to.' Nate was genuinely worried about her, Tara's breathing was irregular, her body beset with tremors as though she had Parkinson's or motor neuron disease...or both. God, don't die, he pleaded guiltily, not yet!

'Okay Nate,' she eventually said. 'The kid...he was uh, forceful, direct and I remember he never blinked, never stopped staring at me. I felt like he was inspecting me, looking inside me, seeing what made me tick.' She rubbed her wrinkled brow with both hands, leaving the flesh deathly white. 'And from nowhere this kid, boy, whatever, threatened me, turned his back and seemed like he no longer gave a toss whether I was there at all. His attitude changed like that...and I don't know why.'

Holy crap, Nate pondered, who was this kid? His mind started to fill with crazy images, some of them pushing him a little off balance. 'Changed to what...what did he say?'

'He said we were lazy, uh...unexplainably haphazard. Science was mentioned, something about disdain for, um...cerebral nuance.'

Nate was blown away, nibbling on his lip, then chewing it hard, 'what do you think he meant by that? I mean, I get the words but what the hell right?'

'I don't know,' Tara said, wiping beads of moisture off her forehead, 'I got the impression he sort of took it all rather personally. He didn't move, didn't raise his voice, uh, barely changed expression but I could sense it. I could feel the heat in his eyes, uh, the temperature of his displeasure, uh...on my skin. He spoke of global divisions, that's right...our want for warfare...conflict.' Tara raised her arms slowly above her head, clasping her hands in front of her chest. She pulled her eyes closed, steepling her fingers, then opened them suddenly. 'The boy said it was puzzling and at odds with...I think he said something like probabilistic outcomes. I couldn't help myself. I asked him if he was well, like God...you know, because what he said just added up...and I came out with it. Despite what he looked like, his words implied an intimate investment in Earth...in us,' Tara said, sucking in a flesh-wobbling breath, the memory visibly upsetting her. 'He didn't bother to answer the question but eventually said he was part of a race of beings that watched things very closely.'

'You actually thought he was God,' Yoshi said, gasping, 'the boy?' He glanced at Nate stupefied, lifting his eyebrows as far as they would go.

'Now I think he's the devil,' she said, hissing with intent. 'No God would do this to someone.' Tara glanced at her left arm, then the other, jiggling the chicken-fat flesh. 'Jesus, I can't look at myself.'

'Continue,' Nate said gently, not sure what to say. He felt like a callous brute but they needed to get it all.

Tara licked her lips. 'Then he told me I couldn't leave, that I would have to stay in this place forever. He tilted his head forward albeit a little mechanically which was the only body movement I ever saw. I think I panicked...like my heart almost stopped. I demanded to know where I was, why I couldn't go outside, you know, why I was a prisoner. He said I couldn't survive outside, can you believe that?' Tara was getting excited and stopped abruptly, knowing she couldn't sustain it, her words hanging in the air while she breathed in short takes, eventually recovering herself. 'I completely freaked out, started screaming for what seemed like minutes. On one side was space, I could see what seemed to be arm's length stars, and the other was a rocky landscape a bit like Mars but grey and forbidding. I must have fainted because I woke up on the ground and saw the boy with his back to me. I spoke to him, ended up yelling at him, even swearing at the little prick, and not just swearing, but full on, well you know...abuse really. I think that's where I screwed up because he was vindictive, I was sure of it¬ even before then.' Tara's eyes were wide beneath her jelly eyelids. 'Then he turned to face me with the bluest eyes you could imagine. He said he didn't care what I did, go, stay, whatever and then he turned his back and ignored me, so I got up, flipped the bird, walked back to the wooden door and stepped through.'

Nate was listening to her speak and it was the young Tara, her voice was different but she spoke exactly like Tara used to, just slower and with a lower pitch typical of a pensioner's larynx. It was depressing looking at her because there was just no way back, she'd lost her youth, her personal years, her life in a heartbeat. All by going through some prosaic wooden doorway that was without doubt anything but that.

This thing clearly had a nasty streak, the evidence was right in their face and it scared the living hell out of them. Because if this cold, perfunctory kid was part of a race that was "watching things closely", then the scenario was possibly way worse than the shitstorm they were already in.

Tara's lips were trembling, the wizened skin around her eyes shaking almost in step. 'When I was standing at the wooden door I heard him say something…with a little more emphasis.' She peered at Nate with age-clouded eyes.

'What?' Nate pleaded. Spit it out, he begged silently.

'He said something about unproductive, empty space, that information is the answer.'

Nate stared at her blindly, confused, fighting to assign meaning to it. 'Did you question him…like what it meant?'

'No, I wished I had but I wanted out of there so badly I just pulled open the door, walked straight through,' she said, peering at him like someone begging to be spared the guillotine. 'And here I am Nate, a haggard old turd who swapped a few harsh words, a raised digit maybe, for the best sixty years of her life. Great trade huh?' Tears fell again and this time she just left them.

Nate wondered how you consoled someone like this, deciding heavily that it was beyond his rather limited emotional skill set. 'So you think he did that because you flipped the bird and called him a few choice names?' No way he thought, but Christ, if it was true, *vindictive* wasn't strong enough. This individual was a fucking techno terrorist and the implications of an advanced Kardashev capability with such a damaged mindset…well he was rock solid on that being as bad as it got.

Nate was intrigued by her belief that this creature was angry with humanity as a collective, because we hadn't progressed in the right way, maybe hadn't developed as others might have. The whole concept sounded like trumped up fantasy but he freely admitted that humans had no wider perspective, so sorting fact from fiction was founded solely on the wiring of the human brain…back to that infuriating chestnut again. Nate conjured an odd thought, reckoned it put the whole thing in perspective, maybe confirmed what we were missing. He pictured a common garden variety snail and framed the notion in his mind. Is a "fast" snail still slow? Sounded daft but it was an intriguing thought experiment, because if a fast snail and slow snail existed in isolation they would make assumptions using their "snail logic", but would never know for sure because any connection with others is absent. Neither race of snails would ever know which one they were. Someone else, maybe someone that watches things closely would need to decide, casting their critical eye across all snails in the galaxy…or even the Universe.

Nate imagined two snails, one about to break the finishing tape, one barely beyond the starting line, it sounded like lunacy but what if we had been inordinately slow and were just blind to it? Apparently this irritating little upstart had a wider view, had been watching with a perverse, sneering interest. The message they'd been sent played on his mind and had been since they'd unravelled it. Failure. Seriously, who would send such a prosaic and insulting message, the callousness, the sheer bluntness surely spoke to the cold, unemotional mind of the sender. And pressing the point further, the sender appeared to have the power to do pretty much anything it liked in a technical sense, including removing colossal masses with not the slightest eddy of molecular dust left behind.

An uneasy perplexity invaded Nate's mind, the guarded half-statements from the kid, the message, all the events that had occurred courtesy of the Spheres, all the ducks in his prefrontal cortex were lining up. And in his mind, humanity was being surveyed heavily, scrutinised, and the interim result, the scorecard, the benchmarking, maybe even the teacher's comments looked anything but promising. In fact it might be such a bummer that flunking, even expulsion seemed a real possibility.

'Who was this kid?' Yoshi asked directly, 'you say he was human, was there any indication he might have been, you know, something else?'

'Well he looked human,' Tara said openly. 'He seemed physically like us but mentally less so, the intensity, the colour in his eyes varied when he spoke. Maybe that's a display of emotion for whatever kind of thing he is,' she said hoarsely, coughing lightly, adding, 'I think it took the form of a human to put us at ease but I honestly have no idea. What I think I remember might be right or wrong or somewhere in between.'

'Maybe their true form would really freak us out,' Yoshi said, staring fixedly at Nate.

Tara nodded, 'yes I believe you might be right.'

Nate got through to Jack at the Johnson Space Centre and as expected, Mission were sceptical, settling on grudging acceptance after they shared some of the more in-your-face detail. The truth became self-evident after some harried encouragement got Tara in front of Houston by Skype, leaving absolutely nothing to the imagination. No special effects, Tara assured them reluctantly, adding it was just a thanks-for-coming gift from a malicious, spiteful fuck of a creature.

Like Nate, Jack felt things were becoming less and less germane with the world they took for granted, almost like being shoved into the quantum world where things just didn't make sense, objects fizzed in and out of existence in a madhouse of uncertainty, ruled by multiple states without the slightest inkling of probabilistic outcomes, unless someone bothered to look. Nothing in this hyper-dimensional asylum had any of the rigour of the true-blue world they'd left behind.

Tara would soon be airlifted to St Vincent's Hospital in Sydney for a battery of physiological tests to see if there were any cellular clues that might tell them what really happened to her. Hopefully they might find out how old she really was, eighty or ninety…maybe even in the hundreds.

28. The Big One

"The mind is a universe and can make a heaven of hell, a hell of heaven." ~ *John Milton*

'Jesus H Christ,' Harry said, bug eyed, 'aging half a century in…that time? Maybe it would've been better not to come back at all.' He tried to get his head around what it would be like being a vibrant, sexy young woman and in a finger snap, look at me - a haggard old buzzard. Harry struggled to come up with a worse scenario that didn't involve death or complete disability.

Ageing was something the human mind grudgingly accepted because it happened slowly enough so the changes were absorbed into the cerebral cortex, much like a daily flat file update. It didn't mean you were happy with it but you had a long and gentle downslope of more of this and less of that…reluctant acceptance Harry thought. Tara had none of that indulgence, she just fell off a vertical cliff, plummeting from fresh and ripe to ancient in the equivalent of a heartbeat.

Vic depressed a pushbutton to start the APUs for an OMS burn to ease them into a circular parking orbit around Earth. Thrusters would pitch and yaw the craft, RCS would burn off enough momentum to hit the right corridor, taking them within spitting distance of the Spheres, once every Earth transit. Space without the Moon was a harrowing reminder of the power and capability, the possible motives of whatever or whoever might be close on their doorstep.

'Y'know it's a must to get off Earth,' Harry said, 'because in the not too distant future that is going to be a goddamn nightmare, blistering hot one side, brass-monkey the other.'

'Sounds lovely,' Skylar said, 'nothing we'll need to worry about I guess.'

'…you mean because we should be smart enough to fix it by then or we won't be around because of our friends?' Harry quizzed, grimacing, quickly realising the folly of his words.

Sky's throat convulsed with an involuntary swallow. 'Well I meant you and I and the rest of us will have lived and died actually.'

'Oh,' Harry said nonchalantly, 'yep right.' Just what she didn't need, a reality check.

Vic maintained a distant, melancholy look. 'It's sad, all the Moon junk…just gone.' His eyes were locked on the empty dimensions of Earth orbit. 'The Apollo descent modules, Duke's family photo at Descartes, the Surveyors, Luna's… vanished into thin…well, space I guess.'

'Vic?' Sky said, staring at him intently, surveying his face carefully. 'I've been thinking about the other-us we saw.'

He glanced over and his face thawed a bit. She'd shown zero interest in anything apart from herself in days so it was nice to hear her talking about the mission, albeit a part that made him feel like hurling. He reckoned Sky looked a bit different too, more normal, the shadows under her eyes less obvious, looking less like a nutter, more like Sky.

'I think we eventually find the answer…that we do find a solution,' she said, nodding. Vic and Harry were paying attention now, looking at her with less derision, a little more curiosity. 'Maybe we work out how to use the Spheres, how to shift across time to the right point, send a message to ourselves to meet at L1. Maybe the only way to beat it is right now, in our time, after that, well…we're screwed.' Sky tipped her head to one side, straining for ideas as she spoke, 'but something must have gone wrong, it didn't work, we, they, just ran out of time.' Sky exhaled noisily. 'That message had more to it I'm sure, like how to stop them, maybe who these bastards are.' She slitted her eyes, skipping them from Vic to Harry, 'but we, did something wrong or maybe they stopped us part way through.' Sky's brow creased as she tried to piece her broken thoughts together.

'Why the convoluted method of transmission…if that was really us in the future, why would we use it?' Vic said, conceding there had to be a hell of a lot they had no idea about.

Harry gave an overblown sigh, 'Vic my friend, do you honestly think anyone has the remotest on that?' He crooked his head, giving him a glassy stare.

'It's a question I've been battling with,' Sky said, 'it has to be related to the Spheres, not us…not our choice, no way.' Her words fell away into silence.

Harry stroked his beard, a beehive of knots and tangles, reminiscent of a mountain man, not a spaceman. There was an almost imperceptible shake of his head as he gazed at Sky. 'This paradox horseshit is giving me a headache. I don't think it's the answer but it's worth thinking—'

'No, you and Sky might be right,' Vic interrupted, rubbing a deepening line on his forehead. 'After all, that was us and they knew things we didn't know. We need to understand more about the Spheres, and then do a better job than Sagan 2.0 did.' He wondered miserably how many attempts it might take till we got it right…Sagan 58.0 maybe…or worse, Jesus, he felt ill.

Out of the blue, Sky told Harry they'd only be allowed to go home when the risk to the planet was dealt with, causing a sharp intake of breath. When Harry picked himself figuratively off the floor, Sky volunteered in a voice full of intent that she realised it and accepted it, so they better get on and deal with it. He was certain the downhill slide would continue toward mental oblivion, so the unexpected words caught him out, telling himself, whatever, he'd take it for as long as it lasted.

Sky was busy devising a plan to analyse each Sphere, grab any intel they could and maybe itemise, map and compare whatever they managed to collect. Essentially do in some small part what kid-thing said he'd been doing to intelligent life on Earth. Examining, watching…scrutinising.

Sky initially thought the idea was nuts, still did actually, but it was gnawing at her, demanding attention. Slowly, by degree, she continued to evaluate it, mainly due to a complete lack of options. Grabbing at straws it most certainly was but at least it was definitive action and Sky knew she had a hell of a lot to make up for, and if going home meant sending these godforsaken objects on their way, well, insane or not, every idea had to be torn asunder and tested. Just maybe, one might lead to another that was more right than the one before. That was her motivation because success meant going home to her daughter and her fractious psyche had finally figured it out and embraced the bigger picture. If they gathered enough interlocking pieces and aligned them just so, maybe it would free them from these things and allow them to return to a free planet. It was lunacy, she freely volunteered it but it was her lunacy and anyway, the logical, prudent approach had delivered exactly fuck all, so an alternate, offbeat approach could hardly screw up their strike rate. So bring on left field, she said to Harry and Vic…the reckless, wild, the illogical even. Putting the atmospheric objects aside for the moment, there were six Spheres left in orbit and this was where Sky knew the real banality kicked in hard, but she didn't give a toss. The equation was simple; "success equalled home", so doing was better than sitting on your goddamn hands.

What if some sort of code was the answer, entered in a certain sequence, perhaps by Sagan approaching them in a particular order? She shook her head, hmpfing and sneering at the deeply humanistic thought process. Punch 'em in right, you disarm the death sequence, punch 'em in wrong and…well, fuck me, she brooded, imagining instant dissolution like the Moon. It sounded rudimentary and way too terrestrial, but she soothed herself by knowing it was something, maybe a smidge more than nothing. After all, the odds of the peculiar strategy being right were vanishingly small, but they weren't zero…doing nothing was zero. At the least they might extract something decisive about the objects, which might lead them in another direction, somewhere more promising, so whatever happened, it would be time spent productively, offering the faintest spark of hope.

One of the many questions that grated on their subconscious was the issue of predestination. The Sphere's covet to evade a deliberate, frontal approach favoured the "fluid thesis" as did the way they dragged them in from time to time. So the when and where of entry seemed to be stage managed, which might mean topological spacetime was crucial to the objects in some unknown way. On that score they had nothing more than dodgy guesswork, pissing in the wind Harry said, an on-coming one at that. It wasn't pretty.

Harry glanced at Sky thoughtfully, lifting an eyebrow agreeably. 'You know Sky, I'm totally in because nothing makes sense and this is the closest thing to sounding like an option I've heard in a week. It's nuts, whacky, but hey.' He threw his arms in the air, grunting. 'Bring it,' he said, happy to have something, even happier to have Sky back, even if the reprieve was temporary. No way he was going to say no, despite the harebrained nature of her so-called plan.

'It's, something,' Vic said, 'information is key, so your number thing is as good as any.' Vic rolled his shoulders, stretching muscles, breaking into an ironic smile. Fuck me, he chuckled, is she talking about a PIN number…seriously?

***

Eyeing each other they realised with trepidation that they could be looking at the future-them they saw at L1…in waiting. For a moment they stared wordlessly, mulling it over, knowing they had to gain knowledge the other version didn't have, even if it was simply how to dispatch the entire message once they got what they needed. Like Sky had said, the plan to avoid the wrath of the Spheres probably had to be executed early, any later and maybe it was too late. So he assumed, older-them needed to engage with younger-them to instruct, guide, lead the way, perhaps push them toward the salvation Sagan 1.0 had to execute to make all this go away…with information. Which was key.

'Sagan. Flight, do you copy?' They were punched back to reality by Jack's voice which sounded shrill and harsh.

'Copy,' Vic said, praying the news wasn't too bad. Jack's tone rarely varied by a semi-tone and for those in the know, a variation beyond that was a chilling insight.

'Uh, Vic…hang on…Pete, quiet!' He snapped, coming back to them. 'We have a situation here Vic,' he said with a detectable tremor. There were voices in the background, some talking to Jack, others yelling, some sighing, others more ominous. Normally they could hear vague back and forth chitchat, but there was none of that. Harry knew something historic was up. Bad historic.

'Um, okay,' Jack said, gathering himself, 'the thirteenth Sphere has gone along with its, uh…gravity entanglement.' They could hear his heavier than normal breathing through the VOX mic. 'The connection was with J-Jupiter.' He said Jupiter with a shaky exhalation.

Oh shit, Vic screamed to himself, splintered thoughts muddling his thinking as he sweated over the import of the Jovian monster to their tenuous little family.

'And, uh…Jupiter?' Harry said with forced calm, tasting gut acid. If the plump sentinel went, he was certain they were in the worst shit imaginable. Unlike the Moon, which we could live without for a long time, Jupiter's loss would be catastrophic. A myriad of voices joined in an amorphous mix of chatter and unmeaning on the other end.

'It's still there,' Jack came back loudly, trying to be heard over the racket. 'We've got Keck 2, SALT and AAT locked on it 24/7. Let's just fucking hope and pray it stays that way.' He spat the expletive in grim emphasis, summing up the mood perfectly.

If Jupiter went the way of the Moon then the hand of these others would be proven, the smoking gun…proof en evidence. The kicker was why didn't they just get on and do it, just do to Earth whatever the hell they'd done to the Moon. What was the reason for taking the scenic route, surely it would be more humane to just execute their end game. And that was the other twist, because maybe humane wasn't part of the plan.

***

Griffin came scuttling back from DoD's makeshift bunker looking deeply agitated. The rest of his executive troops were in step behind him, a gaggle of puffing, flushed faces in dark suits. Jupiter was on borrowed time if recent history was any guide, leaving them with the unnerving sense of a looming catastrophe, one they were powerless to control. But that was forgotten, at least right now, because something else had happened closer to Earth that needed their full attention.

Griffin's unease morphed into a dark, malicious glare that zeroed in on Jack. 'We got a call from our Canuck friends in British Columbia,' he said, 'didn't know they were still fucking alive up there.' He glanced at Picton-King. 'Anyway, they've had their, er…what was that telescope Hillier?'

'Dominion Radio Telescope.'

261

'Yeah that's it, they had it gun-barrelled on the object above Deadhorse and guess what?' He stared vacantly at Jack and Pete who both gazed stiffly back. 'It's chattering…the damn thing has started squawking in radio frequencies.'

Jack's eyes widened, glancing at Pete who was gawking at Griffin. 'What…like talking, data…is that what you mean?'

'Just noise, a modulating carrier wave apparently. Every science team is on it, the Sit Room, POTUS have been briefed along with everyone that needs to know around the country.' Griffin was about to continue when his cell rumbled. Grabbing it from his pocket he glared myopically at the sender. 'Price from Princeton,' he snarled, frowning and exhaling in a burst. His whole demeanour grew in severity as he absorbed the message. Griffin shook his head irritably, cursing under his breath. 'Says there's a mirror sideband buried in it which has vestigial structure. Goddamn this jerk, how many times…who speaks shit like this?' He scowled at his phone as though it had the power of mind, 'does he seriously think I need to know all this? Just the facts I told him, just the facts, stow the detail.' Griffin sighed. 'Anyway,' he said, squinting at the text, 'he's talking about superposition of some signal on the carrier wave. My world is suddenly full of nerds and geeks speaking this crap, just merrily assuming that everyone gets it.' He arrowed his gaze at Hillier and Ballard and they nodded obligingly.

Griffin's phone rumbled again. 'Oh for Christ's sake,' he growled, 'Price again. What the hell is wrong with him?' Griffin's head snapped up as all hell seemed to break loose around him.

Jack peered around, edging back, baffled by a sudden ocean of sound that spread through the FCR as though a dissonant orchestra had started playing in every corner of the MCC. Tones were sounding, music, melodies were playing and a hundred variations of incoming data tones exploding like corn in hot oil.

Ballard was speechless, gawping blindly at the sea of confused faces buried in their devices, tapping, reading, trying to get a handle on what was happening. The entire Mission Control team were peering in his direction, most of them holding their phones up, flabbergasted.

Jack was stunned by the email he'd opened and the crazy looking image attached to it. Ballard and Griffin held their phones toward each other and then at Jack, the image was identical. Everyone in the Flight Control Room received the same attachment seemingly at the same time.

The apparent intrusion of a higher power into the FCR left the room unnervingly still, a cold shiver running through Jack, head to toe, sensing something supernatural invading one of NASA's main arenas. It was like time had slowed down, what was flat, now uphill, the world oddly angled somehow. He closed his eyes as tight as he could, reopening them, heart still pounding.

Ballard fumbled around, queasy in the stomach as he inspected it, face watchful as he waited for whatever might be coming next.

Pete scrutinised the prosaic little image. 'I don't get it,' he said, feeling goose bumps on his arms. Look at the, uh…ID.'

<Known Sender>

'Jesus,' Jack said, 'known sender…what the hell?' He stared uneasily at it, dizzy, confused.

'Shouldn't that be unknown,' Griffin said, completely thrown by the strange message.

'I'm no electronics expert,' Pete said, 'but cellphones don't have the functionality to make that reference. Known sender isn't part of their fuzzy logic, If it's known it's either been keyed in or a call's been received before, and then the message has a name…not just frigging known.'

'Yup, sounds right,' Jack said, taking a lingering glance at the words on his cell. 'Christ, here we go again, he told himself, sifting sanity from bullshit.' Jack's eyes burnt as he ran over the facts as they were, coming up against the familiar double-brick wall.

Griffin's cell toned in his pocket. 'Is this guy actually fucking serious?' He snarled, answering and speaking before Price could utter a word, 'Look, everyone here got the—' Griffin stopped talking, clearly having been cut off mid-sentence. After some frustrated grunting he drew a deep breath, staring at Ballard without expression. 'Jesus, okay, yes, call me, straight away.' he pocketed his cell and suppressed the need to scream. 'Well, I'm not sure what to say,' he said, rubbing the back of his hand across his forehead so hard it left a red mark. 'That's one for the history books,' he said, scowling at Jack and added, 'as if we needed another screwed-up entry.'

'What?' Ballard spat like a rifle shot, jigging up and down, readying himself for the chaos of briefing half a dozen exec teams from Washington to New York.

Griffin thrust a thunderous face forward as he spoke. 'Everyone in the United States received the same goddamn email at the exact same time. Damn near everyone has this ridiculous electronic image.' He sighed sharply at the odd image on his cell. 'Price thinks everyone on the planet with a device or app received it…cellphone, email, Facebook, Twitter, Instagram, Tumblr…you name it, this thing has penetrated them all like a fucking techno-virus.' His face was flushed as he chucked it around in his head, coming up with nothing but a blinding ache near his temple.

'From the, uh…Spheres?' Ballard asked, looking cautiously from Griffin to Hillier.

'Oh Christ,' Griffin spat, 'you think?' He thumped his forehead with a fist. 'Of course it's from them. Who else…your mama? Jesus, get a grip.' He shook his head dismissively at him.

A brief shadow swept over Ballard's face but he held his tongue. He wanted to crush Earl's skull but remained still and silent, maintaining discipline, for the moment.

'But what is this image?' Picton King said, peering at it, turning his phone through every angle, nose almost on top of it. 'It's a poor resolution something, not sure what…stick figures maybe?'

'Blocks,' Hillier offered, 'like that goddamn game, what's it called, where you change the shape of the whatsits so they all fit together?' He was pinching his nose, racking his brain.

'Tetris,' Jack said. It kind of looks like it if you close one eye but I don't think so…it's a stretch.' Jack jerked his head back sharply. 'Christ, what am I saying…why the hell would Tetris be sent to the greater population of Earth?' They were losing their minds, he was sure of it. 'Look, we can't strike anything out but seriously, keep thinking.' He chuckled under his breath, deriding the idea of aliens sending a Tetris image around the globe. For God's sake, he mocked silently, intelligence was clearly bottoming out.

Griffin was wondering what sort of halfwits were working in US Defense, starting with the knob who somehow got the gig as Secretary of State. Some things you just keep quiet on . 'Price and his team and every other crew in the US are working on it,' Griffin said curtly, 'deconstructing it, seeing what it's made of. If there's something there they'll find it.' Griffin glanced at Ballard disdainfully, 'hey, maybe it's just another chickenshit exercise that goes nowhere.'

'There's meaning in it,' Jack muttered idly, 'if we can't find it, well, remember the word…failure? If we don't find something then…well?' He stared at Griffin gravely, lapsing into silence, pulse hammering the side of his neck, fevering over the enigmatic little picture.

The military execs glared at him, then at each other, seemingly agreeing with the sentiment.

'Jesus,' Griffin heaved, softening his gaze, blinking quickly a few times. 'We gotta make this happen…find something.'

All of them were peering at their devices in silence, weighing it up, why it had been mysteriously dispatched to every cellphone, IP address on the goddamn planet. Even the astronauts aboard ISS got it through their OPALS laser comms system. Every server, every cell base tower around the globe received it in a thunderous, synchronised explosion of data.

Intriguingly, odd looking as it was, there appeared to be very little to get excited about.

'Shit,' Pete said, squinting harshly, expecting something profound…getting the equivalent of a peanut butter and jelly sandwich. 'Seriously, it just slips further off the grid, right? I mean…a few poor resolution squares stuck together?' He snorted sharply through his nose, sneering at the simplicity of the inane attachment. 'Why bother…if they were going to send something, send something! Maybe we should show them the Mona Lisa or The Last Supper, stick it up 'em.'

Griffin's cell rumbled again, Griffin frowned, mouthing "Price", his expression darkening into a furious scowl, causing a vein to appear in his neck like some inflamed Frankenstein scar.

Nodding and growling several times he tried to get a word in, but eventually gave up, thanked Price distantly and thumped his cell on the desk.

'This science stuff is a total headfuck,' he said, scratching the side of his heavily pored nose. 'They've isolated the data that makes up the image.'

'What data?' Jack asked, feeling his pulse quicken.

'Bunch of decimals apparently,' Griffin said glibly.

Jack tipped his head, 'hang on…not binary? Aren't images composed of binary?'

'Fuck me,' Griffin grunted, 'can you see me okay son…who do I look like?'

Jack was tempted to call him a muttonhead or a twit but he gripped his loins, held onto it.

Griffin added, 'he said the picture's based on decimals, that's what Price said, he was a little surprised but it's not without precedence he said.'

Pete looked up a little startled. 'Um,' he mumbled, thinking it through, 'it could be similar to something we mucked around with at MIT, a lot of us did, to show the flexibility of base-two over base ten, uh…the last one is decimal. I'd ask why the hell they'd use something so redundant, but they've got runs on the board, right?' He eyed Griffin mischievously and couldn't help himself. 'The decimals are converted into a different base system, or radix, between one and thirty-six.' Pete was sciencing it deliberately, doing his best to wind the prick up, adding some cream, 'it's sort of like "modding" decimal into binary to produce an image, using ones as anything odd, zeroes as even, stuff like that.' He could see Griffin turning a ruddy shade of crimson, breathing like an aging locomotive. 'Then it might, say, apply black to zero and green to one, building an image, although not a very detailed one.' He racked his brain, wondering what else it could be but had nothing, just the question of why? If it was the old converter, the fact he was familiar with it was strangely ironic.

Griffin inhaled roughly, about to give Pete both barrels when his phone pulsed again. Raising his cell he saw a text from Price with the data. 'Okay, so here's the numbers beneath the image.' He passed his phone around. 'You boys need to see what you can come up with…looks like shit to me but I'm not the fucking expert here.' He pushed his head at Pete, raising both eyebrows, calling him a smart-arse son of a bitch with his eyes.

3516481421369040502000003

'Christ,' Hillier barked, 'they're not primes, are they, uh…Pi?' The suits looked at him vacantly, brooding over the numbers blindly.

Jack knew instantly what they were, any NASA tech worth their salt would know. It started with three which would suggest Pi to the untrained, but no way it was that, the second decimal was wrong, and so too most of the rest of them. This was something else entirely, something intriguing.

Griffin saw his knowing smirk, pursing his lips. 'Jack, you swallow the fucking canary?'

'Yep, well I mean no, but I reckon your teams will already know the answer.'

'My cell ain't ringing.' He held it up and waved it around.

'Well it will.'

'So…good or bad?'

'Well that's to be seen sir because the numbers are only part of it. The interesting part will come later. The picture sent to every corner of the globe looks like it's composed of, wait for it…GPS coordinates, you know, lat and longitude.'

Griffin rubbed his chin doubtfully. 'You sure, like you're positive about this?' Griffin said, lowering his brow to emphasise the gravity of the question.

'Pretty sure,' he said, looking him straight in the eye. 'I reckon these numbers are pointing to a piece of real estate on Earth…not in space and not multiple locations this time.' He stiffened his posture, breathless at the prospect of finally decoding a single, maybe definitive piece of information.

Griffin's cell rang and he grabbed it from his waist pocket. After a few seconds he yelled, 'yes Price we know what they are. Get about finding what it's pointing at.' He hung up, called him a cocksucker and placed his phone on the desk again. 'Find the spot so we can brief the country…in case they don't know already. Find the spot!'

Pete dashed to his workstation, scrolling manically through his NASA location devices, the Dec/RA app for position in space and the SatTracker for terrestrial location. 'I'm guessing it's not south or west because there's no minus sign…right?'

'Let's go with it, if it looks wrong we try the other way. One of them will be right.'

'Yep, okay, good.' Pete entered the coordinates in the SatTracker using the compass designations they'd decided on, apprehension crawling up his spine like a spreading wave, screaming out for the numbers to lead somewhere…God forbid, to be insightful.

35.1648142N 136.90405020000003E

Pete was about to punch Locate, seeing the sea of faces staring at him expectantly, studying his every move, watching his fingers trembling on the console.

'Hit the goddamn button,' Griffin demanded, mopping his brow with a sleeve.

Pete pressed it and held his breath, exhaling in a rush as he read the bewildering result. The name of the city, country and the street address appeared boldly on the screen. It wasn't some backwoods nothing like the others, nor was it a singularly significant part of the planet, or at least as far as they could tell.

'Oh for the love of…and this means what?' Griffin said, raising a hand and waving it angrily, stepping forward for a closer look, mystified by the address.

2-17-1 Sakae, Naka-ku, Nagoya Japan 460-0008

'Ja-fucking-pan?' Griffin spat, gazing with focus at the screen. Why he was so surprised he wasn't sure. For whatever reason, he'd expected it to be continental United States, personal bias he figured, but still…Japan? Where the hell was Nagoya anyway? Some island he assumed, whole damn place was islands wasn't it?

'Get it up,' Jack said eagerly, 'finally something real, an actual street address,' he said in a voice sunk to an awestruck whisper. The other Spheres were out in the country, pretty much as far from civilisation as possible, but this was a city…metropolitan.

'If this is a goddamn McDonald's, I'm going to take a fucking Howitzer to one of those Spheres,' Griffin said wryly, trying to mask his growing unease. Nothing, and he meant nothing, had gone to plan or expectation so far and he felt deeply fatalistic about the same bullshit continuing.

Pete saw the location and visibly winced, composing himself with a clearing cough, typing the street address into the browser. As the nature of the location became clear, there was a collective intake of breath. Pete clicked on the top-rated website, already fevering over its significance. 'Well, um…it's a planetarium sir, specifically the Nagoya City Science Museum, largest astronomical planetarium in the world it says on the blurb.'

All the military heavyweights gawped in Pete's direction, waiting impatiently for some ideas as to why they'd been steered toward a bloody planetarium…in Japan no less.'

Huffing and puffing, Griffin, paced around, tight as a wire. 'You're sure that's it?'

'Dead centre, this is it,' Pete said, so wanting to tell this jerk to chill out. 'At least we figured it out…score one for us right?' He said, sneeringly.

Griffin ignored him. 'Why a planetarium? He said, eyeing Jack deadpan. 'Ballard, Hillier,' he said, raising his voice aggressively, 'brief everyone…you know the drill. Get the intel out there, see what comes back. Joint Chiefs, POTUS needs to know, priority one. Hillier, speak to the Kremlin, UNGS, the world probably knows but let's get on the front foot with this. Oh and tell Boris to pass this on to Putin.' He raised a middle digit and a single hairy eyebrow.

The military execs bustled from the FCR, heading to the makeshift war-room to dispatch the latest data to the need to know list. Jack and Pete were left swinging in the wind, contemplating the rather weird location their friends were nudging them toward. Jack was baffled not only by the oddly circuitous behaviour but by their complete lack of consistency, because this time it wasn't binary or even ASCII text, this time it was an image coded in decimals that led them to a bloody planetarium no less. What the fuck was high in his mind.

Jack eyed Pete sceptically, studying him carefully for a moment. 'All that effort,' he said, pursing his lips, 'I mean, if it actually took any of course, to send it all the way around the globe.' He winced. 'Sending it deliberately to nearly every man and woman on the planet and what do we get?' He sighed, frustrated. 'Looking at it logically, you'd reckon it had to be epic, but it seems so nothing, on the surface at least. The fact the damn thing's in Japan and has some visual link with space might be a little hopeful I guess.'

'Jesus you're the smart one,' Pete said sheepishly, 'I'm with you on the space thing, they project stars and planets and this one is crazy…totally state of the art.'

'So why are they so keen for everyone on Earth to know about it? Like I said, is there something on the star map for us, maybe it's a fucking pirate map, you know, X marks the spot?' His tone was mocking but his eyes were steely, searching for a grain of meaning.

Pete knew failure hadn't been avoided at all, they'd gotten the broader detail but no way they had the real detail…the reason for the invitation to downtown Nagoya.

'And what's so damn special about the set-up in Japan,' Jack said. 'These things are dotted across the world and they chose Nagoya. It might be a good one but—'

'I've been there Jack, it's not just good, it's spectacular. Come over and check it out.' Pete showed Jack the website, flipping through the images of the astonishing space combo, pausing on the first external shot of the place.

'Oh fuck me, you must be joking,' Jack said slowly, widening his eyes, then squinting at the unexpected image. 'The resemblance, Jesus…it's uncanny. You see it, right?'

Pete felt his pulse rising. 'Yeah of course, but that can't be it…no way it can be just that.'

Jack squashed his mouth up, 'maybe they've taken a shine to it, found a bed-buddy.'

'It's a fair coincidence,' Pete agreed, looking closer.

'This is big Pete, has to be.'

The spatial coordinates provided by the now world famous image was indeed centred on a planetarium. It was the largest, most advanced of its type in the world with fibre-optics providing retina quality renderings of stars, planets and damn near everything else that called the Milky Way home. Intriguingly, ironically, it was all housed inside a massive silver sphere patterned on the outside with perfect geometric rectangles.

'So we've been directed to a man-made sphere by an alien-made Sphere. How incredibly odd,' Pete mused quietly.

'At the moment…it's meaningless,' Jack said, 'but the so-called thinkers are on it so maybe they'll finally come up with something.' Jack's eyes became cold and hard, debating whether it would ever happen. Four hundred of the top minds across the country had come up with the grand total of squat. Jack was mystified these science prodigies hadn't found at least something, some meagre whiff of anything resembling pay dirt. That was something else no one had an answer to…their baffling lack of answers. It bugged him because it seemed wrong which in itself seemed perversely right.

Maybe Nagoya was part of the puzzle, Jack thought, a modern manufacturing hub in Aichi, smack bang in the middle of Japan's largest island, Honshu. Was there something unique about it, a distinction that set it apart, made it unique? He felt the stirrings of another headache as tangled questions started stacking up in his brain.

'Well I see it's world famous for its Tebasaki.' Pete said, staring deadpan at his laptop.

Jack glanced at him curiously, 'So, what is—'

'Grilled chicken wings, deep fried and smothered with a mouth-watering seasoning, according to the JNT site anyway.'

Jack rolled his eyes, 'you idiot…keep digging my friend,' he said, giving a small half smile, salivating on the inside, thinking how welcome a bucket of chicken wings would be, chuck in a serve of fries too. He licked his lips and refocussed.

Jack was studying the similarities between the backcountry objects and those in geosynch orbit above it, struggling to understand the relationship with the enigmatic Japanese dome. Maybe it was a red herring, maybe it wasn't, perhaps it was super critical. Jack sighed long and hard. 'Fuck me,' he breathed, chewing his lip. Pete saw the cold smile and spots of colour in his cheeks. 'This is killing me,' Jack said wearily, pushing his head up and down in a stretching motion, puffing his cheeks out. He felt a sharp ache in his throat, wondering idly if he'd caught a virus. A week in bed, even in hospital, a bloody nuthouse would do, all of it having a lovely soothing ring to it.

'So, um…let's go over it one more time,' Pete said. 'We have an image composed of numbers that aren't just numbers. They turn out to be coordinates leading to a planetarium that looks pretty darn similar to the crazy object that probably sent us the image. And then add in the coordinates to L1 and the message and everything else, seriously, I've said it before…this is a fucking madhouse.'

Jack smiled crookedly, nodding. 'You know it Pete.'

***

Nate looked back at the imposing line of Ospreys with their props folded back like massive grounded insects. Military personnel had taken up stations about a hundred metres from the MVs, facing outward with LSAT rifles fixed at their waist as though an imminent threat was milling around in the Transantarctic Mountains.

'…they reckon we're in Afghanistan? Yoshi said wryly, glancing around, wondering where the sky full of warplanes was at. 'We're in the middle of nowhere trying to do something for, uh…everyone, who the hell'd be a threat?' He scanned the horizon again, more seriously. 'Do they have intel we don't?'

Nate rolled a shoulder, 'they'd never tell us anyway. It'd be need to know if they did, it's just how they roll, although some of these terrorist groups are seriously messed up, so who knows.'

Yoshi and Nate had carte blanche approval from the Secretary of Defence through the Joint Chiefs and POTUS to effort any numerical inputs they saw fit, until or more likely if, Nate thought, they got word from Mission to effort something different. Their larger role was to implement strategies agreed on by the genius-tanks but all they were getting was the drawn-out sound of crickets, leaving them pretty much on their own. Nate was with Jack, the lack of input from the ground teams was inexplicable, almost as though there was a conspiracy of silence. Nate knew it was absurd but the nagging feeling was persistent. They'd had so much time, the best brains on the planet, it was almost as though the planet's higher thinking had been nulled somehow. What they did know was that coherence, logic or meaning was painfully absent, all they had was silence and obtuse messages.

'Okay!' Nate said emphatically, gazing at the tablet in front of him. 'We know it gets Pi, and the Spheres are well, spheres so that makes perfect sense, right? Maybe too much sense…perhaps it's too obvious,' Nate said pensively, squashing his brow. 'Maybe lateral thinking is the way to go, you know off-script.' Yoshi looked at Nate sideways, jaded by the endless guessing. Nate paused only long enough to collect his thoughts, 'we could try Bijective, Negabinary, Fibonacci, Pascal's, Negative or Signed bases…but do you know how many frigging numeral systems there are? We'd be here for years trying them all, hoping one might be right, that we magically stumble over it, assuming there is one that does the job, or is impactful at all.' Nate was proffering opinion and arguing himself down, then repeating the same painful process, staring into thin air, drained and pretty sure it would all eventually come back to Pi…but he wasn't completely sure.

Yoshi grimaced 'uh…it has decimals of Pi running all over it Nate so why would it be anything else?' Der, he felt like yelling, his deeper mind warning him that the numerals could be just a ruse to mask the real fix.

'Yeah, we assume it's still Pi but look at it, it's just a blur.' Nate gazed at it, cupping his brow doubtfully. 'It could be The Colonel's secret bloody recipe but we can't assume, we need to temper logic a little bit.' He gave a forced smile, nodding tensely at Yoshi.

'Whatever though, until we decide it's a no go, let's stick with it,' Yoshi said. 'Leave the other options as that…redundancies in case we need them.'

267

Nate was suddenly unsure about everything, squinting at the haze of numbers. 'Have you, considered that these things aren't being directed by anyone?' He stared off in the distance somewhere, mulling it over.

Yoshi pushed the idea around in his head, intrigued and fearful, debating whether that might be good or bad, having no idea.

Nate rubbed his gloved hands together, 'like they, uh…might be an intelligence in themselves, created to spread through space, maybe like Von Neumanns, advanced, maybe sentient in their own right?' His eyes sparkled with wonder, mouth curled with a hint of dread. 'Perhaps they pull out resources, self-replicate, just keep on going, overwhelming everything they find. You know, arrive, do their work, move on.'

'Do their work?' Yoshi repeated nervously, breathing a little quicker. 'I guess that's the million-dollar question…what is their work?' His face drew into a serious frown. 'You don't suppose they eat whatever they find to create new Spheres do you…like moons, ice, planets?' His eyes widened. 'People perhaps?' His breath was now bursting in and out in streams of vapour.

'I don't see any new Spheres…we're losing, not gaining,' Nate said, contemplating the end-game, thinking worst case scenario, conjuring endless darkness in his mind. Nate stared blankly at Yoshi, admitting there was bugger all they could do about any of it, irrespective of what the truth turned out to be. 'So how does kid-thing fit into it?' Nate mused curiously.

'Well, maybe they generated him,' Yoshi suggested, 'to be an emissary, you know, so they can deal with us on a personal level, to interact and converse without scaring the bejesus out of us.' He rubbed his eyes, massaging them gently with his knuckles. 'Although from what Tara said, his demeanour could hardly be described as diplomatic or calming. More like some fucking alien Riddler right?' He flashed a worn-out grin at Jack who forced a smile in return, tight, unconvincing.

Nate ground his teeth back and forth, clearly frustrated as he plumbed his mind, eventually cleaving his mouth apart, drawing a breath. 'What if we give 'em what they gave us, binaries in ASCII format, just come out with it. Something like, oh I don't know…what the fuck do you want?' He threw his arms in the air theatrically. 'Just bloody get it out there. Surely it's worth a shot. Start with the bleeding obvious, work backwards from there.'

Nate was unsure, 'that's, well, sort of a plan I guess.' Barely, he told himself. DoD and NASA had selected his team, that was fine, but doing all this in isolation? That was never the deal, he'd gone into this expecting reams of help from across the country and the world, so where was it? Instinct told him all was not well, every fibre in his body uneasy, agitated…suspicious.

Yoshi snapped his fingers at Nate, 'no time to drift off…so it's an idea I guess…do we need approval?' Yoshi said, nervous about arbitrarily applying such a goofy plan.

'I'm not waiting two hours for an inevitable *your call*. Get it up, let's give it a crack, that's the brief.' Nate sighed gently, throwing Yoshi a reassuring smile, hiding his trepidation, taking a stride over to the table and sitting down with a grunt. Nate tapped out some keystrokes on the laptop, bringing up the ASCII Text>Binary converter.

Yoshi felt ashamed when he gawked at the juvenile nature of what they were sending, looking at the words again and agreeing it was farcical, barely passing the test for intelligence. Just get it out there he sighed to himself, we'll start basic, work upward, downward, sideways from there. Winging it was one of the few options they had, and this bullshit right here qualified summa cum laude. He typed in the words, leaving out the F-bomb. Maybe it was the way to go, he concluded, cautiously clicking on Binary Value. A flood of numerals appear that looked ridiculously long.

011101110110100001100001011101000010000001100100011011110010000001111001
01101111011101010010000001110111011000010110111001110100001000000110011001110010
011011110110110100100000011101010111001100111111

'Lot of numbers for one sentence,' Nate said. 'Plug 'em in, see what happens.

Yoshi nodded, agreeing it was a shitload of numbers for six stupid words but hey, it was worth a shot. 'So, a long hold for one, short for zero, right?'

'Yup,' Nate replied. 'They should be smart enough to work it out. Depends whether they're interested, whether they want to listen, whether they give a crap.'

Yoshi felt like he was performing some sort of bizarre alien choreograph and after a few minutes he was done, got up, stepped back and felt his right arm flushed with blood, aching.

Yoshi eyed Nate thoughtfully. 'Tara said kid-thing reckoned we were a disappointment.' He slowly shook his head, frowning, 'I mean, seriously, what is it to them, are they like keeping score…on everyone?' He smiled thinly but there was an undercurrent of fear, unease certainly. 'Hey, maybe if you don't achieve a decent rating its good night, finished, done. It's a visit from the Headmaster and bit by bit you get pulled to pieces, packed up, filed away, ready for some other up and comer to slip in and have a shot.'

Nate gave a sharp, bemused snort, chuckling nervously, 'beware the low score right?'

They sensed a low-pitched vibration, something throaty, resonating in their bones, jangling their insides. It wasn't long before it became a bowel-shaking clamour, gradually joined by a different, pulsing sound. Nate instinctively looked to the sky, thinking it might be an Osprey returning from wherever the hell it dropped the bodies off to. No, the sky was clear and anyway, it was all wrong, too deep even for an MV22. The military personnel were staring like Muppets in their direction, standing sessile like toy soldiers.

Suddenly, the Sphere exploded in blue light, tinting the entire landscape for as far as they could see, even extending to the ragged peaks of the Mountains in the distance. The U-shaped valleys, the moraines, troughs, the kames were painted with an almost phosphorescent sapphire glow, intensely beautiful and fearfully supernatural.

***

Griffin got a phone call from Sydney's St Vincent's Hospital an hour ago, receiving the first tranche of results on Tara's condition. Under normal circumstances it would have been news without peer, but in these times of almost counter-intuition, well, it was intriguing but not off the scale. Tara's initial medical workup was, to say the least, a little off. She had been probed and analysed by a team of genetic programmers and molecular biology whizzes, and to put it mildly, they'd had the time of their lives. Spirited theories were flung around over pots of coffee, boxes of jelly donuts and a hell of a lot of whiteboard scribbling and arguments. But bottom line was that none of them had ever seen anything like it. The results were, in the lead programmer's words, fucking awesome. He'd followed that up with a profanity filled reference to it being impossible and how they could possibly have screwed up the tests. They'd re-run the Pluripotent stem tests and various other controls a dozen times…the inexplicable results were scientifically, definitively verified.

Her treating physician, Dr Bart Halverson removed his glasses and placed them on his desk, telling them with the graveness of a Presidential Decree that her biological age was two hundred and sixty years with an error margin of three point six years. Griffin's response was predictable, swearing into the phone in a cloud of spittle, calling him a fucking whack job and hanging up. In the back of his mind he believed it, but Griffin's military mind discarded it by reflex. Steeling himself, he rubbed his eyes, straightened his tie and called him back, having a much more tolerant conversation. Halverson carried on excitedly about something called DNA methylation, which he assured him, spoke to age very accurately. The only thing Griffin was assured of was that Dr Nerd spoke a very different language, but he quickly got the thrust of what he was saying.

Verified or not, none of them could wrap their brains around it. How the hell could someone age the best part of three centuries in the space of a few puny minutes Earth time? Most of them got the nuts and bolts of time dilation and relativity quite well. That is, if you arrowed into space at close to the speed of light, Einstein's special relativity says that one day in ship time could equal years back on Earth. Same with black holes, if you dropped far enough into the gravity well, without getting caught of course, one day in there could be the best part of a decade back home. But it wasn't like that, and it wasn't like Tara went forward or backward in time like Becker and his team did, this was way, way different. She'd stepped through a wooden door and returned to Antarctica almost eight times older than she was when she'd left a few minutes earlier. Halverson and his crew were adamant that the UV damage and oxidation they'd detected in the tests meant she had to actually live the years. That is, day after day of UV exposure and bodily function, digestion and the like, so the question was obvious, the implication thunderous. Where had she been? Tara thought she'd just aged in the blink of an eye but perhaps a very long life indeed had been hers, and she simply had no memory of it.

***

Jack had been trying to raise the base at the Pole for five minutes but comms were a complete boner. Griffin had the Pentagon try and raise the military commander on the Osprey's two-way with the same result. Nothing at all, no static, no acoustic noise, certainly no voice.

Jack saw Griffin flinch as his cellphone rang, then check himself. 'Griffin,' he snapped into the phone, pondering if it could possibly, perchance be good news. Just once he groaned to himself. His phone had been the conduit for some seriously screwed up news so no one was thrilled when the damn thing sparked to life. Jack stiffened, seeing his expression darken. Griffin gave an exaggerated 'Jesus Christ almighty,' and slapped the phone in Jack's hand, eyeing him grimly.. It was the NASA Administrator, Matt Jenson, his voice, sleep deprived at best.

What Matt said next was his worst nightmare and in the seconds it took for his words to escape, Jack's world imploded into shards of light that swam in front of him. In his mind it was game over. Earth and everything she sustained was doomed, not immediately and maybe not even because of what he'd said, but it cast in stone the course they were on. The end of the road was now clearly sign-posted, bold black words screaming "Death and Extinction Ahead" and they were stuck in an old clunker with no steering wheel, no brakes and no hope.

'You still there?' Jenson whispered lamely.

'What do we do? What in the name of…what do we do?' Jack spluttered, feeling his brain slowing, a dead stall not far away.

'Tell Griffin, he needs to brief the President,' Jenson said, hanging up abruptly. He had no bloody idea what they could do, absolutely no idea at all. Nothing was his best guess.

Jack handed Griffin his phone, barely able to hang onto it.

'Well?' He demanded, his heart rifling, like it wasn't in the place it was supposed to be.

Jack felt almost concussed, trying to think through a thickening haze, 'um, Keck 1 scope in Hawaii reports that Jupiter has, well…gone.'

Griffin stared at him, the only sign of life being a slight raise of his left eyebrow, a twitch in his cheek. 'Oh Christ!' Griffin finally screamed, looking blankly at Ballard. 'It's not like we didn't expect it but shit, shit!' He punched his phone, lurching away, head bent slightly forward. Ballard and Hillier followed him, barely inches behind, leaving Jack and Pete peering at one other, sharing the horror of a global death sentence no one could escape.

The loss of Jupiter was sort of anticipated but it still remained squarely in the hidden recesses, the horrible place where never-can-happen things bubbled and gurgled like a hideous witch's brew. Now it was apparently hard-wired into Earth's history like the world wars and George Washington's fucking birthday. To have it actually happen, to be elevated to F-A-C-T, well, Jack could see the whole shebang was devolving into devastating, shambolic absurdity.

'The thing about it is that it didn't just vanish instantly,' Jack said, fighting to keep himself together, 'it sort of uh, faded and then, poof, gone entirely.' He gazed incredulously, lifting one eyebrow higher than the other. '…according to Matt, the Keck feed showed it coming apart, vanishing, over a period of about sixty seconds, until all that was left was like that bright bit on those old TVs when you turn 'em off.' Jack felt his pulse becoming erratic. 'All sixty-three of its moons

270

are still there,' he added croakily, 'motherless…just wandering around up there, goddamn nomads in space…for the moment.'

Pete gasped loudly. 'What could do that?' He squeezed his eyes shut, appalled and in the same breath, awed. 'How do you do that to something so immense…and leave nothing behind? Pete seemed to wobble as he wrestled with something that irrational. 'The Moon is unexplainable…but Jupiter is so much more. It's like, a thousand Earth's…right?' Pete closed his eyes again, feeling the futility of their plight settle heavily in his gut.

'So…what's next then?' Jack muttered, tapping his forehead audibly. Pete was wondering the same thing. Polar ice, the Moon, Jupiter…it utterly beggared belief.

'They're, uh…getting bigger,' Pete said faintly.

'What do you mean?' Jack quizzed distantly, seeing Griffin browbeating Ballard and Hillier about something, pointing his finger at them like a dagger.

'The things that've gone…they're getting bigger…more massive.'

Jack shortened his gaze, narrowing his eyes, '…they are, indeed they are,' he said knowingly, before freezing abruptly. 'If that's a pattern, the next one is—' Jack paused, looking through the ponderous window panel at the Sun as it beat down on the space centre. It was Sol, their life-giver, the heart and soul of the solar system. If the pattern continued…he felt beads of sweat on his lip, wishing he could just blank out his thoughts, countering it with the Sun's lack of entanglement which should mean it was safe…right? Wrong, he slammed back, knowing the folly of applying anything that implied consistency or conforming to expectation.

Pete's mouth had dropped open, 'if they keep getting bigger it's not going to end well.'

'Oh shit…master of restraint,' Jack said acidly, 'these rumples in space, the corridors of gravity or whatever, we have no idea where they go but we know they're out of system.'

'That's what O'Donnell from JPL said.'

'Okay, so why are the Spheres here, near Earth when most of the targets, the majority of them, seem unrelated to us?' Jack stood facing the window, 'are there other poor sods out there being treated the same by these arseholes?'

Pete's face brightened slightly, 'hey…what if they're about to, um…maybe they'll push off, motor away to some other shit-out-of-luck planet.' He was nodding softly, leaning toward Jack.

'Wishful,' Jack breathed, 'time will tell. I don't think so but I damn well hope so.'

'Maybe they're everywhere,' Pete said, 'every intelligence gets a set of Spheres.'

Jack gave a brittle laugh, wagging his head numbly.

Pete watched as the Government huddle in front of them broke up and Griffin came muddling back. 'Okay, POTUS and his so-called chief science advisor want us working on two fronts.' He lifted his chin, curling his mouth facetiously. 'Everyone thinks he's a fucking genius but it's a no-brainer. Why POTUS has faith in him I'll never know, he's such a snivelling twat…must have something over him, no way he's there on merit,' Griffin sneered sniffing loudly. 'Maybe Willard's been screwing around, Mason found out and that's his payback.' His features drew into a malicious leer, then quickly reset. 'Anyway, the first is working on shutting the things down which we've got going on with Sagan in orbit and the teams in Antarctica, and around the country. Second, we need to know what the Jupiter event means for us short term and once we know definitively, we'll clue you in. We're assembling the best from around the US at Stanford for a, bit of a shindig. Hillier and I are relocating to The Pentagon with the rest of the POTUS team as part of Project STRATA.'

With that they turned on their heels and with no hint of farewell, exited Building 30 along with their security team, heading for the helipads and immediate extraction.

Sagan had slipped into the Hubble field of view, only a few hundred clicks from the remaining five objects in space, gradually transiting east and dipping below Earth's horizon.

Pete felt some comfort that the best minds in the States would be in the same place at the same time, focussed on the same event. Unravelling implications was great, but for all intents and purposes they were like a newborn kitten raising a tremulous paw at a cornered lion. 'Without Jupiter will Earth's…will any orbits be stable?' Pete said uncertainly, thinking he sort of knew the answer but planetary physics, Newtonian stuff, wasn't really his gig.

'Orbits aren't the problem I don't think,' Jack said thoughtfully. 'Remember Shoemaker-Levy…the comet Jupiter ripped into pieces? It's more that sort of thing, its gravity protects us, without it we're a hell of a lot more exposed, but even that's not the worst of it,' Jack said, peering up broodingly through the panoramic window at the sky, losing himself in thought.

'What?' Pete prompted abruptly, seeing him zone out.

'Asteroid belt,' he said quietly, 'it's only there because Jupiter's there, um…was there I mean.' He sucked a breath into his lungs, shaking his head vigorously, 'without it the Sun'll be lord and master so we're gonna be in a world of hurt soon enough. I'm no expert but I reckon we're in serious trouble.' He stopped and thought about it, 'if we had a decent way to divert these things it might be different but we've got nothing but hot air and empty promises.' he said, shrugging his shoulders almost in resignation. 'You and I and everyone else at NASA have been banging on about it for how long? The sodding planet is powerless.' He clutched at his neck, scratching his Adam's apple roughly, sniffing irritably. 'What's the point having kick-arse NEO programs that can identify a bogey, plot its fucking course to the centimetre, then have no way of fending the damn thing off? What a short-sighted, stupid approach.' Jack curled his lip sourly, frustrated by a political system that had effectively doomed the planet through its self-serving, myopic focus. 'It's like being able to find every piece of gold on the planet and having nothing more than a beach spade to dig it up.'

'There's always something better to spend the green on,' Pete said, 'and now it's come back to bite us on the arse like we always knew it might.'

'Let's wait and see what these so-called geniuses come up with…that should be worth waiting for.' Jack's cheerless grin hid a fathomless dread, a knowing that whatever they did wasn't going to mean squat.

***

'We'll be closing on the Sphere in twelve minutes,' Vic said, checking the RRS data.

'Sky, which one?' Harry rifled. He really didn't think it mattered, "cause all the fuckers looked the same" he'd said gruffly, certain it was nothing more than a lottery, no guarantees, apart from there being no guarantees. It was only the Spheres positions in space that set them apart. Maybe it meant something, maybe it didn't but if it did, they were clueless until they sampled a few.

They'd spoken to Jack about it and he'd left it up to them, coming clean on what they already knew, he couldn't add dick from Earth. The off-hand, almost casual announcement about Jupiter blew their minds, Earth, the solar system, all the bits and pieces were seemingly eroding like an eraser across a pencil sketch.

Sky glanced at Vic in surprise. 'Y-you actually want me to choose?' She said, doing a partial double take. 'I wouldn't know where to start, what to use as criteria, a baseline— '

'Just pick a bloody Sphere,' Harry snapped. 'None of us has a clue and it's no time for statistical analysis, just a blind guess will do, maybe we'll get lucky.'

She peeped through the glass panel. 'Okay, the one at the very top there, that looks— '

'Oh God not that one!' Harry cried. Sky snapped her head around, eyes wide.

'Kidding,' he shrilled, flashing a toothbrush grin. 'The top one it is. Vic, at your pleasure.'

Vic gripped the hand controller and deflected it for an RCS burn to pitch Sagan toward the chosen bogey near the top of the inferred structure.

'Approach at orbital headway, target is fifty metres from contact,' Harry said carefully. 'Before we barrel on in, give it a chance to react.'

'Copy. Contact fifty seconds, five hundred metres.'

Sweet potato, Harry mulled vaguely, that was the striking colour as they approached, a faultless match. He despised the taste of the beastly vegetable, so the analogy was apt he reckoned, distasteful, the both of them.

'Hundred metres…eighty…sixty…' A final puff of hydrazine was expelled from the fore RCS vents to null velocity, bringing Sagan to a halt relative to its target. They were literally eyeballing the Sphere but slipping off to the side as Vic fought to establish complimentary motion using the starboard Verniers. The polar orbit was inexplicably stable for the Spheres but required a small, constant burn from Sagan to keep them close. 'Okay we're uh, stable with a burn rate of oh point four kilos.'

None of them could see any movement. There was no patterning on the surface, no ripples, just a mirror surface free of any visible imperfection. Still no reflection of the craft though, stars yes, Sun yes, Sagan no. Did it distinguish natural from created?

'So how long do we wait?' Sky said, breathing deeply, seeing there was no identifiable reaction, as though it didn't want to know them.

'I honestly thought it might pull us in,' Harry said. 'We've never entered one by choice, so whether we can just sail on in, well— '

'Are we ready?' Vic asked impatiently, fixing his gaze on Sky. It was time to take this thing by the scruff of the neck and give it a decent shake. Vic punched out a kiss of gas, inching Sagan forward until it penetrated the envelope, which it did without resistance.

They punched into the Sphere, then into space with instantaneous velocity, Vic immediately seeing stars everywhere, passing them like cars on a busy highway, whole galaxies - spirals, ellipticals, irregulars - began whizzing past as Sagan arrowed into the vacuum. Everything was there in a seeming role call of celestial bits and pieces. Skylar felt panic return in a gut-wrenching rush, wrestling blindly with the scope of what was all around them. Massive black holes were guzzling dust and debris, colourful supernova remnants were everywhere, gorgeous nebulae, spinning neutron remnants, quasars, blazars, magnetars, comets, glorious molecular clouds and every other object imaginable were right there beyond the window panel, implausibly close. So many, so quickly she gasped, baffled as to how it could all be squashed into their diminutive field of view.

Sky could tell they were slowing down, seeing a distant spiral galaxy start to slowly gain form ahead of them and the background motion of stars and matter braking dramatically. There was no inertia though, no sense of additional weight as they presumably lost speed, without the slightest nod to Newton's laws of motion. The galaxy ahead gathered detail, it's beautifully symmetrical and loosely wound arms beckoning them in a rainbow of colour and harmony. They were almost upon it, maybe two thirds of the way from the centre of the galaxy where they could see a cataclysmic inferno as a colossal blackness guzzled matter in an orgy of fire and chaos. Among the stuff of the spiral now, clouds of gas and dust were everywhere, an enveloping mist, pinpricked with dazzling points of light. One star loomed brighter through the background of sparkling dust, a gorgeous yellow flame, front and centre. The nature of the star became suddenly and breathtakingly obvious, Vic saw it immediately, blowing out a sharp breath, openly staring, spellbound. It was crazy, mind blowing, almost inconceivable in scale.

Sky was struggling like a CPU burdened with too many tasks, awe-stricken, blood pumping wildly as she fought to take everything in. 'What—, 'she paused and breathed in and out shakily, 'would it take to construct…that? It must have more stuff in it than the star.' She murmured an expletive under her breath, aimed at the floor of the shuttle.

Harry stared at her dumbly, guessing they were in for another irritating Q&A session where "A" didn't exist, would probably never exist and "Q" was just a fucking pain in the arse. That said, he tried to imagine the living space on the object, knowing it must be hundreds of billions of square kilometres, probably way more, engineering on the highest level imaginable. Whoever, whatever had done it had taken what they had and not only completely redesigned it but shipped in solar system loads of material from God knew where to extend it! And by extend he reckoned they were talking billions of times over. 'Fuck me,' Harry murmured, almost allowing "how " to escape his lips but managing to wedge his mouth closed before it got out.

Below them it presented as some incredibly robust material, completely encircling a yellow star that nestled in a cavity not much bigger than it, at its centre, some hundreds of millions of kilometres distant, Harry assumed. It was an almighty solid, metal wheel, very clearly populated, with its life-giver smack bang in the bull's eye of the structure. The synergy with the objects they'd seen in Antarctica and elsewhere was palpable to the eye. This star, like the Spheres, was nestled in the centre of the silvery plates girdling them, extending out to the extremity of the system. Sky's thoughts were like molasses – stodgy and dense, making her feel like heaving over the aluminium benchtop she was clutching, feeling drugged and dizzy as she surveyed the absurd cosmic design.

The disc looked thin but Vic knew that was only relative to its ridiculous breadth because it must have been hundreds of clicks from top to bottom…maybe a lazy billion or so across. Sky couldn't avoid the numbing sensation that the orbital dimensions of the star had simply crystallised into some gargantuan metal ocean. Vic was peering at the star as it slowly moved below their side of the disc to the other side, watching light gradually receding across the disc as night started to fall on their side of the implausible pinwheel, the dark shadow of space slowly consuming it.

As soon as light from the star disappeared, the "night" sky lit up, several bright white discs appearing, some close, some distant, all moving across the face of the mighty metal surface at height.

'Moons,' Harry said. Not a question, more a statement, not that anyone gave a shit about his pathological hatred for empty questions.

Vic glanced around, 'over there,' he said abruptly, 'where the star came from…see the mirrors?' He studied it closely, assuming they reflected light from the star onto the moons, following them as they transited across.

Sky's head was snaking everywhere as she grappled with the surreal vista. 'I can see oceans, maybe lakes down there,' Sky said, wiggling and squirming in her chair. Vic continued to marvel at her change in mindset. A day ago she was on the verge of a grand mal meltdown, would've gladly murdered both of them and flown the shuttle herself if it got her a way home, but now…well, just in time he reckoned 'cause he was ready to jettison the other one into the vacuum.

Harry had a faraway look in his eyes. 'Did this galaxy look, uh…sort of familiar on the way in,' he said, 'and the star?'

'Yep,' Vic said, already harbouring the same idea he knew Harry was wrestling with.

'I didn't want to say anything,' Sky said, 'and I still don't.' Her mind was spinning in shrinking circles, approaching a similarly numbing conclusion.

'Look at the facts,' Harry said, '…same galaxy type, similar location on a spiral arm, by the look of it, same G-type yellow dwarf star, right? It's not proof by any stretch because we know how vast all this is, but it is, interesting.' He furrowed his brow, throwing it around, discarding it, then conceding it was a possibility.

Sky caught his gaze and held it. 'Could it really be…the Sun…in a few million years maybe? More to the point,' she said in a sunken whisper, 'is that us down there…Earth…humanity?'

Harry allowed himself a broad smile, splitting his beard like a ripped broadloom, 'I bloody hope so, because it means we've worked out a solution to all this, um…shit.'

Skylar was still shifting in her seat, frowning, unconvinced. 'I'm not sure that's it. Do you remember what Tara said about that kid? He said he was disappointed with us, you know, we hadn't fulfilled our potential, or words to that effect.' Sky paused, staring blankly at them. 'Maybe this is a glimpse of what we should've done, where we should be…shoving it in our face, showing us how messed up our decisions have been as a collective.' Her eyes went cold, 'this may not be in our future at all…maybe it's a different future,' she said, her face paling as she finished speaking, deeply uneasy with the implications of her own words.

Vic's eyes were closed, knowing it was all guesswork. 'Okay, so aside from flipping us the bird, telling us how backward we are, is there any learnings from this place?' Vic said, not seeing a goddamn thing. 'It's fine to show us this, but what do we take from it…clues, insights, what?'

'Maybe we're not supposed to take anything from it,' Harry said impatiently. 'Like you said Sky, it's just these fucking alien sycophants, maybe that's the game plan, to humiliate us, you know, penance for poor behaviour.' His mouth twitched with a faint smirk. 'We have no idea what might motivate an alien species…we don't, we can't,' he said, raising his hand and waving it irritably. 'Their whole sorry philosophy could be based on stupid mind games, thought experiments, cruelty, nothing can be ruled in or out,' he said, flashing a miserable smile.

Sky looked appalled. 'Jesus, thanks for the motivational speech Harry.

'Well I'm not here to serve up bullshit or kiss anyone's arse. We can have opinions, you guys love guessing, but at the end of the day it's not worth shit. The truth is out there, it's the eating that'll define it.'

'So, eating shit, is that the deal?' Sky said, crossing her arms.

'Eating humble pie when they send you the same way as Jupiter, that's what,' he said, glaring at her briefly, grinning spitefully.

'Okay, chill,' Vic said, raising his voice. An explosive outburst was the last thing they needed because it might send Sky back from where she came, and that wouldn't be good for anyone.

Harry saw it from the corner of his eye, knowing what it was before he turned. 'Here we go again folks,' He said monotone, seeing the familiar orange mist rain through the shuttle, growing into a fog so opaque they couldn't see their hands in front of their face, and then instantly clearing.

'Holy…so no journey back, just straight out, snap of the fingers stuff,' Vic said curiously, seeing Earth in all its sapphire glory below them. 'These things really are incredible…magic right?'

'Yep, magic, pure and simple,' Harry agreed wanly. 'So, we got what from it Skylar…you know, the one you chose?' He was still grinning, softly.

'Well not much. There was a message I think but I don't see how it helps us.'

'I'll say it again,' Harry said, 'I don't think there was anything to get.'

'Yeah well, if we take that attitude we may as well bend over and kiss it all goodbye,' Sky said, sighing heavily. 'Jesus Harry, we have to assume there's a way out of this…we have to.'

Vic had his headset on, about to try and raise Jack on the S-band.

Harry wasn't sure one way or the other but he hoped to hell Sky was right, or at least not completely wrong.

***

Paul Bloom, the Acting Assistant Secretary of Defense, had lines of sweat glistening on his upper lip, as he pondered the events that roped him into this godawful gig. It was like they wanted a volunteer and everyone took a step back and there he was, hanging there like a damn fool, blowing in the wind. He swore under his breath as he, stared at the real-time horror story in front of him.

He was standing at the head of the Annenberg Auditorium at Stanton U in Pasadena, about to address a gathering of astrophysical luminaries, the lot of them gawking at him in various states of tedium and impatience. Some serious players were in residence, gathered under the authority of the US President and ferried here, some forcibly, by several dozen CIA and DIO operatives and a fleet of daunting Piasecki choppers.

Bloom gazed over the sea of VIPs, heaving an anxious sigh. Seated around the massive table was a smorgasbord of brand-name scientists: a Guggenheim Fellow, a Duffield Professor, a Scientist in Residence, an Emeritus Laucasian Professor and a trio of other world-renowned physicists and planetary astronomers, not to mention a couple of irritatingly outspoken exobiologists.

The room was a cacophony of noise, blended voices that summed to little more than white noise. Bloom detested scientists and he knew most of them hated Government types so it didn't auger well for an affable meeting. When they were interviewed or soapboxing their maddening theories, they were brilliant and incredibly insightful, but in a group of their peers, mother fuck, he thought sullenly, recalling what he'd seen so far. Most were inclusive but some were little more than self-seeking mercenaries, intolerably self-centred, despite the global stakes that seemed to be on the line.

He felt like screaming at them, calling them a pack of narcissistic arseholes, and that's where the meeting was at, getting nowhere fast, in fact, it seemed that none of these so-called geniuses had any definitives about Jupiter at all. They sort of knew what the impact of losing it might mean, but everyone almost to a man or woman contradicted the other and it was escalating from disagreement into personal insults. So far it was a waste of time, his role as facilitator pretty much a failure, making him feel like running through the open door with not a care in the world about destination.

Within the confines of the room were many of America's best minds yet they were struggling to draw anywhere near the conference objectives, that is, agreed, locked down scientific truths. Every planet's orbit would be impacted, but for Earth it would be small because Newton's Law determined that Jupiter was simply too far away to inflict any major damage, at least in the short term. There was a pseudo-consensus on that, as there was around the harmonics of the Jovian asteroid belt. With Jupiter now a memory, the Sun was the guiding force for billions of asteroids and that meant everyone unfortunate enough to be in the inner solar system was in a serious pickle.

Several players used their scientific insight to the fullest, regaling the group by referring to God as the only one who could save them now. That was the size of it, the smartest people on the planet had few answers apart from the bleeding obvious and a few religious citations and cheap credits thrown in to button the whole lot down.

The asteroid belt was now a major threat to the planet. No one knew exactly where the pieces of rock would end up, but modelling was the next imperative using Einstein's general relativity, specifically the "matter tells space how to curve" bit, to determine likely transit lines. NASA's Dawn spacecraft was currently orbiting Ceres, the largest of the asteroids, hopefully giving up some data for accurate computer modelling to start, allowing the speed and direction of a great many asteroids to be predicted and plotted, giving Earth early warning of any potential death chunks. And of course then there were the moons of Jupiter, all of them shuffling tirelessly toward the inner solar system…all sixty-three of them.

Some were the size of Mercury.

So, it was the general conclusion that the loss of the dappled titan would eventually reach out with tens of millions of asteroids motoring toward the zone of warmth, and Earth had little hope of avoiding contact. And by contact it was implied that meant obliteration of all things. It was simply a matter of probability, and the odds were massively stacked against it. Earth was being fired on by a canon full of buckshot and there was simply too many of them, from a few metres across to virtual worlds that were right now streaming toward the cavernous gravity well of the Sun.

NASA had their Near Earth Object programs on maximum alert with every scope running their automatic pointing, imaging and analysis around the clock. The Catalina Sky Survey, Pan-STARRS, NEOSSat, LINEAR, Spacewatch and NEOWISE were scouring space to gun barrel any incoming extinctors or smaller pieces of talus that might be on a parabolic course for Earth. The best part was that everyone understood the darkly humorous paradox that existed and no one knew it better than Pete and Jack at NASA. Earth barely had more than harsh language to throw at anything they identified, so the voice of many around the world was…why the hell are we even looking? That was the consensus from the mass media and they'd absolutely nailed it.

Concepts for dealing with space chunks were many and varied, some serious, some less so, others almost comical. There were nuclear strikes and kinetic interceptors to nudge them of course, or maybe paint them in bright colours to increase push from solar radiation. Or how about a solar sail, gigantic mirrors or attaching a honking big rocket to steer the fuckers away? All these ideas sounded at least a little hopeful but none of them were in any shape to help because they were little more than scrawlings on a whiteboard.

These others had taken Jupiter knowing it would spell the end for Earth… for all life on the planet. The question was on everyone's lips, already shouted around the globe, on the streets and at the highest levels of Government. If they wanted us gone, why didn't they just get it over with and pull the fucking trigger? For some unfathomable reason, it seemed like the pain was being prolonged.

The Stanford crew were scheduled to continue working on the Jupiter Event for the next week but the preliminary upshot from one of the greatest scientific get togethers of all time was that Earth had little chance of surviving and perhaps it had none.

29. Genesis

"I don't paint dreams or nightmares, I paint my own reality." *~ Frida Kahlo*

The thing in front of them looked like nothing they could possibly have imagined, conveying one overall, spine tingling sensation – sharp. Connie was peering at the thing through the deeply recessed porthole of the AVP, Becker floating behind her, similarly struck by the piece of alien architecture seemingly eyeballing them from only a few thousand metres away.

'How utterly odd,' she said, pulling her hands through her hair, not taking her eyes off it, befuddled by its appearance.

Before them was a grey sphere maybe ten clicks through the middle with a surface that looked densely ribbed, intricately cut by a series of ridges and valleys that ran around the surface of the object at an angle of about thirty degrees, as viewed from the AVP. The most unnerving feature wasn't its size or the unusual surface patterning – it was the three-hundred-and-sixty-degree mass of translucent, acicular needles that spread from its curvature and into space like protective barbs.

'If I told you it made no sense what— '

'It must make sense to whoever created the damn thing,' Connie interrupted, glancing at the O2 pressure gauge showing slightly less than fifty pounds 'We've got thirty minutes of air,' she said, staring at him uneasily. 'We either sit here and run out of air or we give that thing a prod.'

'I say we sit here and die,' Becker muttered, winking nervously, 'but that's just me.'

'You idiot,' she grunted.

'Go…take us in closer…slowly.'

'Thanks for the heads up, I'll take it onboard.' She rolled her eyes, moving over to the Nav Panel by gripping and gently pushing off the wall and the ESU unit. Connie grabbed the joystick, thumbing the pressure throttle for the aft thrusters. All they needed was a single spurt and they were on their way.

'Shit, too fast!' She barked to herself, countering it with a brief fore burn to null some of their momentum. 'Okay okay,' she breathed, 'five metres…better.' Connie swiped sweat from her forehead with a finger, watching it float away into the cabin. Interesting, she thought absently as she watched them drift away like soap bubbles on the wind. Everything in nature wants to be a sphere, that's where the balance is. If you have enough mass to create a decent gravitational field, or tiny and fluid enough, then Mother says you have to be a sphere, no arguments, that's just the way it is.

'Uuum, uh…Connie, what is that?' Becker said unsteadily, half knowing what it might be as it orbited the heavily bristled Sphere, seeing it inexplicably slip into view.

'Holy mother—' Connie said, a hand flying to her chest, 'I-It's a goddamn Soyuz…what is it…what the hell?' She gawked at it for a while, speechless, scared by its apparent demise. It's broken hatch…solar panels all busted up.'

'Whatever happened, they're dead, whoever was in there, they're gone…along with the air,' Becker said.

'Does that mean, you know…Jesus, why is their hatch hanging open like that? Did they bolt in their suits or were they, um, spirited out?' She gazed at Becker goggle-eyed, confused.

'Focus, don't screw this up,' Becker said, his hands cold and moist with sweat.

She forced herself to watch the partially crushed craft loop below the strange horizon, vanishing among an endless forest of sparkling, spiny bilges.

'Time to contact?' Becker asked firmly.

'Uh, twenty-five hundred metres…four minutes.'

'Bring it up short, let's not just barge in like we own the place.'

'Seriously, who do you think you're talking to?'

'Just saying,' he said defensively.

'Don't.' She said, turning to the avionics panel, monitoring their approach, heart pounding, eyes searching for problems. Slowing the craft further, they slipped to within a hundred metres, reducing speed to zero with two brief puffs of propellant at fifty metres. The AVP was now motionless in space only a few ship lengths from the seemingly razor-sharp terminations that shone perilously in the dingy glow.

'You know if this thing decides to up and go we're not in a good place,' Becker murmured, peering ominously at the thing in space.

'I'd worry more about running out of air, suffocating,' Connie said, working frantically on a solution, peering back at Soyuz which had reappeared, wondering what messed up strategy they'd decided on because it sure as hell hadn't worked, leaving a broken craft, probably two dead cosmonauts. Swallowing visibly, she put it out of her mind, focussing on the prickle-beast ahead.

'We can't get to it,' Becker said, stating the obvious. Connie gave him a sideways glance, the slightest sweep of amusement on her face. 'Always on the ball,' she said.

Whatever,' Becker said, shrugging, 'but this thing is nuts, why would it need protection, like protection from what?' He gulped, staring vacantly, hoping the steeples were some uber-complex apparatus, rather than a means of warding off something neither of them cared to imagine.

Connie narrowed her eyes on the tip of the structures but was struggling to focus. They seemed to vanish at the terminus rather than taper, so getting a sighter on them was nigh on impossible. 'They're like a centimetre wide, tapering to…dunno, visibly nothing at the top. I don't think sharp does them justice.' She envisioned them ending with a single molecule right at the apex, the concept of *"contact will cause injury"* taking on a brand-new level of hurt she was sure.

'It's a fucking cactus on steroids,' Becker offered intuitively.

Connie's breasts were rising and falling in quick succession as she struggled to draw breath in the anorexic atmo of the AVP, cabin pressure falling to single figure PSI. 'Twenty minutes,' she said, sweeping a hand across her moist forehead. 'We've got O2 canisters which'll give us another thirty minutes or so.' Her voice fell away as she sank into dark resignation, tears welling behind her eyes, accepting that there was no hope of rescue in this most ridiculous of places.

'Oh that's just great,' Becker murmured, gazing vacantly. 'An extra thirty minutes…gee, a whole thirty?' He offered with consternation that melted into a despairing headshake.

Numbers on the life support pressure gauge dwindled further into the yellow as they grudgingly followed its progress. Connie searched for options as she did a three-sixty, scanning the cabin, reaching out and abruptly grabbing the hand controller, initiating a small as possible forward burn, then countering with another from the aft.

'Christ,' Becker shouted, having no idea what she was trying to do. 'Are you actually trying to puncture the craft? Because you might wanna discuss it – '

'No, I'm trying to save the fucking craft, and us,' she barked, saliva punching away from her lips, propelled by the inertia of the explication.

The gigantic bilges were now just metres away and neither had any doubt that simple contact would shell the craft and they'd be ripped through the hull into space, eviscerated on the way through maybe, finished off by the pressureless nightmare beyond.

'Three minutes, give or take,' Connie said in a whisper, staring down at her boots as an uncomfortable warmth spread from her neck into her face. They could sense the loss of air pressure in their thickened lungs, between the ears, in their oxygen addled minds. Each of them cradled an atmosphere canister with a facemask, but neither could help wondering why…, a few additional, lousy minutes, a few thousand breaths. Connie stared at Becker dovelike, sadly silent, knowing a unpleasant death was staring them in the face. The warmth was displaced by an ice-cold panic rising up her spine, squeezing her heart, making it pump so hard it seemed like her whole body was pulsing in some sort of restless sympathy. She was struggling with the idea of losing existence, peering at the razor-edged needles beyond the window, whichever way she turned, death stared back.

Connie floated her way back to the Nav Panel and Becker watched her vacantly as she went, having given up any attempt at false bravado. With a facemask strapped to her face she was breathing as calmly as she could but losing the battle, contemplating what she was going to do. Joystick firmly in hand Connie locked the chair restraints, gesturing to Becker to hang onto something. He suddenly realised what she was going to do.

He pulled his facemask off long enough to yell, 'don't, you'll break the fucking hull. You're not trained to fly this thing.' Suffocating was one thing but feeling the rip of the vacuum, no way she'd take the risk of that happening. Becker had nothing, insanity perhaps?

She shrilled something unintelligible back at him, eyes like a caged cat, flitting from the Nav panel to Becker, then outside at the object. 'Hang on to something.' Connie said, gunning the engines and initiating a one hundred percent burn with what little prop remained. 'I'm not gonna float around here like a dumb fuck, waiting to run out of 02.' Becker's grip on the panel wall slipped and he was thrown toward the front of the ship as it thumped away from the sharpness. Becker saw her eyes fixed on one of the Nav displays, concentrating hard while the AVP bucked and shuddered.

Connie had armed the small fore-mounted thrusters to spray the Sphere with burnt hydrazine, which sent the pod hurtling in the opposite direction. She then shut off the burn, immediately engaging aft verniers to slow them, then bring them back in, sending Becker toward the back of the pod this time. Jesus, she's actually gone bonkers he thought quite seriously, grabbing at the handle on the equipment locker to right himself. Fucking female drivers, his pathetically misogynist brain registered as he watched in astonishment.

'Christ,' Becker said slowly, gaping at Connie for a moment, not believing what he was seeing. 'H-how could you know that? He said, still peering at the sight unfolding in the vacuum.'

'I didn't, I had no idea, but it made sense,' she murmured, just as surprised as Becker, taking shallow slurps of air. 'Maybe we have learned something along the way.' Connie turned fully toward it, properly studying what they were coming upon. She felt like all the blood had rushed to her head, making it tight and sore from accumulated pressure. The sight was nuts.

All the bilges were already part way into the body of the Sphere, disappearing much like a snail's antenna might disgorge and dwindle into its wrinkled body. After a minute or so the object was free of appendages, and apart from the oddly ribbed surface it was similar to the other objects they'd seen…just way bigger.

Connie was breathing thickly through her facemask, realising it meant little. If they couldn't get inside and find something to breathe they were cooked, now down to ten minutes of air left if they stayed calm.

'Do it,' Becker said, feeling numb. 'Go!'

Connie spurted the pod forward using both front and rear propellants to variously impel and impede until it was only a few metres from the intricately convoluted curvature.

'Um, you might want to take a look,' Becker said, seeing that she was glued to the velocity and ranging display.

'We're not moving Becker—' Looking up, she stopped talking, eyes growing like duck eggs. She whispered, 'oh wow.'

'I guess it sees us,' Becker offered thinly.

The massive object was changing colour from a submarine grey to a slightly dirty orange and then it started to gently spin, gathering momentum and rotating on a steeply inclined axis. No surprises there, she thought, focussing on their approach. Angular momentum was their thing. Must be important, Connie mused, feeling dizzy and distant, detached.

Becker turned to her and studied Connie closely, conceding that her brief piloting experience was all that separated them from a rather grisly end, and possibly from any life at all. Seeing her limpid brown eyes scan the Navigation panel he prayed, rolling his eyes slowly to the roof of the AVP, clenching everything.

'Ten metres,' she said staccato-like, '…five…t-two…'

The tiny pod touched the Sphere and met not the slightest resistance, not a surface of any kind or even a mild spring zephyr. As the pod descended into it, an observer outside would have seen the Sphere's original colour return, the rotation stop and the dense mat of bilges return in all their sharp-as-hell glory. The massive object flickered briefly, flickered again, then slowly faded, finally vanishing into the darkness of the vacuum.

***

They assumed they were in space somewhere but even after allowing their eyes to adjust, there were no stars, no scattered light, nothing. Connie felt panic in her chest as the suffocating darkness enveloped them and seemed to have no end. They had an hour's battery life in the pod to feed light and propulsion but only a few minutes of air so the electrics were a non-issue. Don't need light when you're dead, Connie brooded absently. She tasted burning stomach acid, fighting to swallow it, instead coughing and seeing her own death scribbled in front of her like a child's crayon drawing, fluorescent, horrible.

Taking small irregular breaths, they knew it would buy them maybe minutes, their O2 bottles now harrowingly light. Connie sensed heat growing in her sternum, a faint trembling in her cheeks as her demise took root in her mind. 'Fuck it,' she said dully, starting to sob, almost soundlessly in squeaks of pain, her shoulders shaking as she fought to stifle it. 'This is not how it's supposed to end Carson.' She stared at him, boring into him with massive chocolate eyes. 'It's not my time...not our time.'

Despite everything, Becker did a double take. 'Carson?' He said, slapping a hand against his cheek. 'Shit, you never call me that...this is serious, right?' He tried to smirk but his facial muscles closed down before he got half way there.

'Idiot,' she breathed faintly, smiling sadly at him, nodding minutely. Connie was about to tell Becker she was sorry for all the crap she'd piled on him over the years, but snapped her mouth shut, instead popping her eyes wide open, seeing a bright light on the wall, like the Sun had just poked through clouds after a thunderstorm. Swivelling around clumsily in zero-g they peered forlornly through the lead-glass portal.

'Holy sweet fuck,' Becker said, gripping his forehead.

They'd seen it before but the scale of what was around them still looked totally unreasonable.

'Is this good?' Becker croaked, praying.

Connie mumbled something as she gazed at it, like Becker, pleading for something life-giving. Irrespective, the overwhelming emotion was relief because they needed no convincing that this had to be better than suffocating in the dark.

'Is there any, um...end to it? Becker's eyes roamed around nervously, absorbing the view that was sort of familiar but still morbidly overwhelming.

Connie pushed her head around, taking in the monstrous chamber they were motoring through, much like a mosquito with a planet all to itself. In front of them was a dull space crammed full of the squat barrel shaped objects they'd seen before, looking pretty much the same but there were differences she thought, feeling a prickling sense of unease. Connie wasn't absolutely sure but the overall view seemed a bit off. They were lined up in the same geometric formation and like the other chamber it appeared to go on forever. Maybe it was just her sleep and oxygen deprived mind playing tricks, but still, the question remained, why were there so many of these trite looking objects?

'That's it,' Connie said sluggishly, fighting to slow her breathing down, at the same time wondering if there was air outside, or pressure of any kind.

Her head was blocking Becker's view outside. 'What?' He said but was met with silence. 'Hello?' He raised his palms and eyed her warily. 'You said "that's it"...what's it?

'The objects are closer, that's why it looks different.' She turned to him, 'so it could be the same place we saw from Sagan and the objects have been drawn closer, or it's a different chamber.'

281

'Brilliant, and I give a shit because?'

Connie snapped her mouth shut, crumpling her nose, 'Jesus, maybe this is the sort of thing we need to be noticing, trotting out our finer intelligence, it could be part of whatever's going on.'

He saw the fire in her eyes, 'okay, I get it.' Becker said, treading warily.

'Finer intelligence,' Connie repeated, looking at Becker's vacant dial, almost barking out loud but too scared to waste precious oxygen.

'I hope there's air out there,' Becker wheezed, 'if there is or isn't, how do we know?'

'There's no airlock so it'll be a one timer if we find out there's not.' She scraped her forehead with a knuckle, thinking it through, 'why would there be air, unless there's something here that, well…needs it?' Connie stared at him quizzically, then peered anxiously through the porthole.

'We need it,' Becker said softly.

The AVP was edging closer to what they took to be the bottom of the chamber, eventually touching it with a slight bump. Connie had known for a while she wasn't piloting it, the pod was moving forward of its own volition, controlled by an external force with no onboard prop burn. She didn't say anything because she didn't want to think about it, couldn't do anything about it.

'Uh…touchdown I guess,' Connie said, turning to Becker, placing her arms out to steady herself. Bizarrely, she could feel the weight of her tongue and lips as though they were suddenly leaden. 'Hey…do you feel that? Jesus, we're getting gravity.' She felt woozy and lightheaded, heard her too-slow voice and was almost convinced it was someone else, but could now stand and move pretty much as she would back home on Earth.

'Seems about one gee,' Becker said, chewing on the coincidence, figuring it wasn't a coincidence at all.

There was a dull cha-chunk behind them and a banging sound of metal on metal that echoed harshly in their ears. Connie's heart lurched wildly and spinning around she saw the hatch hanging open, her face touched by a gentle punch of atmosphere. She managed a small, shaky grin and Becker returned it with a smile that spread his face like a hot-dog bun, his face rapidly darkening, picturing the crushed Soyuz.

'Who, uh, opened the hatch?' Connie said suspiciously, squinting narrowly at the spring-loaded handle. It had been pulled, turned and the positive locks separated. The question remained…by who or what?

'Does that mean they want us alive…I guess that's good right?' Becker said haltingly, having a nagging feeling there was way more than just arcane shapes out there. 'Well I guess they want us out of the pod,' he added, peering at the yawning hatch, shooting Connie a watchful glance.

'Well let's not piss them off then.'

'After you milady,' Becker said lightly, tipping an invisible hat toward the open door.

Stepping cautiously, they entered into a reasonable sized gap between an endless white wall and the first of the columns and rows of cylinders. She knew the hatch didn't release itself…someone, or thing had to have done it. She felt it in her gut, the queasy sensation that she might actually vomit over the alien surface. Wouldn't that be a wonderful first offering, she thought, appalled and a little amused. On behalf of the human species…damn it, hang on, then ralph on the ground in front of them in a disgusting display of human regurgitation. Maybe they'd think it was our idea of a generous welcome. Forget the handshake, she mused wryly.

Becker peered closely at the wall, conceding that it looked like a regulation plasterboard job on Earth – a little off-white, flat lustre, no standout texture or detail. Had to be more to it he reckoned, moving his eyes along the ponderous barrier, his mind peeling open at the prospect of what might underpin it. Becker tilted his head forward, gazing intently but still seeing little of interest, just banal paleness. Tentatively poking at it he swiftly withdrew his index finger just in case, eventually sticking his finger in with intent, stunned as his finger penetrated without resistance to a depth of about a centimetre, feeling something tingling on the tip of his pinkie. It was like pushing through liquid but there was a distinctly firmer surface beyond, not unyielding but harder, like set gelatine, firm but malleable. It was the first real touch of their stuff, first contact, he scoffed silently, surveying the surreal landscape seemingly stretching on forever.

'Did they pressurise all this…for us?' Connie asked disbelievingly. 'I mean, look at it, the size of this place is off the scale, it's absurd.'

'They might just breathe the same stuff,' he angled his head up, awed by the criss-crossing lines of cylinders, seeing them condense into a solid mass as distance spiralled, visually to infinity.

The sheer number of the things was disconcerting to the eye, worsened Connie was sure by being outside the ship this time, at the whim of whatever might be milling around out there, beyond the horizon. Inside Sagan it was different but outside, here, she felt vulnerable and had an uneasy sensation similar to vertigo. It was the unnerving possibility of meeting something neither of them would be able to cope with, coupled with the daunting dimensions spiralling around them, both eating her up, filling her with unsettling thoughts.

'D'you reckon we're still inside the thing with the barbs all over it?' Becker said, 'or maybe we've been shunted somewhere else…like to their planet, one of their planets?' He looked bewildered, turning slowly in a full circle.

Connie gawked at him, 'who knows, but wherever we are we might as well show ourselves around. We sort of pushed our way inside so I don't think we're here for some grand revelation.' She clenched her jaw and regarded him speculatively. 'I mean it's not like they chose this place for us,' she said, peeking around and second guessing herself immediately, questioning whether they'd truly exercised free will, mulling over what they might find if they looked long enough and far enough, sensing a deep-seated urge to sprint back to the AVP, re-arm the hatch and hide inside its small but reassuring superstructure.

Becker was stamping gently on the floor, noticing how unyielding it was, an interesting contrast to the strange, energetic pliability of the walls. Kneeling on aching knees, he prodded at it like he did the wall, seeing it light up where his fingers touched it. He stood up with a painful groan, scraping his boot across it, watching it spark, seeing plumes of particles, the dusty output dwindling and vanishing. 'Hmmmm,' he said, fascinated, legs trembling as he widened his gaze toward the sky.

Connie was about five metres in front of him, getting as close as she could to the cylinders without actually touching them. 'Why that shape, I mean cylinders…it's odd, right?' She said softly, taking small steps to change her perspective. 'Apart from these things, everything's spherical, yet we have this chamber or, um, chambers crammed full of strange gun barrel shapes.' Connie was eyeballing one of them just below eye-level. There was a ten-centimetre space above and below it, allowing her to see both ends of the cylinder, hopeful there might be an open throat but not really surprised when she saw a solid surface. The cylinders were as black as space and totally homogeneous apart from some vague markings that were so small she could barely make them out. Grey figures on a black background. Connie knelt, peering myopically at them. The markings were right at the limit of her vision.

Connie's hand flew to her chest, her voice rising as she spoke, 'Becker…these are digits.' She had finally resolved the series of figures from a few centimetres away. 'It's binary like we saw before, but, uh,' she edged even closer, 'these are different.' After a moment, she conceded that it wasn't surprising, more of the same really, but these were so damn hard to see.

Walking over, Becker could barely see anything past a suggestion of a smudge on its surface. He didn't even try and read them. 'Okay Sherlock, so what do you reckon?'

She smiled coldly 'do you remember the binaries Vic saw from Sagan when we were in the other chamber?' Becker gazed blankly at her. 'Anyway, these are way more indistinct, the others were bold black numbers on a white background, remember?'

'Yeah,' he said idly, having no recollection. Bold black…what? He thought impatiently.

'These are way subtler,' Connie said, gazing solidly at the next cylinder, then the one next to it. 'The digits are numbers I guess…big numbers. I'm no expert on Base 2 stuff but I know zero is on the right, bigger numbers on the left, Vic told us that.'

'Okay, so how big?' Becker said, vaguely recalling the numbers they'd sighted in the other chamber. And, maybe the other chamber was just a different part of the one they were in.

'Every one of these barrel-things has a number,' Connie said with a glimmer of excitement, staring up and across, spellbound by the sheer scale of what was around them. ''See this one here?' Becker moved his head closer, seeing some of it, peering at her quizzically.

'You know I wear reading glasses, right?' He said, raising a sarcastic eyebrow.

She looked at him disdainfully. 'Oh Christ, I thought they were a fashion accessory, you mean they actually have glass in them?' Her dark eyebrows arched mischievously. 'Look whatever…see here?' She pointed at Becker's smudge, 'it's got twenty-seven binaries, and there's ones in the left-hand columns.' She whispered the last part of the sentence. 'This place isn't just big…it's huge.' Her heart was pounding, a little giddy as profuseness grew a new leg. Connie kept circling a single, harrowing idea. If these cylinders were in any way "bad", well, there were probably no words in any language to describe the shitiness of their situation.

110101000010101010010011110

Becker stared at the numbers, then back at Connie with an impatient sigh. 'And?' He eventually added brusquely, irritated with the math that was coming back to haunt him.

Connie scowled, 'Jesus, just don't, that number is more than ten billion for God's sake.'

He snapped back to attention, half offended, half smiling. 'So…why so many?'

'You seriously think we can know that?' She said, breathing sharply through her nose, burying a flash of anger, thinking of Harry. 'Who knows, maybe they're an energy source.' Crazy, off-grid scenarios flashed through her mind…how would an advanced Kardashev race energise itself…dark matter turbines, antimatter reactors, black hole dynamos, maybe some crazy entropy converters, maybe some of them, probably none of them. Just perhaps that's why there's so many she pondered, maybe they were in the company of some galactic power source for a billion…wait, a trillion worlds. For us it didn't register but it might be desktop tech for this lot. Connie wondered if the human mind would even recognise their technology as technology. Vic always held that supreme advancement would likely bring an almost melancholy simplicity with it, and surveying their new home, it made more than a little sense.

'If they're all numbered, they have to be different in some way,' Connie said uncertainly, knowing on Earth it made perfect sense, but here in the nuthouse, well, sense was generally absent.

'Maybe what's inside is different,' Becker offered, staring at the closest object, fighting to distinguish it from the ones around it. To his eye they were all mirror perfect copies of each other. Prosaic, austere nothings. On Earth, if you found one, you'd probably think nothing of it…push it to the side of the road and move on.

Connie met his gaze squarely. 'You've finally made sense, my God Becker, look at you.'

'Steady, this stuff's not really my thing, I'm working into it slowly, uh…you know.'

She gave a wry snort, turned on her heels and set off up the narrow passageway between wall and cylinders. After a few minutes of cautious plodding, Connie caught something higher up, in the corner of her eye, a marginal contrast amid the sameness. Thrusting her head forward she blinked deliberately and cupped her forehead to focus…was it even there? A pulse of light flashed behind her. Whipping around, she saw the residual light on her retina, back home she would've described it as a camera flash.

'Shit,' she blurted, eyes pushed wide open, '…you see that?' Her finger was goring the air nervously, 'over there.'

'Er…higher up,' Becker said falteringly, holding his arm out stiffly so it was about fifty degrees from the perpendicular. 'There…maybe.'

Connie started pacing, eyes roaming up and down the line of cylinders, having no idea what she was looking for. Something different she guessed but there was just geometric repetition everywhere – rows, columns of bundled objects occupying space, seemingly doing nothing, they were dormant perhaps, dead even. The things extended everywhere the eye could see until the haze of distance made them look first like solid rods, then completely formless like a tremendous storm cloud everywhere above them. There was no movement, no noise, just the fearful echoing of their words and footfalls as they moved.

Becker was following closely behind Connie, puffing like an asthmatic, struggling to maintain contact. 'You know we…have to drink so I hope whoever they are…have some inkling of our…um, biological needs.' He was grunting as he walked at what he considered breakneck speed.

'Agreed, but do they give a toss?' Connie said, eyeing him narrowly. 'Look at recent history, ask yourself. *Not* I would venture.'

'They let us in when we were running out of air,' he said weakly, not sure if that's what actually happened but it sure seemed like it.'

'Or did we just activate some auto-function by punching it with burnt prop?'

A flicker of despair ran across Becker's face as he listened, slouching his shoulders. 'Jesus Christ, throw me a bone, something to hang onto. Is it too hard to be glass half full for a minute?'

'As a matter of fact it is,' she said curtly. 'Half full, half empty, facts are facts. Face it, they may not even know we're in here.' Connie was glaring now, carving up her own words. If that was the case then they were screwed without possibility of reprieve.

'No way there's anything in here to keep us alive,' he said, 'it's totally fucking sterile…we might as well be stuck in a tin can.

Connie's face hardened as she pondered an expletive ridden offensive but saw how exhausted he was, fatigue obvious in the pockets under his eyes. She took a deep, rattling breath instead, massaging her forehead, two fingers became three. She changed tack. 'Why the hell is there an atmosphere in here? It doesn't make sense. Either it's for us or for them…for whomever, whatever populates this place.' She peered up and around, pulling at an eyebrow. 'This should be vacuum if it was free of biology…I mean, what would be the point of burning up energy to keep this place pressurised?' She stared at Becker, pulse racing, knowing in her core that she was right.

'Where are they then?' Becker asked, nervous about Connie's use of the term *"whatever"*.

'Dunno…like I said, maybe it's for us; the place is empty, except for these cylinder things.'

Becker didn't appear sold on the idea, cocking his head around nervously, his body motionless but eyes in constant reptilian motion. 'No one home…er, I hope.'

'Oh for the love of…this is a colossal chamber, we can only see so far. Maybe they're milling around beyond the horizon, like in the millions.' Connie paused because she was spooking herself and by the bug-eyed expression on Becker's face he was even worse off. Poor sod looked like he'd seen his own death certificate spread out like an evening newspaper. 'Relax, you'll blow a valve,' Connie said with a gentle note of humour in her tone.

'Should we be looking for a way out?' He said, ignoring her. 'I vote a thumping big yes. There's nothing for us here…to survive on I mean.'

'A way out to what?' She asked, pausing to think, guessing it was the logical move, to at least look around. 'Let's see what we can find, maybe what these cylinders are and in the process, a way out, a way in, food and water…whatever.'

Becker rubbed his gut, feeling it gurgle and cramp painfully. 'I seriously need to eat, I mean it, my stomach is eating itself. First Mars, now this, are these arseholes trying to tell me something?' He grabbed at his rapidly diminishing gut, smirking thinly, sizing up how long they could sustain themselves on thin air and inane questions.

'Yeah, the whole thing is about you, a fat blaster…that and fitness, the walking and the like.' She lifted her hands in a derisive gesture, 'Christ, it's been a day and a bit, you'll be fine,'

'Whatever smart arse, I'm slowly dying here.'

'We're all slowly dying, deal with it.'

His face flushed. If he wasn't so tired he would have rapped back at her, but he barely had the energy to stand up let alone pitch a battle with Captain Surly. Fuck it, he thought miserably, glancing up at the enigmatic objects, pondering death by starvation again.

Connie admitted she felt an irresistible urge to consume…food, fluid, it didn't much matter what form it came in. A tender prime rump covered with crisp, salty fries lurched in and out of her mind like an erotic fantasy, leaving her hot and flustered.

Collapsing roughly to the floor with their backs against what they assumed was the outer wall, they faced the cylindrical forest, breathing heavily, perspiring fluid they couldn't afford to lose.

Becker's face was ashen despite being hot and uncomfortable. 'I'm done Connie,' he said, grunting loudly, rubbing his fingers crudely across his forehead, swishing sweat away from his brow.

Connie wrinkled her nose, infuriated by Becker's stupid noises. 'How the hell can walking make you puff like that? God you're so out of condition,' she sighed. 'How long since you even thought about exercise? And I don't mean bending your elbow at the bar or flicking through the contents of your wallet.' She threw him a hostile glare.

'Jesus, get to the gravy stroke, call me a fat prick and get it over with.'

'Consider it said,' Connie grumbled, staring right at him.

'You know how long it takes to run my goddamn business?' Despite being drop dead tired Becker felt his defences rise. He came across as brusque and hard as nails but he was surprisingly delicate when it came to body image. Always had been. In fact bad boy Becker was as sensitive as a tubby teen in a tight outfit.

'Well by the look of you, you better damn well find time or you'll keel over and die. Good luck will only take you so far.'

He looked at her blankly, curling his mouth into a veiled threat. 'I'll take that on board. Just put the end of the fucking world on hold and I'll go punch out some laps, how's that?'

'Better,' Connie said more softly, losing focus as she gazed straight ahead. Something was different, a few hundred metres up ahead, to the right of where they were sitting. Narrowing her eyes, she kept her head completely still, certain there was a variation in the sameness, like a cut diamond among a sea of glass.

'Becker, you see that white cylinder?'

He followed her outstretched arm, taking on the comical look of a man with a white cane straining desperately to read the newspaper fine print. 'I can see a paler something, yes I think so,' he said, but wasn't entirely sure. Becker didn't want to look like a complete dick so he played along.

Connie got up and started power walking down the corridor, leaving Becker behind. If a white one existed, she reasoned there must be more, maybe some she could closely inspect.

'Oh great,' Becker moaned, seeing her motor away, 'wait up,' he slurred, struggling to his feet, groaning all the way. 'Fuck me,' he grunted, plodding after her.

Connie saw a pale object at roughly head height not too far away, feeling her heart jerk in her chest. 'Yes,' she shrilled, not sure why she was excited, but something different amid the mass of uniformity had to mean something. The human-logic chestnut reared in her mind again. Wrong, right …who knew? The more they looked the more they might square the imponderables away.

Connie slowed to a crawl, started inching up on it, eyes riveted as she approached, as though closing on a hair sensitive IED. Surveying it closely, she slumped her shoulders, frowning impatiently at it. Same as the black ones save for the bone white colour. Still cautiously approaching, she pointed her head forward, concentrating all her senses on it, probing, listening, even smelling. Slowly, her eyes widened. 'Hang on…the number Becker,' she said, heart pounding even harder, 'it's shorter…way shorter.'

10101101110011111100000

'It's only a few million, There's a shitload more black than white if I'm reading this right.'

Oh Der, Becker thought, glaring at her furiously, breathing loudly, feeling pressure behind his eyes which was always a precursor to him losing it. Was she serious? Here he was on the verge of collapse, maybe death and she was droning on about numbers as if they actually meant something. Numbers! What the hell was the game plan here…survival or research? He was thirsty, weak, stone motherless starving, and she was talking math.

'Look Brainiac,' he snapped abruptly, 'this means squat to me, and you don't have a hope of finding an answer, like ever. So you've found a white one, seriously Connie, whoopee fucking doo.' He ground his knuckles together with a threatening glint in his eye. 'Of course there's less of them…just look around.'

Connie turned to Becker with contempt, 'I realise you're intellectually challenged and I accept that. Let me say this clearly so you can get your head around it.' She paused momentarily. 'If we don't solve whatever's going on we're probably finished, not just you and I…maybe all of us.' She tapped her temple gently with a finger. 'That's everyone you've ever known, throw in your future grandchildren as well. We're shit out of options here Becker…we need to thread the needle and find something.' Her eyes were cold and deadly serious. 'This may be all horribly vapid to you but it's what we've been dealt so we need to get on and find a way.' She spun away, surveying the view around her for anything suggesting a clue, sensing the futility despite her bluster.

Becker hated to admit it but whilst he felt chastened and a little irritated, he was mostly impressed. She was a strong woman, he'd known that since day one, but her presence of mind in this ridiculous situation was quite inspiring despite his fatigue. He was ready to give up, sit back down, refuse to budge another inch but he felt the smallest dram of hope return.

'Okay…so what next?'

'We keep moving until we can't,' she said firmly.

'I think I was there half an hour ago,' he said, smiling and grimacing simultaneously.

'You'll be fine, c'mon let's go.' Her face was a mask of stone, all business, humourless.

'You a drill Sargent in a different life?' Becker quizzed flashing a defiant grin.

'Funny. Move,' she snapped with a ghost of a smile.

'Been possessed by a surly alien maybe?'

'Possessed by a want to live, now fucking move that arse Becker.'

Dropping his mouth closed he got to his feet without a groan this time, continuing up the seemingly endless path between the mighty cylindrical peaks towering around them. They peered around in silence for anything that might be of use, any break in the geometric sameness, but saw nothing but depressing monotony, infinite repetition with only the rare intrusion of a different colour.

It seemed less and less likely that this prosaic habitat would be something where creatures would exist, creatures of any kind, intelligent or not. Their first guess was that it was some energy producing hub, or perhaps it was industrial, manufacturing, engineering even, maybe a combo of several or all, or more likely none of them. The inscrutable question echoed inside Connie's head without any hope of favour. If she was right about their level of sophistication then everything would operate without intervention, that would be a given. So, her guess was they were here by intent, and for some inexplicable reason they had been spirited to this mysterious metal world for a reason.

After another hour, their pace had slowed to a point where they were barely moving, resting every few minutes now a physical necessity imposed by burning muscles and a depressing, enervating lack of nutrients. They continued scanning the cylinders around and above them, searching for the tiniest hint of a bigger picture.

After another ten minutes of tortuous trudging Connie caught something in the distance, glinting in the light, appearing more luminous than anything she'd seen. The dark cylinders seemed to absorb light rather than reflect it, but this whatever it was in the distance sparkled like cut crystal. Becker was fifty metres behind her, providing a constant stream of groaning and panting that was irritatingly audible as though he was right in her ear. Glancing over her shoulder she could see his pallid features, waiting to hear the thwump of his dead body hitting the ground at any time. The poor bastard was almost on his knees, willing himself forward on shaking knees.

Connie slowed to a dawdle as the cylinder came properly into view. It wasn't far above head height and was distinctly gold in colour, very different from the others. The standout object was actually a proper colour rather than the no-colour or every-colour embodied by the billions of other objects around them. It was like a hunk of pure gold had been carefully turned on a lathe into a perfect cylinder. Stopping in front of it she waited for Old Man River to grind his way up to her.

'You seeing this?' She pointed slightly above her head.

'Whoa,' he puffed raggedly, 'that's my c-colour baby…glorious…gold!' He fell to the ground, leaning back against the wall.

'Get up, read this, it's too high for me.'

'Oh, so now I'm needed. Thanks…means a lot to an old geezer like me.'

'Just take a look, it might be important.'

Becker pushed his back up the wall, moaning all the way until he was sort of standing, wobbling, but standing. 'Outta the way shorty,' he wheezed, gently fending her away.

'You're on such thin ice…you have no idea.'

He smiled thinly, standing as tall and still as he could, looking intently at the numbers.

'Read them out…slowly.' Connie demanded without a trace of levity.

The numbers were so small it took every ounce of focus but after a minute he reckoned he had them. Wiping his eyes with the back of his hand Becker blinked several times, concentrating, inhaling small puffs of air. He read them out very slowly, '…zero, zero, zero—'

0000010011010101

Connie grunted curiously after he'd finished, not surprised, but surprised that her logic held up. 'The number is small…these cylinders are rare, it's less than fifteen hundred I think,' she said with a glazed, puzzled look, lowering her eyebrows, 'if there's so few of them then they must, uh…have something unusual, maybe have something important inside…right? She felt her face tightening, knowing it was all hopelessly moot. 'Or maybe what it does is different to the others in some way.' She finished with an impatient snort.

'If only we had a fucking can opener,' Becker said with a twinkle of mischief.

'Hilarious.' Connie said. 'We need to keep moving, our life-span in here is, um…short.'

'No shit,' he shouted with energy he didn't know he had, raising his arms, brandishing his palms. 'Go,' he said, 'I'll be behind you somewhere. A thud means I'm dead.'

She regarded him briefly, this time grinning broadly. 'I'll remember that.'

Something was at ground level ahead, a darkness near the wall this time, away from the cylinders. 'Up there,' she said urgently, pointing the way. Connie stopped and turned to him, wincing, 'oh God what am I saying?' She chastised herself, knowing he was a bee's dick from being legally blind with distance. 'Anyway,' Connie added testily, 'there's something up there.'

Becker was irritated, variously frowning and squinting Magoo-like, and with a mocking sigh offered her a one-finger salute because he did see something. It was part of the wall where it met the floor, moving, writhing sort of, although he knew that might be a figment of his dodgy eyesight.

Adrenaline pushed them a little quicker, stepping with intent now, moving toward it, but it was less than they'd hoped for. Motherfucker, Becker screamed silently, eyeing the thing fearfully.

'Oh…w-what is this?' Connie said, staring with mouth agape, tongue slightly exposed. 'It's…it's…is it?'

Becker joined in, murmuring broken nothings, a little more horrified as it sunk in. 'This is bad, does this mean, er…you know—'

Connie swallowed hard, battling to control an overpowering urge to retch. Was this really their fate? She averted her eyes, goggling back at Becker, ready to give the whole bullshit need to live thing up. 'We're fucked,' she almost sobbed, moisture warm behind her eyes. 'Look at them Becker. Damn it…I thought there was a way out.' She felt like collapsing, giving in to the tears, allowing the hopelessness flight, relieving the ache in her brain.

'There's always hope,' Becker said weakly, shifting his eyes from the horrible mess, not convincing himself one bit.

'No, if it happened to them, why would it be different for us? Something opened our hatch right…so where are they?' Connie turned jerkily in a full circle, ready to scream, feeling a withering contempt for the bastard race that she thought might be making careful notations and calculations, perhaps granular assessments in some pristine piece of shit laboratory.

'Fucking hell,' Becker snarled. Was this seriously what was to come…that they'd be in this shitbox forever?

A few metres in front of them, a sight presented itself like something from an Egyptian history book. Sprawled in front of them were pieces of equipment and clothing that looked so out of place strewn among the geometric purity and clean floor lines. At her feet was a pair of thick white gloves, presumably neoprene rubber she guessed. Further up, discarded untidily, was an antenna headset and a bottle with "O2" printed on it in bold black letters. Other stuff was lying further away, Connie could see a dirty arm and glove assembly and something that looked like a large grey backpack with all sorts of things sticking out of it.

'This is insane,' Connie said, pointing to a cracked, scuffed helmet lying next to the wall. Their eyes were drawn to the sight ahead like fire ants to a skunk beetle, no longer needing any clues to work out what it was.

Two bodies were slumped against the wall about two metres apart, appearing for all money like Egyptian mummies, as though they'd been dead for centuries but hadn't rotted. Seemingly they had just "aged" without putrefying due to a lack of bacteria or maybe the removal of the atmosphere…either before or after death. One of them was still wearing a ripped pressure suit with "Sokol-KV2" embossed on the left breast.

Becker was nauseated, trying to choke back a full-blown shudder as he gaped at what resembled a ghastly anthropological exhibit. Their flesh was like wrinkled leather, tan coloured with specks of mahogany and black, internal organs had collapsed, leaving tissue paper skin hanging like hessian bags above. The one without the pressure suit was in bad shape, ragged chunks of flesh missing from his limbs, dirty yellow bones exposed beneath, Becker immediately thinking shark attack. Connie was now seriously considering how they might end it if this bullshit just went on and on. Starvation, dehydration, it was a bitch of a way to go. Suicide was a distant comfort, lying in the back of her brain like a dormant jumping jack. The question of how could come later.

The cosmonauts had clearly succumbed, in Connie's words, "a fucking eon ago", comparing them to Amenhotep who was thousands of years old, but these buggers were Soviet cosmonauts, no way they were more than fifty years old.

'How long?' Connie said in a hoarse whisper, fighting to avoid seeing her own demise reflected by the withered corpses in front of her.

'They look like aged leather for Christ's sake, how long would that take?' His face was twisted with revulsion as he spoke, lips pulled down about as far as they could go.

'Hundreds, has to be, it doesn't matter, in this environment, maybe thousands.'

'So, they got, deposited here that long ago?' His heart was thudding uncomfortably.

'Shifting through time isn't a big issue for this lot, in case you hadn't noticed.'

He looked around, up, across, into the distance, searching for anything that made sense. 'So, uh…how did they get from the Soyuz into here…their craft is like…outside.' His face was crinkled like a crushed beer can.

Connie ignored him, as she rolled scenarios around in her head, discarding all of them, knowing something had to be right, no doubt one of the billions beyond her imagination. 'You know, maybe we've been sent back or even forward in time, how do we know we're still in our time? We don't…can't.' She sneered bitterly, slitting her eyes. 'I fucking hate this place,' she said, wrapping her arms tightly around herself, 'it sucks in here.'

Connie finally summoned the nerve to edge up to them and survey them closely, eyeing the skin-hugging Soviet space garment that was also weathered and worn, like an overused tank top.

'He's been um…eaten,' Becker finally decided, pointing briefly to the other fellow, trying to come up with a more acceptable scenario, but eaten it was.

'Well, only a little bit,' Connie said humourlessly, following the pattern of bites.

Becker winced, peering at the wounds that were more than just wounds. 'Well, he's missing that…and that,' he mumbled, poking the air in the direction of the yuck bits. Clearly, they were the result of some desperate gnawing. They both knew the truth.

'Jesus, they were that desperate…when he died, him over there started eating him.' Connie walked away a few steps to compose herself.

'Well, hopefully he was dead,' Becker said, averting his gaze.

Connie nodded in agreement. 'So, where the hell does that leave us?'

Becker placed his eyes on Connie, eyeing her slowly from head to toe until she arched her eyebrows and placed an ominous hand on her hip.

'Can I help you?'

'Just checking out the menu,' he sighed, curving his mouth into a tight smile, unable to help himself.

Connie blew out a massive breath. 'You'll be first to drop Becker and trust me, every part of you is safe.'

'As I expected,' he chuckled quietly, tapering into silence.

'You know, I bet they thought they'd get out too,' Connie said, 'poor bastards ended up mummified, is that seriously what we've got coming?'

Becker was holding his sides, looking pained. 'Why would they give us atmosphere, open the hatch, encourage us in here just to watch us die like insects in a fucking jar?'

'Maybe because they can, perhaps that's the whole point…it might even be the end-game. It's screwed up but this might be what they enjoy, maybe it's their scientific protocol, watch others struggle, see what they do, see how adaptable they are…might even give them their jollies.'

'Thanks,' Becker spat, wagging his head slowly, conceding she may be right. He edged closer to Connie, looking a little sheepish. 'I know I've been a bit slack, third wheel stuff and all, but this, uh…sort of makes me wanna step it up a bit,' he said, peering at the decay and the bite marks, the devastated flesh. Well that was a start he supposed, at least he got the words out.

'I'm in too,' Connie said, looking and sounding equally determined.

'Let's just get away from this shit. Poor pricks, no way they deserved this,' Becker said, imagining things he wished he hadn't.

After another hour, movement had degenerated into an uncoordinated loping. It was simply more of the same, click after click of bland black cylinders, they hadn't seen another white or gold one in all that time, although what that mattered they weren't sure.

'My feet are numb Becker, these Baffin's feel like they're full of thumbtacks.'

'I thought they were your come fuck-me shoes Con,' he said with a brief guffaw.

She screwed her mouth up, sniffing. 'Fuck you…how's that?' Connie was in no mood for his irritating Beckerisms.

'Trying to lighten the mood is all,' he mumbled, drawn quickly back to the sombre reality of where they were, his heart bouncing as he revisited the fate of the Soyuz boys.

Connie needed water, knowing Becker needed it even more. They weren't in danger of imminent death but they were rotten thirsty, aching all over and damn uncomfortable.

'Hey!' Becker sputtered from behind, pointing to the right, over Connie's shoulder near the wall. She stopped, swung slowly around and froze, her face shaken flat like an ironed bedsheet. What the fuck, was her immediate brain scream, paling as she grappled with the bizarre visual.

She stared dumbly at an ebbing, flowing something that was making a sort of slopping sound like wet cement turning over in a mixer. After an uneasy silence they stepped cautiously forward, initially thinking it might be a crack in the superstructure, which made about as much sense as anything else they'd seen to date. Like zero. Its geometry was peculiar, not a sphere, not a cylinder, not a jagged wound in space, it was sort of like a lenticular patch of decades old sump oil embedded in the wall somehow, writhing and oozing as though driven by a herculean gale. Moving closer, they could sense an attraction, some sort of inertia gently compelling them forward, pulling at them like a bar magnet on a block of iron. A sense of comfort consumed her when she watched it squirm, leaving Connie with a feeling that her emotions were being managed, remotely controlled, but she couldn't bring herself to analyse it or care, she just knew it was happening, wanting the hell out of this place. The decision was made and Becker was clearly onboard too. Fuck it, no way he wanted to stay in here and end up like the two freeze-dried Soviets.

'Connie, let's go, we need to go.' He grabbed her hand, peeking closely at her.

'Yes,' Connie said matter of factly, staring mindlessly at the darkness, wondering if the cosmonauts had been afforded a similar way out. Maybe they'd refused the offer for some inexplicable Soviet reason.

Edging forward virtually as one they touched the edge of the roiling darkness, feeling not the viscid wetness they expected but simply a jolt of energy that pulsed briefly inside their heads, something fizzing against their clothing like a static buildup was discharging on contact. Inching onward, they wormed their way through disconcerting dimness, gravity loosening its grip then yielding completely. Weightlessness had them floating unimpeded in whatever nebulous half-world was around them. The glow from the entrance was still behind them, a narrow slash ever so slowly closing in on itself like a healing gash. Connie felt a wave of tidal panic as darkness became everything, blacker than black, a repugnant, rayless coffin. Trying to scream, her mouth was useless and in a moment of frenzied horror she realised there was no sensation from her neck down, she couldn't move, speak or do anything apart from think. Adjusting to the blackness, she saw pinpoints of light, stars she realised, all around them, not just stars but galaxies, gas and dust clouds, everything that made up space…just like before. Eyeing Becker, she saw the same inscrutable paralysis, his eyes flicking around as he fell through space, presumably fighting to make sense of the madness around him. Good luck she thought, distantly with a hazy, faraway feeling of death and detachment.

Their uncontrolled tumbling had them facing each other for a brief instant and it was then that it struck her, making her want to scream out loud, sob hysterically, both, but she couldn't raise a molecule of movement, sensing her sanity sloughing away like spent bullet casings. She wasn't breathing and worse, her heart was dead in her chest, but her brain was alive, struggling under the craziness, and how in the sweet fuck did she have thoughts when there was nothing vascular to drive them. Every fibre in her body screamed it's not real!

Floating in what seemed like the vacuum of space, open to heat and cold, they felt nothing, no bodily fluids trying to squirt through skin, no pain, no ruptured eyeballs, no discomfort. Their bodies were unperturbed by the most ferocious environment imaginable, a stroll in the park, oh…but she was physically dead. This was an illusion she reasoned, but for what end? Was there an intuitive learning to take from it, and like everything else…the aching question remained… why?

Without a kiss of inertia, they started accelerating vanishingly fast, evidenced by distant objects screaming past them, entire galaxies in front were now behind them, everything material was sling-shotting past them in a blended blur of light, broken into a blinding kaleidoscope of colours.

Galaxies were piling up in the centre of their view, everything slowly accreting, falling in on itself, moulding itself into a perfect gravitational sphere below them, and inside was everything.

Locking eyes on the scene below, it struck Connie that she was looking at a curvature surrounded everywhere by empty space. It seemed like there was a Universe and beyond it a second expanse of nothingness surrounding it, sort of like vacant room for it to grow into. Unsurprisingly, it made no sense because the Universe was spacetime itself and grew its own dimensions as it expanded so there was no edge or end to it, let alone anything "beyond". So, what the hell? She had no time to mull it over because she was approaching what looked like a sheer wall…a fucking wall in space no less, right in front of her, drawing her forward. The great wall of space she said to herself dreamily, waiting to die.

***

The flow of numbers started on Earth two hours ago and this time they were designed to be straightforward, no encryption, no fussing over meaning, no serious intellect needed. The only smarts required was Binary 101 and then a way to convert them to Base Ten, decimals that is, so Joe Six-pack on Earth would have little problem. Buried in the numbers was something simple, harrowingly explicit but still with an element of mystery. To most, it was a firm nod to the darkest fears they'd harboured since the visitors arrived on their doorstep.

Enough people were plugged into social media to ensure that much of the globe were quickly clued into the frugal transmission. The precise details weren't spelled out but the gist of the message was clear to even the most technically challenged and mathematically clueless. Once again, it seemed that humanity's fixation with connectivity was being hijacked and used against them, but it only seemed that way. Popular belief that the World Wide Web and global radio comms were being hacked was wrong. It wasn't Internet or wireless radio delivering the message, it was something completely without scientific explanation. The question of why and how went even deeper, now a global pandemic generating forty billion messages a day.

Two hours ago, Jack and Pete started receiving streams of zeroes and ones on their phone, out of nowhere. Pete was on a call when the first ream of digits arrived. Jack checked his cell and there they were, coming just as fast. The transmissions matched perfectly, clearly a single-source comms, sender unknown this time, and bizarrely, if that word still possessed any veracity, they weren't Internet derived. They were simply bold white figures streaming over the face of cellphones globally, in a single or double line depending on your screen size. Cellular and other mobile devices still worked fine, phone, text, email, apps, no problems. It was business as usual apart from the line or two of anomalous math that seemed to have no quantum basis for being there.

YouTube was heavy with videos that defied belief. People were deconstructing their phones piece by piece, crushing them under bricks, running over them with cars. Some were dropped from great heights, their owners scampering down stairs, cameras still running while they inspected the results. No matter what torturous destruction was meted out, the numbers just kept on rolling. Shattering the glass into dust was the only way to stop them. In the words of billions around the globe, uttered wide-eyed with a despairing headshake, the adjective that was losing every shred of substance: Impossible. The first two letters were being forcibly pried away.

One of the remaining techs from the new SLS Shuttle programme told them what they already knew, described with a storm cloud of expletives. The tech guy from the Orion Team seemed to know what he was talking about, data from a text message zaps its way from your provider's tower to the control channel of your cellphone and only then do you get an SMS in whatever language your phone decodes it in. Having something cycle constantly over the soda lime or Gorilla Glass of your cell…well, he said, that was a complete head-fuck, like trying to fart Mozart's Piano Concerto. It defied any natural law you cared to choose, he growled, confirming he was talking about the cellphone thing, not farting Mozart. Tech-guy snorted cynically, blurted something about motherfucking magic and stormed off, clearly miffed that he didn't have an answer.

Everyone in the Johnson Space Centre, all eighteen thousand people at NASA, were receiving identical numbers on their devices. Not long after that, media centres globally reported that every device was getting the same zeroes and ones, cellphones, tablets, laptops, desktops, TVs…the lot. Even cinemas were getting it, right there on the big fucking screen, IMAX and all. Whoever was sending the numbers was going to significant pain to make sure everyone on the planet had a bird's eye view of it. And they weren't inert like the others, these were cycling every second with an

292

unmistakeable pattern, pulsing and beating like a human heart, presenting themselves in a sequence, the very first one being nineteen digits in length, a prime number.

1111010000100100000

Within a few minutes of receipt, the answer to the numerical riddle was soaring around the globe, courtesy of every phizog of the social and unsociable media. The first binary number received by more than seventy-five percent of the population was half a million. Exactly five hundred thousand. No tens, no hundreds, just a nice balanced number. Identifying it was one thing but…so what? Well that was quickly answered a few minutes later when it sort of "woke up", became active and started cycling ever so steadily, reducing by one, then two, three, four, five and so on, once every second. Now it had counted down to four hundred and ninety thousand plus change.

Digits were binary but they were spelling out consecutive, reducing decimals every second and if the pattern continued it would reach zero in a little over five days. The implications winged around the planet like carpet nukes, a surgically positioned projectile that hit right where awareness and mind lived, where humanity was stored. Already grappling with the annihilation of planets, moons and pieces of Earth, the social order of the planet was being systematically shelled and forced to its knees. Wherever the greater population cared to look, there was a countdown clock staring back with a grim promise. The daily, hourly, every moment smartphone infatuation was now an invidious nightmare, an unnerving reminder of the coming of what most assumed was hammer time.

Global infrastructure was dissolving in the face of the forbidding promise from space. The only remaining jigsaw piece was religion and it wasn't just intact, it was everything across all spiritual bandwidths, Christianity, Islam, Hindu, Buddhism and a hundred other sub-beliefs. The promise of another life beyond this was the only thing holding sway, because this one might be grinding to halt. What had been a possibility to some, a probability to many, was now an absolute to most. And the world was already dying because of it.

***

Jack was frowning hard as he paced down the main corridor of Building 30 with Pete right behind him. They'd just video-linked with Griffin and his entourage in Pasadena and it hadn't gone well, the entire dynamic had tilted badly. Fucking capsized and sunk was Griffin's booming summary, looking as grave and surly as they'd seen him. Hardly surprising, Jack conceded, considering the state of the nation, the impotence of the country's formidable military and Griffin's failure to do shit about it.

Peering into the FCR high security room, Jack looked forebodingly at the group that remained in residence, distraught by what he couldn't see. They'd only been gone an hour and everything was, well…a lot roomier. Doubtlessly reflective of greater society he thought glumly. Instead of a hundred and twenty flight controllers, shift managers, tech personnel and security staff, there were maybe thirty people milling around, seemingly doing nothing in particular. Faces were brooding, pain and melancholy broad-carved, most appearing vacant and spent, emotions smoothed away. Small groups were dotted around the room, some hunched over cellphones, gazing wordlessly at the numbers sloughing away. Security was nowhere to be seen. Anyone was free to wander in, do whatever he or she liked in the high security area, an absolute contravention of standing orders.

Jack shook his head and sighed dispiritedly. 'Christ, it's a fucking ghost town,' he said, surveying the sad looking NASA HQ. 'Did they all just up and leave, like…together?'

'Dunno,' Pete offered distractedly, shocked at the walk out, the piss poor show of support in the hallowed hall. Taken aback though he was, he got it. Making family a priority was the only thing left…for most.

Jack watched Pete intently, thinking hard. 'I've never seen Griffin so downcast, so pessimistic. He's a bulldog, you know, always on.'

293

'Ordinarily it'd be a good thing but yep, he gets it as much as anyone.'

'Can't blame him…five days, Jesus,' Jack said, clearing his throat with a hack. 'Makes it hard to get up for anything, to think about anything except what happens when this thing ticks down to…you know.' His voice sank to a hoarse whisper.

'We don't know what'll happen at zero-time… we think we do but …it could be anything.'

'Christ Pete, you reckon it might be what, a countdown to some glorious, insightful event? Or "hey just kidding, had you going, right?" I mean, for fuck's sake get with the—'

'Well you never—'

'Do the bloody math, Jupiter, the Moon, I think we can safely assume it's not a humanitarian mission.'

'I just don't think we should give up. There's still time and where there's time, well, right?'

Jack exhaled in a rush. 'I know, it's just…when people like Griffin start rolling over it makes you wonder whether it's worth it, makes you reassess. Should we be home with family? I mean, are we actually making a difference here?'

Pete murmured agreement, 'only way we can add value is here, so I'm staying, try and save my family. It mightn't do any good…but maybe it will.'

'That's what I thought until I saw Earl's dial,' Jack grumbled, gazing off in the distance.

'Not something I wanted to see,' Pete agreed, 'people like that don't break easy.'

Jack swallowed, coughing weakly, 'Griffin was seriously conflicted, couldn't get his head around it. Like he said, why don't these pricks just act, get it over instead of the bullshit prep work?'

'Yup, kept banging on about it, so did Ballard. Why give us all this warning, glimpses of our own demise…why the torment?'

They looked at each other warily, knowing what the other was thinking.

'Psychological warfare,' Jack said firmly. 'Torture, torment, pain, suffering…call it what you like but these fuckers are waging a battle on the most unlikely front imaginable. And it's working. You've seen the reports…it's goddamn end of the world stuff out there…who needs North Korea?'

'Griffin's an example in point, it's working on the highest level, against the very people orchestrating the defence of the planet…if you can call it that.'

Jack ambled over to the panoramic window, staring out at the brilliant sunshine, wondering if the curtain fall for this incredible place was only a handful of days away. Surely it couldn't be, four and a half billion years in the making…five days to go? 'Fuck me,' he muttered, rolling his eyes down to the burnished tiles, trying to expunge horrible visions of apocalypse, or worse. Vanishment was the word that came to mind, it had to be added to the dictionary but then he remembered dismally how short time might be. *"Everything we took for granted",* he mused pitiably, from a book to a blade of grass to the molten core of the planet, all of it might soon be gone. Not even a memory because that required human life to endure. 'Why do it?' He repeated sharply, suddenly feeling desperately lonely. 'Like Griffin said, why not just gun barrel us, pull the trigger, be done with it?'

'Has to be part of the plan,' Pete said, glancing at his cell, 'this countdown is fast-tracking decay…they don't have to physically do anything to bring us down. Our whole premise for society is building a tomorrow or at least planning for it. If that's not there, the human mind is cactus, no way it can cope, the whole shooting match loses its appeal.' Pete eyed Jack gravely, a rueful scowl crossing his face. 'It becomes an hour-to-hour thing, just surviving, and religion, faith takes over as the only imperative. The rest is, well, shit…civilisation doesn't have a ghost of a chance.'

'So, they give us some graphic examples of annihilation, like the Moon and Jupiter, then beam a countdown clock to every terrified soul on Earth,' Jack said, feeling his jaw tense and his body follow suit. 'I mean, is that their colonisation handbook? No nukes or death rays, just a mental battle that plays on the frailties of young societies…easy as shelling peas.'

'And then they take the planet,' Pete said, 'zero resistance, zero damage to the planet.

Jack felt a shiver run up his spine, 'can that seriously be it?'

'In five days we'll know I guess.' Pete said, shuffling back to the window.

Jack gazed over at the TV that still showed CNN Live proudly displaying a timer converted to decimal dutifully counting down like remaining time at the Superbowl. 129:15:5

Pete's brows arched into a scowl. 'If they took the ice from Antarctica in a surgical block then they could remove us the same way. No need to send us around the twist first. if colonisation is the plan…no way. It doesn't add up, it's possible but…oh Christ,' he said, angry and exasperated.

Jack nodded agreement. 'We could be completely wrong with everything,' Maybe not better but maybe a scenario we hadn't considered.'

'Yeah,' Pete breathed, feeling his heart thud, envisioning death by a thousand cuts at the hands of whoever, whatever was pulling the puppet strings.

30. Unimaginable

"Sometimes an unimaginative mind can imagine the most unimaginable." ~ *Munia Khan*

The polar Sphere was mesmerizing. Nate and Yoshi watched as it radiated colour, the light flowing across the metal surface and stopping dead at its edge, then flowing back on itself like a King tide. There were some sort of particles suspended in the light that ebbed and flowed like ocean waves but they never strayed a millimetre beyond the plate, maybe forbidden to do so at some quantum electric level. Nate could hear the radiance start crackling like a campfire just before it exploded in a flood of colour in every direction, forming an instantaneous vision of forest around them. Nate gazed at it, pretty certain it wasn't just a vision, it looked surreal but it also looked as real as it got.

'Rainforest,' Yoshi shouted instinctively.

'You think?' Nate said, lifting his eyes and surveying the stunning biodiversity suddenly served up around them. Densely storied trees with thick, malformed branches surrounded him, all of them sprinkled with intricate ferns and mosses with gnarled underbrush and brambles everywhere. Fallen logs, masses of tangled ivy and berry bushes were all over the place, the floor of the forest crammed with plant decay and dotted with colourful fungi. Seeds and pods were strewn about like corn feed, and there were animals too, three deer in the distance, mice and lizards only metres away, spiderwebs spun between trees ahead. The scent of earth and rotting wood, the wildflowers, animal smells and the scent of pine was strong on the breeze, feeling the kiss of falling leaves nuzzling them as they fell in the thousands from the roof-top canopy to the ground.

Bewildered by the profuseness of what had been a desolate rockscape only minutes before, Nate inhaled the perfumes and aromas, looking in every direction at a mature, luxurious forest that would have been at home anywhere on Earth, except here in the cold wastes of Antarctica of course.

Yoshi contemplated how a perfectly real looking, smelling forest could crystallise from nothing on these barren volcanic rocks.

'Our guests can clearly do whatever they want,' Nate said, 'and make it look pretty damn good. It has to be a, er…hologram I think, albeit a kick arse one.'

'No, it's real,' Yoshi stated firmly, 'the sight, sound, the smell, the touch. This is real Nate…it's amazing.' Yoshi picked up some leaves, threw them in the air. 'Hologram my arse,' he jibed. 'I can't see it from here but I know it ends at the plate's border.' He could just make out one of the Osprey's between the leaves and the branches. The plate was some sort of cathode for the Sphere he figured…maybe like a TV receiver is to a transmitter.

Yoshi heard the same crackling sound, seeing the forest collapse to nothing in a scintillating lather of vanishment. In a few seconds, there was nothing but the metal plate sitting dispassionately atop naked Antarctic bedrock, harsh brown, desolate. 'Christ,' Yoshi barked, 'that happened right?' He spun around and despite himself, looked to see where the damn thing had gone.

Nate glanced at him, 'Why did it happen? That's what you should be asking…that's the answer we need, why the hell did they manufacture a forest then erase it?'

Looking around, everything appeared to be in order. The Ospreys were all there in their compact configurations, military personnel were still milling around the edge of the metallic plate inanely. Had they even seen the jungle? Sure as hell didn't seem so. There was no reaction at all, no confusion or rush to engage them in a debrief. His heart rate punched a little harder.

An unsettling rumbling started beneath their feet, raising every hair on their bodies as some sort of energy saturated the air, a pins and needles sensation brushing their skin abrasively.

'Oh Christ, here we go,' Nate said, ready to run into the mountains, to take his chances with the leopard seals and penguins.

Nate gazed distastefully at it, struck by the sensation that it was angry although he assumed that was just his humanity showing. After all, colour was hardly a mathematical indicator of state-of-mind, or so he hoped because this time it was every conceivable tone of red, from crimson to vermillion to amaranth and burgundy.

Staring into the hypnotic light Yoshi realised how exhausted he was, and not just that, he was hungry, thirsty and his legs were wobbling with fatigue, almost compelling him to sit down to avoid collapsing. Jerking his head back abruptly, his pain vanished into the freezing air because something was there, in the light. He yelped, shuffling back a step or two, peering closer at the Sphere, holding his chin as he wrestled with what was in front of him. Both of them were unconsciously edging backward as a shadowy figure started pulling itself together about ten metres in front of them. The unexpected chimera conjured itself, right where the forest had been.

Yoshi's pale northern skin further drained of colour as he stood dead still, battling to ignore the quivering in his chest, pushing his head nervously forward, squinting to see what it was, his breath catching high in his throat. Moving slowly forward, the thing was resolving into a crisp image.

Nate made an odd howling sound as the shock forced something more primal than language from his mouth, his face filled with incredulity as his hands dropped loosely to his sides. He couldn't have been more shocked if he'd seen George Washington, in his broadcloth suit with eagle buttons, emerge from the light on a horse.

A few metres in front of them a woman dressed in business attire, maybe forty-five years old, was perched on the polar metal, staring fixedly at Nate like a night-owl, unblinking.

'Wh-who are you?' Yoshi stammered, unable to remotely comprehend who or what she might be or what the hell she was doing here. They were both expecting one of their alien protractors but what they got was prosaically human, visually at least.

She ignored him and continued staring magnetically at Nate with amazingly luminous green eyes, like sparkling aventurine.

'Who is this, um…person?' Yoshi whispered to Nate through a tight-lipped mouth, without moving his head or eyes. He noticed she hadn't taken her eyes off Nate, leaving him frozen, for all money looking like a plastic dummy.

Suddenly the woman moved her head forward. 'JJ,' she purred, holding her arms out and walking slowly up to him, smiling warmly all the way.

Yoshi gasped sharply. Nate still didn't move, rejecting it because it couldn't be, but there she was, seemingly flesh, blood and real. Nate was dizzy, couldn't breathe, clenching his toes so hard he thought they might break off in his shoes. Could he say the words settling on his tongue, burning like acid? In the back of his mind he knew it wasn't, but Jesus, a forest from nothing…and now this?

'Uh…m-mum?' He eventually said, pushed off-balance by the roaring sound and muddled words in his ears. The light around him surged.

'Of course it's mum, she said, raising her hands reassuringly. 'How have you been JJ? You look good.' She grinned broadly, sizing him up with her hypnotic eyes.

Holy God, Yoshi thought, peering in bewilderment. 'So, uh…where does JJ come from?' He said faintly.

'Long story,' he said, 'TV show I used to watch, guy was like me apparently.'

Yoshi nodded vaguely, watching Nate study her, taking in every detail.

God, can it be her? He shook his head hard. Of course it can't, they must have ripped her out his memory somewhere, fabricated her, like the forest, but she looked so real…so young.

'Y-You died ten years ago,' he said shakily, taking a deep breath to try and steady himself, 'cancer in the lung, you, uh…remember?' Nate surveyed her intently, watching her facial expressions, seeing the little dimple in her cheek when she smiled. And the wrist, he could see the scar from the broken glass she'd needed stitches for a lifetime ago.

'Come here honey,' she said lovingly, looking him up and down again, walking a few steps and gathering him in, hugging Nate tight. Oh Christ he said to himself, feeling the emotion well up, she even smelt like his mum. He tried to stifle it but couldn't, and started choking up, telling himself it couldn't be true but succumbing because real or not this was her in every conceivable way - sight, smell, sound …, she, it was perfect. Whoever had done it had gone to great pains and done their homework well. The question of how made his brain hurt because this was no hologram, it was a real, living, breathing person.

'Why are you here? Yoshi said firmly.

Nate shot him a frown. 'Jesus, play nice…go easy.'

'It's okay JJ, I understand,' she said softly, almost harmonically. There was a gentle, musical note to her voice.

'How are you here?' Nate said, desperate to hear her take on how she could be here. She was cremated and her ashes scattered over Nicholas Lake, her DNA fried, scattered to the wind. No coming back from that he thought darkly. Did they seriously expect him to believe it was her…just back for a fucking visit? Nate chewed on it a bit. Maybe they just wanted to personalise something, figuring she'd be able to get the job done a little better, and perhaps they were right.

She'd gotten primary lung carcinoma from a lifetime of smoking and decayed in front of him in the space of months. A vibrant, beautiful woman, reduced to a wrinkled, hairless bag of loose clothing dumped in a hospital bed for a month before she died. Her last days were wretched as her pain resisted the opiates pumped through her IV bag like common saline. She died suddenly one day as he held her hand - a mercy killing by the Doctors he was sure. He remembered his guilt at the joy he felt when she'd gone, but any decent life, one actually worth living had ended months before.

Looking at her standing on the metal plate at the South Pole, Nate saw his mum as she was before the cellular beast had taken its interminable grip. She looked incredible.

'I'm here JJ, that's all you need to know.' She smiled, with an air of anticipation. 'Do you remember our trip to Broken Hill when the damn pipes in the wall shuddered at the same time every morning…we cracked up every time right?' She was giggling in her same stilted way, wiggling her nose like Samantha from Bewitched.

Yoshi was going to say "good times" but checked himself, knowing what a sham this was. 'You died,' Yoshi blurted, feeling like it needed to be chucked out there because this was going nowhere. 'Do you remember dying?' The words were macabre, but they were relevant.

Her features suddenly hardened, the openness collapsing as she puckered her brow. 'I remember realising I was dying but desperation changed to acceptance and peace, I have that same feeling here. I wonder where I've been for the last ten years but I really don't care. I'm here now.'

Nate raised a hand and rubbed a finger across his mouth. 'Yes, um…but why are you here?' He said anxiously, meeting her eyes without blinking, becoming impatient. 'There is a reason right?'

She looked at him with a strange expression, part confusion, part something else…surprise maybe. 'I was about to say I don't know JJ, but I realise I do, it's just come to me. I have a message.'

A complex set of lines appeared in her forehead, giving the impression she was concentrating fiercely on something. 'You must understand what it means to be you,' she said, her lips pulled tight, making them look a little blue from want of blood.

Staring, they waited for her to continue, urging her on with their eyes but nothing came. Yoshi wondered if he should shake her…put a coin in the slot, he thought, stifling a smirk. She continued gazing vacuously with zero sign of any mum personality.

'What do you mean by—'

Nate was cut short when she suddenly started up again, seemingly without knowing he was even talking, '…here is where your dilemma begins,' she said, her eyes growing more luminous, 'you have developed so poorly, so inexplicably below expectation,' she paused again, 'you must demonstrate value to the Collective, coherent math, expansive technology. We cannot help you more than that.' Her face suddenly melted, brows arching, eyes piercingly alive, maliciously accusing. 'Your species deserves no moral treatment,' she said venomously, suddenly breaking out of whatever trance she'd been in, her hands flying to her forehead, palms covering her face.

'I'm so sorry JJ,' she sobbed. 'I don't know where that came from…but I know it's true, you are all in great peril.'

Yoshi watched Nate as she was talking, seeing the knowing scrawled on his face like signed execution orders. Their species was in deep trouble, now depthless quicksand they didn't have the smarts to haul themselves out of. *Shit.* Literally.

'Is that all?' Yoshi demanded loudly, 'can you recall anything else, more detail…any idea why the math is needed…clues, anything? I mean seriously, there has to be more.' His eyes were pleading for something meaningful. Yoshi reckoned the answer lay with string theory, maybe spacetime widgets, internal relativity or even loop gravity. If they could sort the corn from the husk, then maybe unification was possible, the dream of quantum gravity might become a reality. Was that what they meant by coherent? All of it was just guesswork, theories that couldn't be tested so what hope was there? Despite all the promise and hope, they delivered only frustration time after time…failure. There was that word again. Humanity's search for a Theory of Everything was just that, failure. If he was able, he would have raised both hands in the air, hoisted the white flag and resigned his pursuit for the mind of God…so where the hell did that leave humanity?

Nate was caught on one thing. 'You said "more than that". That you'd assisted us I mean. So there have been clues among all the…um, events, is that right?' He raised his eyebrows, peeling his eyes open, begging for a morsel of insight or acknowledgement.

She looked at him urgently, saying, 'I need to go. My time here is done.'

'Clues?' He repeated, 'is that what you meant? That there was something…somewhere?'

'I need to go,' she repeated slightly louder, firmer.

Looking at her stony countenance he could see she'd tuned out. She was a dead stick, eyes dull, clearly out of time, nothing left to give. That said, Nate didn't want her to go. He wasn't an idiot, but truly and honestly, he didn't give a rat's ass about the finer details. She looked like her, sounded like her, smelled like her, had all the expressions, habits, even scars for God's sake. She or it had been custom built with a level of care he couldn't comprehend, and a purpose now apparently discharged.

So another useless message was delivered to the blue world savages who apparently lacked the mental spark to save themselves. Nate and Yoshi felt a little guilty even though whatever they hadn't achieved, and ostensibly should have, was utterly beyond their control. They felt unwanted, soiled, bio-trash that seemingly failed what was apparently reasonable expectation.

She walked back to Nate and hugged him, kissing him tenderly on the cheek. He hugged her back generously, kissing her goodbye. 'I love you JJ,' she purred softly. Reaching out he grabbed her hand as she walked away, losing it as she retreated toward the light, a shadow, then she was gone.

'Well, that's something you don't see every day,' Yoshi said, managing a tentative smile.

Nate continued staring at the Sphere, swallowing the lump lodged tightly in his throat, feeling empty and sad. There was no joy in seeing his mum because it wasn't her, it just dredged up long forgotten memories he'd slowly learned to live with…and would now have to do so all over again.

On the face of it, the message was as terrifying as it was useless and short. Humanity had to prove itself to some "Collective" and to do it they needed something they quite simply didn't have, and worse, wouldn't have for God knew how long. It was utterly beyond them, they might be decades, centuries away from acquiring the knowledge for Grand Unification, and if Hawking were to be believed, maybe they'd never get it. Bizarrely, it seemed their lack of focus on hard science might be their undoing. Nate's whole demeanour was growing in severity, how the hell were they supposed to know that science was such a pivotal galactic imperative

'I got the impression we didn't make the grade,' Yoshi said. 'That we just don't have the right stuff…to join this so-called Collective, whatever it is.'

'Why don't they just leave us alone?' Nate spat, feeling a headache flare. 'Maybe we don't want to join a frigging Collective. I mean, by "Collective" they mean civilisations right…a bunch of 'em that share what…some sort of communal share point, a galactic cooperative?' Nate's face was darkening further, brows squashing tight. 'Well, we're not fucking interested,' he said resentfully, balling and unballing a fist as he spoke.

'Doesn't sound like there's much of a choice,' Yoshi said in a murmur. 'I don't think they're asking, I think if you're not in…well you're um, out, and out means right out, I think.'

'What if we just say no…tell 'em we're not interested in their bullshit boys club?'

'I don't think there's anything to decline Nate. Sounds like we're not getting an invite in the first place,' he said tightly. 'I reckon we're on the blacklist, the good-for-nothings as it were…the backwoods relative you never invite to a party 'cause they're dumb as shit, grope the girls, spill the drinks—'

'Yeah, well screw 'em,' Nate said, spitting the words venomously.

'I reckon we're stranded…no lifeboat,' Yoshi said forlornly, wondering what the finer detail of this so-called Collective was.

'Pretty much,' Nate said, 'like you said, if you're not in you're out, as in *gone* I think. His face was a wrinkled mess, contemplating their tenuous foothold on existence.

'Damn it,' Yoshi said, weighing up the nature of "out", sick in the gut, darkly fatalistic.

'Get Jack on comms, tell him about this stuff. This message such as it is needs to be sent to every wank-tank around the country…the world. It's probably worth dick but we gotta follow rules. Hey, who knows, maybe we just saved the world?' He winced in pain, wagging his head numbly, craving a bar stool, a whisky, even a smoke. No point worrying about the hateful fucking C-word now he figured.

Yoshi was in the process of downloading everything to Jack when he saw the Sphere firing up again. 'Oh for God's—,' Yoshi started, heat flushing through him, angry at the never ending, senseless carnival ride. 'Jack, we've got more action happening, I'll have to get back to you.' He acknowledged, wished them luck somewhat coldly and disconnected. Yoshi had little doubt things were escalating, it'd only been minutes since the last event and here it was happening again. Fucking great, he thought, his chest tingling as he pored over the reasons for the sudden return to action.

This time there were no pretty lolly shop colours, the light was simply white. Yoshi guessed they'd eventually find out what the colours meant. Every hue in the rainbow would eventually get a gig if this continued. Yoshi whispered, 'Bring it,' more anxious than he cared to admit. His legs started trembling violently as he saw shadows within, vague obscure motion suggesting animation, movement, twisting in the breeze. Lengthening shadows, scrabbling limbs, monstrous shadows started congealing into something their minds construed as hideous.

Two figures moved skittishly onto the metallic landscape, peering around anxiously, ending up gazing directly at Yoshi and Nate from a few metres away. They both had expressions speaking to some level of insanity, wild eyed, gawking at each other like animals who'd just managed to evade a predator.

Yoshi had seen enough, 'who are you? Identify!' He belted the last word at them like a rifle shot.

In front of them were two beings, clearly visible as the light dissipated into the freezing air of the tundra. A man, a woman, motionless, apparently stunned by where they found themselves. The new arrivals were frantically puffing condensing vapour into the air, slowly calming themselves, continuing to survey their location, eyeing Yoshi and Nate curiously.

31 Information

"A sum can be put right: but only by going back till you find the error and working it afresh from that point, never by simply going on." ~ *C.S. Lewis*

'Okay Sky, which one this time kiddo?' Harry said, fanning the air, not really caring what the answer was because he didn't think it made any difference. 'Eeny-meeny-miney-moe perhaps? A more scientific principle…well, it's as good as it gets,' he said, scowling impatiently, irritated.

Sky glanced furtively over her shoulder at Harry who was standing behind her. 'I say we choose one of the two central Spheres. The ones that gave us the numbers…the binary, at least we know they're active in all this.' She was still contemplating the update they got from Jack. Jupiter just up and vanishing on them. The words hadn't registered, the concept so hollow it just skated around without finding a way in, like a roulette ball on a wheel that never slowed. The biggest planet, a thousand Earths, gone in a heartbeat, apparently fading out like a dying flare. Forgetting the whys for a moment, she swerved unnervingly. From what they'd seen, their tech capabilities seemed to put biblical gods to shame, if they could erase Jovian sized worlds without the need for explosive power then…was anything beyond them? And what about the implications of Jupiter's gravity wellbeing no more, Vic knew the entire solar family was at risk, including the precious seed below them and it still grabbed him by the balls and gave them a damn good tweak every time he rolled around the meaning of *end game.*

'Anyone have a problem with either of them?' Vic quizzed, 'they're rotating on a pretty steep axis so we'll go with the one that presents easiest when we get there.'

'Whichever,' Sky said, eyeing them with the trembling expression of an agitated cat.

'Gun it commander,' Harry offered, his mouth curving into a veiled smirk.

'Easy, or you can drive,' Vic said, grinning mildly as he deflected the hand controller for a simple translational manoeuvre. pushing them toward the nucleus of the Sphere.

Sky was listening intently, trying like hell to smile, most of all, to maintain self-control, but it was only a poorly constructed ruse hiding a morbid state of anxiety. Nothing had really changed inside her head. Dying up here was an unrelenting source of horror but if they didn't meet the threat head on, Earth, home, people, family…it might all be gone.

Vic had the shuttle on the doorstep of the objects within a few minutes. The grace and choreography of the rotation was a sight to see, an alluring harmony had the golden Spheres spinning around an invisible central axis as though they were atomic particles manacled by an implacable nuclear force. Nodding briefly at Harry he said, 'okay, let's do it.' As he ignited the aft verniers.

Sky felt her body stiffen as they closed on it, staring owlishly at the glowing curvatures - maybe one was salvation, the other a million times worse than hell. Flashing across her mind was her daughter's face. Goddamn it, she thought dismally, her heart banging like a drum. Skylar tried the Sama-Vritti breathing thing Vic taught her but it did nothing but make her dizzy. And now she felt the agony of a cramp in her thigh, suddenly straightening her leg to avoid it. The objects loomed large, two tremendous ball bearings, spinning, swinging like atomic qubits from a mighty quantum computer. As they inched closer, a shiver ran through Sky; she was, convinced these things were more evil than any of them imagined.

***

'This is Griffin, we on?'

'Yep, we got you,' Jack confirmed, seeing a clear image of the Stanford University Braun Auditorium drop into view on the massive screen at Mission Control. On the left was the Hubble feed and next to it was the image of a room crowded to overflowing with the best minds in the country, as well as Griffin and his Government cronies who looked distinctly out of place.

301

'This is Blake Norris,' Jack recognised the voice as the Principle Investigator for LINEAR.

Griffin looked up at the ceiling mounted camera and said, 'Jack we have eyes on JPL, Mission and LINEAR but you'll have us and only be able to hear LINEAR. That's the best we could do…apparently.' He shot a scowl at Picton King who gave a brief shrug, rolling his eyes disdainfully.

The NASA facilities and Stanford were linked for the final stages of the debate on the *"Implications of Major Planetary Loss"* which had been going for a week but was now expected to provide some definitive intel. Scholars of note, many of eminence from around the country were still in residence, together with numerous Heads from the Agency's network facilities at Stennis, JPL, Toulouse, Cape Town, Toyama, Ningpo and Gorki. The director of the Astrophysical Council was there as were four members from the SSEC, five controllers from NEOWISE and Pan-STARRS, chiefs from the National Science Foundation, the Science Advisory Committee, FEMA, the UN Security Council and the National Security Council. The auditorium was bristling with tension and formality with a rarely seen combination of Government and intellectual heavyweights.

The LINEAR Near-Earth Object programme was NASA's best practice deep-field survey that dealt with potential death chunks bigger than a click in size. It was run by MIT's Lincoln Lab, using the best global tech available, namely the electro-optical sensors built for the US Air Force Space Surveillance Agency. Its findings were truthed by other organisations, most importantly, Pan-STARRS, NEOWISE, Spacewatch and the Catalina Sky Survey. Every resource was focussed on the asteroid belt, trying to spot objects that might be transiting toward Earth, potentially striking at some point along its year long solar passage.

Geoff Rhodes walked to the podium at the head of the monstrous table, testing the mike with a flick of his finger. All seemed in order as he grunted, feeling the tap-tap of his pulse rising in his throat. Jack could see sweat beading on his top lip. Poor bastard, he thought, having to speak to and more to the point, control this room full of ballistic egos. Paul Bloom had tried it for the first three days and he was, in his own words, "ready for the straps and rubber room."

'Welcome gentlemen to the topic of Jupiter's loss to the solar system,' Geoff started, 'and the implications in the short term…for Earth…for us.'

'Jesus,' Jack whispered to Pete, 'building the drama much?'

Pete winked at him with a half-smile, 'and that's just the opening remark.'

Geoff continued after a brief pause, 'I'll start with a summary, then defer to Blake for some expert detail on what NASA has found. I need to remind you all as a matter of formality that the President has classified this intel as Code White, Level 10. If anything is verbalised, documented, disseminated by any means inside or outside these walls, the new, uh…Global Terror Act comes into play. As you know there's no reasonable doubt here, just gaol.' He stopped for a breath, the words of caution hanging in the air. 'Sorry to be so harsh but, uh, well…you understand. If any of what we're about to discuss gets out, then the world will be even sorrier for it.' Glancing around the room he added, 'we all okay with that?' Tough shit if you're not he thought distractedly.

There was an audible murmur through the mike. Jack nudged Pete, raising an eyebrow, whispering, 'they've found something?' Pete shook his head vacantly, keeping his eyes forward.

'Whatever it is…it's gotta be big,' Pete eventually said, feeling a coldness in his throat as his brain threw up partial images, hellish scenarios. How many ways can you die, he brooded.

Geoff dragged in a deep breath, straightening his bearish shoulders, awkwardly clearing his throat. 'So Jupiter and the Moon have been removed by means and motivations we don't understand. We are currently efforting analysis and trials in Antarctica, in space through shuttle Sagan and with expert driven think-tanks across the country, including here at Stanford.' Geoff cleared his throat and continued in a slightly more ominous tone.' It's Jupiter we're concerned about most. The loss of its deep sweeping abilities and control over the asteroid belt are likely the reason we're here at all…the reason we exist as a species.' Taking a sip of water, he let go of the glass before he'd rested it back down and it landed with a loud ca-chunk, spilling water onto the pulpit. 'Shit,' he blurted before he could stop himself. 'Ah…er, sorry about that.' Geoff wiped his forehead with the back of his hand, offering a shaky smile. He continued, annoyed by his lack of composure. 'Okay, so the asteroids that were in gravitational harmony with Jupiter have come under the primary care of the Sun and are…as we speak, moving toward the inner solar system, searching for balance.' He raised his hands and pulled them in toward his chest, 'they will end up, we suspect, in a zone bounded at its closest between Mercury and Venus and at its most distant from the Sun, somewhere between Earth and Mars. It'll tighten up over the next thousand years or so.'

One of the Soviet scientists from Gorki broke in, '…these er, asteroids will swing in and out of this zone, maybe a bit further until they find equilibrium with the masses…yes?'

'Yes, that's exactly what will happen,' Geoff replied quickly.

'Okay, so we're wood ducks for centuries,' the Russian stated firmly, looking down at his tablet, already tapping away.

'Pretty much,' Geoff conceded, silently thanking the Soviet prick for stating the obvious.

The noise through the mike was much louder this time. All of them knew the asteroid belt was in a different gravitational free-fall but to have it confirmed within the confines of the Stanford Auditorium added weight to the pronouncement.

'Christ,' Jack said quietly. 'What's the punch line to all this?' He wished to God this session would wind up, it was torture.

'Okay,' Geoff said heavily. 'I'm going to hand over to MIT for specifics on what we've observed and calculated so far. Blake, it's all yours.' Geoff sat down, wiping his brow with two knuckles, glad that some other poor schmuck had to deal with the rest of the hurt.

Blake was a brilliant astroscience scholar. He sucked at public speaking, but as LINEAR's head honcho he had all the facts. It was his turn to scrape his boot across the mound and suck it up.

'…um, thanks,' he started uneasily, looking distinctly ill at ease. 'The news, er…isn't good gentlemen,' he said. 'It's not as bad as it could be but, well, it's bad enough. There are several waves of asteroids heading broadly toward the Sun and by implication, toward the inner planets.' He took a lingering breath, fighting to null the shakiness in his voice. 'We've used every resource we've got, running them around the clock, primarily the Catalina Smith and Steward Observatory in Arizona, Pan-STARRS Discovery 'scope in Hawaii, the Las Cumbres Observatory in California.' Blake's voice was becoming slurred as he struggled to keep it together. No sleep for two days took a toll on vocal cords. 'Our largest CCD cameras have been working twenty-four-seven since it happened.'

'That's mighty impressive,' Geoff said, pinching the bridge of his nose, 'but cut to the facts, time is something we…look, just get to it Blake.' He sensed the impatience of the group by the growing background noise.

'Oh, er, sure,' he said sheepishly. '…um, so we've identified two objects that have a ninety-one and ninety-four percent likelihood of intercepting the forward projection of Earth on its solar …'

'English Blake for God's sake.' Most of the scientists knew the deal anyway but there were non-science types present, Government, Diplomats, UN and the like. If their pained expressions meant anything, they were struggling to understand what he was droning on about.

'Right then, you know best Geoff,' he said with a brittle smile. 'The two objects will almost certainly impact Earth and do so remarkably quickly. Both are travelling at around a hundred kilometres per second, which we can't explain. The entire mass of rock and debris from the asteroid belt is travelling as though it has, um,' he paused, searching for simplicity, '…like it's received a colossal gravity assist from something out there, something we can't see or detect in any wavelength, using any remote sensor, here or in orbit.' Blake took a sip of water, replacing the glass carefully, hand visibly shaking. Peering back up, he blinked several times, drawing out a long sigh. 'If there's something up there responsible for the sudden velocity it's nothing we've encountered before. If it was something massive like a black hole or even dark matter we'd detect its effect but there is nothing…just regular space.' He steepled his fingers, rubbing his nose, studying the flurry of activity in the massive auditorium.

All the brilliant minds in the room were scribbling on pads, typing on tablets and laptops, looking up and down or gazing around to gauge reactions, maybe try and see what others were thinking. Silence finally returned as they pondered what seemed like a complete nonsense.

'Rocks, debris and planetoids are approaching on parabolic trajectories but so far only two are predictively modelled to strike.' Blake's eyes widened noticeably, 'and when I say *only* I use the word most advisedly because they are depressingly world ending.' His face paled 'The Dawn spacecraft is in orbit around Ceres, the largest asteroid, we're moving its camera to get some vision.'

'How big are we talking?' Jack asked tentatively, 'the two that are going to hit I mean.' His mind raced with visions of dying dinosaurs and a burning, expiring planet.

'Right,' Blake blustered, shifting papers around on the podium. 'The two have been previously described and named, 434-Hungaria and 243-Ida...and they are fifty-eight kilometres and twenty-seven kilometres in diameter...respectively. They're goddamn monsters Jack.' Geoff gazed down and pulled his shoulders back, clenching his jaw so hard the muscles in his neck stood out.

It wasn't unexpected, it was just the mundane declaration of extermination that was so numbing. The sheer magnitude of the killers was mind blowing, and taken with the inexplicable countdown, the vanishment of planets, the obtuse messages of failure, the whole screwed up scenario was simply a mind fuck. The world was ending, the only question was... what would strike first.

Like a rising tide, the noise returned and quickly became overwhelming, questions, accusations, statements of doom drifting in the air like wedding confetti.

'Jesus...Gentlemen please!' Geoff shouted as he got to his feet, glaring at Blake, urging him on. Get it the fuck over with he said silently, jutting his jaw toward him.

Blake nodded stoically. 'We have twenty-nine days to impact, uh...first impact,' he said croakily, finishing off the verdict of extinction to the crowd, together with a decent timing on the probable curtain fall. 'These are S and E Type asteroids, so we can expect the worst possible damage.'

Not that it mattered a goddamn iota, Jack thought miserably, at that size and speed, even loosely aggregated comets or fairy dust would be an extinction level event let alone a conk-buster made of metal and silica. They would bludgeon Earth with a force belonging to the Gods. Their impacts, individually would be devastating. Together, one after the other, they would be utterly catastrophic, planetary wrecking-balls that would rid Earth of every form of life including bacteria. His heart felt heavy in his chest as he grimly debated whether their world would even be here when the rocks arrived.

Jack saw Griffin stand up roughly and move to the mike. 'Avoidance strategies...NASA? He said, raising his voice fiercely. 'What've you got?'

Blake's voice became audible as the noise slowly retreated. He rubbed his chin and briefly tugged an ear. 'I-I don't think you understand sir,' he said, confused, 'there is no strategy for anything larger than a few kilometres and even then they're theoretical and have little chance of success. We've got nuclear explosions for short range, kinetic impacts for long range, ion beams, focussed laser, solar sail...but these assume we have months or years to prepare. And sir, ignoring time available for a moment, we have zero answers to things of this magnitude.'

Griffin shot him a killer glare, tilting his head ominously. 'Surely there's something,' he demanded, scowling at him, then scanning the faces of the scientific gathering scornfully.

'Zero chance,' Blake confirmed evenly.

'Jesus Christ, you NASA boys reckon you're the smartest people on the planet...and you have nothing? What is it that you people spend twenty billion a year on?' He looked at Blake with his best Griffin comply or die stare. Most around the table wondered who this ignoramus was.

'Mr Secretary,' Blake said gravely,' there is absolutely nothing we can do, except pray. We don't have the tech to deal with this type of threat. These things are beyond us. If we were a bit further along technically maybe we'd have a chance.' He rubbed his nose nervously, watching Griffin taking short steps back and forth, grunting and pulling at his tie. In for a penny, Blake thought dryly, continuing, twisting the knife in Griffin's gut, 'but we are royally screwed I'm afraid, bar an unforeseen change in trajectory. Remember the asteroid that killed the dinosaurs?' Griffin stared back deadpan. 'Well that was ten clicks through the middle, these things are six times bigger, coming in ten times quicker, made of way harder material.' The noise of blended voices evaporated again, the silence rich with fear, black, desperate, inescapable.

'God almighty,' Griffin said bleakly, 'what do we do? What damage will these things do?

'I'll field this Blake,' Geoff said, waving Blake back to his chair. He turned deliberately to Griffin, 'what damage you ask? Well, we've modelled it on our Pleiades computer which we had built with your twenty billion a year,' he rolled his eyes at Griffin who gazed back unimpressed. 'Anyway, it will be total, doesn't matter which one hits or if both hit or only one hits, everything's gone. It will be total sterilisation, the entire web of life will be gone, tsunamis, oceans boiling away, global volcanism, ozone layer destroyed, atmosphere vaporised.' He crossed and uncrossed his arms, running a hand across his face. 'The planet might survive but it'll be line-ball and if it does it'll be deader than dead for millions of years, maybe more.'

Griffin stayed silent, eyes lost behind a brow that jutted out unnaturally. He turned abruptly, glaring at Hillier. 'Go tell POTUS in person, tell him. Take a chopper, land on the fucking White House lawn if you have to.' He released a shuddering breath and spoke a tone lower. 'Get DoD approval Jim or you'll get shot out of the sky.'

He looked squarely at Geoff, losing any sense of calm, pointing with an index finger. 'I don't wanna hear that there's no solution. You find a way, you hear me?' He said, almost screaming. 'Norris, get your people on it, priority one, gang-bang the data, cut it up, rip it apart, then put something together, find a fucking way…something.' His face was flushed red, spotted with anger. 'What the hell are we going to tell our people…how do we sweeten this godawful bullshit?' He pursed his mouth sourly and sighed, picking at his top lip. 'We have no countermeasures so do we just bloody invent one, make it up, tell 'em it's under advisement, under control, that we're dealing with it?' His eyes were visibly straining in their sockets, seemingly ready to drop out and hit the floor. 'Anyone with a decent scope will be able to see these rocks. Goddamn comet hunters will put their trajectory together soon enough, what do we do then?' He snarled, still glaring at Hillier, then Ballard then Picton King with murderous intent. They stared back like idiots without comment, too terrified to speak for fear of putting their foot in it. This sort of decisioning or even idea rendering was way beyond their pay grade, definitely beyond their mental capacity. 'Why are you still here Hillier, I thought I told you to go! Fucking move it, POTUS, now!' Griffin stormed out of the room with his entourage of execs and minders forming a gaggle behind him. Only Hillier was in front of him, fairly sprinting out the door, running as fast as his short, squat body would allow, grunting and panting all the way. The door finally slammed shut with a hinge-rattling crash.

'Christ,' Jack whispered under his breath, watching the tormented expressions on those at Stanford. There was little left to say, so few bothered talking. Most were motionless in their seats, gazing at each other vacuously, shaking their heads despairingly.

Geoff thanked all those present and terminated the video link. All three camps were left to ponder the extinction of humanity.

***

Sky watched in horror, the idea of what might be inside or beyond, consuming her, as was the vexing news Jack had passed on to them earlier. Both were bubbling around, making her feel a little lopsided, sort of counter-weighted too much to the left. As the object loomed she thought anxiously about Tara, wondering how she could possibly have given birth while she was in there. The Doc from St Vinnie's hospital, Halverson, reported quite matter-of-factly that physiology workups concluded that she'd given birth at least once and maybe even twice. She'd been a busy girl apparently.

Tara had no memory of anything except the creature, yet she apparently left a son or daughter, perhaps both inside the Sphere, and presumably a partner of some description. Of course, it was more likely to be an artificial scenario… that in itself posed troubling questions about what she'd given birth to,

Sky felt a chill just thinking about it, a skin crawling shudder. The boy-creature apparently looked human but Tara had suspected it was all a ruse, just some physico-fabrication to assuage our primitive fears. Could she have birthed some hybrid part-breed, an experimental half human, half alien something with some dark clandestine purpose? Maybe it was fully alien or had a sprinkling of humanity mixed in like raspberry coolie, the hideous questions kept scraping across Sky's brain like glass-paper… painful, impossible to ignore.

They were treating Tara with an experimental Alzheimer's drug, AC253-B to try and get some of her memory back but they weren't confident. Her prefrontal cortex was very quiet under stimulation, meaning her memory centre was likely in poor nick. Skylar batted around the idea of losing all memory of her daughter and it made her feel like retching, although she conceded that no memory meant you'd have nothing to miss…but it was still a morbidly distasteful idea.

Vic warned them to brace as Sagan came within a few metres of impact. They had been in a semi-synchronous rotation with the object before inching cautiously inward, hitting it dead centre and rather than passing through it, seemed to stay within its ample curvature. They had occasional glimpses of the Sphere's silica-like surface from the main window, seeing beyond and into an incredibly dense cosmos. Space was pumped with matter wherever they looked except straight ahead where it was perversely dark and featureless. To the sides, above and below the front window panel there were stars everywhere, crammed together, a traffic jam in space, with every conceivable colour and tonal variation of the rainbow, a spectacularly rich stellar canvass, profuse beyond words.

They had a pretty good idea where they were, they weren't novices in this *show-and-don't-tell* caper anymore; the colossal bottleneck of glowing matter and gas was pretty much a giveaway. They were central to a galactic nucleus, no doubt about it, the final proof, a gargantuan black hole lying dead ahead, consuming everything around it, in a feeding frenzy, devouring stars, planets, gas and debris from a mind-blowing accretion disk that was blindingly luminous. It wrapped around its equator like a colossal version of Saturn's rings, broken only where matter was plummeting into the maw of the beast, heated to incredible temperatures.

Their direction of travel made it pretty clear where they were headed. 'We're s-still inside the Sphere, right?' Skylar said, her eyes swollen as she peered at the vista beyond. No way Sagan could withstand the exotic cocktail of gravity and radiation. They were a fair way distant but she knew that wouldn't last, most thankful they were cocooned inside the object.

Harry stared wordlessly at Vic for a moment, adrenaline making him buzz head to toe. The most enigmatic object in the Universe and here he was, eyeballing one…a fucking colossal one.

'Are we going in?' Sky stammered, searching Vic's eyes, her legs wobbly despite zero-g.

'Oh, we're going in alright,' he said. 'Everyone has a pad and a pencil, anything of, uh,' he searched for the right word, '…interest, get it down.'

Harry's mouth took a sarcastic twist, 'are you shitting me?' He shot back, 'We're going in there and you want us to write down anything of interest? I need a bigger piece of paper.'

Vic gave an impatient hmmmff. 'Okay, how about anything that presents as—, ' he paused again, lowering his eyebrows before shaking his head. 'God, I don't know…something suspicious, unusual, anything you reckon might point us in a better direction, how's that Harry?'

'Great,' Harry said. 'But I don't think there's anything in there apart from black hole junk, infinite gravity, firewalls, photon spheres, deadly radiation, stuff like that.'

'Maybe there isn't, maybe there is, and if there is, we need to be frosty and get it down. We won't know what we're looking for, until we see it…so pay attention.' Vic eyed him seriously, trying to read his expression. 'We're up here for our country, for the world and humanity Harry, pretty sure you're onto that.'

Harry grunted and saluted caustically, picked up his pencil and made stabbing motions toward Vic that ended with a broad grin. 'Maybe I'll plot some graphs as well, a nice column one, or a pie,' he mumbled, 'yeah, a pie chart, show the number of stupid questions thrown around by you lot.' He placed the pencil behind his ear and told him he was ready to go.

They appeared to be moving away from the particle disc at about seventy degrees to the perpendicular, transiting almost directly upward relative to its seemingly endless ring plane. Without the slightest kiss of inertia, the Sphere came to a halt and started back in the opposite direction, coming down almost directly into the bulls-eye of the black hole that was everything in front of them.

'This thing…er, how many solar masses Vic?'

'Jesus…billions,' Vic spluttered, hypnotised by vision of the blinding accretion disc retreating sideways, the oily blackness swelling in front of him as they closed the distance ridiculously fast. It was a solar system sized edge to space, sucking the galactic nucleus like a cosmic leach, dragging in stars by the hundreds and a lot more besides.

Skylar was unmoving, staring like a porcelain mannequin as they aligned themselves with the starloads of infalling material, punching straight down, through the horizon of no return. They rapidly arced away from the boiling stream of white-hot plasma being sucked down for as far as they could see, like Daniel 7:10, an endless river of molten gold and silver. Vic knew it was being drawn by the infinite curvature that was the root cause of all they could see, nature's most unlikely offspring.

They swept into an area that looked no different from normal space, like they were in a completely starless cosmos but that was it, there were no bizarre causality violations, infinite stretching or even boiling sparks of Hawking radiation. Looking as far back as the window panel would allow, they could see a tight curvature of starlight rising above them as though the outside Universe was squashed into an observable sphere.

Vic watched Sky's eyebrows turn sharply downward as she tried to make sense of what was out there. 'This ain't your regulation black hole,' Vic offered, 'it's the Godzilla of singularities. The bigger they are the less tidal forces, and one this big you could probably go EVA and wouldn't be any different from space in Earth orbit.'

'A-Amazing,' she whispered faintly, seeing a dim light appear from the depths of the darkness, brightening quickly ahead of them, suddenly everywhere all at once. Sky still hadn't moved as they penetrated the horizon of light, nearly having a seizure when she saw what was unfolding beyond. Her eyes grew until the tiny criss-crossing red veins were exposed for all to see.

'What in the n-name—, ' she mouthed almost silently, her voice falling away. 'H-How?' None of it should be here, not in a black hole. They'd seen some sights along the way but this one pretty much took the gong for the most outlandish.

Harry ripped the pencil from behind his ear. 'Let me get some clues down, on your teeny piece of paper here.' He glanced at Vic musingly, pondering it for a second or two. 'Remember, the brat said this Collective were disappointed in us, so maybe this is, um…maybe they are just showing us, sort of like we thought,' Harry added, wincing, feeling indignant and above all, deeply confused.

Below them was something so thunderously expansive, it fairly hit them like a knuckled punch. Peering straight out they could see part of an incredibly busy solar system with an array of Earth-like planets revolving around a tremendous sphere of light, star-like in appearance, but somehow a little off. They counted ten planets close to them, but there were thousands of others in the near and far distance, probably many more they couldn't see. All of them were blue and white, unambiguously alive, all in ultra-close orbits, ringing the pseudo-stellar object for as far as they could see, gently rotating as they moved.

Skylar looked at the picture and didn't have to be told there was something wrong with it. 'That's, uh…not a star, is it?' She mewed almost kitten-like, eyes almost hanging out of her head.

'uh…no,' Harry said, trying to make sense of it himself. 'Not a star, not here, no way,' but then he checked himself, there were planets, so most everything was possible he guessed. Harry snorted, picturing Jim Morrison sunning himself on a beach chair…because it was no more fanciful, maybe less so, than the absurdity being served up in front of them.

'It's the singularity, providing what a star normally would…ridiculous… insane, somehow they've stabilised gravity waves to create an amazingly harmonic environment.' Vic stated.

Harry grinned, 'and it's all green Sky. They've tapped into an unlimited supply of clean energy forever…no carbon tax required.'

'That's all wonderful Harry but how do they get out…like into space…not even light can escape.' Sky's forehead was wrinkled with effort as she chewed on the baffling nonsense.

'Maybe they don't need to,' Vic said, 'There might be millions or billions of planets in here. Once you're in, you're in, or maybe there's wormholes or who knows what that gets 'em out.'

Sky looked gravely at Vic, 'okay so how do we get out?' Nothing escapes a black hole, she knew that was law, but reckoned it might have lost its fidelity, or maybe gained an extra meaning, a new gospel according to who, she wasn't sure.

Vic shrugged and smiled knowingly. 'I reckon they've got it covered.'

Harry's breathing was getting louder, his face reddening, creasing with anger. 'All this stuff is wonderfully impressive, but let's cut to the chase here,' he said, giving a jarring clap of his hands. 'We've seen the disk habitat and now this…stirring stuff, right?' He lifted a cynical eyebrow. 'Far and away beyond anything we're capable of, or even reasonably imagined as possible. You say there's clues to a solution…well I say frogshit.' Harry was rigid, finger-tapping his hip. 'I don't know who that kid was but what he said resonates with what we're seeing. Like I said before, this is the sort of stuff we were supposed to achieve, he said we were screw-ups so maybe that's the reason for this chickenshit tour, to show us drop-outs how it's supposed be. But then that digs to the real issue in all of this.' Harry gazed into the air, eyes unfocussed, pensive. 'Why, oh why go to the trouble of rubbing our noses in it, what's the purpose, you know, for an advanced race?' He was breathing in short bursts, nostrils flaring with effort, beard in constant motion. 'I mean if we didn't make the grade, maybe help us or fail us, but seriously, why show us what we don't have a snowball's hope of achieving in a million lifetimes?' Harry knew he was asking questions with no hope of answers, breaking his own cardinal rule in the process, but fuck it he thought. All bets were off, torn up, erased…whatever. This was now officially a trailer load of steaming horseshit.

Vic looked at him, 'no answers Harry, there's no answers— '

Skylar was having none of it. Her face was suffused with irritation and she said loudly, 'that's crap Harry, we've achieved amazing things, the last hundred and fifty years we've gone from riding bareback on horses to landing on the Moon...sending craft to Mars…the outer planets.' She shook her head, not having any of it. Disappointment my arse, she thought angrily.

'But that's just it Sky,' Harry said, raising his hands expressively, 'we've assumed our evolution has been gob-smackingly fast but we've had zip to compare it to. It's the one-planet mentality…it's dangerous.' He scratched at his neck fiercely. 'Without any relativity, how do we know we aren't actually dumb as shit in the grander scheme? I reckon both civilisations we've seen, the disc-hab and this one are around the same age as us. We've talked about this Kardashev scale that speaks in millions of years, but what if it's supposed to happen a lot quicker than that?' Harry's face softened into passive vacancy as he pondered the odds, the likelihood that humans were seriously backward.

Sky was blinking rapidly, scowling at the floor. 'So, what…in the bigger scheme, we're retarded?' She asked incredulously, not wanting to believe it but conceding there might be a slice of something in it. She gulped…maybe more than a slice, but surely not the whole fucking pie.

'Maybe Sky, maybe. Without any reference or perspective, we'll never know.

Vic looked at Harry suddenly, 'we're moving again,' he said quickly.

'You sure?' Harry asked, not seeing anything that suggested motion.

'I can feel it. Whenever these things move there's a sensation, like fizzing in my ears, really faint. Focus, see if you get it too.'

Sky frowned, closing her eyes tightly, '…um, nothing,' she said after a few seconds.

'Nup,' Harry growled. 'You on something we don't know about?'

He offered a thin smile. 'Guess my brain's more sensitive than yours... not as thick.'

'Oh, so that's what you think?' Harry's mouth curled up wryly.

'Saying it like it is.'

'Prick,' he said, his face ceding to a beard splitting grin.

The singularity was behind them now, providing a front row view of the cosmos beyond the event horizon. Everything was shovelled into the middle of their view, same as they saw on the way in, a sphere that contained everything, including, incredibly, that was behind them.

'Jesus...the entire Universe in a single frame,' Skylar said, breathing in the unnervingly hybrid view of space. Situation normal when gravity has the strength of a few billion Suns.

They were moving faster, punching through the sparking, fizzing lightshow playing out just inside the event horizon, and without a sideways glance they pulsed back into the Cosmos proper.

Harry's eyes sparkled. 'Hah! Laws, constants, physics...screw you!' He shouted, raising a middle finger and sounding, looking every bit the neo-science nutbag. His expression stalled, growing serious as he recalled something. 'You remember the other thing the kid said that seemed odd? When Jack said it I thought nothing of it, but Tara reckoned every one of his words were carefully chosen. 'So, when he said something about wasted space, he meant something specific...I mean, that's probably right isn't it?' Vic nodded, Sky looked unsure, 'I thought he meant that we hadn't spread our wings, but now, um, I'm not so sure.' Harry said, pondering an empty cosmos.

'You're gonna have a stroke...take it easy,' Vic said a little mockingly, seeing the canyon lines on his forehead. 'You're the one championing the "no questions unless there's a theory" right?'

Harry shrugged, grunting through his teeth. 'Well I do have a theory,' he said. 'You've heard of the Fermi Paradox, right?' He nodded at them, explaining it anyway, '...so unless Earth is crazy odd there should be ETs running around everywhere 'cause our system is younger than a lot of others in the Galaxy.' They both nodded, aware of the little Italian's scientific idiom. 'Was Creature commenting on the nature of all this?' He motioned with his arms out and up, 'that the Universe isn't very productive, doesn't have what it needs to be friendly to life...to intelligence...on a larger scale?'

'That's a long bow Harry,' Vic sighed heavily. 'Pretty sure it was a commentary on us but hey, who knows?' Vic had heard enough, smiling weakly as their view of the Universe disappeared behind a rolling orange mist.

Skylar was gob-smacked at what Harry was suggesting. Tara even referenced the word God when she spoke of Creature, even asking him the question. On the face of it, the idea seemed utterly preposterous. But if the clue he'd given was that... well fuck me she thought dispiritedly, overwhelmed. The statement could be taken a dozen different ways and every time she re-ran it, something different showed its face. Sky decided to park it, gazing out the window as the orange stain shimmered a bit, then drew back like a curtain, revealing a beautiful blue Earth below them. They weren't far from the Spheres, groaning when she looked closer, shaking her head repeatedly as she surveyed the horror. 'Oh Jesus...oh God,' she moaned pitifully, looking up at Vic with huge doe-like eyes. 'Oh God,' she breathed again.

'What Sky?' He blurted, pulling his head away from the forward window.

'There's...four gone,' she moaned, 'remember, five was Jupiter.'

Harry counted them and felt a wedge in his throat contemplating the chilling notion of their family shrinking even further. At least Earth was still there, and the Sun was still shining in the forward window panel. He didn't dare give life to that nightmare, returning to Earth orbit to find it empty. No planet, no people, no Moon, no Sun...just them and a big fucking lonely Universe.

'Sagan, Flight, do you copy?'

Vic heard the urgency in Jack's voice, gulping instinctively, troubled by the intent.

'Shit,' Sky spat, 'I don't wanna know Vic, don't answer...I'm telling you, no more.'

Vic glared at her impatiently. Throwing his headset on he said, 'we have to answer, we can't leave Houston hanging. 'Copy Jack, what do you say?'

32. Return

"The intention that man should be happy is not in the plan of Creation." ~ *Sigmund Freud*

'Um, I'm Nate, this is Yoshi…w-who the hell are you?' He said sizing up the intriguing arrivals from the Sphere. Nate was stunned by the appearance of the duo, initially unsure what they were or whether they were even human. Watching them intently he took in every detail, looking for tell signs that might give them away as not quite human, but he detected nothing.

'Hello?' Nate said timidly, seeing them just standing there, gazing back almost comatose.

'Er, yeah, sorry, 'Carson Becker, this is my side-kick Connie.' She glared at him, muttering a mixed insult and profanity under her breath.

Yoshi exhaled loudly, expelling every scrap of air from his lungs into the freezing atmosphere. His expression softened, '…crap, from the shuttle, right? We were with Jack at JSC when you disappeared into that thing.' Nate's heart slowed from a gallop, realising these were no aliens, but never say never he reminded himself. Probably just a matter of time, maybe not here but somewhere, sometime, they'd put in a showing, he felt sure.

Last time they were heard from was at L1, a million clicks away, under normal circumstances that would need some serious explanation, of course now, well, it didn't need any.

Nate peered fixedly at Becker, eyeing him up and down. 'So, what happened up there, like how did you end up back here, the Pole, where you started right?'

Becker had been surveying the rugged mountains in the distance, suddenly spinning his head toward Nate, hearing the words and muddling over the meaning. He stiffened and glanced skittishly at Connie, both frowning deeply at each other, trying to reconcile the ridiculous conundrum.

'You're fucking joking, right?' He said, heart pounding, suddenly breathless, conceding with a gasp that he recognised the volcano-like silhouette of Mt Kirkpatrick to the East.

Nate filled them in on the harrowing event at the foot of the world, completely blowing their unsuspecting minds and then he moved on to everything else they'd missed, the Moon, Jupiter…the inscrutable kid-thing which nearly struck Connie dead where she stood. The connection was clear, the implication was terrifying. They lowered themselves to the ground, hyperventilating, clouds of white vapour everywhere, rich with expletives. It would take time Becker said disbelievingly, Nate mindful it was the last thing they had, rubbing an eyebrow nervously, knowing what needed to be done. 'Er, Becker, Connie,' he said suddenly, 'can you give us a minute?' I uh, need to talk to my comrade here about some camp details. Nothing important but HQ said it was restricted intel, some Army protocol thing.' He battled to keep his voice level and free of suspicion.

Becker's jaw was set square. 'Okay, well, we're not going anywhere,' he offered.

Connie eyed Nate closely, holding her tongue, enjoying the afterglow of exiting the hellhole that defied human experience on one hand, and on the other, well, fuck me she thought, just the end of the world. 'Yeah, fine, whatever,' she said without interest, gazing around at the beauty of the unclad continent. She peered into the sky and thought *Moon* and felt instantly sick.

Yoshi was puzzled as he fell in step behind Nate, knowing something was up.

'Christ, you get it don't you? You have to have a bad feeling about this. How do we know, I mean, is that really them?' Nate mumbled in a voice that was barely a hiss in the back of his throat.

'What the hell?' Yoshi whispered with intent. 'Are you okay…like feeling okay?'

'I'm fucking fine,' he spat sharply, quietly. 'Focus. Remember the other-them they gabbled on about at L1, the debrief with Jack…the craft they saw?'

Reading between what Nate said, the words finally wormed into his brain. 'Oh shit, surely you don't think— 'Yoshi's brow was so twisted it had lines that had their own lines.

'It's a possibility,' he said, 'and we know they were shit scared about it.'

'Why would they do it, I mean, what would going back achieve?' Yoshi asked, struggling to believe he was even having the conversation.

'That's the thing, nobody can know, maybe it's to do serious mischief, lay groundwork for something to come. If they got rid of any of their doubles, wouldn't that get rid of them as well? There's fucking paradoxes everywhere.' His eyes were wide, pupils pinpoint, stony.

'Well whatever the motivation, no way it could be good news, for anyone.'

'Damn right. No way…no way.'

'So, what do we do?' Yoshi muttered, glancing over at Becker and Connie as casually as he could. He could see them looking out in the direction of Mt Kirkpatrick, talking, and to his mind, looking mighty suspicious. Every now and then they would glance back at them, then back at the mountains. Yoshi wrung his hands and rubbed his brow, sliding a slow hand over his jaw. What were they talking about? Yoshi tried to listen but there was just the drone of the transantarctic wind.

Nate peered over Yoshi's shoulder, surveilling them closely. 'We don't know them well enough, that's the problem. If they revealed traits, information, anything out of character, how would we know, we'd have no idea.'

'Jesus Christ, I'll say it again,' Yoshi said irritably, 'what do we do? You brought it up, what's the answer if we somehow realise it's not them. You know, if they pull out a doomsday weapon, aim it right at us?' He grinned stiffly only a few inches from his nose.

Nate bit his lip and raised his shoulders, 'look we'll just have to watch them closely.'

'And if they do make a move?' Yoshi said, genuinely puzzled, bordering on disbelief. 'I can't believe we're talking about this, but if they make a move, whatever that even means, what are we supposed to do?' He looked at Nate aghast, 'I might be Japanese but I know zero about martial arts, fighting, stuff like that.' He grinned but it was a flash, melting into the freezing air.

'Okay, okay, I get it. I just think we need to know it's a possibility, stay alert, know that things mightn't be as they seem.'

Yoshi's eyes rose like moons. 'Do we…should we tell Jack?'

'If we suspect something, otherwise no. He's got enough shit on his plate with those suits hanging off him like fucking barnacles.' He shot a quick glance at Becker. 'Let's get back.'

'You know Nate, the thing is, if they are um, not what they seem, then us over here, by ourselves, will make them mighty suspicious.'

Nate met his gaze, his face hardening, conceding how right Yoshi was.

'So, this is Antarctica?' Becker said incredulously, taking a slow, deep breath as he looked around, exhaling in a rapidly fading plume. 'The glaciers…just…gone. We were on bedrock last time we were here, but—, ' He paused and craned his head straight up, 'Jesus, there was a couple of kays of ice above our heads.' Turning slowly in a full circle he surveyed the heavily incised, unfamiliar landscape that was so unlike the polar Popsicle he'd left behind. 'This is crazy, not one goddamn icicle left. Does it even snow here anymore…blizzards and the like?'

'Not once so far,' Yoshi said, pursing his lips in thought. Not only had the glaciers gone but so too the almost daily ice falls. The National Weather Service told Jack that all was in order, the moist systems from the lower lats still fed into this place so the absence of ice was another confounding mystery. These others must have done something to the climate? Changing local weather wasn't an apocalypse but it did make one anxiously revisit the notion of "a thousand cuts".

'Such a beautiful place,' Connie whispered, gazing at the raw landscape, so alien, so remarkable. It was still damn cold, that hadn't changed, which begged the same galling question, why the hell hadn't any ice fallen?

'It's great if your idea of beautiful is a barren, freezing wasteland,' Becker said, looking at Connie sideways then up at the jagged highlands.

Connie glared at him, massaging an eyebrow, feeling her blood rise. 'You lack any appreciation of the finer things you know that? This place is gorgeous, look, open your damn peepholes.' She pressed a hand on the back of her neck, pushing her lips together.

'No, this place is freezing, dead and perverse, it's a nightmare, look around you.'

'You're a nightmare,' she said, gritting her teeth, lamenting his pitiful ignorance.

'Well it's one up on where we came from I'll give you that.'

Connie's face mellowed, feeling a shiver as she recalled the most horrific, mystifying nowhere imaginable, fighting to box the memory up where she couldn't get at it, but it was still there.

Nate smiled as he watched them trade insults. Despite the rancour and occasional hostility, there seemed to be a shared connection between the two. No way these were alternates, he thought, conceding in the next breath that artificial memories had to be considered. Rubbing cold stubble on his chin, he winced at the never-ending number of covert scenarios that might be in play.

Connie was certain they'd think she was barking mad but with an iron effort, a deliberately serious tone, facts only, she relayed the story of the chamber crammed with the mundane cylinders. Then in a stuttering, stumbling voice, she followed with their sanity testing violation of space as they rode the vacuum, searching for the least whacked-out words but ending up calling themselves *"conscious corpses"*. It echoed around them, sounding like the biggest bucketload of fish guts imaginable, convinced they couldn't believe it. Not breathing, no heartbeat, yet full animation, that was some serious stuff to digest…and believe. Their blank expressions and soft-boiled eyes confirmed it, they didn't even mention the possibility of it being a dream. Enough shit had happened in the last weeks to make the most tin-pot, hair-brained event seem plausible.

Connie said urgently, 'we need to report to Mission…you have comms right?'

'Sure.' Nate motioned them to the canopied area, gesturing with an arm.

'So, uh…what's the security for?' She quizzed, spying the armed military milling around the periphery of the plate, in her words, like the "fucking National Guard."

'No idea, Defence Secretary's idea.'

'Hardly going to be trouble down here,' Becker said a little uncertainly, 'is there?'

'Nah, unlikely but the world's pretty much done,' Nate said soberly, 'it's an unholy mess out there, anarchy across nearly every city, every country.' His mouth stretched down grimly, 'populations everywhere are panicked, society's going the way of the fucking dinosaurs… the Spheres, the Moon, Jupiter…killer asteroids were the final straw—'

Connie's eyes sparked, blinking rapidly a few times, 'hang on, say what…asteroids?'

'Oh right, uh…we might have missed that one,' Nate said, in the same breath wondering what he would have done if they did know, because they couldn't have. If these two were alternates their game plan was well and truly on song he mused uneasily.

'Hello… what?' Connie asked, heart pumping harder to keep pace with her breathing.

Nate wondered how he should proceed, glancing at Yoshi who pushed a shoulder up, silently urging him to get on and do it. 'Uh, well…Jupiter's gone and the asteroid belt is unstable, the whole lot is coming toward the Sun, toward us,' he said, shrugging lamely.

The language hit their brains, bounced off, then piled up with enough weight to sink in.

Yoshi thought they may as well get it over with, 'we have two headed our way and there's no hope according to Jack. Us, everything else…we're done. The bigger one will pulverise the planet…send it back to the archaic.'

Connie moaned, senses thickening like treacle. 'No hope at all…as in zero? Is that what you mean? What about collision avoidance stuff, do we have no way of— '

'Zero.' Nate confirmed coldly. No point sweetening the truth, it was what it was.

'And this was released to the public?' She asked incredulously, eyeballing him wildly.

'No of course not but there's enough dickhead astro-nuts out there to find anything that's coming our way.'

Becker was dazed, a thousand thoughts arrowing through his brain, exploding like a line of squibs. He knew the Spheres were threatening a grim finale but now they were facing odds of zero, was the end of everything already written? 'How long?' Becker said feebly, 'how long have we got?'

'Two weeks or so,' Nate replied, averting his eyes, feeling the pain all over again.

'Oh great…coupla' weeks,' Becker said vaguely, gawking at Connie who wore such a pitiable expression it sent a tremor through him. They gazed at each other open mouthed, galvanised by the horror of those few, brief words.

'So, what are you doing here?' Connie eventually asked Nate, trying to expunge the portents of death and destruction from her mind.

'Trying to turn this piece of shit off. You know they reckon you started all this…by screwing around with it in the first place.'

'We already figured that out,' Connie said ruefully, 'thanks for putting it like that though, cuts through the bullshit.' She looked at Becker, then at Nate, 'so that's what they're saying … we're the ones who fucked up the world. That we're the, uh…new Oppenheimer… destroyer of worlds?'

'Something like that, yeah,' Nate said, a smirk running briefly across his face. 'Actually, Creature claims you were compelled to find this thing because some random timeline had been met, and then I guess curiosity did the rest, you pumped it full of numbers and away it went.'

'Compelled?' Becker splurted. 'Are you serious…compelled? He repeated doubtfully, breaking into a wry smile, pretty sure it was hogwash.

'Compelled by greed maybe, self-indulgence, self-love definitely,' Connie said, eyes gleaming, 'no one had to force that on him, he was just following Becker instinct. You know, a dog digging up a bone, a deer crapping in the woods, it doesn't know any different, just does what it does…look, see, eat, shit.'

Becker shook his head testily. 'Seriously do you ever consider not unloading on me? Remember, there wasn't actually any rhodium here despite what it looked like on the Grav maps.'

'Oh, for God's sake, get a grip. That is so irrelevant it's not even funny…you thought it was there but it was just this goddamn metal plate,' she said sneeringly. 'Whatever the hell it was, you wanted it!' She snorted at his pathetic attempt to deflect blame.

'The bloody specimen's what started this,' Becker blurted defensively. He thought about it for a couple of seconds, conceding the compelling part might be right. It was within their capabilities. 'Maybe it was an elaborate plan to hook us in,' he said, puckering his mouth uneasily.

Connie snorted even louder this time, ending with a derisive chuckle, 'yeah that's right,' she said sharply, 'an alien race stuck a rock in Antarctica, made sure you not only got hold of it but you chased it all the way back to the Pole like the third little pig. And all so you could stumble over the anomaly like a drunken cowboy. Shit,' she snapped, staring at him like he'd grown a hump, 'can you be more of an idiot?' Connie didn't care if it was true, there was no way she was going to swallow it. Not while Becker was standing in front of her pretending to be all wide-eyed and innocent. The Nate fellow was right, Becker was like Oppenheimer, simple as that. Clearly not in intellect but in what he'd unknowingly set in motion. Connie knew she was almost as complicit as he was in setting off what seemed to be nothing short of a countdown to apocalypse.

In his own mind Becker was blameless. Chasing a dream, that's all it was, and while it was technically illegal he didn't see how he could be held responsible for the ridiculous chain of events that followed. Who could have predicted it…but compelled to do it? He was the first to reject that as absolute dribble. Obsession, desire, the want for fame had driven him, not some alien race with mischief on their minds.

'Nate, can you get on to Jack?' Connie asked, scowling at Becker who was still looking all innocent and hurt. That crap needed to be stowed, the priority was letting Jack know what they'd seen up there. Cryptic, unmeaning though it was, that was the deal they'd agreed to. Full disclosure.

'Sure,' Nate said walking over, picking up the headset, radioing Mission in Houston on the UHF SatCom uplink. He tried three times, on each occasion getting nothing. Twice more got the same irritating, confounding noise. 'Sounds sort of like thermal static but we're in the coldest place on Earth,' Nate said, bewildered. 'Um, well, the upshot is that comms are down.' He tried to come up with reasons for Houston's silence, maybe a Borealis event although he knew there hadn't been a single one since the de-icing, or so said his intel briefing. If precipitation had somehow been nulled then hey, charged particles from the Sun, no problem. Outta here.

Nate glanced at Yoshi. 'Take Connie and get our friends from Langley to raise Jack on their AR Modular setups. They've got tactical units in the Osprey's,' he said, 'automatic band switchers so they should be able to sort something out.' He still felt uneasy.

Yoshi and Connie had already started off toward the tilt-rotors, camped just beyond the edge of the metal dish.

***

Earth had stopped being Earth more than a week ago. Jewel of the solar system it may have been but now it was a pallid facsimile of its former glory. The colour, the joie de vivre had been sucked out of it almost overnight, entire populations grappling with the brutal knowledge that end-time was imminent and its most palpable harbinger was barely a stone's throw away in space. Social order was fading by degree, infrastructures that supported human civilisation were creaking under the weight of a planet mostly divorced from its core behaviour.

Commerce had pretty much shut up shop along with every other field of endeavour, taedium vitae was gripping the globe…no one gave a shit. No interest, no incentive, no future. With zero-time looming, there was no motivation to do a thing that looked even a week in the future. Complete loss of purpose changed the daily footprint of every person on Earth. Apart from eating and loved ones, the future was the reason to get out of bed, to go to work and provide, to learn and better one's self, find a partner, have a family. These were the fruitful, mind-consuming things that staved off the natural obsession with dying. But that was all gone now. All that was left was death.

With the future peeled away, the world was a playground for street zombies. Thugs and murderous automata were everywhere, crime was anywhere you cared to look and food supplies were already growing short. Normally law-abiding citizens were stealing, maiming and worse to provide for their own.

Religions, fundamentalists, sects, cults, theologies and more, the planet was corner to corner with End-Time noggers, internet bloggers, Judgement Day zealots, adorning nearly every street, every newspaper, saturating social media to the exclusion of just about everything else.

The twin leviathans would strike Earth at incomprehensible speed. Regular asteroids might be expected to impact at twenty clicks a second but these were screaming in at many times that, promising an extinction level event like no other.

Parents agonised over their children, mentally imaging them for the journey, praying for an afterlife, knowing their futures were measured in cosmic heartbeats and soon to be erased by a couple of feeble specks in the night sky, if not before by methods unknown. Their children, their children's children and the thousands of future generations would all be snuffed out, courtesy of an alien imperative that defied comprehension.

The obliteration of human culture and anything that fell under the blanket of civilisation was virtually complete. By the time Earth's atmosphere was tapped, should they last that long, there would be precious little left to destroy.

***

'All comms are down,' Yoshi shouted when he thought he was within earshot of Nate. 'Military boys are the same, have no idea why.' His face darkened, 'well there is one idea but I don't think it's the reason.' He glanced at Connie who looked away, rubbing at strands of tangled hair.

'What are they saying?' Nate said, feeling the back of his neck start tingling. Three from three he wondered anxiously? Radio would be yet another ignominy.

'Equipment's fine, they ran self-test routines, they came back okay.' Yoshi paused, gazing at Nate.

'Well?' He snapped abruptly. 'So, what's the goddamn theory?'

Yoshi looked him straight in the eye. 'That everyone's gone.' He didn't break his gaze, seeing Nate visibly swallow, not believing it but admitting it was possible. Had these others gone from de-icing to de-humanising, to eliminating in some sort of biblical reckoning?

Nate's forehead churned with lines. 'Gone?' He repeated Yoshi's word apprehensively. 'Then why would we be here? If everyone's gone we'd be gone…right?'

'Bullshit,' Becker yelled, 'you, can't be serious, can you? You don't believe they're— '

'Well it's possible, but no I don't believe it,' Nate said. 'Logically if the rest of us were gone, we'd be outed too. Just because we're isolated wouldn't make a difference would—, ' he paused, drawing his brows together, grinding his jaw. 'Maybe being isolated down here, uh…saved us.' He rubbed his forehead with a thumb, 'shit, who knows…everything's a big fat maybe.' Nate paced around, taking short mincing steps, grimacing, breathing erratically.

'Maybe all that's left is people in isolated areas, Arctic, Greenland, etc.' Connie muttered. 'Remember, the Spheres in the atmosphere are all at high and low lats, maybe that means something.'

They peered at Connie, not believing there was any veracity in it, but twitchy all the same.

Nate snapped his head around, struck by a thunderous thwacking sound from one of the Osprey's turboshaft engines firing up. The Rolls Royce powerhouses were throttling up to VTOSS speed and in a few seconds the twin rotors, the colossal triple blades had it in the air, pounding away from the base. She watched the nacelles rotate ninety degrees to jet mode, powering it over the rocky peaks above. Despite their perilous situation, Connie couldn't help but be impressed, the damn thing was fucking awesome.

'Well I guess we'll know soon enough,' Yoshi said, watching the craft vanish behind the mountains, 'although it'll take 'em days to get to Australia and back, if they decide to come back.'

Becker peered at the remaining aircraft, relieved to see no other activity. There were just military guys standing around, doing nothing in particular. 'Hopefully they don't all decide to pull up stumps,' he said restlessly, not relishing the idea of being stranded in this barren hellscape.

'You'll be fine Becker,' Connie soothed with a bemused smile, 'if they leave I'm sure they'll take you with them, you're way too valuable to leave here.' She twisted her lip at him, finishing with an acid grin, melting further into an unfriendly stare.

'I don't think any of us want to be stuck out here with just this.' He gestured in a sweeping motion with one arm, pointing toward the rather flimsy supply tent.

'Always the team player,' she said unsympathetically, 'should have known better.'

'Glad you finally recognise that,' Becker said, nodding his head firmly.

'I recognise that you're full of— '

'Shit!' Nate said loudly, ending Connie's sentence dramatically. 'We need to start working on the object. Enough bickering,' he said seriously, 'you two should just slug it out, get it the hell over with.' He shot a disarming smirk at Connie and a cautionary scowl at Becker. She was cute in her little polar outfit, Becker was just an insufferable bore.

'No way,' Becker said flippantly, 'any fight, she'd win, I wouldn't lay a glove on her. She does that Japanese self-defence crap.' Nate grinned knowingly at Yoshi who glared back, pushing his chin up, ignoring the sarcasm.

'And don't you damn well forget it,' Connie said emphatically, zipping her parka right up to her chin and pressing her lips tightly together.

Nate's research told him that blinding ice storms gathering from nowhere and life threatening wind-chill were a constant threat in this formerly harsh land. It used to possess a hundred deadly faces but since the madness had begun in earnest, much of that had just vanished along with the ice. Still freezing and desolate, it was way less lethal to the underprepared. Now, with temperatures dropping and winds rising, Nate felt like things might be on the downswing. And he didn't think it had anything to do with the high latitude season change marching their way. There was a higher force in command. He walked with intent to the comms area, grabbing two backpacks. 'Becker, take that bag, let's go…we need to move. Weather's closing in so time might be short.'

Connie couldn't help but puzzle over the apparent disorganisation, she'd heard no talk of tactics, just that they needed to do something. Sounded anything but a crack strategy. 'So, what's the plan?' She asked Nate directly as they strode toward the centre of the dish. 'Is there a plan?'

He looked her up and down, raising an eyebrow. 'What's our plan?' He repeated quizzically. 'What, so you can decide if you want to hang around?'

Connie stopped walking and made a hmmmff sound through her nose, 'okay smart arse, what was the brief from HQ?' She stared at him with distaste. 'How's that…comprendo?'

Nate looked straight ahead, 'well, it's not much more than I already told you. We try and deactivate it, turn it off, power it down or just destroy the damn thing with explosives.' Connie's eyes bulged, then swept over his face, stunned at the unexpected declaration of war. Nate powered on, leaving her behind. 'We have unconditional approval from Griffin, he's the Secretary of Defence, to effort anything we've reasonably thought through, agreed by all parties. We need to try and synch with this thing, understand it where we can, use what we already know.' He turned around and lowered his chin toward Connie, 'so yes we have a plan of sorts, but we need to start thinking because it's, well…nothing if not fluid.'

Connie shuffled back a step or two, mulling frantically over his words, expelling her breath in a spray of pale fog. Are you fucking serious…destroy it? 'Are you on the level, do you honestly believe you can blow that thing apart?' Connie eyed the object closely, certain it wasn't even made of material as they'd define it, then shifted her eyes back to Nate, incensed by the insanity. Did these idiots think this thing was pieced together in Wisconsin, built from army-issue steel and aluminium? If they were looking to really piss it off, then trying to kill it was absolutely the way to go. Her face was burning despite the cold. If all these events, including this one, were a high-end test of humanity's ingenuity and we roll out a barrel full of firecrackers to solve it, well God help us all, she thought bitterly. We could truly kiss our arses goodbye if that screwy military scenario came into play.

'That's a contingency only…a backup,' Nate said, backpedalling awkwardly. 'If we try everything we have and don't get a result we, uh…blow it up, or like you said, we try to.'

'But blow it up how?' She repeated in a blur, feeling her mind swim. The idea was mad, irrational at best. Connie was confident a nuke would barely knock the shine off it.

'We've got Semtex…plastic explosive, five kilos of it…in there.' He pointed a finger at the bag Becker was holding. 'Enough to level a city block.'

Becker froze, eyes snow coning out of his skull as he stared blindly at what he was holding. 'Semtex what? You're joking…in here?' He peered at the bag again, swallowing hard, nearly gagging. 'I thought it was food…water. Jesus.'

'Don't drop it,' Connie said loudly, stifling a laugh but quickly growing serious, realising she'd go up with him if it went off.

'Shit,' he said, glaring at Nate. 'You might have told me I was carrying a fucking bomb.'

'Relax,' Nate said without much conviction, 'without the detonation cord it's quite safe.'

Connie had heard enough of this backwoods trollop. 'This is nuts,' Connie moaned, crossing her arms tightly across her chest. 'This will not impress them, whoever the hell them is. Anyway,' she said forlornly, pausing, her heart-shaped face the colour of fresh snow, 'the asteroids - does it really matter what we do down here, they're going to do the job right?' She was blinking rapidly, rooted to the spot, her face sagging.'

Nate stared at her for a long moment. 'What we do know is that nothing about any of this is predictable. 'Things might change Connie and if they do, this becomes pretty damn important.'

'And the bomb?' She mewed, barely audible.

'Like I said, it's last resort stuff, a failsafe, so let's try and turn this thing off before we need to, um…you know.'

'Failsafe you say,' Connie scoffed softly. 'Nothing safe about it, can never happen.'

***

Standing next to the small hemisphere were four patently nervous human beings, eyes wide behind their polar visors as they moved in stilted steps, wind whipping grains of loose rock painfully against exposed skin on their face. They were grouped tightly together on the alien slab, surrounded by the steeply chiselled nakedness of New Antarctica. The really puzzling part of the picture were the twin Spheres, one large, one small, sitting idly in the middle of the dish, their perfect curvature a glaring contrast to the stark erosional landforms around them.

Yoshi unzipped one of the backpacks, grabbing a stack of prints untidily stapled together. 'Ten thousand digits of Pi, should be enough,' he chirped, grinning proudly. 'We've also got the deepest numbers that exist, the last thousand digits extracted by the ETD Project, eighty trillion decimals down you know.' Pulling out a laptop computer he set it on the ground, powering it up.

Yoshi's eyes glazed, then focussed sharply, 'um, what is this?' He gaped at his computer screen as though seated in a crowded restaurant, his laptop suddenly breaking into a porn movie for all to see.

Nate glanced over, eyeing the bewildering activity. 'Holy shit,' he blurted, 'is it connected to SatNet?'

'No.'

'Apps open?'

'Of course not,' Yoshi snapped irritably, 'it hasn't even finished loading to the Start screen. Jack hadn't told them about the countdown clock. It was what it was, knowing, not knowing, no difference in the end. Distractions, further decay of morale had to be avoided.

Sitting boldly on the screen was a single line of numbers, zeroes and ones, that changed ever so slightly each second.

'Get Jack,' Nate commanded loudly. 'Get him!'

***

'Christ,' Nate moaned after terminating the Satellite link with Jack. All of them had been wondering how it could possibly get any worse, now they knew. That's exactly what had just happened. It had just gotten fucking worse. The world had been served with an all-points bulletin to cease and desist as a species. A convenient, go-anywhere countdown clock had been lovingly provided, in case Earth didn't know how completely screwed we were. Some believed otherwise but most accepted that zero time on the clock was genuinely zero time for Earth. If these others wanted to kill the human spirit, demolish the planet's infrastructure then they had done a bang-up job, planned it to a tee with singular perfection. Nate thought the clock might at least give them a way to measure their success. If they actually achieved something maybe the binary counter would stop, disappear even, perhaps start counting upward. Damn, that would be satisfying he said to himself, knowing the chances were probably numbingly remote.

'So anyway,' Connie frowned, 'back to Pi…do we just chuck 'em in, see what happens?' She said, rolling her eyes briefly, 'is that the grand plan here?'

'Yep,' Nate said, ignoring the sarcasm. 'One by one until something happens or we decide we're wasting our time.' He eyeballed her, wondering what insightful ideas she had to offer.

'Great plan,' she said contemptuously. 'Well thought through.' She felt like shouting NOT at the top of her voice to the world, letting it echo across the rocks, just managing to hold it in.

'And you would suggest what? Nate asked evenly, 'we're open to anything you've got.

Her face relaxed and she sighed. 'Oh Christ, I just meant that…I have nothing alright, it's just that it seems like we're not thinking creatively enough, there has to be more…where are the ideas?' She looked frustrated, rubbing her cheek, glancing sidelong at Becker, scowling. There were genius teams dotted around the country, institutions like Cornell, Princeton, where was their intel…their ideas? It was like a conspiracy of disinformation, strike that she thought, of no information. Their lack of insight, lack of anything was utterly inexplicable because these people had opinions on everything - theories, concepts, models, speculations. All they got was puzzling silence which like most everything else added up to something riddled with peculiarity.

'We know it reacts to Pi,' Nate said, 'that's all we know but maybe that's all we need to know. We might be trying to outsmart ourselves if we look more left field and use something less obvious.' He nodded thoughtfully, 'we've already tried just about everything from a numbers standpoint - Fibonacci, rationals, Hypercomplex, p-andic, Conway's, Knuth's, primes, Transfinite, Nilpotent, Quadratic...I mean, do I need to go on? Nothing else has traction with this thing. It only wants Pi.' His stare was pained but his eyes were bright and thoughtful. 'It's like a shark that'll go nuts with blood in the water. Pi seems to be, uh...well, blood to the Sphere.'

Connie glanced at Becker with a crooked smile. 'Just like you Becker, it only wants pie.'

He turned his head slightly, a ghost of a grin straying across his face. Bring on the goddamn Semtex, he said to himself. Take Connie's smart-arse mouth and the objects out for good. Plus, this number crap sounded like it might take forever. His vote right at this moment, peering at Connie's pious mug, was to jump straight to the back-up plan. Shock and awe all round he figured, grinning darkly on the inside.

'So Pi it is,' Nate said without much confidence, kneeling down and studying the printed sheets. 'We're up to Pi decimal thirteen...only a few hundred trillion to go,' he said, anxious to get going and see where it took them. 'Take these, get on with it, you know the drill, push and release till you get to the right decimal.'

'I think I can manage, I'm Japanese remember? I don't do martial arts, hate Anime, but by Christ I do math...it's a sight to see,' Yoshi said, smiling thinly, ambling over to the small hemisphere with a bunch of prints that were flapping in the gentle breeze. He dropped to the ground, palming the object seven times, dutifully waiting the prescribed twenty seconds. Then he did it nine times, then three, two and so on, feeling his hand start with the pins and needles already.

'I'll take the next shift, then you Becker, then Connie. We'll keep going for as long as we can, then break for food, assuming we don't get some action beforehand.'

'I'm hungry now!' Becker said, smacking his lips loudly, like he was blowing a raspberry.

'Christ, maybe the fate of the world, and you're thinking of your stomach?' Connie said. 'Seriously, you have such self-involvement issues.' She turned and walked away a few steps.

'Yep, one of the issues is not starving to death in this place.'

She clenched her toes, stifling a response, almost chuckling. Becker was sometimes irritating, always arrogant but he was also annoyingly likable. That was pretty much the size of it. The guy told it like it was, rarely bothered with pleasantries or political correctness. Reminded her of someone else she confessed grudgingly.

'I'll go get you something,' Nate said, 'we've got dried fruit, nuts, that'll have to do.'

A perceptible distress washed over his face as he leered at Nate. 'What, no pizza? He glanced at Yoshi. 'What about Raman noodles, you said you were Japanese right?'

'Fruit and nuts Becker,' Nate repeated curtly. 'Take it or leave it, we don't run a bloody restaurant down here.'

'I'll take it...with a beer or glass of red, you choose,' he said smirking boyishly at Connie who was watching Yoshi punch in the numbers.

Nate was walking toward the supply tent when they heard the distant screaming in the direction of the highest peaks, Mt Markham he reckoned, but Nate saw nothing. It sounded like the roar of jet engines but it wasn't the Ospreys, the note was all wrong. He stared uncertainly at Connie, silently asking the question. Watching it approach, they were too stunned to move. Becker was sure of one thing, they should already be running.

***

'Jack, this is Sagan, we copy you just fine.' Vic ignored Skylar, answering the hail from Houston. Cutting yourself off from the world wouldn't make a zac of difference. Fate was fate, whether you knew about it or not.

'Good to h-hear your voice Sagan,' he said, sounding agitated.

Vic hesitated for a second. 'What's happening down there?' He said, 'you sound, er—,' he paused, looking at Harry who nodded. Skylar was waiting in white-knuckle terror for Jack to spill it. It was obvious by his tone that something had happened… something seriously messed up.

'Two things.' Jack said gravely, taking a deep, calming breath of air. Sky's body tensed, she was scared, not for her but her daughter, Earth…her entire family. Please don't be too bad she pleaded, knowing it was going to be, without a word needing to be spoken.

Jack just went straight to it. 'Two asteroids are incoming on a course that will impact Earth in twenty-seven days.'

Skylar's face crumpled, imploding into a network of dark lines. 'Oh Jesus,' she said, seeing Vic's expression dim into something unreadable. 'Where…will they hit?' Skylar said in a dull whisper. Her body was a steel rod, waiting for the beginning of an unbearable hell.

'Did you get that Jack?'

'Yep, got it, 'um it doesn't matter where they hit,' Jack said as gently as he could, for what reason he didn't know. 'Their speed, size, composition…nothing will be left.'

'Oh God, this isn't happening,' Sky gripped her head. 'Get me back to Earth, fucking now!'

'Steady,' Vic said firmly, raising his hands in supplication. She was moaning and they knew she was right at the precipice, the proverbial gates of reason, hanging on by a single pinkie.

'Okay Sky, just wait, hear him out.'

'Countermeasures?' Harry shouted, knowing the answer but going through the motions for Sky. After he'd said it he realised it would be cold comfort.

'None. Speed, mass, time to contact leaves us with no viable strategy.'

Great question Harry said to himself, pursing his mouth, having absolutely no idea how to appease her. She was rocking gently back and forth, looking for all the world like a nutter from Angels Institute. There was genuinely no hope now, irrespective of what they did up here. Their journey was over. Skylar would get her wish to go home, before home met an inglorious end in a few short weeks, maybe a damn sight sooner.

'Okay Vic, it's academic but what's the second thing you spoke of?'

'The eleventh Sphere has gone,' Jack said coldly, 'and, um, well…it's taken something with it, something kinda big.' His voice evaporated slowly, leaving the chilling words hanging there. He added under his breath, incredulously, 'and if you think nothing made sense before…prepare yourselves because this makes all that's gone before it seem like too much mustard on your fucking hot dog.' He spat the last few words like he was hawking up a swallowed fly.

Terrified silence hit the Sagan end of the S-band. Roaming glances, eyes swollen with fear. Too much mustard? Vic thought about it emptily, how was that even possible, what could possibly trump the lunacy they'd seen by such a margin?

'What J-Jack?' Vic stumbled, suddenly sounding and looking desperately fatigued, dark circles sandbagging his eyes.

The static peeled away and Jack took a rasping breath through the intercom. 'The eleventh Sphere was entangled with something off-system,' he said. 'We didn't know what it was…but we do now. It was apparently connected to blackbody radiation…er, the cosmic microwave background.' Jack's voice fell away as he waited for the avalanche. If they put two and two together they might get nine because the suggestion, the implication broke every natural law in every text book you cared to name. Not bent them or skirted around them, snapped them at right angles like tinder dry kindling.

Harry's mouth opened and then slammed shut, went slack, his face drained of colour, now ashen and sickly looking. What? He grimaced and shrugged at Vic who was staring blankly at the comms unit, not knowing which of his busted thoughts he should ponder more deeply, to pose as a question. His face was pounded blank, then broke into a frown so deep the lines in his forehead seemed to generate shadows. If this was going where he thought it was, based on previous events, then Jack was understating it badly. This was seriously, unexplainably, universally fucked up. Sky's head had dropped into her hands again, zoning out, battling interminably to shut the noise out.

'How can you possibly know that?' Harry shouted so Jack could hear him through Vic's headset. His tone was uncomprehending. Was he going to get the glib answer he expected?

'Because it's fucking well gone,' Jack said bitterly, knowing that'd get them, lock, stock and mind-numbing barrel.

'What's gone?' Vic said quizzically, not ready to accept it. His mind was whirling, trying to find a way around the insane paradox.

'The CMB is no longer there, it vanished from all our detectors after the Sphere went. All the probes, WMPA, WISE, Herschel, Planck sent alerts to NASA and ESA. It's like a fucking call centre down here with all the beeping and buzzing.

Vic's mouth was twitching as he ground his jaw back and forth. 'For God's sake, this is,' he stopped talking, shaking his head briefly, '...have you crunched the math on what you're telling us? Do you realise how—' he repeated the pause, searching for the right word, '...impossible that is? I mean, that word's been thrown around every which way but...you get it right? The fucking laws of physics say so, like all of them.' He continued muttering inaudibly under his breath, one hand curled over his head, desperately thinking it through.

'We get it. All of us get it. If the CMB vanished it'd take fourteen billion years for us to find out. Einstein, Relativity, everything we deify as LAW says so...there's no wiggle room with these things.' Jack's rapid breathing was more pronounced now.

Becker was wagging his head numbly, eyes roaming around the group. 'Can someone kindly tell me what a CMB is?' He said impatiently. 'I don't wanna seem like the dunce of the group, but well...hello?'

Vic tore his headphones off. 'It's the left-overs from the Big Bang,' he said brusquely, 'microwaves that fill the sky everywhere in the infrared. It's like Jack said, they're about fourteen billion light years away...a halo that's everywhere,' he said, clenching and unclenching his fists in front of his face, throwing his headset back on. Becker continued staring at him dumbly, wondering when the explanation would start.

'You there Jack?'

'Yep. Got nowhere else to go.'

'It's, uh...not April fool's is it?

'I wish...oh how I wish,' Jack murmured soberly. 'What is happening out there Vic?'

'You know I've been thinking this for a while,' Vic said thoughtfully, 'Sam Treiman was wrong...not just mistaken but balls-up wrong.' Vic realised he wasn't, but on the face of it that's how it seemed and it irritated the shit out of him.

'The physics Prof from Princeton you mean?'

'Yep, Treiman's theorem. "Impossible things usually don't happen". What he meant was that they can never happen ever, because there's natural laws that forbade it. "Impossible" is empirical, not subjective, relative or the least bit fucking malleable.'

'Well he got it wrong like you say,' Jack said ruefully.

'Oh God, listen, he was spot on,' Vic said. 'What's wrong is that something's up which is completely beyond us.' He stared down at his hands, slumping.

Sky looked up, uncomprehending. 'S-So how have we even detected this when it should take all those years to reach us?' There was a quaking in her voice and her eyes seemed to tremble in their sockets like loose ball-joints. Sky recalled the bizarre journey where they appeared to be traveling FTL, believing it was just some anomalous visual effect, but with the CMB thing, well, maybe it was spot on real. But they weren't talking simply FTL here, which was hard enough to concede, they were talking instant transmission she assumed, no speed limit, no E=MC2. According to Einstein, energy told mass how to move and how space should curve, but in this case it was doing absolutely fuck all. Space was fine but mass and energy weren't saying shit to anyone and were now criminally at odds, seemingly doing whatever the hell they liked. It was dead-set anarchy and for the speed of light, it was open slather.

Vic peered around tentatively. 'Maybe…you know, what we've taken for granted all these years isn't right, could that be it? Perhaps that's why we haven't been able to unify the laws, get gravity to marry with quanta, because the laws were wrong to start with.' He was grabbing at straws, sweating, deeply muddled. Vic coughed, clearing his throat, drawing a long breath, 'but that makes no sense either, because everywhere we look the laws stand up, experimentally they're perfect, time after time, everywhere.' The story of his life, the things his mind relied on as bedrock, were collapsing around him, attacking his sanity, and maybe that's exactly what Creature and his cronies wanted.

'So, physics isn't what we thought it was,' Harry repeated, flicking his fingers through his beard, utterly gobsmacked. 'Or maybe they can screw with the laws that make space what it is.' He paused to dissect his words, thinking furiously, 'speed is governed by the Higgs Field right?' Vic you know more about this stuff…perhaps they can turn it on or off in certain places, fiddle with the speed of light as a result. You know, make it so radiation gets everywhere at once instead of taking the long way around.' Knowing damn well it didn't, he looked vacantly at Vic and said, 'sound reasonable?'

'Fuck no,' Vic said wearily. 'Although how in the name of all things godly do you pick apart the quanta of space? I mean I won't use the word Treiman but, well…you get the drift.' He looked at Sky who still had her eyes tightly closed, fists clamped against both her temples.

'So, let me get this straight…these creatures are vanishing things piece by piece, making hellishly sure we know about it,' Harry said with a sinking sensation. 'They're not just coming in and exterminating, they're mowing down the neighbourhood, near and far, holding each piece up like a trophy…the whole severed heads on a pole thing, to scare us out of our fucking minds.

'Vic, uh…tell Jack we're coming home. We're done up here,' Harry said woodenly.

Sky wiped tears from her eyes and cheeks, eyes pushing wide. 'Yes, take us home. We need to…all of us.' The tears flowed again, rolling gently away from her eyes.

'Jack, you hear that?'

'Yep, got it,' he said. 'Runway 33, we'll let Kennedy know. They'll be waiting. You know, red carpet and all…if anyone's still there of course.'

'Yeah, no one left to roll it out right?' Vic scoffed tiredly. It'll be good to get home.'

Jack said softly, 'you've been amazing up there, I mean that. Target data for de-orbit is being uplinked now. GPCs will be good to go…one minute.'

'Copy,' Vic said, throwing his headset aside, glancing at Sky. 'Ready?' He smiled wanly.

'Yes, yes, yes!' She sobbed, angling her chin up and brushing away tears, setting more of them free into the cabin.

'Make it so,' Harry piped.

'Okay,' Vic said as he typed deliberately on the CRT keyboard, waiting a few seconds before giving an inflated sigh. 'Okay, OMS gimbal test, uh…looks good,' he said, picking up the rotational hand controller and making a slight deflection with his fingers. 'RCS burn, uh…atmospheric interface in fifteen. Vic turned the RHC, reorienting Sagan, pitching up forty degrees, rolling slightly for wings level, yawing to hit the correct glide slope to Kennedy. The digital autopilot did the monitoring and watched their Deltas, ensuring they were diving into the correct thrusting corridor. Earth wheeled in front of them until it was beneath the belly of the vessel, directly front on. 'TIG on my call,' he glanced at Harry, 'Entry switch checklist?' Vic said, lifting an eyebrow.

'Nah you can wing it, attitude looks great.

'Okay then,' Vic said lightly. Entry roll mode off, landing PC to on.' He was struggling with fatigue, snapping his head to stay focussed. 'Throttle to auto, body flaps, elevons to manual.'

Harry was trying to feel enthused about returning to a planet that Jack told them was a full on fuck up. But that would be solved beautifully he brooded, because there were country-sized slabs of metal and rock on its way to expunge every one of its many points of issue. It would be sterilised more completely than a petri dish dipped in a bucket of Ethylene.

Grabbing the control stick, Vic pushed it firmly down. 'Ignition,' he said, feeling the immediate kick of inertia as they punched into the gradually condensing coming together of space and atmosphere.

Harry had no family, or family he gave a toss about. The wife had done a runner with Sarah, his surviving daughter, a decade ago. Now he didn't know her, and his parents were gone, died long ago. Reflecting on their death, one soon after the other, his mind was dragged back to the abhorrence they were facing, the death of an entire species, an intelligent race with all its artistic and technical creations, hard fought philosophy and science. Everything would be gone in a heartbeat, erased as though it meant nothing, gone with not an atom left over to show that it ever existed.

They dipped into the atmosphere, igniting space in an almighty blast furnace of crimson, yellow and orange as the shock wave and growing particle storm tried to burn through the nanocarbon hull. The abrasive colours were everywhere, burnishing space and glowing incandescent around them. Entry interface came and went, the beautiful blue of the atmosphere, mahogany of the continents surging up at them.

'Sagan, Jack, copy? His voice boomed from Mission Control as radio silence ended.

Skylar snapped her head around like a cracked whip. 'Just go,' she shouted, max it, get to Kennedy.' Sky bit her lip, trying to hold back the tears, stunned that they'd actually made it home, hoping Jack had no more bad news, sensing the futility.

Vic grabbed his headset and shoved it on his head. 'Vic, what?'

'Four more Spheres…gone, all off system, connections, uh…unknown. Every orbiting Sphere has gone plus one in the atmosphere…only six left.' Jack's voice was shrill in the intercom.

Vic lowered his chin to his chest and seemed to sag a bit, shifting around in his seat uncomfortably, pondering four. It had been one at a time, now four of them at once. He mumbled 'fuck' to himself. 'Does it matter Jack, I mean, should we—,' he was going to say give a rat's ass but held onto it, peering at space, wrestling with the loss of stuff that was family…for billions of years.

'Just thought we'd let you know is all,' Jack said coolly. 'Things are going to go and soon, but you're probably right, we're just observers, nothing we can do.' His voice cracked as he finished talking. 'Come on home guys.'

Vic gazed at Harry blankly, both knowing what the other was thinking. No way it was going to happen, not now.

Skylar sighed, visibly deflating in front of them. 'Thank you,' she wheezed, repeating it with a faint smile and heartfelt, 'thank you Jack.'

Vic turned to her seriously. 'We'll land at Kennedy but Harry and I are going back.' Sky was about to jump in but Vic held up a hand. 'He didn't ask, he didn't have to. On Earth we're worse than useless, up here we're slightly more than that.' Sky closed her mouth, turning to the window panels, seeing their minds were made up. Whatever, she thought distantly, that was their deal, she was pumped to be heading home to her little girl, even if it was just to say goodbye.

Sky shot Vic a joyless smile. Happiness, pleasure…all the positive emotions that made Homo sapiens human were already extinct, chewed up and spat out by what was looming large from space, and counting down on the egg timer. But at least she was going home to spend the last pieces of existence with Alysha. That was all there was and it was enough, but it didn't lessen the agony of her child's life being cut so tragically short.

33. Forgotten

"Secrets are never so dangerous as when they've been forgotten." ~ *Natalie C. Parker*

Tara remained in a private room in the Cardiac Care Unit of St Vincent's Hospital in middle Sydney. The city was pretty much a ghost town, decimated by looters as the population reacted to the news. City streets were now eerily quiet, the only noise the swirling of rubbish in the wind, sweeping between abandoned buildings. Sounds of traffic, the rumble of the underground had been missing for over a week. The Harbour Bridge was derelict, the grounds of the Opera House barren apart from a few stray dogs and flocks of gulls and pigeons.

For the past week, the hospital had been crammed with the wounded and dying but the ER sat quiet, mostly deserted. Everyone had fled to the relative sanctuary of their homes in the 'burbs or beyond. The desolate urban scene made for a perfect rendering of post-apocalyptic life even though the crack of kismet, in whatever form it came, was yet to arrive. The human reaction was shameful but hardly unexpected, after all, most conscious species would suffer similarly if it knew existence was ending and they had not a dollop of power over their fate.

The scene from her first-floor window was chilling. In her moments of clarity, she tried to be grateful for having lived so long but with almost no recollection of her life within the Sphere there was just heartbreak, wrapped in a hazy shroud of self-pity. She knew her personal years had simply wasted away, squandered somewhere in the whimsy of space and time. Consciousness was assembled not just from the quanta of electrical sparks in the brain, but from a jigsaw of memories, and hers were simply missing, apart from her younger years that were hobbled by the mists of old age.

Jeff Rogan from FEMA was in the room with two of his field agents, busy covering the two mirrors with tarp and tape. Griffin's standing orders from POTUS was to get something from Tara that might insight, in his carefully chosen words, "what turned her into a fucking swamp donkey." Having met with POTUS, the Joint Chiefs and a few close White House advisors, Griffin had regained a little faith, believing they might still be able to save themselves, although what it was based on no one had a clue. Blind faith they assumed but he was the boss and anyway, they didn't need much of a lead, they needed to believe.

Halverson came striding into the room with his medical team who had been managing Tara around the clock on DoD orders. She was being treated with various Alzheimer drugs, brain protein treatments and a few experimental serotonin/dopamine cocktails. A special mix of liraglutide, aducanumab and AC253 was showing promise, prompting a few flashes of deeper memory. Tara was taking doses just shy of lethal to an individual so old, but tough shit, Griffin had said coldly, it was a course of action sanctioned by the President. The needs of the many, Halverson was told tersely, making him feel slightly better about himself, although he was still tending more toward the hypocritical than the Hippocratic. He hoped like hell the healing gods would understand.

'Oh Christ,' Tara groaned when she saw Halverson step through the door carrying a bag of goodies. Dragging out several sets of X-rays he slapped them on the lightboard across from her bed, peering myopically at the images of her brain, pacing back and forth on the carpet in a circuitous two-step. 'Look at this,' he said excitedly, using his pen to point to a part of her brain. 'This is the PET scan from earlier, see the purple?' He had, disconcertingly, a toothy grin like a backwoods idiot.

Tara nodded slowly. 'Okay…you gonna explain it,' she said wearily. Can't be bad, she figured because he was so damn upbeat.

'This here is the prefrontal cortex and hippocampus…it's starting to light up. It's becoming more active,' he said, grinning again, rubbing his greying moustache. 'That doesn't mean memories will come flooding back but it's a promising sign.' She looked unimpressed, glaring back at him as if to shout *what's in it for me?*

'Jesus, I might have less time than Earth does…so all this matters how?' She said bitterly, the scowl deepening, her wavering voice worsening.

Tara was sick and tired of being poked, prodded, having her blood taken, the endless MRIs, PET scans, taking pill after pill of who the hell knew what. Rogan looked at the Doc, nodding, Halverson briefly returned it, cautiously.

The FEMA agent spoke as gently as he could. 'The Doctor has said that asking questions might assist recovery, it might help you unlock something.'

'That's right, Halverson said, still nodding as though he had early onset Parkinson's. 'So Tara, the agent will ask questions and you just do your best to answer them. The Secretaries of State, Defence, the President are looking for anything, and I mean anything, that might help us.'

'Well if you put it like that Peter…go your very hardest,' she said, managing a testy smile that vanished quickly.

Tara's parents were ushered from the room under mild protest as Rogan and his helpers drew seats beside her bed. The Doc needled some Klotho protein into her IV fluid, turning the sodium mixture a pale urine yellow.

After ten minutes, they got the okay from Halverson to proceed. Not an interrogation FEMA had assured the Doc, just a few targeted questions. Rogan glanced at one of his colleagues. 'Make sure you're getting all this. Griffin wants the audio, all of it.' The agent nodded placed. his phone on the table, turning on the voice memo app, giving Rogan the thumbs up to let it rip.

'Okay Tara,' Rogan started, 'you said you didn't age while you were inside, it was only when you came back that you turned…er, well, into, what you are now.' Fuck he thought, shuddering at his insensitivity, not the start he'd hoped for.

'Relax, I'm not blind you know. I've seen myself too many times to give a shit anymore. Nice of you to cover all the mirrors up but you really needn't have bothered. She glanced at Rogan thoughtfully. 'I only have a few broken memories so I'm not sure how much help I can be.'

'It is what it is,' he said, 'just give us what you have.'

'My, uh…first memory was being inside something that scared me, a bright light in my face and under me, I could see my insides,' she said, shaking her head distastefully. 'All these disjointed images I have seem so dream-like, nebulous…I'm not even sure they're real, with all the drugs…maybe they're not.' Her face turned even sadder.

'They're not hallucinogens,' Halverson said, 'quite the opposite really.'

Tara nodded impassively. 'I recall, much later, getting an idea what the bright thing did.'

Rogan pushed the phone closer. 'Go on,' he said in a whisper, his eyes widening.

'One of them spoke about not ageing, not to me personally, but I overheard words, although I have no idea where or how. I can't remember it all but I remember they made no sense at the time.'

'They spoke in English?' Halverson blurted in shock, 'you could actually understand them?' He'd expected visual memories but not much more, certainly nothing spoken, at least in a language that made any sense.

'Oh yes,' she said, 'just like you and me, perfect English.'

'Jesus,' Halverson blustered, standing up and taking a couple of steps backward, composing himself, then sitting down carefully. 'What words, uh…what were the words?' He craned his neck closer, swallowing hard. Shit, he thought, startled, the old bat might actually have something.

Tara was visibly concentrating, her eyes pulled tightly closed, a steely frown digging hundreds of wrinkles into her already furrowed brow. She looked so painfully old and frail, Rogan couldn't believe she was still drawing breath. "Fossil" was never more apt, the old lady from Titanic had nothing on her, in fact she was barely a hatchling he thought with a muffled snort.

She took a sudden rasping breath of air. 'The words were, um…something about genes and the like. I recall some sort of environmental immunity such and such, turning ageing on and off.' She glanced at Rogan who was looking up at Halverson for help.

'Well I, er…guess that makes some sense,' he said a little out of breath. 'If they can control the things that age us, turn it on and off then whammo I suppose, you grow to maturity and stay young forever. If there's perfect replication of cells every time and they can repair oxidation, cell damage, then I guess that'd do the trick.' He raised a palm to his forehead and probed it thoughtfully with a finger. 'Easier said than done mind you, the reality would be ridiculously complex on so many levels. I mean, if we're reading it right, methylation and apoptosis, this is, uh…flicking the switch on immortality. It's a genetic programmer's wet dream.'

Rogan stood up and walked the Doc over to the wall. 'Just easy on the immortality stuff okay…she's been whacked with the ageing stick so I don't think that's gonna be helpful.'

'I was just— '

'Just be careful,' Rogan said impatiently. He said almost inaudibly, 'I doubt they were showing her how to use the fountain of youth. Look at her.' Rogan gave the Doc a lingering look and left him by the wall, returning to Tara, sitting back down, smiling stiffly at her.

She looked at him suspiciously. 'Everything okay with you boys?'

Rogan nodded, breathing out a 'yep, no problems,' and squirming in his seat. 'Um, so what did they look like?' He said, eyes wide as cue balls as he waited for the response.

She ignored him or simply didn't hear him, going off on a different tack. 'Their language was like nothing I'd ever heard before, but certain familiar words started creeping in after a while. I eventually just seemed to get it. I'm not sure it was English, but I know I understood it,' she said, dragging in a couple of weary breaths then closing her moth-wing eyelids. 'And what did they look like you ask?' She did hear him after all, opening her eyes as wide as her limpid skin would allow.

'Yes,' Rogan said, nodding gently. Come on you old nutter, he felt like screaming.

Tara stared directly at Rogan with age-clouded eyes. 'They looked just like us,' she said breezily, 'they were human and apart from the children, were all around the same age, maybe thirty, twenty-five perhaps.' A smile quivered on her lips, turning her cheeks into a hive of heavy wrinkles.

'Shit,' Rogan exclaimed. He'd expected the profound and gotten the prosaic. Humans were doing this, humans? But how could that— '

'Maybe they just looked human?' Halverson interjected.

'Yes, maybe,' she volunteered, seemingly expecting the question. 'You could well be right, but they definitely seemed human enough. Perhaps I've blocked their real form out…how would I know? Like I said this is vague, fractured, muddled.'

'Okay, let's stay on track,' Rogan said. 'Do you know where you were, was anything familiar?' He was speaking too quickly, getting excited, his face hawkish and severe.

Halverson glared at Rogan deliberately. 'Take it easy Rogan, one at a time for God's sake. You're not dealing with a teenager here.'

'You know I can hear you right?' Tara said, offering a lopsided smirk. 'I'm old, not deaf.' She cackled briefly. 'Anyway, I remember little of my surrounds, I've thought about it at length, nothing is clear. I know it was a small planet with close horizons, three large moons and there were two bright stars in the sky…close together. I was kept in a house with a high roof and everything else like something here on Earth. I wasn't allowed outside, that I remember. And I don't remember eating, sleeping, going to the bathroom…how about that for strange?' She lifted a sparsely haired eyebrow, cupping her mouth. 'I've strained, I've really tried but there's nothing else there, and the concept of time is almost absent, I mean, it seems like I was there for maybe a week but obviously, well, you know—, ' she trailed off and tugged on an age spotted ear, shutting her eyes and taking forever to open them again. Rogan wondered if the old bugger had gone for good. Tara looked deathly pale as her face went vacant. She licked her lips and slurped at the air, fighting for breath.

Rogan mouthed "the baby" at Halverson and he nodded almost imperceptibly.

'So, Tara…what do you remember about the, uh…baby?' He said, staring fixedly at her, holding his breath. Was she going to freak out? There was no immediate reaction but the flinty expression and tightly puckered mouth suggested she was wrestling with it.

'Almost nothing I'm afraid,' she said without emotion. 'I remember seeing her tiny face, then she was removed, I never saw her again.'

'So it was a girl?'

'In my mind, it was but I don't know…it's based on a single memory, a still image much like a photo in my mind,' she said, closing her eyes again.

'And you, uh, had a partner?' Rogan quizzed cautiously, 'you know, to get pregnant? He said it with a twinge of embarrassment.

'I don't know, but I think I remember why they wanted me to have her.'

Rogan waited…and waited. 'Why?' Rogan urged, 'why Tara?' He felt like shouting in her wrinkled ear, maybe getting a hearing horn and bellowing into it.

'I heard them say it. My baby was for some sort of data extract. I don't know the exact reasons but it was to do with some, um, sequences that weren't evolving right. They spoke of things that made no sense. Sorry to use the "something" word so much but they were like something-something algorithms, fundamental data…DNA I assumed.. I never heard anything about the Spheres or anything happening out there.' Tara shut her eyes again, letting out a long, exhalation like a death rattle. 'I'm not feeling well,' she murmured, putting the back of her hand gently on her forehead.

'Okay that's it guys, give it a rest.'

'Just one last question Tara, did you know who you were when you were there?' Rogan posed, 'that you were from Earth.'

'No I don't think I did, I didn't know who I was or where I was from until I came back through the Sphere. And I think the young boy might have been trying to protect me by saying I wasn't, uh…allowed to leave,' Tara said, puffing between barely parted lips, sweat beading her lightly moustached upper lip. 'It was like he knew what would happen if I left, although that's a wild guess of course.' She let out a soft gasp.

'So he might have had some empathy for you…for us?' Rogan asked directly, wondering if finally they might have gotten a molecule of meaning.

'Look, I'm sorry, it's all guesswork…these are memories. I'm not even sure they are memories at all…some might be, others mightn't be,' she offered with a sigh. 'Oh, I just remembered,' she said, touching her forehead with an index finger, 'he also said, if I remember right, that the teams we had working, ah…on a solution wouldn't succeed. I had no idea what he was talking about, if I did I would have pressed the point.'

Rogan looked puzzled, 'how could he know that?'

Tara's tilted her head up, 'wait, I think he said, wouldn't be allowed to succeed…there was a help in there somewhere too I think.' She looked muddled, clearly labouring with her mind. 'Not allowed to help maybe…I don't know, maybe that's right.…or not.' She laid her head back, staring vacantly at the ceiling, lungs rattling with each breath, one eye watering copiously. She closed her eyes and this time didn't re-open them.

***

Rogan picked up his cell and closed the voice recorder. Making a few keystrokes he sent it on to Griffin, signing off for the night. He was done. This was his last night on the job, he hadn't told anyone, never intended to. The world was shutting down and he was heading home to be with his family for whatever time they had left. Nothing Tara had given them seemed of any immediate value, and worse, he wasn't the least bit sure they weren't just the ramblings of a demented old snuffer high on a cocktail of experimental medication. Maybe the whole lot was just a dream with absolutely no material basis whatsoever. The Government had no ideas, no strategies and certainly no answer to any of the chaos on Earth, let alone uncovered anything insightful about the enemy. Griffin and his cronies could go fuck 'emselves, he'd done his bit and wanted to die on his own terms.

34. Revelation

**"At the dawn of man, many words of inspiration.
At the end, there will be words of revelation." ~ *Toba Beta***

'W-What is it Nate?' Connie said, peering wide-eyed at the massive cloud or fog bank or whatever was approaching them at break neck speed from the western highlands.

'Ice storm!' He screamed, struggling to be heard over the roar of the wind that was suddenly all over them. 'Get back to camp!' Nate yelled, flourishing his arms wildly as he started driving into the wind. It felt like he was pushing through a Boeing wind tunnel full of thumbtacks.

'What about the equipment…the explosives?' Becker shouted at Yoshi. Hardly the time for the mother of all explosions he thought uneasily as he ploughed into the icicle ridden storm.

'Leave it,' Yoshi yelled after him, wondering the same thing, 'it'll be fine.' He had no idea apart from Nate saying it needed a detonator.

The storm was whipping in from the Mt Kirkpatrick highlands, whistling inversion currents, buffeting the landscape in cyclonic waves that were inexplicably shallow to the ground. Above the narrow hell-zone, the weather was fine, two degrees Celsius, nary a breath of wind.

It was a chilling game of back one, forward two as they fought their way to the tarped area that looked ready to yield completely. Thankfully it was oriented the right way to avoid being demolished and blown off the former glacier and ingloriously into the Amundsen Sea.

'Jesus, the ice,' Connie said, craning her head around wildly, seeing nothing but a shrieking, blinding blizzard everywhere, 'where's it been?'

'Dunno where it's been,' Becker screamed, 'but it's back…making up for lost time.'

'Sleeping bags now,' Nate said gravely. 'This isn't survivable out here,' he shrieked, 'get in!' He could feel the temperature peel away, knowing it was at least fifty below, freefalling.

'Do it!' Becker screamed, peering desperately at Connie and Yoshi.

They were exhausted and freezing, their movements torpid and clumsy but they managed to stuff themselves in their heavy Gore-Tex cocoons in under a minute, zipping them right to the top with only their goggles sticking out. Huddling together near the back of the tent, next to the comms station they listened fearfully to the pounding blizzard lash everything around them.

'Definitely making up for lost time,' Becker yelled to Connie through the fur of his bag.

She grunted at him, all wide eyes and eyebrows. Nate felt like he was inside an aircraft engine, the noise was so terrifyingly loud it convinced him that the end of the world had come early.

After half an hour of unremitting chaos, the storm started to lose some of its grunt and twenty minutes later it was gone, replaced by almost perfect serenity. Peeking out they could see a dim blue sky, the Sun poking through thinning clouds near the horizon, and they could hear nothing but beautiful silence. Unzipping themselves they wriggled out of their sleeping bags and ambled to the edge of the camp, greeted by a surprising sight, but in the general scheme of things, pretty routine.

Nate shuffled a few steps forward, turning to survey everything around him. 'Hmmm, I'll try to be surprised but you know what…this is about right.'

'Yep,' Becker said, 'still pretty cool though.'

The winds had delivered a landscape layering dose of ice to the area, transforming the chocolate coloured rocks into a brilliant white icefield. The metal dish was free of snow, ice or anything white at all. The frozen landscape licked at the edges of the plate but didn't touch it.

'I saw ice falling on it when we were running back to base,' Connie said, 'I know I did, I felt it on my cheeks.' They all nodded in synch, having witnessed the icy downpour falling around them as they sprinted for safety.

'Melted?' Becker pondered out loud.

'Melted, dissolved, sublimated…who knows,' Yoshi returned, but this plate is clearly an ice-free zone.' He shot them a grin, happy to have survived nature's icy onslaught, guessing it might mean that things were returning to normal.

Another day, another event, another fucking mystery, Nate lamented, rubbing his mouth with a gloved hand. He sighed and watched his frigid exhalation disappear into the icy air, seeing not a single cloud in the sky, just a burnished Sun looking determined to set behind the exposed landscape of Marie Byrd.

***

'Okay,' Nate said, still unsure about the way forward they'd chosen, but doing it anyway. 'Um, so, let's get on and do this.'

They were going to try and power down or destroy the anomaly. Or perhaps, they thought, to inadvertently excite it into something worse than the current horror show they had going on, unsure how much worse it could get, vanishment, Nate assumed, grimacing...that'd be worse. With a sense of trepidation they realised by feeding it Pi they just might take it to a new level of animation, perhaps the antipathy of what they were trying to achieve, maybe throttling it up instead of down, accelerating their fate and bringing it forward to right now. The sinister thoughts were always close but they had to press on and execute their half-arsed plan, hope they didn't fuck the world up right here and now.

Nate stooped over Yoshi, 'do a couple hundred then I'll take over. It'll be like arm day at the gym,' he joked thinly.

Yoshi offered Nate a fleeting smirk and started pressing the small object, watching the blur of light continue flashing over its surface, assuming the amorphous haze of white was still Pi, but the reality extended to everything they could imagine, and way more. Yoshi grinned wryly through rising heartburn, picturing it as some clandestine unification theory written in the Queen's English, cycling over and over, but the reality was that it was just spinning white light.

Connie watched the military camp, fearing the worst. 'Shouldn't that 22 be back by now?' She continued gazing at the three aircraft that sat limply like gigantic beetle bugs in the near distance. 'It's been three days, the trip should take less than two right...there and back?' She stared directly into Nate eyes, searching for an answer that might settle her queasy stomach.

'Yes well, that's right,' Nate admitted reluctantly. 'Maybe they had mechanical issues, couldn't get fuel, um...decided they weren't needed back here. Perhaps they were requisitioned elsewhere, humanitarian mission perhaps.' He paced around a bit, smoothing his crumpled parka.

Connie watched him as he fidgeted. 'Or maybe there was no one there so they just kept going, looking for someone...anyone...and they couldn't. I mean, the purpose of going was so they could come back with intel.' She held her breath, blinking owlishly. 'They're military Nate, they've got their code, they wouldn't do that.' Her eyes were searching for a reasonable scenario.

'Just hang tight,' he soothed, 'no point guessing.' Nate had similar fears but figured siding up with Connie wouldn't jack their morale any. If they weren't coming back there was nothing any of them could do about it. Suck it up, move on, that was about the size of it.

Noise wafted over the metal plate from camp, zapping and fizzing like a faulty power line.

'Damn it,' Nate blurted, already running back to camp, realising what it was. 'Comms unit,' he said, a little off-balance as he ran.

Connie watched him dash off, heart jumping in her chest, pleading silently, running falteringly on drunken legs. She shook her head hard, desperate to null her mind, conceding how unlikely it was that their random idea had worked.

Nate grabbed the mike, pushing the Talk button. 'Jack, is that you?' Barely audible static is all they got. 'Shit, where is he?'

'Take your finger off Talk,' Connie snapped.

'Oh shit, right.'

'…you there, do you read?' came the voice. It was Jack, loud, bold, distinctly edgy.

328

'It's Nate…I've got Yoshi, Becker and Connie with me.'

'Thought we'd lost you for good…wait…what?' Jack said shrilly, pausing and taking a sharp breath. 'Say again…you have, uh…Becker and Connie?'

'Here in the flesh, courtesy of the anomaly apparently, spat them out all shiny and new here at the Pole.'

'Hello Jack,' they said almost in unison.

There was another pause, background murmurs and static, as Jack was presumably picking himself up off the floor. 'Jesus Mary and…we'd er, given up on you…um, shit, sorry about that,' Jack said, puffing as he spoke, struggling to organise his thoughts into coherent words.

'Understandable,' Connie said straight up, looking at Becker and raising an eyebrow.

'Prick,' Becker said with a loud snort, chuckling to himself.

'Should I ask what happened in there…at L1?' Jack asked with a note of awe in his vocal tone. 'Or is that for another time…anything that might help us?'

'Another time and no,' Connie answered. 'We've replayed it over and over, there's nothing, just a bunch of questions to add to the million or so others we've collected over the journey.'

'Okay, understand. Um, your Osprey crew won't be returning,' Jack said in a suddenly sympathetic tone. 'The Pentagon got a call from Pendleton, they were on comms when they were overrun at the RAAF base in Glenbrook over there in Australia. They thought the place was deserted so they dropped to refuel. Two of them were killed, the third was on comms when they think he went the same way.'

'Oh Christ,' Connie moaned,' realising that with Jack on line, the pilots killed at Pendleton, it meant most everyone was still out there. She couldn't help feel a twinge of happiness, burying the guilt, but given the rotten prognosis for the planet she wasn't sure why either emotion surfaced. It was involuntary, hard-wired, life, hope she reminded herself with a dull wag of the head.

'Christ, poor bastards,' Nate sighed. 'What the hell's going on out there?' He'd seen enough on cable news before it went off line to realise how bad it was, only way to get was worse.

'We've got a mob outside the gates here, maybe a thousand, maybe more. They're expecting some sort of miracle from NASA, you know, send something up, destroy the threat, we're fucking miracle men apparently.' He exhaled sharply through his nose. 'Media's almost done, TV, radio, printed. Social media's through the goddamn roof as you can imagine. Internet and cellphone towers are still operational but when they go everything'll be dark…zero media, zero intel. Stay where you are, you're in the best place, long as you've got food, water, the more isolated the better.'

'Are you safe?' Nate said a little indifferently, too exhausted to take on any more misery, sick of the incessant voice in his head that was telling him to pack it in. Yes it was probably hopeless and getting it over with had some perverse attraction, but he still had a dram of resolve to resist the pull of surrender. Just in case.

'Yeah we're okay, we've got security fences, everything's locked down, but hey, it won't stop 434-Hungaria right?' He sighed, deep and guttural, going on for several seconds. 'Given what's happened, I'm not sure we'll even make it to that, we may be gone before they arrive.'

'You mean the countdown or some nutjob with his finger on the button?' Nate queried.

'No, no, well maybe, but… you wouldn't have heard,' Jack said candidly. Four more Spheres disappeared a day ago, they had off-system connections with, er…very deep objects.'

Connie felt like she was starting to come unglued. Her heart jack-knifed in her chest, making her feel giddy. Putting fingers in her ears wasn't beyond her, nor was running and putting distance between her and the infernal comms unit. The futility was devastating because whatever was coming at them would get her and every other living soul, there was nowhere to hide. Everything she could think of or imagine was totally, numbingly academic. Glancing grimly at Nate, her breath wedged in her throat, seeing Yoshi still manfully pumping decimals of Pi into the damnable object. He was frantically pressing, waiting, repeating with eyes pulled wide, hoping forlornly for a result. Poor blighter. It was mindless, useless, and she felt caustic humiliation churning in her gut. Failure.

'By deep what are you saying?' Nate stared at the comms unit, unmoving, with the mike pressed to his mouth, holding it hard enough to expel the blood from his knuckles.

'Well okay, hang onto something,' Jack cautioned, 'the CMB has gone, and the Hubble Ultra Deep Field has gone.'

Nate's face was blank as he tried to process the improbable sentence. 'Hang on,' he murmured, 'this was a time of major galaxy formation so there has to be …'

'…Nate, park your brain for a sec okay, forget what you think you know,' he said impatiently. 'Don't think, just listen and know what I'm telling you is true.' There was an elongated pause, making them wonder if the line had been cut. Nate forced his mouth open, shutting it when Jack's voice came back. 'All of those deepest galaxies are no longer there. Remember, these were the ones dating pretty much all the way back, almost to the beginning of time, some of the very youngest, most distant galaxies Hubble ever found. And of course the CMB…well that's the left overs from the birth of fucking time.'

Nate had parked his brain for long enough, he was puffing with effort, unable to forget what he knew, as Jack had so blithely suggested. 'But there should be something there…what am I missing here Jack?' He could actually feel his blood draining deeper into his body to feed his vital organs that were in overdrive.

'No, you got most of it. And that's what's missing, something. We've had Keck 2, Kitt Peak, the VLA, Hubble ACS and Nicmos running confirmations and follow up in every part of the sky, every EM wavelength, both hemispheres and they—'

'And you found what?' Nate interrupted, unable to remain silent as his brain rebelled with tangled thoughts that made no sense. It all felt surreal, bogus, made up, the sense of veracity that everyday life possessed seemed to be slipping away, degrading into some fantasy world bereft of constants, laws or even the vaguest hint of solid ground.

'As at yesterday,' Jack said, 'there was nothing in space beyond a redshift of two-point-two…that's about five billion light years away. I've spoken to Lloyd at JPL, you remember him, well he explained a few things. The part of the Universe we can see is about fourteen billion light years in any direction, but beyond that, according to him, space is expanding faster than C, so it's beyond our view, like forever.' His voice was ripe with disbelief. 'If you ask Lloyd, the real size of the Universe is forty-five or so billion light years in any direction.'

'So you're telling us this why?' Nate said, fighting to control his breathing that was gunning in perfect synch with his heartbeat.

'Well, if that's the case we've lost eighty billion light years of spacetime, assuming the dropout continues across the particle horizon.'

Nate's hand suddenly opened, letting the mike drop so it hung from the cord a few inches above the ground, swinging back and forth, making a swishing sound in the otherwise dead silence of the camp. Everyone stared at it wordlessly. It was like an insidious fantasy being dragged up the rabbit hole, compelling him to almost pinch himself to make sure he was properly awake.

Nate turned his head slowly to look at Connie, a little unsteady. Yes, Earth was up against it, they got that, it was hideous, but the true scale of it might be so much bigger, stretching the limits of the human condition to get a handle on it, to process it, let alone accept it.

Nate grabbed the cord and swung the mike up into his hand. 'Do you mean that mass and space have gone?' He stared at the mike, 'not just planets and stars and stuff but actual space…the vacuum?' His eyes stared into thin air, watching bright sparkles fizzle in the air.

'Lloyd is certain of it,' Jack said briskly, 'and it's no longer expanding. Space, or what's left of it, is contracting, he's seeing blue shifted light everywhere…nothing is red shifted anymore…nothing.'

'Oh for…you are shitting me,' Nate wheezed over the top of Jack's explications. No more redshift. He felt a primeval need to find shelter, to hide or run, put acreage between him and the fucking comms unit, the Pole, Jack, everything.

'…Lloyd surveyed the Virgo Supercluster on Saturday,' Jack said, clearly deeply on edge now, voice quavering, '…every part of it, that's nearly fifty thousand galaxies, they're coming toward us, not expanding with space anymore but shrinking with it, and, um…speed is increasing incrementally. Yesterday away…today toward.' Jack stopped and they could hear him taking deep breaths, trying to compose himself. 'Stating the obvious…everything is escalating rather rapidly.'

'Mother of God,' Nate breathed disbelieving, 'everything is so—' he glanced furtively at Connie, '…I'm not sure what words to use…fucked up is getting old.' His head was throbbing. 'So our reality is just sloughing away,' he said woodenly, turning his head to Yoshi, rolling his eyes to the sky, 'like some freakish erosion that is utterly—,' he baulked at using the word. 'Oh fucking hell,' he offered instead, closing his eyes.

'An unholy understatement,' Connie groaned, unable to wrap her mind around the language Jack had so bluntly thrown at them.

Nate's voice was a semi-tone lower, 'you said, *"as of yesterday"*, is there an update?' Did it really matter, he screamed to himself after the sentence escaped into the freezing air? Connie glared with naked contempt, bemused by his apparent want for more torture

'You sure you want me to go on,' Jack asked earnestly, 'maybe you should be focussing on what you're doing down there. It is what it is Nate, knowing, not knowing, makes no difference, your words.'

'We've got Yoshi out there efforting that. Go ahead Jack…just do it, get it over with.' He turned away from Connie, tensing, waiting for it, entertaining his darkest thoughts as he did.

'The total effect of the four Spheres has taken us down to around five hundred million light years…the Laniakea Supercluster is now the most distant object out there, beyond that, well…there's nothing.' They could hear something like priapic breathing through the intercom. 'And by nothing I mean no matter, no space, no time. Zero dimension.' Jack's sinking heart was obvious in his tone.

Nate's and everyone else's most grievous contemplations were crystallising in a dizzying rush. The contraction…the vanishing was continuing and worse, there were plenty of Spheres still up there, presumably still entangled with the scraps of spacetime that remained. He felt his mind yield a little more, because things were now officially beyond the feeblest, candle-lit thread of hope.

Becker was peering around with the same pained look of befuddlement he'd worn for the last twenty minutes, fighting to collect enough words he understood to construct a question. 'With, uh, everything coming in…does that mean there's an end out there somewhere…an edge?' He stared mindlessly, almost trancelike, as mysterious concepts were force fed into his mind.

Connie eyed him like a puppy who'd soiled the brand new sofa. 'Oh good God, is that what you took from Jack's words?' She eyed him up and down sourly, seeing his hangdog expression.

Nate said calmly, 'no edge. Spacetime is all there is, there is no beyond…like tramping over Earth, no matter how small or big it is, you'll eventually come back to where you started.' Nate chucked it around as he was speaking, admitting he wasn't totally sold on the idea. If it was small enough, like really itty-bitty, maybe there had to be an edge, he wasn't sure. If there was though, what neoscientific nothing was on the other side…beyond the reality of the stars, the galaxies and the space? Nate stewed on the awesome concept. He pictured what might happen if one was able to zip around faster than the inflating Universe when it first sprang forth, and you managed to kiss its hyper-expanding margin…what then? Nate was gobsmacked by the concept. Would you pass through it, be annihilated by it, or was it an inviolable barrier between physics and some crazy zero-dimensional abstract? Maybe it was a rolled up selection of dimensions not observable from "here", just like string theory predicted. Or was it just reality within, nothing without, as most academics sternly maintained. He wasn't so sure, and now that this seemed to be all playing out in reverse but at a relative snail's pace, Nate's question was becoming more relevant and devastatingly tantalising.

After a long pause Becker shook his head and blinked a couple of times, saying, 'okay, I think I get it.' He shot Connie an injured expression, itching his nose with a stiff index finger, sending her a palpable message.

'Right back at you,' she muttered. 'I'd ask you what you got because we need a bit of slapstick right now, but I won't.' She turned anxiously to Nate for long seconds, bunting questions around, battling to manage her heart rate, partly because of a desire to unload on Becker. 'It's not the how anymore, that doesn't matter, they're doing it and it's real. It's always been the why right? She peered deeply into his eyes with the slightest tremor in her top lip. 'Why would they want to do this? I can't get it out of my head.' She pushed hair back from her forehead, touching her throat delicately, feeling the stubborn thudding of her heart, undiminished. 'These things, these creatures must be utterly incomprehensible…like on a cognitive level I mean. This is torture…cutting off bits until we die, and it's not like we've done shit to them,' she said, feeling a flush of heat. 'Maybe just by being, by existing and not excelling on some purely scientific level, is enough to earn their wrath. We would never torture other creatures like this.' Connie swallowed and bit back tears of despair and outrage.

Nate lifted a single dubious eyebrow, 'like we do to lower animals you mean?' He said pointedly, seeing her misery but saying it anyway.

'We don't torture for torture's sake Nate. We kill for food and we—' She stopped, thinking it through, seeing Nate shaking his head ever so slightly.

'Oh for Christ's sake, wake up and smell the bloody methane…of course we torture. Just because animals aren't intelligent by our criteria, they suffer. Jesus, you just have to look at them to know that,' he said, regarding her quizzically. 'We shoot, hunt, maim, carry trainloads of cattle thousands of miles, drag 'em off, slaughter them. We squash thousands of hens in cages so they can't move, medical testing, vivisection, seal clubbing, whaling…I mean, do you need me to go on?' His eyebrows were as high as they could go, vanishing under his motley fringe, aghast at her ignorance.

'But we're intelligent,' she said forlornly not sure her argument was valid any more.

'Are we?' Nate said sharply, 'want me to repeat the list, doesn't sound intelligent to me.'

'That's bullshit, most of it's done for a reason, it's not just indiscriminate killing.' Connie looked down at her feet and shuffled, feeling even less sure now.

'These whatever-they-are,' Nate said, 'may be so far up the evolutionary ladder that it's like us to mice or a mound of inch ants. And how guilty do you think we'd feel if we killed a mouse or knocked over an anthill and slaughtered millions of the little buggers? Most of us would feel nothing, and this might be exactly what we're dealing with…it's all relative I guess.'

Connie held a hand to her neck, spreading her fingers fearfully, admitting it made too much sense. 'So we're the inch ants,' she said dismally, 'and they're taking our anthill apart, piece by piece.'

'Yeah, okay…but why would they destroy their own anthill,' Becker said sceptically, 'we're all in the Universe together right? You say they're super advanced? They sound dumb to me.'

'I don't think it's their anthill,' Nate offered softly, knowingly.

'I was thinking that too,' Connie said, unsurprised by Nate's offering, as mad as it sounded.

Becker stood dumbly, hand holding his chin, frowning. 'Okay, so you're saying they're from a different universe?' He stood there waiting for a giggle, a disarming smile maybe.

Nate looked him straight in the eye, deadly serious. 'Yeah, I am.'

Walking out of the comms area they started out to where Yoshi was keying in numbers but he wasn't there. Nate's heart jumped, he couldn't see him anywhere.

'Yoshi!' Becker yelled, the echo from the highlands screaming back at him.

'Oh for…he's fucking in there,' Connie bawled, pointing a trembling finger at the Sphere.

'But we didn't see any light,' Becker said, wondering if they'd missed it somehow.

'It's bright out here, unusually so. It might have gotten lost, maybe it was infrared or UV, or even none…we can't pretend to know how these things work.'

Yoshi's prints were lying on the ground near the Sphere, slowly breaking free of the single staple, scattering in the gentle breeze.

Connie squinted into the highlands, willing him to appear, knowing better. 'It's the only answer,' she conceded. Her stomach clenched painfully as she agonised over his fate…and who the next victim might be.

332

Becker collected the scattered pages, seeing they were crossed nearly all the way up the first page. The last one had a circle rather than a cross with an exclamation point next to it. *Yel*

He'd written *"Yel"* next to it with a pen line going straight off the page. 'Jesus, check it out,' he said.

Nate was pacing around manically. 'That decimal he punched in…must have produced a yellow light.'

'Yep, that's what it looks like.'

'He was supposed to come tell us,' Becker said, 'not just up and walk in like he fucking owns the place.'

'He didn't just walk in,' Nate fired back, 'no way he'd do that. I think it was like Tara, he was lured in, unconsciously, subconsciously, whatever…but not just because he felt like it.' He cocked his head at Becker, wondering if anything actually percolated in that thick head of his.

Connie was of similar mind, turning to Becker, quirking her lip in disdain, 'give Yoshi credit, he's no fool, unlike some.'

'Some…uh, like you right?'

Nate rolled his eyes, seeing the need to play intermediary, 'what number decimal is that Becker, the yellow one?' He said it loudly, to drown them out or at least distract them for a bit.

'Uh…one hundred.'

'Whoa,' Nate blurted, contemplating the symbolism of the number. What odds that a symmetrical number such as that would bring first response? Ten to the second power which pulled his mind to base two numerology. Was two a theme? Nate's face grew serious as he tried to connect the dots but wasn't sure the dots were any more than fantasy because twos and squares and integers were pretty much diametrically opposed to spheres…Euclidean versus non-Euclidean math as it were. Trying to sort chaff from the wheat, he admitted that wheat might very well be absent altogether. Nate's brain was screaming out for hooks and connections as he weighed up a hundred…was that number special? It was the first number with three digits, his face melding into a puzzled frown. So he had one hundred and three this time, something clicking in his brain, but it was ill defined and definitely a stretch, an obtuse leap of faith.

Everything about the Spheres involved cutting through dimensions of spacetime to reach another place or time. The objects were, among other things, dimensional triggers of some sort…doorways past and future, to places with crazy physical laws, somewhere no laws seem to exist. Maybe three referred to non-time dimensionality? Nate was sure if he stretched possibility and simplicity any further they would snap clean through. In the back of his mind he knew the most complicated numbering systems had done nothing, so he figured, what the hell? Seemed reasonable in his mind but reasonable simply meant it had odds of more than zero.

'Let's try a hundred powered to the number of spatial dimensions, so a hundred to the third power….that uses both numbers. Find the millionth decimal of Pi Becker. And also do it using four dimensions of spacetime, a hundred to the power of four, a hundred million. Find that decimal too.'

Becker stared blankly at him like he'd been smashed in the face with a saucepan. 'Are you shitting me?' He folded his arms against his chest and frowned. 'How many fucking numbers do you think I have here?' Becker waved the wad of paper in his face, flapping it loudly.

'Oh, right, sorry about that.' He slapped his forehead with his palm, 'use the laptop we're connected to Wi-Fi on the Iridium network. Search for Pi Numerator, Connie, give him a hand.'

She jimmied apart the Mac, opening the search engine. 'Let me help Becker,' she said, nodding playfully, 'technology isn't your thing, I understand that.'

'I can type a bloody sentence.'

'Of course you can, what about spelling?' She smirked, winking.

'What would I do without you?' He groaned wearily. 'Just get the goddamn numbers.'

'I'm with you Becker,' Nate said, 'Connie, play nice, now let's move, give me the first number.' Nate paused to consider the game plan before proceeding. 'Maybe three is pointing us to dimensionality but then we're supposed to extend the idea and think a bit deeper, like including higher dimensions beyond our traditional four.' The whole lot sounded prosaically banal but anything was worth a shot, at least it had some marginal basis to it, slightly better than numbers from a chocolate wheel or picked out of a bloody hat. Slightly.

Connie looked past the binaries still counting down on the screen and glanced up, confused. 'Are you…there's no way you can put in millions of digits, obviously you're not, but, uh…you can't just skip to them because it won't know what number in the sequence you're pointing to. There's only options one through ten you know.' Connie looked puzzled, grimacing, hoping he'd thought it through… a little better than it seemed.

'Thanks for the remedial math,' Nate said, nodding his head in mock gratitude. 'I'm a Laucasian Professor.' He grinned at her but there was no humour, just a steely resolve.

'Okay genius, so the plan?' She pushed her palms toward Nate.

He ignored the bait. 'We chuck in the binary equivalent,' Nate said. 'We know it understands base two so we input binary for a million, pause, then follow with the decimal. Binary to identify position, decimal for Pi.'

'Sounds like a plan,' Becker said, it made at least some sense to his math impaired brain.

Connie admitted it sounded sort of okay, fringe, out there, but passable. 'Okay then, just checking you know what you're doing.'

'What's the decimal Becker, the millionth?' Nate asked.

'Er…one.' He said uncertainly, then re-checking the Pi Converter on the web portal.

'And the other one…a hundred million?'

Jesus, wait on, um…shit…this is going slow. I hate that little colour wheel. Okay, uh…they're the same, both of them are one. One million and a hundred million are both one,' he said, bending his neck forward, checking again, satisfying himself that he was right.

Connie was watching old man Becker squinting at the screen, having no confidence in his dodgy eyesight. 'You absolutely sure blindy?' Connie said, suppressing a Magoo-inspired blast.

Becker frowned, unconvincingly. 'Completely sure, eyesight is bang on thanks.'

'Well then, same number, what are the odds? Nate said curiously, 'and in format they're binaries as well as a decimal,' he added, chewing his bottom lip, contemplating the intriguing coincidence. So much for distinct formats, ain't happening,' he said, eyes burning as he muttered 'one hundred…one zero zero,' scratching his chin thoughtfully with three fingers and a thumb. 'Okay,' Nate said. He was going to do this himself. 'Long hold for one, short for zero, pause ten seconds then one pulse for the Pi decimal. Piece of cake right?'

Becker and Connie watched him do his stuff, unmoving, unblinking, waiting for something to happen. After a minute, Nate stood up, edged back a couple of steps, watching it hawk-like. 'Nothing,' he declared after a minute. 'Strike a million off the list but honestly, does it have any idea what we're trying to do?' Now that he'd done it, it seemed even more off-beat, a little embarrassing. He stared down at his feet, rubbing his darkly shadowed eyes.

'Maybe you'll piss it off trying to shortcut it,' Becker said vaguely.

'More than it already is?' Connie spluttered. 'You keeping up with the apocalypse?'

'Okay, so piss it off more then,' Becker said, maybe that'll…I don't know, win its respect.'

Connie studied his face and wagged her head in dismay. 'Look, we've got no idea whether any of this even registers with it, let alone how it might interpret it, it's all guesswork.'

'Can't make it much worse,' he offered glibly.

She was so sick of hearing it. 'We might make it happen a lot quicker and in my book, that's way worse,' Connie said, banging her foot silently on the alien metal.

Becker took a short breath, 'oh, well let's be careful then,' he said defiantly, holding both palms up in a "slowly slowly" gesture. 'Go harder, go slower, which is it?'

She muttered some unsavouriness under her breath, turning away sharply.

'Right, time for the second iteration,' Nate said hopefully, groaning as he knelt down and started the task. He completed twenty-seven variable hold presses followed by an elongated pause, then one pulse, firstly defining the Pi decimal position, then the actual Pi numeral. Nate finished, pulling back a few steps, watching as the white blur on the small object stopped dead.

'Shit,' he yelped, stumbling forward this time, seeing twelve lines of numbers, static and bold on its surface, luminous white against the black background. No one dared to breathe or make a sound, everything was still, no wind, no noise, just the endless frozen landscape, two alien Spheres and a trio of jittery humans trying desperately to mollify the strange visitor to their shores.

A wall of dissonant noise abruptly shattered the silence and all hell seemed to break loose around them in a disorienting surge. The large Sphere pulsed once in an almighty starlike burst and as it dulled, a mathematical rendering appeared, a series of numerals, perhaps a reply Nate thought dizzily, maybe an answer to what he'd so unceremoniously dumped into the smaller object.

'Jesus, you did it,' Becker screamed, throwing his arms up in a victory "V".

'We haven't done shit, who knows what it's up to,' Connie spat, scratching at her cheek,

'Well, whatever we don't know it's bad…yet.'

'Probably a coincidence,' Nate said, 'a hundred million's a nice number but it might be simply responding to our touch…it's a fair bet,' he conceded, cold-smiling almost apologetically, doubting whether any of their ideas were logical in the broader sense, uncomfortably aware that his tinkerings were based on little more than a mountain of flimsy self-justification.

Nate edged up to it cautiously, skittish about what might be watching him, surveying the intimidating sequence of numbers. He murmured something indistinct, awestruck, eyeing it from a few feet away. 'That's a big arse number.'

10110101111001100010000011110100100000000000000000

The small hemisphere was now generating a low humming sound, resuming its blur of what they assumed was numbers, giving the impression it was cycling much quicker than before, although they agreed it was hard to tell. After a minute or so it slowed, coming to a halt, like before.

'What the hell?' Nate said, fumbling with the zip on his parka, sweat moist on the back of his neck as he watched its demeanour change again.

'Are we maybe, um…interrupting its train of thought?' Connie said in a murmur.

'Seems like it…but I'm sure it has set protocols,' Nate said, grinning faintly, 'don't reckon confusion would be one of 'em.' He bent down over the small Sphere and looked closely for the first time, taking a piercing breath.. 'H-Holy…Mother of God,' he uttered, leaning closer to the numbers sitting fixedly on the face of the object. His eyes grew wide, 'What in the name of Jesus and—' Spires of light danced behind Nate's eyes as he gaped at the surreal scene. From about a quarter of the way across the surface of the small Sphere, the twelve parallel lines of Pi decimals changed…oh and how they changed! The rows of decimals had joined themselves into patterns, and for the first time, the numerals weren't just random junk mindlessly pursuing one another toward infinity. His mind was blinded by the sudden pattern in the chaos and his immediate thought was bullshit, that it couldn't be real but his higher brain held sway. Somewhere in the depths of his consciousness, it made a molecule of sense as it stared back at him like a child's whiteboard doodling.

'Uh…Nate?' Connie murmured, looking from the small sphere to him then back again several times, deafened by a growing ringing in her ears.

Nate had no words. He blinked at it blindly as though gazing at an abstract painting, scrapping to find reason amid the madness. He pushed forward slightly, studying the normal Pi decimals that all of a sudden morphed into something else entirely, slightly less than a quarter of the way across. If he was right, the implications were so off-script that it was beyond, well…just beyond, that's the best he could come up with. He couldn't slow his brain enough to corral the idea and crack it open, to wrest comprehension, ramification.

'It can't be,' Nate whispered, finally evacuating some breath, 'h-how can it be?' Colour vanished from his face. He was expressionless, mouth slack and drooping like a corpse.

Connie's neck angled forward weirdly. 'Is that like…what I think it is?'

'I guess it's still Pi,' he said, coughing to clear his half closed throat. 'I mean, it could be just something they've thrown in, but with everything's that gone before it, the sheer significance of PI in all this…I don't think so. Those, uh…figures are part of the equation, part of the solution to Pi,' he added almost inaudibly, eyes wide like headlights.

Connie's mind was buzzing as she studied it more closely, gobsmacked by the idea that dividing the perimeter of a circle by its diameter and eventually, after sifting through the promise of infinite transcendentals, getting these composite images. It was nuts… way worse than simply crazy, it defied every splinter of terrestrial logic, putting it squarely in the realm of stupor or hallucination.

Nate looked vacantly at Connie, 'I don't know I just don't…I have no idea,' It sounded like delusional mumbo-jumbo but the way the random numbers melded into the compositional images somehow ticked every neuron in his brain. This was how it was, this is how it had always been, since forever…we just hadn't dug far enough to find out.

Connie couldn't take her eyes off them. She had the unbalancing sensation that one plus one was now the verified product of seven. Everything had the distinct impression of being wrong.

The patterns were in basic shapes composed of zeroes and ones carefully purposed to imitate upright lifeforms. For some unfathomable reason, the abyssal regions of Pi had a clear design that included the only decimals that were also the sole members of the binary language. These multipurpose digits, the zero and ones, upright and horizontal, were the artist's tools in sculpting the tantalising figures that sat pregnantly in front of them. The other decimals were discarded as useless even though they could've been joined together to render the images. This meant something, Nate felt sure, but how they were supposed to use it was a total mystery. Maybe the binary monster splashed over the large Sphere like a soliloquy would provide some perspective, a gram of meaning.

Nate was so tired he was stay upright, but he forced his eyes over to the larger object. If this was really Pi, it had stick people in it and whether they were humans or something else, they were derivatives of the purest mathematical sobriety in the Universe – the inner workings of a circle, or in three dimensions, a sphere. It quite simply didn't get any simpler. Divide that by that, you get this. Oh, and if you dig deep enough you get all the philosophical trimmings as well. There was no arbitrary assignment of numbers with Pi, you didn't get to choose the ones that make up a pattern, it simply was what it was. If you plucked them out of a hat enough times, you'd eventually get what you wanted, but these were empirical and without favour, unchosen because they were Nature herself, silently waiting for whoever took the trouble to calculate it into the well of infinity.

Nate was staring down at his hands, understanding the data was entangled in the quantum foam of spacetime at the instant of creation, along with every other harmonic law and constant that made our stuff friendly to life. Slowly, he drew a surrendering breath through his nose, envisioning Pi, the God number, pondering what other glorious, maybe insidious significance it had.

Nate threw his hands up. 'Pi is everywhere Connie…on Earth, the Moon, Pluto, the most distant fucking object you can think of. And….get this, it somehow knew about these lifeforms, maybe us, maybe others that wouldn't blunder along for billions of years.' He looked harried. 'In what reality can that be possible? What degree of pre-tuning are we talking about here The numbers are upright and horizontal, I'm not even sure tuning is a strong enough word.' He rubbed an eye with the heel of his palm. 'I mean, if this is to be believed, the laws were designed so these things had to emerge,' he said, stabbing at the chicken scratchings, '…is there any other answer?' He held his stomach, feeling an uncomfortable looseness, stung by a bunch of half-ideas running across his brain, but one stood head and shoulders above the rest, and it was pretty damn obvious. It wasn't difficult, it was in your face, it was just accepting it as even a vague possibility that was gut-wrenchingly hard.

Nate turned away, mentally cooked, glaring back at the ominous number that was adorning the larger Sphere like a rather garish neon sign.

35. Irreducible

"I beg you take courage; the brave soul can mend even disaster." ~ *Catherine the Great*

When Yoshi woke, he wasn't sure how long he'd been out, finding himself on his feet in a rather strange circular compound. He swore to himself quietly in Japanese, gazing at the unexpected surrounds. His calf and thigh muscles ached, leading him to wonder how long he'd been standing there or how far he'd walked, his mind still thick with *just-woke-up* stupor.

The place had high walls made from something resembling hardened clay. In places, pieces had crumbled to the ground and shattered, leaving angular slabs scattered at the base of the wall like talus. Familiarity or deja-vu, he wasn't sure, but something about this place piqued his deeper brain.

He yelped as a pulse of adrenalin shook him properly awake. With a shudder strong enough to make him stagger, Yoshi realised he was on the wrong side of the Sphere, the horror of Tara filling his mind with chilling images of cellular devastation. Christ, he screamed silently, spinning around, seeing no escape, at least not in the direction he'd come from. Glancing at his skin, he sighed gratefully. He knew exiting might be the twist that saw him spat out as a wizened supercentenarian.

The thought of spending decades in this this place hit him hard, maybe he'd be frozen in the flecks of time before humanity's extinction, living a century or so in the almost zero time it took caesium to vibrate between two energy states back home on Earth. 'Fuck,' he said, peering down at the ordinary looking ground, scraping his boot across it, half expecting to expose something metallic underneath. To his surprise though it was just typical track hardened dirt with a layer of orangey grit caked over the top. Shallow striations looked like someone might have swept it with a stiff broom.

'Oh, what is this?' Yoshi murmured, rearing back, spying a bunch of plastic looking chairs in the near distance, very Earthly, very unsettling. The chairs were arranged in what he counted as twelve rows, as though they were set up for a reception, a cheap-arse wedding perhaps. It all seemed inexplicably out of place, familiar but misplaced in the extreme.

Yoshi angled his head back, looking up for the first time, almost gagging at the vivid purple sky so close above, seemingly chock full of electrical currents and seething eddies. Higher up, ragged orange clouds stormed across a heavy sky, filtering the light from two striking stars that from his perspective, hung in the sky in an intimate embrace.

To Yoshi's eye, the whole place looked like a Middle Eastern setting apart from the crazy atmosphere that spoke clearly to an off-world location, having the feel and visual of a planet in a very different, probably distant star system. He dwelled on the possibility of being lured to this place for the same reason Tara was. As far as he could tell, taking stock of everything he'd seen and heard back home, he reckoned he was screwed, maybe dead or coming back older than Otzi the Iceman.

Something caught Yoshi's attention off to the side, a contrast against the pale seats and ochreous walls. 'Fuck,' he blurted taking a rasping breath as he studied the unexpected figure,. It was a person but not just any person, it was human in appearance, a boy, a teenager maybe. By his appearance, clothing, countenance, there was no doubt in his mind this was Tara's "kid" she'd spoken about with such disdain, the harbinger of her unexpected descent into the most extreme winter of life.

Whatever the kid was, he looked just that, a fairly typical high school teenager, sporting clothing in basic black that was so dark he couldn't make out any detail apart from his outline, contrasted by the white chair and limonitic wall behind him. His stare was intense, intimidating, exuding a hint of expression although Yoshi found it mostly unreadable. It might have been displeasure he decided, or irritation, seeing one of his eyebrows ever so slightly lowered, but the rest of his face was fixed and impassive. Whoever, whatever this was, Yoshi sensed an unspoken flavour of maturity beyond his youthful appearance. This was no kid, he was convinced it was one of them and intuition told him that the kid's guise was barely a molecule deep.

Yoshi sensed an uncomfortable tingling near his left temple, blood surging beneath his hairline, clearly going somewhere in a hurry. Then a voice, directionless, Yoshi naturally assuming it wasn't the kid, he ran his eyes around the compound, seeing no one else, just him and Creature.

He heard words in perfect, unalloyed English, telling him that "they should already be megaparsec". Yoshi was startled because there was absolutely no bearing to the voice, left, right, behind…in front. They just fell between his ears as though delivered by headphones supplying data remotely to his Wernicke's brain. He was intrigued by his use of not just human language but human terms and definitions, guessing they had done their prep-work well, briefly considering they may have some other more clandestine handle on terrestrial affairs. Yoshi tried to respond with a question but there was nothing there, no sensation, no voice. No matter what he did he couldn't compel any air through his voice box…not even a squeak, a peep or a grunt. Breathing was fine, in and out, easy as, but his larynx had shut down, been shut down. Mother fuck he thought desperately, feeling a gag reflex in his throat. Creature had no intention of letting him speak or to engage so he'd simply switched him off, applied some bio-mute button, letting him breathe but not speak.

Minutes passed and nothing happened except the incessant shining of those blue eyes, no blinking, no movement, no suggestion he was getting anything Yoshi was thinking. Was he really toying with him, maybe enjoying watching him squirm, thinking ant hill, recalling Nate's grim analogy. Yoshi imaged words in his mind, thought them as carefully as he could, syllable by syllable, letter by letter but Creature just sat there, like a metal statue. Pious little shit was his final frustrated brain spurt, instantly regretting it. Maybe he wasn't ignoring me, he just couldn't get anything I was thinking. Yoshi averted his eyes, mulling over blue-eyes' ability to grasp Earthly explications. Before he decided anything, he was hit with a flurry of left-right whacks to the side of his head, the volume dizzying. Turn it down, he screamed silently, holding his temples, palms flattened against his head.

'Save yourselves or not,' kid-thing toned without any identifiable inflection. Stilted and a little tinny, the voice lacked the normal human rhythm, his eyes burning in multifarious shades that might have embodied emotion, but the face, the inflection remained polished marble. 'Information is key,' he said, moving his upper body ever so slightly, 'physics is a redundancy.'

Yoshi shuffled sideways, swaying, holding his throat, recalling Tara saying something similar, the information bit anyway. Frowning, he contemplated the *"physics"* piece of the puzzle, did this kid think that meant something to him because he was seriously off the mark if he did. In his mind's eye, he'd already marched up and told the brat to fuck off and leave him alone…leave them all alone, and having thought it, he questioned his sudden bent for aggression. Yoshi had no idea how it might be possible, but did evolution on Earth somehow create humans differently to others? Maybe it tipped in the wrong mix, emotions, psychological makeup, decisioning, just piss poor across the board. He immediately called bullshit because evolution was nothing more than a broad genetic process selecting better mutations to go forth and multiply, to make a species stronger, better, more resilient. They were Earth's fruit, ripe, unripe or simply buds that fell off the twig too early maybe.

It hit him again, the vibration spread through his jaw, aching like a serious dental infection.

Creature was staring unblinkingly, eyes a threatening shade of ice blue melding abruptly to darker midnight. 'Your inability to identify your own existence through math defines you as a species,' he said through a tightly closed mouth. Yoshi lowered his eyebrows, searching for meaning. Failure seemed to be the main take out from whatever strange commentary he was embarking on.

The words rang in his head, trailing off in a diminishing echo, then coming back stronger, deeper. 'Everything within your grip of science is peripheral to what is common insight to your peers.' He remained utterly still, without a breath of emphasis or movement. 'You failed to see that your world is not explainable in purely physical terms.'

The stories relayed by Becker and Connie flashed across Yoshi's mind, causing him to reel back a few steps. All the inconceivable absurdity that played out in space, it sounded like metaphysical bunkum, but was Creature actually alluding to it? Because that sure as hell wasn't explainable purely with physics, at least as they knew it, in fact it was the antithesis of physics, seemingly defying nature itself. Picking at his chin, he mouthed *"peers"* to himself, mulling over the word Creature had used. An incredulous stare grew on his face as he wrestled with the kid's spurious role in the bigger picture. Clearly his kind were of significant import, it was just the degree and scale that remained a mystery. Could it be that they were some ascendant collective of minds with a central purpose in some cryptic higher order… maybe they had an overarching role in the Galaxy or even beyond, his mind ached as he tried to know things that were profoundly unknowable.

Yoshi saw motion and froze as kid-thing slid gracefully up from his chair, walking fluidly toward the metal looking gate at the far end of the compound. Opening it, he glided slowly outward, toward what appeared to be a volcanic black beach, and a bit further on a tinted ocean looking a little like orange Kool aid, stretching glass-like to a close, dim horizon.

He stopped but didn't turn, standing ramrod still. 'Your higher thinking is a baffling source of frustration that has no precedent within the Collective.' He seemed to pause and droop a little. 'The trouble you have caused me is incalculable.'

In a few seconds Creature was gone with only the sand, the waves and the dusky sky remaining.

36. Pi

"If people do not believe that mathematics is simple, it is only because they do not realize how complicated life is." ~ *John von Neumann*

'God almighty,' Connie whispered, eyes mortared to the luminous characters, still battling to sift reason from the implausible patterns hiding deep inside nature. Nate was unmoving next to her, panting in shallow, vaporous bursts, goggling at the tiny stick figures spread across the small hemisphere as though they were holding hands in some bizarre human conga line. After the last of the figures ended there were half a dozen zeroes on each of the twelve lines, terminating at the right-hand extremity of the small curvature. Pi effectively came to a close with these neohuman renderings, finally supplanted by zeroes, Pi being finally squared away a few billion kilometres into the decimal miasma. Irrationality evaporated, transcendentalism discarded, and finally a polynomial solution to π was presented to those proficient enough to arrive there, which he seriously doubted included them.

Nate was sitting on the metal surface in a daze, deep in thought about what was so innocuous before them, apparently the answer to one of the greatest scientific divides in history, did Pi ever end? Well yes indeed it did, and with it an unambiguous sign that intelligent life was part of the grand plan. That there was a fucking grand plan!. Life, presumably intelligent life was inevitable, determined through some extraordinary process before the Big Bang was deliberately unloaded. Nate was light headed, the knowing was soul-changing, but it was only part of it.

Becker was in his regulation state of wide-eyed confusion, peering awkwardly at Nate, hoping for an explanation, all squashed eyebrows, ruminating desperately in his own awkward way.

Nate had never been unsure about anything in his professional life, even his first look at abstract algebra was a candy run, understanding it with ease inside a day, ascending to a virtuoso within a month. He debated whether any of this meant anything in terms of disabling the Sphere. He had no idea, but one thing stood above all the baffling confusion, what they had been shown, in a broader sense, was a devastating epiphany, absolutely life changing for any student of science. Anyone, anywhere he corrected, student or not, every walk of life, no matter how brief that might end up being. Nate saw it unbricking everything down to the very footings of science, philosophy, divinity, the most astonishing scientific insight of all time and hammer time for humanity was looming in the sky like a second Sun.

Becker had lost patience and asked the question loudly in frustration. ' What the hell does it mean…for the real world? In layman's language, not scientific blather.' he gawked at Nate.

'Well, you know as much as we do,' Nate said. 'According to that.' He jabbed at the air, 'the end point is an even eight hundred trillion decimals in. That's where nature closes shop and sticks up the piss off sign. It's so mind numbing that it should close out with stick men and— '

'Or women,' Connie interrupted tersely, '

'Yes of course, or women,' Nate acknowledged softly.

'What do these stick things mean?' Becker interjected, wishing more than anything he'd paid more attention to math instead of hooking up with girls, swapping stupid notes like an oversexed teen. Wait, he frowned, that's what he was, but eyeing Nate he thought, nah, no way, math was code for geeks, losers, Coke bottle glasses, no sex. Screw that, he'd happily stay the math stooge.

'For the love of God Becker,' Connie snarled, 'have you not been listening to anything Nate's been saying?' She'd seen him zone out. 'Sorry about him,' Connie offered irritably. 'Just hold the idiot questions, leave it to the adults.'

He looked away, breathing in heavily, holding it, then exhaling slowly in a trail of white vapour. 'So, you know exactly what's happening here right? You're an expert, that's all I want to know, you're an expert.'

'I'm not a frigging expert, but I listen.'

'I'm listening but this is…um, difficult.'

Damn it she thought, feeling like a pit-bull terrorising a poodle…a tiny black woolly one.

'Okay, fine, I agree, it's crazy difficult to get your head around. I'm just as, uh…the questions…lack of insight, I'm with you on that.' She smiled knowingly at him.

'Thanks,' he returned vaguely, exhausted.

Nate watched them with interest, seeing the odd dynamic grow another leg. What was it with these two? He pondered the point quizzically for about the tenth time. They should just hook up, get it the hell over with. 'That's fine…it's all good,' he soothed. 'We're can't all be math geniuses. Anyhow, these stick men or women have been here forever.'

Connie wore an incredulous look, 'Hang on,' she said pensively, 'so we or something like us was foretold before anything was anything?' It was an obvious question but no-one had broached it front on. 'H-how can that be?' She peered unseeingly at him, mystified, clueless, trying to read the expression in his eyes, desperate for the genius he advertised so freely.

'Is it us? That's the first question,' Nate stated, 'like you said, it could be others, some other bipedal creatures but personally, I think it's us…humanity, Mankind. I mean, they've drawn back the curtain, shown it to us, and, we are on Earth.' He raised his hands, drawing a grating breath.

'So um, correct me if I'm wrong,' she continued, softly shaking her head, 'you measure the outside of a circle, divide it by its diameter, and eventually…you get selfies…of us?' She rubbed her temples, pressing her eyes tightly together…to keep it together.

'That's it in a nutshell,' Nate said gently. 'We exist in the bowels of the most basic constant in the Universe. Crazy much? You fucking bet your arse, but there it is.'

'Created,' Becker rattled under his breath. 'You mean God, right?' He looked dazed, His eyes were bulging as he formed the words, then grew even wider after they'd fallen out of his mouth.

'It's these others,' Nate said slowly, 'it has to be them, they're the ones.'

'So is this the clue we've been seeking, you know to solve whatever it is we're supposed to solve, to stop all this?' 'Connie asked doubtfully, 'is this what we need?'

'I don't know…I mean, if it is, what do we do with it?' Nate was puzzled, Situation normal Becker grunted to himself, resigned to never knowing anything, like fucking ever. Facing away from the group, Becker turned back hastily, grabbing Nate's shoulder, shoving him harshly in the direction of the highlands and pointing with an outstretched palm. 'We need to go,' he said urgently.

Nate immediately saw what was coming and groaned. 'Oh, crap,' he said harshly, watching and listening, knowing only too well what was storming toward them from the northeast.

They could see a wall of clouds and ice screaming down the face of Mt Markham and they could hear it, roaring like a dozen B52s. The wind was on them already, the ice not far behind, crackling and pummelling rock as it burst toward them.

Sprinting back to camp they had to hunker down before the katabatic nightmare hit, hoping it didn't tear through their flimsy woven canopy. They managed to wriggle into their sleeping bags, beating the lethal cyclonic fingers by maybe a minute, the temperature falling forty degrees in the time they heard the first crackle of icefall. This time the sky was anthracite black with bone-splitting thunder on the back of blinding sheets of lightning.

Connie swam over to him using her arms and legs inside her sleeping bag to wriggle over. She ended up face to face with him about a foot apart, eyes as wide as he'd ever seen them, irises fully exposed, clear and perfect. She edged her head up so she could speak over the fur lining. A horrendous ripping sound rose above them as the entire canopy of the base broke away, revealing a visibly boiling sky, pitch dark and riddled with high altitude lightning.

'Fuck,' Connie screamed, feeling herself being pushed along the ground by cyclonic wind, covering her face with her gloves to keep the icicles from pounding into her. She disappeared into the darkness outside, followed by Becker and Nate who were powerless to resist the polar frenzy. All they could do was curl themselves into balls and hope they didn't die.

37. Reduction

"A thing is not necessarily true because a man dies for it." *~ Oscar Wilde*

Vic and Harry had returned to earth orbit a day ago after landing on Runway 33 and disembarking their rather eager passenger. Before she could take a step, Sky stopped dead in her tracks, melting into a puddle of pent up emotion. The DoD under Griffin's direction had spirited her daughter Alysha to the Kennedy Space Centre in Florida, meeting her mum at the bottom of the shuttle stairs, jumping into her, tears pouring down her face. Sky almost gobbled her up, squeezing the air out of her, so happy, but despairing that their sense of destiny was so pitiably flimsy.

It was distressing and at the same time poignant for Harry who still grieved for his son, watching them as they fused into each other's arms. Before she walked off, Sky paused and turned slowly, gazing up at the cockpit of the mighty ship and mouthing a heartfelt "thankyou", wiping away tears as she smiled, her face collapsing with sadness.

Harry wondered if maybe Todd was alive in one of those other "maybe" universes that existed beyond their shrinking dimensions. Perhaps he was there, in a place where decisions were different, where doors slid the other way, shifted, skating off to the park. Anyway, right or wrong, it gave him a little comfort as he watched Sky playfully grabbing her daughter and kissing her, seeing them walk off, hand in hand toward the massive US flag adorning the front of the space centre. He lamented being in the universe where his son was dead. 'Fucking typical,' he murmured to himself.

Sky and her daughter highlighted to all of them what they'd be losing when the rocks hit or the others finished their work…kids, love, the emotionally beautiful side of humanity, all of it to be vaporised, vanished in a heartbeat.

Vic wondered about their hasty decision to return to orbit, reckoning a few days spent on Earth might've been the right thing to do. It was a screwed-up mess but still, it was home. Vic looked at Harry lazily, 'you know, it would've been so easy to rip back the parking brake on the old girl.'

Harry nodded distractedly, not really caring one way or the other. Had the Spheres remained where they were, Earth bound it probably would have been, but things had changed several days ago. All the Spheres had just up and left at the same time, motoring slowly through the clouds, offering some brief hope that maybe the bastard objects were leaving for good. It was short-lived and depressingly wrong as they resumed their familiar resting place high above Antarctica in the same geostationary orbit. They just sat there, rotating languidly, stacked one above the other, not bothering with any semblance of deeper structure. Earth was now biding its time, waiting for the Spheres to wink out, one by one, or maybe all together, taking their entangled masses to hell with them.

Plastered vividly across the planet's technology, the global egg timer had dwindled to sixteen hours and pocket change, the event to play out at the strike of zero was anyone's guess, most accepting it would be devastating for Earth. The converse argument was that logic expected a grisly outcome so maybe the presumption was actually off the mark because counter-intuition seemed to be the new cosmic norm. So, the considered upshot was fuck knows, the single, only source of proof would be in the eating.

Harry still held the unshakeable belief that they could save the planet although the longer it went on, the harder it became to hang on, futility going the way of entropy, or that's how it would have been, all things being equal. Now it was descending into the realm of blind faith, as the countdown swept nearer to zero and the island sized rocks thundered past Mars, close enough to be imaged perfectly by the GeoMars Orbiter. And that's where he was now, he knew in his gut there was a way, but he didn't think they had time to find it, so he half-doubted the decision to be up here but where there was life there was always the feeblest heartbeat of hope. He quite simply needed to believe.

Vic terminated comms with Jack. 'We're down to three Harry…three of 'em left,' he said. 'Nothing else has gone but it's a given, like night follows day.' His face was drawn with fatigue, deeply uneasy, thinking hard, seeing nothing but the inevitability of extinction.

'Yup,' Harry said as casually as he could. 'Jack'll let us know. Won't be long now,' he muttered a little more grimly than he meant. Like Vic, he was drained and pretty much resigned to his fate apart from a shred or two of blind hope.

They had a month of food supplies, plenty of hydrazine and unlimited noble gas to power the Magneto. Good or bad, they weren't sure, but it meant they could remain in orbit until zero-time did its work, or the sledgehammers from space bashed the door down. If they were "lucky", they would still be here when the rocks flashed inward, sightseers with a most unfortunate view, the kinetic energy released when they struck making Chicxlulub look like a fourpenny bunger.

Vic was shifting uncomfortably in his seat, mumbling inaudibles under his breath, doing a fine impersonation of Harry, basically looking like a nutjob. His mind was stuck in a dark rut, running a never-ending loop on what might be dealt to Earth and its apparently defective intelligence. They'd be the final duo, stuck in a tin can, the pitiable remnants of spaceship Earth, a miscarried sentience found to be quite simply not up to it. Vic blew a rush of air through his nose, batting around the horror, visualising the suffering in his overworked mind. They'd be up here living, such as it was, while everyone on Earth would be dead or dying, directly from the impact or slowly cooking from the radiant heat of burning continents and boiling oceans. With a bird's eye view of hell, basically a horrific molten apocalypse leaving nothing alive, what then? He pondered the point grimly.

'So, uh…what do we do when Earth is, uh…you know?' Vic asked, still finding it hard to accept this reality. 'I mean, what do we do then?' He ran his hands through his hair, staring blankly.

'So, you think we have no hope?' Harry asked, surprised by the apparent surrender.

'No, I was kidding…yes I think we have no hope,' he flashed back. Vic's voice was caustic and grave, eyes roaming the cabin aimlessly.

'Jesus,' Harry croaked, feeling the last kiss of hope vanish into the ether. His old mate was positive to the last in any situation, at least outwardly, and it hit him hard. 'Well I guess we stay here, watch our home get wiped out by the rocks, if the frigging hourglass hasn't already done its work. If it's rocks, it'll be purgatory down there for thousands of years, if it's the, uh…other, well, spin the fucking wheel, right?'

The comms unit belted to life with belching static, gradually resolving into Jack's voice, his tone dire. No surprise there Harry thought. Muscles in his jaw and face tightened like piano wire.

'Sagan, Vic, copy back. Jack's voice was pure steel.

'We have you,' Vic said hesitantly. 'What's happening?' He was too damn tired to absorb any more doomsday prophecies. 'Just give us some decent news.' Vic held his breath, turning his shoulder to the comms unit and closing his eyes, feeling his heart skip a couple of beats.

'Shit,' Jack murmured sullenly, 'there's no good news. I'm here with Pete, that's it, everyone's gone – we're running the whole goddamn show down here. Pete and I and a couple of others at JPL are all that's left of NASA. Even the military have gone, the suits, techs, admin left an hour ago, after the last event, like rats from the fucking Andrea Doria. They just walked out the door…didn't even bother to tell us. Arseholes,' he spat angrily.

Vic reckoned Jack was probably close to doing the same thing, walking out the door with Pete, closing Johnson down for good. He sounded out of breath, puffing through his words, clearly under serious duress, very un-Jack like.

Flicking the lights to night setting, he looked miserably through the window panel at space outside, immediately wishing he hadn't. A pathetic sound like a dying animal rose from his throat as he roamed the window, searching for something and clearly not finding it. Vic mumbled something almost closemouthed, jerking his head around, staring back at Harry with a glazed look of disbelief.

'What? Harry asked sharply, seeing that space did look different but he couldn't nail it and then he tried mightily to control an urge to retch. There was way less light, less stars…less everything.

Vic's jaw was loose but suddenly snapped shut. 'Fuck me,' he forced out in a dull whisper, 'Andromeda's gone…Mag Clouds too. They should be right there,' he pointed weakly left of centre, then upper right, turning straight back to him, ashen and dazed. 'But they're not. See Sirius and Canopus, they're marker stars but they're marking shit now.'

Harry heard Jack 's shaken voice through Vic's intercom. 'Everything's gone.'

Vic glanced at Harry, locking eyes wordlessly, bewildered because they could clearly see stars in the sky. Less stars but still stars. Mass and space were still out there, they were fucking sitting in it for Christ's sake.

'What do mean everything?' Vic shot back, we can— '

'Jesus, everything but our Galaxy is gone,' he said feebly. 'The Universe isn't our, er, Universe anymore. Goddamn it,' he wheezed, 'it's only a hundred and fifty thousand light years across. That's it…that's the whole gig.' His voice fell away into silence, the words hanging there painfully. Jack continued, winding up with a shrill breath. 'Hubble and Keck and a bunch of other scopes caught images of things switching off…vanishing like a fucking power grid failure, it utterly defies anything you can throw at it.' Jack was panting, sounding desperate, resigned to a fate that seemed pretty clear. 'Hercules went, then Leo, Hydra and up the line it went, all gone with instant transmission.' Jack inhaled loudly. 'It's…it's…I don't what it is, but the speed of light seems to have been reset to …infinity I guess…and that right there simply cannot be… no way, no how.'

Vic glowered at Harry, plumbing his addled mind. 'It'd screw everything else up, all of physics would be busted wide open…the whole bloody lot, sub-atomic states all the way to gravity.' His eyes were shining as he mulled over the devastating paradox, every one of his internal organs pulsing uncomfortably. 'Nothing would survive intact, equations would be ruined, quantum mechanics DOA, infinities everywhere, reality junked.'

Jack exhaled noisily into the mike. 'I've got a paper from Stanford, and yes, it would muck everything up, no way it could exist like this. Something's deeply, deeply amiss here,' Jack said emphatically, taking a moment to catch his breath and gather in his spiralling thoughts. 'If the square of the speed of light becomes infinite, Einstein's equations go pear-shaped really quick. Everyone is absolutely bullish on it because we're left with a Newtonian Universe that we absolutely cannot exist in.' Jack cursed under his breath as he continued reading the report. 'Uh…space should be as bright as the Sun from galactic light, well briefly, because electron orbits would break, meaning atoms are gone, obviously we're gone…stars detonating everywhere because of altered fusion, no past, present, future…I mean, fuck me, do I need to go on?' He seemed to be waiting for an answer, but there was just stunned silence. 'The upshot is that it becomes stone cold dead, period, every law says so but, hey…apparently they don't count.' He turned away from Pete, shaking his head at the floor.

'…it's nuts,' Harry said, smoothing his beard around his mouth. 'We're seeing none of that obviously…it's pretty normal apart from the vanishing.' His, voice was thick with doubt, suspicion.

'And there's the quandary,' Vic said, '…why aren't we seeing it, hang on, forget that, why are we even here to debate it, that's the real twist right?' His eyes were swollen and red, narrowed to slits as he fevered over how they were alive in this nuthouse.

'So, the speed of light has been retouched without effecting anything else,' Vic murmured, feeling his head swim with flaring light.

'Which is, say it with me, *impossible*,' Jack muttered cynically.

'Of course it fucking is,' Harry added venomously, combing his brain for anything, finding nothing but red-hot nerve endings.

'Well apparently not,' Vic said. 'Could they possibly be so advanced that they can grab the vacuum by the, uh…scrotum, unpick it, then sow it back together again just so, like, however they want…bypass stuff we assume is hardwired as nature?'

They could hear Jack hack out a cough. 'Well, we're never gonna know.' He said, finally clearing his throat. 'Let's park it because things are getting bloody skinny out there.'

'And there's still three of them left,' Vic said bleakly. 'That'll take the rest of what's out there right?'

'Well…probably,' Jack replied coolly. 'That's what we're thinking, Stanford tells us what's left isn't stable, can't be, in its current form. There's enough mass and gravity in the remains to make everything crunch together pretty damn fast. Dark energy only pushes the Hubble constant over huge distances, no way it could do the job with a single pathetic galaxy. Yet fuck me if it doesn't get even worse…nothing in the Milky Way is blue shifted or red shifted anymore. Light isn't being stretched or squashed, I don't need to tell you what that means.' Pausing the onslaught for a moment, he scratched absently at his arm, breathing in and out forcefully. 'Well I'll tell you anyway…gentleman, every star, every planet, every goddamn molecule that's left out there is motionless, as though a handbrake has been pulled up to the hilt.' His voice went down a semi-tone, ominous. 'They have not the slightest idea why, because it cuts across every scientific law that exists. Go figure, but I guess it's sort of lost its shock value, right?'

'Go figure indeed,' Harry said wanly, wondering how much more demented this could get, pretty much convinced there was no cap.

Vic and Harry peered wordlessly through the window of the shuttle, picturing the limits of the Universe that were now so perversely close. Fighting to avoid the vagaries of why, Harry decided he couldn't. It had totally pervaded his consciousness, a cerebral tic that was reproducing itself bunny style, hijacking everything that made him Harry. He hated focussing on chicken shit imponderables but this godless lunacy was so grotesquely off-centre, it simply demanded mindless attention. Since the Spheres appeared in the sky the ensuing events lacked even the most tenuous whisper of logic, openly destroying things proven time and again on Earth, in the deeper cosmos, everywhere humans had been able to look. Hubble's Ultra Deep Field studies and SpARCS remote MACS cluster had imaged the first stars to emerge after creation…every law, principle and theory, Einstein, Newton, Hubble, Planck…it all held up perfectly every time. Consistency of Nature, that which was now nowhere to be seen, was everywhere in the human Universe, all the way back to the dawn of fucking space and time.

Harry's expression was stark, brooding, steeply uneasy as he hashed over the downfall of their perfectly predictable home. Trying to identify some of the dots, he fought to join a couple of them, but barely found any way into it, grimacing bitterly. He wasn't even sure there were any fucking dots to join. 'If we piece everything together,' he said, 'every event, every journey, is there anything that ties any of it together…on any level? I've mulled it over, chewed on it, rolled it around and guess what, absolutely fucken nada.'

'Yeah…same,' Vic said quietly. 'Is there something core that runs through it because if there is I— '

'There is something,' Harry interrupted, '…that nothing makes a speck of sense, right down to obeying natural laws we took to be proven. So, what does that tell us?' His brow wrinkled into incomprehension.

Vic was blank, his features even darker, 'and that means something's fundamentally wrong, it's all wrong, it doesn't compute.' He lapsed into a short silence. 'Harry…the big picture is full of shit,' he said, spreading his arms out, putting them behind his head and moaning dismally.

'Vic, this is Jack.'

'Oh Jesus,' Vic blurted, clutching an arm to his chest, 'yes...copy.' He rolled his eyes at Harry as the grim reality of another Jack-style explication seemed to be looming.

'Another one gone,' he said, devoid of emotion. 'Just a pigeon pair left.'

Sagan, on the other side of Earth, couldn't see the Spheres but they would soon enough.

'We've got all the 'scopes still manned, we're watching for anything,' Jack murmured, 'there's two left so I guess we've got a bit more time…maybe.' His voice fell into an uneasy, contemplative silence.

Vic finally spoke, shifting back and forth in his chair noisily. 'What do you base that grand assumption on?' He knew the whole lot could go at any time, there were no rules in any of this, that was the one definitive they had hold of.

'Nothing, just a guess,' Jack replied absently.

'Okay, fair enough,' Harry said from the background.

'Er, Vic, hang on a minute would you,' Jack said distractedly. There was a pause, they heard some muted voices in the background, some of it becoming louder, shouting from somewhere. 'Pete's got JPL on the line about Keck, I'll, uh...get back to you.'

Vic wasn't sure he wanted to, but he did it anyway, turning cabin illumination back to night setting. As he peered out, Harry heard a massive intake of breath, an involuntary spasm, his own unconscious reaction to what his eyes were ferrying to his brain. Or more to the point, wasn't conveying to his brain. 'Jesus Christ, this is it,' he breathed, pulling his head back sharply. 'It's coming...quickly.' Vic's mind was swimming, his vision pulsing in time with his heartbeat as he studied space outside, seeing almost nothing. There was one wretched shining light, that was it. He half expected to see some shimmering wall of exotic something careering toward him that would end in implosion, reality simply vanishing, gone forever, everything, everyone, gone without a trace.

Getting up from his seat Vic half shuffled, half staggered over to the window panel, peeking reluctantly at a hundred and twenty degrees of space. His hair was hanging in oily bunches over his crinkled forehead, eyes straining for detail, desperate for more than he could see. 'Procyon, Centauri, Capella, Jesus...Vega, Betelgeuse...for fuck's sake, Harry they're gone.' He turned to him, gasping, moisture welling in his eyes. Despite it all, he simply couldn't help it, a career astronaut and cosmologist, in love with space since he was eight, awed by the simple extravagance of it all. It was like a horrible, involuntary abortion, everything he cherished, torn away and discarded like trash. He gave a disbelieving headshake. It couldn't be...but it was, the reality was staring bleakly back at him.

'Vic, you still copying? Jack said.

Harry's head erupted in pain, the ache extending temple to temple as wave after wave of hurt struck him, maybe an aneurism he thought despairingly. Bring it, he groaned silently, tensing for Jack's words. It was happening, he knew it. Evaporation, wondering vaguely what it would feel like, vainly trying not to listen to Houston.

'Go Jack...what is it?' Vic said, resisting the urge to drive his fist through the comms unit.

'The solar system is it.' His voice was ice, running down on the last few words like a dying battery. 'There's nothing else,' he said with a derisive snort. After a moment's uncertainty, Jack added, 'funny...we used to think Earth was the centre of the Universe, Aristotle and his mates,' he droned, 'if you dissented you were burned at the stake. Well fuck me if the old bastard wasn't spot on, we're now the centre of the whole shebang, geezer just called it early.' Jack was chuckling grimly.

'No shit,' Vic said, 'we're up here you know, we've got our eyes on what isn't.' He could feel death now and it evoked a feeling so hopeless that some small part of him welcomed it, just to get it the hell over with. The waiting, the imagining was horrible.

'All our planets are still there,' Jack said, 'and hey, there's two Spheres left and neither GRACE or GOCE can detect any gravity waves anywhere, so shit, maybe we'll be, uh...okay.' His words were hopeful but his tone spiritless, belief close to zero.

'Are you actually on the level?' Vic said, too tired to tell, assuming it was just blind hope. 'We can't survive like this because spacetime ends beyond, what...the Oort cloud? Christ, like you said, it can't be stable, but it's in some kind of baffling stasis, which could change, probably will change, just a matter of time.'

'Yeah,' Jack muttered numbly, 'anyone's guess. And by the way, space ends on the other side of Neptune, not the Oort cloud.'

Vic closed his eyes, visualising the crumbling state of their everything.

'All the other's had gravity waves?' Harry asked, 'every one of them, right Jack?

'Yep,' he said dully.

'So, if the remaining ones don't have them, then you might be right,' Harry said with the tiniest spark in his eyes.

Vic raised his chin disdainfully, 'so, what…they're the welcoming committee…hey, sorry about your Universe…took it a bit far. Motherfuckers,' he said with a snarl.

Harry examined Vic's resigned expression, feeling like he'd been thrust into some reverse role-playing parody. He was Vic, Vic was he, positive suddenly deeply negative. Harry sighed 'yeah they are fuckers.'

'More than fuckers,' Vic shot back, laying his head back on the seat, shutting his eyes again. 'Shit,' he said to no one, opening them and peering at the single point of light outside, Saturn he figured, the only light in their view of the sky, the single pathetic object left, one of eight in the Universe. The name made him blurt with contempt, *Universe…give me a fucking break*, he said to himself, gasping angrily at the name it no longer deserved. It was space, that was it, not much of it either.

'I think we should just go,' Vic said, 'I want to get a look at the, uh…look I know about no edges trust me but there has to be a shrinking horizon, I mean, what a singular opportunity,' he said absently as fragmented images and models, pretty pictures of expanding space smacked him. All the textbooks, all the millions of pages of data, it bordered on comically wrong…certainly sadly out of date. Despite their likely fate, the ruination of most everything that defined him, the scientist in him still burned strong. 'All is lost,' Vic said calmly, 'so why the hell not?' He stared at Harry with the strangest expression.

Christ Harry wondered, looking closer, who is this guy? 'Okay, so if there is this horizon, the other side is a nothing, zero space, zero time, not much room for us, right?' He raised his eyebrows quizzically, knowing it went without saying.

Vic chewed his bottom lip and returned Harry's gaze deadpan. 'If things were different I'd say we were out of our fucking minds but now I say this without condition, what do we have to lose?'

'Okay…do it,' Harry said, shrugging, 'we're useless here, so might as well satisfy a curiosity before we…whatever.' His beard parted slightly, shooting a small, tentative smile at his comrade, wondering how their lives could possibly have come to this ludicrous juncture.

Jack could barely utter more than a dull croak, he just told them to do whatever felt right because life would be over soon enough, theirs and whatever other folk might have existed in the deeper cosmos.

'OMS Vic…fire it the hell up,' Harry barked, smiling lunatic style. 'Let's see what this baby can do.' Vic counted down to the hydrazine punch that would soon be overtaken by Mag drive to thump them outward toward the edge of existence.

38 Re-Entry

"If you wish to make an apple pie from scratch, you must first invent the universe."
~ Carl Sagan

Like the blizzard before, it abated quickly, retreating up the highland slopes and enveloping Mt Kirkpatrick, leaving the lowlands clear and disconcertingly still. Surprisingly, they were none the worse for wear and unzipping themselves from their sleeping bags they gazed around, seeing nothing unusual. The metal dish was shiny and around it the ice formed a wall that curved inward, seemingly without any support at all, about four feet high.

'So, the dish has a field of some sort over it,' Connie said, seeing how the ice had gathered against it at the edges. 'Sort of like a protective sheath, made of um—?' She gawked at Nate who was moving his head around to find some perspective.

'Yep, God knows what, and even he mightn't know, wouldn't know I'd venture.'

Add something else to the list,' Connie mumbled, looking high and low but seeing nothing.

Walking out toward the object, Nate was going to plug in the exact sequence of ones and zeroes that formed the humanoid images, see if it did anything, still thinking it was a little lame but determined to do it anyway. 'Shit,' he yelled like a gunshot. 'Jack.'

'What?' Connie panicked, spinning around wildly, wondering if Jack had suddenly appeared from the ether. 'What the hell are you— '

'We were supposed to update him, anything of er, note. I think what we have here is both of those.' He lifted his hands emphatically, talking louder. 'Talk to Jack, give him the lowdown, I'll start getting these numbers in.'

Connie wrestled with her heartbeat that was surging in her chest as she wandered toward the comms unit, taking deep, hitching breaths. She hoped comms was down, because knowing or not knowing mattered not, hoping to see SatCom machine-gunned by the rock-hard ice.

Becker inched past the backpack full of Semtex, unable to avoid an involuntary wince, conscious of there being enough plastique stuffed in it to obliterate a city block and then some. A suicide bombers wet dream, he mused nervously, shivers running up his spine, imagining the damage it would do out here, not to the object maybe, but to anything human certainly.

Nate headed to the small hemisphere with his laptop under his arm, gently setting it on the ground. Copying the Base 2 numerals into Notepad he enlarged them for easy viewing, errors couldn't be tolerated, it had to be bang on the first time. He reckoned if they had any chance of this working, messing up one number would be enough to ruin the whole lot. If this was a screwball test of sorts, maybe that was part of it, attention to fucking detail! Tara's kid apparently reminded her of a pretty typical High School student although trending more toward an arrogant, dismissive little piss-ant. Not too different from some of the brainless nobs he'd know at school, but that aside, there was something intriguing in there somewhere. A congruence that seemed worthy of deeper analysis but he had no time to think, they needed to get moving with the numbers. Maybe he'd pick it apart a bit more later…if there was a later, he chastened miserably.

'Okay Becker, read 'em out slowly, carefully, we can't screw this up. Pushing the laptop over to him he knelt next to the object. 'Christ,' Becker blurted, seeing the countdown numbers still fizzing across the face of the search engine, pregnant with a bleak promise they were trying to break.

'We better hurry, time's, uh…counting,' Becker said. They both gazed at the screen wordlessly as the numbers rearranged themselves every second, heading south.

1111110100 1000000

The sky was still a ruddy twilight courtesy of the polar summer, the poor old Sun bobbing just above the southeastern horizon like a twenty-watt globe. Despite the fleecy, thermal layering in their clothing, they were constantly cold, every frigid breath and pale exhalation reminding them where they were.

Rubbing their hands together vigorously to loosen stiff fingers, Becker and Nate kicked off a careful choreography of reading numbers and placing pressure on the alien machine. Despite the cold, it soon had them sweating, in Nate's case, aching from the same repetitive motion. Becker felt the pressure of screwing up, Nate the pain of lactic acid build-up in his arms but after twenty minutes it was over and they took a few weary steps backward, waiting, praying for something to happen, to maybe click into place like the cylinder pin on a tumbler lock.

Nate glared at the objects daring them to do nothing. 'Shit,' he murmured through laboured breathing.

'Maybe it's a good thing,' Becker said upbeat, 'turning if off…disabling it is good, right? But how would we know if it's off?'

'Well for a start maybe those numbers might stop ticking,' he said, clenching a fist and releasing it, 'maybe everything would just, you know, return.'

Becker leered at him, rolling his eyes uncomprehending. What the hell was he going on about. How do you undestroy something, especially things so insanely massive? Short of going back in time there was no way, but he conceded it wasn't impossible…incredibly, they'd lived it, although hardly of their own volition.

Waiting in silence, only their pounding hearts in their ears, they watched it for several minutes without moving. Becker turned to the bag stuffed with Semtex and gulped, guessing it was quickly becoming time for The Pentagon's backup plan. Connie would never agree to it but she didn't have to because the knuckleheads in Washington had signed off on it in a heartbeat. Can't stop it, can't understand it…kill it. Implementing the "Seoul strategy" was okay to save a population under threat, but what of the consequences when duelling with an off-world device? Can't understand it took on a catastrophic level of import. None of the suits had addressed it, or cared.

Nate glanced at Becker, 'it's probably gonna be Semtex time so best you be ready for that.' He could see that options were gone, the countdown was still counting and oblivion continued to loom from multiple points of the compass, all crosshairs firmly centred on Earth.

Half way back to base they heard and felt a familiar bone-shaking sound, guttural, like a sound system grinding out bass from close range. Spinning around, they saw something a little unexpected, giving them the slightest whiff of hope. Soft silvery light so much gentler than its previous guises was flowing from the Sphere like a dense gas and maybe it was, drifting to the ground and rolling across the metal dish like dry ice or thick mist, licking at the edges of the plate but going no further. The inglorious noise stopped and breathless silence returned, not the slightest zephyr of a breeze. Nate was sure it should be windier where they were, central to what used to be a sprawling glacier but it was either a piece of shit blizzard or calm and beguiling. No way that was anywhere near normal for Antarctica, it was far and away the windiest continent on Earth, at least it used to be.

Connie came ambling through the mist, her feet cutting swathes through it as she went. Becker could see she was upset, the tiny head shake, the upturned lips and moist eyes sealed it.

'Jesus H motherfucker,' Becker groaned as if in serious pain. Nate thought she looked cute in her blue snow pants and thick red parka, the big black boots just capped it off. Bulging beneath her clear goggles though was a petrified set of almond eyes.

'You, speak to Jack?' Nate said, rocking back slightly.

She threw her arms out roughly, 'I hope this activity you've got going here is getting somewhere,' she said, pausing for a breath, 'because we have no time,' she said fearfully, ogling the silvery light, sensing its pull. Nate could see the light reflected in her big brown eyes.

'For God's sake,' Becker said, thrusting his chin forward, 'just spit it out, what'd he say?' His fists were clenched so tight by his side his fingernails were cutting his palm.

She slowly turned her head to them, giving the impression she'd been drugged, eyes still huge, mouth partially open, tongue ever so slightly exposed.

'Jack told me, pretty casually really, that it's a fire sale up there…in space,' she said brokenly, sighing. Connie shrugged, then her shoulders slumped, tears coming and slipping slowly down her cheeks like glycerine. 'Everything must go…is going.'

'Jesus, it's okay,' Becker soothed, 'we'll find— '

'It's not fucking okay and never will be…not now, tomorrow, ever,' she said, dragging a hand up and down her thigh. She eyeballed Nate, 'you know what's left out there?' She lifted one arm straight up and it trembled in the soft light. 'Well…Puniverse, that's the name, there's us poor pricks, the Sun, a few planets, asteroids…that's it.' Connie shook her head grimly as she sank to her knees, tears falling and mingling with the alien metal as her face twisted horribly, sucking air in shoulder heaving moans. Looking up at Nate, she said limply, 'we've lost the lot beyond Mars.'

Nate's head thrust upward involuntarily. 'Mother of God,' he whimpered uselessly, living in hope that maybe the vanishing had stopped but sensed how futile it really was. This was…he searched for the right word and couldn't find it. The whole thing had a sense of make-believe, like a fictional character finding life, walking up to you on the street and slapping you heartily on the back. Way, way worse he told himself wretchedly.

Starting out the size of an electron, Nate knew the Cosmos would soon enough resume its birth state and a few femtos later, would simply cease to be anything at all. Strangely, he was confronted by a wizened, smiling face, an emotional nod to his Nanna back in Plympton, reading some crazy-arse fairy story to him about Chicken Little. This bespectacled little guy was convinced the sky was falling and had to rush off and tell the Lion, and so on and so forth until there was a madhouse of hysteria and panic. He always thought it was so lame but here it was, Chicken fucking Little was crystallising around him in a dizzying boyhood rush. The end of the story was grim because Little and his doe-eyed mates were eaten by a cunning fox. It was doing his head in.

***

The comms unit beeped slowly four times. Connie heard it and froze like a floodlit rabbit, heart pounding relentlessly against her breasts. No one bothered to speak, they just fought wordlessly with emotions, welling like molten rock, terrified of further noise from Jack.

Nate started walking toward camp, there was no hiding from it. Connie sat down on the cold ground, staring at the gorgeous highlands in the distance. 'Wow,' she mewed distantly, focussing stoically on the stunning chocolate and cream landscape of Marie Byrd, purring at the snow-covered ground that was not so long ago home to colossal plates of grinding glacial ice. Now it was home to a godforsaken alien machine that was part of something profoundly unforeseen, forcing not just humanity but the whole caboodle to its knees.

Connie held her breath as she watched Nate wind his way back to them, stopping a few times, peering down then starting again, clearly deep in thought, seemingly uncertain whether to even come back. He hacked out a gravelly cough, laying a probing hand on his forehead as he spoke. 'It's coming,' he uttered mechanically. Nate was about to use the word Universe but he kept it in, agreeing with Connie, it was a misnomer now. What was around them wasn't that…it wasn't a galaxy, even a solar system, it was verging on…he pulled his eyes closed and did his best to null his thoughts. He eyed them blankly, his sagging features sending a clear message that it was done, over, finished.

Connie averted her eyes, she'd seen enough. Glancing up at the dim sky she half expected to see something chasing down at them from above, a hideous black sky that would spell out the last seconds of existence. She felt body and mind slowing, syrupy thoughts mashing together, battling to draw air. Her mind swam briefly until she fell untidily to the ground with an inglorious thwump. Becker didn't take his eyes from Nate, didn't even see her drop, he heard her, knew what had happened, but reckoned it might be for the best.

'How fast?' he murmured, but Becker felt like screaming at the unfairness of it, convinced he was about to go the same way as the Universe…imploding into the deepest vacancy.

'Hubble was looking at Mars when it went,' Nate said, 'Jack and Pete got a close-up view of it vanishing, and well, it was apparently quite bizarrely incredible.'

Becker was puffing out clouds of white vapour as he flicked over image after image in his mind, all of them dark, deathly, leaving him numb.

'The planet went slowly,' Nate mumbled disbelievingly. 'It just ate it like the phases of the Moon until it was all gone…no more red planet.'

Becker finally bent down, groaning all the way, rolling Connie on to her side. She gradually came around and staggered to her feet, still punch drunk, eyes groggy and swollen. Standing like steel caricatures they variously studied, scanned or stared vacantly at the alien objects, every card they could think of had been played and all they got was an ocean of dots, seemingly without prospect of being joined, filled in, or connected in any way.

Becker sighed dejectedly, 'why bother?' he said thickly. 'Do we seriously think we can change what's going to happen? Everything's gone. We're done…we're out of time.'

'So we just wait to die, is that it? Connie challenged with little vitality, agreeing, but refusing to concede. 'Man up for God's sake, miracles happen.' Her face said otherwise but she wasn't going to let him curl into a ball and give in. Pussy, she thought savagely, flashing a cold smile.

Becker searched her face quizzically. 'So you're waiting for a miracle…expecting a miracle, well…we're truly screwed 'cause it ain't coming.'

'I'm not expecting shit but we're fresh out of ideas so what's left?'

'Not waiting for a miracle is what's left.'

'And you suggest what plan of action? I'll grab a pen if you have something.' She nodded at him contemptuously, tilting her head, making a buzzing sound with her lips.

'I've got nothing but I'm thinking.'

'Really, thinking?' She waved her hand dismissively.

'Well, it's what we have,' Becker said thinly, feeling beat, '…we just think, and by think I mean you guys take the lead.' Becker smiled and bowed his head in a gesture of concession.

Nate nodded bleakly at Connie, siding with Becker, pretty much resigned to failure. A sphere of space some eighty-five billion light years across had all but packed up and vanished…what chance of it stopping now? He felt dizzy and weaved on the spot a bit, catching himself.

'Look this isn't much,' Connie said, 'and I don't, uh…like it, but I think maybe—' She was still mulling it over, heart pounding wildly at what she was entertaining. 'I don't think anything's coming out, and no way it's off…you know, inactive.' She blinked owlishly, looking into Nate eyes, her stomach tightening as she ruminated on what needed to be said. 'I think maybe one of us has to go in.' She raised her arm uncertainly, pointing directly into the maw of the object, her legs shaking violently. Looming death or not, the idea of entering the machine, chilled her on a level that poked every fear and phobia she had, and there were many.

Becker surveyed her curiously, 'well, that's something I guess, but who wants in…to enter?' They stared pensively at the Sphere and the weird radiance, admitting they were seriously unimpressed by the idea, but none of them had anything else, apart from the other strategy. So it was doing nothing, losing everything or go on in, play the odds and see what was lurking beyond the stark grey curvature. Becker had a sudden image, puerile and human, imagining butting heads with some steeply bohemian figure inside as he hailed him gustily with a "don't be shy human, step right up…spin the wheel…everyone's a winner!" Christ, he thought, pinching an eyebrow.

The horrors inflicted on Haigh and Tara were front and centre as they tossed the idea around, fending off ghastly images of being sliced in half like a watermelon or living some shadow life and returning a wizened apricot, none of it painting the object as a vacation destination of choice.

'I think we need to do it,' Becker said solemnly. 'It's the only way…the only option, apart from doing nothing…I guess we should give up on the miracle.'

Nate pursed his lips, nodding his head seriously, tentatively agreeing but harbouring grave trepidation and concerns.

'Okay…so let's draw straws,' Connie murmured, staring at her feet. Becker looked at her perplexed. 'Seriously, I'm not drawing against you Connie. This place is on borrowed time anyway. Unless there's something in there for us we're done, so I'm the one…I'll go.' He immediately wondered what he was saying but it was a reflex. No way he wanted in there but letting Connie go was worse.

She wrestled with it for a few seconds, knowing instantly that Becker had it pegged. What was the point of staying here and dying in a big crunch, not knowing whether it would be quick, slow or even humane. Maybe going inside was better. All things considered, it didn't sound like it was any worse.

Connie gazed at Nate emptily, then at Becker, feeling warmth behind her eyelids. 'I'm co-coming too,' she said, her voice catching in her throat. I can't let you go alone you oaf, you know how you are in confined spaces.' Connie threw him a smile, veiling a deep, dark uncertainty.

Grinning, he wiggled his eyebrows, 'okay then, we go. The best exploration team there was…now we're trying to save the world.'

'Well, we screwed it up so only fair we try and fix it I guess.'

'I messed it up,' Becker said emphatically, 'you just called shotgun on the whole thing.'

'Yep,' she smiled, 'you fucked it up.'

They stared at one another with unspoken affection, nodding almost imperceptibly. This was it, right here, now and they knew it.

Connie wasn't sure whether to laugh hysterically or cry, or even cry hysterically and laugh, a sting of tears behind her eyes told her it was coming so she bit her lip, struggling to hold them back. The tears were wet on her cheek, she saw Becker watching her curiously, eyeing her closely. Yes, I have fucking feelings she felt like shrieking, a shudder running up her spine and into her neck. For some reason, she had the unnerving feeling that this time, inside would be much worse than before.

'I'll stay on comms,' Nate said, flushed with guilt, 'y'know, in case we get something from Jack.' He was grateful not to be making the trip.

Becker and Connie glanced at each other, and in unison turned toward the Sphere, her intake of breath loud and sharp, flesh crawling, every instinct screaming at her to run. She had to forcibly talk herself down, grabbing Becker's hand, pushing herself through the billowing mist until they were at the foot of the great machine. Her heart was thundering, beating harder than she thought it could, her brain fabricating grisly pictorials of hell that might only be a few arm's lengths away.

'Go through as one.' Nate said anxiously, recalling the Haigh incident, screwing his nose up as he remembered the hideous smell of his blood.

Putting his arm tightly around Connie's shoulder they stepped into the light as one, crossing the alien threshold and promptly vanishing.

Nate was watching with focus, seeing them well after they fell into the light, their shadows remaining, then dwindling to nothing. Breaking his gaze, Nate rubbed his hands together, shivering in the cold air, taking in the false dawn to the west. The Sun sat just to the side of Mt Markham, fixed like a dim lighthouse near the darkened horizon. Glancing back at the Sphere he watched the radiance peel off until it once again fell into darkness. He paced back toward camp to check in with Jack and give him an update, for all the good it would do, and of course check whether he had any good news. 'Ha,' he spat out loud, scoffing heartily at the idea, offering an exhalation of derisive vapour in the direction of the comms unit.

39. Beyond

"Mathematics doesn't care about those beyond the numbers." ~ *Dejan Stojanovic*

"I think we are just insects, we live a bit and then die and that's the lot. There's no mercy in things. There's not even a Great Beyond. There's nothing." ~ *John Fowles*

Sagan was heading directly away from Earth and the Sun as fast as its Mag engines would push it, currently maxed at two hundred and twelve thousand clicks per hour. Pretty good for fucking failures Harry mused bitterly, flipping a middle finger in his mind. Jack had passed on news of Mars demise and that the good old Universe now ended somewhere between the fence and the corner shop.

Vic and Harry were fixed to the shuttle window, waiting for what… they weren't sure. In fact they had absolutely no idea, not a theory, maybe a few spurious guesses, that was it, death certainly. Would it be some exotic boundary ready to swing the gate shut on the incredible playground that was space? Vic was frantically trying to connect a bunch of scattered ideas from his higher brain but all he got was a collapsing black bubble with them cowering like cornered animals in the middle…watching, expecting to die, like any sentient creature, hoping desperately to live.

Vic was pulling some concepts together, ruminating on some fringe NASA stuff he'd heard and read over the journey, remembering negative bag parameters, anti-masses, colour-flavour bodies, counter-vacuums or maybe screwy hyperons or Casimir effects and Bose-Einstein goodies. Of course, it might just be the prosaic termination of spacetime, no exotic matter or anything required. Exhaling loudly, his mind threw up a whimsical yellow sign pointing outward, boldly warning anyone who happened upon it, "Caution - Space Ends Ahead". The bowel churning fear of actually coming upon the end of everything was surprisingly mixed with feelings of almost euphoric awe.

Harry swivelled his head lazily to Vic. 'So, explain to me how it can be contracting at such a slow rate?' He squashed his eyes, squinting at Vic suspiciously. 'First it was in some sort of steady state, now it's shrinking, but not much faster than we're travelling, based on Jack's latest.' Harry pushed his head up and down as though stretching sore muscles. 'Like you said before there's enough mass to make what's left implode like that right? Harry snapped his fingers. 'So, here's another example of things we have no words for,' he said blankly, 'something else that's just plain wrong.'

'It's all wrong,' Vic groaned, 'nothing's made sense since day one. Good old physics is yesterday's news. This can't be happening but there you go, look around, it's happening. Maybe now there's not enough mass for an implosion…but applying laws and expectations ain't gonna do.

'C'est la vie,' Harry said. 'Add it to the pile my friend.'

'I'm getting sick of that fucking pile, but, um…what if we apply Occam's razor…what do we get?' Vic asked, steepling his fingers in front of him.

'The simplest explanation? Maybe we're dealing with some R&D megafuckers who can needlepoint every single natural law, and don't give a toss about doing it because the universe they're in is safe and snug.' Harry's expression hardened as he gummed away on it, looking out to space, reckoning he might be close to the mark.

***

Sagan was a million kilometres from Earth, between somewhere and nowhere, the view indescribably lonely, sad and forlorn because nothing was out there, not a single burning ember in the sky. Venus, Mercury and of course Earth and the Sun were out there but weren't in their field of view. The killer rocks and all the other shrapnel from the asteroid belt were probably out there too, but that was it. Apart from this pitiful roll call of matter, space was dead and getting smaller and deader with each heartbeat.

Vic was grinding his jaw with serious intent. 'You know, this whole edge thing…I'm not sure. Remember I said the Cosmos we used to know couldn't have an edge?'

Harry nodded slowly, grinning impatiently. Captain Theory returns with a brave new vision. Just give it up, he moaned to himself, knowing full well he'd keep going even if he swore at him square in the face. 'The Universe was a four-dimensional spheroid, right?' Vic said as a statement of fact. 'So it didn't matter where you were on the sphere, you still had fourteen billion light years of observable space in front of you, or behind you or whatever. But it's not like that anymore.' He stared through the window. 'It has to be different now, it has to be small enough to have scale and structure.'

Incoming comms caught him off guard. 'Sagan this is Jack, you copy Vic?'

'Uh…copy,' Vic said, gulping instinctively at the sound of the S-band.

'One left,' Jack said mechanically. 'You may as well turn around and come back…whatever you want to do,' His voice collapsed into silence.

'You think that's it?' Vic murmured, hardly surprised at Jack's sentiment.

Jack took a loud, deep breath and paused. 'Sun's gone Vic. We're in darkness, living on residuals. The electrical grid across the planet will collapse in a week.'

Vic felt horror hit him like a ten-ton iron block, the futility, the pure hopelessness of their plight setting hard in his brain. The ducks had just lined up in a perfect row, showcasing the worst kept secret. Oblivion was the end game, now unambiguously penned in planet-sized letters, engraved boldly on the ragged face of the planet. Nearly five billion years of nuclear burning erased in a heartbeat. Any flimsy thread of faith had vanished, now they genuinely had nothing.

'Oh God,' Vic groaned, wringing his hands, resting his head on the hard leather of his seat.

Harry's head had fallen sideways, also now laying on the back of his chair, gazing high into the air. 'That's it, game over,' he chuckled strangely, sucking his mouth into an amused pucker. 'How do you reckon the after-match presser will go?' He bugged his eyes out at Vic. 'Oh, y'know, we tried our best, everyone's hanging tough, we can still make the playoffs, next week's another game…I don't think so, it's a fucking wipe out.'

Vic was doing his best to ignore Harry's nonsensical yabberings. 'Do we go back, keep heading out…what? He considered the options knowing none were any good.

Harry's mouth had re-set in a forbidding line, eyes dull as phosphorus. 'Does it honestly matter?' He mumbled dismally into his beard. 'Jesus Christ Almighty…the Sun? Wake up. I'm too old for this shit.' Harry paused and lapsed into silence, lamenting the awfulness of life in a state of perpetual darkness, living, albeit briefly, with the absolute certainty of death, extinction of all things. There wouldn't even be starlight let alone a Moon to light the sky. And once electrical grids started failing, well, he couldn't even conceive of the catastrophic nightmare that would create. Panic like he'd never felt welled in Harry's throat as though a railroad spike had been hammered in to the hilt.

If it hadn't already, Mankind would devolve into a species without order, groping around in the dark, devoid of any of the tenets that mark a civilisation. Harry felt a twinge of thanks at being stuck so far away from the house of horrors, cradling his head, straining to think about anything other than the gruesome descent of his home planet.

Peering ahead, they could see faint arrows of light dancing at the limit of their vision like countless, fizzing sparks. Vic considered jumping on the altazimuth scope but knew whatever it was would be on them soon enough. Shards of light were everywhere in their forward vision, brightening until they melded into something resembling a complex lightning storm, an intricate web of fine electrical charges appearing to have underlying geometry. It was energy no doubt, but what energy?

Vic's heart took an almighty beat. 'My God,' he gasped, seeing billions of tiny fireworks growing brighter around them.

'It has to be it, the end of everything,' said Harry. 'Full RCS gimbal,' he added quickly.

Vic spun around to him, 'I'm not turning, we're going in, out or whatever the hell happens when we collide with that thing,' he said, staring back at the approaching light storm, feeling an unexpected emotional reaction to what he was seeing that he hadn't felt it since Sunday school.

Harry lowered his eyes, lifting his palm up and dropping it. He really didn't care one way or the other, growling, 'do it,' in monotone.

Vic doused power, continuing momentum toward the sparkling, convulsing wall of energy that was falling toward them, presumably the barrier between dimensionality, space and time...and zero anything. Looking closely, he saw intricately filigreed eruptions, discharges, all colours, arcs of light sparking everywhere, overwhelmingly beautiful, terrifying.

'It's amazing,' Vic breathed, watching it surge toward them, gathering more and more detail as it did. The boundary, envelope, whatever, was now almost on them, resembling a tremendously complex circuit board trading electrons chaotically, viewed at almost zero distance.

Harry's bewilderment was total, heart erratic, thudding in his chest, blood booming in his ears. The boundary of their pocket reality was so close he could see discharges sparking between countless spheres that formed part of the fabric of the barrier itself, presenting like tiny, sparkling jewels. It was a fleeting glimpse though because as soon as Harry saw it, a thundering shudder pushed them hard against their seat restraints.

'Wh-wha-t?' Vic couldn't believe he was still conscious. Contact should have been fatal because it was surely the terminus for reality, beyond which there was nothing left to exist in...no space, no room. Retaining consciousness didn't seem to be an option. He got that impossible meant little now but it had to be relevant here, he told himself, searching blindly for something that made a speck of sense. Being beyond the edge would mean existing in no space at all because what was left wasn't the size of an electron or even a quark. It was truly zero.

They watched "space" or whatever the hell it was outside, erupt with dazzling points of energy in a million places at once, rocking the ship as though Sagan was in a vertical re-entry.

Vic's eyes roamed the cabin, then outside wildly, seeing nothing but dull whiteness beyond. Space had gone, their space that is, they'd seen white space before but this was different.

'Er...well maybe we're inside the uh...boundary,' Harry said, breathing the words through a mouth as thin as a pencil line, gritting his teeth, hanging onto his seat with a death grip, waiting to die. Sagan was being thrown around, knocked sideways, pushed down, then up, like a Moon-rover ride on the Aeria highlands, all clunk and bump on less than adequate shocks.

Vic caught a flash from the corner of his eye. 'Ohhh whoa...Harry, look,' Vic said, seeing what was inside the shuttle, feeling the ill-defined emotion he felt before intensify.

Harry released his restraints and edged toward the front of the shuttle, eyes massive and round like a possum in torchlight. 'Fuck,' he said emphatically, instinctively rearing away from it.

Webs of what seemed to be static electricity arced through the cabin, condensing into sheets of fizzing energy, surrounding Vic like a halo, although he felt no sensation when they touched his suit. Harry wondered if the spark-things were electricity or even energy at all. The sheets of light gradually coalesced from all corners of the flight deck, twisting into a solid sphere of blue light, growing to envelop the centre of the cabin. It then set about pumping like a heart muscle, radiating strings of something undreamed of, Harry guessed.

Vic's face spoke in a final goodbye, a mask of deathly resignation. Harry's gave him a two-finger salute and ghostly smile trembling over his lips, an almost imperceptible pleading on his face.

A dissonant thump broke the side bulkhead away from the window panel. The shuttle came apart in slow motion without any suggestion of force or decompression, it simply yielded at its strut-riveted seams. Vic and Harry found themselves floating in the void, meandering aimlessly in dim light, watching broken pieces of the shuttle drift slowly past, moving deeper into the pallid emptiness that was bereft of anything resembling structure or detail. The ether was smooth and featureless for as far as they could see. Harry sensed no pain, strangely felt no fear despite their predicament. He had the impression they were drifting not through space but through an atmosphere because he was starting to feel gravity. Now there was wind rushing up at him. All he could see below was a mildly phosphorescent aura, as though he were freefalling through a solid wall of St Elmo's fire. Vic was nowhere to be seen. The fact he wasn't breathing hadn't even dawned on him.

40. The Collective

"I was walking among the fires of Hell, delighted with the enjoyments of Genius, which to Angels looks like torment and insanity." ~ *William Blake*

Connie glanced around sharply, seeing with a half-hearted sense of relief where they were. Third time's a charm she mused uneasily. The question of why was more intriguing because this time, she had an inkling of what this place might be.

They found themselves standing in the middle of a featureless circle, maybe thirty metres in diameter and around it were endless rows and columns of cylinders she and Becker were now quite familiar with. They could see they were aligned with the centre of the circle, radiating outward and upward like spokes from a mighty cogwheel. That's where they were standing, central to the cogwheel, standing in what they took to be the bullseye of the entire, overwhelming structure.

'Could be a hell of a lot worse I guess,' she whispered, hearing her voice harsh and metallic, echoing in the eerie silence. The cylinders were everywhere but there was still that unnerving sensation of space.

Becker was stroking his throat, grimacing, 'is this just more of the same?' He asked, remembering the mummified Soviets, the hunger, the exhaustion, 'there was nothing here last time...so what's changed?' Becker was peering around, thinking *same old bullshit*.

Connie started to answer but let her mouth drop closed, hearing a noise somewhere in the distance. Jerking her head around, her heart started hitting her soft palette mercilessly. She put a shaky finger to her lips, whispering softly, 'ssshh.' They were footsteps, Connie was sure of it but they'd stopped, now there was just more spooky silence. Then they started up again, a pad-padding noise, much fainter this time as though whoever, whatever it was, knew they were there, listening.

'Wh-where?' Connie said almost silently, breathing in measured gasps. She couldn't tell where it was coming from because every sound bounced off the metallic cylinders.

'There,' Becker muttered, pointing over Connie's shoulder. He pushed at the air with an index finger. 'Oh fuck it,' he said loudly. 'Come out we know you're there, Jesus we're not deaf.'

'Shit,' Connie yelped silently, her mouth running dry, brain firing off a hundred ghastly thoughts, every muscle tensed head to toe, like fencing wire. 'Becker is that you?' Connie's eyes met Becker's, bulging at the familiar sonorous tone, holding her hand over her heart, waiting for it to slow, completely blown away.

Yoshi came striding out from behind the third row of cylinders, looking exactly as he had when he'd entered the Sphere days ago, the same stupid grin plastered across his face.

'Yoshi!' Connie screamed, running up to him and grabbing him in a massive bear hug, a mixture of joy and relief. 'Thought you were dead,' she loosened her grip, allowing him to breathe.

'That's about as close as I've come...suffocation.' His face split into another boyish grin. 'Seriously, it's great to see you, both of you, thought maybe I'd never see anyone again.' His grin wrinkled into a more sombre expression.

Becker grabbed his hand, shaking it madly. 'Good to have you back kid,' he said enthusiastically.

'So where've you been?' Connie asked keenly. 'You been here all this time?'

Yoshi's brows were so heavily creased it actually looked like he'd aged inside the Sphere but he was just thinking hard. 'I saw that same kid, uh...thing as Tara in some odd Middle Eastern setting,' he said brokenly, recalling what seemed like a distant memory. 'All dust, high clay walls and a crazy arse sky with twin Suns. If they were trying to put me at ease, well score one for their failure right...I mean, do I look middle-eastern?' He smirked but the sentiment was serious.

'I don't think they give a crap about making us feel comfortable,' Connie said, 'quite the opposite, seems to be their game plan.'

Yoshi swallowed, continuing nervously. 'I ended up walking through some doorway, fully expecting death, worse maybe, and hey, I'll take this as a pretty good result.' He turned his head, then returned his gaze to Connie. 'Although this place is way beyond weird.' For the first time Yoshi looked properly at his surrounds, visibly tightening his jaw as he did, looking puzzled as his eyes made their way around the chamber. 'What the hell is this pl— '

Yoshi was chopped off mid-sentence by another noise to their right, a different, more complex tap tap-tapping sound, floating everywhere in the chamber. Something was coming toward them although it sounded like it had more than two legs, a bit like the sound a large dog might make. Not bipedal was Connie's brain scream, picturing some forlorn creature suffering a similar godless fate. The adrenaline coursing through her limbus made it difficult to think, to stand without wobbling. She glanced with clear distaste at Yoshi and Becker, this could be about to get very ugly indeed.

'Oh you have to be shitting me,' came the vaguely familiar voice. 'Becker and Connie, Jesus Christ, in the goddamn flesh.' Vic and Harry were clearly not believing what they were seeing.

Connie reared back instinctively as they came toward her, 'holy shit…I shouldn't be surprised I guess, but…where's the shuttle, how did you—'

'Totally ridiculous,' Vic said, furrowing his brows, then softening them, 'we thought you were gone, or at the very least sent somewhere else…permanently I guess.'

'Well, we're back,' she said with a fleeting smile, 'how did you get here?'

'You wouldn't believe it, Vic said flatly, 'not sure we do really,' he glanced at Harry, 'and to be honest we're not sure how we got here.'

Harry looked around 'What about you, from L1, you just got spat out here?'

'Oh, we've been around Harry, just know it. We came here from L1, got shunted back to ground zero, then back here again, Groundhog style, you know. What does it mean…something, nothing?' She peered at Vic for a few seconds, feeling good to see his face again. 'So, your ship?'

'Gone,' Vic said. 'Busted up, drifting in…not sure what the right word is now…space is wrong.' He gazed at Connie miserably, 'it's all just about gone, space I mean.'

They gazed at Vic and Harry without expression, knowing it was coming but completely torn by confirmation. Connie gasped, a bitter breath, glancing at Becker who was staring at the floor numbly, unmoving. It was a while until someone gathered the energy to speak, Becker finally breaking the silence, looking squarely at Vic. 'So, uh…you survived how?' He asked shakily, wondering how the hell they survived a shuttle crash.

'Dunno…it was totally surreal,' Harry said, gripping his fists like he was about to pray, not sure how to relay the bizarre encounter. 'We met up with an, er…edge, horizon, boundary, call it what you want, and keep the laughter to a minimum,' he said with the barest grin, 'the, uh…end of everything.' He clasped his hands over his head, closing his eyes and shaking his head. 'It was sparking away like some crazy electrical grid, then things got sort of messy.' Harry drew in another lingering breath, surveying their faces. 'Everything was strangely slow and gentle, then, bam, we fell through some sort of atmosphere…came to over there,' he pointed at the first few rows of cylinders.'

'Well what I do know is that this place is getting crowded,' Connie said, debating the curious get together, a sense of unease rolling in her stomach. 'So why are we all here,' she said, 'as a collective… we've been brought here deliberately, grouped together for a reason right?'

Harry looked at her narrowly, five minutes he'd been here and already a stupid question without hope of answer. He knew there was stuff all else to do, damn tired of that argument as well.

'Hang on, so…what is this place?' Yoshi said, finally completing his question from earlier,. 'These objects, so many of them.' He was stunned by the sheer volume of what was around him.

'We know a little bit, Connie said, 'like they're numbered and there's billions of them.' Yoshi was listening bug-eyed, sifting the words for meaning, awestruck as he gazed at the cylinders. 'We've seen three colours, they're mostly black, some white, a few are gold.

'And the colours mean?' Yoshi asked, immobile, 'no idea right?' He continued studying the endless rows around him, seeing a few white ones nestled in with the black.

'I have a theory but it's only a theory,' Connie said, her heart rising in her throat, knowing what they'd think. 'It's based on something we, something we saw…which I, uh, won't go into.'

'Okaaaay,' Vic prompted slowly, 'out with it.'

'Um,' she paused, not sure she should continue but, the time for restraint had truly passed. 'Your theory…what is it?'

'Well, ah…we think these objects aren't anything to do with tech as we'd define it, you know, power sources and so on,' she said, drawing and holding a lungful of air. 'I think they're vessels for artificial realities, for universes like ours.' She maintained her stony gaze at Vic, waiting for a reaction, the gasps of derision, explications, profanity and the like.

Everyone was deathly still, frozen, leaving the words hanging in the air, puzzling over the idea Connie seemed to be stating as a declaration of fact. 'You fucking what?' Harry eventually blurted, staring at her slack-jawed with teeth exposed through his gnarled beard. He waited for the smirk which didn't come. 'You're actually serious about this…you believe what came out—?' Harry was gaping at her with absolute focus, eyeing her like a hawk, almost daring her to keep it up.

'Completely,' she said without hesitation

'But how, I mean, look at them,' Yoshi said, gasping. 'It makes no sense.' He was squinting at them, frowning, it was insanity.

'So, hang on,' Harry said, raising a palm defensively. 'You're saying that everything a universe is, was or will be, has been created and is evolving inside that thing.' He twisted his jaw, adding, 'that thing?' Harry poked sharply at the nearest cylinder, figuring it was big enough to hold maybe a few kilos of dirt. Dumb broad he thought to himself, she's tripping. 'Fuck off,' Harry said harshly, 'all that space wrapped up in these things? Come on…seriously…think about it!'

'I agree,' Connie said with the briefest smile, 'it makes no sense but we've seen what they can do. They're obviously dimensional architects of the highest order so think about it…why not?' She'd had enough of this beat around the bush crap, glaring at them with contempt. 'Oh Jesus, pull your heads out of your arse, broaden your fucking minds, it's insane yes, absolutely, but it's possible because we've all seen impossible how many times?'

Vic hadn't said anything but it was coming as he battled to organise his thoughts into something more than a chaotic jumble. Finally pushing his head up from the floor he eyeballed Connie. 'I know you have reasons for thinking it, based on whatever experiences you had, but are you honestly saying that our Universe, such as it is, is here in this place, and we're no longer in it?'

Yoshi barked something in Japanese, his eyes flashing around the chamber, pondering location. If it was in here, then the Cosmos was no more special than any of the other billions, crammed into this place like a goddamn battery henhouse.

'Yes,' Connie said, 'it's a possibility…I think it's in here somewhere and they created it.' She ran her hands nervously through her hair, pulling at a knot, 'and apparently now they're uncreating it.' She glanced at the others, flustered, wondering where in God's name they went to from here, puzzling over the relevance of the G word she'd used in her mind.

Yoshi was still glancing around wildly, baffled. 'If these are, you know, universes, then why is there such a massive bunch of them?' His face was a strange mix of wonderment and trepidation as he weighed up the nonsense.

Harry fumed. 'Stop asking shit we can't answer!' He said, grinding his jaw back and forth, causing his ragged beard to move in aggravated sympathy.

'Yeah no worries,' Becker said. 'So why are we here?' He stared brazenly back at him, not giving a rat's ass about his psychotic aversion to curiosity. He'd have to suck it up like a big boy.

'Good one Becker, keep pushing, see where it gets you.'' Harry's face was tight and tense, waiting for him to go just a little further, his left fist tight and shaking in a clear promise of what it might bring.

'Just back off Bowden, worry about your goddamn numbers.'

'Must be nice being an idiot,' Harry shot back. 'Not a worry in the world, all teddy bears and rainbows up there ain't it?' Harry touched a finger to his temple and twisted it.

Becker was a little taken back by the palpable dislike burning in Harry's eyes. Psycho was the first word that came to mind, go fuck yourself the second, but he held onto both. Having some hillbilly punch-up in the middle of the chamber would be a rather inglorious display for anyone who might be taking an interest.

It was a strange, unsettling clip-clopping sound that was loud and harsh, like steel tip boots on ceramic tiles, echoing around them. Once again, it made the exact location difficult to pinpoint.

'If it's a fucking horse I'm out of here,' Becker said with a shaky smile.

'You idiot,' Harry said humourlessly, 'although you'd at least have some company…you know, a mental equal.'

Connie glanced at Becker, elbowing him hard in the ribs to stave off a punitive strike. He grunted and shot her a hurt look. 'Hey…Jesus, easy,' he moaned, rubbing his chest.

'Aww…you okay baby?' She teased, struck by a perfect mental image of Joe that came from nowhere. Connie shook her head to erase it. Surely not she chided herself, guessing at best it would be a brief hello and goodbye, but she'd take it.

Cocking her head, she listened intently, her brain throwing up unnerving teasers of some primeval horror, tall and erect, covered in spines, drooling saliva as its sabreous claws scraped across the floor toward them. She shuddered, pondering the odds of it being the ugly fucker from ancient Mars, back to get her for real this time. She stared at the spot where she thought the sound was coming from, seeing nothing.

***

Nate noticed the dimming light and thought it strange. At first he assumed it was the Sun sliding below the horizon, pushing Antarctica toward its frigid winter. Then he thought more deeply, no way, he tempered, watching a strange dusk fall across camp, stretching gradually upward to the highlands. Nate turned and peered quizzically, stopping dead, frozen like a snowman. He narrowed his eyes, bringing his hand to his forehead to block out what little light there was. '…the fuck is going on?' He murmured, seeing a mystifying chunk missing from the solar photosphere, as though the Moon were passing in front of it, much like a regulation eclipse. But it'd been a week since the Moon was taken from the sky. Unease was fusing into panic, chest tightening. 'What?' He gasped, trying to figure out what he was looking at, having no answer apart from the hideously obvious. Holding his jaw, he tried to kill a scream in his throat as he watched a dark divide creep across the star like a necrotic cancer. Everything behind the black line appeared to be dissolving, there were no fragments, flares or exploding plasma, it was simply turning into, um, he thought idly how to describe it…into space. That was it he thought, it was being replaced by space, empty space.

Hearing something pitiable Nate realised it was a gurgling from the back of his own throat, an involuntary wail that washed over the metallic landscape, an awful echo of despair. The entire star was gone, like Jupiter, the Moon, it had simply been rubbed from the skies. Five billion years of stable nuclear burning had simply disappeared, the vanishing taking it with the ease of a pencil mark erased by a stroke of rubber.

Perfect darkness hit the landscape, and in a moment of clinical terror, Nate knew that daylight would never come again. He'd witnessed the curtain fall on humanity right there in the sky, the horror hitting him with a rush of hopelessness so strong he sunk to the ground on useless legs, holding his head with one hand, hearing the thudding of the Ospreys massive rotors as they fled. They didn't even bother to tell him, just up and left, leaving him with no possibility of escape. Can't blame 'em he said to himself coldly, nothing mattered now, life, death, nothing. Apart from lights on the receding aircraft and the LED's on the comms unit, darkness was as complete as starless space.

359

Nate was sprawled on the ground like a polar castaway in unrelenting night, yet it should have been a cool summer's day.

After muddling around in the dark with his pocket torch, Nate finally located the switch for the battery powered lights that lined the edge of the canopy. They were there mainly for blizzard conditions, would last a day…maybe. After that it was endless darkness, temperatures hostile beyond belief, followed by a most disagreeable death.

A Sunless Earth would quickly start to unravel, made worse at the poles where stored heat was almost zero. In short order, the atmosphere would start to freeze out, collapsing as a pretty frost then solid sheets of ice, covering the land and the frozen oceans like Jupiter's ice ball moon, Europa. Of course, by then the vanishing would have completed its work, or the asteroids, sterilisation, so its irrelevance was as total as it got.

How many ways? Nate wondered. Earth was fucked on so many levels it went way deeper than the most absurd depiction of apocalypse, almost humorous in the grimmest of ways.

Nate had terminated comms with Jack, confirming zero impact from anything he'd done, coming as no surprise because he realised how facile his decisioning was. Jack was indifferent, coolly passing on the news, telling him that every observation from every major telescope in Australia, the US, China and Russia confirmed that nothing had changed, the steady implosion continued to be real. They'd briefly bid each other farewell, knowing they would never speak again, finding little emotion, just fatigue, acceptance, enduring bewilderment.

Nate took the Lumens torch and walked out to the Sphere, standing right next to it, as close as he could get without actually touching it. For the first time, he really eyeballed it from only a step away, peering at its surface, squinting in the artificial light. He was overwhelmed by a sudden hatred, scoffing at his pitiable lack of mind. It probably painted him, humanity, for what they were, way too emotional, frequently irrational and all too often, hysterical beings. Nate rolled it around in his panic thickened mind, wondering if a holistic response might have been the answer. Instead of each country doing their own thing, flipping the bird to their neighbour, they should've been trying to solve it as a global collective, fusing all the intel, presenting a united front. Logically that would have delivered something a hell of a lot better than the fractured hash-up they'd managed to engineer. The United Nations was in the background, predictably failing and confirming its reputation as an impotent, poorly planned reflection of humanity's disdain for global accord. If the UN had teeth, some binding protocols, a decent set of balls, it might have been different, but it was underfunded, under-resourced and just fucking underwhelming.

Focussing on the surface of the object lit up by his Lumens, Nate hunched over, searching for any detail on its curvature. The surface had the colour and lustre of obsidian, jet black, vitreously reflective, the smoothness of glass when he wiped his hand across it, feeling the hair on his arm react to a slight static charge. When he moved his hand the other way it was rough, like a cat's tongue.

Nate flinched, seeing something appear in the centre of the light. 'what the—?' He mumbled in a whisper, taken aback, but holding his ground. Peering closer, he watched the thing pulse with a regular beat. 'Wh- what?' Nate breathed the word almost silently. In front of him was a single dot, perfectly round, blinking on and off with a period of about half a second. 'No fucking way.' Nate moved his neck around, gawking at it from every angle. Was it waiting for him to do something, give it something, a command maybe? A goddamn equation, algorithm, words…should he thump it? If he had a front-end loader he'd dig the fucker up and roll it into the ocean, imagining Error 404 Page Not Found gradually forming on its indignant surface. He gulped, succumbing to mindless paranoia but hey, no Sun, certain death…losing it completely was quite reasonable he told himself, feeling sweat, freezing cold between his shoulder blades.

Knowing what he was about to do, Nate already felt ridiculous, but there was no one around, so fuck it. He took a shaky breath and started talking, posing a number of pointed questions as though it had the power of mind, was fluent in human language. No one could rule it in or out, the objects could be programmed automata but equally they could be deeply intelligent, intuitive, able to comprehend and communicate with the outside world in any number of ways. Despite his desperation and steely dread, he felt like a moron, watching the white dot continue blinking in front of him like a mindless abstraction, totally unreactive to his presence. Or maybe the piece of unholy shit was simply mocking him, offering false hope…taunting him with a sense of opportunity but providing no way to engage. Nate felt his face grow hot with humiliation and wanton anger, recognising a deep need for vengeance.

Veins were throbbing in his neck, fists clenched, teeth bared, 'you fucking rotten bastard,' he yelled like a madman, jutting his chin out aggressively. Nate stuck his index finger up at it. Then he thumped the tormenting dot and was instantly flung backward onto the metal, sprawled untidily on the ground, groggy, instantly sore. Rousing himself gingerly he struggled back to his feet. 'Shit,' he coughed, looking himself up and down, thick clothing sparing him from serious injury, his entire right-side tingling from the force of the shock. He knew the bastard wasn't off or even dormant, it was just waiting in some stealth mode, conserving energy, biding its time.

Nate brushed himself off, the rage coming back as he glared at it, knowing what he needed, strike that, what he wanted to do. Godless garbage he fumed, he was going to blow the prick out of the ground. He had four kilos of Semtex, a decent length of detonating cable and a deep fucking yearning to inflict injury. It wouldn't help their plight any but it'd sure as hell give him a boost. Grabbing the backpack he pulled out the vacuum pack of explosives, cautiously tearing apart the polyvinyl envelope in the weak light. He held the red bundle behind his back, approaching the Sphere hesitantly, wondering if it might identify him as a threat. Carefully, he brought the package to the front, kneeling slowly, gently pressing the red plastique against the black curvature where it met the metallic plate. He imagined what the explosive so close to his head was capable of. It was of no great import though, he'd come to terms with dying a few days ago.

Nate shaped it like plasticine, pushing, forming it into a snaky line about five centimetres thick and thirty centimetres long, looking like the crimped surrounds of a brightly coloured pie. Eat at your peril he mused darkly, hoping it gave the machine a serious case of heartburn.

Nate edged back, still bitten by a desire to punish, and he cared nought if it was only by attacking one of their drones or whatever the hell they were. As a show of intelligence, it was as bad as it got, but for feel good value it was off the bloody scale.

Grabbing the detonator cord he laid it out, walking slowly, pace by pace back to basecamp. It was laced with granules of PETN and would literally blow up when it was lit. There would be no slow burn here, just bam…gone.. Nate taped some blasting caps to the cord, running the wire back to a safe distance behind the equipment lockers. 'Duck arseholes!' He yelled insanely, picking up the detonator that would trip the cord. A part of him knew he was losing his mind, but the part making the poorly conceived decisions was grinning maliciously, wringing its hands together wickedly.

Before he had a chance to fire the charge, a low whirring noise started up ahead of him. He searched for detail but it was just an apron of darkness beyond his feeble torchlight. Whatever, he thought, pointing the light down to the blasting caps. All of a sudden his world exploded in colour, everywhere blanketed by light, brilliant, dazzling, overtaking stone dead darkness. In the first split second, he hoped the military had returned for him because anywhere was better than here, losing the idea as soon as it hit him. Nate couldn't steady his breathing, panting in the freezing air, condensing breath everywhere, seeing the Sphere in all its irritating, awful glory.

'Oh, you have to be—' Nate breathed, seeing the object transforming the metal dish into a blood coloured nightmare. The crimson daylight was unwavering, the sight utterly surreal, evoking an odd feeling, part dread, part awe with something else he couldn't define. Reverence maybe, visions of hell perhaps, both he decided absently. To his mind the photons looked like light captured beneath the event horizon of a black hole, infinitely red shifted and bereft of energy.

Had he called its bluff he wondered, on the verge of being destroyed, had it relented, offering something up, maybe an option to Semtex…to injuring it, killing it even? If he did manage to blow it to bits it would feel great and hey, score one for humanity, but realistically…his mind trailed away into blankness. He didn't think chemical explosives would even knick it given what they'd seen of these things. This hyperphysical object was conceivably a tesseract or even a glome that stretched way beyond their simple three-and-one dimensions. It was hardly going to be broken down by phenylstyrenes and citrates no matter how destructive their combination might be on Earth.

Nate gently placed the detonator on the ground and walked back to the Sphere, peering at the light as it gushed to the edge of the plate, then back on itself as though it were something more than just light. A stiff breeze was strangely warm on his face as he threw around his limited options. Nate was sure it could compel him inside like the others but maybe it didn't want to, or perhaps couldn't for some reason. He had to play the odds, he didn't want to, but it was the right thing to do, and reuniting with Connie was a vague possibility… and that made him smile on the inside.

Having made the call, Nate took a deep breath to clear his mind, walking straight ahead, wanting to get it over with. As he did and just before he touched the light storm, a thought mashed into his mind and started ping- ponging. What if this thing was conscious and possessed a steely survival instinct, maybe it would promise anything to avoid being harmed, and what might the rotten reality be? He decided to retreat, rethink it, but he couldn't move, there was an irresistible pressure behind him and now it was physically edging him forward. 'Fuck you!' He screamed, feeling himself being jostled forward against his will, unable to resist, forced into the nucleus of light as though an iron fist were locked in the small of his back. The more he struggled the firmer he was steamrolled forward. Nate looked around wildly, knowing his fate was set so he relented, stepped forward and fell headlong into the Sphere and started falling through complete darkness.

41. Showdown

**"Here lies one from a distant star, but the soil is not alien to him,
for in death he belongs to the universe."** ~ *Clifford D. Simak*

The shadow was indistinct but it quickly assumed a form that was disturbingly familiar to some. Yoshi was aghast, feeling a shudder sweep through his body. 'Oh shit,' he spluttered under his breath, 'the fucking kid.' Warning spasms flared as he recalled the horror of voice-lock, remembering what he'd told him, information is key. Whatever, whoever it was, this thing made him want to bolt.

A teenager to the human eye, it was his chilling countenance, the dark delivery of his words, made with such bleak authority that painted him as anything but human. Creature stood at the edge of the circle, studying closely, eyeballing all of them. The face was blank but thin eyebrows formed an almost straight line, giving a mild suggestion of annoyance. His arms were still by his side, not a flicker of movement anywhere on his body apart from the eyes.

'Jesus Christ,' Becker whispered, looking at his sullen face. 'Who is this little punk?' Connie elbowed him, putting a finger to her lips. 'Ssshh,' she said quietly, clutching her hands in front of her, memories of Penang firing back at her. Like Yoshi, every fibre of herself screamed get the fuck out. This was the same kid from a decade ago, looking exactly the same, down to eyes, face, clothes, hair, even shoes. Connie fingernailed felt a tremor rise in her chest, tensing every muscle deliberately, fighting a brain-haze dizziness, as though her thoughts were frozen.

Creature was dressed as Yoshi last saw him, black clothing, no joins, no buttons, no breaks in the material, certainly nothing that resembled a crease. He was covered neck to toe, making his face look pasty pale, accentuated by deathly blue lips, seemingly lacking a decent flow of blood. For all intents and purposes, he was a schoolboy, albeit dressed like a funeral director in need of a decent meal and some rays. Like his coiffed hair, the shoes were black and glossy, blending seamlessly into his black trousers. The overall impression was of a seriously strange individual, made worse by the circus freak eyes and the expression that whilst mild, carried an unsettling suggestion of disdain.

Creature's eyes seemed to be calculating every detail, appraising them coldly. To the human eye he didn't appear the least bit impressed with what he was seeing.

Yoshi was shocked when he started speaking because his own experience was so different, so, well…vile. It was some sort of one-way non-verbal exchange, presumably through his audial cortex, his Wernicke brain he guessed, detail unknown.

The boy spoke without moving any other part of his face, all of it remaining strangely immobile as though set hard like a pale cream alabaster. 'So, you are the ones who have tried to save this world.' He voice was clipped, crisp English with the very slightest hint of a British intonation. Vic was aghast when he spoke, flinching, startled. The voice was deep and mature, like a male well into his twenties. He'd expected something more adolescent, a higher pitch, or at least less polished and assured, but that was based solely on his appearance and none of them were sold on that. Still, the expectation was so disparate to reality, it was troubling, a little unbalancing.

Harry was the first to speak, 'it's not just us, most of the planet is fighting,' he said, glaring at him head on, puzzling over the identity of this individual. 'So…is there an answer to it all?'

Creature stared vacantly with burning blue eyes, silence his measured response.

'Who the hell are you?' Becker boomed in an echoing avalanche, 'show us who you are you coward,' he added savagely, giving him his best Becker scowl.

'Jesus, take it easy,' Connie said urgently under her breath, 'we might be able to negotiate with this kid. We need to keep him on side or at least not totally piss him off.' Her mouth twisted into a warning, staring him down.

Becker blinked at her uncomprehendingly, 'are you nuts,' he shot back, trying to keep it down, 'on side…which part of him is on side?' Becker shook his head in mock disbelief. 'Destroying worlds, stars, galaxies…on side…is that what you think?'

'We need to try to get him on side you oaf,' she said a little less emphatically, surely, they had to roll the dice for the sake of what was left. This arrogant alien-child caricature was literally all they had, so they needed to hold their emotions, for Becker, insults, in check.

Creature was studying Connie and Becker, listening to their words. There was no break in his mask of stone but the eyes continued to hammer away in various shades of blue, like dense and less dense fluids warring for position.

'Who am I?' creature repeated slowly. 'I am like you, human by definition but a different species, a different type of human.'

Vic frowned, puzzled by the statement. Type…what did that mean, was it simply a turn of phrase? They all thought it was an odd description but who knew how this thing's mind worked, but creature used the word human which was an Earthly designation, like binary and decimal.

'Is, uh…this what you really look like?' Connie asked as gently as she could, checking her rising anger, 'to us you're a human boy…is that what you are, as a different species, a child?' Like the others she wanted to grab his pasty white throat and squeeze it until he came clean on the murderous sideshow they had going on. But slowly-slowly Connie tempered, conscious of the need to play it carefully. She glanced at Becker and did a double-take, seeing his face squashed and suffused with blood, pretty sure cautionary words would hold him back only so long.

'My real form is as you see it but I am not a boy as you would define it,' he said without inflection. 'We manage ageing so external form is not a reflection of age.'

Connie drew in a whistling breath, leaning forward, slack jawed. 'Manage ageing?' She repeated slowly, picturing the locked gates of Nirvana loosen a bit. 'H-How?' She stammered, scratching at her mouth, wondering if this kid would part with any of their deeper secrets.

Becker whispered in her ear, 'we need to ask him why…why are they doing it, removing your wrinkles can come later.'

She drew her lips into a tight smile. 'Slowly,' she said with a brief flourish, 'let's try and get him talking, he seems to want to talk.'

My God, Harry thought, this little shit is amazing, they'd apparently decrypted the fountain of youth. His frown deepened. 'So how old are you sonny?'

'Harry!' Yoshi said, throwing an arm out, looking mortified, 'please.' Despite their perilous position, dissing the race with the crosshairs on Earth was still a bad strategy.

Creature studied Harry for long seconds, giving no hint of further displeasure.

'Older than your species,' he said without shifting his gaze.

'O-k-ay,' Harry said haltingly, rolling his eyes and bunching his beard up. Holy shit, he said silently, no wonder they've achieved what they have. We've gone from horse and cart to space travel in a hundred years, what would this lot have accomplished in such an absurd time frame?

Becker was looking seriously aggravated, pacing back and forth, eyes wild, darting at the cylinders, the kid, back at the group. 'Enough of this history crap, why are you doing this...why are you here?' His flush was now burnt, bloody anger. 'You realise what's happening out there…right?' He really wanted to end with bastard or some other more cutting expletive, but managed to check himself.

Connie waved Becker back, fixing on the kid. 'An entire race is about to be wiped out.' The hate was heavy in her tone, forgetting her on-side strategy, admitting it was never going to hold. Like Becker, all she could see was an insolent little prick eyeing them distastefully, like something sticky he'd picked from the bottom of his shiny black shoes.

Creature voiced slowly, 'this is the first time — ,' he paused, maybe for reflection or perhaps balking at the words, '…that I have failed. That is why I am here.' He raised his chin slightly and looked down on them. 'We are forbidden to interact, but I have put the Code to one side so I can inspect this humanity of yours.'

Becker snorted loudly. 'You fucking what?' He said, on the verge of springing at him. 'Is this little prat serious?'

'Becker!' Connie snapped, shaking her head sharply, 'he's not a bloody kid, he just looks like one. For Christ's sake he's older than us as a species you oaf— '

Vic was watching the kid intently, mystified and intrigued, heartbeat ramping in his chest as he hung on the peculiar words. 'Inspect us how?' He said, a little disconcerted by the evocative phrase, sweat moist on his palms. Restitution or retribution he brooded, clearing his throat quietly.

'You have rightly assumed that the objects around you are dimensional constructs, created by the Collective, ones within my personal portfolio.' A satisfied flicker seemed to stir in his eyes, although none of them had a clue what that meant. 'I exist wholly to engineer the growth of technical life that exceeds what has gone before it. Time and complexity are key, these are the aims of GD.'

'GD?' Vic repeated softly, taking a quick intake of breath. 'It only needed one more letter, an "O", in the middle of it and well…crap he said to himself, fighting to keep his heart in check. His eyes opened as wide as they could go, peeling back as he threw the words around.

'Genesis Directorate,' Creature said, his eyes churning with beguiling colour.

They were all looking at him, confused, awed, the scope of their advancement painting a disturbing picture with humanity stuck somewhere in the fine print - loincloth mud humpers at best.

Connie felt punch-drunk, lowering herself to the floor, parking her thoughts, battling to clear her mind. They were all as good as dead, their reality essentially devoured, so why was he here…and what did inspect mean? Maybe he was some bohemian Maître D' sequestered to usher them through the doors of the departure lounge, before the gate finally swung shut.

Creature's eyes were the Tyndall blue of a snow wolf, sharply intelligent, calculating, evil, Connie was bored, listening to him droning on about himself and his unrivalled achievements, She was stunned by the strange off world being standing so close because it actually had a lot of Becker in him, self-involvement, conceit, arrogance…it was mind boggling.

'Test results decide status and role within the Collective,' Creature continued, regarding them impassively. 'My vessels displayed an amplitude of progressive complexity, timelines down, science up, reinvesting learnings, bringing peerless advances. My research and standing stood me apart.' He finished with his brow lowering ever so slightly toward his molten blue eyes that were firing majestically. 'Until I created you,' he said, pushing his chin up even higher, for the first time displaying a bona fide emotion as though he was describing an execration like Ebola or Progeria, pulling his lips back, exposing the end of a horrible blue tongue, cold blooded like a desert lizard. Connie saw his revulsion, making her shiver, steeling herself to resist the urge to get away from him.

The sense of disobedience was palpable, being dumped on as they were by this creature for not ascending to some perverse standard that none of them, anyone on Earth had a clue about. Despite it sounding so unwarranted, it still hurt, made even more offensive by the augury of their lassitude…a pale faced schoolboy from the stars.

Vic could see broken sprays of light distorting his vision as he pondered what Creature was saying, that humans had the same fundamental standing as electromagnetism, gravity or gluons, pre-determinations that were stitched into the vacuum, much like a very complicated recipe that had to come out just so, or it was a one way trip to the trash can.

Their *everything* was little more than a tabletop experiment gone awry. Vic imagined setting the gravitational constant to this number, the strong nuclear to that number, electro to this…oh and yes, the sentient beings that'll scrape themselves together from all the fine tuning…well, let's set them to this. And while we're at it, let's tinker with Pi so we can really screw 'em over later on, you know, when they're conscious and can really feel the pain. Vic peered closely at kid-thing, scratching his jaw, feeling things he shouldn't, trying manfully to kill it, but the dogged sense of awe was there. Despite the madness and the horror, it couldn't be ignored, it was pure, hard-wired human emotion.

The ability to hatch a set of creation numbers and predict what would come of them across a Universe of such absurd age, complexity and volume…how does one do that? Vic's scrambled mind couldn't comprehend how astonishingly difficult it would be to make sure the machine worked at all, that the endless layers of quantum physics and gravity worked in tandem to keep it chugging along, let alone ones that grew lavish existential outcomes. The possibility of that being anywhere near a truism was a cerebral showstopper, the tightening in Vic's throat growing into a firmly lodged boulder that almost stopped him drawing breath.

Connie awkwardly clambered to her feet, watching Creature's expression darken as he studied the beings huddled in front of him. If what he said was true, then he was their, what…maker? Seemed about right, she guessed, and incredibly, he despised them for screwing up his "perfect track record", for not living up to his expectations. Connie took a couple of sharp, shallow breaths, muddling over the madness, feeling queasiness turning into a need to empty her stomach violently.

Creature ended in a clipped monotone, seemingly staring between them or through them with a burning gaze, an unreadable expression. 'It was unacceptable and unexplainable.' he stated.

Becker's face flushed again, worse this time. *Unacceptable?* He chewed heavily on the boorish remark, breathing loudly, grinding his teeth, feeling heat rising in his body.

'Come,' Creature said crisply, walking up one of the aisles to their left, surrounded by cylinders on every side.

'Do you have a name?' She asked as politely as she could muster, knowing she was addressing a serial killer.

'No,' came the curt reply.

Connie glanced at Becker who was muttering something, jaw set hard, eyes slitted. She could see he was going to lose his shit, wondering how long it'd take before he took a roundhouse swing at him. Christ, this thing might just lift a pale pinkie and erase him where he stood.

Vic was watching the cylinders above him as they walked in single file up the imposing corridor, an isthmus between oceans of carefully arranged objects that stretched outward and upward, seemingly to oblivion.

Creature came to an abrupt halt, moving his head slowly upward, the cylinders cycling downward toward them, rapidly changing positions. In front of him at eye level was a bone white cylinder, a clear contrast with the black ones surrounding it. He regarded it with a slight curl of his mouth, which seemed to confirm it was the human Universe. Paradoxically, which hardly seemed a strong enough word, Connie mused, it was being ogled by its inhabitants from outside their own universe. Staring mutely at it, she sensed what it was like when none of the circuits in your head connected like they used to. Standing in the chamber, gazing at the featureless white vessel that held their reality, the contradiction was complete. It couldn't be, no way it could…but it was.

Creature cast a spiritless eye upon it, the image not lost on any of them, breathtaking, soul shattering, the maker of everything, the architect of life, beholding his artistry with a slightly dirty sneer. It struck Connie again, it was that feeling of being unworthy, she couldn't help it, but in Becker's case, it just pissed him off, in his whispered words, making him ready to rumble…and talk smack to the little prick.

'So, you're saying that everything we ever knew was, um…inside this…thing?' Vic breathed, sweating profusely. 'In this?' He repeated, pointing at it with a trembling finger, an uncomprehending stare. 'Goddamn it,' he said slowly, barely opening his mouth. His eyes looked ready to blow as he gently picked at the stubble on his chin, studying the smooth, creamy surface.

Becker's face was clouded, then serious. 'Hang on, so we're looking at our own Universe,' he said, 'someone explain that to me?' He tilted his head from the perpendicular, failing to register a single thought that didn't instantly dissolve into unmeaning.

'To put it simply, we can generate anything we choose. Laws are no more than keystrokes.'

'Oh well if you put it like that,' Becker said, his face screaming what the fuck? Moving his head forward, he said to Connie, 'is he, it, serious about that blather?'

'These objects, this expanse was created for you,' Creature said, 'so you can see what I do, how much I have done. All these domains are just numbers without external physicality.' He peered down at the white cylinder, 'yours is the only white-status since my first days of programming. He looked up, around, 'you are an aberrant outcome.'

'So, we're being dismantled?' Vic said suddenly. The words sounded nuts but they were straight from his brain, no thinking.

Creature appraised him with focus, 'we normally retract the program but I made it— ' he paused and for the first time, seemed to really search for a word, 'more unpleasant for you.' The sneer deepened slightly as he surveyed them.

'You vindictive little fuck,' Becker snarled, 'you screwed things up and then you take it out on us...are you completely insane? This was your fault, not ours, you're supposed to be— '

Connie punched Becker's shoulder with such force he grunted and exhaled loudly.

'Hey!' He groaned, holding the spot she whacked, 'he's got it coming...this is bullshit, look at him, like he bloody owns the place.'

Harry snapped his eyes to Becker, thrusting his head at him ominously, 'you keeping up?' He said sharply, flicking his gaze around, 'he does own everything you twat.'

Creature ignored them and started pacing back to the circle where they'd first come together, all of them falling in line, struggling to keep up as he powered away. Vic sunk to the back of the group, stewing over the words, knowing enough to realise Creature didn't waste them. Once they got back to the circle, he would ask his question, see what came of it. Their lives were done, he accepted it, they all did but he wanted something, closure perhaps, at least some insight. More unpleasant, that's what he had so coldly declared. Could it be that depressingly simple? On a whim, make it more unpleasant and then wipe away a civilisation, a Universe? If that was the truth then he was more beast than creator.

Before Vic could open his mouth, Yoshi beat him to the punch 'I met you before...you said information was key, you claimed physics was part of it but not all of it, um...not enough to understand the bigger picture.' He looked around nervously. 'So...what'd you mean by that?'

Screw that, Vic thought, way too general. 'You mentioned program,' he said quickly. 'Retract the program, you said.' He raised both eyebrows deliberately, mouth gaping like a sideshow clown, waiting for the ball to be dropped in...if he got a ball at all.

Creature looked almost amused, then something akin to smugness spread across his pale, fresh face. 'In some ways you show genuine insight but it is not sustained, poorly focussed. Most civilisations your age have colonised many star systems, re-engineered what was theirs, advanced to much of their galaxy, understanding precisely the nature of their universe.'

'So, what's up with your stupid countdown clock?' Becker snapped, glaring hatefully at him, 'is that why we got it, so we knew when it was all going to end...you know, teach us a lesson?'

'You deserve it all,' creature said tonelessly, turning away abruptly.

He actually doesn't give a shit, Becker said to himself disbelieving, not an iota of give a fuck. Ending ugly was the only way this thing could finish, but Becker bided his time, longing to attack him. Would it work, no, but what was the downside? He couldn't see one.

Vic slumped his shoulders, conceding the awful truth. To think we'd always thought our advances were so rapid, innovation, invention, technology...sprinting up the ladder of science. Vic was dumbfounded to think that in the bigger scheme of things, humans weren't very intelligent at all, in fact from what Creature was telling them, they were the dunces in the corner of the room with the paper hat on.

Becker had taken enough insults from this trumped up dirt-bag. He knew he wasn't just a kid, but Becker lived his life in the visual and couldn't get past his stinging arrogance, reluctantly tuning back to the kid's blatherings.

'The vessels we create are algorithms, simulating what you so blithely call reality, lines of code defining how its components interact, complexify, evolve.'

Connie knew blood was draining from her face as he spoke, struggling to draw in a wavering breath. 'S-Simulated?' She whispered shakily, her legs unsteady beneath her, glancing poker-faced at Vic then Harry. Yoshi was staring like a tree frog, eyes wide, fixed, unblinking. Connie's body was tensed head to toe, juggling the nouns and the verbs in her head.

Vic turned to her, 'he's uh…he's not describing a physical process,' he said, peering over at Creature, thinking revelation, pretty sure a major jigsaw piece had just snapped into place.'

'You, your world, your Universe, all the universes, are manifestations created by our genesis code.'

'Oh fuck me!' Harry said loudly, mystified, sensing his mind giving way.

'For you it is perfectly real,' Creature added. 'Reality is relative.'

Yoshi lifted an arm and was studying it feverishly, moving his head back and forth, opening and closing his mouth slightly as he concentrated. Reconciling Creature's words with the reality of his flesh was impossible. He was squinting, poking, prodding, wrestling with the stark reality…or was that unreality. Finally looking up, he said, 'so, um…let me get this right, I'm not real, is that it…I'm just something executed by a CPU?' His breath was shallow, mind suddenly drugged. Blowing out loudly, he said, 'well I sure as hell feel real, look real…right?' His eyes narrowed, voice sinking to a whimper of disbelief, Yoshi stewed on it, ideas, images way beyond crazy filling his mind, making it difficult to see. *"Double click for a new civilisation, or right click and select New Universe to start over"*. Fuck me he thought, squeezing his eyes shut. They'd been insulted, degraded, bullied and were now reduced to a few lines of code, a smart-mouthed overlord and a shitload of processing power.

Yoshi wasn't sure if he felt like exploding with laughter or collapsing and crying. He eyeballed the kid then broke off, sitting on the ground, mumbling incoherently in Japanese.

Connie was finger tapping her thigh manically, straining to get her head around what manner of computing power they possessed to create it all, a working Universe, a machine with billions of trillions of planets, stars and everything else to populate it. But most of all, to make it seamlessly real, indistinguishable from what they'd assumed was Nature. To top it off, they hadn't just made our Universe, they'd made billions of others, she lamented dizzily. It was so far beyond mind-blowing, and on the most ridiculous scale imaginable. Strike that she thought, *unimaginable.*

'You searched for answers and in an inexplicable act, claimed that vibrating strings was the best candidate.' He looked at Yoshi deliberately, almost admonishingly as though he couldn't believe humans had concocted such a load of trollop. 'You asked what my reference to information meant. It was looking more deeply to solve the unification of physics, the fact that you couldn't bring together the small and the large should have led you to the answer, as it did with others, your peers.' Pausing again, he looked slowly, purposely from one to the other until he'd passed eyes across all of them individually. Surveying his flock Connie thought, wondering if he could tell what they were thinking. Was his research still in play here, sifting through their thoughts, gathering, compiling?

'Vibrating strings of energy were wrong, lines of code were right,' he said, staring coldly. 'Information is the building blocks, zeroes, ones, yes, no, these are the irreducible elements, giving rise to your so called fundamental particles.' Creature stepped forward with a rhythmic stride, pulling his shoulders back and standing straighter. Connie wanted to edge backward but resisted, not sure if her legs would move if she tried, debilitated by having her entire life ripped from under her. 'I was certain you would deliver GD's best results.' He paced slowly around, watching them wordlessly, conveying displeasure as teacher might to tardy student.

Becker was pacing back and forth in small staccato movements, curling and uncurling his fingers, staring at Connie who herself was peering at Vic, searching for anything that might add context, which now seemed beyond hope. Harry was trapped in hell, strangled by ideas that had no right to be set forth as fact or truth, or even a vague possibility. His heart took a massive, single beat as he visualised what was actually running his deeper cellular processes. Nothing! Well, something he acknowledged, but sure as hell not what he thought, at least not on a finer scale. He glanced at the others suspiciously, surveying himself up and down with a brand-new set of eyes. Code. Harry reckoned they'd heard enough, nothing else really mattered. Digital beings. Yes/No. Enough said.

'Unification would always be a mystery until you accepted what was right in front of you. It was the answer to everything,' he said, spreading his fingers at his side, a motor skill they hadn't seen before. 'Yet you simply failed to recognise it.'

That's it, his mind shrieked, the brakes yielded, Becker saw nothing but blinding sparks in front of him, adrenaline driving him toward the creature, face contorted with murderous intent.

'Becker, no!' Connie screamed but it was too late. He had had finally lost it and was going to beat the little prick to death if he could.

When he was close enough Becker took an almighty swipe at the kid and with no surprise to Vic at least, his arm went straight through him and he wound up in an untidy heap on the floor. 'What the—?' He shouted, looking up sheepishly from the ground.

Gazing down at him, the kid had a vague look of knowing on his face. 'I would not be so stupid to come here in person,' he said, peering at Becker, giving no hint of surprise, then looking back at the group. 'The more I reviewed you the more I failed to understand your deficiency. It was irreconcilable with the program, impossible I believed.' Harry listened to him use the word impossible and allowed himself a wry smile, seeing a flicker of irony in Vic's eyes as well. They'd given up on the word, but Creature was using it to describe them. The twist in the tale was darkly pleasurable. Becker's mouth twitched, watching Creator try and work them out and coming up short.

'Who's a fucking failure now?' Becker said, insult intended. Connie made a shooshing sound but her elbow was out of reach so he ignored her. 'You made us but can't work us out…sounds like a serious issue you got there.' Fucking idiot he thought with the deepest satisfaction, smirking and giving a pleasurable grunt.

'You were the problem,' Creature said slightly louder, 'my base code drove everything but it was you— '

'Bullshit,' Becker said, almost spitting at him, not giving a toss anymore. Creature didn't react, pausing only momentarily.

'Somehow free will stepped outside the algorithm and I am…yet to determine how that could happen. It has never happened…before.'

Welcome to our world, Harry breather, chuckling, because even this inscrutable being was confused, seemingly losing a little composure, asking things no one could possibly answer. Useless questions now spanned civilisations, universes he thought, what hope did he have? Harry shook his head pitifully; the meaningless quizzing was everywhere around him…in the literal.

It suddenly hit Vic that they were dealing with a hard-core psychopath. This card carrying nutjob had written the code, set every constant and law in the Cosmos yet blamed us for not fulfilling his expectations, when all they'd done was evolve in synch with whatever godforsaken program he'd written. It was an oxymoron of epic proportions, yet this purportedly advanced individual didn't see it, or did and flatly refused to accept it.

Despite initially rejecting it, all of them started to wonder where it might have gone wrong for humanity. If what Creature said was true then every one of his programs, apart from us had been successful and evolved to minimum expectation, and most a hell of a lot more than that. It seemed incomprehensible that everything could run so seamlessly from evolution to scientific enlightenment and physical mastery. Absolute tosh Connie reckoned, but she paused reflectively. If we were all based on lines of code, programs, maybe the free will he spoke of was more strictly defined in others, behaviours way more consistent. It made sense because wouldn't they behave, that is execute in line with instructions? Like an Asimov robot, there were things allowed, things inviolably off limits, but with us that was completely missing the mark, humans were free to make whatever choices they liked, do whatever they wanted, without restriction.

Free will was apparently restricted, even nulled by these hyper-geeks but like Milton who was handed too much kindness, this kid had seemingly fumbled the flask and dropped the whole goddamn lot into the human mix. Our program was supposed to be his pièce de résistance, yet apparently it was a bust. Whatever the reason, it was a no-brainer that humanity were screw-ups given the one-dimensional criteria they were being measured against. If it took unwavering scientific focus then we were hobbled before the game even started, there were so many competing emotions in play, they were virtually unending. If we were vying with citizens of the supermassive black hole or artificial ring system then it was hardly surprising we didn't stack up. She couldn't help another pang of regret and yes, a touch of shame as she pictured comparisons stuck ingloriously on a whiteboard somewhere, imagining a depressing line graph with years since inception on the X and science/tech status on the Y. Humanity would be flat lining while others would be heading off the scale like Everest and Death Valley. There'd be a big fat delta line showing the embarrassing stagnation of the human condition.

Creature looked at Becker unrelentingly, boring into him, seemingly speaking to him in particular. 'There were no clues that could have saved you. I ignored the Code because I wanted you to deal with the pain of termination before your program was exited. I make no apologies.'

Christ, Connie thought grimly, this whatever he was, was a megalomaniacal freak, clearly not rating us as life at all…value literally zero. 'Uh, by exited,' Connie said, feeling a depthless weight in her chest, 'you mean pulling the plug, right?'

'Closing the program, yes.' He confirmed coldly. 'Discarding it.'

'Jesus Christ,' Becker wheezed sharply, feeling his muscles tense involuntarily. He looked for 'Control-Alt-Delete,' he murmured, fingering his temple, contemplating the horror of instantaneous loss of existence. His pulse bounced in his neck. Maybe we'd be saved in the History bar somewhere he mused sadly, feeling like chucking himself on the mercy of the Court. Looking at the callous indifference on the kid's face, he could see there was absolutely no favour there, equally certain the Humanity program wouldn't find a home anywhere near the Favourites Bar. Just junked in the Trash, then emptied and permanently washed away into data nihility.

. Program Close? Connie had a mental image that almost made her gag-reflex empty her stomach all over the pale alien floor

Vic gaped at Harry unseeing, heart pounding, struggling to get his head around the idea of everything being a program inside the mother of all motherboards, a few lines of code, universes of processing power.

'So instead of just closing us down you led us into a game we never had a chance of winning?' Connie asked, throwing a contemptuous glare, no longer caring what he thought. 'You are a shameful excuse for a, what did you call yourself, human? You say we failed because we've exercised free will, well you're nothing but a two-bit…murderer.' Connie's lip was quivering as she lowered her head, staring at her hands, then the floor, eyes tearing up. Digital tears she mooned, wiping her eyes and glimpsing the moisture, like all of them, her self-image destroyed forever.

Connie realised with a thump followed by a sharp pain in her chest why this thing was so lacking in anything remotely close to give-a-shit about their welfare. We were just a bunch of numbers, a few lines of programming code, nothing more. We weren't life, we were just an experiment living an artificial life and like the billions of others, he would've pulled the plug as easily as we would've laid baits to knock off a few billion white ants. And worse, we weren't just insects, we were insects he reviled because of what we hadn't done. Shit, she thought with miserable certainty, their plight was truly beyond the faintest flicker of hope. Connie knew it with as much free fucking will as she'd ever known in her life.

Creature stood stock-still in appraising silence for some minutes, then surprised them by responding to Connie's fiery accusation. 'Yes,' he said stonily, 'you never had a chance but I gave you hope. I amended your program and you chased life, never considering the data you were seeing was actually what makes your world work. You just failed to look deeper, kept searching for particles, strings and other similar non-information. You didn't need to unify your theories, you needed a brand-new vision. It was most disappointing,' Creature said without intonation but with full intent of the impact of his icy words.

Becker glared right at him, clenching his fists, realising the kid wasn't actually here so the pent-up rage was going nowhere. The pressure in his brain, the want to kill was dizzying and he felt suddenly faint, grabbing at Connie's shoulder to stop himself dropping to the floor.

'Jesus,' Connie said, almost collapsing under his weight. 'Get it together.'

'God-Devil,' Becker muttered distantly, directing it quietly at no one.

They looked at him blankly, nodding, taking his meaning. Becker had it penned beautifully Vic thought. This so-called research scholar from some godforsaken Genesis Directorate was both maker and destroyer, life-giver, life-taker and he could do it without regard, on a whim, without the slightest pang of remorse. Exterminate a civilisation, no problems…just let me wash up for dinner first love. But there was a rotten irony to it all, because without the God-Devil, we would never have been and Vic could see the numbing conundrum. For the first time, he even felt empathy for this killer, for he was the only reason any of them had ever drawn a breath. But the empathy was steeply tempered, because now he wanted to take everything away. Digital or physical, humanity was fiercely self-cognizant so to Vic there was no distinction. Like Creature said, the universes they simulated were indivisible from reality so Mankind's grip on life and death, capacity to know terror, feel love and every other life shaping emotion was as real as it got. If they were so damn smart how did they not get that, or maybe they did, and if they did, he wasn't sure which was worse.

Vic had been stewing on something since he'd laid eyes on the freak and with a break in transmission he chucked it in. 'So where are you from,' he said more urgently than he'd intended, 'where did you, uh, start out?' He smiled shakily, shrugging, wondering if he'd get anything back.

Creature drew his granite eyes to Vic, locking on like a hard-dock. What he said was lucid but unfathomable. 'I am from Earth.'

All of them heard the others' intake of breath, a sharp "uh", echoing around them, followed by silence as their minds scrambled over the mountainous peaks of disbelief. It was a claim no one expected, rattling around like a mental gumnut trying to find a like shaped hole to drop into.

'Mother fuck,' Becker exhaled, racking his brain, touching his forehead, quickly deciding there wasn't anything there. Connie and Harry waited for anything that might add context to his claim. Yoshi was frozen to the spot like a Donatello sculpture.

'Originally our home was identical to yours in every way.'

'Okay, so your programs simulate your own planet…Earth?' Vic struggled to spill the words through a mouth barely wider than a pencil mark. It sounded wrong because Earth was their planet, he wasn't sure whether he felt defensive or jealous, definitely deeply uneasy.

'Not always but frequently we do, it is compelling seeing the homeland as it once was, to conduct research in a familiar domain. Your universe was programmed to be identical to ours, every asteroid, planet, every star, every galaxy.'

Vic watched him cautiously, squashing his nose up. 'So, your planet was called Earth…why does ours have the same name, I mean naming is arbitrary surely?'. He glanced back at Creature, 'uh…isn't it? Vic wasn't certain of anything anymore.

'Code updates,' Creature said crisply. 'We are allowed certain minor updates across the journey. They do not materially effect the original program or the few things deliberately left open.' His eyes shone with extra layers of colour as he finished the sentence. 'I say again that your algorithm left no scope for what you ultimately became.'

'So, like I said, you fucked it up kid,' Becker said, waving his arm unceremoniously, rubbing it in, nodding at him caustically.

Creature turned, taking a half step toward him, then stopping abruptly. 'Is that your opinion?' He asked blandly.

'That's what I know.' Becker spat vehemently.

'Yep,' Connie said firmly, 'you built the damn code so what other reason can there be? I mean, seriously, are you in denial?'

'Twat,' Becker murmured, shaking his head, looking up at the forest of cylinders above him. This creature might be an apex intelligence that could effectively redouble magic but Becker reckoned he was still dumb as shit.

'I don't make mistakes,' he said. 'You transcended limitations of the code, make no mistake, reasons will be isolated and rectified in the next iteration and results will be as expected in the first run.'

'So I'm guessing this re-run won't include us? Vic said matter of factly, realising how redundant the question was…how fucking awful it was.

'No. It will start over, a new program initiation.'

'Big Bang, right?' Connie murmured, mulling over the cold, clinical name he'd given it…*program initiation*. Christ, this individual was a stone-cold cyborg.

'Yes. Big Bang,' he confirmed impassively.

'Out with the old, in with the new,' Becker said in a low guttural growl. 'Well, there you go. That's it then.' Becker pushed his head skyward, wondering how the hell life got so screwed up. This creature had designed humans and their Universe like a complex Baumkuchen, got a thumbs down from the judges and was going to bin us like spoilt left overs, every last one of us, down to the last atom, virtual particle, cosmic ray, space…time. Our everything was balanced on the flimsiest kiss of data and once it was withdrawn, everyone, everything would just wink out of existence.

'So how do you know you're not living in a simulation?' Vic asked pointedly, trying to find a flaw in his cocksure attitude, catch him off guard maybe.

Creature's brow showed a mild hint of rising, almost imperceptibly. 'We are,' he replied, with a lulling, almost hypnotic note this time.

Vic stared at him wide eyed, feeling a shiver of panic. It wasn't the response he'd expected. Was he taking the piss…would he even know what that meant? No way, Vic reckoned, this kid had the EQ of rendered steel.

Creature's air remained unchanged, standing in silence, looking above them, ostensibly staring into thin air.

Vic clasped his hands over his head, speechless, blinking as though he had a serious facial tic. Simulated by a frigging simulation. Seriously? He had nothing, no thoughts, no voice. There was no future so fuck it.

'Wait, how do you know that?' Becker said, puckering his mouth cynically, 'been visited by a little shit in black clothes who calls himself God?'

The kid turned directly toward Becker, pushing his lower lip forward a bit. His mouth compressed almost into nothing then released quickly. 'I do not call myself God,' he said with an urgency and intent that made Becker inch back a few steps.

'Way to make God-kid angry Becker,' Connie whispered close to his ear.

The fact that he could be annoyed by words gave Becker a buzz. Suck it up arsehole he felt like screaming at him, but Connie's almond eyes narrowed furiously, making him think twice.

Harry lifted his face out of his hands. 'But there had to be an original.' He felt the madness fishhook into his mind. 'You know…the chicken and the egg,' Harry said to Vic, barely audible. 'There must have been a naturally evolved race in a naturally evolved universe somewhere…like first, I mean, you can't create yourself from nothing, right?' Harry summoned a brittle smile.

Creature watched them coldly, the set of his chin a little different. 'Data may be the natural state of matter.' There was an unhurried pause. 'The fact that we are capable of simulating it is immaterial. Simulating a simulation is no different from simulating a non-simulation, both are quite interchangeable if done correctly, reality is solely in the eye of the beholder.'

Becker wrinkled his nose up, letting out a quick breath of air, wondering what this jerk was droning on about. He got bits and pieces of it but it was geek in its most unalloyed form.

'High intelligence is the reproductive mechanism for universes,' Creature toned, causing them all to refocus, 'they inevitably create other universes whose future intelligences will do the same thing, continuing up a never-ending line of creation.'

'Oh fuck me,' Becker murmured, taking a bemused breath, 'now we're a bloody sex organ.'

Connie couldn't stifle a momentary giggle. 'I've called you a dickhead before Becker.'

He glanced at her, dissolving into a wry smile. 'And now you know for sure,' he said, giving an exasperated sigh.

****

Looking at the forest of cylinders, Vic realised with awesome clarity that each one was a separate universe, some probably like ours, some completely different, but all with stars, galaxies and life, some with beings looking just like us. They'd be living their lives, working, having families, many probably unaware that their entire existence was no more than a few specks of coded nonsense. Even though this place was just a mock up so they could get their heads around Creature's so-called body of research, it did the job well. He broke his stare with a sharp head flick.

Glancing at Vic, Harry said, 'there's still one Sphere out there?'

'Last time we checked,' he said wearily.

'So, the last one is for Earth…right?' Harry mumbled, looking toward Creature narrowly.

'We are inside the final object,' he said, the wall nearest them clearing and below them the strange brown land of new Antarctica stared back, where the Spheres had been so happily occupying a synchronous orbit. It was soul crushing. One left.

'We are just in time,' Creature said with the slightest kiss of enthusiasm. They couldn't see his face but they were sure it would carry a shadow of self-satisfaction. Becker's need to somehow get even, to avenge humanity, had him doing an irritating two-step on the alien floor.

Connie's face was crimped with agony, clenching her teeth tightly together as she expelled a horrified grunt. Despite the inevitability of it all she still couldn't believe this thing was going through with it. 'So, y-you actually intend finishing Earth off…our Universe…completely?' Her nose was squashed with disbelief, two parallel lines digging mercilessly into her forehead.

'Soon,' he said, continuing to face away from them.

'You can't do it you bastard,' Becker said stiff armed. 'Just undo what you've done and we— '

'It is already done,' he said firmly and empirically, as if speaking about incidentals that were of little import. As far as the kid saw it, he was the artist, the copyright owner and could do whatever the hell he wanted without restriction, regulation, repercussion. Again, Vic thought grimly of the bigger picture. Creator, ruler, destroyer.

It was so beautiful, Connie thought, fingering the silver ring on her finger, seeing everyone else staring out with her, pushing around the same gruesome thoughts. To think of the gorgeous blue pearl as a few lazy lines of code was so, uh…fucked up would have to do. It cut across human consciousness like a chainsaw. She peered closer at the planet in lonely silence, wondering how their reality could be promulgated inside the alien equivalent of a CPU? It was too much to accept she told herself emptily because it looked so real and she guessed in a sense it was, Creature had said so too. Eye of the beholder, and anyway, information might be the only "reality" there was, sure the particles and forces were still there, but on a much finer level it all came from a simple nod or a shake, a yes or no, data that sat way, way down under… detectable only by the most scientifically savant. Connie puzzled over her feelings, the sensations, emotions, pleasure, pain, love – agonising over what nuance lay at their base, perpetrated in some prodigious math beyond the Cosmos. But her thoughts were clear on the main idea. If something is simulated with a processor, be it an atom, an apple or a human, or even an entire universe, if it's done just so, then it was indistinguishable from what one might unwittingly call the real thing. It was just a question of tech and computing power, just like the kid, the God-Devil had said. Connie shed a tear as she beheld the beauty of the gorgeous blue pearl, Earth.

Suddenly looming toward them was a massive potato-shaped asteroid, moving relatively slowly, certainly not as Jack had reported. But speed was never going to be the problem because this was a monster. Connie and the rest of them watched as it hurtled past them, rotating slowly as it out-gassed ferociously, colliding with Earth off the southern tip of Australia, almost right under them.

The atmosphere wasn't even a minor inconvenience as it peeled back the crust of the planet, thundering into the iron rich gristle of the upper mantle. 464-Hungaria was a Pacific island chunk of primeval rock delivering a terminal strike, hurling trillions of tonnes of rock and debris into the sky, violently ejecting the atmosphere into space. The life-giving envelope was reduced to a colourful torus of spinning gas trailing Earth like a cometary tail, bleeding colourful nitrogen and oxygen into space. The thermal pulse boiled the oceans, forging rings of bubbling tsunamis kilometres high, engulfing everything on the planet. The devastated surface was peppered with pieces of crust flung into the stratosphere, returning as an apocalyptic meteor storm setting the planet ablaze. The sky was already darkening, morphing into a smoke-filled Venusian nightmare, slowly veiling the molten firestorm. All life, down to microbes and viruses, was gone in a moment of apocalypse like no other in history. And the worst thing, did it matter? No.

'Jesus God,' Connie dribbled, watching horrified as Earth was pulverised by the corpus of ancient, mangled iron. The madness of their maker was gaining clarity as they drew in the barbarity of his ploys to inflict misery on the humans that had so pained him.

Everything they'd ever known was gone in a heartbeat, and despite what they'd learned, this was real, the kid was a fucking lunatic, no one would convince them different.

Becker was still struggling to control his emotions recalling his earlier embarrassment of striking out at thin air and falling on his arse. His breathing was getting progressively louder as he considered what this race had inflicted on them, peering miserably at Earth, now a dirty coffee colour with the crimson glow of a newly volcanic surface just visible beneath.

'D-Dead as,' Connie mumbled, wrestling with sobs that threatened to overwhelm her.

'...just gone,' Harry added quietly, seeing Connie biting her lip, blinking back tears. He glared at Creature with undisguised hatred, teeth glistening in the corner of his mouth.

'So what now?' Becker said. 'What's the next party-trick? We have nowhere to go so what're your plans...um, with us?' His fury melded into apprehension and he gulped instinctively, recalling Connie's chilling words about pulling the plug, convinced the bastard-in-black wouldn't think twice.

'You cannot exist beyond the program,' he stated clinically. 'When it closes you will close.' Creature's wan expression remained, he'd passed a death sentence on them all without the slightest breath of regret. 'That's the way it has to be,' he added with his clipped, adolescent voice.

'Is that right?' Becker said, snarling angrily. 'Man up, appear in person and I'll show you how it has to be.' His feet were wide apart, clearly threatening violence, on what was anyone's guess.

'Just leave it,' Vic murmured, husky with fatigue, 'look, it's done...it's over. We've got nowhere to go.'

Connie was hiding behind her hands, desperately wanting to avoid the hideous sight of dying Earth. The planet was choking on smog and ash, being pummelled by chunks of rock re-entering the now anaemic atmosphere as crimson, vapour trailing meteors. They were the last humans in the Universe, virtually the entire human race had just been wiped out in front of them. Cosmic genocide, she screamed silently, peeking tearfully at the planetary debacle below, so wrong, so horrible yet they were powerless to do a thing about it. Creator had finally raked his eraser across the page, the torture was over, hammering one implacable, non-negotiable home:

Underperform as a species at your peril.

42. Genesis Code

"Creation and destruction are two ends of the same moment. And everything between the creation and the next destruction is the journey of life." ~ *Amish Tripathi*

In Nate's mind, he exited the Sphere in the same instant he'd entered it, stumbling out onto a small metallic landscape. There was no deathly vacuum, fires of Hades or simple corporeal dissolution, the pumping of his heart gradually quieting as he surveyed his new location curiously.

'…interesting,' he muttered faintly, pausing to examine the almost featureless, yet strangely familiar visage. It was Mars, it had to be – the salmon skies, anodyne Sun, chocolate boulders, orange and primrose dunes stretching to the close horizon. A small potato-like object caught his eye as it screamed overhead, Phobos he knew. The realisation sunk in quickly, something that knew him well was generating this oddly pleasurable sojourn. If they wanted to sway him, maybe impress him then this was definitely part of the journey. Of course breathing the pallid ether of carbon dioxide with an air pressure close to nought was impossible. Gravity on Mars wasn't much better either, yet he was taking guttural breaths and felt his normal weight, just like home. In fact he was strolling and breathing, enjoying the warmth like he was smack bang in downtown Chesterfield USA. Definitely could be worse. Glancing around, every muscle in his body suddenly tensed.

Nate saw a shadow in the distance, maybe a kilometre away, not far from where the horizon dipped away precipitously. Wandering slowly up to it, as he got closer, he felt like dropping to his knees but resisted. Someone had done their research very well indeed.

'Sweet Mother of— ' he trailed away under his breath. He sloughed through dusty dunes, dodging rocks until he was only an arm's-length away, like a dumbstruck child gazing at his pop idol. The two cylindrical TV cameras were still there and the corroded dish continued to point skyward toward the defunct orbiter, coated with sand and grit. The shiny metal arm lay dead, fingers resting on the surface, partially buried by an advancing dune. He touched the little sailing ship from Earth, remembering his boyhood dreams, following its incredible journey every day in the newspaper. Only a handful of years after Apollo he was sure this was a massive step toward landing a man on Mars in the next decade. What a fucking crock he brooded, picking up its lifeless limb, pushing it back so it rested on the craft. Nate stared at its plutonium heart - its RTG - that sat dead behind the windshield, having long ago powered everything he'd seen from distant Earth.

Surely he hadn't been brought here simply to meet up with his old pal Viking. After all, he'd tried to blow the Sphere off the face of the Earth which omened rather poorly for this to end in anything but torment.

Nate snapped his head around, seeing a distant figure emerge from the rocky landscape, becoming clearer as it ambled across the desert toward him, seemingly having come from beyond the short horizon.

Nate yelped, recognising the figure as his mother…again. He stared openly, wondering why she'd been summoned back to him, feeling his heartbeat rising in his chest.

'Hello JJ,' she said urgently, 'we have a problem I need to speak to you about.'

Nate saw immediately there was something odd about her. Movements were stiffer and she was straight down to business, no pleasantries, emotional hellos or loving chit-chat. Nate wasn't sure if he should be grateful or terrified. Mars, his Mum and the Viking lander were all here, someone was going to serious pains. Clearly, they'd rummaged through his Hippocampus and grabbed bits and pieces, cornerstone memories, experiences. If they wanted info from him why not just grab it while they were in there digging up the memories? He had no answer to that one.

'Um…who has a problem Mum?' He asked softly, the knot in his stomach returning.

She hadn't blinked, moved or taken her eyes off him since she'd arrived and this time, her voice came with no animation, just stone-cold urgency. 'The group who manages the Genesis Programme has a problem they'd like your help with,' she said.

Nate continued peering, scratching his forehead. 'Er, I have no idea about any of that…what program?' He was taken aback, 'who wants my help?' Nate was flustered, 'how on Earth can I possibly help them?' Some of her words seemed to add a little weight to a bunch of chaotic thoughts he'd been playing around with for a while. They'd been building in his brain, brick-by-brick and maybe this was the mortar to join all the nonsense together. He closed his eyes and ran over what he knew, the experiences with the Spheres, what he'd heard from others, and this friendly "Mars", all adding to the idea that on first reflection seemed barmy. As a vague student of some of the more left field implications of quantum chromodynamics he had a decent head start on most. The binary numbers, the seemingly broken laws of physics and now what his Mum said about a *"Genesis Programme"*. Well he was pretty sure it was all about faking reality. Clenching every muscle he could, Nate considered slapping himself, but settled for rubbing his face firmly with both hands.

'Okay, go on,' Nate said uncertainly, examining his Mum who looked a little ill, eyes puffy and fatigued, age lines crossing her face. If she was a simulation, shouldn't she be a perfect copy of the original like before? Strange, he told himself, rubbing his mouth harder.

'They believe one of their principal designers has breached the Code but his data is inaccessible. The Code dictates all programs be accessible to GD but it has been deeply encrypted by a programmer. They know you are soldier code to the program.' Her eyes bulged unnaturally. 'They need your help.'

Nate rubbed his forearm across his face, conscious of a growing pain behind his eyes. The penny suddenly dropped inside his head like a massive flash-bang, making him reel. Some rogue programmer was engineering all this, all the baffling events in space…to space. He'd had his suspicions about the Universe well before these others and their inscrutable Spheres arrived. Everything about it was too perfect, balanced on something finer than a razor's edge, so incredibly tuned in favour of life it couldn't be by chance. But a program? Well that was a little, uh…surprising.

Nate looked at the elderly woman who seemed frail and unsteady on her feet. 'Do you know you've already been here? I hate to say it but he did a much better job in, um…making you,' Nate said, puzzled, noticing there was none of the finer detail like the facial dimple, the scar on her wrist and the voice was wrong, much too young for her rather haggard appearance.

'He is astonishingly gifted so that is no surprise,' the woman offered. 'We are all able to create spacetime simulations but he is levels ahead in producing complex biology. We ask you to explain what he is doing.' The robotics were suddenly gone as she stared with vivid, pleading eyes. Emotion was being generated to compel a positive response, he got that.

Nate raised an eyebrow. 'Well, he's been taking our Universe apart piece by piece, changing the laws of physics to suit himself, tormenting us, killing, things like that.'

'Go on,' she voiced shakily, her face collapsing further into complex lines.

'Go on…seriously…do I need to go on?' He said impatiently, 'he's erasing everything in chunks, animate, inanimate…the lot.'

She stared at him vacantly, unblinking, head angled in a strange way.

'We're left with a pathetic nothing, barely bigger than Earth.' Nate's voice sunk to a dull rasp on the last few words.

The woman tilted her head back level with him and spoke firmly, eyes suddenly stony. 'He must be stopped.' She paused, lowering her eyebrows as though working hard on a problem. 'The program must be amended to comply with the Convention on Genesis.'

Nate looked at her,. 'So, okay, what is it…this convention, can you tell me?'

She hesitated as if waiting for instructions and after a few moments said, 'why of course.'

She spoke the words formally, describing each of the five cornerstone protocols, explaining each one slowly and deliberately as if reading carefully from a page of notes:

Digital realms are designed to insight scientific evolution and relativity of intelligent life
Programmed life allows consciousness to exist in otherwise null environments
Successful programs self-perpetuate, Convention 2
Programmers may not reveal their presence to programs
Programmers may not amend initial codes beyond scripted limits (Clause 24)
Program termination only by closure codex

Nate grunted almost mockingly through the last three. 'Well he's, uh…bummed out on several of those,' he said, feeling a prickle of unease stir in his spine as he pondered the import of what they wanted him to do. 'So, uh…what's the plan?'

'You will go to him and tell him that he must—'

'Hey hang on. You want me to go and confront him?' He said, staring incredulously. 'You're kidding right…why can't you do it, I mean why can't they do it? He's not going to listen to me, no way he will.' He bit his lip until it throbbed, feeling his fingers go cold. Nuh, he said to himself, fucking kid's a nutter.

'We cannot do it JJ, it would breach the Convention. Your reluctance is understandable, however we are unable to enter your world, and that's where he is. He is inside one of the Hubs and has several of his programs with him, so we are prevented from interfering.'

'Why the hell would he listen to me?' Nate demanded again. 'He'll dismiss me, ignore me, maybe worse. Why would he acknowledge me?' He took a deep breath, as he imagined negotiating with this individual.

'Tell him Fyoderov knows his crimes, he will be removed from GD if he fails to comply.'

'And what am I asking?' Nate said, hunching his shoulders a little, accepting that he was being asked to have a good old chinwag with an entity that was essentially god and the devil…wrapped up in a creepy black package. No worries he thought, grabbing a fistful of dishevelled hair. Piece of piss. Might serve morning tea as well, he mocked to himself, dry laughing.

'Tell him that 10111010111001111110010011101100 must be reset to its last point of full functionality. You don't need the number, he will know the program.' She stepped back, looking at the Sphere, holding an arm out.

'The Hub is ready for you JJ,' she said gently, with an expression of pure steel. 'Remember what I said, it is very important to you.'

'Are you coming?' He asked, hoping for support but knowing better.

'No, I need to stay.' With that she turned on her heels and walked into the desert, marching stiff legged toward the pink horizon.

'Uh, okay but what— ' Nate said louder, stopping, realising the talking was over. 'Holy crap,' he murmured, starting back over the "Martian" dunes toward the light, looking back to get a last glimpse of her, but she'd already gone, vanished into the ether like so much melted snow. Nate walked into the light without hesitation, hoping his destination was as stated. He didn't trust the Spheres, the strange race directing them.

***

Creature looked mildly surprised when a strip of light appeared near the wall like a shimmering desert mirage. Harry gulped, darting his eyes around the group, thinking it might be their mode of execution, beguiled into it somehow and dissolving like ice-cream runoff on the way through. Fucking great he thought, but the slightly open look on the brat's face suggested he was…Harry wasn't sure, uncertain he reckoned, a little taken aback. Walking slowly, almost tentatively over to it, he bent his neck forward, inspecting it closely. The fizzing sound increased in pitch, the colour of the energy darkening to a steel grey and when Nate's body stumbled through and he solidified inside, it was definitely a surprise, albeit muted. Creature froze, watching the new arrival intently as he strode into the light of the chamber, offering a wobbly smile to the group.

377

'Hey!' Becker whooped, 'Jesus, you made it.' The thin smile on Nate's face was replaced by a look of relief, realising he was still alive, looking down at himself, saying, 'yeah, I guess I did.'

'How the hell'd you get here?' Harry said, moving forward, studying him closely.

'Well…uh, I was sent here,' he said, looking uncertainly at the kid who stared back at him, total concrete. Just as Nate thought, the kid was the rogue programmer and he looked dead-set scary. Young he may have been but everything about him, the entire package, was mature and malevolent.

'Sent?' Connie repeated, frowning, her face quizzical, confused.

'Friends of Fyoderov.' Nate said as firmly as he could, pausing to gauge the reaction. Creature was standing only a few metres away, studying them like a cat might eyeball a mouse before it pounces and rips it apart. He had the suggestion of a crease in his forehead, mouth slightly open, revealing an upper row of bright white teeth.. It was gone before they could get a decent look.

'Fyoderov?' Creature repeated with a note of urgency. It was the first time he'd ever phrased anything as a question. 'How is that possible?' They heard him whisper, presumably to himself. His portfolio of programs had recently been examined, the best in the Directorate. The program he'd hidden was undetectable. Promotion to the big-chair of the most prestigious discipline in the Directorate was his to take, so why had Fyoderov sent this soldier to him…from his portfolio?

Nate found it difficult to look at him without trembling, desperately fighting it because this was genuinely last-ditch stuff. He balled his fists so tightly his knuckles cracked. 'Fyoderov knows, 'I was returned to give you this message;. 10111010111001111100100011101100 must be reset to its last point of full functionality' Nate fixed his eyes on Creature's forehead to avoid the eyes. He took a quick peek, noticing with dismay that Creature was staring back blankly, hardly the reaction he wanted. 'They will exit you from the Directorate and the Collective if you refuse,' Nate said, breaking eye contact and gazing into the distance, pleading with his heart to slow.

Creature didn't move or speak, simply glaring at them like a deranged Howdy Doody puppet. His eyebrows suddenly tensed and straightened as he seemed to wrestle with the best way forward to minimise damage, realising his irrational want for vengeance may have tripped him up. 'I should have just ended the program,' he said impassively, turning sharply and ambling away.

'Where's he going? Becker quizzed, causing Harry to grunt tersely. Connie assumed the kid needed *"think time"* to try and extricate himself from a situation he hadn't anticipated.

'Man, that was awesome,' Becker gushed, grinning broadly, feeling some energy return. 'So this directorate, they're like his...boss?' He rubbed his hands together, thumbs in the air. 'They want him to reset everything, holy shit,' Becker said effusively, giving him a firm nod, 'we're not out of the game…right?'

'Wasn't my idea I assure you, but maybe we're not,' Nate said. 'He's broken the Code, like really fucked it up. There's some serious conflict with this, uh…whatever they are.'

'Shit, he's coming back,' Becker said, eyeing him warily as he sauntered back more slowly than he'd walked away. His face was stone cold vacant, eyes unblinking, little volatility in his stark blue irises. Creature walked toward the wall, faded and vanished from the chamber.

Connie grabbed onto Becker, waiting for the rest of them to simply fade away as well.

After a minute of terrified silence, Becker said, 'uh…so what now?' His head was jerking around, conceding they were probably alone in the chamber. 'Is he seriously gonna comply?'

'I can't imagine the prick yielding to anyone,' Connie said, 'but we don't know how serious the threat was, hopefully to him at least, it was life and death.' They could see snarl lines dig into her brow. 'His whole rotten existence seems to revolve around status within that Directorate, hopefully they take him down, lock him up for good.' A look of amusement flickered across Connie's face, visualising him in handcuffs and ankle chains, giving a deep, gratifying sigh.

Looking at Earth, Connie's stomach cramped as she grieved for their beautiful world, now veiled by dirt, smoke and dust, surrounded by a diffuse orange blanket of rock and debris extending all the way to deep orbit. Earth was as dead as it was ever going to get.

43. Recovery

"Sometimes to return is a vulgarity." ~ *John Fowles*

'Jesus Christ,' Joe said as softly and respectfully as he could muster. This guy was borderline insane, like clinically, he was sure of it. He felt like barking dumb-arse straight at him, but it wouldn't do a zac of good. 'Are you listening to any of this Carson?' Joe said, feeling hot, really wanting to be somewhere else. He'd watched the big guy zone out for the best part of thirty seconds, he wanted to grab him and shake him violently, hopefully snap him back to the real world.

Becker shook his head hard, peering around, widening his eyes, then narrowing them, trying to focus. Connie was next to him, elbow hard on the boardroom table, hand on her chin, looking equally perplexed. Joe turned his head impatiently. 'Um, you guys okay?' he said, dwelling quizzically, a little ill at ease at the sudden zone out. Goddamn it, he thought, the biggest, dumbest decision of their lives and they were half fucking asleep.

Connie shifted her head up at Joe with the biggest Doe eyes he'd ever seen. She was staring at him, unblinking, seemingly a world away. My God, she muddled to herself, it was Joe. Glancing around, her heart started thwumping in her throat as she stared vacantly at her surroundings. With a jolt, she woke up properly. Oh my, she said to herself, feeling a sense of elation mingled with something darker, sitting heavy and languid in her gut. They were back, she got it, but why did she have memories of events that would never take place? Connie felt like squealing, hollering, falling to her knees, but something made her suppress it so she clenched her jaw, tightening her throat to lock it inside. Play it cool she said to herself several times, surveying the room, finishing up looking at Becker who not surprisingly looked a little off. Can't blame the old geezer she thought…it'd been a hell of a ride. Clearly Joe was none the wiser. Dead Joe, it was so incredible, thank God, it appeared that he had no idea.

'Connie, tell him how nuts the idea is, the Company, the investors, you have a wider responsibility here,' Joe said, gazing at her briefly, surprised by her sudden lack of fight. 'Does anyone get it? I mean, you could go to gaol, right?' His eyes were bugging out of his skull, urging her to back him up, to do the wildcat Connie thing and give it to him between the eyes.

'Well…er, um, yeah I suppose he could,' she said trying to muster some steel. 'Yes, you could go to gaol, can you imagine how messed up that would be?' She smirked knowingly at him, nodding. 'Although I think you'd be quite popular inside, with your little orange jumpsuit.' She was smiling now, a glint in her eyes, throwing him an exaggerated wink.

'Ease up,' Becker said in mock disgust, holding an arm outstretched, waving his palm. 'Joe, can we have a minute?'

'Er, sure,' he said. Joe wanted out anyway, the boardroom had turned into a bloody nuthouse. Corporate suicide anyone, what about gaol or bankruptcy…maybe a side order of personal immolation? He should just keep walking he thought miserably, out the door, up Martin Place, book himself into a nice quiet room at Sydney General, maybe the psych ward, requisition some calming meds. If the GraviMet data came back positive, Becker would be impossible, more impossible, it'd be a horror story, demands, nightmare deadlines, and then the risks he didn't even want to start poring over.

Joe moved quickly from the room in case Becker changed his mind, clicking the door closed and speeding off, muttering under his breath as he motored up the corridor. As he did he weighed their strangely casual response to the risk of losing the lot, everything they'd built over the last decade. Becker didn't deserve the Company, Joe firmly believed that. He was just shit lucky to stumble over Aladdin's frigging Cave in the middle of the desert which funded anything he could dream of for the rest of his born natural.

Connie felt like she'd banged her head on something hard, sparkles of spots and dots appearing in front of her eyes. She gave a clearing shake of the head, gazing at him, surveying his face, frowning. 'You remember...right?' She whispered the words with a quaver, eyes widening, head bending toward Becker.

'Of course, Jesus, yes,' he murmured forcefully, grinning slowly. 'That little shit actually did what he was told, he fixed his stupid program.'

'Careful what you say,' she said, smiling cautiously, 'we are the program remember.'

Cocking his head to the side, Becker glared. 'Yeah, you're right, as much as I'd like to forget it...ain't gonna happen.'

'Never,' she agreed, twisting her lips up on one side, shrugging with her mouth.

'We're back in November sometime,' Becker said, glancing at the digital diary on his desk, smiling with a big toothy grin. 'As screwy as it sounds, we've been...well, I guess reset is the word. His smile waned, erased as his mind wrestled with the memories. From everything to nothing and back again. Full fucking circle he mused, wanting to burst out in triumph, the joy stifled by something immovable in his throat.

'I'm not sure,' Connie said gravely, suffering the same prickle of unease. 'How do we remember, why do we remember?' Her eyes were wide like a predatory bird. 'I don't get it. We shouldn't remember what hasn't happened, what won't happen. I feel like I'm going nuts here...this is effect before cause. We're on Earth before the events...so I guess it's the whole digital thing. It doesn't have to be logical, it just has to be written in base code.' The new physics, Connie brooded, gasping under her breath, weighing up the nonsense she reckoned Earth would grudgingly come to accept as Grand Unifying Theory. Of course explaining it in equation form would be nigh on impossible, but at least it would bridge the long sought dependency between quantum mechanics and gravity. The glorious answer was...there fucking wasn't one! In the next breath she felt a deep seated certainty that Earth could never be allowed to know the truth.

'Joe didn't seem any the wiser,' Becker said in a soft voice. 'Wonder why us, not him?'

Connie seriously doubted it but said, 'maybe he was playing it cool, you know not sure if we remembered.' She shook her head almost imperceptibly.

'What if we ask him and he really doesn't know, we'll sound bonkers,' Becker said. 'But maybe he's in the same boat.'

'Perhaps he doesn't remember because he died, wasn't around when everything reset.' Connie knew they could debate Joe forever when laying clues in front of him would be way easier.

'Anyway, leaving Joe aside, we can't tell anyone. I don't know where the sensation comes from but it's like the idea's printed on my brain, the old indelible ink thing.'

'Yeah, same,' Connie said. 'Tell no one. I feel it,' she said, chuckling softly. 'Not ink Becker, more like computer code. Data telling us what to think through trillions of connections, interactions, switching.' Connie reckoned it might be spot on. Perhaps what Convention demanded.

'Okay, so that's it then,' Becker said, 'our secret.'

'For the moment,' Connie murmured, zipping her mouth with two fingers, 'we tell no one, everyday'll get easier,' she promised. 'Despite all the source code stuff, all the madness, we are truly, consciously alive.' She had a gleam in her eye. 'It might be based on code, numbers, qubits, fucking raspberry jubes but their processing power and, um...despite his words of hate, they've built a perfect reality...a perfect us.' Her pupils were dilated, eyes glazed as her mind raced. 'And like the freak said, maybe the suitcase universe is the only one kicking around, the other one, the so-called natural one might be just a humanistic pipe dream. I mean no one has ever been able to explain how the big bang came along so is it really that nuts? It's gone from downright unexplainable to a total head fuck. That's progress I guess.' She smirked, looking back at Becker, lifting both shoulders and holding.

'Jesus that was impressive, you were fluent right there, no gaps or stutters, I feel way better now.' He cocked an eyebrow, puckering his mouth, finishing with a gentle, mocking sigh.

Connie raised a single finger to her eye and smiled thinly. 'Thanks Becker, I mean that.'

44. Compliance

"If it can be destroyed by the truth, it deserves to be destroyed by the truth." ~ *Carl Sagan*

Fyoderov was seated with his assistant in front of Minan, who was also seated, about three metres away, looking mildly uncertain. The Directorate Administrator looked about twenty-five years, Minan about sixteen, members of the Consort a mix of ages, nothing over forty or under fifteen, courtesy of their wizardry with the telomeric clock, allowing them to deftly side-step organic decay forever. Simulated they may have been, but their technical artistry allowed them to grip and rip, seizing the vacuum and tweaking the inner syntax of their own base program. Virtual universes were spawned to run their monolithic processors, tapping energy from gaggles of them, supplying infinite quantities of cyberpower. The first law of thermodynamics was simply a speck of code easily pushed aside - if you had the know how to design inflation with the right glob of matter, energy screamed into being from nothing. Should they have a want, they could re-create Earth from day one so that every event was identical to theirs, every weather event, every animal, every footstep, every growl, meow or word spoken, and it was no more difficult than math 101…simply a matter of knowing.

'Minan,' Fyoderov started, 'I say with deep regret,' he paused, studying him, '…this is the first violation since the First Dozen was established.' Minan's face was acutely intelligent, watching Fyoderov intently. 'You will right your wrong with expedience, you must reinstate the program to comply with each Article of the Code.' He frowned ever so slightly at Minan. 'Do you understand our orders?'

'Of course,' Minan replied immediately, acknowledging the judgment icily, thankful it wasn't a great deal worse. He was certain GD were unprepared and weren't entirely sure how to deal with it, sensing conflict in the Controller's manner, less conviction than he expected.

Fyoderov recited the numerical coordinates of the program, dismissing him with a brief flourish.

Whilst he had no choice under law, Fyoderov was strangely ambivalent about the orders he gave, not because they weren't in synch with the Code but because the orders seemed inconsistent. He sensed a growing need to review the Code in light of Minan's violation. Fyoderov struggled with the decision because in this instance, implementing the Moral Code by working backward didn't seem to give the same ethical result as it did when it worked forward.

Minan would not be expelled from the Directorate, losing their best and brightest right now was not an option they cared to exercise. The needs of the few outweighed the needs of the many, and that twisted logic was simply how it had to be.

Minan paced down the featureless white corridor, tapping a small device crimped tightly around his ring finger, a personal GUI interface with GD's data processors that translated Genesis codes into activation events. The device appeared recreational but it connected him to the inner tech of the research hub, the twenty-four state Terbium, Planck scale processing loops, possessing the post godly ability to trigger creation events every femtosecond for as long as they pleased. Given that a femto was to a second as a second was to thirty million years, their capability was a billion-fold beyond anything covered off by throwing the God word around. Should they lift a finger with desire, they could launch a hundred trillion universes in less than the blink of an eye. God should be so lucky.

Minan was sorting through some sensations that had been gnawing at him since he departed the human world, a strange, hollow quality, something he hadn't felt for so long, leaving him continually replaying events in his mind. Like Fyoderov, Minan was conflicted but it was for a different reason. These humans had wormed their way into his psyche like a blight, but now, well…his feelings had changed unexpectedly…dramatically. It was the temper and intensity, the personality of their resistance, they were spirited, bold and while it was difficult to admit, he was impressed on some level, certainly intrigued. The outcome from billions of soldier species had never gone so wrong, so utterly counter to expectation…and revealed such potent qualities. They were a disappointingly backward race for their age but something was growing in him he was struggling to deny and finding difficult to define.

Minan regretted afflicting the Becker and Connie programs like he had but it was too late to stop, the course of action was done and locked, the only outstanding action was execute. Minan disabled his emotions and the distractions drained from his mind. He had much to do. If he didn't enact GD's orders it would be an inglorious and abrupt end to his career, and for a being with an unlimited life span that was a very serious problem indeed.

Minan fleetingly visualised the program designate 101110101110011111100010011101100, ignoring Gen Mode, choosing Paradigm Erasure, having already reset the program so it recovered seamlessly at a date before Timer Activation. A few additional amendments were injudiciously thrown in, but nothing impactful to the orders from GD. Their wishes, indeed their judgment would be executed as ordered. Minan paused briefly then visualised what he wanted. The program closed, dispatching instantly for assessment to a deactivation division of GD. It was age-old thinking but it remained true through thousands of millennia, the greatest failures yielded the richest learnings.

Recovery had brought the Universe back to everything it had ever been. The Cosmic leftovers from the Big Bang were everywhere again in glorious infrared. The Virgo Supercluster with its million galaxies was back, along with trillions of black holes, quintillions of stars and planets, molecular clouds, dirt and dust and all the other celestial trimmings. Jupiter and the Moon were there, the asteroid belt back home under the loving care of the Jovian giant, and the Sun burning bright in the skies, warming the luxurious third seed that held the only intelligence in the Cosmos, a rare and extraordinary world indeed.

A hundred billion cubic light years was a mighty playground for one sentient species, providing almost unlimited possibilities for it to evolve outward. Time was the only thing it didn't have. By the Maker's intent, potential was a given, but to prosper and remain in the game, it had to find the global wherewithal to unlock its technical destiny quicker than it ever thought it had to.

Like other genesis scholars at GD, Minan benchmarked his work against Collective best practice, and like any decent, disciplined house of learning it set minimum performance limits. Many species would make the cut but some would fail while others would go on to glorious, illimitable futures. Those falling below the median profile would be sent packing and were dealt with in line with the minutia of the Moral Code. Ascending to the Maker's non-negotiables, his imperatives, his ego, was the quintessential meaning of life…and death.

***

Connie was racking her brain, trying to figure out the best way to tackle Becker to the ground, talk him out of his hair-brained mission and make it sound like she meant it…assuming the gravity data still came back positive. They had no idea if it would. Was the anomaly still under the ice? She thought yes, Becker thought no but Connie was convinced, picturing the fucker still ticking grimly on their existence.

As she peered at him, debating the right way forward, all the lights in the room went out, emergency evac lights punching on, providing a dim blue glow, ghostly and fearfully unsettling.

'What the hell?' Becker barked almost as one word, spinning around to Connie. 'Power failure,' he said, wincing as he looked up at the dull downlights. He had a harried, wild appearance, shaking his head in the half-light.

Connie was drawn to a chilling sight behind him, her mouth falling open, every physical process in her body slowing. Her lips fell downward, exposing a few shining teeth as she gazed terrified beyond the boardroom window. 'I-it's not over,' she said, forcing it over the gravel in her throat. 'Oh God,' she uttered hoarsely, not believing it, believing it, blood draining from her face as she searched for detail beyond the window.

Becker turned and saw, his face went blank as he peered bleakly, at what… he wasn't sure.

Connie shortened her gaze, locking eyes with Becker. 'It's nothing…I mean nothing…there's nothing out there.' She raised her arms slowly, placing her hands around her face, staring at him, slapped by the chill of a single thought…the kid was still fucking with them.

Outside the boardroom windows they could see nothing, no light, no contrast, not the slightest suggestion of anything beyond. It was late afternoon in a G10 city normally crammed to the hilt with sound, motion, people, cars everywhere in a peak hour crush of human activity. Now there was zero, the only light coming from the evac bulbs that were starting to flicker, seemingly ready to pack it in.

Connie sensed an involuntary moaning in her throat as she sweated in the dim light, heart pounding on her spine. 'Oh, Christ Becker, once evac goes I think…we go.' He grabbed Connie and she buried her face in his chest, both grasping each other tightly as the lights continued to flicker ominously, casting shadows on the walls around them.

Becker could see the horror misting in her eyes, feeling hopelessness screaming in his ears. 'I'm so sorry Connie,' Becker murmured vaguely, 'I-I can't save you.' He felt his composure cracking.

Connie grabbed him even tighter. 'No one can save us,' she gasped, trying to strangle a sob but failing, her chin and cheeks trembling violently. Becker held her shoulders, trying to sooth her with useless whispers.

'I, uh…you know Connie…know that,' he muttered as he ground his jaw to kill the tears. 'Know that,' he added with barely any sound.

'O-Oh G-God,' she sighed again, the words almost unintelligible as the evac lights died completely, darkness everywhere like plunging into a vat of crude oil. Becker suddenly released her and she reached out, flailing the air for him, 'Becker, come back,' she pleaded despairingly. 'Please…come b-back.' Her voice trailed into a low moan, arms still fanning in front of her, finding only empty space.

The evac lights punched back on and Connie could see that Becker had gone. It was just her and the empty boardroom. Connie silently sunk to the floor, lights dimming to a barely perceptible glow, then shutting off with a grim thud.

Connie was trembling in the dark, knowing everything was gone. She was the last of her species, left in whatever this pit of suffering was. A single piercing scream rose from her throat, a blood curdling wail of anguish and resignation – the final cry of humanity.

*****

Program Close should have taken the lot in a heartbeat but it hadn't because the Creator hammered the nail in a little bit further. In the last seconds he did things he hadn't expected.

The program was reinstated, and it brought back the virtual Universe in all its former majesty, across billions of light years. Then the plug was pulled and the program erased - the Earth, humanity and everything else was brought to an instantaneous end to comply with Article 6 of The Genesis Code - No Notice of Termination. Order had been restored. Almost.

Afterword

Renewal

The outpouring of energy started as the smallest, brightest speck imaginable, exploding in every direction at many factors of C, virtual spacetime flashing into existence in an orgy of hot, dense energy made from the simplest cyber elements. Evolution had yet another chance to machine the advancement of mathematical widgets through a glorious Kardashev algorithm...and come up with a sentience worth keeping.

It wasn't in the same place as the human universe because spatiality had no meaning, there could be duality of volume, either negative or positive but no usable space in the true sense. It was merely space in non-space, clusters of data with extreme virtual dimension but no real dimension, billions of light years to the beholder that might swim in a drop of water. The cyber-energy buzzing and fizzing with electron states was one of a million creation events happening right "now".

The Universe inhabited by the humans had been terminated for failing to meet minimum requirements, by an embarrassing margin. This was another of Minan's algorithms. Human deactivation had been completed, there were no errors of design but still the emergent structure had evolved perilously unencumbered, undone by free will and doomed before it started. This new domain was an optimised human design, identical in program but compiled a little differently. As Minan surveyed the initiation of the new program his anticipation was obvious to those who knew him and understood his steep desire for perfection. In time, he would see the results, as he would the other billion domains he had in his Active Project Portfolio, although he held special hope for this one in particular

Learnings from the legacy human habitat were high in his mind and never again would he invade one of his own programs. The impact on him was more than he had anticipated, there was something about them that stayed with him, it was difficult to define, the best he could come up with was loss. The sensation was mildly unpleasant when his emotions weren't nulled but he refused to live in that frozen world permanently.

Minan had decided to preserve two of the humans from the failed algorithm. Through a simple translocation process, he copied them into a different universe, closing the originals while maintaining their base-data and closing the loop. It wasn't the program per se that was of interest because that was just math. Minan's conclusion was that they had transcended or in some way defied their own source code, acquiring excessive self-volition, a peculiarity never seen before, something no one in GD had an answer to quite yet.

So, assessing these virtuals further seemed to be worth considering, despite breaching the Code again and placing his position at GD in serious peril. But the need to do so surpassed even the fear of expulsion. Science and learning wasn't the only reason for saving them, he understood that and perhaps it wasn't the real reason at all. Having spent virtual time with them, Minan felt an odd mix of empathy and intrigue. Something inside him spoke loudly, telling him that saving a couple of specimens might be the right thing to do.

So, he did.

The chosen two were comfortable for the moment.